NB

UNDER FIRE

W.E.B. GRIFFIN

G. P. PUTNAM'S SONS
NEW YORK

This is a work of fiction. Names, characters, places, and incidents
either are the product of the author's imagination or are used
fictitiously, and any resemblance to actual persons, living or dead,
business establishments, events, or locales is entirely coincidental.

G. P. Putnam's Sons
Publishers Since 1838
a member of
Penguin Putnam Inc.
375 Hudson Street
New York, NY 10014

Library of Congress Cataloging-in-Publication Data

Griffin, W. E. B.
Under fire / W. E. B. Griffin.
p.   cm.
ISBN 0-399-14788-8
1. United States—History, Military—20th century—Fiction.
2. United States Marine Corps—Fiction.   3. Korean War,
1950–1953—Fiction.   I. Title.
PS3557.R489137U53   2002   2001048245
813'.54—dc21

Printed in the United States of America
1   3   5   7   9   10   8   6   4   2

Book design by Jennifer Ann Daddio

Maps by Jeffrey L. Ward

UNDER FIRE

PROLOGUE

In 1944, Vice President Henry A. Wallace was perceived by many—perhaps most—highly placed Democrats to be a genuine threat to the reelection of President Franklin D. Roosevelt.

He was cordially detested by the Republicans—and many conservative Southern Democrats—both for his liberal domestic policies and his unabashed admiration of the Soviet Union.

Perhaps equally important, the poor—and declining—health of President Roosevelt, while carefully concealed from the American public, was no secret to many Republicans, including their probable candidate for the presidency, Governor Thomas E. Dewey of New York.

There was a real threat that Dewey might make it an issue in the campaign: "Roosevelt, if reelected, probably won't live through his term. Do you want Henry Wallace in the Oval Office? Or me?"

Wallace, it was decided, had to go.

For his running mate, Roosevelt picked Senator Harry S Truman of Missouri, who, while an important senator, was not part of the President's inner circle.

It was a brilliant political choice. Truman had earned nationwide recognition for his chairmanship of a Senate committee investigating fraud and waste by suppliers of war materials. "The Truman Committee" was a near-weekly feature on the newsreels at the nation's movie palaces, showing a nice-looking man visibly furious at contractors caught cheating the government and the military officers who'd let them get away with it.

And he couldn't be accused of being antimilitary, either, for he had served with distinction as a captain of artillery in France in World War I, and he had retired as a colonel from the Missouri National Guard.

The Roosevelt-Truman ticket won the election in a landslide. Vice President Truman appeared with Roosevelt at the inauguration, and then was more or less politely told to go away and not make a nuisance of himself while Roosevelt and his far-better-qualified cronies ran the country.

During the first eighty-one days of his fourth term, President Roosevelt met with Vice President Truman twice, and they were not alone on either occasion.

On the eighty-second day of his fourth term—April 12, 1945—while vaca-

tioning in Warm Springs, Georgia, with a lady not his wife, Franklin Delano Roosevelt died suddenly.

That made it urgently necessary to bring President Harry S Truman up to speed on a number of matters it had been decided he really didn't have to know about, including a new weapon called the Atomic Bomb.

And to tell him of some disturbing theories advanced by the intelligence community—most significantly the Office of Strategic Services (OSS)—that Josef Stalin had no intention of going back to Mother Russia to lick his war wounds, but rather saw the inevitable postwar chaos as an opportunity to bring the joys of communism to the rest of the world.

There had already been proof:

The U.S.S.R—which was to say Stalin—had forced the King of Romania to appoint a Communist-dominated government; Tito's Communists had assumed control of Yugoslavia; Communists were dominant in Hungary and Bulgaria (where a reported 20,000 people had been liquidated). In Poland, when Polish underground leaders accepted an invitation to "consult" with Red Army officers, they had been arrested and most of them had then "vanished."

And Stalin had made no secret of his intentions. Shortly before the end of the war, the OSS reported, he had told Yugoslav Communist Milovan Djilas, "In this war each side imposes its system as far as its armies can reach. It cannot be otherwise."

President Harry S Truman had been in office less than a month when—at 2:41 A.M. on May 8, 1945, at General Dwight Eisenhower's Reims, France, headquarters—Germany surrendered to the Allies.

Three days later, on May 11, 1945, Truman abruptly ordered the termination of Lend-Lease aid to the U.S.S.R. But then, on the advice of left-leaning Harry Hopkins, Truman made what he later acknowledged was a major mistake. To assure Stalin of American postwar goodwill, he kept silent about the "vanished" and imprisoned Polish leaders, and then recognized the "new" Polish government in Warsaw as legitimate, although he knew that it consisted almost entirely of Soviet surrogates.

In July, Truman met with Stalin at Potsdam, Germany, outside Berlin. Truman came away convinced that Roosevelt was wrong: "Uncle Joe" could not be treated like a difficult senator and bribed with a couple of highways and a new post office in his hometown; he had every intention of taking over the world.

Truman returned from Potsdam, thought it over, and ordered that the atomic bomb be used against Japan. Use of the bomb would, he reasoned, primarily, save the lives of the 500,000 American servicemen whom the military experts expected to die in a "conventional" invasion of the Japanese home islands.

It might also, Truman hoped, convince "Uncle Joe" to behave. Only a fool or a maniac would risk war against a nation equipped with the most devastating weapon ever developed.

On August 6, 1945, Hiroshima was literally obliterated by an atomic bomb. On August 8, the Soviet Union declared war on Japan. The next day, as the Red Army marched into Manchuria against the Kwantung Army, which could offer only token resistance, a B-29 dropped a second atomic bomb on Nagasaki.

On September 2, 1945, aboard the battleship USS Missouri, in Tokyo Harbor, Japanese foreign minister Shigemitsu Mamoru, on behalf of Emperor Hirohito, unconditionally surrendered the Japanese empire to General of the Army Douglas MacArthur, the officer Truman had designated as Supreme Commander, Allied Powers.

Even before the official Japanese surrender, senior Navy and Marine officers knew—again, substantially from reports of OSS agents in China—that the civil war in China, between the Communists under Mao Tse-tung, and the Nationalists under Chiang Kai-shek, was a threat to world stability that the United States was going to have to deal with, and that the Marines would most likely be sent there to do the dealing.

Less than forty-eight hours after the surrender, a warning order was issued to the Marines—who had been gathered together in the III Amphibious Corps, and who had been training for the invasion of the Japanese home islands—to prepare to move to China.

In October 1945—a month later—Truman, by Presidential Directive, "disestablished" the Office of Strategic Services (OSS).

The joke whispered around Washington was that it was the only way Truman could see to get rid of William J. "Wild Bill" Donovan, who had headed the organization since its birth—also by Presidential Directive—in June 1942.

Donovan, who had won the Medal of Honor in France in World War I, had been a law school classmate of Franklin D. Roosevelt, and a lifelong crony. While there was little doubt that it was an effective tool of war, it—and Donovan—was cordially detested by the military establishment, and there is little doubt the very senior brass encouraged the new Commander-in-Chief, whenever they had his ear, to quickly put it out of business

Whatever the reasons, the OSS—its detractors said that OSS meant "Oh, So Social"—was "disestablished" and the vast majority of its 12,000 men and women almost instantly released to their civilian pursuits. The very small percentage of OSS personnel who were members of the "regular" military establishment were returned to the regular Marine Corps, Army, and Navy, where they were most often greeted with less than wide-open welcoming arms.

Truman, who was never reluctant to admit he'd made a mistake, had by the early months of 1946 decided he'd made one in killing off the OSS.

By then, Soviet intentions were already becoming clear, and the bureaucratic in-fighting of the newly "freed" independent intelligence services of the Army, Navy, and State Department had made it clear that the nation did indeed need a central intelligence agency, whether or not the various Princes of Intelligence liked it or not.

Truman, in yet another Presidential Directive, gave it one. He "established" the Central Intelligence Group and the National Intelligence Authority. Then, in 1947, he pushed through the Congress, a bill making it law. The Central Intelligence Agency was born. Possibly as a sop to the regular military establishment, and possibly because he was singularly qualified for the post, Rear Admiral Roscoe Hillenkoetter, USN, was named first director of the CIA.

On March 5, 1946, in a speech at Fulton, Missouri, British wartime Prime Minister Winston S. Churchill said, "From Stettin in the Baltic to Trieste in the Adriatic, an iron curtain has descended across the Continent."

That was certainly true, but it wasn't Soviet Russia's only iron curtain.

There was another one in Korea, a peninsula extending into the Yellow Sea and the Sea of Japan from the Asian continent. It had been ruled, rather brutally, by Japan since 1895.

Almost casually, when the Soviet Union finally agreed to enter the war against Japan, it was decided that the Soviets would accept the surrender of Japanese forces in the north of Korea, and the Americans in the south. The 38th parallel divided Korea, just north of Seoul, into roughly equal halves, and the 38th parallel became the demarcation line.

Immediately upon moving into "their" sector of Korea, the Soviets put in power a Korean Marxist named Kim Il Sung, and promptly turned the 38th parallel into an iron curtain just as impenetrable as the one in Europe.

The Soviet government expected that Japan would be divided as Germany had been, into four zones, each individually controlled by the Four Powers—France, England, Russia, and the United States. But that wasn't going to happen.

The English and French presence in occupied Japan was negligible. Japan and the Japanese economy were in ruins. Japan could not be levied upon to support an occupation army, because they simply didn't have the wherewithal. And the English and the French, themselves reeling from the expense of World War II, simply couldn't afford to pay for an Army of Occupation of Japan. The English were having great difficulty with India—which wanted out of the British Empire—and with the French, in what was known as Cochin-China and became known as Vietnam.

And, of course, the French and English had the expense of maintaining their armies in occupied Germany, now not so much to keep the defeated Germans in line as to prevent the Soviet Union from charging their armies through the Fulda Gap to take over continental Europe.

The British, additionally, were having a hard time supporting their forces in liberated Greece, where Communist forces—primarily Albanians supported by the Soviet Union—were trying to bring Greece into the Soviet orbit. In 1948, the British simply announced they could no longer afford to stay in Greece and were pulling out.

Truman picked up that responsibility, supplying the Greek army, and dispatching Lt. General James Van Fleet and an American military advisory group to Athens. The American anti-Communist battle in Greece—almost unknown to the American public—is considered by many to be the first "hot war" of the Cold War, and the American "advisors," many of whom fought in small groups "advising" Greek units in the lines, as the precursor of U.S. Special Forces.

The absence of British and French forces in Japan made it easier for the Supreme Commander in Japan, Douglas MacArthur—who had no doubts of Soviet intentions, and didn't want his occupation of Japan facing the same problems the Army of Occupation of Germany was facing vis-à-vis the Communists—simply to refuse to permit any Soviet presence in Japan.

The Soviets protested their being kept out of Japan to Truman, who ignored them.

Washington also ignored what was going on in Korea. The American commander, General John R. Hodge, in the absence of specific orders—in fact, any orders—from Washington, took matters into his own hands.

As early as late 1945, he began to establish, first, a South Korean police force, and then a South Korean army. To counter the Soviet surrogate, Kim Il Sung, Hodge permitted an anti-Communist Korean, Syngman Rhee, then living in exile in the United States, to return to Korea.

By 1948, the division of Korea along the 38th parallel was complete. North and South Korea each had a president, a government, and armed forces, and each proclaimed it was the sole legitimate government for the whole country.

The sole substantial difference between the two was that North Korea was far better armed—with captured Japanese and newly-furnished Soviet equipment—than South Korea. Fearing that the fiery Syngman Rhee would march against North Korea, the U.S. State Department prevailed upon Truman to deny South Korea heavy artillery, modern aircraft, and tanks, and ultimately to order all but a few hundred soldiers in a Greek-style "Korean military advisory group" out of the country.

Hostility between North and South Korea grew. In the eight months before June 1950, more than 3,000 South Korean soldiers and border policemen died in "incidents" along the 38th parallel.

On January 12, 1950, Secretary of State Dean Acheson outlined President Truman's Asian policy in a speech at the National Press Club in Washington, D.C.

Acheson "drew a line" of countries the United States considered "essential to its national interests," a euphemism everyone understood to mean the United States would go to war to defend.

Acheson placed Japan, Okinawa, and the Philippines within the American defense perimeter. Taiwan and Korea were not mentioned.

Five months later, on June 25, 1950, the North Koreans invaded across the 38th parallel.

I

[ONE]
Aboard Trans-Global Airways Flight 907
North Latitude 36 Degrees 59 Minutes, East Longitude
143 Degrees 77 Minutes
(Above the Pacific Ocean, near Japan)
1100 1 June 1950

"This is the First Officer speaking," the copilot of Trans-Global Airways Flight 907 said into the public address system microphone. "We are about to begin our descent into Tokyo's Haneda Airport, and have been advised it may get a little bumpy at lower altitudes. So please take your seats and fasten your seat belts, and very shortly we'll have you on the ground."

Trans-Global Flight 907 was a triple-tailed, five-months-old Lockheed L-1049 Constellation, christened *Los Angeles.*

The navigator, who wore pilot's wings, and who would move up to a copilot's seat when TGA accepted—next week, he hoped—what would be the eighteenth Constellation in the TGA fleet, did some calculations at his desk, then stood up and murmured, "Excuse me, sir," to the man in the jump seat.

The man in the jump seat (a fold-out seat between and immediately behind the pilot's and co-pilot's seats) looked over his shoulder at him in annoyance, finally realized what he wanted, muttered, "Sorry," and made room for the navigator to hand a sheet of paper to the copilot.

The navigator made his way back to his little desk, strapped himself in, and put on his earphones, in time to hear:

"Ladies and gentlemen, this is the first officer again. I have just been advised by our navigator—this is all subject to official confirmation, of course—that it appears that a very, very favorable tailwind in the last few hours is probably going to permit us to again set a world's record for the fastest regularly scheduled commercial flight time from San Francisco to Tokyo, with intermediate stops at Honolulu and Wake Island.

"The current speed record is held by a TGA Constellation flown by Captain M. S. Pickering, who is our captain today. If our computations are correct, and are confirmed by the appropriate authorities, TGA will be delighted to send each of you a certificate attesting to your presence aboard today. Keep your fingers crossed."

Captain M. S. Pickering turned and looked at the man in the jump seat.

"You'd better get in the back, Dad."

Fleming Pickering—a tall, large, well-tailored, silver-haired, rather handsome man who was, as he privately thought of it, *One Year Past The Big Five Zero*—nodded his acceptance of the order and moved to comply with it, although he had really hoped he would be permitted to keep the jump seat through the landing.

He wasn't wearing earphones and had not heard a word of either of the copilots' announcements.

He left the cockpit, musing that they were now starting to call it the "flight deck," and then, when he saw his seat and seatmate, musing that while there was a good deal to be said about the benefits of crossing the Pacific Ocean at 325 knots, there were certain drawbacks, high among them that if you found yourself seated beside a horse's ass when you first boarded the aircraft, you were stuck with the sonofabitch for the rest of the flight.

It was different on a ship; you could avoid people on a ship.

Had been different on a ship, he corrected himself. Passenger ships, ocean liners, were as obsolete as buggy whips. There once had been fourteen passenger ships in the Pacific & Far East fleet. Now there was one.

Pickering nodded politely at the horse's ass in the window seat, sat down beside him, and fastened his seat belt.

"Up front, were you?" the horse's ass inquired. "I didn't know they let passengers go in the cockpit."

"My son is the pilot," Pickering said.

"And I guess if you're the pilot, you can break the rules for your old man, right?"

"And I work for the airline," Pickering said.

"No kidding? What do you do?"

"I'm in administration," Pickering said.

That was not the whole truth. Trans-Global Airways was a wholly owned subsidiary of the Pacific & Far East Shipping Corporation. When the *Wall Street Journal,* in a story about Trans-Global, mentioned P&FE, it used the phrase "privately held." The Pickering family owned P&FE, and Fleming Pickering, pater familias, was chairman of the board.

"So you're on a business trip?" the horse's ass asked.

"That's right," Pickering said, smiling with an effort.

That wasn't exactly true, either.

While it *was* true that he was going to Tokyo to participate in a conference between a dozen shipping companies—both air and what now had become "surface"—serving the Far East, it was also true that he was going to spend as little time as possible actually conferring with anyone. He was instead going to spend some time with a young couple—a Marine captain and his wife—who were stationed in Tokyo. He had never told either of them, but he regarded both of them as his children, although there was no blood connection.

When Pickering had been a young man, being groomed to take over P&FE from his father, Captain Richard Pickering, his father had told him over and over the basic rule of success as a mariner or a businessman: *Find capable subordinates, give them a clear mission, and then get out of their way and let them do their jobs.*

Fleming Pickering had capable subordinates who knew what he expected of them. And—very likely, he thought, because he did not get in their way and let them do their jobs—they did their jobs very well; in his opinion, far better than their peers elsewhere in the shipping business

They would do the conferring in Tokyo, and he would not get in their way.

What had happened was, the previous Wednesday, Chairman of the Board Pickering had, as was his custom, arrived at his San Francisco office at precisely 9 A.M.

It was an impressive office, occupying the southwest quarter of the upper (tenth) story of the P&FE Building. In some ways, it was museumlike:

There were four glass cases. Two of the four held precisely crafted models of each of the ninety-one vessels of the P&FE fleet, all built to the same scale, and each about two feet in length. There were tankers, bulk-carriers, freighters, and one passenger liner.

The other two glass cases held far larger models. In one was a six-foot-long, exquisitely detailed model of the clipper ship *Pacific Princess* (Richard Pickering, Master), which had set—and still held—the San Francisco–Shanghai speed record for sailing vessels. The other glass case held a thirteen-foot-long model of the 51,000-ton SS *Pacific Princess* (Fleming Pickering, Master), a sleek passenger ship that had set—and still held—the San Francisco–Shanghai speed record on her maiden voyage in 1941.

Hanging on nearly invisible wires above the clipper's glass case was a model of a Chance Vought CORSAIR F4U fighter aircraft. It had been built by the same firm of craftsmen who had built the ship models, and, like them, was correct in every detail. The legend "MARINES" was painted in large letters on the fuselage. Below it was lettered VMF-229, and below the cockpit window was the legend "M.S. Pickering, Major, USMCR" and nine small representations of the Japanese battle flag, each signifying an enemy aircraft downed by Major Pickering.

Suspended above the glass case holding the model of the SS *Pacific Princess,* there was a model of the Trans-Global Airways Lockheed Model L049 Constellation *San Francisco,* a four-engined triple-tailed airliner, in which TGA Chief Pilot Captain Malcolm S. Pickering had set two world's records, one for fastest commercial aviation flight between San Francisco and Honolulu, and the other for fastest commercial aviation flight time between Honolulu and Shanghai. The latter record was probably going to be on the books for some time, because the Chinese Communists were now in Shanghai, and American airlines were no longer welcome to land.

Behind the chairman's huge, antique mahogany desk, the huge wheel of the clipper ship *Pacific Princess* and her quarterdeck compass stood guarding an eight-by-twelve foot map of the world

Every morning, at six A.M., just before the night operations manager went off duty, he came up from the third floor, laid a copy of the more important overnight communications—"the overnights"—on the chairman's desk, and then went to the map and moved ninety-one small ship models, on magnetic mounts, from one position to another on the map to correspond with their last reported position.

The previous Wednesday morning, at 9:01 A.M., Chairman of the Board Pickering had taken a look at the map, read the overnights, poured himself a cup of coffee, and with that out of the way was, at 9:09 A.M., where he had been the day before at 9:09 A.M., and would almost certainly be tomorrow, at 9:09 A.M.

That is to say, bored stiff and without a goddamned thing to do for the rest of the day.

Unless one counted the Second Wednesday Luncheon of the Quarterback Club of the Greater San Francisco United Charities, Inc., and he hadn't even wanted to think about that.

Captain Richard Pickering had been right on the money about that sort of thing, too. *"Flem,"* his father had counseled, *"the trouble with giving people something is that, since they get it for nothing, they tend to consider it worthless."*

Fleming Pickering had long ago painfully come to conclude that what Greater San Francisco United Charities—and at least six other do-gooding or social organizations—wanted of him was his name on the letterhead and his signature on substantial checks, and in exchange they were willing to listen politely to his suggestions at meetings, while reserving and invariably exercising their option to ignore them.

At 9:11 A.M., Mrs. Helen Florian, his secretary for more than two decades, had announced over the intercom, "Boss, Pick's on line three."

Pickering, who had been sitting with his feet on the windowsill, watching the activity—there hadn't been much—in San Francisco Bay, spun around, and grabbed the telephone.

I am, he had realized, *in one of my "Boy, do I feel sorry for Poor Ol' Flem Pickering" moods, and I don't want Pick picking up on that.*

"Good morning," he said cheerfully. "What's up?"

"Mom still in New York?" Pick asked.

"I think today's Saint Louis," Pickering replied. "You know your mother."

A picture of his wife of thirty years—a tall, shapely, silver-haired woman with startlingly blue eyes—flashed through his mind. He missed her terribly, and not only because she made him feel as if he were still twenty-one.

When Fleming Pickering had heard the sound of trumpets and rushed off to the sound of musketry in World War II, Mrs. Patricia Foster Pickering had "temporarily" taken over for her husband as chairman of the P&FE board. Surprising everybody but her husband, she had not only immediately gathered the reins of authority in her delicate fingers, but pulled on them with consummate skill and artistry.

When he'd come home, there had been some talk of the both of them working at P&FE, but Patricia had known from the start that, if their marriage was to endure, she would have to find something to do other than share the control of P&FE with her husband.

The temporary chairman of the board of P&FE had become the chairman of the board of Foster Hotels, Inc., in part because she was the only daughter of Andrew Foster, majority stockholder of the forty-two-hotel chain, and partly because her father—who had wanted to retire—had made the cold business decision that she was the best-qualified person he could find to run the company.

While Patricia Foster Pickering shared her husband's—and her father's—belief that the best way to run an organization was to select the best possible subordinates and then get out of their way, she also shared her father's belief that the best way to make sure your subordinates were doing what you wanted them to do was to *"drop in unannounced and make sure there are no dust balls under the beds and that the liquid in the liquor bottles isn't colored water."*

Which meant that she was on the road a good deal, most often from Tuesday morning until Friday evening. Which meant that her husband was most often free to rattle around—alone—in either their penthouse apartment in the Foster San Franciscan or their home on the Pacific Ocean near Carmel from Tuesday morning until Friday evening.

While he frequently reminded himself that he really had nothing to complain about—that in addition to his considerable material possessions, he had a wife who loved him, a son who loved him and of whom he was immensely proud, and his health—the truth was that every once in a while, say once a month, he slipped into one of his "Boy, do I feel sorry for Poor Ol' Flem Pickering" moods and, logic aside, he really felt sorry for Poor Ol' Flem Pickering.

"Let's go to Tokyo," Pick said.

"Why should I go to Tokyo?"

"Because your alternative is watching the waves go up and down in San Francisco Bay until Mom gets home," Pick went on. "Come on, Pop. Let her wait for you for once."

It probably makes me a terrible husband, Fleming Pickering thought, *but there would be a certain justice in having Patti rattle around the apartment waiting for me for once.*

He had another thought:

"I thought it was decided you weren't going to Tokyo," he said.

He hadn't ordered Pick not to go to the conference, but he had happened to mention what Pick's grandfather had had to say about picking competent subordinates and then getting out of their way.

"Bartram Stevens of Pacific Cathay is going to be there. Charley Ansley called me from Hong Kong last night and told me. Charley doesn't want him pulling rank and taking over the conference; he asked me to go."

Bartram Stevens was president of Pacific Cathay Airways, which was to Trans-Pacific Shipping what Trans-Global was to P&FE. J. Charles Ansley, who had been with P&FE longer than Pick was old, was general manager of Trans-Global.

Charley didn't call me. There's no reason he should have, I suppose; he was asking/telling Pick to go, and that would be Pick's decision, not mine.

But if I needed one more proof that I am now as useless as teats on a boar hog around here, voilà!

"And if I showed up over there, wouldn't that be raising the stakes?" Fleming Pickering thought aloud.

"With all possible respect, General, sir, what I had in mind—and Charley agrees—is to stash you quietly in the Imperial, but let the word get out that you're there. In case, for example, Commodore Ford just happened to be in the neighborhood."

Commodore Hiram Ford was chairman of the board of Trans-Pacific Shipping.

And that sonofabitch is entirely capable of showing up there and trying to take over the conference.

"This your idea or Charley's?"

"Mine, Pop," Pick said. "Come on! What the hell! You could see the Killer and Ernie. And I'll have you back by next Thursday."

"If you and Charley agree that I should."

"We do," Pick said, firmly.

What the hell. The alternative is watching the waves go up and down in San Francisco Bay until Patti gets home. And it'll do her good to have to wait for me for once.

"I'm with the State Department, myself," the asshole in the window seat announced.

Why doesn't that surprise me?

"Are you really?"

"I've just been assigned to General MacArthur's staff."

"That should be an interesting assignment," Pickering said, politely.

"I'm to be his advisor on psychological warfare."

"Really?"

"I'm looking forward to working with him," the asshole said. "From what I understand, he's an incredible man."

"Yes, I would say he is," Pickering agreed.

And the first thing you're going to have to learn, you simpleton, is that no one works with El Supremo, they work for him.

And the second is that the only advice Douglas MacArthur listens to is that advice which completely agrees with his positions in every minute detail.

[TWO]
Haneda Airfield
Tokyo, Japan
1155 1 June 1950

Fleming Pickering politely shook the hand of the State Department asshole in the window seat—who actually thought Douglas MacArthur would be grateful for his advice—and wished him good luck in his new assignment.

Then he walked forward to the cockpit and stood and waited while Pick went through the paperwork associated with the end of a Trans-Global flight. Then he followed Pick and the rest of the crew down the ladder pushed up to the cockpit door.

Pick waited for him at the bottom of the ladder, touched his arm, and nodded across the tarmac toward two nattily dressed military policemen who stood guard over a well-polished Douglas C-54 that bore the bar-and-star insignia of an American military aircraft, and had "Bataan" lettered on either side of its nose.

"That's MacArthur's, right?" Pick asked.

"It says 'Bataan' on the nose," Pickering replied, gently sarcastic. "I think that's a fair assumption."

"Doesn't look like there's much wrong with it, does there?" Pick asked.

"I think that's probably the best-maintained airplane in the Orient," Pickering said. "What are you driving at?"

"Just before we came over here," Pick said, "I had a call from Lockheed. The military laid a priority on them for a new 1049, to replace the war-weary C-54 of your pal MacArthur. So Lockheed's going to give him the next one off the line, which was supposed to be mine, and which I need."

"He *is* the Supreme Commander, Allied Powers," Pickering said. "And you're just a lousy civilian."

"Spoken like a true general," Pick said, with a smile.

"Yes, indeed, and why aren't you standing at attention in my presence?"

Pick laughed and waved his father ahead of him toward the door in the terminal marked CUSTOMS AIR CREWS ONLY.

Trans-Global's Tokyo station chief was waiting for them outside customs. Pickering didn't know him, but the man obviously knew who he was.

I suppose, as MacArthur is El Supremo of Japan, I am El Supremo of Pacific & Far East. But what does this guy think I'm going to do to him? Eat him alive?

"I'm Fleming Pickering," he said, offering his hand with a smile.

"Yes, sir, I know. Welcome to Tokyo. How was your flight, sir?"

"Very nice," Pickering said. "Did you get the word about how little time it took us?"

"Yes, sir," the man said. "And we should have official confirmation within the hour." He turned to Pick. "Congratulations, Captain."

"Let's hold off on that until we get confirmation," Pick said. "But thanks anyway."

"Captain, Mr. Ansley asks that you come to base operations. Apparently, there's some paperwork connected with certification. . . ."

"I figured there would be," Pick said. "Dad, there's no reason why you have to wait around here for God knows how long." He turned to the station chief. "We have wheels to take my father to the hotel, right?"

"Right outside," the station chief confirmed.

"I'll see you at the hotel," Pick said.

The wheels turned out to be a 1941 Cadillac limousine. Pickering wasn't pleased with that, but realized that saying anything to the station chief would make him sound ungrateful.

"Charley Ansley's told me what a fine job you've been doing here," Pickering said, offering his hand to the station chief.

That wasn't exactly true. It was an inference: *If this fellow wasn't doing a hell of a good job, Charley Ansley would have canned him long ago.*

"That's very kind of Mr. Ansley, sir," the station chief—whose name had never come up—replied, almost blushing with pleasure.

Pickering got into the backseat of the limousine. The station chief waited at the curb until the limousine was out of sight.

This is not the first time I've been driven from an airfield into Tokyo in a limousine. The circumstances were different the last time. The last time, Japanese soldiers and police and ordinary civilians lined the streets, bowing their heads toward the cars of their American conquerors.

I was involved in that goddamn war, literally from the first shots until the last act.

But that was a long time ago, General, and incidentally, General, you're not a general anymore.

On December 7, 1941, wakened by the sound of low-flying aircraft, Fleming Pickering had gotten out of his bed in the penthouse suite of the Foster Waikiki Beach Hotel in Honolulu and watched the Japanese attack on the Navy base at Pearl Harbor.

He had been enraged, not only at the Japanese sneak attack, but also at what he perceived to be the nearly criminal incompetence of the senior military—especially the senior Naval—officers in Hawaii, who he felt had been derelict in allowing such an attack to happen.

He had sailed that night to Seattle, Washington, aboard the *Pacific Princess*, the flagship of the Pacific & Far East fleet, which had been commandeered by the U.S. Navy and was to be converted to a troop transport. Its speed, it was theorized—and later proven—would make it immune to Japanese submarine attack.

Once in the United States, Pickering had immediately gone to Washington to volunteer for service as a Marine again. Brigadier General D. G. McInerney, USMC, with whom he had served—both of them sergeants—at Belleau Wood in France in the First World War, more or less gently told him there was no place in the Marine Corps for him, and that he could make a greater contribution to the war effort by running Pacific & Far East.

It was the second time he had been, so to speak, rejected for government service.

Before the war had involved the United States—but when he had known that war was inevitable—he had been offered "a suitable position" in the "Office of the Coordinator of Information," later renamed the Office of Strategic Services. Swallowing his intense dislike of the Coordinator of Information himself, Colonel William "Wild Bill" Donovan, he had gone to Washington for an interview and found that what Donovan had in mind was a bureaucratic post under a man for whom Pickering had a profound disgust.

Forced to admit that Mac McInerney was right—he was not qualified to be a Marine captain, much less a Marine colonel, which is what he had more than a little egotistically had in mind—Pickering had gone from McInerney's Eighth and "I" Streets office to the Foster Lafayette Hotel, across from the White House, where he was staying in the apartment of his close friend, Senator Richardson K. Fowler (R., Cal.). Once there, nursing his rejection, he had promptly crawled most of the way into a quart bottle of the senator's Famous Grouse.

When Secretary of the Navy Frank Knox had appeared unannounced in the apartment to see Senator Fowler, Pickering had lost little time in sharing with the Secretary his opinion that "the Pearl Harbor admirals" should be court-martialed and that Knox himself should resign. Almost as an afterthought, he told Knox that he would fight the Navy's intention of commandeering the entire Pacific & Far East fleet—they could have the *Pacific Princess* and the other passenger ships, but that's all—all the way to the Supreme Court.

The next day, nursing a monumental hangover as he flew back to San Francisco, he was convinced that his drunken attack on Knox—for that's unquestionably what it had been—had ended once and for all any chance of his ever again serving in uniform.

He was wrong. A few days later, Helen Florian, his secretary, had put her head in his office and announced that Secretary of the Navy Frank Knox was in her office and wanted to see him.

Pickering was convinced that it was payback time for their encounter in Senator Fowler's apartment. Knox was almost certainly going to tell him, with justified relish, that the U.S. Navy was commandeering every vessel in the P&FE fleet and the P&FE building, "for the duration," and that he was to be out of the building by five o'clock.

But that wasn't what Knox had had in mind at all.

Knox said that he suspected—human nature being what it was—that the reports he was getting—and would be getting—from the admirals in the Pacific—men with a lifelong devotion to the Navy—would understandably paint the situation to the advantage of the Navy, rather than as what it actually was.

What he had to have, Knox said, was a cold, expert appraisal of what was going on out there from someone who knew ships, and shipyards, and the Pacific, and wasn't cowed by thick rows of gold braid on admirals' sleeves.

Someone, for example, who had spent his lifetime involved with the Pacific Ocean; someone so unawed by rank and titles that he had told the Secretary of the Navy he should resign.

Within days, a hastily commissioned Captain Fleming S. Pickering, U.S. Navy Reserve, boarded a Navy plane for Hawaii, his orders identifying him as the Personal Representative of the Secretary of the Navy.

Pleased with the reports Pickering had furnished from Pearl Harbor, Knox ordered him to Australia to evaluate the harbors, shipyards, and other facilities there. He arrived shortly before General Douglas MacArthur did, having escaped—at President Roosevelt's direct order—from the Philippines to set up his headquarters in Australia.

Pickering became an unofficial member of MacArthur's staff, but by the time of the First Marine Division's invasion of Guadalcanal, was convinced that his usefulness was pretty much at an end.

Aware—and not caring—that Knox would certainly be annoyed and probably would be furious, Pickering went ashore on Guadalcanal with the Marines.
He offered his services to the First Marine Division commander, Major General A. A. Vandegrift, in any capacity where Vandegrift thought he might be useful, down to rifleman in a line company.

The First Division's intelligence officer had been killed in the first few hours
of the invasion, and Vandegrift—who had come to admire Pickering's brains
and savvy while they were planning the logistics of the invasion—named Pickering "temporarily, until a qualified replacement could be flown in from the
United States," to replace the fallen incumbent.

The day after his qualified replacement arrived, so did the U.S. Navy destroyer *Gregory,* under dual orders from the Navy Department: Deliver urgently
needed aviation fuel to the island, and do not leave Guadalcanal until Captain
Fleming Pickering, USNR, is aboard.

En route to Pearl Harbor, the *Gregory* was attacked by Japanese bombers.
Pickering was on her bridge with her captain when her captain was killed. Pickering, as senior officer of the line aboard—and an *any ocean, any tonnage* master mariner—assumed command of the destroyer, skillfully maneuvering her
until the attack was over, whereupon he passed out from loss of blood from the
wounds he had suffered when the first bomb struck.

He was flown to the Navy Hospital in San Diego, where, as he recuperated,
he decided that his wound would probably spare him from a court-martial, and
that he would quietly be released from the Navy.

He was, instead, summoned to Washington, where, on the Presidential
yacht, *Sequoia,* President Roosevelt not only gave him—at the recommendation
of the Navy's Commander-in-Chief, Pacific—the Silver Star for his valor in
"assuming, despite his grievous wounds" command of the *Gregory,* but informed
him that he had that day sent his name—at the request of Secretary Knox—to
the Senate for their advice and consent to his appointment as Brigadier General, U.S. Marine Corps Reserve. He would serve, the President told him, on
Knox's personal staff.

He soon found out what Knox had in mind for him to do.

Literally hidden in one of the "temporary" wooden buildings erected during World War I on the Washington Mall was the USMC Office of Management Analysis, even its name intended to conceal its role as the personal covert
intelligence operation of Secretary Knox.

Pickering, in addition to his other duties, was named its commander, and
in effect became director of covert intelligence operations for the Navy.

In February 1943, after General Douglas MacArthur, Supreme Commander, Southwest Pacific Ocean Area, and Admiral Chester W. Nimitz, U.S. Navy
Commander-in-Chief, Pacific, had made it abundantly clear that neither would
have anything to do with Colonel "Wild Bill" Donovan's Office of Strategic Services in their theaters of operation, President Roosevelt had solved that problem
by issuing an executive order naming Brigadier General Fleming Pickering,
USMCR, as OSS Deputy Director for the Pacific.

Although Pickering hated the appointment—before the war, he and Donovan had once almost come to blows in the lobby of New York City's Century
Club, and he was still smarting over the insultingly low-level job Donovan had
offered him before the war—Pickering had to admit it was Roosevelt at his
Machiavellian best.

Neither MacArthur nor Nimitz would—or could—protest the appointment. MacArthur had written glowingly to Roosevelt about Pickering's service
in Australia, and Nimitz had personally ordered Pickering decorated with the
Silver Star for his valor on board the destroyer sent to bring him off Guadalcanal.

Pickering had served as the OSS's Deputy Director for the Pacific—which
included, so far as the OSS was concerned, both China and India—for the rest
of the war. The last time he had been in Tokyo had been as a member—arguably
the second senior member—of the team flown into Japan to arrange the details
of the surrender. He had left Japan two weeks later, and taken off his uniform
a week after that.

[THREE]
The Dewey Suite
The Imperial Hotel
Tokyo, Japan
1430 1 June 1950

"I think we did it," Malcolm S. "Pick" Pickering said to his father as he came
through the door. "Made our time official, set another record, I mean."

"Who did this?" Pickering asked, gesturing around the huge, elegantly furnished suite.

"I hope so," Pick said, ignoring the question. "Ford *is* here. It would really
piss him off."

"Who did this?" his father repeated. "Isn't this a bit much for one man?"

"Mom did it," Pick said, just a little sheepishly. "She knows the guy who owns it—or maybe the general manager, somebody at the top—and set it up. I think he owed her a favor, or something."

And what that does is get her off the guilt hook: If Flem is with Pick, and in the best suite in the best hotel in Tokyo, then there's no reason for me to feel guilty about leaving Ol' Flem alone.

"And what time do the geisha girls arrive?"

There was the sound of a gentle chime.

"That must be them," Pick said, smiling.

It was instead a full colonel of the United States Army, in a tropical worsted uniform, from the epaulets of which hung the aiguillette of an aide-de-camp, and on the lapels of which was a shield, in the center of which were five stars in a circle, which was the lapel insignia of an aide-de-camp to a general of the Army.

There aren't that many five-stars around anywhere, and only one in Japan. This guy is El Supremo's aide.

How the hell did he know I was here?

"May I help you, Colonel?" Pickering asked.

"Sir, you're General Pickering?"

"That was a long time ago, Colonel."

"Sir, I'm Colonel Stanley. I'm an aide-de-camp to General MacArthur. . . ."

"I sort of guessed you were," Pickering said, chuckling, waving his hand at the colonel's uniform. He turned and motioned for the colonel to follow him into the suite.

"Colonel Stanley," Pickering went on, "this is my son, Captain Pickering, of Trans-Global Airways, who tells me he has reason to believe that he set a speed record today, bringing us here. We were about to have a drink to celebrate that, and I hope you'll join us."

The colonel shook Pick's hand and said it was a pleasure and offered his congratulations, "but with your permission, General, I'll pass on the drink. It's a little early."

"Relax, Colonel," Pickering said. "I won't tell El Supremo. Scotch all right?"

"Yes, sir," the colonel said. "Scotch would be fine."

Pick went behind the bar.

"Dad," he said, amused, "there's a note here. It says, 'When the services of a bartender are required, please press the button.' Do I press the button?"

"No," Pickering said, flatly. "Is there any Famous Grouse?"

"Your reputation and tastes precede you, General, sir," Pick said, and held up a bottle of Famous Grouse Scots whiskey.

"That all right with you, Colonel?"

"That would be fine, sir. Thank you," the colonel said, and then remembered his mission. He took a squarish envelope from his pocket and handed it to Pickering. "The compliments of the Supreme Commander, General."

Pickering took the envelope and opened it.

The Supreme Commander and Mrs. Douglas MacArthur Request the honor of the presence of

Brig. Gen. Fleming Pickering, USMCR

At

Lunch/Cocktails/Dinner
Whatever is my old Comrade-in-Arms' pleasure
At the Supreme Commander's Residence

At

Whenever you can find the time.
Jean and I welcome you to Japan,
my dear Fleming!!!!!
Just tell the colonel what is your pleasure.

Douglas

Dress

Pickering handed the invitation to his son, who took it, shrugged, and pursed his lips in amusement.

"Like I said, your reputation precedes you, General, sir."

"Colonel," Pickering said. "Would you be good enough to present my compliments to General MacArthur, and tell him that as soon as I know my schedule, I'll be in touch?"

"Yes, sir," the colonel said. "General, I think that the Supreme Commander had cocktails and dinner tonight in mind, sir."

"How do you know that?" Pickering asked, as if the question amused him.

"Colonel Huff mentioned it, sir."

"Good ol' Sid," Pickering replied, his tone suggesting that he didn't think of Huff that way at all. There was immediate confirmation of this: "He's still El Supremo's head dog robber, I gather?"

Colonel Stanley's face—just for a moment—showed that the question both surprised him and was one he would rather not answer directly. He took a notebook from his tunic pocket, wrote a number on it, and handed it to Pickering.

"That's Colonel Huff's private number, sir. Perhaps you could call him?"

"I didn't mean to put you on a spot, Colonel," Pickering said. "I go a long way back with Colonel Huff."

"I understand, sir," Stanley said.

He took a token sip from his drink and set it down.

"With your permission, General?" he asked.

"You don't need my permission to do anything, Colonel. It's been a long time since I was a general. And I understand you must have a busy schedule."

Stanley offered his hand to Pick.

"A pleasure to meet you, sir," he said. "And congratulations on the speed record."

"The thing to keep in mind, Colonel," Pick said, smiling, "is that my dad's bite is worse than his bark."

Stanley smiled, offered Pickering his hand, and left the suite.

Father and son exchanged glances.

"Something amuses you, Captain?" Pickering asked.

"Something awes me," Pick said. "I just realized I'm in the presence of the only man in Japan who would dare to tell Douglas MacArthur's aide that he'll see if he can fit the general into his schedule."

"I like Douglas MacArthur," Pickering said. "And Jean. And I'll see them while I'm here, but I came here to see Ernie and Ken. Now, how do we do that?"

"Something wrong with the limo? Mom set that up, too. I'm reliably informed it's one of the two 1941 Cadillac limousines in Japan. And at this moment it's parked outside waiting to take you to Ken's house."

. "You're not going with me?"

"Charley Ansley wants me to come to the Hotel Hokkaido—that's where the conference is—to make sure all the *T*s are crossed and the *I*s dotted on the certification. *Before* we rub our new speed record in Trans-Pacific's face. He said something about a press conference. I'll come out to Ken's place as soon as that's over." He paused. "Unless you want to go to the Hokkaido with me?"

Pickering considered that a moment.

"I'm not going to show up at the Killer's door in a chauffeur-driven limousine. If you've got his address, I'll take a cab."

"Great. I'll take the limo to the Hokkaido. I laid on a Ford sedan for me. You can use that."

Pickering considered that a moment, then nodded.

He had a fresh thought.

"I didn't think about bringing anything for them."

"There's a case of Famous Grouse in the trunk of the limo. You want me to have it moved to the Ford, or should I bring it when I come?"

"Put it in the Ford."

"You're going out there right now?"

"Just as soon as I shower and change my clothes."

"Pop, remember not to call him 'Killer.' "

"He doesn't mind. I'm one of the privileged few."

"Ernie minds."

"I stand corrected. And you remember to try to look humble at the press conference."

"You know what Frank Lloyd Wright said about that: 'It's hard to be humble when you're great.' "

"He is great. What you are is an aerial bus driver who caught a tailwind."

Pick smiled at his father.

"Wright designed this place, didn't he?" he asked, gesturing around the suite.

"Yes, he did."

[FOUR]
No. 7 Saku-Tun
Denenchofu, Tokyo, Japan
1705 1 June 1950

When the 1946 Ford Fordor pulled to the curb of a narrow, cobblestoned street before a stone wall bearing a wooden sign—"Corporal K.R. McCoy USMC"— the driver practically leapt from behind the wheel, dashed around the front of the car, pulled Pickering's door open, and, smiling broadly, bowed to his passenger.

Pickering smiled at him, then went to the trunk to get the case of Famous Grouse. The driver wrestled it away from him after a thirty-second tug-of-war, and Pickering went to the steel door in the fence, where he finally found a wire loop that might be a doorbell.

When he pulled on it, there was a muted jangling. Sixty seconds later, a middle-aged Japanese woman in a black kimono opened the steel door and, first bowing, looked at him curiously.

"I'd like to see either Corporal or Mrs. McCoy," Pickering said.

It was obvious that she didn't know a word of English.

"Corporal McCoy," Pickering repeated very slowly.

Then there was the sound of a female voice. It was a young voice, and speaking Japanese, probably asking a question.

Pickering took a chance. He raised his voice.

"Ernie?"

There was no reply.

"Ernie! It's Flem Pickering!"

Now the female voice spoke English.

"Oh, my God!"

A moment later a strikingly beautiful young woman, her black hair cut in a pageboy, ran through the door and threw herself into his arms.

"Uncle Flem!" she cried.

Her voice sounded broken.

Jesus, I hope that's happiness!

A moment later, over Ernie's shoulder, Pickering saw her husband. He was a well-built—but lithe, rather than muscular—even-featured, fair-skinned crew-cutted man in Marine Corps khaki shirt and trousers.

"How are you, Ken?" Pickering asked, getting free of Ernie to offer him his hand.

"You're the last person in the world I expected to see, General," McCoy said.

" 'General' was a long time ago, Ken," Pickering said.

There's something wrong here. What did I do, walk into the middle of a family squabble?

"Did I drop in uninvited at an awkward time?"

"Don't be silly, Uncle Flem," Ernie said. "Come on in the house."

"It's just that . . . you're the last person in the world I expected to see," McCoy repeated.

"Pick'll be along in a while," Pickering said. "He just set another speed record getting us here, and he and Charley Ansley are in the process of making it official."

"Great!" McCoy said.

His enthusiasm and his smile seemed strained.

That's strange. You usually never know what he's thinking.

That's the mark—not being able to tell what they're thinking—of good poker players and intelligence officers. And Ken McCoy is both.

What did Ed Banning say that day in Washington?

"It's as if he was born to be an intelligence officer."

Obviously that doesn't apply to poker players or intelligence officers when they're fighting with their wives.

Well, what the hell, married people fight. This is just another example of your lousy timing, showing up in the middle of one.

Ernestine Sage McCoy was the closest thing Fleming Pickering had to a daughter. Her mother and Patricia Foster Fleming had been roommates at Sarah Lawrence. He had literally walked the floor of the hospital with Ernie's father the night she was born.

Although he had never put it into words, Pickering thought of Kenneth R. McCoy as a second son, and he was sure that Pick thought of Ken as his brother. Patricia Fleming *liked* Ken, but she was never quite able to forgive him for marrying Ernie. Elaine Sage, Ernie's mother and Patricia had decided, when both of their children were still in diapers, that Ernie and Pick would—should—marry.

But Pick had met Ken in Marine Corps Officer Candidate School, and become buddies, and then Pick had introduced his buddy to Ernie, and that had blown the idea of Ernie marrying Pick out of the water.

Fleming Pickering had inherited newly promoted First Lieutenant Kenneth R. McCoy when he had been given command of the U.S. Marine Corps Office of Management Analysis.

And quickly learned far more about him than Pick had ever told him, probably because Pick had decided the less said about Ken's background the better.

Ernie had almost immediately announced on meeting Ken that she had met the man with whom she intended to spend the rest of her life, a declaration that had done the opposite of delighting her parents, and Patricia Fleming.

For one thing, he had neither a college education nor any money. That was enough to make the Pages uncomfortable. Learning that "Killer" McCoy was something of a legend in the Marine Corps, and why, would only make things worse.

Brigadier General Pickering had gotten most of the details of Lieutenant McCoy's background from another officer assigned to the Office of Management Analysis, then Major Ed Banning, who was himself something of a legend in the Marine Corps.

Pickering had gotten the details of Banning's exploits first: He had been the 4th Marine Regiment's intelligence officer in Shanghai and gone with it to the Philippines, where he had been temporarily blinded in action against the Japanese. He—and a dozen other blinded men and officers—had been evacuated from the island fortress of Corregidor in Manila Harbor just before Corregidor fell.

When his sight returned, Banning had, perhaps predictably, been assigned to the Office of Management Analysis, where he immediately set about looking for Lieutenant McCoy to have him assigned to the intelligence unit.

He had found Second Lieutenant McCoy in the Naval Hospital at Pearl Harbor, recovering from wounds suffered with the Marine Raiders during their daring attack on Makin Island.

It had taken some doing to pry the details of McCoy's background from Banning, who felt—and said—that they should be allowed to remain obscure. But finally Pickering had gotten Banning to open up.

Then Captain Banning had met then-Corporal K. R. McCoy in Shanghai. He had been appointed "in addition to his other duties" to serve as defense counsel for the accused in the court-martial case of *The United States vs. Corporal K. R. McCoy, USMC.*

There were several charges, with murder heading the list.

As the case was explained to Captain Banning, a tough little corporal in one of the line companies had knifed an Italian Marine to death, and damned near killed two other Eye-Tie so-called Marines in the same fight.

It never was said in so many words, of course, but what would be clearly in the interests of the Marine Corps would be to sweep the international incident as quickly as possible under the diplomatic rug. To that end, if Banning could get the troublemaking corporal to plead guilty to the lesser charge of manslaughter, the colonel, "on review" would reduce whatever the sentence was to a relatively mild five to ten years in the Portsmouth Naval Prison; he could be out of prison in two, maybe three years.

Before actually going to see McCoy, Banning first went over the official reports of the incident and the evidence. There was no question at all that one Italian Marine had died of knife wounds, and that McCoy had wielded the knife. Then he went over McCoy's records. He learned that McCoy had enlisted in the Corps at seventeen, immediately after graduating from high school in a Philadelphia industrial suburb. He hadn't been in trouble previously, and had in fact made corporal in a remarkably short time, before his first enlistment was over. Normally, it took six to eight years—sometimes even longer—to make corporal.

Finally, Banning had gone to see Corporal McCoy in the brig, and had seen that McCoy was indeed a tough little streetwise character. And smart, but not smart enough to realize the serious trouble he was in.

A conviction for murder would see him sent to Portsmouth for twenty years to life.

McCoy, making it obvious that he trusted Banning not quite as far as he could throw the six-foot, 200-pound officer, his tone bordering on the offense known as "silent insolence," had rejected the offer.

"No, thank you, sir, don't try to make a deal for me for a light sentence, sir. With respect, sir, it was self-defense, sir, and I'll take my chances at the court-martial, sir."

Banning admitted to Pickering that he had managed only with an effort not to lose his temper with the insolent young corporal.

"But it wasn't stupidity, General," Banning said, now smiling about the incident. "McCoy was a step—a couple of steps—ahead of me."

"How so?" Pickering had asked.

"When I got back to my office, there was a message asking me to call Captain Bruce Fairbairn. Does the general know who I mean?"

"The English Captain Fairbairn? The head of the Shanghai Police?"

Banning nodded.

"And the inventor of scientific knife-fighting," Banning said. "And the Fairbairn knife. Does that ring a bell, General?"

"I've had drinks and dinner with Fairbairn several times in Shanghai, and I've heard of his knives, of course, everyone has, but I've never seen one."

"The third one I had ever seen I had seen that morning," Banning said, with a smile. "When examining the evidence against Corporal McCoy."

Pickering had thought: *Now that he understands that he has no choice but to tell me all about Killer McCoy, he seems to be enjoying it.*

"I didn't want to believe it was a Fairbairn," Banning went on. "Fairbairn didn't sell his knifes. He issued them to his policemen, and only after they had gone through his knife-fighting course. When I saw the knife McCoy had used on the Italian, I decided, on the very long shot that it was a Fairbairn, that McCoy had stolen it somewhere."

"And he hadn't?"

"When I called Fairbairn, he very politely said that he thought he should tell me that if the Marines persisted with the foolish notion of court-martialing McCoy, three of his policemen were prepared to testify under oath that they had seen the whole incident, and that McCoy had done nothing more than defend himself."

"Why hadn't they come forward earlier?"

"Fairbairn—the Brits can be marvelously indirect—said that his policemen 'were prepared to testify under oath' that they had seen the incident. . . ."

"Which is not the same thing as saying they had seen it?"

"Yes, sir."

"Well, was it self-defense or not?"

"McCoy—later, when I had come to know him well—told me it was self-defense. I believe him."

" 'Had come to know him well'?" Pickering quoted.

"I went to the colonel and told him that not only had McCoy refused to plead guilty, but also that Fairbairn's police were going to testify for him. Under those circumstances, there was no way the incident could be swept under the rug."

"So there was no court-martial?"

"No court-martial. McCoy even got his knife back."

"Was it a Fairbairn?"

"It was, and he'd gotten it the same way Fairbairn's police got theirs, by proving he knew how to use it."

"How did he get to know Fairbairn?"

"There was a high-stakes poker game every Friday night at the Metropol Hotel."

"He was only a corporal," Pickering said. "Major, I used to be a corporal. I never played poker with officers."

"McCoy was a very unusual corporal," Banning said, smiling, "as I quickly found out when he was assigned to me."

"Assigned to you?"

"The colonel took pains to make it clear that there had better not be another incident involving Corporal Killer McCoy."

"That's why they called him 'Killer'? Because he killed the Italian?"

"That was the beginning of it, I suppose, but it really stuck on him after he wiped out, practically by himself, a reinforced platoon of Chinese 'bandits' working for the Kempae Tai." The Japanese secret police. "There were twenty bodies in that 'incident.' "

"How did that happen?"

"When he reported to me—and he didn't like that; he liked being in the weapons company, where he planned to be a sergeant before his second hitch was up—I told him frankly that all I expected of him was to stay out of trouble until I could figure out something to do with him. He was obviously, I told him, not going to be of much use to me. I was the intelligence officer, and someone who didn't speak Chinese or Japanese obviously couldn't be of much use."

"And he spoke some Chinese?"

"He told me he could read and write Cantonese and Mandarin, plus Japanese, plus French and German and even some Russian, but was having trouble with the Cyrillic alphabet."

"And could he?"

"Natural flair for languages. Maybe natural is not the right word. *Supernatural* flair, maybe. *Eerie* flair."

"So you put him to work?"

"I had to do so without letting the colonel know," Banning said. "So what I did was send him on the regular truck convoys we ran between Shanghai and Peking, and other places. They took anywhere from five days to a couple of weeks. McCoy would disappear from the convoy for a few hours—or a few days—and have a look at what the Japs were up to. God, he was good at it!"

"And the Chinese 'bandit' incident?"

"The Kempae Tai would hire Chinese bandits to attack us whenever they thought they could get away with it. They particularly liked to attack the convoys. The Japs paid them, and what was on the trucks was theirs. They made the mistake of attacking one that McCoy was on. He and a buck sergeant named Zimmerman were waiting for them with Thompsons. And they were very good with Thompsons. The 'bandits' left twenty bodies behind them. McCoy and Zimmerman loaded them on trucks and took them to Peking. That, sir, is where 'Killer' got his name."

Pickering had not yet told Banning that Lieutenants Pickering and McCoy were friends, but he had Pick in his mind as Banning spoke of Killer McCoy.

It meant, of course, that when Malcolm S. Pickering had been in his first year at Harvard, starting to work his way through the pro forma resistance to copulation of the nubile maidens of Wellesley, Sarah Lawrence, and other institutions of higher learning for the female offspring of the moneyed classes, McCoy had been a Marine in China; that when Pick had been earning a four-goal handicap on the polo fields at Ramapo Valley, Palm Beach, and Los Angeles, McCoy had been riding Mongolian ponies through the China countryside keeping an eye on the Imperial Japanese Army at a considerable risk to his life.

"How did he get to become an officer?"

"The Corps put out the word to recommend NCOs for Officer Candidate School. I thought McCoy would make a fine officer. The colonel saw sending him to the States as a good way to get him out of Shanghai. I think I was the only officer in the Marine Corps who thought he would get through officer training."

"He had some trouble getting through," Pickering said. "With some officers who didn't think a corporal with no college degree should become a Marine officer."

"How do—?" Banning blurted, and stopped.

" 'How the hell do you know that'?" Pickering finished the uncompleted question. "My son was in his class; they became quite close. They are quite close."

"Well, he got through," Banning said.

"And then he volunteered for the Marine Raiders?" Pickering asked, but it was more of a statement than a question. He knew that McCoy had been a Raider.

"Yes, sir. But not quite the way that sounds."

"I don't understand. . . ."

"McCoy's language skills—and his China service—came to the attention of the G-2," Banning said. "He decided McCoy was just the man he was looking for."

"As an interpreter, you mean?"

"No, sir. To keep an eye on Colonel Evans Carlson, the commander of the Marine Raiders."

"Now, that I don't understand," Pickering said.

"There were a number of officers in the Marine Corps who thought that Carlson had dangerous ideas," Banning said. "And some who suspected he was a Communist."

"My God!"

"So the G-2 called McCoy in and asked him to take that assignment."

"I knew McCoy was in the Raiders," Banning said. "But I didn't know about this."

"He came back from the Makin Raid—where he was hit, by the way—and reported that Colonel Carson was not a Communist. And then I found him in the hospital in San Diego and had him transferred here. He was hoping to stay with the Raiders, but he belongs here."

"Yes, I'm sure he does," Pickering replied.

"It's . . . as if he was born to be an intelligence officer," Banning said.

"It sounds that way, doesn't it?" Pickering had agreed.

II

Ernestine Sage McCoy spoke to the woman who had come to the door in the wall—in what sounded to Pickering like fluent Japanese—and very quickly, before McCoy had finished making Pickering a drink, a plate of hors d'oeuvres appeared.

"Welcome to our home, General," McCoy said, touching his glass to Pickering's.

"General is a long time ago, Ken," Pickering said. "What I am now is a figurehead. You know what a figurehead is? The wooden-headed figure on the bow of a ship?"

There was dutiful laughter.

Not only dutiful, but strained.

Neither one of them is in a laughing mood.

Christ, I must have walked in here just before she was going to throw a frying pan at him. I wonder what the hell he did?

Or what she did?

Pickering relayed the love of his wife, and told her that Patricia, the last time he heard, had been going to have dinner with her father and mother in New York, and Ernie said to give Patricia their love when he got home.

"How long are you going to stay in Japan, General?" Ken McCoy asked.

"Three or four days, no more."

This was followed by a painful silence.

Pickering searched his mind for something to say, and found it:

"I thought I'd look around," he said, and added, "The last time I was here, I arrived five days before the war was over."

"I remember," McCoy said.

"Five days *before* the war was over?"

"Right."

"I never heard that story," Ernie said.

"You said," McCoy said, and for the first time there was a suggestion of a smile on his face, "that it was the first time El Supremo ever asked for an OSS intel report."

"First and only," Pickering said.

"Tell me about it," Ernie said.

At least it will break the silence.

"Major McCoy and I were on Okinawa," Pickering began.

And the first word out of your mouth is a disaster, reminding him, reminding them, that he was busted back to captain after the war.

". . . and Sid Huff . . ."

"Who?"

"MacArthur's aide."

"He still is," Ernie said.

"So I heard," Pickering said. "Anyway, Sid showed up on Okinawa, from Manila, where El Supremo was at the time. He announced that MacArthur wanted me to go in on the first plane. Of course, he couldn't phrase it that simply. . . ."

" 'General,' " McCoy said, accurately mimicking Huff's somewhat pompous manner of speech, " 'it is the Supreme Commander's desire that you proceed to Tokyo with the initial party . . .' "

"Very good, Ken," Pickering said, chuckling.

"What happened, sweetheart," McCoy said, "is that El Supremo originally intended to send Huff, but changed his mind at the last minute and told him to ask the Boss here . . ."

Sweetheart? That means he's in the doghouse. I wonder what he did. Or she thinks he did.

"Darling, let him tell the story."

"Darling"? That doesn't sound like a grossly annoyed wife.

"He won't tell all of it, baby," McCoy said. "Huff couldn't make up his mind whether he was unhappy at being denied the chance to be on the first plane to land in Japan, or happy. There was a lot of talk that the Japs were out of control, and the first Americans to land might get their heads chopped off. In that case, Huff figured better that the Boss's head roll . . ."

Sweetheart? Darling? Baby? These two aren't fighting, at least with each other. What the hell is going on?

"I will give Colonel Huff the benefit of the doubt that he was disappointed at being denied the chance to be on that C-46," Pickering said.

"What's a C-46?"

"Curtiss Commando. Two-engine transport," McCoy replied.

"But what C-46?"

"I don't remember the date, exactly, but it was after we dropped the second atomic bomb, and the Emperor decided to surrender, August fifteenth, 'forty-five, I think."

"15 August 1945," McCoy confirmed.

"My husband remembers every date he's ever heard, except two," Ernie said, smiling at McCoy. "Our anniversary and my birthday."

Whatever he did, he's apparently forgiven.

"So on the twenty-sixth, I remember that date, it had been decided to send in one airplane, to Atsugi, on the twenty-eighth, to get the lay of the land," Pickering went on. "I thought about going, but decided against it. There were better-qualified people than me who should have gone."

" 'General, it is the Supreme Commander's desire that you proceed to Tokyo with the initial party . . .' " McCoy parroted again.

"So I went," Pickering said. "We left Okinawa at oh dark hundred . . ."

"Oh four hundred," McCoy corrected.

"And flew into Atsugui, where the Japs met us with bowed heads."

"I would have guessed there was a fifty-fifty chance that something would happen," McCoy said.

"Proving, of course, that K. McCoy, the perfect intelligence officer, has in fact made a bad guess at least once," Pickering said, chuckling. "Absolutely nothing happened. I got in a car—an old English limousine, not a Rolls, something else—and a Jap drove me to the Imperial Hotel, where I reserved a wing for Major McCoy and other deserving OSS types, soon to arrive from Okinawa. . . ."

McCoy and his wife exchanged glances.

What the hell did I say to cause that?

What the hell is going on?

To hell with it. All they can do is tell me to butt out!

"Will somebody please tell me what's going on here? What's wrong?"

"Sir?" McCoy asked.

Too innocently.

Pickering looked at Ernie. She looked close to tears.

"What's up, honey?" Pickering asked, gently.

She looked between Pickering and her husband for a moment.

"They're throwing us out of the goddamned Corps, Uncle Flem," she said. "That's what's up."

I can't have heard that right.

"I didn't get that, honey," he said.

"They're throwing us out of the goddamned Marine Corps," Ernie said, clearly. "We're being shipped home. They're taking Ken's commission."

"What the hell happened?" Pickering asked.

"He wrote a report that nobody liked," she said. "And refused to change it."

"A report on what?"

"He won't tell me," she said. "But I know it's about Korea."

Pickering looked at McCoy.

"They're throwing you out of the Marine Corps? You're not talking about a court-martial?"

"I'm talking about a TWX from Eighth and Eye," Ernie said.

A TWX was a teletype message. Eighth & Eye meant Headquarters, United States Marine Corps, which is at Eighth and I Streets in Washington, D.C.

"A TWX saying what?" Pickering asked.

" 'You are relieved of your present duties and reassigned to Camp Pendleton, California, effective immediately. You are being involuntarily released from active duty as captain, USMCR, effective 1 July 1950, and are advised that an evaluation of your records is under way to determine in which enlisted grade you may elect to enlist, if that is your desire, following your separation. I have the goddamned thing committed to memory."

"This is hard to believe," Pickering said.

"Isn't it?" she said, bitterly.

"I shouldn't have to say this," Pickering said, "but whatever I can do to help, I'll do."

He said it first to Ernie, then looked at McCoy. McCoy looked at him, but it was impossible to read what the look meant.

Then McCoy got out of his chair and walked out of the room.

"He doesn't like it that I told you," Ernie said.

"Hey! I'm glad you did. You're family, Ernie. You and Ken."

She smiled wanly at him.

McCoy returned a moment later, carrying a leather briefcase. A handcuff on a steel cable hung down from it.

I haven't seen one of those in a long time.

What the hell is the matter with the goddamned Marine Corps? Ken McCoy is the best intelligence officer I ever met, and that includes Ed Banning.

McCoy set the briefcase down on the coffee table before the couch on which Pickering was sitting, worked the combination lock, and took from it a half-inch-thick stack of paper fastened together with a metal clip. He handed it to Pickering.

The document was covered with a sheet of manila board on which were printed three diagonal red stripes at either end of the words TOP SECRET.

"What's this?" Pickering asked, as he started to flip through it.

The second page, which had TOP SECRET printed at the top and bottom, answered his question:

TOP SECRET

Document No. NE/May50/2333   Copy *3* of *4*
Duplication Forbidden

**Naval Element
Headquarters
The Supreme Commander for Allied Powers
Room 2022 The Dai Ichi Building, Tokyo, Japan**

(APO 901/FPO 3347, San Francisco, Cal.)

23 May 1950

SUBJECT: Intelligence Evaluation/Korea

TO: The Supreme Commander, Allied Powers

ATTN: Major General Charles A. Willoughby

1. Forwarded herewith is "An Evaluation Of Probable Hostile Action Within Ninety Days Against the Republic of South Korea by the People's Democratic Republic of Korea".

2. The Evaluation, and Attachments I through VII, were prepared primarily by Captain Kenneth R. McCoy, USMCR, of Naval Element, Hq, SCAP.

Edward C. Wilkerson
Edward C. Wilkerson
Captain, USN
Chief, Naval Element SCAP

One (1) Enclosure as follows:

Evaluation, Subject as above, w/attachments:
I: Summary, Agents' Reports
II: North Korean Order of Battle (Including Strength),
Infantry Units
III: NKOB(IS), Artillery Units
IV: NKOB(IS), Armored Units
V: NKOB(IS) Motor Transport
VI: NKOB (IS) Aviation Units
VII NKOB Depots, POL, Ammunition
VIII:NKOB: Logistic facilities (Rations, Medical, POW
Compounds, Misc.)
IX: Chinese Communist Order of Battle (Including
Strength) Infantry Units Within 300 miles of North
Korean Border
X: ChiComOB Artillery Units Within 300 miles of NK
Border
XI: ChiComOB Armored Units Within 300 miles of NK
Border
XII: ChiComOB Motor Transport Within 300 miles of NK
Border
XIII: ChiComOB Aviation Units Within 300 miles of NK
Border
XIV: ChiComOB Logistic facilities (Rations, Medical,
POW Compounds, Misc.) Within 300 miles of NK Border

TOP   SECRET

"Jesus Christ!" Pickering said when he'd read the transmittal letter. "Are you sure, Ken?"

"About as sure as I can get, General."

"Is that the report?" Ernie asked. "Do I get to see it?"

"No, baby. Sorry. It's classified Top Secret."

"Ken, I haven't had a Top Secret clearance—any clearance—in years. Why are you showing this to me?"

"Maybe you can do something with it," McCoy said.

"I don't understand," Pickering said. "I don't understand any of this. 'Do something with it'?"

"I can't get it past Willoughby," McCoy said, simply. "Which means it won't get out the Dai Ichi Building, and somebody at Eighth and Eye should know what's coming down."

Major General Charles A. Willoughby, who had been General Douglas A. MacArthur's intelligence officer in the Philippines and throughout World War II, was now performing the same function for him in the grandly named Office of the Supreme Commander Allied Powers, which was really the Army of Occupation in Japan.

Pickering had had more that one run-in with General Willoughby during the Second War; several of them had involved McCoy.

That sonofabitch again!

"He give you any reason, Ken?" Pickering asked, but before McCoy could reply, he asked, "Where did you get this?"

"I stole it," McCoy said, simply.

"And what's going to happen to you when it turns up missing? My God, Ken, you just can't make off with Top Secret documents!"

"You can if the document doesn't exist. That one doesn't. There's no longer a record of it."

"Let me get this straight," Pickering said. "You prepared this evaluation?"

"Yes, sir."

"On your own, or officially?"

"The Korean part officially. The Chinese part on my own."

"And you submitted it to this Captain Wilkerson?"

"And he sent it up to Willoughby. And the next day Wilkerson called me in and told me (a) I was relieved; (b) the evaluation didn't exist; (c) I should start packing."

"Why?"

"I can only guess," McCoy said.

"Guess."

"Remember when there was no possibility of guerrillas in the Philippines?" McCoy asked.

It had been the official position of the Supreme Commander, Southwest Pacific Ocean Areas—MacArthur—that it was absolutely impossible for any American guerrillas to function in the Japanese-occupied Philippine Islands.

"Before you went ashore on Mindanao and established contact with General Fertig, you mean?"

They were both smiling.

Goddamn it, why are we smiling? If that's what's going on, it isn't funny.

"I think it's entirely possible that Willoughby has just assured El Supremo that there is absolutely no risk of trouble in Korea," McCoy said. "And doesn't want his opinion challenged by a captain. I can't think of any other reason. . . ."

"But what if you're right?"

"The evaluation doesn't exist. The worst scenario for him is to say he was completely surprised by what happened, and strongly hint that he was let down by incompetent junior intelligence officers."

"But your evaluation . . ."

"Doesn't exist," McCoy said.

Pickering looked at his watch.

"Pick's liable to walk in any minute," he said. "We can't let him know about this."

"Why not?" McCoy asked.

"You'll show it to Pick and not to Ernie?" Pickering challenged.

McCoy went to Pickering, took the report, and handed it to his wife.

She had just begun to read it when the bells tinkled.

"You go," Ernie ordered. "I'm reading this."

Pick Pickering came into the room a moment later.

He and McCoy embraced.

"You may now call me 'Speedy' Pickering," Pick said. "It's official."

Pickering handed him the sheet of notebook paper on which Colonel Stanley had written Colonel Huff's private telephone number.

"Call Colonel Huff, identify yourself as Captain Pickering, calling for me— for General Pickering—and say that I would be honored if General and Mrs. MacArthur would join me for cocktails and dinner at the Imperial—"

"Boss, El Supremo never goes to the Imperial," McCoy interrupted. "Or anywhere else, either, really."

"So I read in *Time*," Pickering said. "Make the call, Pick."

"What the hell is going on?" Pick asked.

"Make the call, and then we'll bring you up to speed," Pickering said. "But for a quick answer, it seems like old times."

[TWO]
No. 7 Saku-Tun
Denenchofu, Tokyo, Japan
1805 1 June 1950

The Japanese housekeeper came into the room and said something in Japanese to Ernie Sage McCoy.

"Colonel Huff for you, Captain Pickering," Ernie translated. "There's an extension by Ken's chair."

"Huff is calling to say that Supreme Commander and Mrs. MacArthur would much prefer that you come to the Embassy," Ken McCoy said.

"Probably," Fleming Pickering said, with a smile. He followed Pick to the telephone on the table beside Ken McCoy's armchair.

Pick picked up the telephone.

"Captain Pickering," he said.

He held the phone away from his ear so that his father could overhear the conversation.

"This is Colonel Huff, Captain."

"How are you, Colonel?"

"Captain, I relayed General Pickering's invitation to the Supreme Commander. He asked me to get word to General Pickering that he and Mrs. MacArthur would much prefer that the general come to the Supreme Commander's quarters for cocktails and dinner. Is that going to pose a problem for the General?"

"I'll have to ask him, Colonel. Would you please hold?"

It was not the reply Colonel Huff had expected. This was clear in his voice as he said, "Of course."

Pick covered the microphone with his hand, then whispered, "How long are we going to make him wait?"

"Sixty seconds," Fleming Pickering said, with a smile. "Sixty seconds is a very long time when you're hanging on a phone."

Pick put the telephone on his shoulder, holding it in place with his chin, and then pushed the button on his aviator's chronometer that caused the sweep second hand to start moving.

Sixty seconds seemed like a long time. Ernie Sage McCoy shook her head and smiled at her husband.

Finally Pick took the telephone from his shoulder.

"That will be fine, Colonel. What time would General MacArthur like my father to be there?"

"The Supreme Commander's limousine will be at the Hotel Imperial at 1900. Would that be convenient?"

Fleming Pickering touched Pick's arm and shook his head, "no."

"Dad's not at the Imperial, Colonel."

"Oh?"

It was obviously a request for information. Pickering shook his head "no" again.

"And he has a car," Pick said. "I'm sure he would prefer to have it with him. I don't know what his schedule is after dinner, but I'm sure there will be something."

"The Embassy at 1930, then," Huff said. There was a tone of annoyance, slight but unmistakable, in his voice. "Would that be convenient?"

"If something comes up, Colonel, I'll call. But I feel sure Dad can meet that schedule."

"Thank you very much, Captain."

"Not at all, Colonel."

Pick hung the phone up.

"How'd I do?"

"You annoyed Huff. There will be a reward in heaven," Pickering said.

Ernie Sage McCoy, smiling, shook her head again.

The maid reappeared almost immediately, and delivered another message in Japanese.

"Another call for Captain Pickering," Ernie translated.

"I'll bet I know who that is, Ken," Fleming Pickering said, and when he had McCoy's attention, went on in a credible mockery of General Charles Willoughby's pronounced German accent: " 'Ven der Supreme Commander says he vill send hiss limousine, Cheneral Pickering *vill* ride in der limousine, or I vill haf him shot!' "

McCoy chuckled.

Pick picked up the telephone.

"Captain Pickering," he said, then: "Oh, hello, Uncle Charley. What's up?"

There was a pause.

"Oh, hell, I thought you forgot about that. And there's no way I can get out of it?"

Another pause.

"Okay. I'll be right there. But see how short you can make it, okay? I want to have dinner with the guy who married my childhood sweetheart."

He chuckled and hung up.

"Charley Ansley says 'Hi, Ernie,' " he said.

"And?" Ernie said.

"There's going to be a press conference, and the entire future of Trans-Global Airways depends on my being there."

"Why don't you take Ken and Ernie with you," Fleming Pickering said. "And then out to dinner."

He could tell from McCoy's face that he didn't want to go. And from Ernie's that she did.

"Honey?" she asked.

"Sure, why not?" McCoy said.

[THREE]
The Residence of the Supreme Commander, Allied
Powers
Tokyo, Japan
1930 1 June 1950

The two impeccably turned-out Army military policemen at the gate to what had been the U.S. Embassy compound and was now the residence of the Supreme Commander, Allied Powers, who had been at Parade Rest—standing stiffly erect, with the hands folded on the small of the back—came, very precisely and very slowly, to attention and very slowly raised their hands in salute as the 1941 Cadillac limousine approached the gate.

They held the salute until the gate opened and the limousine passed through, before very slowly bringing their rigid hands down from the forward lip of their chromed steel helmets and returning to Parade Rest.

The motions were artificial, more like ballet movements than a military gesture—

Like, the passenger of the limousine thought, somewhat unkindly, *like those clowns standing in front of Buckingham Palace in those comic opera bearskin hats.*

What's that all about? Does El Supremo think he's the Mikado? They already have an emperor of Japan, I just drove past his palace.

Yeah, but the truth of the matter is, that ridiculous emperor doesn't have any power, and this one, El Supremo, does.

He is the Supreme Commander, Allied Powers.

He sends for the Emperor—I saw that in the newspaper—and the Emperor comes. Jesus Christ, Douglas MacArthur is the king of Japan.

Watch your temper, Fleming Pickering!
You're here to help Killer McCoy, not to tell El Supremo what a pompous ass he is.

There were a second matched set of MPs standing at either side of the door of what had been the U.S. Ambassador's residence, and they, too, repeated the slow-motion salute as the limousine pulled up before the building and an officer—a major in the regalia of an aide-de-camp—came quickly down the shallow flight of steps.

He pulled the passenger door open and stood at attention.

"Good evening, General Pickering," he said. "The Supreme Commander expects you, sir. If you'll be good enough to come with me?"

"Thank you," Pickering said, got out of the limousine, and walked into the residence ahead of the major.

Colonel Stanley, who had come to the Imperial Hotel, was waiting for Pickering in the main corridor of the building.

"Good evening, General," he said, offering his hand. "The Supreme Commander and Mrs. MacArthur are in the library."

"Hello, Colonel," Pickering said.

Stanley pushed open double doors, stepped into the center of the opening, and announced:

"Brigadier General Pickering, U.S.M.C.!"

The only thing missing is four clowns in purple tights blowing trumpets with flags on them.

A white-jacketed steward—obviously a Filipino, but not the Philippine Scouts Master Sergeant Pickering remembered as MacArthur's personal servant—stood almost at attention before a sideboard on which bottles, glasses, and silver bowls of ice, lemons, and maraschino cherries were laid out.

MacArthur stood with his wife and three officers at the far end of a long, rather narrow table on which sat a silver-flowered bowl. Pickering knew two of the three officers, Major General Charles A. Willoughby and Colonel Sidney Huff. The third officer, a stocky, somewhat pale-faced major general, he had never seen before.

He missed and looked for Lieutenant General Richard Sutherland, who had been MacArthur's chief of staff throughout World War II, until he remembered reading that Sutherland had been returned home for unspecified reasons of health.

Sutherland, Willoughby, and Huff—and their underlings—had been "The Bataan Gang," MacArthur's intimate circle.

If that two-star is here, with the Bataan Gang, he must be Sutherland's replacement.

"Fleming, my friend," MacArthur called in his sonorous voice. "How wonderful to see you!"

Pickering walked along the table toward him.

"It's good to see you, General," he said, offering his hand.

Jean MacArthur stepped close, offering her hand and then her cheek.

"Jean, you look wonderful," Pickering said, as he kissed her cheek.

"General," Willoughby said. He was a large, imposing, erect man.

"General" came out "Cheneral." *I wonder if Ol' Charley knew that, behind his back, he had been known—and probably still is—as "Adolf" and "Der Führer."*

"General," Pickering replied, then turned to Colonel Huff.

"Good to see you, Sid," he said. "How are you?"

"General," Huff said. His smile was strained.

"And you don't know General Almond," MacArthur said. "Ned took Dick Sutherland's place as chief of staff."

Almond offered his hand.

"I've heard a good deal about you, General," he said.

"If you've heard it from these two," Pickering said, indicating Huff and Willoughby, "then I deny everything."

Jean MacArthur laughed. MacArthur smiled, and so did Huff and Willoughby, but for them it was visibly an effort.

A photographer, a middle-aged master sergeant, appeared, holding a Speed Graphic camera.

The subjects of the photography were posed in three different positions: all the officers standing together, with MacArthur and Pickering in the middle; MacArthur and Pickering standing together; and MacArthur, Mrs. MacArthur, and Pickering with Mrs. MacArthur in the middle.

The photographer left and the Filipino steward served drinks. Pickering was not offered a choice, but when he sipped at his whiskey and water the taste was familiar.

Somewhere, obviously, it has been filed away that Pickering, Fleming BG, USMCR, likes Famous Grouse whiskey.

"Old times, my dear Fleming," MacArthur said, raising his glass.

"Old times, General," Pickering repeated.

"I was just telling Almond," MacArthur said, "that you were in Australia when, having been ordered from Corregidor, Jean and I and the others arrived."

"I remember it well," Pickering said.

"What I remember was that you were a Navy captain," Jean MacArthur said, "who I remembered as a friend, as a merchant marine captain in Manila. And then you went to the Guadalcanal invasion, and the next time I saw you, you were a Marine general officer. I never quite understood that."

"Either did I, Jean," Pickering said. "There were a lot of us who received commissions in the services for which we were clearly not qualified."

"Now, that's simply not true," MacArthur said. "You were a splendid officer. Your contributions, not only to my campaigns, but to the entire war effort in the Pacific, prove that beyond any question."

He turned to General Almond.

"General Pickering was not only deeply involved in the planning of my invasion of Guadalcanal, but went ashore with the first wave of Marines to make that landing . . ."

That's not true.

I was involved in the planning, but only because I knew shipping and the practical knowledge of the subject on the part of most of the logisticians involved—Army, Navy, and Marine Corps—was practically nonexistent.

And I was not in the first wave of Marines to land on Guadalcanal, or the second, or the third. I didn't go ashore until I heard that the MCCAWLEY *was about to sail away, leaving the Marines on the beach, and I realized that I couldn't live with myself if I sailed with her. Then I went ashore.*

". . . where General Vandegrift immediately put him into the breach as his intelligence officer, to replace an officer who fell in action . . ."

Well, that's true.

". . . and, when leaving Guadalcanal on a destroyer," MacArthur went on sonorously, despite grievous wounds, Pickering assumed command when her captain was killed in a Japanese attack . . ."

It wasn't anywhere near as heroic as you're making it sound. I was on the bridge when her captain was killed; I'm a master mariner; and when a ship's master can't perform his duties, the next best qualified man takes over. That goes back to the Phoenicians. That's all I did.

". . . for which he was decorated at the personal order of Admiral Nimitz," MacArthur continued.

And I've always wondered if Nimitz didn't regret having done so, when Roosevelt shoved the OSS down his throat on my back.

"And of the many Distinguished Service Medals it was my privilege to award, Fleming, I can think of none more deserving than yours."

What did the Killer say about the DSM? "It's the senior officers' Good Conduct Medal, awarded to rear-area chair-warmers who have gone three consecutive months without catching the clap."

"That's very kind of you, General," Pickering said. He turned to General Almond. "What happened was that Secretary of the Navy Knox wanted me to do some intelligence work for him, and decided that I could do that job better as a Marine."

"You were never a Marine, previously?" Almond asked, surprised.

"In the First World War, I was a teenaged Marine buck sergeant," Pickering said.

"And in the First World War, as a teenaged enlisted man, General Pickering was awarded the Navy Cross," MacArthur said, almost triumphantly, as if winning an argument. "I really don't understand you, Fleming. Modesty is certainly a virtue, but denying that you're not every bit as much a soldier as anyone in this room is simply absurd." He paused and then drove home his point. "You're one of us, Fleming. Wouldn't you agree, Willoughby?"

"Yes, sir, I agree," General Willoughby said.

"Huff?"

"Absolutely, General," Colonel Huff said.

"You're all very kind to think of me that way," Pickering said.

And there is absolutely no chance of me getting MacArthur alone for a minute to talk to him about McCoy and the North Koreans. These three are going to be here all night—this is obviously a command performance for them.

I could, of course, ask him for a moment alone, and bring up the subject. But that would make it clear that McCoy had gone "out of channels," and the fact is, I shouldn't know what I do. McCoy still thinks of me as "his general," but he's wrong. I'm not his general, and he should not have shown me that.

Jesus H. Christ! What the hell am I going to do?

[FOUR]
Conference Room B
The Hotel Hokkaido
Tokyo, Japan
1715 1 June 1950

Charley Ansley was waiting for Pick in the corridor outside the hastily rented room in which a tablecloth-draped table had been set up facing four rows of folding chairs.

When he saw Ernie Sage McCoy and Ken McCoy with Pick, he smiled. He had come to know both well in the early years of World War II, when, at Fleming Pickering's request, he had given them the use of his cabin cruiser in San

Diego. Housing in San Diego at that time had been in very short supply, and absolutely unavailable to couples who were not legally joined in matrimony.

He had been at their wedding, when Ken came home from a hush-hush mission in the Gobi Desert with brand new major's leaves on his uniform.

"God, it's good to see you," he said, extending his left arm to embrace Ernie as he extended his hand to McCoy. "How's my favorite Marine?"

"I thought I was your favorite Marine," Pick said.

"No, you're my favorite Trans-Global pilot, and not only because you are going to go in there and smile, and be modest, and restrain your well-known tendency to be a wiseass."

"Nice to see you, Mr. Ansley," McCoy said, smiling.

"Maybe not 'Uncle Charley,' like the prodigal son here, but at least 'Charley,' okay?"

McCoy nodded.

"Pick," Ansley asked, "do you think your father would mind if I called the Imperial and had them set up a bar, and hors d'oeuvres, in his suite?"

"Yes," Pick said, simply, smiling.

"The public relations guy says he'd like to get him involved in this, and I know damned well he wouldn't come here."

"No, he wouldn't," Pick said.

"So you're saying I shouldn't do it?"

"No, I think it's a good idea. What I said was he won't like it, and I agree that he wouldn't come here except at the point of a bayonet. But if I have to go in there and be charming and modest, the least the old man can do is smile at the press and whoever."

"The charm comes easily," Ernie said. "It's the modesty that gives him problems."

"Thank you, Killer, for taking this forked-tongue female off my hands," Pick said.

"Don't call him 'Killer,' goddamn you!" Ernie snapped.

"It's okay, baby," McCoy said.

"We're ready for you, Captain," a man in a gray suit said.

"And now, I think Captain Pickering will take a few questions," the man in the gray suit announced. "And then we've got cars arranged to take everybody to the Imperial for a little liquid courage."

Predictably, Pick thought, the questions were predictable:

Q. (Fat little bespectacled fart) Isn't this really showboating? Putting the passengers in danger?

A. The safety of our passengers is our primary concern; we have not and will not increase any risk to them.

Q. (Tall, thin, pasty-faced. Was probably a classroom monitor in high school) But speed records imply racing, racing is by definition dangerous, so how can you say this wasn't dangerous?

A. The aeronautical engineers of the manufacturer, Lockheed, and our own aeronautical engineers have come up with what they call an "envelope." It sets forth the conditions in which flight is safe. Airspeed, engine rpm, that sort of thing. We were never "out of the envelope"; if we had been, the record wouldn't have counted.

Q. (Pasty-face follow-up) But then why try to set speed records?

A. We didn't *try* to set a speed record. We tried to bring our passengers here as quickly—and comfortably—as possible within the safe-flight envelope. We did that, and it happened to set a speed record.

Q. (Nice-looking. Great boobs) Aren't you a little young to be a captain?

A. Excuse me?

Q. (Great boobs follow-up. Nice face, too) The popular image of an airline captain—especially of one making across-the-ocean flights like this one—is, oh, forty-ish, fifty-ish, gray temples, a look of experience.

A. I must be the exception to that rule.

Q. (Nice boobs, plus nice teeth in a very nice mouth, follow-up) How did you get to be a captain? Did you fly transports or bombers when you were in the service?

A. No, ma'am, I did not fly multiengined aircraft, bombers or transports, in the service.

Q. (Nice boobs, face, teeth, nice *everything,* follow-up) Then how did you get to be a captain so young?

A. My daddy loaned me the money to start Trans-Global.

Q. (Nice, better than nice, everything, follow-up) I don't think you're kidding.

A. Boy Scout's honor, ma'am.

Q. (Nice *everything* follow-up) Who's your daddy?

A. His name is Fleming Pickering.

Q. There's a rumor floating that he's in Tokyo. True?

A. (Man in gray suit) We're going to have to cut this off, ladies and gentlemen, we're running out of time. Thank you, ladies and gentlemen. The cars are waiting in front of the hotel, and will wait at the Imperial to bring you back here.

"Except for that crack about your daddy loaning you the money to start the airline, you did very well, Pick. I'm proud of you," Ernie said, as they walked along the street to where Pick had parked the Ford.

"Thank you, ma'am."

"Is that crap really important?" McCoy asked.

"According to Charley it is. It sells seats, and that's the name of the game."

"Hey, Captain Pickering, hold up a minute!"

Pick looked over his shoulder to find the source of the female voice. Nice Everything was coming down the sidewalk toward them.

Nice legs, too. Damn nice legs.

"Believe it or not, that was a legitimate question," Nice Everything said.

"What was a legitimate question?"

"You are—at least you look—too young to be an airline captain."

"I don't think I caught the name," Pick said.

"Jeanette Priestly, *Chicago Tribune*," she said, giving him her hand.

Nice, soft, warm hand.

"My friends call me 'Pick,' " he said. "These are my friends, Captain and Mrs. McCoy. Ken and Ernie."

"Which one's Ernie?"

"I am."

Nice Everything turned to McCoy.

"You're also a pilot?"

"I'm a Marine, not a pilot."

Jeanette turned to Pick.

"The public relations guy told me why you didn't fly 'multiengine' planes when *you* were a Marine," Jeanette said. "You should have told me. It would have made a great lead: *'Marine Fighter Ace Sets Trans-Pacific Airliner Speed Record.'* "

"You have to understand," Ernie said, straight-faced, "that when you look in the dictionary under 'modest,' you see our heroes' picture."

The two women smiled at each other.

"And so was the question about your father being here legitimate," Jeanette said. "I'd really like to interview him."

"I don't know about an interview," Pick said. "But if you want to come with us to the Imperial—presuming the old man is back from dinner—I'll introduce you."

"Dinner with MacArthur, right?" she asked.

Pick didn't reply.

"Hey, I'm good at what I do, too," Jeanette said. "Yes, thank you ever so much, Captain Pickering, I would love to go to the Imperial with you."

"And afterward, how about dinner?"

"If I'm in a good mood—and getting to talk to your daddy would put me in a very good mood—I would be delighted."

[FIVE]
The Dewey Suite
The Imperial Hotel
Tokyo, Japan
2245 1 June 1950

In the limousine on the way to the Hotel Imperial, Fleming Pickering had consoled himself with the thought that while he had absolutely no idea what to do about McCoy's predicament, he didn't have to face him right now with that announcement. What he was going to do now was have a drink—maybe two, but certainly one really stiff one—and fall into bed.

Sometimes, perhaps even often, he went to bed facing a problem that seemed to have no solution and when he woke in the morning—for that matter, sometimes at three A.M.—he had found one. He couldn't explain it, except perhaps to wonder if the brain continued to work while one was asleep, but it happened, and with a little bit of luck it would happen tonight.

He heard the sound of a party as he walked down the corridor toward the Dewey Suite, and as he felt for his key, was surprised to realize that it was coming from his suite.

What the hell?

He had just put the key in the lock when it was opened for him by a white-jacketed Japanese barman.

Pickering looked quickly around the room and saw there were two dozen or more people in the living room, including Charley Ansley and the station manager who had met them at the airport, and whose name he still didn't know. After a moment, he recognized Pick's copilot on the flight.

The record-setting *flight. That's what this is all about. Charley's throwing a party for the crew, the people who run the operation in Tokyo, and, more than likely, for the press.*

Seeming to confirm this, there was a bartender now behind the bar, and another white-jacketed Japanese was walking through the room carrying a tray of hors d'oeuvres.

Jesus! Just what I need! Like a third leg.

He saw Pick paying rapt attention to a tall, graceful brunette, and then, surprising him, he saw Captain and Mrs. Kenneth R. McCoy, USMCR.

Pick and Charley Ansley saw him at the same time, and Ansley, a portly man in his fifties who combed what was left of his hair over the top of his skull, started toward him.

"Hail the father of our conquering hero," Charley said.

Pickering smiled, hoping it didn't look as insincere as it felt, and put out his hand.

"Good to see you, Charley," he said.

"This was the best place I could think of do this . . ."

They don't have party rooms at the Hotel Hokkaido?

". . . and even if they did, you probably would not have come over there, and I would have had to invite Bart Stevens, which I didn't want to do."

"It was a good idea, Charley," Pickering said.

"How did things go with MacArthur?" Charley asked.

"He's an amazing man," Pickering said.

"If you're talking about the Supreme Commander," Pick said, "Jeanette here would be ever so grateful for details."

Pickering had not seen Pick and the lanky brunette walk up.

"Jeanette, this is my dad," Pick went on. "Pop, this is Jeanette Priestly."

She put out her hand to him.

"Pick tells me you just had dinner with General MacArthur. True?"

"Miss Priestly, I feel morally bound to tell you that one—especially if one is a very attractive young woman—should never trust anything my son says."

"True or not?" she pursued.

"Jeanette's interest is professional," Pick said. "She's a reporter."

"Chicago Tribune," she furnished.

"It was a private dinner between old friends," Pickering said. "General MacArthur said nothing newsworthy."

And even if he had, despite that brilliant smile you're flashing me, did you really think I would tell you?

"Whatever General MacArthur says is newsworthy," she said, with a smile.

"How did it go, Pop?" Pick asked.

"A trip down memory lane," Pickering replied.

"Just you and MacArthur and Mrs. Supreme Commander?"

He's doing this to get on the right side of the girl. Well, why not?

"We had drinks, first," Pickering said. "General Willoughby, Colonel Huff, and MacArthur's chief of staff, General Almond. I'd never met him before. It was just the MacArthurs and me for dinner."

"What did you think of General Almond?" Jeanette asked.

"He's an army officer, a senior one, and he must be competent, or he wouldn't be MacArthur's chief of staff. Nice fellow, I thought. And you may quote me, Miss Priestly."

"There's a story going around about General Almond," she said. "I'd love to know if it's true or not."

"I really don't think I want to hear the story," Pickering said, rather coldly. "Isn't that what they call muckraking?"

"I know nothing but nice things about General Almond," she said. "But his previous—to being chief of staff to the Supreme Commander—claim to fame was that he had one of the two Negro divisions in Italy during World War II."

"I don't think I follow you," Pickering said.

"Are you being diplomatically dense, General?"

"Please don't call me 'General,' Miss Priestly, it's been a long time since I wore a uniform."

"Sorry," she said, and then smiled at him. "You make it sound like something you're ashamed about."

"I meant to imply, Miss Priestly," Pickering said coldly, "that 'General' is a title of honor to which I am no longer entitled."

Well, aren't you the pompous ass, Fleming Pickering?

Goddamn, she made me mad.

And, I think, on purpose.

Get the old fart mad, and he's liable to say something he shouldn't.

"And I don't know what 'diplomatically dense' means," Pickering said.

"That's when you pretend not to understand what someone has just told you."

"I understood that General Almond commanded a Negro division in Italy. I don't understand the significance of that."

"Really? Or is that diplomatic density?"

He didn't reply.

"Is this history lesson boring you, General?"

He looked at her for a long moment before replying.

"No. If you wanted to get my attention, you've succeeded. Please go on."

"Okay," she said, then waited as Pickering grabbed a wandering waiter.

"Famous Grouse, double, water on the side," he ordered.

"Yes, sir."

"Two," Jeanette said.

"Three," Pick said.

"Oh, what the hell," Charley Ansley said. "Four."

"Please continue, Miss Priestly," Pickering said.

"You can call me 'Jeanette,' " she said. "What should I call you?"

" 'Sir' would be nice."

Charley Ansley chuckled.

"Score one for sir," Jeanette said. "The game ain't over . . ."

"Until the fat lady sings?" Pick offered.

"And half a point for Little Sir," Jeanette said.

Pickering chuckled. Jeanette smiled at him.

That smile she meant.

"We're waiting, with somewhat bated breath, for your history lesson, Jeanette."

"Okay, sir. Consider the end of World War Two."

"Sir was on the first plane to land in Japan," Pick said.

"How fascinating. Next time, raise your hand before you interrupt me."

"Score one for Jeanette," Pickering said.

"We have two five-stars, Eisenhower in Germany, specifically in Frankfurt, and El Supremo here. Each has a three-star chief of staff. Ike had Walter Bedell Smith, who had been his chief of staff throughout the European war, and MacArthur had Sutherland here."

"Okay," Pickering said.

"Just before he died, Roosevelt appointed another three-star, Lucius D. Clay, a heavy hitter who had been in charge of Army procurement throughout the war, to be deputy military governor of Germany under Ike. When Ike went home to be chief of staff, Clay replaced him as Commander-in-Chief, Europe. Truman gave Clay a fourth star, and sent him a succession of three-stars to command Seventh Army."

"You've done your homework, obviously," Pickering thought aloud.

"I work hard at what I do for a living, sir. Like you, sir."

Pick chuckled.

"Walter Bedell Smith, known as 'The Beetle' for reasons I can't imagine, went home with Ike. First, he was made DCSOPS . . . You know what that is, sir?"

Pickering shook his head, "no."

"Deputy Chief of Staff for Operations," Jeanette said. "Then Truman named him Ambassador to the Soviet Union. Now there's talk of naming him Director of the Central Intelligence Agency to replace Admiral Hillenkoetter."

"This is all very fascinating, Jeanette," Pickering said, smiling, "and I'm sure that somewhere down the road, you'll make your point."

"Yes, sir," she said, smiling back. "Now, at *this* end of the world, we had General of the Army Douglas MacArthur, and his chief of staff, Lieutenant General Richard Sutherland. General Sutherland went home for 'reasons of health'—and I'd love to know what was behind that. He thereupon disappeared from sight. No job in the Pentagon, nothing."

"Maybe he was ill," Pickering said.

"Maybe," Jeanette went on. "Leaving one three-star here under MacArthur, Lieutenant General Walton H. 'Johnny' Walker, who commands the Eighth Army. I don't suppose he was at dinner tonight?"

Pickering shook his head, "no."

"Not surprising. He is not a member of the elite, otherwise known as the 'Bataan Gang.' "

"There is a point to all this, right?" Pickering said.

"One would logically assume, wouldn't one, that the five-star Supreme Commander in Japan would be entitled to the same sort of staff as the five-star commander-in-chief in Europe?"

"One might."

"A four-star, like Lucius Clay, would be appropriate, no?"

"One would think so."

"Failing a four-star, then a three-star, right?"

"That would seem logical."

"And failing a three-star, then a hotshot two-star with lots more stars clearly on his horizon. Max Taylor comes to mind. So does I. D. White."

"Who?" Pick asked.

"Max Taylor commanded the 101st Airborne Division; White commanded the 2nd 'Hell on Wheels' Armored Division. He would have liberated Paris if he hadn't had to let the French pass through his lines to get the glory, and he had his lead tanks across the Elbe River and was prepared to take Berlin when Ike told him to let the Russians do it. It's a sure thing that both of them will get a third star, a good chance that they'll both get four, and even money that one or the other will be chief of staff of the Army. And what better way to learn that trade than by being chief of staff to MacArthur?"

"That would seem to make sense," Pickering said.

"So who does the Army—which means Eisenhower, onetime aide to MacArthur—send to the Supreme Commander? Edward M. Almond, whose claim to fame was commanding one of the two Negro divisions in Italy. With-out much wild acclaim, by the way. He did his job, but he wasn't a hotshot. I don't think he's even a West Pointer. I think he's either VMI or the Citadel."

Mention of the Citadel made him think of Colonel Ed Banning, one of the finest officers he had ever known.

"And you've drawn some sort of a conclusion from this?" Pickering asked.

"If I were Douglas MacArthur, I'd think I was being insulted."

"If Douglas MacArthur thought having General Almond assigned to him was insulting, General Almond would not be his chief of staff," Pickering said.

I don't believe that; so why did I say it? MacArthur's reaction to insults is to ig-nore them. He knew damned well they called him "Dugout Doug," and pretended he didn't. It wasn't fair, anyway. He took stupid chances by staying in the line of fire—artillery and small arms—when he should have been in a dugout.

"Huh!" Jeanette snorted.

"And what's wrong with VMI and the Citadel?" Pickering challenged. "George Catlett Marshall went to VMI. And I personally know a number of fine officers who went to VMI and Norwich."

"Point granted," Jeanette said. "I. D. White went to Norwich. You don't see anything petty—not to mention sinister—in Almond's assignment to MacArthur?"

"Nothing at all."

Why did I say that? I believe the story that MacArthur, when he was chief of staff, wrote an efficiency report on Marshall, then a colonel, saying he should not be given command of anything larger than a regiment. There was really bad blood be-tween the two. One of Marshall's acolytes—maybe even Eisenhower himself—could have repaid the Marshall insult by sending him a two-star non–West Pointer whose sole claim to fame was commanding a colored division.

But I'm not going to admit that to this woman, this journalist.

Why not?

Because it would air the dirty linen of the general officers' corps in public, and I don't want to do that.

Why?

Because, I suppose, I used to be called General Pickering. I guess that's like Once A Marine, Always A Marine.

But my fellow generals can be petty. Stupidly petty.

El Supremo refused to give the 4th Marines the Distinguished Unit Citation for Corregidor, even though everybody else on the island got it. When I asked him why, he told me the Marines already had enough medals.

And Charley Willoughby is stupid enough, and petty enough, to ignore McCoy's report—have it destroyed—because it disagrees with his assessment of the situation. Or admit that he didn't even have an assessment. Captains are not supposed to dis- agree with generals, much less point out that generals have done their job badly, or not at all.

What the hell am I going to do with that report?

And what the hell can I do to help McCoy?

"From what I've seen of General Almond, General," McCoy said, "he's as smart as they come."

Pickering was surprised that McCoy had volunteered anything, much less offered an opinion of a general officer.

Why did he do that?

To tell me something he thought I should know?

To challenge this female's theory that there was something sinister in Almond's assignment?

And why, if he likes Almond, didn't he take his report to him, bypassing Willoughby?

Because that's known as going out of channels, and in the military that's like raping a nun in church.

Pickering looked at McCoy.

And had another thought:

Almond must have a hard time with Willoughby, even though the G-2 is under the chief of staff. Not only does Willoughby have MacArthur's ear, but he's the senior member of the Bataan Gang, who can do no wrong in El Supremo's eyes.

"Jeanette," Pick said. "Now that you've talked to Sir, are you going to live up to your end of the bargain?"

"What bargain was that?"

"Dinner. I'm starved. The last thing I had to eat was a stale sandwich on the airplane."

"A deal's a deal," Jeanette said.

"Dad, do you want to go with us?"

"I've eaten, thank you. And I'm tired. The restaurant here's supposed to be pretty good."

"Ken says he knows a Japanese place," Pick said.

Jeanette Priestly put out her hand to Pickering.

"It was a pleasure meeting you, General," she said. "Maybe we'll see each other again sometime."

"It was my pleasure," Pickering said.

[SIX]
The Dewey Suite
The Imperial Hotel
Tokyo, Japan
0140 2 June 1950

Both father and son were surprised to see the other when Pick Pickering entered the living room of the Dewey Suite. Pick had assumed that his father would have long before gone to bed, and his father had assumed more or less the same thing about his son: that at this hour, Pick would also be in bed—Jeanette Priestly's bed.

"Still up, Pop, huh?" Pick asked.

"No, what you see is an illusion," Pickering said, getting out of an armchair and walking to the bar. He picked up a bottle of Famous Grouse. "Nightcap?"

"Why not? Just a little water, no ice," Pick said, and walked toward his father. Pickering handed him a drink.

"Ida M. Tarbell turned you down, huh?" Pickering asked.

"What? Who?"

"Ida M. Tarbell, the first of the lady muckrakers," his father explained.

"Her name is Jeanette Priestly," Pick said. "And yes, since you asked, she turned me down."

"I can't imagine why," Pickering said.

"She said I was good-looking, charming, intelligent, dashing, and rich, and under those circumstances, she obviously could not take the risk of getting involved."

Pickering smiled.

"She really said that?"

"That's almost a direct quote."

"Well, I knew from the moment I saw her that she was an intelligent female," Pickering said. "Sometimes, as I suppose you know, that's a ploy. Telling someone who was is good-looking, charming, et cetera, 'no' may in fact be step one in a hastily organized plan to get you to the altar."

"I don't think so," Pick replied, seriously. "I don't think she wants someone in her life."

"But you are planning to see her again?"

"I don't know, Pop," Pick said, still seriously, his attitude telling his father that the Priestly girl, either intentionally or not, had gotten more of his son's attention than most young women ever did.

"What are you going to do about the Killer?" Pick asked.

"I've been sitting here thinking about that."

"And?"

"There's really two problems," Pickering said. "Ken getting reduced to the ranks . . ."

"Sonofabitch, that makes me mad!"

". . . and his report. Whatever the Killer is, he's not a fool. If he thinks the North Koreans are going to start a war, the odds are that they will."

"So?"

"I just sent Dick Fowler a radiogram, telling him I have to see him the minute I get to the States, and asking him to call the office and let Mrs. Florian know where he is."

Senator Richardson K. Fowler (R., Cal.) a somewhat portly, silver-haired, regal-looking 67-year-old, once described by *Time* magazine as "one of the three most powerful members of the World's Most Exclusive Club," was one of Fleming Pickering's closest friends.

"I was sort of hoping you could get to MacArthur at dinner," Pick said.

"So was I," his father replied. "But it . . . just wouldn't have worked. He would have backed Willoughby, and been pissed with me. Not that that would bother me, but it would certainly have made the Killer's situation worse."

"I had—just now, as I headed home, with my masculine ego dragging on the ground—what may be a disloyal thought."

"What?"

"Fuck the Marine Corps. If they don't recognize what they've got in the Killer, don't appreciate what he's done, and want to bust him down to sergeant, then fuck the Marine Corps."

Pickering looked at his son for a moment before replying.

"I had a somewhat similar thought," Pickering said. "Ken doesn't need the Marine Corps to make a living."

"He doesn't want to live on Ernie's money," Pick said.

"Ken is a very capable fellow. He would do well at whatever he put his mind to. And I think they've come to some sort of understanding about her money. The furniture in their house—did you notice?—didn't come from the Salvation Army."

"And what did the guy say? 'Money may not be everything, but it's way ahead of whatever's in second place'?"

Pickering chuckled.

"Have you got a place for him in Trans-Global?"

"I thought about that, too. Yeah. Sure. There's half a dozen places where he

really could do a job. The problem is that he would think it was charity." He
paused. "God *damn* the Marine Corps!"

"It's not *the* Corps, Pick," Pickering said. "It's some chair-warmer in the
Corps who has caved in to whoever here decided McCoy was a thorn under
MacArthur's saddle blanket, and for the good of the Corps has to go." He
paused. "If General Vandegrift was Commandant, I could—I would—go to
him. But I don't even know who the present Commandant is."

"Cates," Pick furnished. "You didn't know?"

"Cliff Cates?" Picking asked. Pick nodded. "I didn't know, but I do know
him. He commanded the 1st Marines when we landed at Guadalcanal. And
didn't make much of a secret he thought Vandergrift could have done a hell of
a lot better in picking a replacement for the Division G-2 than your old man."
He paused. "But he's a good Marine. A good officer. I think he'd see me—
more important, listen to me. I'll ask Dick Fowler what he thinks."

Pick nodded.

"I didn't ask Ken when they're actually going home," Pickering thought
aloud.

"The day after tomorrow, with us," Pick furnished.

Pickering looked at him in surprise.

"It sort of came up at dinner," Pick explained. "The Killer excused himself,
and came back in a couple of minutes and said his boss—some Navy captain—
had given him permission to return to the States on commercial transportation,
which means us. I guess the sonofabitch figures the sooner he gets the Killer out
of Japan, the better for him."

"And when are we going home?"

"Day after tomorrow. Trans-Global Airways, as you should know, Mr.
Chairman of the Board, operates a thrice-weekly luxury service flight schedule
in both directions between San Francisco and Tokyo."

"And is this thrice-weekly luxury service making us any money?"

"Yeah. A lot more money than we thought it would, at first."

"Don't say anything to Ken about this conversation," Pickering said.

"No. Of course not. I'm going out there tomorrow to help them pack."

"I'll go with you," Pickering said.

"What if he asks you what you're going to do?"

"He won't," Pickering said. "He trusts me to do whatever I think is appropriate, even if it's nothing. He didn't come to me about his getting busted back
to the ranks—that's not his style. But he thinks there's going to be a war, and
that somebody should give the Corps a heads-up."

"Pop, do you think he's stupid enough to take the bust? To be Staff Sergeant—or Gunnery Sergeant—McCoy?"

"I don't think he thinks there's anything for a gunnery sergeant to be ashamed of."

"Either do I, but the Killer should be a colonel, not a fucking sergeant."

"If he gets out, it will be because he thinks Ernie would be uncomfortable as a gunnery sergeant's wife. Not that she wouldn't try to make it work . . ."

"God damn the Marine Corps!" Pick said, bitterly.

"Let's see what happens, Pick, after I talk with Dick Fowler."

[ONE]
Office of the Deputy Chief for Officer Records
Office of the Assistant Chief of Staff, G-1
Headquarters, Camp Pendleton, California
0705 7 June 1950

Major Robert B. Macklin, USMC, parked his dark green 1949 Buick Roadmaster sedan in the parking place reserved for the Deputy Chief of Officer Records, walked around to the front of the frame building, and entered.

Major Macklin knew that people sometimes said, not unkindly, that he looked like an actor sent by Central Casting to a Hollywood motion picture set in response to a request for an extra to play a Marine officer. Major Macklin was not at all unhappy to have people think he looked like what a Marine Corps officer should look like.

He was a tall and well-built, thirty-five-year-old, not quite handsome, fine-featured man who wore his brown hair in a crew cut. There was a ring signifying his graduation from the United States Naval Academy on his finger, and the breast of his well-tailored, short-sleeved, summer-undress tropical worsted shirt bore a rather impressive display of ribbons attesting to his service.

They were topped with the Purple Heart medal, testifying that he had shed blood for his country and the Corps in combat. His Asiatic-Pacific service rib-

bon bore stars indicating that he had participated in every World War II campaign in the Pacific.

There were two enlisted men just inside the door. One was Staff Sergeant
John B. Adair, USMC, who had had the overnight duty of Charge of Quarters,
and the other was PFC Wilson J. Coughlin, USMC, who had had the overnight
duty as driver of the 1949 Chevrolet staff car, should that vehicle be required
in the discharge of Staff Sergeant Adair's duty.

When Staff Sergeant Adair—who was short, squat, starting to bald, and did
not look as if he had been sent over from Central Casting to play a Marine
sergeant—saw Major Macklin, he popped to attention and bellowed, "Attention
on deck!"

PFC Coughlin popped to attention.

There were only two ribbons on PFC Coughlin's shirt, but Staff Sergeant
Adair's display was even more impressive than Major Macklin's. His was topped
by the ribbon signifying that he had been awarded the Silver Star Medal. Adair
also had the Purple Heart, but with two clusters, indicating he had been
wounded three times.

Very privately—although he knew his opinion was shared by most of his
peers—Staff Sergeant Adair thought Major Robert B. Macklin was a chickenshit prick.

"As you were," Major Macklin said, and marched through the outer office
of the G-1's office into the Officer Personnel Section, and between the desks of
that section to his office, which was at the end of the room.

He put his fore-and-aft cap on a clothes tree and sat down at his desk. The
desk was nearly bare. Macklin liked to keep things shipshape. There was an
elaborately carved nameplate he'd had made for a package of cigarettes in
Tientsin, China, after the war. There was a telephone and a desk pad of artificial leather holding a sheet of green blotter paper. There was a wooden In box
on the left corner of the desk and an Out box on the right corner of the desk.
The Out box was empty. The In box contained a curling sheet of teletypewriter paper.

Major Macklin opened the upper right-hand drawer of his desk and took
from it a large ashtray, which had a box of matches in its center. He placed
this on the right side of his desk, then went back into the drawer and came
out with a straight-stemmed pipe and a leather tobacco pouch. He filled the
pipe, carefully tamping the tobacco, and then lit it with one of the wooden
matches from the ashtray. Then he returned the tobacco pouch to the drawer
and reached for the teletype message, which had apparently come in
overnight.

ROUTINE

HQ USMC WASH DC 1405 6 JUNE 1950

TO COMMANDING GENERAL
CAMP PENDLETON, CAL
ATTN: G-1

REFERENCE IS MADE TO MESSAGE HQ USMC DATED 27 MAY 1950
RELIEVING CAPT K.R. MCCOY FROM NAVAL ELEMENT HQ SCAP
TOKYO JAPAN AND ASSIGNING HIM TO CAMP PENDLETON CAL FOR
SEPARATION FROM ACTIVE DUTY.

SUBJECT OFFICER, ACCOMPANIED BY HIS DEPENDENT WIFE,
DEPARTED TOKYO JAPAN FOR CAMP PENDLETON VIA COMMERCIAL
AIR 4 JUN 1950. EN ROUTE TRAVEL TIME ESTIMATED AT
NINETY-SIX (96) HOURS.

SUBJECT OFFICER'S SERVICE RECORDS ARE CURRENTLY BEING
EVALUATED BY ENLISTED PERSONNEL SECTION, G-1, HQ USMC
TO DETERMINE AT WHAT ENLISTED RANK OFFICER WILL BE
PERMITTED TO ENLIST, SHOULD HE SO DESIRE, AFTER HIS
SEPARATION FROM COMMISSIONED STATUS. PRIOR TO ENTERING
UPON TEMPORARY ACTIVE DUTY AS A COMMISSIONED OFFICER IN
1941, SUBJECT OFFICER WAS CORPORAL, USMC.

ON ARRIVAL AT CAMP PENDLETON CAPT MCCOY SHOULD BE
COUNSELED BY AN OFFICER OF EQUAL OR SUPERIOR RANK
MAKING CLEAR TO HIM THE FOLLOWING:

HQ USMC DOES NOT WISH TO ENTERTAIN ANY REQUEST FOR
RECONSIDERATON OF HIS RELEASE FROM ACTIVE DUTY AS A
COMMISSIONED OFFICER. HE WILL BE SEPARATED FROM THE
USMC NOT LATER THAN 30 JUNE 1950.

IT IS THE INTENTION OF THE G-1 SECTION USMC TO
DETERMINE AT WHICH ENLISTED GRADE CAPT MCCOY MAY ELECT

```
TO ENLIST ON SEPARATION AT THE EARLIEST POSSIBLE TIME.
SUCH DETERMINATION WILL BE FURNISHED BY TELETYPE
MESSAGE TO G-1 CAMP PENDLETON, AND IT IS ANTICIPATED
THIS WILL OCCUR BEFORE 30 JUNE. ON RECEIPT OF
ENLISTMENT OPTION, CAPT MCCOY WILL BE OFFERED THE
OPTION OF IMMEDIATE RELEASE FROM ACTIVE DUTY FOR THE
PURPOSE OF ENLISTING IN THE USMC; OR OF IMMEDIATELY
BEING SEPARATED FROM THE NAVAL SERVICE TO ENTER
CIVILIAN LIFE. SHOULD CAPT MCCOY ELECT TO DO SO HE MAY
REMAIN ON ACTIVE DUTY UNTIL 30 JUNE 1950.

CAPT MCCOY HAS TWENTY-NINE (29) DAYS OF ACCRUED LEAVE.
HE SHOULD BE OFFERED THE OPPORTUNITY TO GO ON LEAVE
STATUS IF HE SO DESIRES UNTIL HE ACCEPTS OR DECLINES
REENLISTMENT IN THE GRADE TO BE OFFERED, OR UNTIL 28
JUNE 1950 WHEN ABSENT PRIOR SEPARATION AS OUTLINED
ABOVE HIS SEPARATION PROCESS MUST COMMENCE.

FOR THE COMMANDANT:

ROSCOE L. QUINCY LT COL USMC
ASST CHIEF OFFICER PERSONNEL
OFFICE OF THE ASSISTANT CHIEF OF STAFF, G-1
HQ USMC

ROUTINE
```

Major Macklin puffed thoughtfully on his pipe as he considered the message, then read it again to fix the details in his mind.

Although this was not mirrored on his face, Major Macklin had an emotional reaction to the message. He was surprised at its intensity.

At 0735, five minutes after Lieutenant Colonel Peter S. Brewer, USMC—a short, muscular, thirty-seven-year-old—who was Chief of Officer Records and Major Macklin's immediate superior, had entered his office, he saw Major Macklin in the open door of the office, waiting for permission to enter.

He waved him in.

"Good morning, Macklin," Lt. Col. Brewer said. "Something?"

"Good morning, sir," Macklin replied. "I wondered if the colonel had seen this?"

He handed Brewer the TWX from Eighth & Eye.

Brewer read it, then looked up at Macklin to see what he had to say about it.

"The phrase about encouraging this officer to take leave before he's separated, sir."

"What about it?"

"Sir, I'd like to find something for this officer to do around here, so that he wouldn't have to take leave."

"Why?"

"Sir, I know this officer. May I speak frankly?"

Lt. Col. Brewer made a "come-on" gesture with his left hand.

"Sir, McCoy was commissioned when the Corps really needed officers. And, frankly, he was one of those who never should have been commissioned."

"Why not?"

"Well, sir, he lacks the education to be an officer, and . . . this is difficult to put in words. He doesn't really understand the unwritten rules on which an officer has to pattern his life. He's not an officer and a gentleman, sir, if you take my meaning."

"Where are you going with this, Macklin?" Lt. Col. Brewer asked.

"I know McCoy well enough to know he's living from payday to payday," Macklin said. "You know the type, sir. Not a thought for tomorrow . . ."

"OK, so what?"

"My thought, sir, is that if McCoy doesn't take leave, he'll be paid for it when he's separated. Whether he leaves the Corps or reenlists, I'm sure that he'd like to have—is really going to need—a month's pay in cash."

Lt. Col. Brewer considered that a moment, first thinking that it was really nice of Macklin to take an interest like this—he didn't seem the type—and then considering what he was asking for.

The Eighth & Eye TWX had said McCoy "should be offered the opportunity" to take leave; it didn't make it an order.

"Sure," Lt. Col. Brewer said. "Why not? Have him inventory supply rooms or something. There's always a need for someone to do that."

"And, sir, with your permission, I'd rather not have him get the idea we're doing this out of—what . . . pity, I suppose, is the word."

Brewer considered that for a moment.

"Handle it any way you think is best, Macklin."

"Yes, sir. Thank you, sir. With your permission, sir?"

Lt. Col. Brewer gave Major Macklin permission to withdraw with a wave of his hand.

Major Macklin returned to his office quite pleased with himself.

"Killer" McCoy getting himself booted out of the Corps was really no surprise. The miserable little sonofabitch should never have been a commissioned officer in the first place. I'm only surprised that he lasted as long as he did.

Having him assigned here, under my command, for his last twenty-nine days as an officer is really poetic justice. I owe him.

An officer and a gentleman would never have done to a brother officer what that lowlife sonofabitch did to me. And got away with.

Until now.

The next twenty-nine days are mine.

It's payback time.

As he sat behind his desk, he had another thought that pleased him even more:

If he does accept whatever stripes Eighth & Eye decides he's worth, and enlists—and how else can he earn a living?—maybe I could arrange to have him stationed here.

"Reduced to the ranks"? I'd like to see the sonofabitch busted down to PFC. And with a little luck, I might be able to do just that.

[TWO]
Through With Engines
Near Carmel-by-the-Sea, California
0905 7 June 1950

As Trans-Global Airways' Flight 637, Luxury Service Between Tokyo and San Francisco, began the last (Honolulu–San Francisco) leg of the flight, Fleming Pickering had taken advantage of Ken McCoy's visit to the rest room and had brought up the subject of Through with Engines to Ernie Sage McCoy.

Through with Engines was the more-or-less 110-acre Pickering estate near Carmel. On it was a large, rambling, but not pretentious single-floor house, designed to provide as many of its rooms as possible with the best possible view of the Pacific Ocean; a boathouse; a small airplane hangar; a small cottage for the servants; and a shedlike building used to house the grass-cutting—and other estate—machinery and a garage. None of the buildings—or the Pacific Ocean—could be seen from the road.

The land, which at the time had held only what was now the servants' cottage, and the boathouse had been the wedding gift of Andrew Foster to Patricia, his only daughter, on her marriage to Fleming Pickering. The house—actually the first four rooms thereof; eight more having been added, often one at a time, over the years—had been the gift of Commodore Pickering to his son Fleming on the occasion of his successful passage of the U.S. Coast Guard examinations leading to his licensing as an Any Ocean, Any Tonnage Master Mariner, his right to call himself "Captain," and his first command of a Pacific & Far East vessel.

It was originally used by the young couple as somewhere they could go for privacy when he returned from a voyage, and Patricia had almost immediately pointed out that, since there were no street numbers, and nothing could be seen from the highway, the place needed a name. And it also needed signs to inform the public that it was private property.

Patricia Foster Pickering had thought her husband's suggestion of "Through with Engines"—the last signal sent from the bridge to the engine room at the conclusion of a voyage—was rather sweet, and told him she'd see about having a sign made.

"You'll need a lot more than one sign," he had replied. "I'll take care of it."

She thought that was sweet, too, until, on her next visit to what she thought of as "the beach place," she found the road lined at 100-yard intervals with four-by-eight-foot sheets of plywood signs, painted yellow, red, and black, reading:

PRIVATE PROPERTY

THROUGH WITH ENGINES

NO TRESPASSING UNDER

PENALTY OF LAW

They had come from the painting shop of the P&FE maintenance yard, and consequently were of the highest quality, and designed to resist the ravages of storms at sea.

It had taken Patricia most of Pick Pickering's life to get rid of the signs and replace them with something a little more attractive—and a little less belligerent. One original sign survived, and was now mounted on the wall of what she thought of as "the playroom," and her husband referred to as the "big bar," there being another—the "little bar"—by the swimming pool.

"Honey," Fleming Pickering said to Ernie McCoy, "I just had a great idea. Why don't you stay at Through with Engines while Ken's at Camp Pendleton?"

She smiled at him, but there was an *I know what you're up to* look in her eyes.

What the hell, when in doubt, tell the truth.

"It won't be much fun for you down there, Ernie," he said. "And Patricia—if she's not already back—will want to see you."

And want to talk to you, especially after I tell her about Ken being reduced to the ranks. It's absolutely true that she thinks of you as a daughter. And talking to Patricia would certainly be a very good thing for you.

"I go where Ken goes," Ernie said. "But thanks, Uncle Flem."

"Have you considered that he might want you to stay at Through with Engines?"

"Pick said that, when he offered us Through with Engines," Ernie said. "Your minds run in similar paths." She paused, then repeated, "I go where Ken goes."

"OK."

"Pick's going to fly us down there in his airplane," she said. "We're going from the airport to Through with Engines, spend the night, fly down to San Diego—North Island Naval Air Station—in the morning. Pick will then run the girls out of his suite in the Coronado Beach, and turn it over to us."

"I didn't know," Pickering said.

"That way, I'll have a little time with Aunt Pat," Ernie went on. "The Pickerings are taking good care of the McCoys, Uncle Flem, and the McCoys really appreciate it."

"Ernie, I don't know how much good I'll be able to do Ken," Pickering said.

"I know you'll do what you can," she said, and then Ken had appeared in the aisle and he changed the subject.

Pick's airplane was a Staggerwing Beechcraft, so called because the upper wing of the single-engine biplane was mounted farther aft than the lower. It was painted bright yellow, and there was a legend painted in script on the engine nacelle, "Once is Enough."

"I'll bite," Ernie McCoy said, pointing to the legend after her husband and Pick Pickering had rolled the aircraft from the hangar behind the main house of Through with Engines. "Once what is enough?"

"Once under the Golden Gate Bridge," Ken McCoy said, smiling at her.

"Mom's father gave me the Beech when I came home from the Pacific," Pick said. "It used to be Foster Hotel's. Now they have an R4D. Together with a long 'once is enough' speech. So I had it painted on the nacelle."

"Once what is enough?" Ernie said.

"I told you, baby," McCoy said, smiling at her. "Once under the Golden Gate Bridge."

"He flew this under the Golden Gate Bridge?" Ernie asked, incredulously.

"With poor George Hart with him," McCoy said, chuckling at the memory.

"At the time it seemed like a splendid idea," Pick said.

"George had just gone to work for the Boss," McCoy said. "Colonel Rickabee decided the Boss needed a bodyguard, so I went to Parris Island and found George in boot camp. He'd been a detective in Saint Louis. . . ."

"Still is," Pick said. "I saw him there a couple of months ago. He's twice a captain, once in the cops, and once in the Corps Reserve. He's got an infantry company."

"I didn't know that," McCoy said. "Anyway, one day George is a boot, and the next day he's a sergeant bodyguard protecting the Boss, and the day after that, the Boss collapses—malaria and exhaustion; that was right after he was hit on the tin can leaving Guadalcanal, and they made him a Brigadier—in the suite in the Foster Lafayette in Washington and winds up in the hospital. Rickabee sends George out here to tell the lunatic here that his father's going to be all right, and the lunatic here loads him in this—which he stole from his grandfather for the occasion, by the way—and flies under the Golden Gate. George told me he prayed to be able to go back to the safety of boot camp on Parris Island.' "

"Hart was with your dad all through the war, wasn't he?" Ernie asked.

"All the way, right to the end. He was even on the plane when the Old Man went into Japan before the surrender," Pick said. "Good man, George."

"And you got away with it?" Ernie asked. "You flew under the bridge, and got away with it?"

"I was a newly rated Marine aviator," Pick said. "With probably two hundred hours' total time, and therefore convinced I could fly anything anywhere . . ."

"By the skin of his teeth," McCoy said, "and with the considerable assistance of Senator Fowler."

"I don't like the look in your eyes, Pick," Ernie said. "Nothing smart-ass with the airplane today, OK?"

"Nothing could possibly be further from my mind," Pick said, smiling wickedly.

"She means it, Pick," McCoy said. "Nothing cute with the airplane."

Pick looked at McCoy, surprised at his seriousness.

"Ernie's pregnant," McCoy said. "This is the fourth time; the first three didn't—"

"Jesus H. Christ!" Pick said. "Jesus, Ernie, you didn't say anything. . . ."

"The first time, I told everybody, and everybody was really sympathetic when I miscarried," Ernie said. "Like it says, 'once is enough.' "

"You're the only one who knows," McCoy said. "Don't make us sorry we told you."

Pick looked between the two of them for a moment.

"Would congratulations be in order?"

"Nice thought," Ernie said. "But a little premature. Wait six months, and have another shot at it."

[THREE]
North Island Naval Air Station
San Diego, California
1400 8 June 1950

"North Island," Pick Pickering said into his microphone. "Beech Two Oh Two."

Pick was wearing a flamboyantly flowered Hawaiian shirt, yellow slacks, and loafers without socks.

Ernie McCoy was sitting beside him, wearing a dress. Pick had refused, considering her delicate condition, to let her defer to the rule that men sat in the front of a vehicle—wheeled or winged—and women in the back. McCoy, wearing his uniform, was in the back with the luggage that wouldn't fit in the baggage compartment.

"Civilian aircraft calling North Island. Go ahead."

Ernie could hear the conversation over her headset.

"North Island, this is Beech Two Oh Two, VFR at 4,500 over the beautiful blue drink, about ten miles north of your station, request approach and landing, please."

"Beach Two Oh Two, North Island is a Navy field, closed to civilian traffic. Suggest you contact Lindbergh Field on 214.6."

"North, Two Oh Two, suggest you contact whoever has the exception to the rules book, and then give me approach and landing."

"Hold One, Two Oh Two."

There was a sixty-second pause.

"Two Oh Two, North."

"Go ahead."

"North clears Beech Two Oh Two to descend to 2,500 feet for an approach to Runway One Eight. Report when you have the field in sight."

"Roger. Understand 2,500, Runway One Eight. Beginning descent at this time."

"Aircraft in the North pattern, be advised that a civilian single Beech biplane will be in the landing pattern."

"North, Two Oh Two, at 2,500, course one eight zero, I have the runway in sight."

"Two Oh Two, North. You are cleared as number one for a straight in approach and landing on Runway One Eight. Be advised that high-performance piston-and-jet aircraft are operating in the area."

"North, Two Oh Two, understand Number One to One Eight. I am over the outer marker."

"Two Oh Two, North. Be advised that Lieutenant Colonel Dunn will meet your aircraft at Base Ops."

"Thank you, North."

There was no headset in the back of the Staggerwing, and McCoy had not heard the conversation between the North Island control tower and Pick Pickering. And because he was in the rear of the fuselage, when the airplane stopped and he heard the engine dying, he reached over, unlatched the door, and backed out of the airplane. When his feet touched the ground, he turned around and was more than a little startled to see a light colonel standing there wearing the gold wings of a Naval aviator, a chest full of fruit salad, and a displeased look on his face that, combined with the fact he had his hands on his hips, suggested he was displeased with something.

Probably Pick. This is a Naval air station, and you're not supposed to land civilian airplanes on Naval air stations.

Captain McCoy did the only thing he could think to do under the circumstances. He saluted crisply and said, "Good afternoon, sir."

At that point, recognition, belatedly, dawned. It had been a long time.

Lieutenant Colonel William C. Dunn, USMC, who carried 138 pounds on his slim, five-foot-six frame, returned the salute crisply.

"How are you, McCoy?" he asked, and then stepped around McCoy to assist Mrs. McCoy in leaving the aircraft.

"Oh, Bill," Ernie said. "What a pleasant surprise!"

"You're as beautiful as ever," Lieutenant Colonel Dunn said, "and as careless as ever about the company you keep."

Pick Pickering got out of the airplane.

"Wee Willy!" he cried happily, wrapped his arms around Lieutenant Colonel Dunn, and kissed him wetly on the forehead.

Second Lieutenant Malcolm S. Pickering, USMCR, had been First Lieutenant William C. Dunn's wingman, in VMF-229, flying Grumman Wildcats off of Fighter One, on Guadalcanal. They had become aces within days of one another. Dunn had gone on to become a double ace. The Navy Cross, the nation's second-highest award for valor in the Naval service, topped Dunn's four rows of fruit salad.

Dunn freed himself from Pickering's embrace.

"You're a disgrace to the Marine Corps," Dunn said, failing to express the indignation he felt was called for, but did not in fact feel. "My God, you're not even wearing socks!"

"*I* don't have a loving wife and helpmeet to care for me," Pick said. "How's the bride?"

"About to make me a father for the fourth time," Dunn said, "and unaware I'm on this side of the country."

"What are you doing here—on this side of the country—and *here?*"

"*Here,*" Dunn said, gesturing to indicate the airfield, or maybe southern California, "because I need to borrow, beg, or, ultimately, steal Corsair parts from our brothers in the Navy, and *here here*—" he pointed at the ground "—because when I landed I called the Coronado to see if you might be in town, and they said you were expected about now. So I checked with Base Ops to see if they had an inbound Corsair. The AOD was all upset about some civilian airplane about to land. I knew it had to be you."

"As a token of the Navy's respect for the Marine Corps reserve, I have permission to land here in connection with my reserve duties," Pick said. "It's all perfectly legal, Colonel, sir."

"I've heard that before," Dunn said.

"Ken's reporting into Pendleton," Pick said. "We all just came from Japan—and on the way over, immodesty compels me to state, I set a new record. . . ."

"The most violently airsick passengers on one airplane in the history of commercial aviation?" Dunn asked, innocently.

McCoy laughed.

"Those who have nothing to boast about mock those who do," Pickering said, piously. "But since you ask, there is a new speed record to Japan."

"Inspired, no doubt, by a platoon of angry husbands chasing the pilot?" Dunn said.

McCoy laughed again.

"You understand, Ernie," Pickering said, as if sad and mystified, "that these two—Sarcastic Sam and Laughing Boy—are supposed to be my best friends?"

"The way I heard it, they're your only friends," Ernie said.

"Et tu, Brutus?" Pick said.

Dunn laughed, then turned to McCoy.

"What are they going to have you doing at Pendleton, Ken?" Dunn asked.

"I really don't know, Colonel," McCoy replied.

Dunn didn't press McCoy. As long as Dunn had known him—and he had met him on Guadalcanal—he had been involved in classified operations of one kind or another that couldn't be talked about.

"Captain McCoy," Pick said. "If you would be so kind, go into Base Ops and call us a cab while the colonel and I tie down the airplane. We have to eat, and the food is much better at the Coronado Beach than in the O Club here."

Pickering walked around the nose of the Staggerwing to where Dunn was really stretching to insert a tie-down rope into a link on the wing.

"Bill, so you don't say anything in innocence. . . . What the Killer's going to do at Pendleton is make up his mind whether he wants to go back to the ranks."

"Jesus Christ!" Dunn said, in surprise. "I thought he at least would be the exception to the rule. . . ."

"What rule?"

"Commissioned officers have to have a college degree," Dunn said. "I've lost four pilots in the last three months to that policy. But I thought they'd make an exception for somebody like McCoy."

Pickering had not heard about that policy.

But if I let Wee Willy think that's the reason the god damn Corps is giving him the boot, I won't have to get into the Killer's "There Will be a War in Korea in Ninty Days or Less" theory. Which, of course, I can't anyway.

"I guess not," Pickering said.

"Is he going to take stripes? Or get out?"

"I don't know. I don't think it would bother him to be a gunny, but Ernie . . ."

"Well, at least they don't have any kids to worry about," Dunn said.

"No, they don't."

Dunn looked at him thoughtfully.

"Pick, I can easily get a field-grade BOQ. If things would be awkward at the hotel."

"Don't be silly. There's plenty of room, and I think having you around will be good for both of them."

"What the hell is McCoy going to do outside the Corps? It's all he knows." Pick Pickering threw up his hands in a gesture of helplessness.

Then the two of them started to walk toward Base Ops.

Lieutenant Colonel Dunn was having thoughts vis-à-vis Major Pickering he did not—could not—share with him.

I love Pick, I really do. But the cold truth is that he is a lousy field-grade officer. A superb pilot—a natural pilot—and as far as courage goes, he makes John Wayne look like a pansy.

But, my God, he's a Marine major, and he lands at a Navy field barefooted and dressed like a Hawaiian pimp in an airplane that he once flew under the Golden Gate Bridge—I got that incredible tale from George Hart, so it's absolutely true.

I will, therefore, not tell Major Pickering that we have an old comrade-in-arms at Camp Pendleton that just might be able to turn the G-1 around about reducing McCoy to the ranks, and failing that, will certainly make his passage through the separation process at Pendleton as painless as possible.

If I told Pick, he'd hop in a cab, go out to Pendleton, in his Hawaiian pimp's shirt and bare feet, march into the general's office, and begin the conversation. "Clyde, you won't believe what a fucking dumb thing the Corps has done this time"...

Well, maybe it wouldn't be that bad, but it would be outrageous and thus counterproductive, and therefore I will not tell him what I'm going to do.

Not, of course, that there's much chance that I will be able to do anything at all.

[FOUR]
Office of the Deputy Commanding General
Camp Pendleton, California
1520 8 June 1950

Captain Arthur McGowan, USMC, aide-de-camp to the Deputy Commanding General, a tall, slim twenty-nine-year-old, put his head inside the general's door.

"General, Colonel Dunn's on the horn," he said.

"I was getting a little worried," Brigadier General Clyde W. Dawkins, USMC, replied. He was a tall, tanned, thin, sharp-featured man who had just celebrated his fortieth birthday.

He signaled with his index finger for Captain McGowan to enter the office, close the door behind him, and listen to the conversation on the extension telephone on a coffee table.

General Dawkins waited until McGowan had the phone to his ear before he picked up his own.

"I was getting a little worried, Bill," General Dawkins said. "Your ETA was noon. Where are you?"

"At the Coronado Beach, sir."

"I sort of thought you would be at Miramar," General Dawkins said.

The Miramar Naval Air Station was the other side of San Diego—about fifteen miles distant.

"Bill," the general went on before Dunn could answer, "you're not going to tell me Pickering's involved in this little operation of yours?"

"No, sir. But I'm in the suite. So's Pick. And until three minutes ago, so was Killer McCoy. And his wife."

General Dawkins was familiar with "the suite" in the Coronado Beach Hotel. Its fifteen rooms occupied about half of the fourth floor of the beachfront hotel, and was permanently leased to the Trans-Global Airways division of the Pacific & Far East Shipping Corporation.

At one time, before World War II, it had been leased to the Pacific & Far East Shipping Corporation for the use of the masters and chief engineers of P&FE vessels, and to house important passengers of the P&FE passenger fleet.

During World War II, on a space-available basis, its rooms had been made available to Marine and Navy officers with some connection to P&FE, or the Pickering family personally. That, in turn, had evolved into "the suite" becoming the unofficial quarters of Marine aviators, especially those who had served with VMF-229 on Guadalcanal, when they were assigned to—or passing through—one or another of San Diego's Marine and Navy installations.

General Dawkins had many fond memories of the suite, and usually the first one that came to mind was of the harem of stunningly beautiful girls at one wartime party who had gathered like moths at a candle flame around Tyrone Power and MacDonald Carey, both of whom had put their Hollywood careers on hold to serve as Marine aviators.

Sometimes he remembered the party where the star had been the actor Sterling Hayden, who'd been a Marine officer, but in the OSS, not an aviator.

Now General Dawkins regarded the suite as a time bomb about to explode. The final evolution had been into where the Marine Reserve aviators stayed when in the area, at the invitation of Major Malcolm S. Pickering, USMCR.

Although it had not come to General Dawkins's official attention, he had no reason to doubt the rumors that, especially during the two weeks of summer training many Marine Corps Reserve aviators attended in the San Diego Area, considerable quantities of intoxicating spirits were consumed by them in the suite, in the company of young ladies who, despite their beauty, were not the type one took home to meet one's mother. Or one's wife.

"No kidding?" General Dawkins said. "Give him my best regards. McCoy, I mean."

"Actually, sir, I'm calling about McCoy."

"First things first, Bill," Dawkins said. "There is at this moment in Hangar 212 at Miramar eight crates. . . ."

"Yes, sir, I know."

"I don't know, and don't want to know, what they contain."

"Sir, they will be picked up first thing in the morning. My Gooney-Bird lost the oil pump in the port engine, and was delayed in Kansas City. Its ETA here—North Island—is 0500 tomorrow morning. Figure an hour to fuel it, and I'll have it on the deck at Miramar at 0630, and with any luck at all, I'll be wheels-up from Miramar at 0730."

" 'I'll be wheels up'?" Dawkins parroted. "You'll be flying the Gooney-Bird?"

The Gooney-Bird was R4D, the Navy/Marine version of the Douglas DC-3 twin-engine transport.

"Yes, sir. I came out here in a Corsair. One of my kids will take that back."

"And you don't think anyone will wonder why a light colonel is flying a R4D?"

"I thought the Navy might be less prone to question a lieutenant colonel, sir," Dunn said.

That's probably true. But the real reason, Wee Willy, that you'll be flying the R4D is because you don't want one of your officers catching the flak if this midnight requisition of ours goes awry; you'll take the rap. You're a good officer, Dunn.

"If you're not wheels-up by 0830, give me—or Art McGowan—a heads-up, and I'll start the damage control."

"General, I really appreciate—"

"Save that until you're back at Beaufort," Dawkins said. "Save it until two weeks after you're back at Beaufort."

"General, even with cannibalizing, I can only get fifty-five percent of my Corsairs in the air—"

"I seem to recall, Colonel, your mentioning this before," Dawkins interrupted him. "And, to save a little time here, ensuring that you will be wheels-up at Miramar with these crates aboard by 0830 tomorrow, let's change the subject."

"Yes, sir."

"Tell me about the Killer," Dawkins said.

"He's being reduced to the ranks," Dunn said.

"That goddamn college-degree nonsense again?"

"Yes, sir."

"Oh, Jesus, Bill."

"Yes, sir."

"Well, I've had a shot at it, but I don't think I'll be able to do much good. All I get is the same speech—there's no money, we have to reduce the number of officers, and one of the elimination criteria is education."

"Yes, sir. And actually, I think it's too late to help the Killer. He was ordered home from Japan, to Pendleton, for separation not later than 30 June."

"We're going to wind up with an officer corps consisting mainly of college graduates who can't find their ass with both hands," Dawkins said, bitterly.

"General, what I was hoping you could do is spare the Killer as much of the separation nonsense as possible. It has to be a humiliation for someone like the Killer to be told the Corps doesn't want him as an officer anymore."

"What the hell is he going to do as a civilian?" Dawkins asked, rhetorically.

"Well, in the sense he doesn't need a job, he's a lot better off than some of the people caught in the reduction."

It took Dawkins a moment to sort that out.

"Oh, yeah, that's right. His wife has money, doesn't she?"

"Her father is chairman of American Personal Pharmaceutical," Dunn said. "I understand there are two majority stockholders: Ernie McCoy's father, and Ernie McCoy."

"That much, huh? I'd heard something, but I had no idea she had that kind of money."

"And even if that wasn't true, the Pickerings, father and son, would make sure the Killer doesn't go hungry."

"And I think we can presume that when General Pickering heard the Corps was giving the Killer the boot, he did his best to see that it wouldn't happen."

"I'm sure he did, sir."

"And couldn't help, either," Dawkins added, bitterly.

"It doesn't look that way, sir."

"So what can I do for the Killer, Bill?"

"Maybe have a word with the G-1, sir. Speed him through the process."

"Done, Bill," General Dawkins said.

"Thank you, sir."

"When does he report in here?"

"He's on his way out there right now, sir."

"Then I'd better get off my ass, hadn't I? Make sure you're wheels up by 0830, Bill, or we're both liable to be reporting to the G-1 for involuntary separation."

"I'll do my best, sir. And thank you, sir."

"Have a nice slow flight across the country, Colonel," General Dawkins said. He hung up the telephone and turned to his aide. "Get the car, Art."

"Aye, aye, sir."

[FIVE]
Office of the Assistant Chief of Staff, G-1
Headquarters
Camp Pendleton, California
1545 8 June 1950

The usual practice when one of Camp Pendleton's general officers had business to transact with the G-1 was that the G-1, who was a full colonel, went to their offices. Thus, the G-1, Colonel C. Harry Wade, USMC, was surprised to hear someone bark, "Ten-hut on deck"—a command given only when someone senior to the senior officer on duty, in this case Colonel C. Harry Wade—came into the building.

Wade looked through his open office door to see what the hell was going on and saw Brigadier General Clyde Dawkins marching purposefully toward his office, trailed by his aide-de-camp.

Colonel Wade rose quickly to his feet.

"Got a minute for me, Harry?" General Dawkins asked, as he entered Wade's office.

"Good afternoon, General," Wade said. "Of course, sir. Can I offer you some coffee?"

"No, thanks," Dawkins said. "I'm coffee-ed out. Art, will you close the door, please?"

Captain McGowan closed the door.

"I'm not sure, Harry," General Dawkins said, "whether this is what you could call 'for the good of the Corps,' or personal. But I'm here."

"How can I help, sir?"

"This goddamn college-degree nonsense has just gotten one more damned good Marine officer."

"We've talked about that, General," Wade said. "If this is a special case, I'll get on the horn to Eighth and Eye. But I think I can tell you what they're going to say."

"Yes, I think I know, too," Dawkins said. "I think it's too late for anything to be done about this."

"Yes, sir?"

"Does 'Killer McCoy' mean anything to you, Harry?"

"I've heard about him. He made the Makin Island raid, didn't he? With Major Jimmy Roosevelt?"

"The Makin Island raid, and a hell of a lot else," Dawkins said. "During the war, the Killer spent more time behind enemy lines than most people you and I know spent in the Corps."

"Yes, sir. I know who he is. I've never met him."

"You're about to," Dawkins said. "He's on his way out here from Diego for involuntary separation. He's a captain. He used to be a major. They took that away from him, and now they want to send him back to the ranks."

"I don't know what to say," Colonel Wade said. "You could tell me this college-degree thing is stupid, but you'd be preaching to the choir."

"I want his passage through your separation process greased," Dawkins said. "And I don't want him to suspect it was greased because somebody feels sorry for him."

Wade did not reply directly.

"What the hell can a man like that do on civvy street?" he asked, as if of himself.

"I just found out he's the opposite of hurting for money," Dawkins said. "For whatever consolation that might be. His wife owns a large chunk of American Personal Pharmaceuticals, and the rest of it is apparently owned by her father."

"In other words, he's in the Corps because he wants to be," Wade said.

"Exactly," Dawkins said. "And now he's getting the boot. I want that exit to be as painless as possible."

"With your permission, sir," Wade said, "I'd like to get Lieutenant Colonel Brewer in here. He's in charge of involuntary officer separations."

Dawkins thought that over for a moment.

There was no question in his mind that Colonel Wade would relay his desires to the lieutenant colonel. But it would take only another couple of minutes of his time, and the lieutenant colonel would have no question in his mind what the Deputy Commanding General wanted.

"Good idea, Harry," Dawkins said.

Colonel Wade walked to his office door and opened it, and spoke to his administrative assistant.

"Sergeant, run over to Colonel Brewer's office and tell him I'd like to see him right now."

"Aye, aye, sir."

"And if he has a file on a Captain McCoy, tell him to bring that with him."

"Aye, aye, sir."

Three minutes later, Lieutenant Colonel Brewer entered Colonel Wade's office, carrying a large manila folder on which was lettered "MCCOY, K.R. CAPT USMCR."

He was visibly surprised to find the deputy commanding general resting his rear end on Colonel Wade's desk.

"You know the general, of course, Brewer?"

"Yes, sir," Lieutenant Colonel Brewer said. He had met Dawkins for no more than two minutes when reporting aboard Camp Pendleton.

"That's McCoy's file?" Dawkins asked.

"Yes, sir."

He offered it to Dawkins, who took it.

"The general is interested in seeing that Captain McCoy's separation from the Corps be conducted as expeditiously as possible," Colonel Wade said.

"Yes, sir. I understand."

"You understand what?" Dawkins said.

"Sir, Captain McCoy's reputation precedes him," Lieutenant Colonel Brewer said.

"You bet your life it does," Dawkins said, "but there is something in your tone of voice, Colonel . . ."

"Sir?"

"What exactly do you know about Captain McCoy?" Dawkins asked.

"Well, sir, from what I understand of Captain McCoy, he was lucky to be retained on active duty as an officer as long as he was."

"Anything else?" Dawkins asked, softly.

"Sir, as I understand the situation," Colonel Brewer began, slowly, having sensed that he was marching on very thin ice, and having absolutely no idea why that should be, "Captain McCoy was commissioned from enlisted status in the early days of World War Two when the Corps was desperately seeking officers."

"And we commissioned practically anybody who could see lightning and hear thunder?" Dawkins asked.

"Yes, sir."

"Anything else?" Dawkins asked.

"Well, sir, it's come to my attention that he's . . . uh . . . in a financial position where he would be better off to spend his last twenty-nine days in the Corps on duty, rather than on leave. So that he could be paid for his unused accrued leave on separation, sir."

"And what would you have Captain McCoy doing on his last twenty-nine days of active service, Colonel?"

"Well, sir, as I'm sure you know, there's always something an officer can do. Inventory supply rooms. The Exchange. That sort of thing."

"Colonel," Dawkins said. "Listen to me carefully. I'll tell you what you are going to do vis-à-vis Captain McCoy, who is at this moment en route here. You will immediately receive him in your office. Ninety seconds after you receive him in your office, he will depart your office on leave until the last day of his active service as an officer. When he reports back here on that last day of service, you will have arranged for the hospital to give him his separation physical examination on a personal basis—that is to say, it will take no longer than sixty minutes. If the hospital has any problem with that, have them contact me. When Captain McCoy has his separation physical in hand, you will personally hand him his final pay and his travel orders to his home of record, and wish him well in his civilian career. You understand all that?"

"Yes, sir," Lieutenant Colonel Brewer said.

"See that it happens, Harry," Dawkins said to Colonel Wade.

"Aye, aye, sir."

"Come on, Art," General Dawkins said to Captain McGowan, and walked out of the room.

[SIX]
Office of the Chief for Officer Records
Office of the Assistant Chief of Staff, G-1
Headquarters
Camp Pendleton, California
1610 8 June 1950

"You wanted to see me, Colonel?" Major Robert B. Macklin, USMC, inquired of Lieutenant Colonel Peter S. Brewer, USMC, from Brewer's open office door.

"Come in, Macklin," Brewer said, "and close the door."

"Yes, sir."

"About this Captain McCoy, Macklin . . ."

"Yes, sir?"

"I want to make sure I have this straight in my mind," Brewer said. "From what you told me, you served with him. Is that right?"

"Yes, sir."

"Where was that?"

"I was on several occasions stationed in the same places as McCoy, sir, but I don't know if that could be construed as 'serving with' him, sir."

"For example?"

"The first time I ran into McCoy, sir, I was in intelligence in the 4th Marines in Shanghai, and he was a machine-gun section leader in one of the companies. I knew of his reputation there."

"Which was?"

"Sir, I . . . uh . . . I'm a bit reluctant, under the circumstances . . ."

"This is just between you and me, Macklin. Let's have it."

"He was known as 'the Killer,' sir. He got into a knife fight—a drunken brawl, as I understand it—with some Italian Marines, and killed one of them. I was surprised that he wasn't court-martialed for that, and even more surprised when I was an instructor at the Officer Candidate School at Quantico, when McCoy showed up there."

"I see."

"At the time, knowing what kind of a man he was, I recommended that he be dropped from the officer training program. I just didn't think he was officer material, sir."

"But he was commissioned anyway, despite your recommendation?"

"Sir, the Corps was desperately short of officers at the time, scraping the bottom of the barrel. The Quantico sergeant major, for example, was a sergeant major one day and a lieutenant colonel the next."

"Really? What was his name? Do you remember?"

"Yes, sir. Stecker. Jack NMI Stecker."

"You serve with McCoy anywhere else, Macklin?"

"When the OSS was formed, sir, there was a levy on the Corps for officers with intelligence experience in China. And/or who had some knowledge of Oriental languages. Both McCoy and I were assigned to the OSS. He had some smattering knowledge of Chinese, I believe."

"And that's how you came to understand his personal characteristics, his 'payday-to-payday' philosophy of life?"

"Yes, sir. I suppose it is. May I ask—?"

Brewer put his hand up to silence him.

"I hardly know where to begin, Major Macklin," he said. "Let me start with Brigadier General Jack NMI Stecker, holder of the Medal of Honor, under whom it was my privilege to serve when he was special assistant to General Vandergrift, when he was Commandant of the Corps. You weren't suggesting, a moment ago, that he was something like Captain McCoy, someone who really shouldn't have been an officer in the first place, much less a lieutenant colonel and ultimately a brigadier general, were you?"

"No, sir. General Stecker was a fine Marine officer. But, if I may say so, he was sort of the exception to the rule."

"Not like McCoy, is what you're saying?"

"Not at all like McCoy, sir."

"Would you be interested to learn that whatever other problems Captain McCoy has at the moment, paying the rent is not one of them?"

"Sir?"

"I just came from Colonel Wade's office, Macklin, where I very much fear I left General Dawkins with the impression that I don't know what's going on around here."

"Sir?"

"Both General Dawkins—who is obviously personally acquainted with Captain McCoy—and Colonel Wade—who had a somewhat different opinion from yours of McCoy's service to the Corps even before we had a look at his records—are convinced the Corps is making a stupid mistake in separating Captain McCoy from the service."

"I can only suggest, sir, that the general and the colonel are privy to information about Captain McCoy that I'm not."

"You didn't know that he was both wounded, and decorated for valor when the Marine Raiders made the Makin Island raid?"

"That never came to my attention, sir."

"Did it ever come to your attention that Captain McCoy was awarded the Victoria Cross by the Brits for his service to the Australian coastwatcher service?"

"No, sir, it did not."

"How about his award of the Distinguished Service Medal for his having established a weather station in the Gobi Desert in Japanese-occupied Manchuria?"

"No, sir."

"There are several possibilities here, Major," Colonel Brewer said, almost conversationally."

"Sir?"

"One of which is that you are the most stupid sonofabitch ever to wear the insignia of a Marine major. Among the others are that you are a lying sono-fabitch with a personal vendetta—for reasons I don't even want to think about—against Captain McCoy."

"Sir—"

"Shut your mouth, Major," Brewer snapped. "Until I make up my mind which it is, and what I'm going to do about it, you will report to the Head-quarters Commandant for an indefinite period of temporary duty. I don't know what else he will have you doing, but you will start by inventorying every company supply room on the base. You are dismissed, Major."

[SEVEN]
The Director's Office
East Building, The CIA Complex
2430 E Street
Washington, D.C.
0930 9 June 1950

"The Director will see you now, Senator," the executive assistant to the Director of the CIA said, and held open the door to an inner office.

Senator Richardson K. Fowler and Fleming Pickering rose from a dark green leather couch and walked toward the office.

Rear Admiral Roscoe Hillenkoetter, a tall, imposing, silver-haired man, came from around his desk with his hand extended.

"Sorry to have kept you waiting, Senator," he said.

Pickering and Fowler had been in the outer office no more than three minutes.

In holders behind the admiral's desk were three flags: the national colors, the CIA flag, and a blue flag with the two stars of a rear admiral.

"Thank you for seeing us on such short notice, Admiral," Fowler said.

"Anytime, Senator, you know that," Hillenkoetter said, and extended his hand to Pickering.

"This is my very good friend, Fleming Pickering," Fowler said.

"How do you do, sir?" Hillenkoetter said. "What is it they say, 'any friend of . . .' ? I'm trying to place the name."

"I'm chairman of the board of Pacific and Far East Shipping," Pickering said.

That, too, rings a bell, but no prize. There's something else. What?

"First, let me offer coffee," Hillenkoetter said, "and then you can tell me how I can be of service."

A younger woman than the admiral's executive assistant appeared with a silver coffee service.

There was silence as she served coffee.

Pickering, Pickering, where have I heard that name before?

Oh, yeah!

Pearl Harbor. Right after the attack. He was a reserve four-striper; Navy Secretary Knox's personal representative. Abrasive bastard. Thought he knew everything, and didn't like anything the Navy was doing. Or had done.

And after that, what?

He was in the OSS. He was the deputy director of the OSS for the Pacific. Or was he? The OSS guy was a Marine brigadier, not a Navy captain.

Admiral Nimitz liked the OSS guy. Maybe there's two Pickerings—brothers, maybe.

What he is after, a job?

The young woman left the office.

"You were the assistant director of the OSS in the Pacific," Hillenkoetter said. "Isn't that right, Mr. Pickering?"

"*General* Pickering was the assistant director *for* the Pacific," Fowler corrected him.

"Excuse me," Hillenkoetter said. "*For* the Pacific."

"Yes, I was," Pickering said.

"General Pickering has just come from Tokyo," Fowler said.

"Is that so?"

"Admiral, before we go any further," Fowler said. "If you have a recorder operating, please turn it off."

"I beg your pardon?" Hillenkoetter asked, surprised and indignant.

"If you have a recorder operating," Fowler repeated, "please turn it off."

Hillenkoetter didn't reply; he didn't trust himself to speak.

Who does this arrogant sonofabitch think he is, coming into my office and telling me to turn off my recorder?

"Franklin Roosevelt had the Oval Office wired to record interesting conversations," Fowler went on, amiably, reasonably. "I have no reason to believe Harry Truman had it removed. If I were in your shoes, I'd have such a device. I suspect you do, and I'm asking you to turn it off. There are some things that should not be recorded for posterity."

Hillenkoetter felt his temper rise.

Like a senator pressuring me to give his buddy a job, for example?

Who does he think he is?

He thinks he's a power in the Senate. He knows *he's a power in the Senate. Ergo sum, one of the most powerful men in the country.*

Hillenkoetter pressed a lever on his intercom box.

"Mrs. Rudolphus, would you please turn off the recording device?"

"Yes, sir," Mrs. Rudolphus replied.

Her surprise was evident in her voice. One of the reasons the admiral had kept Senator Fowler waiting was to make sure the recorder was working.

One did not let one's guard down when a senator—any senator, much less Richardson K. Fowler (R., Cal.)—called one at one's home and asked for a meeting at your earliest convenience, say, nine o'clock tomorrow morning.

"Thank you," Fowler said.

Hillenkoetter didn't reply.

Fowler looked at Pickering and made a *give it to me* motion with his index finger.

Pickering took a fat business-size envelope from his interior jacket pocket and handed it to Fowler. Fowler handed it to Hillenkoetter.

"Take a look at that, Admiral, if you would, please," Fowler said.

Hillenkoetter opened the envelope and took out the sheaf of paper.

"What is this?"

"Before we talk about it, Admiral," Fowler said, "it might be a good idea for you to have some idea of what we're talking about."

Hillenkoetter's lips tightened, but he didn't reply. It took him three minutes to read the document.

"This would appear to be an intelligence assessment," he said finally. "But there's no heading, no transmission letter. Where did this come from?"

"I had my secretary excerpt the pertinent data from the original," Pickering said.

"From the original *official* document?"

Pickering nodded.

"Such a document would be classified," Hillenkoetter said, thinking out loud. "Secret, at least. How did you come into possession of the original?"

"The original document was prepared by an officer who worked for me during the war," Pickering said. "I believe what he says in that assessment."

"I've seen nothing from our people there, or from General MacArthur's intelligence people, that suggests anything like this," Hillenkoetter said.

"That assessment was given to General Willoughby," Pickering said. "Who not only ordered it destroyed, but had the officer who prepared it ordered from Japan."

"That sounds like an accusation, General," Hillenkoetter said.

"It's a statement of fact," Pickering said.

"Why would he do something like that?"

"God only knows," Pickering said. "The fact is, he did."

"And the officer who prepared it, rather than destroying it, gave it to you? Is that about it?"

"That's it," Pickering said.

"General Willoughby is not only a fine officer, but I would say the most experienced intelligence officer in the Far East," Hillenkoetter said.

"Does the name Wendell Fertig mean anything to you, Admiral?" Pickering asked.

Hillenkoetter searched his mind.

"The guerrilla in the Philippines?" He smiled, and added, "The reservist who promoted himself to general?"

"The guerrilla in the Philippines who, when the Army finally got back to Mindanao, had thirty thousand armed, uniformed, and organized troops under his command waiting for them," Pickering said. "During the war, he forced the Japanese to divert a quarter of a million men to dealing with him."

Hillenkoetter, his face showing surprise at the coldly angry intensity of Pickering's response, looked at him and waited for him to continue.

"Before, at President Roosevelt's direction, I sent a team of agents into Mindanao to establish contact with General Fertig, General Willoughby, speaking for MacArthur, stated flatly that there was no possibility of meaningful guerrilla operations in the Pacific."

Hillenkoetter took a moment to digest that.

"I gather your relationship with General MacArthur was difficult?" he asked.

"Anyone's relationship with General MacArthur is difficult," Pickering said. "But if you are asking what I think you are, our personal relationship was—is— just fine. I had dinner with him and Mrs. MacArthur last week."

"And did you bring this . . . this *assessment* up to him?"

"General MacArthur's loyalty to his staff, especially those who were with him in the Philippines, is legendary," Pickering said. "I know Douglas MacArthur well enough to know that it would have been a waste of time."

"And, I daresay, he might have asked the uncomfortable question, how you came to be in possession of the assessment in the first place?"

Pickering didn't reply.

"The officer who gave you this assessment should not have done so," Hillenkoetter said.

"Is that going to be your reaction to this, Admiral?" Pickering asked, coldly.

"Someone dared to go out of channels, and therefore what he had to say is not relevant?"

"Easy, Flem," Senator Fowler said.

"I didn't say that, General," Hillenkoetter said.

"That was the implication," Pickering said.

"I'll need the officer's name," Hillenkoetter said.

"I'm not going to give it to you," Pickering said, flatly.

"I can get it," Hillenkoetter flared.

"If you did that, Admiral, this whole thing would probably wind up in the newspapers," Senator Fowler said. "I don't think you want that any more than we do."

Hillenkoetter, while waiting to hear that the recording system was functioning, had gone over the CIA's most recent "informal biography" of Fowler, Richardson K. (R., Cal.) and was thus freshly reminded that the senator owned the San Francisco *Courier-Herald,* nine smaller newspapers, six radio stations, and five television stations, including one radio station and one television station in Washington, D.C.

"This is a matter of national security, Senator," Hillenkoetter said, and immediately regretted it.

"That's why we're here, Admiral," Pickering said.

Hillenkoetter glared at him, realized he was doing so, and turned to Fowler.

"What is it you would like me to do, Senator?" he asked.

"At the very least, light a fire under your people in Japan and Hong Kong and Formosa and see why they haven't come up with an assessment like this," Pickering said.

"I was asking the senator, General," Hillenkoetter said.

"What General Pickering suggests seems like a good first step," Fowler said. "Followed closely by step two, which would be keeping me advised, on a daily basis, of what your people develop."

"Senator, my channel to the Senate is via the Senate Oversight Committee on Intelligence. I'm not sure I'm authorized to do that."

"Well, I certainly wouldn't want you to do anything you're not authorized to do," Fowler said, reasonably. "So what I'm apparently going to have to do is go to Senator Driggs, whom I had appointed to the chairmanship of the Oversight Committee, and ask him to give you permission to give me what I want. I think Jack Driggs would want to know why I'm interested."

"Another option would be to bring this to the attention of the President," Hillenkoetter said.

"Whatever you think is best for all concerned," Fowler said. "I'm going to have lunch with President Truman at half past twelve. Would you like me to bring it up with him then?"

They locked eyes for a moment.

"Senator," Hillenkoetter said, "I mean this as a compliment. You really know how to play hardball, don't you?"

"I've heard that unfounded accusation before," Fowler said.

"May I speak out of school?" Admiral Hillenkoetter asked.

"I thought I'd made it clear this whole conversation is out of school," Fowler said.

"With all respect to General Pickering, and his former subordinate, the officer who prepared this assessment, I'm having a great deal of trouble placing much credence in it."

"See here, Admiral—" Pickering flared.

"Flem, let him finish," Fowler said sharply.

"For one thing," Hillenkoetter went on, "I can't believe that General Willoughby would suppress something like this, and for another, as I said before, I've received nothing remotely approaching this assessment from my own people in the Orient."

"So?" Fowler asked.

"On the other hand, it comes to me not only from a . . . *the former* . . . deputy director of the OSS for the Pacific, but via a senator, for whom I not only have a great deal of respect, but who apparently believes there is something to the assessment. Under that circumstance, I will immediately take action to see what I can find out myself."

"How?" Pickering asked, sarcastically, "by sending Willoughby a radio message?"

"Flem, goddamn it!" Fowler said.

"By dispatching my deputy director for Asiatic Activities—your replacement, so to speak, General—over there as soon as I can get him on a plane, with instructions to—what was your phrase, General? 'light a fire'?—*light a fire* under our people in Hong Kong, Taipei, and Seoul to *refresh* their efforts."

"All right," Fowler said.

"It would facilitate things if they could talk with the author of this," Hillenkoetter went on, tapping his fingertips on the assessment. "To do that, I'd have to have his name."

"Flem?" Fowler asked.

Pickering thought it over.

"No," he said, finally, "for a number of reasons, primarily because everything he knows is in the assessment. What they would really want from him is his sources, and I don't think he'd be willing to tell them."

"We're supposed to be on the same side, General," Hillenkoetter said.

"I'm not entirely convinced of that, frankly," Pickering said. "Anyway, my . . . friend . . . would not give up his sources unless I told him to, and I'm not willing to do that. At least, right now."

Hillenkoetter shrugged.

"I may keep this, right?" he asked, tapping the assessment again.

"I've been thinking about that," Pickering said. "Could I have your word that you'll use it to pose specific questions—about the order of battle, that sort of thing?—I mean, that you won't turn it over as is to your people? They wouldn't have to be rocket scientists to figure out who wrote it if they had the entire document."

"And we wouldn't want that to happen, would we?" Hillenkoetter asked. "It might wind up in the newspapers."

Fowler smiled.

"You have my word, General," Hillenkoetter said. "And would you agree, Senator, that we don't have to worry the President about this just now?"

"Not for the time being," Fowler said, and rose from his chair. "Thank you, Admiral, for your consideration, and for seeing us on short notice. And I'll expect to hear from you shortly, right?"

"Absolutely," Hillenkoetter said, and offered his hand to Pickering.

"It was a pleasure to meet you, General."

"Was it really?" Pickering asked.

Hillenkoetter laughed, a little uneasily, and walked Pickering and Fowler to his office door.

As he watched them walk through his outer office, there was an unexpected bulletin from his memory bank.

Christ! The Gobi Desert weather station. The OSS—Pickering—put that in, in the middle of Japanese-occupied Mongolia. Nobody thought he could do it, much less keep it up. But he did, right through the end of the war. The B-29 bombing of the Japanese home islands could not have taken place without it. And we're still using it.

Whatever else Pickering may be, he's no amateur.

Maybe there is something to this assessment.

But why would Charley Willoughby sit on it?

He became aware that Mrs. Warburg, his executive assistant, was looking at him, waiting for orders.

"Call Mr. Jacobs, please, Mrs. Warburg," he said. "Ask him to come up as soon as he can. And call transportation and start working on tickets for him to Hong Kong."

"Yes, sir," she said.

He started to close his office door, but she held it open.

Then she stepped inside the office and closed the door.

"Admiral, the tape recorder didn't get shut down," she said.

He looked at her.

"There was something in your voice when you said to shut it down," she said.

"You heard that conversation?" he asked.

She nodded.

"No, you didn't, Martha," he said. "And I want you personally to get that tape, shred it, and burn it. And make sure there are no copies."

"Yes, sir," she said. "Do I get to read the assessment?"

"It's on my desk. You can read it, but I want zero copies made."

"Yes, sir."

"You did the right thing, Martha," Hillenkoetter said. "But this . . . situation . . . is extraordinary."

"Yes, sir," Mrs. Warburg said, and walked to his desk to read the assessment.

IV

[ONE]
The William Banning House
66 South Battery
Charleston, South Carolina
1630 17 June 1950

When they saw the Buick station wagon pull to the curb, both "Mother" Banning and her daughter-in-law, "Luddy," rose from the rocking chairs in which they had been sitting. Mother Banning folded her hands on her stomach. Luddy Banning clapped hers together, producing a sound like a pistol shot, and then, a moment later, a dignified, gray-haired black man in a gray cotton jacket appeared from inside the house.

"Ma'am?"

"Stanley, our guests have arrived," Luddy Banning said. "Please inform the colonel, and send someone to take care of their car and luggage."

"Yes, ma'am."

Mother Banning and Luddy Banning were the mother and the wife, respectively, of Colonel Edward J. Banning, USMC, who was both commanding officer of Marine Barracks, Charleston, and Adjunct Professor of Naval Science at his alma mater, officially the Military College of South Carolina, but far better known as the Citadel.

Colonel Banning was a graduate of the Citadel, ('26) as his father ('05), grandfather ('80), and great-grandfather ('55) had been. On April 12, 1861, Great-Grandfather Matthew Banning had stood where Mother and Luddy Banning now stood on the piazza and watched as the first shots of the War of the Secession were fired on Fort Sumter.

He had then gone off as a twenty-five-year-old major to command the 2nd Squadron of the 2nd South Carolina Dragoons. When released from Union captivity in 1865, the conditions of his release required him to swear fealty to the United States of America, and to remove the insignia of a major general from his gray Confederate uniform. For the rest of his life, however, he was addressed as General Banning, and referred to by his friends as "The General."

Grandfather Matthew Banning, Jr., had answered the call of his friend Theodore Roosevelt and gone off to the Spanish American War as a major with the First U.S. Volunteer Cavalry. Family legend held that Brevet Lieutenant Colonel Banning had been one of the only two First Volunteer Cavalry officers actually to be astride a horse during the charge up Kettle and San Juan Hills. There was a large oil painting of that engagement in the living room of the house on the Battery, showing Brevet Lieutenant Colonel Banning and Colonel Theodore Roosevelt leading the charge. For the rest of his life, he was addressed as Colonel and referred to by his friends as "The Colonel."

Matthew Banning III elected to accept a commission in the Cavalry of the Regular Army of the United States on his graduation from the Citadel in June 1905, the alternative being going to work for his father in one or another of the Banning family businesses. He had been a first lieutenant for twelve years when the United States entered World War I in 1917. When the Armistice was signed the next year, the silver eagles of a full colonel of the Tank Corps were on the epaulets of his tunic, and a Silver Star and two Purple Hearts were on the chest.

With the Colonel still running the family businesses, Colonel Banning III remained in service after the war, even though it meant accepting a reduction from colonel to major. By 1926, he had been repromoted to colonel, and on the parade ground at the Citadel had sworn his son, Edward J. Banning, into the United States Marine Corps as a second lieutenant upon his graduation from the Citadel.

Like his father before him, Matthew Banning III had been addressed as Colonel for the rest of his life, and referred to by his friends as "The Colonel."

The Colonel lived long enough (1946) to see his first grandson, and his son—with the eagles of a Marine colonel on his epaulets—assigned as a Professor of Military Science at the Citadel.

For a while, the likelihood of either thing happening had seemed remote. For one thing, Edward Banning had not married as the next step after graduating from the Citadel, as had all his antecedents.

He was thirty-six, a captain serving with the 4th Marines in Shanghai, before he marched to the altar, and that only days before he went to the Philippines with the 4th Marines, leaving his White Russian bride in Shanghai at the mercy—if that word applied at all—of the Japanese.

Captain Banning was blinded by Japanese artillery in the Philippines and evacuated by submarine. His sight returned, and he was given duties he would not talk about, but which The Colonel understood meant Intelligence with a capital *I.*

Once, on the piazza of the house on the Battery, just before he went—for the fourth or fifth time—to the war in the Orient, then Major Banning confided in The Colonel that, realistically, he held little hope that he would ever see his wife again. There had been no word of her at all.

And then, in May of 1943, when by then Lieutenant Colonel Banning was "somewhere in the Pacific" there had been a telephone call from the Hon. Zachary W. Westminister III (D., 3rd District, S.C.), a Citadel classmate.

"Matty, you sitting down?"

"No, actually, I'm not."

"Matty, ol' buddy, you better sit down."

It didn't sound as if ol' Zach was going to relate bad news about Eddie, but The Colonel had been worried nevertheless.

"I'm sitting, Zach, now get on with it."

"I just came from meeting with the President," Congressman Westminister began, "and I can only tell you a little. . . ."

"Get on with it, goddamn it, Zach!"

"When you get off the phone, you go tell 'Lisbeth to change the sheets in the guest room. Your daughter-in-law will shortly be arriving."

"My God!"

"And if you still have a crib in the attic, you better dust that off, too. She's coming with Edward *Edwardovich* Banning in her arms."

"You're telling me there's a baby?"

"Edward *Edwardovich*—how 'bout that?—Banning. Born August 1942, somewhere in Mongolia."

"Goddamn, Zach!"

"When I know more, I'll be in touch. The President just gave the order to put the two of them on a plane from Chunking."

Elizabeth Banning didn't say anything, of course—she was a Christian gentlewoman—but The Colonel knew that once the situation changed from Ed having married some White Russian in Shanghai who would probably never be heard from again, to having Ed's White Russian wife and their baby about to arrive at the house on the Battery, she naturally had concerns about what she would be like, how they would fit into Charleston society.

The former Maria Catherine Ludmilla Zhikov had come down the steps from the Eastern Airlines DC-3 looking far more like a photograph from *Town & Country* than a refugee who had spent seventeen months moving across China and Mongolia in pony-drawn carts, pausing en route for several days to be delivered of a son.

Her Naval Air Transport Service flight from China to the United States had been met at San Francisco by Mrs. Fleming Pickering, who transported her and the baby to the Foster San Franciscan hotel where the proprietors of the in-hotel Chic Lady clothing shop and the across-the-street Styles for the Very Young baby clothes emporium were waiting for her.

"I knew the moment I laid eyes on Luddy that she was a lady," Mrs. Elizabeth Banning said at the time—and many times later.

"If I had arrived in Charleston looking like I looked when I got off the plane in San Francisco," Luddy Banning said later—after The Colonel had gone to his reward, she herself had become "The Colonel's Wife" and Elizabeth Banning had acceded, much like Queen Elizabeth's mother, to the title "Mother Banning"—"Mother Banning would have had a heart attack. Thank God for Patricia Pickering."

Behind her back—not derisively or pejoratively—Luddy Banning was known as "the countess," not only because she had a certain regal air about her, but also because a Citadel cadet doing a term paper on the organization of the Russian Imperial general staff had gone to The Colonel's Russian wife for help with it.

The colonel's Russian wife, while perusing one of the cadet's reference works, had laid a finger on the name of Lieutenant General Count Vasily Ivanovich Zhivkov, and softly said, "My father."

That announcement had taken no longer than twenty-four hours to become common knowledge among the cadets of the Citadel, another twenty-four hours to circulate among the faculty, and another twenty-four hours to reach the houses along the Battery.

Luddy Banning descended the wide stairs and walked down the brick sidewalk through the cast-iron fence to the Buick and waited until Captain Kenneth R. McCoy, USMC—who was wearing a yellow polo shirt and khaki trousers—got from behind the wheel, then wrapped her arms around him.

"Our savior," she said, seriously.

"Ah, come on, Luddy!"

"You were our savior, you will always be our savior," she said. "Welcome to our home!"

She kissed McCoy twice, once on each cheek, and then went around the front of the Buick and embraced Ernie.

"How nice to see you again, Major McCoy," Mother Banning said, offering him her hand.

"It's Captain McCoy, ma'am," McCoy said. "It's good to see you, too."

"Well, I'll be damned," a male voice boomed from beside the wide staircase. "Look what the tide washed up!"

Without realizing he was doing it—literally a Pavlovian reaction—McCoy saluted the tall, stocky, erect, starting to bald man, who had a blond eight-year-old boy straddling his neck.

"Colonel," he said.

"Goddamn, Ken, you of all people know me well enough to call me by my name."

He walked quickly to McCoy, his hand extended to shake McCoy's, then changed his mind and embraced him.

"It's good to see you," McCoy said.

"Come on in the house, Stanley'll take care of the bags and the car. I think a small—hell, large—libation is in order."

He looked at his wife, who was coming around the front of the car with her arm around Ernie McCoy.

"Hey, beautiful lady," he called. "Welcome to Charleston."

"Hello, Ed," Ernie said. "Thank you, it's good to be here."

They all went up the stairs as Stanley, the dignified black man, and a younger black man came down the stairs.

"I put the wine in the sitting room, Colonel," he said to Banning.

"Just the wine?"

"No, sir," Stanley said. "Not just the wine."

"Good man, Stanley."

"These glasses are . . . exquisite," Ernie said, as Ed Banning poured champagne in her engraved crystal glass.

"They've been in the family a long time," Mother Banning said. "We only bring them out for special people."

"Thank you," Ernie said.

"The general bought them in Europe before the war," Mother Banning said. "On his wedding trip."

Ed Banning saw the confusion on Ernie's face.

"Mother refers, of course, to the War of Secession," he said. "These glasses spent the war buried on the island, which always made me wonder if my great-grandfather had as much faith in the inevitable victory of the Confederacy as he professed at the time."

"Edward, what a terrible thing to say," Mother Banning said.

"Mother, as it says in the Good Book, the 'truth shall make you free.' "

There was polite laughter.

"Speaking of the truth," Banning said. "Let me get this out of the way before we get down to serious drinking. The general called—Ken's and my general, Mother—and let me know what's going on. We're family, in my mind. . . ."

"And mine," Luddy said. "This family wouldn't be here if it weren't for our savior."

"Hear, hear," Banning said. "Anyway, I want you both to know that what's ours is yours, anything we can do to help, we will, and we can either talk about it or not. Your choice."

"I'm going to cry," Ernie said.

"Drink your booze," Colonel Banning said, and then had another thought: "One more thing, Ken. Ernie Zimmerman, the best-dressed master gunner in the Marine Corps."

"What about him?"

"I wanted to ask you before I asked him and Mae-Su down from Beaufort. You want to see him?"

"Wouldn't that be an imposition?" Ernie asked. "Ken and I talked about going down there to see them on our way to California."

"You weren't listening, beautiful lady," Colonel Banning said. He turned to the butler, who was in the act of opening a second bottle of Moët et Chandon extra brut. "Stanley, see if you can get Mister Zimmerman on the horn for me, will you?"

"Mae-Su is my sister, Ernie," Luddy Banning said, in gentle reproof. "She is always welcome in our home."

Master Gunner Ernest W. Zimmerman, USMC, his wife Mae-Su, and their five children arrived at 66 South Battery two hours later. At Mae-Su's insistence, the entire family was dressed in a manner Mrs. Zimmerman felt was appropriate to visit—as she described them privately to her husband—"the ladies in Charleston."

The four males of the family—Father, thirty-four; Peter, thirteen; Stephen, twelve; and John, seven—were wearing identical seersucker suits. The three females—Mae-Su, thirty-three; Mary, six; and Ernestine, three—were wearing nearly identical summer linen dresses.

The dresses and suits had all been cut and sewn by the Chinese wife of another Parris Island Marine—this one a staff sergeant drill instructor—who had gone to the Shanghai Palace restaurant in Beaufort, South Carolina, hoping to find employment as a cook—for that matter, anything at all; she needed the income—on the basis that she had been born and raised in Shanghai.

The proprietor, Mae-Su Zimmerman, was not interested in a cook, but she was looking for a seamstress. The DI's wife—who had met her husband in Tientsin, China, right after World War II—came from a family of tailors and seamstresses. After passing two tests, first making, from a picture in the society section of the Charleston *Post-Gazette* a dress for Mrs. Zimmerman, and then, from the Brooks Brothers mail-order catalog, a suit for Master Gunner Zimmerman, Joi-Hu McCarthy went into business with Mrs. Zimmerman, who became a silent (40 percent) partner in Shanghai Custom Tailors & Alterations, of Beaufort, South Carolina.

Mrs. Zimmerman was also a silent partner in several other Chinese-flavored businesses in Beaufort as well as the proprietor of the local McDonald's hamburger emporium, and the franchisee of Hertz Rent-A-Car.

The Ford station wagon in which the Zimmerman family appeared at 66 South Battery, properly attired for a visit to the ladies, belonged to Hertz of Beaufort.

Luddy Banning and Mae-Su Zimmerman embraced with understated, but still visible, deep affection. Mae-Su had been Luddy's midwife by the side of the dirt road in Mongolia when she had given birth to Edward Edwardovich Banning.

In Cantonese, Mrs. Zimmerman inquired of Mrs. Banning, "Does the Killer know we know?"

"My husband told them," Luddy replied in Cantonese.

"Sometimes I hate the U.S. Marine Corps," Mae-Su said.

"Me, too. But they are married to it," Luddy said.

The children were gathered and ushered up the stairs toward Mother Banning, who waited for them. She told them they all looked elegant, and gave each a kiss and a peppermint candy.

"The Colonel and the Killer are downstairs, Ernie," Luddy said to Master Gunner Zimmerman.

"How is he?"

"Better than I thought he would be when I heard," Luddy said.

"That don't look like no Marine master gunner to me," McCoy said when Zimmerman walked into what was known as "The Colonel's study," although it was in fact more of a bar than a study. "That looks like an ambulance chaser."

That was not exactly the truth. Despite the splendidly tailored Brooks Brothers–style seersucker suit, white button-down-collar shirt, and red striped necktie, there was something about Zimmerman that suggested he was not a member of the bar, but rather a Marine in civvies. He was a squat, muscular, barrel-chested man, deeply tanned, and his hair was closely cropped to his skull.

"Screw you, Captain, sir," Zimmerman said, walking to him, and grabbing his neck in a bear hug.

"How they hanging, Ernie?" McCoy asked, freeing himself.

"A little lower every year," Zimmerman said.

"Help yourself, Ernie," Banning said, gesturing toward an array of bottles in a bookcase.

"Thank you, sir. What are you—"

"Famous Grouse," Banning said.

"What else?" Zimmerman asked, chuckling.

"And we have been marching down memory lane," Banning said.

"Yeah? Which memory lane?"

"Guess who's at Pendleton?" Banning asked.

Zimmerman shrugged.

"Major Robert B. Macklin," McCoy said.

"No shit?"

"I saw his name on his office door when I was in the G-1 building," McCoy said. "I didn't see him."

"That figures, G-1," Zimmerman said. "That chair-warmer is a real G-1 type."

Banning and McCoy chuckled.

"Killer," Zimmerman went on, conversationally, "you really should have let me shoot that no-good sonofabitch on the beach on Mindanao."

Banning and McCoy chuckled again, louder, almost laughed.

"Jack NMI Stecker said I could," Zimmerman argued. "You should have let me."

"I was there, Ernie," Banning said. "What Colonel Stecker said was that you could deal with Captain Macklin in any way you felt you had to, if, *if,* he got out of line. As I understand it, he behaved in the Philippines. . . ."

"That sonofabitch was never *in* line," Zimmerman said. "And now he's a goddamn major, and they're giving you the boot? Jesus H. Christ!"

"Ernie, I told Ken we wouldn't talk about . . . that . . . unless he brought up the subject," Banning said.

"How are you not going to talk about it?"

"By not talking about it," Banning said.

"So what are you going to do? Take the stripes they offer you, or get out?" Zimmerman asked, ignoring Banning.

"Would you take the stripes, Ernie?" McCoy countered.

"I thought about that," Zimmerman said. "Christ, when we were in the Fourth in Shanghai, I was hoping I could make maybe staff sergeant before I got my twenty years in. But that was *then,* Ken. A lot's happened to us—especially you—since *then.* No, I don't want to be a sergeant again, having to kiss the ass of some dipshit like Macklin, or some nice kid who got out of the Naval Academy last year."

"Spoken like a true master gunner," Banning said, chuckling.

Master gunners are the Marine equivalent of Army warrant officers. While not *commissioned* officers, they are entitled to being saluted and to other officer privileges. They are invariably former senior noncommissioned officers with long service, and expertise in one or more fields of the military profession. Their pay and allowances, depending on their rank within the master gunner category, approximates that of second lieutenants through majors.

"What did they offer you?" Zimmerman asked.

"I won't know that until I get back to Pendleton," McCoy said.

"You give any thought to what you would do if you do get out?"

"Fill toothpaste tubes at American Personal Pharmaceutical," McCoy said. "I've got an in with the boss's daughter. I don't know, Ernie. I'm going to think about it on the way to California. Right now, I have no goddamn idea."

"Colonel, you tell him about the island?" Zimmerman said.

"There hasn't been time," Banning said.

"Island?" McCoy asked. "What island? The one where your great-grandfather buried the champagne glasses?"

"As a matter of fact, yes," Banning said. "You know where Hilton Head Island is?"

"Across from Parris Island? To the south?"

"Right. They're starting to develop Hilton Head, you know, put in a golf course, nice houses, that sort of thing. The family's got some property on Hilton Head . . ."

"Like five thousand acres," Zimmerman interjected.

". . . and south of Hilton Head," Banning went on, ignoring him, "the family has an island."

"You own that one? That's where you buried the glasses?" McCoy asked.

"Buried what glasses?" Zimmerman asked.

"Yes, we own it," Banning replied, again ignoring Zimmerman. "And Luddy and I, and Mae-Su and Ernie, have been talking about developing that ourselves."

"Where are you going to get the money?"

"Well, I have some," Banning said.

"And Mae-Su's made us a real bundle, Killer," Zimmerman said. "Mae-Su figures that if we start now, don't get ourselves over our ass in debt, put everything we make back in the pot, starting about 1960, 1961, we'll be in a position to make a killing."

"Why a killing?" McCoy asked. "Why 1960?"

"Mae-Su asked me what a Marine lieutenant colonel has in common with an Army lieutenant colonel and a Navy commander."

"None of the above can find their asses with both hands?" McCoy quipped. "OK. I'll bite, what?"

"They don't have any place to go when they retire. They don't own houses, most of them, and they're going to have to have someplace to go, and they would like to be around their own kind. Plus, they have pretty decent pensions."

"And 1960, 1961, because that's when the first of the World War Two guys can start to retire at twenty years?" McCoy asked.

"Exactly. The buildup started in 1940," Banning said.

"So what are you going to do between now and 1960?" McCoy asked.

"Two things," Banning said. "One: Develop the property on Hilton Head. They're planning to sell houses, et cetera, to well-to-do people looking for a second home or a retirement home. We'll see how that's done, learn how to do it, and with a little luck make a little money, and invest that in the development of the other island."

"What's 'two'?" McCoy asked.

"See if we can come up with some friendly investors, working partners," Banning said.

"And you're loaded, Killer," Zimmerman said. "Think about it."

"My wife is loaded," McCoy corrected him.

"I'm as broke as any other marine gunner," Zimmerman said. "Mae-Su's made a lot of money. *We're* loaded. Not like you and The Colonel, but loaded."

"It's more than the money, Ken," Banning said. "It would be something for you and Ernie to do, all three of us to do, when we hang up the uniform for the last time."

"Like what?"

"You know who's harder to cheat than an honest man?" Zimmerman asked, then answered his own question. "A China Marine, that's who. A graduate of the Bund School of Hard Knocks."

"Most construction, Ken," Banning said, "is done by subcontractors. One firm puts in the sewers, another one the streets, another one the electricity, et cetera. What the builder, the contractor, has to do is make sure—"

"They don't rob you blind," Zimmerman finished the thought for him. "And yeah, I do know what I'm talking about. When we built the last house in Beaufort, the one we're in now, I did the subcontracting. The first house we had, we got screwed by the numbers. This house, believe you me, we didn't."

McCoy suddenly had a thought, from out of nowhere.

When The Colonel said that General Pickering had called and told him what was going on, I presumed that he meant he told him everything. Why I got the boot from the Dai Ichi Building.

But he didn't. He just told him that I was being involuntarily relieved from active duty as an officer. And that's all that The Colonel told Ernie, because it was all he knew.

They don't know what's going to happen in Korea.

I don't know what's going to happen to me after what happens in Korea happens. If it happens before 30 May, will they keep me in the Corps as a captain? Or what? If they offer me, say, gunnery sergeant, and I take it, then what? Go to war as a gunnery sergeant in a line company? But they offer me gunnery sergeant and I turn it down, and get out, they damned sure won't call me back as a captain.

But I'm a Marine, and Marines are supposed to go—what's that line?—'to the sound of the musketry"—not the other way, to build houses on golf courses on islands for well-to-do people.

"Why do I get the idea you're not listening to me?" Zimmerman asked, bringing him back to The Colonel's study.

"I'm thinking, Ernie, I'm thinking," McCoy said.

Then think of something.

"Does The General know about this get-rich-quick scheme of yours?" he heard himself ask.

"It's not a get-rich scheme, Ken—" Banning said, offended.

"Fuck you, Killer," Zimmerman interrupted . . .

"—and yes, he does. He said that whenever we're ready for an investment, to let him know."

"I apologize for the wiseass remark," McCoy said. "I don't know why I said that."

"Because you're a wiseass, and always have been a wiseass," Zimmerman said.

"And with that profound observation in mind, we forgive you," Banning said. "Right, Ernie?"

"Why not?" Zimmerman said.

[TWO]

"We have a small problem," Ernie McCoy said to her husband in the privacy of their room. "I couldn't figure out how to say 'no' again."

"No to who, about what?"

"Apparently, Ernie and Ed are starting some kind of real estate development . . ."

"They told me."

"And Luddy thinks it would be just the thing for us when you get out of the Marine Corps."

"And?"

"They're going to propose at dinner that we go to the island—"

"Which island? I think there's two islands."

Ernie threw up her hands helplessly.

"—to look at it."

"General Pickering apparently did not tell them why I was sent home from Japan," McCoy said.

"I picked up on that," Ernie said. "I almost blew that too, honey."

" 'Almost'?" he parroted.

"They don't know," Ernie said.

"Good. And we can't tell them, obviously."

She looked at him curiously.

"They would try to help," he explained. "Especially Ed Banning, and there's nothing he could do, except maybe get himself in trouble."

"So what do we do?"

"When Luddy proposes we go look at the island, we say, 'Gee, what a swell idea!' "

"They're not talking about much money," Ernie said. "A couple of hundred thousand."

"You know how much I make in the Corps, *made* in the Corps. 'A couple of hundred thousand dollars' is not much money."

"You sign the Infernal Revenue forms, you know what *our* annual income is," Ernie said. "Not to reopen that subject for debate, I hope."

They met each other's eyes for a moment, then Ernie went off on a tangent.

"What I was thinking, honey, is that we don't have any place to go when . . . if . . . you get out of the Corps. Not about going in with them, but this Hilton Head Island place. It might be a nice place to build a house."

"We could probably pick up a nice little place for no more than a couple of hundred thousand, right?"

She didn't reply, but he thought he saw tears forming.

"Baby, I'm sorry," he said.

"It's all right."

"I asked Zimmerman if he would go back to wearing stripes, and he said no, he wouldn't. I had already decided that I wasn't going to either, but it was nice to hear that I wasn't alone."

"I told you that was your decision," Ernie said.

"Yeah. I remember," he said.

"And I meant it," she said.

"I know, baby. But it wouldn't have worked. It just wouldn't have worked. For me, or for you."

She nodded but didn't speak.

"I don't know what's going to happen if I'm wrong," he said.

"About 'the worst-case scenario'?"

He nodded.

"I hope I am wrong," McCoy said. "I hope that there is no war, that I get separated 30 June, that—"

"We could come back here and go in the real estate development business?"

"Either that, or to Jersey, and the executive trainee position your father offered me."

"He means well, sweetheart. . . ."

"I know, and for all I know, I might find Personal Pharmaceuticals a real challenge."

"Ken, for the last goddamn time, that was Daddy's idea of trying to be a nice guy. If I had known he was going to propose that, I would have stopped him."

"You told me that, and I believe it," he said. "But to get back to the point, the worst possible scenario may be what happens. If I'm out of the Marine Corps should that happen . . ."

"You're out, right? There's no way they can call you back in?"

"There was a light colonel, a nice guy named Brewer, in the G-1's office at Pendleton. He had me in his office, and he let me know that he thought it was a dirty deal to 'involuntarily separate' me just because I don't have a college degree. Anyway, I asked a couple of questions, and the answer to one was that the Navy Department has the right to call someone back into the service in a national emergency up to a hundred and eighty days from the date of their separation."

"Oh, God!"

"After that, the separation becomes permanent. The thinking is, I suppose, that after six months, you've forgotten everything you knew. But for 180 days, I'd be subject to recall."

"Maybe they wouldn't want you back."

"Because I'm a troublemaker, and got a final fitness report from Captain Edward C. Wilkerson, USN, using words like 'irresponsible' and 'lacking basic good judgment'? Probably not to intelligence duties—I don't even have a security clearance anymore. Did I tell you that?"

She shook her head, "no."

"But I would be a former Marine captain, presumed to have the basic skills of any Marine captain. I don't think they'd give me command of a line company, but the Corps always needs motor officers, supply officers . . ."

"That's so goddamned unfair!"

"This is the 'worse' that priest was talking about when we got married, 'for better or for worse.' "

"Oh, honey!"

"So what we're looking at, to try to start something new in our life, baby, is 1 December 1951, not the end of this month. Between now and then, we'll just have to hold our breath."

"We'll really be starting something new in our life about then," Ernie said. "If nothing goes wrong again this time."

"Nothing will go wrong this time," McCoy said, with a conviction he didn't feel. "And with that in mind, what the hell, why not, what's a measly couple of hundred thousand, why don't we look for a place on Banning's Island where we can build a house? We can't just sit around waiting for the other shoe to drop. And maybe we'll get lucky."

"Well, maybe not *build* a house," Ernie said. "Maybe just buy one, a small one, until we see what happens."

[THREE]
The William Banning House
66 South Battery
Charleston, South Carolina
1400 24 June 1950

Stanley loaded the basket of fried chicken and "other munchables" Mother Banning had prepared so that Ken and Ernestine—Mother Banning could not force herself to refer to Mrs. McCoy as "Ernie"—would have something to eat on the road, in the middle seat of the Buick station wagon, and then went up the wide staircase to the house to announce that everything was ready.

He had also loaded, in the back of the station wagon, two large, tall, cardboard tubes that The Colonel had prepared. One contained a plat of the Banning property on Hilton Head Island, showing the proposed subdivision, with a triple lot (A-301, A-302, and A-303) marked in red. The triple lot was on a high bluff over the Atlantic Beach—it would be necessary to construct a stairway to the beach, but what the hell, that was better than having the Atlantic Ocean come crashing through your living room in a once-in-a-century hurricane—and when the proposed golf course was built, would have a view of the fairways, far enough away from them to prevent golf balls from crashing into the house's windows.

The second cardboard tube contained a preliminary plat for the proposed subdivision of Findlay Island, which was south of, one-sixth the size of, and shielded from the Atlantic Ocean by Hilton Head.

The thinking was that the sooner they got things rolling on Hilton Head, the sooner there would be money to put into the development of Findlay Island. Moving cautiously, they would be ready in plenty of time for the wave of military retirees that would start in 1960, and grow for the five years after that.

Colonel Banning had made it clear that he wasn't trying to sell anything, that it was just something Ken and Ernie should take a close look at, think about.

There would be plenty of time to do that on the way to Camp Pendleton.

Ken and Ernie had originally intended to spend only a day or two with the Bannings. Then they would have driven to Beaufort, South Carolina, outside Parris Island to spend another day—or part of one—with the Zimmermans. From there, they had planned to drive to St. Louis, Missouri, to spend a day—or part of one—with George Hart, and then from there to southern California.

Instead, after two days in Charleston, they'd gone to Beaufort with the Bannings and spent three days there, in Zimmerman's surprisingly large and comfortable house on the water. Two days had been spent looking at the property on the islands, and on the third, the men had all put on their uniforms and taken a physical trip down memory lane to the U.S. Marine Corps Recruit Training Depot, Parris Island. Captain McCoy had taken his boot camp at Parris Island, and had been back only once since then, when, shortly after he'd returned from the Makin Island raid he'd been assigned to work for General Pickering, and had gone there to jerk Private George Hart out of a recruit platoon to serve as Pickering's bodyguard.

The next day, the McCoys and the Bannings had returned to the house on the Battery in Charleston, and a farewell dinner prepared for them under the supervision of Mother Banning.

With the time spent, they were now going to have to drive straight across the country to San Diego, and put off the visit to George Hart until after McCoy went through the separation process at Camp Pendleton.

Mother Banning surprised her son by going down the wide staircase to the Buick—instead of standing, as she usually did, on the piazza, with her hands folded on her stomach when guests left—to kiss both Ernestine and Ken goodbye.

"Drive carefully," Colonel Banning said. "And give this some serious thought, Ken."

"Yes, sir, we will," Ken said, shook his hand, and got behind the wheel.

At the end of the Battery, waiting for a chance to move into the flow of traffic, he said, "I wish I could."

"Could what?"

"Give it some serious thought. Doing what they're going to be doing looks like a lot more fun than filling toothpaste tubes."

There was a break in the flow of traffic, and he eased the Buick into it.

"Things will work out, sweetheart," Ernie said. "What is it they say, 'it's always darkest before the dawn'?"

He laughed, but it was more of a snort than a laugh.

"What time is it, honey?" Ernie asked.

He looked at his watch.

"A little after 1400," he said.

"You're going to have to get used to saying 'two,' " she said.

"I guess," he said, and added, "Mrs. McCoy, it is now a little after two P.M."

Ernie chuckled.

There is a fourteen-hour difference between Charleston, South Carolina, and the Korean Peninsula. In other words, when it was a little after two P.M. on 24 June 1950 in Charleston, South Carolina, it was a little after four A.M., 25 June 1950, on the Korean peninsula.

> **The North Korean attack against the Ongjin Peninsula on the west coast, northwest of Seoul, began about 0400 with a heavy artillery and mortar barrage and small-arms fire delivered by the 14th Regiment of the North Korean 6th Division. The ground attack came half an hour later across the 38th parallel without armored support. It struck the positions held by a battalion of the Republic of Korea Army's 17th Regiment, commanded by Colonel Paik In Yup.**

PAGE 27

U.S. ARMY IN THE KOREAN WAR

OFFICE OF THE CHIEF OF MILITARY HISTORY

DEPARTMENT OF THE ARMY

WASHINGTON, D.C., 1960

V

[ONE]
The Communications Center
The Pentagon
Washington, D.C.
1710 24 June 1950

The first "official" word of the North Korean incursion of South Korea was a radio teletype message sent to the Assistant Chief of Staff, G-2, Department of the Army in Washington by the military attaché of the U.S. Embassy in Seoul at 0905 Korean time 25 June 1950. It entered the Army's communications system a relatively short time afterward, probably "officially"—that is to say, was "logged" in—in a matter of minutes, say at about 1710 Washington time 24 June 1950.

25 June 1950 was a Saturday. While the Pentagon never closes down, most of the military and civilian personnel who work there during the week weren't there, and only a skeleton crew was on duty.

There was a bureaucratic procedure involved. The message was classified Operational Immediate, the highest, rarely used, priority, and on receipt the senior officer on duty in the communications room was immediately notified that an Operational Immediate from Korea for the G-2 had been received, and immediately sent to the Cryptographic Room for decryption.

The signal officer on duty telephoned the duty officer in the office of the Assistant Chief of Staff, G-2, giving him a heads-up on the Operational Immediate, and informing him that he would deliver the message personally as soon as it was decrypted.

In turn, the G-2 duty officer immediately telephoned the Assistant Chief of Staff, G-2, and caught him at his quarters at Fort Meyer, Virginia.

The Army's chief intelligence officer told his duty officer that he was just about out the door to attend a cocktail and dinner party at the Army and Navy Club in the District, but would stop by the Pentagon en route to have a look at the Operational Immediate from Korea.

Then he called the Chief of Staff of the U.S. Army, and found him at his quarters—Quarters 1—at Fort Meyer. He told the Chief there was an Operational Immediate from Korea, and that he was en route to the Pentagon to have a look at it. And where would the Chief be in case it required his immediate attention?

The Chief said he was going to Freddy's retirement party at the Army and Navy, and since the G-2 was going there, he could see no point in he himself going to the Pentagon. Sometimes, the Operational Immediate classification was applied too easily.

By the time the G-2 reached his office, the Operational Immediate from Korea had been decrypted. He read it, and after a moment ordered his duty officer to see if he would reach the Chief, who was probably en route to the Army-Navy Club, over his car radio.

It was possible, even likely, that somewhere in the Embassy of the Union of Soviet Socialist Republics, or in the Embassy of the Democratic Republic of Czechoslovakia, or in the Embassy of the Democratic Republic of Albania, or elsewhere, there was a man sitting at a radio receiver tuned to the frequency of the police-type shortwave radio in the Chief's car, so the conversation was phrased accordingly:

"Chief, that message we were talking about? I think it might be a good idea if you had a look at it yourself."

"I'm on my way. Thank you."

In the G-2's office, twenty minutes later, the G-2 read the message and reached for the red telephone on the G-2's desk. In twenty seconds, he had the Chairman of the Joint Chiefs of Staff on the secure line.

"Sir, I've got an Operational Immediate from Korea that I think you should have a look at right away."

"OK."

"I think you might want to give the Secretary a heads-up, and with your permission, I'm going to do the same to mine."

"OK. On my way. You're in your office?"

"Yes, sir."

"Meet me in the Ops Room."

"Yes, sir."

"And I'm in the car. You give the Secretary a heads-up."

"Yes, sir."

The G-2 telephoned, on the secure circuit, the Secretary of Defense and the Secretary of the Army, in that order, and gave both the same message:

He had just spoken to the Chairman about an Operational Immediate he had just received from Korea, and the Chairman was en route to the Ops Room to have a look at it, and had ordered him to relay that information to the Secretary.

The Secretary of the Army said he was on his way, and the Secretary of Defense said that it would take him ten minutes to shave and get dressed, and then he'd be on his way.

Before he left his home, the Secretary of Defense called the Secretary of State and said he had no idea how important it was, but there had been an Operational Immediate from Korea, and everybody was headed for the Ops Room to have a look at it, and maybe it might be a good idea for the Secretary to send somebody to the Pentagon, if not come himself.

The Secretary of Defense also called the Director of the Central Intelligence Agency, and on being told the Director would not be available for thirty minutes, got the Assistant Director and told him there was an Operational Immediate from Korea that he thought the Director should have a look at, and that everybody was en route to the Ops Room. The Assistant Director said he would leave word for the Director, and leave for the Ops Room himself immediately.

Less than an hour after that, having read the Operational Immediate in the Ops Room, and assessing other intelligence data available to the Ops Room, it was more or less unanimously agreed that the matter should be immediately brought to the attention of Harry S Truman, President of the United States, and Commander-in-Chief of its armed forces.

The Assistant Secretary of State personally agreed that the President should be informed, but felt that he could not concur in the decision to do so until the Secretary of State had been brought up to speed on the situation and gave his concurrence.

It took another hour to get that concurrence, whereupon the White House Signal Agency was directed to put in a secure call to the President of the United States at his home in Independence, Missouri.

The President took the news almost stoically, and ordered that he be kept up to date on any new developments, regardless of the hour.

The President was not surprised to hear from the Secretary of Defense that the North Koreans had invaded South Korea. He had been so informed three hours previously by the Director of the Central Intelligence Agency, who had received a radio message from the CIA station chief in Seoul, and had immediately decided the President needed to be informed immediately, and had done so personally.

[TWO]
Blair House
Washington, D.C.
2205 25 June 1950

"Unless someone can think of something else we can do tonight," President Harry S Truman said, "I suggest we knock this off. I suspect we're all going to need clear heads in the morning."

The men at the conference table—the Secretaries of State and Defense, the Chairman of the Joint Chiefs of Staff, the Army and Air Force Chiefs of Staff, the Director of the Central Intelligence Agency, the National Security Advisor, and several other high-ranking advisors, rose to their feet.

Although there was nothing *wrong* with the conference room in Blair House, it was not as large, nor as comfortable as the conference room in the White House. If there was still a conference room across the street in the White House. In 1948, it had been discovered that the White House was literally falling down, in fact dangerous. Truman had made the decision to gut it to the walls and rebuild everything. In June of 1950, the reconstruction was two years into what was to turn out to be a four-year process. The last time the President had looked into the White House, it was a gutted shell.

The President had cut short his vacation in Independence and flown back to Washington—in Air Force One, a four-engine Douglas DC-6 known as the *Independence*—early in the afternoon.

His senior advisors had been waiting for him in Blair House, the *de facto* temporary White House, where the Army Signal Corps had set up a teletype conference facility with General MacArthur in the Dai Ichi Building in Tokyo.

It was essentially a closed, state-of-the-art radio teletype circuit, where what was typed in Washington was immediately both typed in Tokyo and displayed on a large screen so that everyone in the room could read it. And vice versa.

MacArthur had furnished the President what he knew—not much—about the situation in Korea, and the President had authorized MacArthur—after consultation with his staff, and through the Chairman of the Joint Chiefs of Staff—to send ammunition and equipment to Korea to prevent the loss of Seoul's Kimpo airfield to the North Koreans, and to provide Air Force and Navy fighter aircraft to protect the supply planes. MacArthur had also been authorized to do whatever he considered necessary to evacuate the dependents of American military and diplomatic personnel in Korea from the war zone, and to dispatch a team to Korea to assess what was happening.

Truman had also ordered the Seventh Fleet (which was split between the Philippines and Okinawa) to sail immediately for the U.S. Navy Base in Sasebo, Japan, where it would pass into the control of Commander, U.S. Naval Forces Far East. COMNAVFORFE was subordinate to the Supreme Commander, Allied Powers, so what Truman had done was to take operational control of the Seventh Fleet from the Commander-in-Chief Pacific (CINCPAC) and give it to MacArthur.

Until they knew more about what was going on, there was nothing else that anyone in the room could think of to do.

Except for Admiral Hillenkoetter, the CIA Director, and he was considering his options to ask for a few minutes of the Commander-in-Chief's time—alone—when the President seemed to be reading his mind.

"Admiral, would you stay behind a minute, please?" Truman asked.

"Yes, Mr. President," the Admiral said.

It is entirely possible, the admiral thought, *that I am about to have my ass chewed for calling him when I got the Seoul station chief's radio. He didn't say anything, but it's possible the Chairman's heard about it, and he would consider it going over his head.*

The Chairman gave the admiral a strange look as he left the room, leaving him alone with the President.

In William Donovan's Office of Strategic Services, the OSS had technically been under the command of the Chairman of the Joint Chiefs of Staff. Donovan had paid no attention to that at all, deciding that he worked for the President and nobody else. Donovan had gotten away with that.

In the reincarnation of the OSS as the Central Intelligence Agency, the CIA was a separate governmental agency, charged with cooperating with the Defense and State Departments, but not under their command. None of the military services, or the State Department, liked that, and they tried, in one way or another, with varying degrees of subtlety, to insinuate that the Chairman of the Joint Chiefs was really in charge. Hillenkoetter was, after all, an admiral detailed to the CIA, not a civilian, like J. Edgar Hoover, Director of the Federal Bureau of Investigation.

The interesting thing, Hillenkoetter often thought, *was that when I was really in the Navy, I thought the CIA really ought to be under the Joint Chiefs. A couple of months in the Agency cured me of that. The only way it can be the* Cen-tral *Intelligence Agency is to be independent, free of influence from any quarter. Things would probably be better if they had called it the* Independent *Intelligence Agency.*

"That'll be all, thank you," to the stenographer, a Navy chief petty officer, who had been taking notes of the conference on a court reporter's machine.

The Chief left the room, closing the door after him.

"Just as a matter of curiosity, Admiral," the President began, "when did you pass to the Chairman the information you gave me over the telephone?"

"My deputy took that radio, Mr. President—by then there were two more of no great significance—with him when he went to the first conference in the Ops Room."

"I didn't tell the Chairman about your call," the President said. "I gave you the benefit of the doubt that you weren't trying to one-up him."

"As I understand my role, Mr. President, I report directly to you."

"Yeah," the President said. "You do." He paused. "Have you had any more radios? Even of 'no great significance'?"

"My Seoul station chief believes Seoul will fall, Mr. President. He is moving his base of operations to the South."

The President nodded but said nothing.

"Mr. President, there is something else," Hillenkoetter began.

"Let's have it," the President said.

"Several weeks ago, on June eighth, Mr. President, Senator Fowler asked for an appointment as soon as possible. The next morning, he came to my office with a man named Fleming Pickering."

Truman shrugged, showing the name meant nothing to him.

"And what did the head cheerleader of Eisenhower-for-President want, Admiral?" Truman asked. "The last I heard, he was not on the Senate Intelligence Oversight Committee."

"The name Pickering means nothing to you, Mr. President?"

"Not a damned thing," the President said.

"He was Deputy Director of the OSS for the Pacific in World War Two. He's quite a character."

"Never heard of him," the President said. "One of Donovan's Oh-So-Socials?"

"Well, that, too, sir, I suppose. He owns Pacific and Far East Shipping, and he's married to the daughter of the man who owns the Foster Hotel Chain."

"And that, obviously, made Donovan decide he was OSS material?"

"Mr. President, President Roosevelt commissioned Pickering a brigadier general in the Marine Corps, and named him, I have been reliably informed, Deputy Chief of the OSS for the Pacific over Mr. Donovan's strong objections."

"The Marines must have been thrilled to have some socialite millionaire shoved down their throat as a brigadier general," Truman said.

"There was not, as I understand it, much problem with that at all, Mr. President. Not only did Pickering win the Navy Cross as a Marine enlisted man in France in World War Two, but he'd gone ashore with the First Marine Division on Guadalcanal, and become—when the G-2 was killed in action—General Vandergrift's intelligence officer."

"He was a reserve officer between the wars?" Truman asked.

Hillenkoetter was aware that Captain Harry Truman had gone into the Missouri National Guard after World I, and risen to colonel.

"He was a Navy reserve captain when he went to Guadalcanal, Mr. President, working as sort of the eyes of Navy Secretary Knox. And when Secretary Knox ordered a destroyer to take him off Guadalcanal, it was attacked, her captain killed, and Pickering assumed command of the vessel, despite his own pretty serious wounds. Admiral Nimitz gave him the Silver Star for that."

"I really am tired, Admiral," Truman said after a moment. "Can we get to the point of this?"

"Mr. Pickering—General Pickering—and Senator Fowler are very close, Mr. President."

"I suppose every sonofabitch in the world has one friend," Truman said.

"General Pickering had just come from Tokyo, Mr. President," Hillenkoetter said, "with an intelligence assessment concluding the North Koreans were preparing to invade South Korea."

"How did he get an intelligence assessment like that? Whose intelligence assessment?"

"He wouldn't tell me, Mr. President, but I have every reason to believe that it was prepared by a Captain McCoy, who was on General Pickering's staff when they were both in the OSS."

"Another Oh-So-Social, this one a Navy captain?"

"A Marine Corps captain, sir. He'd been a major and was reduced to captain after the war."

"I don't have a thing in the world against captains," Truman said. "But wasn't this one out of his league? Captains usually don't prepare assessments predicting the beginning of a war."

"This one did, sir," Hillenkoetter said. "And so far, everything he's predicted has been on the money."

"Why didn't this assessment . . . You're telling me you knew nothing about this assessment?"

"I had never seen it before, Mr. President. And when I read it, it went counter to everything my people had developed, Mr. President."

"Who did he do this assessment for?"

"Captain McCoy was assigned to Naval Element, SCAP, sir. He submitted it to his superior, who passed it on to General Willoughby, General MacArthur's G-2. . . ."

"And?"

"According to General Pickering, General Willoughby ordered it destroyed."

"He didn't place any credence in it?"

"Apparently not, Mr. President."

"And now it turns out this captain was right on the money?"

"It looks that way, Mr. President."

"And when General Willoughby ordered this assessment destroyed, this captain gave it to General Pickering?"

"Yes, sir."

"Who brought it to you? Accompanied by Senator Fowler?"

"Yes, sir."

"Which means Senator Fowler's seen it, knows the story?"

"Yes, sir."

"Which means, if we've just gone to war, and I'm very much afraid that we have, that the story is going to get out that we should have known it was coming, because of this captain's assessment, which MacArthur ignored. My God, it'll be another Pearl Harbor scandal!"

"I'm afraid that's a real possibility, Mr. President."

"And what did you do when this assessment came to your attention?"

"I decided that it deserved further investigation, Mr. President."

"Meaning you sat on it?"

"I sent my Deputy for Asiatic Activities, David Jacobs, to Hong Kong on the next plane with orders to light fires under everybody we have over there to check it out."

"And?"

"Well, there hasn't been much time, Mr. President, but what feedback I got tended—until yesterday—to make me question the assessment."

Truman looked at him for a long moment.

"I appreciate your honesty, Admiral," he said. "Thank you."

He looked as if he was in thought, then asked, "Where is this captain now? What else has he got to tell us that no one wants to hear?"

"That was some of the first feedback I was given, Mr. President," Hillenkoetter said. "Captain McCoy was returned to the United States for involuntary separation from the service."

"Kill the messenger, huh? That sounds like something Emperor MacArthur would do."

"Mr. President, General Pickering led me to believe that General MacArthur is unaware of the assessment."

"How the hell would he know that?"

"He and MacArthur are friends, Mr. President. He had dinner with the MacArthurs when he was in Tokyo."

"Then, since he had it, why didn't he give the damned assessment to MacArthur?"

"The way General Pickering put it, Mr. President, is that General MacArthur's loyalty to those officers who served with him in the Philippines and throughout World War Two is legendary."

"The 'Bataan Gang,' " the President said. "I've heard about that, about them." He paused and looked at Hillenkoetter. "Where is the captain now?"

"I have no idea, sir. In the States, someplace. Maybe at Camp Pendleton, that's a separation center."

"What about General Pickering?"

"He lives in San Francisco."

The President looked at his watch.

"It's half past ten here," he said. "What'll it be in San Francisco?"

Hillenkoetter did the arithmetic.

"Half past seven, Mr. President."

Truman turned the sideboard behind him and picked up the telephone.

"This is the President," he said. "In this order, get me General Fleming Pickering, in San Francisco, California."

He looked at Hillenkoetter.

"Have you got a number?"

"No, sir. And I should have one. I'm sorry, Mr. President."

Truman waved a hand to show that it didn't matter, and turned his attention back to the telephone.

"Start looking for him at Pacific and Far East Shipping. When I'm through talking to him, get me Senator Fowler. I don't know where he is."

He put the telephone back in its cradle.

"If you have the time, Admiral, stick around until I make these calls."

"Of course, Mr. President."

"Do I have to tell you the fewer people that know about this, the better?"

"No, sir."

"You said you sent Dave Jacobs to the Far East. How much does he know?"

"Under the circumstances, Mr. President, I told David that I had reason to question the most recent data I was getting, and wanted it thoroughly checked. I didn't tell him why."

"Don't," the President said.

He pushed a button on a pad on the conference table.

A white-jacketed Navy steward appeared.

"I'm about to have a drink," the President said. "You?"

"Thank you, Mr. President."

[THREE]
The Penthouse
The Foster San Franciscan Hotel
Nob Hill, San Francisco, California
1935 25 June 1950

The chairman of the board of the Foster Hotel Corporation was about to dine with the chairman of the board of the Pacific & Far East Shipping Corporation in what was known as the Foster Hotel Corporation Executive Conference Center. When dealing with the Internal Revenue Service the center was treated as a reasonable and necessary business expense. It consisted of seven rooms atop the Foster San Franciscan, including a large conference room, three bedrooms, a lounge, a sauna, and a kitchen.

When the telephone rang, the chairman of the board of P&FE, attired in a bathrobe, swim trunks, and rubber sandals, was sitting on a stool in the kitchen, watching the chairman of the board of the Foster Hotel Corporation, who was attired in a swimsuit and sandals, and standing at the kitchen stove.

Both executives had just come from the hotel's swimming pool, and on the elevator ride, the Foster Chairman had inquired of the P&FE Chairman what he wanted to do about dinner.

"You know what I really would like is a crab omelet," he replied.

"Good idea. And I think there's a bottle of champagne in the fridge."

"May I interpret that to mean you would not be averse to a little fooling around?"

"Flem, you're supposed to be too old for that sort of thing."

"I'm not."

"Thank God."

A telephone call had quickly produced a one-pound tub of lump crab meat and a loaf of freshly baked French bread from the hotel kitchen. By the time it arrived, the champagne had been opened, and the P&FE chairman—who really didn't like champagne—had brought a bottle of Famous Grouse from the lounge to the kitchen.

When the telephone rang, the Foster chairman had inquired, "I wonder who the hell that is."

Very few people had the number of the penthouse.

"If you picked it up, you could probably find out," Fleming Pickering suggested.

Patricia Fleming turned from her skillet and looked at her husband with what could be described as wifely loving contempt/affection and reached for the wall-mounted phone.

"Hello," she said, then: "Hold on a minute."

She extended the phone, which had a long cord, to her husband.

"Who is it?"

"Another of your legion of pals with a sophomoric sense of humor," Patricia said.

He walked across the kitchen, holding his whiskey glass, and took the telephone from his wife.

"Hello?"

"Brigadier General Fleming Pickering?" a female voice inquired.

"Who wants to know?"

"Brigadier General Fleming Pickering?" the woman asked again.

"This is Fleming Pickering."

"Hold one, please, General, for the President."

Fleming Pickering looked at his wife, who was shaking her head in disbelief at the childish humor of some of her husband's cronies.

"Sure," Pickering said, smiling as he wondered what was to come next.

"General Pickering?" a male voice inquired.

"You got him. Come to attention when you speak with me."

"This is President Truman, General."

I'll be goddamned.

"Yes, sir?"

"General, at four in the morning yesterday, North Korea launched an invasion of South Korea."

"I'm very sorry to hear that, sir."

Patricia Fleming's facial expression changed to one of concern. She pushed the skillet off the fire and went to her husband, putting her head next to his so that she could hear the conversation. She heard:

"There are very few details at this time, but enough to know that it's more than a border incident."

"Yes, sir."

"Admiral Hillenkoetter has told me of your visit to him," Truman said.

"Yes, sir?"

"Who?" Patricia asked. "Admiral who? What visit?"

"I would very much like to see you and Senator Fowler as soon as possible," Truman said. "Would you be willing to come to Washington?"

"Yes, Mr. President. Of course."

"And Captain McCoy. No one seems to know where he is. Do you?"

Well, Christ, Hillenkoetter didn't have to be a nuclear scientist to figure out the only place I could have gotten that assessment was from the Killer.

"To the best of my knowledge, Mr. President, he and his wife are driving from Charleston to Camp Pendleton, probably stopping off in St. Louis on the way."

"You don't know how to get in touch with him?"

"No, sir. I don't. He's due in Camp Pendleton on June twenty-ninth."

"What about in St. Louis? Have you got a number there?"

"Not here, sir, I'm sorry. I'm at home. If they stop off at St. Louis, it will be to see Captain George Hart, who's a policeman, head of the Homicide Bureau."

"They can deal with that," Truman said, as if to himself. "General, if you're willing to come, I'll have someone in the Air Force contact you very shortly about getting you on a plane."

"Yes, sir."

"I would be grateful, General, if this conversation, and anything about your meeting with Admiral Hillenkoetter, did not become public knowledge."

"Of course, sir. I understand, Mr. President."

"Thank you. I look forward to seeing you shortly, General."

"Yes, sir."

"Thank you, again," Truman said, and the line went dead.

Pickering, deep in thought, put the telephone back in the wall rack.

"What the hell was that all about?" Patricia Fleming asked.

"It would appear, sweetheart, that we have just gone to war in Korea," he began.

They had just finished the crab omelet, and Pickering a second, stiff drink of Famous Grouse, when the phone rang again.

Pickering walked to it and answered it.

"Hello?"

"General Pickering?"

"Yes, speaking."

Goddamn it, you're not General Pickering.

"General, this is Brigadier General Jason Gruber, U.S. Air Force."

"Yes?"

"My orders, General, are to get you to Andrews Air Force Base as quickly as possible. How would you feel about making the trip in an F-94? It would mean getting into a pressure suit. . . ."

"I don't even know what an F-94 is," Pickering said.

"We just started taking delivery 1 June," General Gruber said. "It's a follow-on to the Lockheed Shooting Star, the F-80. . . ."

"That's a fighter," Pickering said. "Is there room for a passenger in a fighter?"

"There's room for a radar operator in the rear cockpit. You give the word, I can be at Alameda Naval Air Station in about an hour."

"Where are you now?" Pickering asked, and before General Gruber could answer, asked, "You'll be flying me?"

"I'm at Nellis Air Force Base, and yes, I'll be driving."

"I thought Ellis Air Force Base was in Las Vegas."

"It is," General Gruber said.

"And you can fly here in an hour?"

"If I kick in the afterburners, and I probably will, I can make it in thirty-five, forty minutes."

"My God!"

"The alternative is some kind of transport, General. That, of course, will take a lot longer to get you to Washington. It's up to you."

"I'll need more than an hour," Pickering said. "There's something I have to do before I leave here."

"In two hours, it'll be twenty-two hundred. By then, I'll be refueled and ready to go. How big a man are you, General?"

"Six-one, a hundred ninety."

"And all we'll have to do is squeeze you into a pressure suit, and we can take off."

"How do I get into the Navy base?"

"Alameda will be waiting for you. You're traveling DP, General. Everything is greased. Believe me."

"What's DP?"

"Direction of the President. You didn't know?"

"No, I didn't."

"I'll see you at Alameda, General," General Gruber said, and hung up without saying anything else.

Pickering hung up the telephone and turned to Patricia.

"What was that all about?"

"I'm to be flown to Washington by an Air Force brigadier in a fighter I never heard of. We leave in two hours from the Alameda Naval Air Station."

Patricia Fleming considered that.

"I'll drive you," she said. "It won't take us two hours to get to Alameda, Flem."

"The Air Force guy's coming from Las Vegas. He says he can do that in forty minutes. But I told him two hours," Pickering said.

"Why?"

"I have something—something important—I want to do here first."

"What could possibly be more important than—?" She stopped in mid-sentence, having taken his meaning.

"The same thing I had in mind when we got on the elevator thirty, forty minutes ago," he replied.

She looked at him for a moment, then smiled.

"Oh, Flem, I hope you never grow up."

[FOUR]
The Press Club
Tokyo, Japan
1130 26 June 1950

It has been said that while there just might be honor among thieves, there is absolutely none among journalists, at least insofar as beating a fellow member of the fourth estate out of a story—"getting it first"—is concerned.

But there is a little "scratch my back and I'll scratch yours" cooperative activity among journalists, and so it came to pass that when one distinguished member of the Tokyo press corps got it reliably that an Air Force C-54 was about to leave for Seoul to evacuate American dependents, he told one of his peers.

"That makes us even, right?" he asked, so that things were understood between them.

"Right," the second journalist said, then retired to the privacy of his room to pick up his typewriter and his camera and a change of linen. While there, he remembered he owed a big one to a third journalist, and went to his room on the third floor of the Press Club Building, made sure he was alone, and then brought him in on the C-54 about to leave Haneda for Seoul.

It never entered the mind of any of the three journalists to inform Miss Jeanette Priestly, of the Chicago *Tribune,* of the Seoul-bound C-54. Whatever special courtesies her gender and all-around good looks might otherwise have seen coming her way were more than neutralized by their shared belief that she was one of the more skilled practitioners of their profession, and thus to be treated as they treated any other of their peers. Screw her, in a metaphorical sense, not to be confused with the physical.

The three—who had left the Press Club at different times, one of them by the kitchen door—were therefore disappointed but not really surprised when they met at Haneda Air Base base operations and found Miss Priestly there.

They were disappointed because there would now be four dashing and courageous journalists on the first plane to the war in Korea, not just three, and one of the four was of the gentle sex, which unquestionably diluted the Richard Harding Davis aura of their journey.

Davis was a hero to all three men, who all very privately hoped to emulate him. He had covered every war from the Greco-Turkish through World War I, managing along the way to charge up San Juan Hill with Teddy Roosevelt in the Spanish-American War, and nearly get himself shot by the Germans as a spy in World War I. He then went on to be a highly successful novelist and play-wright.

But there was nothing they could do about the comely Miss Priestly. She was duly accredited to the headquarters of the Supreme Commander, and thus just as entitled as they were to space-available accommodations on USAF transports.

And there was plenty of space. There was no one on the C-54 when it took off from Haneda but the five members of the crew and the four members of the press corps.

As they approached Seoul's Kimpo airfield, the pilot came back into the fuselage to tell them that, since North Korean Yak fighters had strafed the field and were likely to come back, and that since there was a strong possibility that the field had already been captured by the North Koreans, his just-received or-ders were to make a low pass over the field to see if there were any Americans waiting for them, and if not, to go back to Japan.

No, he could not land just to let the correspondents off.

There were Americans on the field, some of them frantically waving jackets to attract the attention of the C-54.

It landed, and the correspondents found Air Force Lieutenant Colonel Peter Scott busily burning documents in Base Operations.

Scott told them things were not as bad as they could be. Seoul had not been abandoned, as reported, and in fact, on direct orders from General Douglas MacArthur, the sixty-odd officers of the Korean Military Advisory Group, and the hundred or so enlisted men attached to KMAG who had evacuated the city, were now in the process of moving back into it.

The journalists asked Colonel Scott how they could get into Seoul, which was seven miles away. He pointed to the parking lot, which was jammed with Jeeps, trucks, and civilian automobiles, including nine recent-model Buicks.

"Most of them have keys in their ignitions," Colonel Scott said.

The male journalists then chivalrously suggested to Miss Priestly that under the circumstances, it behooved her to return to Tokyo aboard the C-54 with the dependents being evacuated, while they went into Seoul. This was really no place for a woman.

Miss Priestly replied with a short pungent sentence that certainly was not very ladylike, but made it clear that she considered herself one of the boys, and had no intention of running away from the story.

The journalists watched the C-54 take off for Tokyo and then climbed into a nearly new Buick and drove into Seoul, where they had little trouble finding the large gray building housing KMAG.

There, Colonel Sterling Wright—who told them he was acting KMAG commander; Brigadier General William Roberts, the former commanding general, having left for a new assignment in the States and no replacement for him having arrived—repeated what they had heard from Lieutenant Colonel Scott at Kimpo: Things weren't as black as they had at first appeared.

For proof of this, he showed them a radio teletype message from the Supreme Commander himself, which said: "Be of good cheer. Momentous events are pending."

Colonel Wright regretted that under the circumstances—KMAG had just returned to Seoul; he would make improvements tomorrow—the only accommodations he could offer the distinguished members of the press would be rather spartan. The men would share quarters, as would he, with the senior officers of his staff, and he would turn over his own quarters to the lady.

Miss Priestly took a shower and went to bed in Colonel Wright's narrow bed.

She was awakened in the very early hours of the next morning by an excited lieutenant who reported that the North Koreans had broken through the South Korean defense lines around Seoul, and that they were going to have to run for it.

Moments later, the North Koreans brought the KMAG compound under mortar fire.

Miss Priestly dressed quickly and went outside the building, where she found Colonel Wright waiting for her in a Jeep. Her fellow journalists, she was told, had already left.

Followed by another Jeep, they raced out of the KMAG compound toward the Han River. They had almost reached the river when a brilliant flash of light and a terrifying roar announced that the bridge had been blown.

Their only escape route to Suwon, thirty miles south of Seoul, where there was an air base, had been cut.

Colonel Wright drove back to the KMAG compound, where he assembled a sixty-vehicle convoy of stragglers and started out to find another way across the Han to safety. After several hours of frantic search, none was found. But they came across a place where small boats could take them across the river.

Wright ordered the vehicles destroyed, and the fleeing Americans made it across the river, and started for Suwon on foot.

About eleven o'clock in the morning, there was a growing roar of aircraft engines. After a few moments, it was possible to identify the aircraft as USAF P-51 fighters. They were obviously strafing Kimpo Airfield, with the obvious conclusion to be drawn that if the P-51s were strafing it, it was now in the hands of the North Koreans.

After a four-hour walk, a Jeep appeared, and Miss Priestly accepted the offer of a ride in it to Suwon. There she found her fellow journalists, two of them wearing bloody bandages. They had been on the Han River bridge when it had been blown.

There were a number of American aircraft on the field, one of which was headed for Itazuke Air Force base in Japan, the closest one to Korea. All four journalists climbed aboard. There was no way that any of them could file their stories of the fall of Seoul from Suwon, and two of them required medical attention.

All four filed their stories from Itazuke. The two wounded men then went to the hospital, and Miss Priestly and the unwounded other one got on another plane headed back to Suwon.

The next morning, as Miss Priestly was trying to find a Jeep or something else with wheels to go see the fighting, a glistening C-54 made an approach to

Suwon and landed. When she saw that it had "Bataan" lettered on its nose, she ran to get a closer look.

Thompson submachine gun–armed military policemen climbed down the stairs, followed by the Supreme Commander himself, and then a dozen general officers, and finally four members of the press corps.

Jeanette Priestly knew all of them. They regarded themselves—perhaps not without some justification; they were the Tokyo bureau chiefs of the three major American wire services and Time-Life—as the senior members of the Tokyo press corps. They were known by their fellows in the press corps as "The Palace Guard" because they covered the Supreme Commander himself, leaving coverage of whatever else happened in Japan to their underlings.

They had obviously been invited by MacArthur to accompany him to Korea—"space available" did not apply to the Supreme Commander's personal aircraft; passage on the *Bataan* was by invitation only.

If the members of the Palace Guard were surprised to see Jeanette Priestly in Korea, it did not register on their faces. But the Supreme Commander himself smiled when he saw her, and motioned her over to him.

There's a headline if there ever was one, Jeanette thought: MACARTHUR IN KOREA.

But how do I get the story out?

"Good morning, Jeanette," he said, offering her his hand. "I wasn't aware that you were here."

"I came yesterday," Jeanette said, and blurted, "and was almost caught in Seoul."

"Seoul will, I am sure, soon be rid of the invader," MacArthur said.

A battered sedan, a Studebaker, not nearly as nice as the Buicks Jeanette had seen deserted at Kimpo, drove up, and Colonel Sidney Huff walked up to them.

"The car is here, General," he said.

"Jeanette, if you would like to wait until I have a chance to assess the situation here," Douglas MacArthur, "you may, if you like, ride back to Tokyo with me on the *Bataan*."

"Thank you," Jeanette said. "That's very kind of you."

I can file from Tokyo just as quick as the Palace Guard can.

"Not at all," MacArthur said. "For the time being, at least, this is no place for a lady."

Jeanette had another unladylike thought, but managed to smile as dazzlingly as possible at him. And then she smiled dazzlingly at the Palace Guard, who were reacting to her being on the *Bataan* as if she were a whore in church.

She waited until MacArthur's small convoy had driven off, and then sat down on the grass by the side of the runway, took her Royal portable typewriter out, and began to type.

```
FOR CHITRIB

PRESS IMMEDIATE

NOTE TO EDITOR AP, UP AND INS WILL HAVE PICS


SLUG MACARTHUR COMES TO KOREA


BY JEANETTE PRIESTLY, TRIBUNE WAR CORRESPONDENT

SUWON, SOUTH KOREA JUNE 27—THE REMAINS OF AN AIR FORCE
C54 DESTROYED BY NORTH KOREAN YAK FIGHTERS WERE STILL
SMOLDERING WHEN THE BATAAN, THE GLISTENING C54 OF
SUPREME COMMANDER GENERAL DOUGLAS MACARTHUR TOUCHED DOWN
AT THIS BATTERED AIRFIELD 30 MILES SOUTH OF THE JUST
CAPTURED SOUTH KOREAN CAPITAL OF SEOUL THIS AFTERNOON.
WEARING HIS FAMILIAR BATTERED CAP AND A FUR-COLLARED
LEATHER JACKET, HIS CORN-COB PIPE PERCHED JAUNTILY IN
HIS MOUTH, GENERAL OF THE ARMY DOUGLAS MACARTHUR
CONFIDENTLY PREDICTED TO THIS REPORTER THAT SEOUL WILL
SOON BE RID OF THE INVADER
```

She looked up from the portable, saw that the Palace Guard had somehow found a Jeep and were obviously intending to join the MacArthur convoy.

She slammed the cover shut on the Royal, jumped to her feet, and ran to it. She climbed over the rear seat just as it started to move.

"Yes, thank you," Jeanette said, beaming. "I would like to go along."

[FIVE]
Washington, D.C.
0905 26 June 1950

The President of the United States came out the front door of Blair House, almost jauntily descended the stairway, and indicated with a nod of his head that he was going to turn right.

Two of the six Secret Service agents on the detail quickly took up positions so that they could precede him; two waited to bring up the tail; and two positioned themselves so that they would be just a few steps behind him. Across the street, two Chevrolet Suburbans started their engines. One moved ahead of the little parade and the second positioned itself behind the tail.

The Secret Service agent heading the parade turned and looked questioningly at the President.

"The Foster Lafayette," the President said. "Senator Fowler."

"Thank you, sir," the Secret Service agent said.

Senator Richardson K. Fowler maintained a suite in the Foster Lafayette. Not an ordinary suite, though God knew suites in the Lafayette were large and elegant as they came, but an apartment made up of two suites, and furnished, the President had learned, with museum-quality antiques.

Fowler was quite wealthy, and unlike some of his peers in the Senate, made no effort at all to conceal it. He considered public service a privilege, and living in Washington, D.C., even as well as he did, as the terrible price he had to pay for that privilege.

The President walked briskly, three times tipping his white Panama straw hat and smiling and waving to people on both sides of Pennsylvania Avenue who recognized him.

The Foster Lafayette Hotel was directly across Pennsylvania Avenue from the White House, the far side—from Blair House—of Lafayette Square. The general manager of the hotel was standing under the marquee beside the doorman, obviously waiting for the President.

The Secret Service agent in the lead again turned and looked questioningly at the President.

"I guess when I invited myself to breakfast, Senator Fowler told him," the President said.

The President shook hands with both the general manager—and called him by name—and the doorman, entered the hotel, walked across the lobby to a waiting elevator, and followed the lead two Secret Service agents onto it.

When the elevator reached the top floor, the President saw that a large, very black man wearing a gray cotton jacket and a wide smile was standing by the open door of Senator Fowler's suite.

"Good morning, Mr. President," he said. "Nice to see you again, sir. The senator's waiting for you."

The President offered him his hand.

"Hello, Franklin," Truman said. "It's good to see you, too."

He followed the lead two Secret Service agents into Fowler's apartment.

Richardson K. Fowler and Fleming Pickering rose to their feet.

"Good morning, Mr. President," Fowler said.

"Good morning," the President said. "Could these fellows wait in your study?"

"Of course, Mr. President," Fowler said.

"It's through there," the President said, pointing. "When I need you, I'll call."

The Secret Service agent was visibly unhappy with his orders to be left alone . . .

"It's all right," Truman went on. "Senator Fowler thinks I'm a threat to the country, but I don't think he's thinking of assassination. Go on."

"Yes, Mr. President," the Secret Service agent said, and trailed by the other, left the room, closing the door after themselves.

The President turned to Fowler.

"You can call me 'Harry,' Dick. We've known each other a long time."

"A long enough time to know better, Mr. President. What is it they say, 'beware of Democrats wearing smiles'?"

Truman smiled, and offered his hand to Fleming Pickering.

"Thank you for coming, General," he said. "And I have to say that for a man who spent the night flying across the country, you don't look very mussed."

"I was very mussed, Mr. President, when we landed at Andrews," Pickering said.

Franklin appeared with a silver coffee set and placed it on the sitting room's coffee table.

"What did you set up for breakfast, Franklin?" Fowler asked.

"A little buffet, Senator. I thought you gentlemen would rather be alone."

"Why don't you move the coffee into the dining room? Then I won't spill it on my new tie."

"Yes, sir," Franklin said, and picked up the tray and carried it into the dining room, with the three men following him.

He set the tray on a table that would hold sixteen diners, then left the room.

"Before we go a word further, it is agreed that this is out of school, right?" Truman asked.

"Agreed, Mr. President," Fowler said.

"Yes, sir," Pickering said.

The President looked at Pickering as if making up his mind about something.

"What is it they say in the Navy, General? 'Let's clear the decks'?"

"It's something like that, Mr. President. But I'm really not a general, Mr. President. That was a long time ago."

"Let's clear that part of the deck first, General," Truman said. "Yes, you are. You are a brigadier general, USMC, Reserve."

Picking was about to argue when he stopped.

Goddamn it, maybe I am. Probably, *I am. I was never* discharged, *in '45. I was* released from active duty and ordered to my home of record.

"And as your commander-in-chief, General, I can order you to keep anything that's said in this room to yourself."

Pickering looked at him but said nothing.

"Unfortunately, I can't order you around, Dick," Truman went on, "as either a senator or a journalist. I can only appeal to your patriotism. We've said—and probably believe—some unkind things about each other, but I don't think you've ever questioned my patriotism, and I certainly have never questioned yours."

"What is it you want, Mr. President?" Fowler asked, coldly.

"I don't want headlines on the front page of every newspaper in the country reading, 'MacArthur Ignored Warning of North Korean Attack,' " Truman said.

"In point of fact, Mr. President," Pickering said. "I don't believe General MacArthur was aware of McCoy's assessment."

"He's in charge over there, General," Truman said. "He should have been made aware of this assessment. He's responsible for the actions—or lack of action—of his subordinates."

Pickering shrugged his agreement.

"We're about to go to war over there," Truman said. "The League of Nations failed because nobody paid any attention to it. Remember when Mussolini was getting ready to invade Ethiopia in 1936? The Emperor of Ethiopia . . . what's his name, Dick?"

"Haile Selassie, Mr. President," Senator Fowler furnished.

"Haile Selassie went to the League of Nations," Truman went on, "and the League of Nations told Mussolini to stop. He knew the League of Nations had no teeth, so he invaded Ethiopia. And the League of Nations didn't—couldn't— do a damned thing about it."

"I remember, Mr. President," Fowler said.

"And so the dictators of the world—Italian, German and Japanese—drew the logical conclusion that since the League of Nations was a joke, they could get away with anything they wanted to do. And that gave us World War Two."

"You think the United Nations is going to be different?" Fowler asked, on the edge of sarcasm.

"For one thing, Dick," Truman said. "We belong to the UN; we didn't belong to the League of Nations. For another, we now face the indescribable horrors of a nuclear war. We can't afford to have the UN fail."

Fowler shrugged, in agreement.

"The UN has just told the North Koreans to get out of South Korea," Truman went on. "If the UN can't make that order stick, the whole world's likely to go up in a nuclear explosion. So the North Koreans are going to have to get out of South Korea. I've decided the United States has to do whatever is necessary see that's done."

"By ourselves, if necessary?" Fowler asked.

"I don't think it will come down to that, but if it does, yes, by ourselves."

"Mr. President, have you read McCoy's assessment?" Pickering asked.

"Admiral Hillenkoetter told me about it."

"McCoy feels that the Army of Occupation of Japan is neither equipped nor trained for combat—that they are facing a superior force."

"He's competent to make a judgment like that?"

"I have absolute faith in his judgment, Mr. President," Pickering said.

"Well, he's been right so far, hasn't he?" Truman said. "MacArthur feels he can 'contain the situation.' I told him to send a team to Korea to see how bad things really are."

For a long moment, no one said a word.

"There're two possibilities," Truman said. "That once the North Koreans understand we're taking action—I've given MacArthur permission to bomb railheads and bridges, that sort of thing—they'll back down, as the Russians backed down in Berlin after we ran the airlift."

"Mr. President, they may have interpreted Acheson's speech, leaving Korea out of our zone of interest, as meaning we would not react."

Truman looked at him, and nodded, and then went on.

"The other possibility is that they—and the Russians, who are behind this—will decide it's the League of Nations and Ethiopia all over again, and keep up their attack. That means the involvement of American ground forces. I think that's what's going to happen."

He looked between Fowler and Pickering.

"After Pearl Harbor, President Roosevelt fired the Pearl Harbor brass—Admiral Kimmel and General Short—for what amounted to dereliction of duty. They hadn't adequately prepared for what happened, and they deserved to be fired. General MacArthur—if we are to believe this young captain of yours, General—has not adequately prepared for what is happening there now. Do I have to explain the problems that would be caused if I relieved MacArthur for dereliction of duty and ordered him home?"

"No, sir, Mr. President," Fowler said.

"If I have to say so, Dick, I'm not talking about political damage to Harry Truman. I don't really give a damn about that."

"Mr. President, I will not make . . . Captain McCoy's assessment and what happened in Tokyo will not be made available to the press," Fowler said.

"Or to, for example, Senator Taft?"

Senator Robert Taft (R., Ohio) who had presidential aspirations, was one of Truman's severest critics.

"I won't tell Bob, either," Fowler said. "Or anyone else. At least for the time being."

"The American people are going to have enough trouble with us going to war in the first place. If we start taking a whipping in the beginning, and it came out MacArthur was warned this was coming and did nothing about it . . ."

"I understand, Mr. President," Fowler said.

"I'm glad you do," Truman said. He looked between the two of them again. "Now I'm getting hungry. I had no appetite at all when I walked in here."

"Mr. President," Pickering said. "I don't want McCoy hurt by what he did."

"I'll tell you what's going to happen to Captain McCoy, General," Truman said. "The Commandant of the Marine Corps has been ordered (a) not to separate him and (b) to have him report as soon as possible to Admiral Hillenkoetter. I declined to tell the Commandant what this is all about, and I'm not going to tell any of the brass, either."

"I don't want him hurt, Mr. President," Pickering repeated. "He's a captain. When people are looking for scapegoats, captains are expendable."

"What Captain McCoy needs is a protector in high places—is that what you're saying?"

"Yes, Mr. President, I guess it is."

Truman looked at him for a moment, then nodded and smiled.

"I was going to save this for later," Truman said, "but we're clearing the decks, right?"

"I don't think I follow you, Mr. President."

"How's your health, General? Could you pass a physical?"

"Yes, sir, I probably could."

What the hell is he suggesting? That I go back in the Marines?

"I think what's about to happen to you, General, is going to happen to a large number of other people in the next few weeks," Truman said.

"Sir?"

Truman walked to a wall-side credenza, picked up a telephone, and dialed a number from memory.

"This is the President," he said. "Get the Commandant of the Marine Corps for me, will you, please?"

It took less than sixty seconds.

"This is the President, General," Truman said. "I understand you're acquainted with Brigadier General Fleming Pickering, USMC Reserve?"

There was a very short pause.

"Please cause the necessary orders to be issued calling the general to active service for an indefinite period, effective immediately, and further placing him on duty with the Central Intelligence Agency," Truman ordered. "It won't be necessary to notify him—he's with me now."

"Jesus H. Christ!" Pickering said.

Truman put the phone down and turned to Pickering.

"Take as long as you need before actually reporting to Admiral Hillenkoetter," he said. "But obviously, the sooner the better."

He smiled at Pickering's obvious discomfiture.

"Can we now have our breakfast?" he asked.

[SIX]
Office of the Deputy Chief for Officer Records
Office of the Assistant Chief of Staff, G-1
Headquarters, Camp Pendleton, California
2330 29 June 1950

Captain Kenneth R. McCoy had learned the legalities of leave as a PFC of the 4th Marines in Shanghai.

Leave is earned at the rate of 2.5 days per month, which adds up to 30 days a year. Leave may be accrued up to a total of 60 days; anything over that is lost. Leave begins at 0001 the first day of leave and ends at 2359 on the last day.

He also believed that whatever was going to happen to him—now that there was a war—was not going to happen after duty hours, specifically, after 1630, on 29 June, the last day of his leave.

When he and Ernie had arrived in San Diego at 1545 that afternoon, therefore, he had gone to the Coronado Beach Hotel, gotten the key to the room from the desk clerk, gone upstairs, had a shower, and then gone down to the bar with Ernie to have a drink and discuss with her the possibilities.

There were several of them, starting with the most likely one, that the war in Korea was so new that there had not been time for the Corps to put into effect any new we're-going-to-war regulations. In that case, Captain McCoy would be separated from the Naval service on 30 June 1950.

It was also possible that we're-going-to-war regulations had been put into effect, and the most likely result of that would be that separations from the Naval service would be suspended either indefinitely, or, as they had been in War II, for the duration of the war plus six months.

It was also possible that while they'd been off seeing Ernie's folks, and the Bannings and the Zimmermans, Eighth & Eye had come through with the determination that ex-Corporal, now Captain, McCoy should be allowed to reenlist in the Corps as a staff sergeant, or a gunnery sergeant, or a master sergeant, and that he would be separated from commissioned service, but not the Marine Corps, and he could volunteer to reenlist as a staff sergeant or a gunnery sergeant, or a master sergeant, and if he didn't voluntarily do so, be retained as a private, USMC, until a determination about what the hell to do about this guy could be reached.

Ken and Ernie had had two drinks in the bar, then walked hand in hand along the beach, and then gone back and had a very nice dinner in the hotel dining room, and then gone to their room and had another shower, this one together, and then fooled around in the conjugal bed until 2215, when he'd risen from the bed, dressed in a uniform, told his wife not to go anywhere, he'd be back just as soon as he'd signed off leave at Pendleton.

Then he'd gotten in the Buick and driven out to Pendleton, arriving, as he had planned, at the office of the Deputy Chief for officer records with thirty minutes to spare.

There was a master gunner and a corporal on duty. The master gunner, a portly man in his late forties, did not bellow "attention on deck" when McCoy pushed the door open. Master gunners rarely—if ever—pay that much military courtesy to lowly captains, especially at almost midnight.

"Good evening," McCoy said. "Where do I sign off leave?"

"What's your name, Captain?" the master gunner asked.

"McCoy."

The master gunner reached for the telephone on his desk.

"Mister, I asked you a question," McCoy said.

There was a tone in McCoy's voice—a tone of command, of *I'm a captain and you're a master gunner, and you will respect that difference in rank*—that the master gunner did not expect.

He had been told by Major Robert B. Macklin to keep an eye out for Captain McCoy, Kenneth R. Out of school, between old warriors, he had told the master gunner that he knew McCoy, that the Corps had finally realized McCoy should have never been commissioned in the first place, and that McCoy had reported to Pendleton for involuntary separation. He had told him further that Eighth & Eye had determined that McCoy should be offered the chance to enlist as a gunnery sergeant on his separation.

That fact—that tomorrow Captain McCoy would either be a civilian or a gunnery sergeant—had influenced the master gunner's decision not to stand up or call "attention on deck" when McCoy had come in the office.

The master gunner now made another decision—based on *right now this clown's still a captain*—and let the telephone fall back in its cradle.

"Sir," he said. "My orders are to inform Major Macklin the moment you showed up here."

"Have you any idea what that's all about?" McCoy asked.

"No, sir, I don't. But if the captain will have a seat, I'm sure it will be cleared up in a couple of minutes."

He reached for the telephone again.

"Get Colonel Brewer on the horn, please," McCoy said.

"Sir?"

"You heard me," McCoy said.

The master gunner made another decision, based both on the tone of the clown's voice and the fact that he was still a captain, and dialed Colonel Brewer's quarters number.

He was aware that McCoy's eyes were on him.

Colonel Brewer answered on the third ring.

"Sir. Matthews. I have a Captain McCoy here in the office. He asked me to call you."

"Finally!" Colonel Brewer said. "Put him on, Matthews."

"Aye, aye, sir," Master Gunner Matthews said, and held out the phone to the clown.

"McCoy, sir," McCoy said. "Sorry to bother you at home."

"I can't tell you how glad I am to hear your voice," Brewer said. "Stay right there. I'll be there in twenty minutes."

"Sir, my wife expects me to be coming back to the hotel."

"Call her and tell her that's on hold; I'll explain everything when I see you."

"Aye, aye, sir," McCoy said, and broke the connection with his finger. He looked at Matthews. "How do I get an outside line? I have to call 'Diego."

"Captain, that phone's for official business."

"You're an interesting man, mister," McCoy said. "Most master gunners I know are anything but chickenshit." He paused. "What do I do? Dial operator?"

"Nine," Master Gunner Matthews said.

McCoy called Ernie and told her something had come up, and he would be delayed; he could call when he knew something.

Matthews took the telephone from McCoy and started to dial.

"You are not to inform Major Macklin that I have spoken to Colonel Brewer. You understand that? That was an order," McCoy said.

"Aye, aye, sir," Master Gunner Matthews said, finished dialing, and when Major Macklin answered, informed him that Captain McCoy was in the office.

He hung up the phone and looked at McCoy.

"Major Macklin, sir, says that you are not to leave the office until he gets here."

"OK," McCoy said.

"Captain, I'm just following my orders."

"I understand."

"Major Macklin led me to understand that you know each other," Matthews said.

"Then you probably have had a fascinating recital of my time in the Corps," McCoy said. "Yes, mister, Major Macklin and I know each other very well."

Matthews met McCoy's eyes.

"Corporal," he ordered. "Get the captain a cup of coffee."

Major Robert B. Macklin, USMC, and Lieutenant Colonel Peter S. Brewer showed up in the office within three minutes of each other, Macklin first. Macklin was in full uniform.

"Attention on deck!" Master Gunner Matthews bellowed when Macklin came through the door.

He, McCoy, and the corporal popped to attention.

"As you were," Macklin said. He walked up to McCoy.

"Where the hell have you been, McCoy?"

"Sir, I have been on ordinary leave."

"I spent several hours on the telephone in a fruitless search for you," Macklin said.

McCoy didn't reply.

"Get Colonel Brewer on the telephone for me," Macklin ordered.

Master Gunner Matthews dialed a number.

After a long moment, looking at McCoy, Matthews reported, "Sir, there is no answer."

"Try it again," Macklin ordered, and then turned back to McCoy. "My orders are to notify Colonel Brewer the moment I have located you."

"Yes, sir."

"In the event I am unable to reach him tonight, I have no intention of letting you out of sight again," Macklin said. "Mister Matthews, is there a cot here?"

"Yes, sir."

"Am I to understand, Major, that I'm under some sort of restriction? Am I under arrest?"

"What you are, Captain, is ordered not to leave this room until I establish contact with Colonel Brewer. I don't know what you've done now, McCoy, but I hope they throw the book at you."

"Yes, sir," McCoy said.

"Attention on deck," Master Gunner Matthews bellowed, as Lieutenant Colonel Brewer came through the door.

Colonel Brewer was wearing Bermuda shorts and a red T-shirt with a gold representation of the Marine emblem covering most of the chest.

"As you were," Brewer said. He turned to Macklin. "That will be all, Macklin," he said. "You can go home now. Sorry to have to have ruined your evening, but this was important."

McCoy looked between Macklin and Matthews.

"Sir," he said. "Mister Matthews had the duty. Major Macklin just got here."

"That's very interesting," Brewer said. "Between now and 0800, Macklin, try to come up with a good reason for your not being here until Captain McCoy showed up as you were ordered to do."

"Sir . . ."

"I'll hear your reasons at 0800. You are dismissed."

"Aye, aye, sir," Macklin said, and with as much dignity as he could muster, came to attention, did a left-face movement, and walked out of the building.

"Sir, can I ask what's going on?" McCoy asked.

"I hardly know where to begin," Brewer said. "But first things first: Matthews, in this order, call General Dawkins at his quarters and tell him Captain McCoy has shown up, and then call Colonel Wade and tell him the same thing and that General Dawkins has been notified."

"Aye, aye, sir."

"Attention on deck!" Master Gunner Matthews bellowed, as Brigadier General Clyde W. Dawkins came into the building.

"As you were," General Dawkins said.

He crossed the room to Captain McCoy.

"Goddamn, Killer, where have you been?" he said, and then he wrapped his arms around him. "Christ, it's good to see you!"

"It's good to see you, too, sir," McCoy said.

"Let me start with the good news. You're not getting the boot. The bad news is that I'm ordered to get you to Washington as soon as possible. To that end, an Air Force F-94—that's a two-seater jet—has been waiting for you at Miramar for the last three days."

"Sir, my wife is at the Coronado Beach. . . ."

"I'm a general now, Killer, indulge me," Dawkins said. "Let me finish before you start arguing with me."

"Aye, aye, sir."

"Your orders are to report here for duty," Dawkins said, and handed him a three-by-five card.

```
Director's Office

East Building,

2430 E Street

Washington, D.C.
```

"Sir, I don't know what this is," McCoy said.

"That's the CIA complex," Dawkins said. "The person you are to report to is Brigadier General Fleming Pickering."

Dawkins saw the look of surprise on McCoy's face.

"Yeah, I thought that was interesting, too."

"What's going on?" McCoy asked.

Dawkins threw his hands up helplessly.

"That's all I know, Killer. Honestly."

"Sir, my wife's at the Coronado Beach."

"So you said."

"And we drove all day to get here."

"OK. You made your point," Dawkins said. He turned to Master Gunner Matthews. "Mister, is there a message form in that desk?"

"Yes, sir."

"I'm going to dictate a message, which you will then type, and the corporal will then take to the message center."

"Aye, aye, sir."

Matthews picked up a pencil and took a lined pad from the desk.

"Priority, Urgent," Dawkins dedicated. "From Deputy CG, Camp Pendleton. To Headquarters USMC, personal attention, the Commandant. Copy to Brigadier General Fleming Pickering, USMC. Captain Kenneth McCoy, USMC, will depart Miramar NAS aboard USAF F-94 aircraft 0800 30 June ETA Andrews AFB NLT 1600 30 June signature Dawkins, BrigGen, USMC. Got it?"

"Aye, aye, sir."

"Captain McCoy," Dawkins said.

"Yes, sir?"

"It is the desire of the deputy commanding general that you and your lovely wife take breakfast with him and his lovely wife at 0630 tomorrow at the Coronado Beach. After which, you will be transported to the Miramar NAS to comply with your orders. Can you fit that into your busy schedule?"

"Yes, sir."

"Then, considering the hour, Captain, I suggest you get moving."

"Aye, aye, sir."

"At the risk of repeating myself, Killer, I don't know what you're up to now, I don't care what you're up to now. But it's damned good to see you."

"Thank you, sir."

VI

Q: Mr. President, everybody is asking in this country, are we or are we not at war?

The President: We are not at war. The members of the United Nations are going to the relief of the Korean republic to suppress a bandit raid on the Republic of Korea.

Q: Would it be correct under your explanation to call this "a police action under the United Nations"?

The President: Yes, that is exactly what it amounts to.

EXCERPT FROM PRESIDENTIAL PRESS CONFERENCE,

BLAIR HOUSE, WASHINGTON, D.C.

30 JUNE 1950

[ONE]
Office of the Commandant, USMC
Washington, D.C.
1430 30 June 1950

"The Commandant will see you now, sir," the master gunnery sergeant said to Fleming Pickering, as he walked to the double doors of the Commandant's office. He knocked, but didn't wait for a reply before opening the door. "Mr. Pickering, sir."

The Commandant was standing just inside his office.

"That's *General* Pickering, Gunny," General Clifton Cates said, in a soft southern accent. "You might want to make a note of that."

Cates was a tall, sharply featured man with an aristocratic air about him.

"Come on in, Flem," Cates went on. "It's good to see you."

"Thank you for seeing me without an appointment," Pickering said, as he took Cates's extended hand. He chuckled. "I was trying to decide whether or not to salute."

"Not indoors, Flem, or while in civilian attire," Cates said, smiling.

"I went to the officers' sales store at Marine Barracks yesterday, to buy uniforms," Pickering said. "No ID card; they wouldn't sell them to me."

Cates chuckled.

"I think the captain there thought he was dealing with a crazy old coot who thought he was a Marine general," Pickering went on. "Later, I realized he was right."

Cates laughed, then stepped around Pickering and opened his office door.

"Gunny," he ordered. "General Pickering's going to need an ID card, and while I think of it, a physical. Set it up to get him an ID card right away, and then call Bethesda and make an immediate appointment for the physical." He paused. "But only after you get us some coffee."

He closed the door, waved Pickering to a red leather couch, and sat down beside him.

"Frankly, I sort of hoped I would hear from you, Flem," Cates said. "Can you tell me what's going on? Right now, I'm just a Marine officer who's obeying his orders and not asking questions about them."

"I hardly know where to start, sir," Pickering said. "This is probably the best place."

Pickering opened his briefcase, took from it a manila envelope, and handed it to Cates.

Cates opened the envelope and started to read. His eyebrows went up and he pursed his lips.

A staff sergeant came into the office carrying a tray with two china mugs of coffee, placed it on the coffee table by the couch, and then left.

"Where'd this come from?" Cates asked, not lifting his eyes from the assessment.

"It was written by a Marine officer then on the staff of Naval Element, SCAP, in Tokyo," Pickering said.

"McCoy, right?" Cates asked. "What do they call him? 'Killer'?"

"Yes, sir."

"I have been advised by Clyde Dawkins—you remember him from Guadalcanal? He had Marine Air Group 21."

"Yes, sir. My son was in VMF-229 in MAG-21."

"Clyde's now Deputy CG at Pendleton. He sent me a TWX saying McCoy left Miramar at 0800 this morning in an Air Force two-seater fighter for here."

"Yes, sir. I had a telephone call from Mrs. McCoy telling me that."

"Now that I think of it, you were supposed to get a copy of the TWX," Cates said, then went off at a tangent: "This thing isn't signed?"

"The original was signed and submitted to MacArthur's G-2, who ordered it destroyed," Pickering said. "The President doesn't want that to get out."

"Then why did you tell me?"

"I thought you should know, sir."

Cates considered that, nodded, and said, "Thank you. That detail will go no further."

"Thank you, sir," Pickering said.

"But I'd like to have this."

"I thought you should have it, sir. That's why I asked to see you," Pickering said, then went on: "What happened was that I was in Tokyo, went to see McCoy, and he gave me that assessment. And told me he was being involuntarily released from active duty. When I got back to the States, I went to see Admiral Hillenkoetter at the CIA, and gave it to him."

"Things are beginning to make sense," Cates said.

"Apparently, after the North Koreans came across the 38th parallel, Hillenkoetter told the President about the assessment. The President called me, and asked me to come here. I got here on the twenty-sixth. The President came to Senator Fowler's apartment for breakfast, got Fowler's assurance that the . . . rejection of the early warning would not get into the press, and then ordered me to active duty."

"Why?"

"I'm not sure," Pickering said. "Possibly to make sure I keep my mouth shut."

"There has to be more to it than that," Cates said. "Out of school, there is some dissatisfaction with Hillenkoetter's CIA. And you were a deputy director of the OSS, weren't you?"

"I don't think . . . Jesus Christ, I hope not. I'm wholly unqualified to run the CIA."

"As I remember it, I thought you were wholly unqualified to be the First Division G-2. And you proved me dead wrong."

Pickering didn't reply.

"Of course, that was when I thought you were a sailor," Cates went on, smiling. "Before Jack NMI Stecker . . . I remember this clearly; we were in General Vandergrift's conference tent, and I had just referred to you as 'that sailor G-2 of ours,' or perhaps that 'swabbie G-2' when Jack stood up, and 'Begging the colonel's pardon, when you and I were at Belleau Wood, so was Pickering. He was a Marine then, and he's a Marine now.' "

Pickering met Cates's eyes for a moment, then said, firmly, "I'm unqualified to run the CIA, period."

"How about to be a new broom in the Pacific, sweeping out the incompetents we apparently have there?"

"That, either," Pickering said.

Cates went off on another tangent.

"Let me tell you what shape the Corps is in," he said. "I was going over the numbers before you came in." He got off the couch and went and sat behind his desk, and began to read from a folder on his desk.

"Total regular establishment strength, as of today, 74,279 officers and men . . ."

"That's all?" Pickering blurted.

"Broken down into 40,364 officers and men in the operating forces," Cates read on, "24,452 in the support forces, and 3,871 in other duties . . . embassy guards, afloat, that sort of thing."

"My God, I had no idea how much the Corps had been cut back," Pickering said.

"In Fleet Marine Force, Pacific—in Camp Pendleton, mostly—we have 7,779 officers and men in the First Marine Division—"

"Only seven thousand men in the First Marine *Division*?" Pickering asked, incredulously.

"The First Marine Division *(Reinforced)*," Cates confirmed, a tone of sarcasm in his voice. "You're used to a war-strength division, Flem, of 1,079 officers and 20,131 men."

Pickering shook his head in disbelief.

"In addition to the First Marine Division, we have 3,733 officers and men in the First Marine Aircraft Wing. That's roughly half the men called for in peacetime. A wartime wing calls for about 12,000 men."

"My God!"

"Roughly, the regular Marine Corps is about one-third of the Marine Corps," Cates went on. "There are 128,959 officers and men in the reserve components. There's some 39,867 people in the organized reserves, ground and air, and another 90,444 in what we call 'the volunteer reserve—individual reservists, in other words; we don't like to think of them as 'unorganized.' "

"Pick, my son, is in the organized reserve."

"I know," Cates said. "I saw his name in the paper a couple of weeks ago, when he set the San Francisco–to–Tokyo speed record, and I was curious enough to check."

"I was on the plane," Pickering said.

"He ever discuss with you why he's in the reserve?" Cates asked.

"I don't think you'll like the answer," Pickering said.

"Go ahead."

"He said all he has to do is show up at El Toro and the benevolent Marine Corps gives him expensive toys to play with," Pickering said. "He really loves flying the Corsair."

Cates chuckled. "I suspect that motivates many of the aviation reservists," he said. "We don't have recruiting problems with the organized aviation reserve; and it's at ninety-four percent of its authorized strength. The ground elements—despite a good deal of recruiting effort—is at seventy-seven percent. Buzzing Camp Pendleton at four hundred knots in a Corsair is a lot more fun on a weekend than crawling through it on your stomach."

"And is the reserve going to be mobilized?" Pickering asked.

Cates nodded. "I would be very surprised if that doesn't happen. That was my motive for filling you in with all this data."

"Sir?"

"Sometime in the next few days, or weeks, someone at the upper echelons of government is going to say, 'Call in the Marines.' That's our job, of course, and we'll go. But someone in the upper echelons of government should be aware that there are not that many Marines available to go. I suspect you'll be in a position to make that point, Flem, and I think it should be made."

"General, I really have no idea what I'll be doing at the CIA."

"Nevertheless, I think it's in the interests of the Corps to make sure you're prepared for whatever that turns out to be."

"I'm not sure I understand," Pickering said.

"Ed Banning worked for you all through the war, didn't he?"

"Yes, he did."

"When I had the 4th Marines in Shanghai, until May 1940, Ed was my intelligence officer," Cates said.

"I didn't know you knew him," Pickering said.

"He now commands Marine Barracks, Charleston, and teaches at the Citadel," Cates said. "Do you think he would be useful to you in the CIA?"

"Yes, sir."

"He's yours. Anyone else?"

"There's a master gunner at Parris Island, also ex–4th Marines, also ex-OSS. Ernie . . . Ernest W. Zimmerman. He speaks Japanese and two kinds of Chinese. I don't know about Korean, but it wouldn't surprise me."

"Spelled the way it sounds?" Cates asked, his pencil poised.

"Yes, sir," Pickering said. "General, I'm a little uncomfortable with this. I may have no responsibilities at all at the CIA and—"

"On the other hand, you may have great responsibility," Cates cut him off. "Let me tell you, between two old Belleau Woods Marines, my greatest concern right now is for the Corps. First, of course, is the beating we're going to take when we go to war understrength and under-equipped. Right on the heels of that primary concern are A and B. A: We'll be sent to Korea, and, once we get there, will be unable, because of the cuts-*through*-the bone economies of Mr. Johnson, to do what people expect the Marine Corps to do." Secretary of Defense Louis Johnson, a Truman crony, had proudly announced he had "cut military excess and waste to the bone." And B: When that happens, when the Corps *can't* do the impossible, it will prove what a lot of people—including our Commander-in-Chief—have been saying, that the United States doesn't need a Marine Corps."

"Truman said that?" Pickering asked, surprised.

"Words to that effect," Cates said. "And unfortunately, I think he really believes the Marine Corps is not needed."

"It's not a pretty picture, is it?" Pickering asked.

"I have faith the Corps will come through," Cates said. "But if I can raise the odds slightly in our favor by assigning three people to you . . ."

"Frankly, I think the best help I could provide will be to talk to Senator Fowler, give him these figures . . ."

"He knows the figures. I think he agrees with Truman."

"He never suggested anything like . . . putting the Corps out of business to me," Pickering protested loyally.

"He's a politician," Cates said. "Politicians never say anything to people that they suspect might be offensive."

Pickering didn't reply.

Cates rose from behind his desk and put out his hand.

"Flem, I have a meeting. They've prepared a draft order to organize a Marine Brigade at Pendleton, and I want to go over it."

"Of course," Pickering said.

"Stay in touch, please," Cates said.

"Aye, aye, sir," Pickering said.

The Commandant's gunnery sergeant was waiting for him in the outer office.

"If you'll come with me, please, General, they're waiting to take your photo for the ID card. And whenever you get to the hospital at Anacostia, they're waiting for you to take your physical. Have you got wheels, General, or should I get you a car?"

"I've got wheels, Gunny, thank you," Pickering said.

[TWO]
Andrews Air Force Base
Washington, D.C.
1305 30 June 1950

"Air Force Eight Eight Three, take taxiway three right to the Base Operations tarmac. You will be met."

"Understand taxiway three right. Do you mean a follow-me?"

"Eight three, negative. Your passenger will be met."

"Got it," the pilot of USAF F-94, tail number 490883, said, then switched to intercom. "You hear that, Captain?"

"I heard it. I don't know what it means," McCoy said.

The F-94 was met at Base Operations by a ground crew, who signaled for it to stop on the tarmac itself, rather than in the VIP parking area, and then rolled a ladder up to the side of the aircraft.

"Thanks for the ride," McCoy said.

"I loved it," the pilot replied. "That was the first cross country I made in a long time without being ordered to watch my fuel consumption."

Not without some difficulty, McCoy unplugged the connections to his helmet, unfastened his shoulder harness, then the parachute connections, and then crawled somewhat ungracefully out of the rear seat and down the ladder.

Two muscular young men in gray suits were waiting for him on the ground.

"Captain McCoy?" the shorter of the two asked,

McCoy nodded.

"Will you come with us, please, Captain?"

"Who are you? Come with you where?"

The shorter man held out a leather credentials wallet for McCoy to see.

"We're Secret Service, Captain."

"You couldn't give me a better look at that badge, could you?"

Visibly displeased with the request, the Secret Service agent again displayed his credentials.

"Okay?" he asked.

"Fine. Now, where are we going?" McCoy asked.

"The car is over here," the Secret Service agent replied. "You have any luggage?"

"It's in the trunk," McCoy said, sarcastically. "And I think the driver's going to want this back."

He started unzipping the high-altitude flight suit.

The pilot came down the ladder and helped him, then climbed back up the ladder carrying the suit with him.

McCoy saw that the ground crew had hooked up a heavy cable to the fuselage. The Secret Service man touched McCoy's arm, and when McCoy looked at him, nodded toward the Base Operations building.

McCoy nodded back and started to walk. He did not think he was being abducted by gypsies to be held for ransom. The Secret Service credentials looked legitimate, and probably were, but that was not the same thing as saying he was in the hands of the Secret Service. When he had been first with the Office of Management Analysis and later the OSS, he had had bona fide credentials as an agent of the Office of Naval Intelligence and as a U.S. Marshal, and had never been either.

These two guys were probably CIA agents with Secret Service credentials. So far as he knew, the Secret Service was responsible for chasing counterfeiters of money and protecting the President. He didn't have any phony money, and he couldn't imagine anyone suspecting him of being a threat to the President.

Their "car" was a black Chevrolet Suburban, with several shortwave antennae mounted on it. They loaded him into the rear, and he heard the door lock click after he got in.

And he knew Washington, so when they headed toward it on Highway 4, which turned into Pennsylvania Avenue before the District Line, he became more convinced that they were headed to the CIA office, which was in the 2400 block of E Street.

They stayed on Pennsylvania Avenue, and when he saw the White House through the windshield, he turned on his seat for a better look.

He didn't get one. The Suburban made a sudden turn to the right, and then before he could orient himself, a turn left into an alley, and then another left and then a right.

And then it stopped, and he heard the click as the rear door was unlocked. The door opened, and the larger of the "Secret Service" agents motioned him to get out.

They were in a courtyard of a house.

"Where are we?" McCoy asked. "What's this?"

"If you'll follow Agent Taylor, please, Captain?" the smaller agent said, and pointed. McCoy followed Taylor through a ground-floor steel door, down a corridor, then up a flight of carpeted stairs, and finally into a small room furnished with a small leather armchair, a small desk, a chair for that, and, on a table against the wall, a telephone.

"Please wait here, Captain," Agent Taylor said. "We'll be just outside."

By now, McCoy was convinced he was in the hands of the CIA, because the two clowns with Secret Service badges were behaving much like the OSS clowns—most of whom, in the beginning, had never seen a Jap or heard a weapon fired in anger—had behaved, copying their cloak-and-dagger behavior from watching spy movies.

He walked to the desk, rested his buttocks and his hands on it, and waited for Spy Movie, Act Two.

The door opened.

The President of the United States walked in.

It took McCoy a moment to believe what his eyes saw, and then he popped to attention.

"Stand at ease, Captain," the President said, offering his hand. "What did they do, sneak you in the back door?"

"Yes, sir."

"How was the flight?" the President asked.

"Very interesting, sir," McCoy replied, truthfully. "It's hard to believe you're moving that fast." And then he had another thought. "Mr. President, my uniform's a mess. . . ."

"There were many occasions, Captain McCoy, when it was Captain Truman of Battery B, that my uniform was, with good reason, a mess."

McCoy didn't reply.

"I've seen your assessment of war in Korea in ninety days, Captain," the President said. "I wanted to have a look at you."

"Yes, sir," McCoy said.

"I don't want you to think before you answer these questions, Captain. I want you to say the first thing that comes to your mind. Understand?"

"Yes, sir."

"Do you think General MacArthur has seen your assessment?"

"No, sir."

"Why not?"

"I think he would have called me in, if he'd seen it."

"Why do you think he hasn't seen it?"

"General Willoughby didn't want him to see it; didn't give it to him."

"Why not?"

"I can only guess, sir."

"Guess."

"He had only recently given MacArthur an everything-is-peachy assessment."

"And that's why he ordered it destroyed?"

"I think that's the reason, sir."

"And you were aware you were defying your orders when you kept a copy?"

"Yes, sir."

"Do you customarily disobey your orders?"

"Not often, sir."

"This was not the first time?"

"No, sir."

"Why, in this case?"

"I knew I had to do something with it, sir."

"You saw it as your duty?"

"Yes, sir."

"And that's why you gave it to General Pickering? You saw that as your duty?"

"Yes, sir."

"And if he had not conveniently been in Tokyo, then what?"

"I would have given it to him in San Francisco, sir."

"Two things," the President said. "First—you're getting this from the Commander-in-Chief—you did the right thing. Secondly, General Pickering is concerned that you'll be in hot water if what you did ever gets out. I hope to ensure that it never gets out, but if it does, you will not be in any trouble. You understand that?"

"Yes, sir. Thank you, sir."

The President extended his hand. "It's been a pleasure meeting you, Captain McCoy. I wouldn't be surprised if we saw one another again."

"Yes, sir. Thank you, sir."

The President went to the door, opened it, and stepped through it.

"Take Captain McCoy wherever he wants to go," McCoy heard the President order. "And take him out the front door."

"Yes, Mr. President," he heard the shorter Secret Service agent say.

By the time McCoy was led to the front door of Blair House and walked down the flight of stairs, the Chevrolet Suburban was at the curb.

He was again installed in the backseat and heard the door lock click.

"Where to, Captain?" the larger Secret Service agent asked.

McCoy fished in his short pocket and came with the three-by-five card General Dawkins had given him at Camp Pendleton.

"Twenty-four thirty 'E' Street," he read from it. "The East Building."

"The CIA compound?"

"If that's what's there," McCoy said.

They were now driving down Pennsylvania Avenue past the White House. McCoy had a change of heart.

"No," he ordered. "Drop me at the Foster Lafayette."

"You're sure? That place is about as expensive as it gets."

"I'm sure," McCoy said.

He was a Marine. He had been a Marine since he was seventeen. Marines do not appear in public in mussed, sweaty uniforms, much less report for duty that way. The Foster Lafayette Hotel had a splendid—more important, very fast—valet service. And he thought he could avail himself of it.

The doorman of the Foster Lafayette was visibly surprised when a Chevrolet Suburban made an illegal U-turn in front of the marquee and a Marine captain in mussed and sweat-stained tropical worsteds got out.

"Thanks for the ride," McCoy said, and walked past the doorman into the lobby of the hotel, and then across the lobby to the desk.

"Good afternoon, sir," said the desk clerk, who was wearing a gray frock coat with a rose in the lapel, striped trousers, and a formal foulard.

"My name is McCoy," he said.

"I thought you might be Captain McCoy, sir. We've been expecting you, sir."

"You have?"

"We have a small problem, Captain. General Pickering left word that if he somehow missed you, we were to put you in the Pickering suite. And Mrs. McCoy called and said that when you arrived, you were to be put up in the American Personal Pharmaceuticals suite. Which would you prefer, sir?"

McCoy thought it over for a moment.

"In the final analysis, I suppose it's safer to ignore a general than your wife," he said. "And I'm going to need some instant valet service for this uniform."

The desk clerk snapped his fingers. A bellman appeared.

"Take Captain McCoy to the American Personal Pharmaceuticals suite," he ordered. "And send the floor waiter to the suite."

[THREE]
The Foster Lafayette Hotel
Washington, D.C.
1730 30 June 1950

The door chimes sounded, and Captain Kenneth R. McCoy, attired in a T-shirt and shorts—from the Foster Lafayette's Men's Shop, and for which he had paid, he noticed, as he signed the bill, *five* times as much as he had paid for essentially identical items in the Tokyo PX—went to answer it, expecting to find the floor waiter with his freshly cleaned uniform.

He found, instead, General Fleming Pickering, USMCR, standing there in civilian clothing.

"The manager of the establishment tells me you ignored another order of mine, Captain, but if you will pour me a stiff drink, I'll let it pass," Pickering said, putting out his hand.

"Ernie called ahead," McCoy said, "and told them to let me stay here. I don't have any money, and I thought it would be better to charge things to my father-in-law, who doesn't like me anyhow, than to you, sir."

"You can put a hell of a lot in one sentence," Pickering said, as he walked into the suite. "First things first, where does your father-in-law—who does, by the way, think very highly of you—keep the booze?"

"In here," McCoy said, leading him to a room off the sitting room that held a small, but fully stocked, bar.

Pickering rummaged through an array of bottles, finally triumphantly holding up a bottle of Famous Grouse.

"I have just been paid a left-handed compliment by a Navy doctor I don't think is as old as you," he said, as he found glasses. " 'For someone of your age, General, you're in remarkably good condition.' "

McCoy chuckled, and took the glass of straight Scots whiskey Pickering handed him.

"Cheers," Pickering said, and they touched glasses.

The door chime went off again.

"My uniform, probably," Ken said, and walked to the door. Pickering followed him.

This time it was the floor waiter, holding a freshly cleaned uniform on a hanger. He extended the bill for McCoy to sign.

"Do you know who I am?" Pickering asked.

"Yes, sir, of course."

"Are you aware there is a standing order in this inn that Captain McCoy's money is no good?"

"Jesus . . ." McCoy said.

Pickering held up his hand to silence him.

". . . issued by the dragon lady of the Foster chain, my wife, herself?"

"No, sir," the floor waiter said, smiling.

"Trust me, and be good enough to inform the manager."

"Yes, sir, Mr. Pickering," the floor waiter said, chuckling.

"And, truth being stranger than fiction, you may start referring to me as 'General,' " Pickering said.

"Yes, sir," the floor waiter said.

"You might be interested to know, further, that for someone of my age, I have been adjudged to be in remarkably good shape."

"I'm glad to hear that, General," the floor waiter said, smiling. "It's good to have you in the inn again, General."

"Thank you," Pickering said.

"I wish you hadn't done that, General," McCoy said when the floor waiter had left.

"One, you said you had no money, and, two, since, having just passed my recall to active duty physical, I am again a general, I will remind you that captains are not permitted to argue with generals."

"Yes, sir," McCoy said. "You've been recalled?"

"By the President himself," Pickering said. "I did not volunteer. He just called the Commandant and told him to issue the orders. When I told the dragon lady, it caused her to shift into her highly pissed off mode. She thinks I volunteered, and then lied about it."

"I never heard you call her that before," McCoy said.

"The kindest thing she said—on the phone just now, before I came down the corridor to find a friendly face—was that I was a 'selfish adolescent who thinks of nothing but his own personal gratification.' "

"Ouch," McCoy said.

"What makes it worse is that I am about as welcome as syphilis at the CIA. Calling me to active duty was not Admiral Hillenkoetter's idea." He paused. "I went to him with your assessment, Ken."

"The President told me he'd seen it; he didn't say how he'd gotten it," McCoy said.

"The *President* told you he'd seen it?"

"They flew me here—from Miramar—in an Air Force jet, a two-seater fighter. When we landed at Andrews, two guys from the Secret Service met me.

They took me to a house—just down the street from here—and put me in a little office and told me to wait. The door opened, and President Truman walked in."

"Blair House," Pickering furnished. "They're redoing the White House from the walls in. That's where he lives, for the time being. What did he have to say?"

"Not much. He asked if I thought MacArthur had seen the assessment, and then—when I told him no, that Willoughby hadn't given it to him—asked why I thought he'd done that. I told him it was only a guess, but I suspected Willoughby had just given him an assessment that said there wouldn't be trouble in Korea. Then he told me that I had done the right thing in giving it to you; that you were concerned I'd be in trouble, and he said I wouldn't. Then he said he wouldn't be surprised if we saw each other again, and left. The whole thing didn't last three minutes."

"Sequence of events: I went, with Senator Fowler, to Hillenkoetter with a sanitized version of the assessment—your name wasn't on it—as soon as I got back from Japan. He said he'd look into it. He asked for your name, and I wouldn't give it to him. The next thing I heard was a telephone call from the President. He said that he knew of my 'visit' to Hillenkoetter, and asked if I would come to Washington; he wanted to meet with Fowler and me. I said yes. He also asked where you were. I said I didn't know where you were, except en route to Camp Pendleton. Two hours later I was in an F-94, and the next morning the President came here, to Fowler's apartment, asked Fowler to keep the assessment, the warning, from the press. Fowler agreed."

"Where'd they get my name?"

"I don't suppose that was hard, Ken," Pickering said. "I also told the President that I didn't want you to get in trouble, and he asked if I meant I thought you needed friends in high places, and the next thing, he's on the phone to the Commandant—personally—telling him to cut active-duty orders on me, effective immediately."

"Because I need a protector?"

"I spent forty minutes with General Cates this morning. He told me that—he *implied*; he's both too much a gentleman and too smart to spell it out in so many words—that there is some dissatisfaction with Hillenkoetter and that it wouldn't surprise him if Truman had me in mind as a replacement."

McCoy visibly thought that announcement over, but his face did not register surprise.

"You were a deputy director of the OSS," McCoy said.

"Who is, and you know this as well as I do, absolutely unqualified to be head of the CIA."

"You couldn't do any worse than this admiral. He should have known this was coming."

"I wouldn't know how to do any better."

"Yes, you would," McCoy said, simply.

"Maybe Hillenkoetter's heard the same thing," Pickering said. "That would explain the ice-cold reception I got over there."

"What are you going to do over there?" McCoy asked.

" *We* have an office in the East Building—that's where Hillenkoetter's office is—four rooms, sparsely furnished."

"In which *we* are going to do what?"

"I think they'll probably want to pick your brains about the North Korean/Chinese order of battle, but I have no idea what I'll be doing except that Ed Banning and Zimmerman are on their way here to help me to do it."

"How did that happen?"

"That was the Commandant's idea. He painted a pretty bleak picture of the readiness of the Corps to fight a war—"

"The First Marine Division," McCoy interrupted. "The First Marine Division, *Reinforced,* at Pendleton, has less than 8,000 men."

Pickering was at first surprised that McCoy knew that figure, but on reflection, was not. McCoy had always been a cornucopia of data; he learned something once, then never forgot it.

"—and is concerned that when the Corps can't pull off a miracle, as it will be expected to do, it will be ammunition for those who think we don't need a Marine Corps."

"How are you and Ed Banning supposed to help about that?"

Pickering thought that over, then said what had first come into his mind.

"Every time somebody says, 'First Marine Division,' we interject, 'which is at less than half wartime strength.'"

McCoy chuckled.

The telephone rang.

It was Ernie.

"Good," she said. "You're there."

"And so is the General," Ken said.

"Aunt Patricia told me. She is something less than thrilled."

"Where did you see her?"

"I'm in San Francisco. With her. I'm on what they call the 'red-eye special,' a midnight flight on TWA to New York. It gets there at seven in the morning. I'll take the train to Washington. Are you going to be there when I get there?"

"Yes."

"Put Uncle Flem on the phone," she ordered, and he heard her say, "Talk to him, Aunt Pat."

He handed the phone to Pickering.

"Your wife," he said.

Pickering raised his eyebrows as he took the phone.

"Selfish adolescent speaking," he said. "Honey, honest to God, I didn't volunteer."

"Whatever you are, you're not a liar," McCoy heard Patricia Fleming reply. "If I get on the plane with Ernie, are you going to be there, too?"

"Yes, ma'am."

"Then I'll see you tomorrow," she said. "Will you still fit in your uniforms?"

"A young Navy doctor told me that I'm in remarkably good shape for my age. Where are my uniforms?"

"I found a couple here in the apartment. Shall I bring them?"

"Please, sweetheart. Thank you."

"How in the world did a couple of nice girls like Ernie and me wind up as Marine Corps camp followers?"

"You have very good taste, maybe?"

McCoy heard Patricia Fleming laugh, and then she hung up without saying anything else.

[FOUR]
Headquarters
Beaufort USMC Air Station
Beaufort, South Carolina
0830 1 July 1950

Colonel Edward J. Banning, USMC, in a fresh but already sweat-stained tropical worsted uniform, and carrying a canvas Valv-Pak, walked into the headquarters building and got his hand up in time to keep the Technical Sergeant on duty from leaping to his feet and bellowing "attention on deck."

"As you were," he said. "Sergeant, is Colonel Dunn somewhere around?"

"Sir, if you're Colonel Banning, he's expecting you."

"Guilty," Banning said. "Where do I find him?"

"Hold one, sir," the sergeant said, and picked up his telephone. He dialed a number, then announced, "Sir, Colonel Banning is here."

Lieutenant Colonel William C. Dunn, USMC, appeared a minute later, wearing a flight suit and holding a mug of coffee in his hand.

"Good morning, sir," he said.

"Hello, Billy," Banning said, as they shook hands.

He reached into his pocket and took out a sheet of teletype paper, the second, carbon copy of what had come out of the machine, and handed it to Dunn.

Dunn reached in the knee pocket of his flight suit and handed Banning a sheet of teletype paper.

"The Colonel," he said, dryly, "might find this of interest. I think I know what yours says."

Both men read the teletype messages:

```
PRIORITY


CONFIDENTIAL


FROM: HQ USMC 1610 30 JUNE 1950


TO: COMMANDING OFFICER
    USMC BARRACKS
    CHARLESTON, SC


INFO: COMMANDING OFFICER
      MCAS BEAUFORT, SC


1. ISSUE APPROPRIATE ORDERS IMMEDIATELY DETACHING
COLONEL EDWARD M. BANNING FOR INDEFINITE PERIOD OF
TEMPORARY DUTY HQ USMC.
2. COL BANNING WILL REPORT TO OFFICE OF THE COMMANDANT,
USMC.
3. TRAVEL BY USMC AIRCRAFT FROM MCAS BEAUFORT, SC IS
DIRECTED. PRIORITY AAAAA. TRAVEL WILL COMMERCE WITHIN
TWENTY-FOUR (24) HOURS.
```

4. NO INQUIRIES CONCERNING OR REQUESTS FOR DELAY IN
EXECUTION OF THESE ORDERS IS DESIRED.

FOR THE COMMANDANT USMC:

WILLIAM S. SHALEY

MAG GEN USMC

PRIORITY
CONFIDENTIAL

FROM: HQ USMC 1610 30 JUNE 1950

TO: COMMANDING GENERAL
    USMC RECRUIT TRAINING DEPOT
    PARRIS ISLAND SC

INFO: COMMANDING OFFICER
      MCAS BEAUFORT, SC

1. ISSUE APPROPRIATE ORDERS IMMEDIATELY DETACHING
MASTER GUNNER EARNEST W. ZIMMERMAN FOR INDEFINITE
PERIOD OF TEMPORARY DUTY HQ USMC.
2. SUBJECT OFFICER WILL REPORT TO OFFICE OF THE
COMMANDANT, USMC.
3. TRAVEL BY USMC AIRCRAFT FROM MCAS BEAUFORT, SC IS
DIRECTED. PRIORITY AAAAA. TRAVEL WILL COMMENCE WITHIN
TWENTY-FOUR (24) HOURS.
4. NO INQUIRIES CONCERNING OR REQUESTS FOR DELAY IN
EXECUTION OF THESE ORDERS IS DESIRED.

FOR THE COMMANDANT USMC:

WILLIAM S. SHALEY
MAG GEN USMC

"I think I know what this is, Colonel," Dunn said, as they exchanged the teletype messages. "The Commandant is holding a convention of real estate tycoons."

"You can go to hell, Colonel," Banning said. "I have no idea what this is all about."

"It might have something to do with what's going on in Korea," Dunn said. "It just came over the radio that MacArthur went over to have a look."

Banning grunted but didn't reply.

"Zimmerman here?"

"He and Mae-Su, in my office. I thought you'd want to go together. Luddy drive you up?"

Banning nodded, and nodded toward the parking lot. "And passed the time delivering lecture 401 on the evils of the communist empire. She's convinced the Russians—excuse me, the *Bolsheviks;* Luddy is a *Russian*—are behind this Korean business."

"And you aren't?"

"Billy, I just don't know," Banning said.

'Well, your chariot awaits, Colonel. Unless you want a cup of coffee or something?"

"I hate long farewells," Banning said. "Let's get the show on the road."

"I'll go get the Zimmermans," Dunn said.

"What kind of a chariot do we have?"

"Gooney-Bird," Dunn said. "Driven by yours truly."

"That's very nice, Billy. But I know you've got things to do around here."

"I could say, 'my pleasure, sir, there's nothing I would rather do,' but being a Marine officer, the truth is that I'm headed for Eighth and Eye, too. I think somebody up there thinks we're going to have a war; they want to talk about mobilization. Taking you in the Gooney-Bird means I can take some of my officers and senior noncoms with me."

[FIVE]
Room 505
East Building, The CIA Complex
2430 E Street
Washington, D.C.
1400 1 July 1950

Brigadier General Fleming Pickering, USMCR, was sprawled somewhat uncomfortably on a chrome framed, tweed-upholstered couch reading the *Washington Star* and Captain Kenneth R. McCoy, USMC, was sitting behind General Pickering's desk, reading *The Washington Post,* when the telephone on the desk rang.

McCoy looked at Pickering for guidance, and Pickering mimed picking up the telephone.

"General Pickering's office, Captain McCoy speaking, sir." He listened, and then added, "Pass them up, please." He put the telephone back in its cradle and looked at Pickering. "Banning and Zimmerman are downstairs," he said.

"That was quick," Pickering said. "Cates told me he would get them assigned here, but that was yesterday afternoon."

He sat up, put the newspaper on the couch, and stood up, looking thoughtful.

"Try to get Admiral Hillenkoetter again, will you, Ken?" he asked.

McCoy consulted a stapled-together telephone book and dialed a number.

"General Pickering calling for Admiral Hillenkoetter," he said into the telephone, listened again, said "thank you," and hung up. He looked at Pickering. "The admiral is not in the building," he said.

"Which means the admiral is not in the building, or the admiral doesn't want to talk to me," Pickering said. He walked to the window and looked out of it.

Escorted by an armed guard in a police-like uniform, Colonel Edward J. Banning, USMC, and Master Gunner Ernest Zimmerman, USMC, arrived three minutes later.

"Colonel Banning, Edward J., reporting as ordered with a party of one, sir," Banning said.

"Hello, Ed," Pickering said. "Ernie, how are you?"

They shook hands all around.

"General," the guard said, "When these gentlemen leave, please have them escorted to the lobby, or call the guard captain, and he will send someone here."

Pickering looked at him a moment, then nodded.

The guard left and closed the door.

"I knew you were coming," Pickering said. "But I didn't expect you so soon."

" 'Travel will commence within twenty-four hours,' " Banning quoted, and handed Pickering the sheet of teletype paper he had shown Billy Dunn at the Beaufort Marine Air Station earlier. "Ernie's got one just like it, with only the names changed to protect the guilty. We went to Eighth and Eye, and they sent us over here. Orders will be cut sometime today placing both of us on indefinite TDY* here."

"Colonel Dunn flew us up," Zimmerman said. "He sends his respects, sir. "Can I ask what's happening?"

"Ernie, I don't know," Pickering said. "But I'm damned sure about to find out." He turned to McCoy. "Look in that phone book, Ken, and see if you can come up with a deputy director, or a deputy director, administration, something like that."

"Yes, sir," McCoy said.

Sixty seconds later, he reported: "There's a deputy director and deputy director for administration. In this building. Shall I try to get one of them—tell me which one—on the phone?"

"Does it give room numbers?"

"Yes, sir. Four-oh-two for the deputy director, four-oh-six for the deputy director, administration."

Pickering walked to the door of the office and made a *follow me* motion with his hand and arm.

They followed him down the corridor toward the elevator, and then Pickering spotted and opened a door to a stairwell.

"It's only one flight down," he said.

One flight down, the door from the stairwell to the fourth floor could not be opened.

"Goddamn it!" Pickering said, and started down the stairwell, taking them two at a time, with Banning, McCoy, and Zimmerman on his tail.

The door from the stairwell to the lobby opened. Pickering started for the bank of elevators, and was intercepted by another guard in a police-type uniform before he could punch the button to summon the elevator.

"Excuse me, sir," the guard said. "May I see your badge, please?"

"I don't have a badge," Pickering said. "None of us have badges. It's one of

*Temporary Duty.

the things I'm going to discuss with either Admiral Hillenkoetter or one of his deputies."

Another guard appeared.

"Sir, I can't permit you to get on the elevator without a badge, or an escort."

"Okay, escort me," Pickering said.

"Sir, I can't do that without permission from the party you wish to see."

"Okay. Get on the horn, call Admiral Hillenkoetter, or his deputy, or the deputy director for administration, and tell him that General Pickering wishes to see him."

"If you'll wait here, please," one of the guards said, and walked to the desk in the center of the lobby.

"How'd you get this far without a badge?" the other guard asked.

"I came down the goddamn chimney like Santa Claus," Pickering said.

Two minutes later, the first guard walked back over to them. He was carrying a clipboard.

"I'll have to see your ID cards," he said. "And then this officer will escort you to the office of the deputy director for administration."

That took another two minutes, but finally all five crowded into a small elevator.

They rose to the fourth floor, and the guard led them down the corridor to an office with a gold-lettered sign reading "Deputy Director, Administration" on the frosted glass of its door.

Inside was a reception room, occupied by a middle-aged secretary. A Navy captain stood beside her desk.

"General," he said. "I'm Captain Murfin, the deputy director for administration. How can I help you?"

"Can we talk in there?" Pickering asked, pointing to the interior office.

"Yes, sir, of course. Can I offer you coffee?"

"That would be very nice, thank you," Pickering said. He followed Captain Murfin into his office.

"Captain, this is Colonel Banning, Captain McCoy, and Mr. Zimmerman. For lack of a better description, they are my staff."

They all shook hands. The secretary delivered coffee in mugs.

"Now, what's on your mind, General?" Captain Murfin asked.

"For openers, I will need, we will all need, identification badges. I'm getting tired of being escorted around by your guards."

"I'll arrange for temporary badges, of course."

"Does that imply you know we won't be around here long?" Pickering asked.

"No, sir. What it means is that I don't know how long you will be here."

"Or what I'll be doing?"

"That, too, General."

"Okay. Let me try to clarify that point. I am here and Captain McCoy is here at the order of the President of the United States . . ."

"So I understand, General."

". . . and Colonel Banning and Mr. Zimmerman are here because they have been placed on indefinite TDY here, to work for me, by order of the Commandant of the Marine Corps. Orders to that effect are being cut today."

"Yes, sir. I suppose I can get you and the captain identity badges, but until I actually have The Colonel's and Mr. Zimmerman's orders in hand . . ."

"Tell me, Captain, is the deputy director in the building?" Pickering interrupted.

"No, sir. He's not."

"And I understand the director is likewise off somewhere?"

"He's at the Pentagon, sir."

"Which leaves you the senior officer on duty?"

"Yes, sir. I suppose I am running the store at the moment."

"Well, Captain, in that case, let me tell you how you're going to run the store," Pickering said. "We are both in the Naval service, and I don't think I have to tell you that a brigadier general outranks a captain."

"Sir . . ."

"What you are going to do, Captain, is immediately take our photographs and fingerprints and whatever else you need to have ID cards printed up for all four of us. Those identity cards will be waiting for us in the lobby no later than 0800 tomorrow morning. You may consider that an order. If the director wishes to discuss this with me—or the deputy director, presuming he is senior in rank to me—wishes to discuss this with me, I will be—we will all be—in my apartment in the Foster Lafayette hotel. Do you have any questions?"

The deputy director for administration considered his reply for at least twenty seconds. Then he said, "General, if you and these gentlemen will come with me, I'll take you to the photo lab."

"Certainly," Pickering said. "And there is one other thing, Captain."

"Yes, sir."

"Please get word to Admiral Hillenkoetter that I will be here at 0800 tomorrow, and respectfully request a few minutes of his time as soon as possible thereafter."

"I'll give him that message, sir," Captain Murfin said.

[SIX]
The Marquis de Lafayette Suite
The Foster Lafayette Hotel
Washington, D.C.
1805 1 July 1950

"I really don't know what to think," Colonel Ed Banning said, popping a bacon-wrapped oyster in his mouth. "I wish I'd known about the Killer's assessment before now. . . ."

"God damn it, are you never going to belay that Killer crap?" McCoy snapped.

"Sorry, Ken," Banning said.

"Never," Pickering said, "at least not among those who know you and love you so well."

"Sorry, Ken," Banning said, sincerely contrite. "It just slips out."

"Forget it," McCoy said.

"As you have forgotten that good Marine captains don't cuss at Marine colonels?" Pickering asked.

"Sir, Captain McCoy begs the colonel's pardon."

"It's OK, Killer, forget it," Banning said.

That caused laughter.

The truth was while they were not drunk, they had been sitting, drinking, in the living room of Pickering's suite—technically, he had commented, his wife's suite; *she* was the chairman of Foster Hotels, Inc.—since 1645, when they had returned from the CIA complex, all the bureaucratic necessities for the issuance of identity cards having taken a little more than an hour.

Some of their conversation had dealt with wondering where the women were; they should have been in the hotel by noon, but most of it had dealt with what was going on, both in Korea and with themselves.

A bellman had been dispatched to the National Geographic Society building, several blocks away, to get a map of Korea—"On second thought, you'd better get half a dozen," Pickering had ordered. "Everything they've got, the coast of China from the Burmese border, near Rangoon, to the Russian border, to the Sea of Okhotsk."

Using the maps, McCoy had delivered an hour-long briefing, entirely from memory, of the disposition of North Korean forces on the Korean peninsula; of Chinese and Russian forces up and down the coast of the Asian continent; of

U.S. Army forces in Korea—there were practically none in Korea—and Japan; and even of Nationalist Chinese forces on Formosa.

He traced the possible routes of invasion across the 38th parallel, and offered his assessment of the probable North Korean intentions.

"I don't think they expected the Americans to intervene, but I don't think that it will have any effect when we do. We probably can't get enough forces over there quickly enough to stop them. What we do send is likely to be pushed into the sea here, in the deep South, around Pusan."

He discussed the possibility of support from Chiang Kai-shek's Nationalist Army on Formosa, and dismissed it as probably not going to be worth very much. And his opinion of the war-fighting capabilities of the Eighth U.S. Army in Korea was anything but flattering.

"Their equipment is old, their training is inadequate, and they don't have any armor to match the Russian T-34s the North Koreans have. The bridges in Japan won't take the weight of an M-26, which is arguably as good as the T-34, so there are no M-26s. The M-24s they do have are light tanks that don't stand a chance against the T-34."

That was frustrating to hear, of course, and so was contemplation of what they were all going to be doing in the CIA.

Banning agreed that it was possible, even likely, that Admiral Hillenkoetter would be fired for not being able to predict the sudden North Korea attack.

"Probably," Banning said, "not right away. If the President is worried about a Pearl Harbor reaction to the attack, the last thing he wants to do is fire the Director of the CIA. That makes what General Cates said, that he's thinking of you to replace Hillenkoetter, make a kind of sense."

"I'm not equipped to run the CIA."

"One scenario is that Hillenkoetter will stay on until you feel you can take over," Banning argued.

The door chime sounded.

"The ladies, I hope," Pickering said, and went to the door.

Patricia Foster Pickering and Ernestine Sage McCoy walked into the room, trailed by four bellmen carrying luggage and cardboard boxes from Brooks Brothers. Both women looked around the mess in the room, and the four Marines, all of whom had their field scarves pulled down, their collars unbuttoned, and their sleeves rolled up.

"I hope we're not interrupting anything," Patricia Pickering said, lightly sarcastic.

"We were getting worried," Pickering said.

"I'm sure you were," Patricia Pickering said, now seriously sarcastic. "If there's any scotch left, I really would like a drink."

Her husband scurried to get her a drink.

McCoy went to his wife and kissed her.

"How many have you had?" Ernie asked.

"A couple," he confessed.

"There is a difference between a couple, which is two, and several, which is any number three or greater."

"Several," McCoy said.

Ernie laughed. "Aunt Pat, I told you. They can't be trusted alone, but they don't lie."

"What's in the boxes?" McCoy asked.

"We went by Brooks Brothers and got you some uniforms," Ernie said.

"Good little camp followers that we are," Patricia said. She went to Ed Banning. "I see that you—*smell* that you—can't be trusted out of Milla's sight, either."

But she kissed his cheek nevertheless, and then Zimmerman's.

"And for lunch we had a hot dog with sauerkraut and a Coke on the side-walk outside Brooks Brothers," Patricia said. "It was good, but it wasn't enough. Plan on an earlier dinner, boys."

Pickering handed his wife a drink.

"Here you go, sweetheart," he said.

"You don't have one?"

"On the coffee table."

"Make it last," she said. "That's your last. I didn't fly across the country in the middle of the night, and then spend the morning in Brooks Brothers and the afternoon driving here from Manhattan just for the privilege of watching you snore in an armchair."

"Yes, dear," Pickering said, mockingly. He was more amused than annoyed, and certainly didn't appear chastised.

Patricia turned to McCoy.

"Say, 'thank you, Ernie, for coming and going to Brooks Brothers for me.' "

"Thank you, honey, for coming and going to Brooks Brothers for me," McCoy said, with a smile.

"You're welcome," Ernie said.

The telephone rang.

Banning answered it, then extended it to Pickering.

"Senator Fowler, sir," he said.

Mrs. Pickering looked annoyed.

Pickering took the phone.

"Hello, Dick," he said. "Come down the corridor and have a drink with us. Patricia just walked in the door."

Fowler's end of the conversation could not be heard by Patricia Pickering, although she tried hard.

"Dick, I really don't want to do that. Patricia is in one of her fire-breathing moods. . . ."

"Hey, don't you listen? I said I didn't want to."

"Oh, goddamn it, Dick. All right. We'll be there in a minute." He put the phone down and looked at his wife. "Our senator wants to see me for a minute. Ken and me. He says it's important."

She didn't reply.

"I owe him a couple of favors," he said.

"Like him getting you back into your goddamn Marine Corps?"

They locked eyes for a moment, and then Pickering said, rather firmly., "Patricia, we'll only be a few minutes. Why don't you order dinner?"

He motioned for McCoy to follow him, and they left the room.

" 'Goddamn Marine Corps,' Aunt Pat?" Ernie said.

"Goddamn Marine Corps," Patricia Pickering confirmed. "He's too old— he's fifty, for God's sake—to go rushing off . . ."

She stopped, looked at Ernie, and started for the door. "I know him and Richardson Fowler. And he's already had enough to drink. You coming?"

Ernie considered this a moment, then shook her head, "no."

"Suit yourself," Patricia Fleming said, and walked into the corridor. After a moment, Ernie followed her.

"We'll be right back," she said.

" 'Goddamn Marine Corps'?" Ernie Zimmerman quoted. "She sounds just like Mae-Su."

"If the Marine Corps wanted you to have a wife, Gunner Zimmerman," Banning replied, delighted at his own wit, "they would have issued you one."

"Luddy's not pissed?"

"Actually, she's not. She would really like me to go over there and start killing Communists," Banning said.

A muscular man in a gray suit stepped in front of Patricia Pickering.

"Excuse me, ma'am," he said. "May I ask where you're going?"

"Not that it's any of your business, but I'm going to see Senator Fowler."

"I'm afraid that's not possible just now, ma'am," he said. "Could you come back in, say, thirty minutes."

"Not possible? What do you mean not possible? Get out of my way!"

"I'm afraid I can't let you pass."

"You can't let me pass?" Mrs. Pickering asked in outrage. "I own this hotel—no one tells me I 'can't pass.' "

Another muscular man walked quickly up as the first Secret Service agent was taking his credentials from his suit jacket pocket, and then the door of Senator Fowler's suite opened.

"Oh, Jesus Christ, Patricia," Fleming Pickering said to her, then turned to someone in the room. "It's my wife."

"Let her in," a voice came from inside the room, and then President Truman appeared in the open door. "Let the lady pass."

"Ladies," Ernie said from behind the second Secret Service agent. "I'm with her."

"Ladies," the President agreed, smiling.

"Good evening, Mr. President," Patricia Fleming said.

"Good evening, Mrs. Pickering," Truman said. "I apologize for this. Won't you come in for a minute?"

He offered his hand to Ernie McCoy.

"Admiral Hillenkoetter told me Captain McCoy was married to a very beautiful young woman. How do you do? You *are* Mrs. McCoy?"

"Yes, sir, Mr. President," Ernie said.

"Hello, Patricia," Senator Fowler said.

"I suspected that my overage adolescent was going to crawl into a bottle with you, Dick, and I see I was right."

"Mrs. Pickering, Mrs. McCoy," the President said, "this is Major General Ralph Howe, an old friend of mine."

"How do you do, ladies?" General Howe said, in a twangy Maine accent. He seemed to be amused.

"How do you do, General?" Patricia said, as she shook his hand.

"I think what we have here, Harry," General Howe said, smiling broadly, "is proof of the adage that behind every great man there really is a beautiful woman."

Truman chuckled.

"Mrs. Pickering," the President said. "I wanted a few minutes with General Howe, your husband, and Captain McCoy. A few private minutes that no one would know about. That's why I imposed on Senator Fowler's hospitality. . . ."

"No imposition at all, Mr. President," Fowler said.

"Can I have them for ten minutes, ladies?" the President asked. "They'll tell you what this is all about later."

"Of course, Mr. President," Patricia Fleming said. "I suppose I have made a flaming ass of myself, haven't I?"

"I suspect my wife would have done exactly what you did," the President said. "Bess suspects that all my friends are always plying me with liquor."

She found herself at the door.

"Again, my apologies, ladies," the President said, and they went through the door.

"And my apologies, Mr. President," Pickering said when the door was closed. "The main reason she's on a tear is that she thinks I volunteered to go back in the Corps, and that Dick Fowler arranged it as a favor."

"If you'd like, I can straighten her out on that," the President said.

"I would be grateful, Mr. President."

"Formidable lady, General," General Howe said.

"I don't think a shrinking violet could run the Foster Hotel chain the way she runs it," the President said. "Now, where were we?"

"I was about to offer Fleming a drink," Fowler said. "Now I'm not so sure that's a good idea."

"I think it is," Pickering said.

"I'll make them," Fowler said. "The usual?"

"Yes."

"For you, too, Ken?" Fowler asked.

"Yes, sir, please," McCoy said.

"To get right to the heart of this," the President said. "When Admiral Hillenkoetter first brought your name up, General, he said that you had first gone to the Pacific as the private eyes of Navy Secretary Knox, and that that had evolved into your being the private eyes of President Roosevelt."

"Yes, sir, that accurately describes what happened."

"I found that fascinating," Truman said. "Although I didn't say anything to the admiral."

"Sir?"

"Until that moment, I thought I had the bright idea all on my own," Truman said. "That if you really want to know what's going on around the military, send someone who considers his primary loyalty is to the President, not the military establishment. General Howe and I go back to France—we were both captains in France. Then we saw one another over the years in the National Guard. In War Two, when I was in the Senate, he went back into the Army, and rose to major general. When this Korean thing broke, he was about the first person I knew I was going to need, and I called him to active duty—to be my eyes in this war."

"I see," Pickering said.

"And when he came down from Maine, I told him about you, about Captain McCoy's assessment, and the trouble he had with it, and we are agreed that your talents in this sort of thing should not be allowed to lay fallow."

"Mr. President, I'm afraid you're overestimating my talents," Pickering said.

"You can do one thing I can't, General," Howe said. "You can talk to MacArthur, maybe even ask him questions no one else would dare ask him."

"Wow!" Pickering said, as Fowler handed him a drink.

"Would you be willing to take on such an assignment?"

"Sir, I'm at your orders," Pickering said.

"Take a look at this," the President said, handing Pickering a squarish envelope. "And tell me if it's all right."

THE WHITE HOUSE

WASHINGTON, D.C.

JULY 1, 1950

GENERAL OF THE ARMY DOUGLAS MACARTHUR

THE DAI ICHI BUILDING

TOKYO, JAPAN

BY OFFICER COURIER

DEAR GENERAL MACARTHUR:

   THERE IS ONE SMALL PIECE OF GOOD NEWS IN WHAT
FRANKLY LOOKS TO ME LIKE A DARK SITUATION, AND WHICH I
WANTED TO GET IN YOUR HANDS AS SOON AS POSSIBLE.

   ADMIRAL HILLENKOETTER, THE DIRECTOR OF THE CIA, HAS
ASKED ME TO RECALL TO ACTIVE DUTY YOUR FRIEND BRIGADIER
GENERAL FLEMING PICKERING, USMCR, AND I HAVE DONE SO. AT

ADMIRAL HILLENKOETTER'S RECOMMENDATION, I HAVE NAMED GEN-
ERAL PICKERING ASSISTANT DIRECTOR OF THE CIA FOR ASIA, A
POSITION MUCH LIKE THE ONE HE HELD DURING WORLD WAR II,
WHERE HE WAS SO VALUABLE TO YOURSELF, OSS DIRECTOR DONO-
VAN, AND PRESIDENT ROOSEVELT.

HE WILL BE COMING TO THE FAR EAST IN THE VERY NEAR
FUTURE, AND I WANT YOU TO KNOW THAT HE ENJOYS MY EVERY
CONFIDENCE AND THAT YOU MAY FEEL FREE TO SAY ANYTHING
TO HIM THAT YOU WOULD SAY TO ME.

SINCERELY,

Harry S Truman

HARRY S TRUMAN
PRESIDENT OF THE UNITED STATES
COMMANDER-IN-CHIEF OF THE ARMED FORCES

Pickering raised his eyes from the letter to the President.

"Is that about the way President Roosevelt handled it?" Truman asked.

"He referred to the general as 'my dear Douglas,' " Pickering said.

"He knew MacArthur," Truman said. "I don't. And I don't think I want to know the sonofabitch."

"Harry!" General Howe cautioned.

"He's an officer in the U.S. Army," Truman said. "Not the Viceroy of Japan, but I don't think he knows that, and if he does, he doesn't want to admit it. And I want you to know how I feel about him, General."

"I understand, sir."

"How do you feel about him?" Truman asked.

"He's a brilliant man—possibly, probably, the best general of our era, Mr. President."

"Better than Eisenhower? Bradley?"

"I never had the opportunity to watch General Eisenhower at work, Mr. President. But I have watched General MacArthur. The word 'genius' is not out of place. But he sometimes manifests traits of character that are disturbing to me personally. He can be petty, for example."

"For example?"

"Every unit on Corregidor but the 4th Marines was given the Presidential Unit Citation. General MacArthur said the Marines had enough medals."

"That's all?"

"His blind loyalty to the Bataan Gang disturbs me, Mr. President."

"That's why you didn't take McCoy's assessment to him?"

"I think his support of General Willoughby would have been irrational, and that very likely would have caused McCoy more trouble than he was already in, Mr. President."

"All I expect him to do is not disobey orders," Truman said. "If he does, I want to know about it. Would that be a problem for you?"

"No, sir."

"Okay. This will go out tonight," Truman said. "I want you to work closely with Ralph here, but you both have the authority to communicate directly with me. If there's a disagreement between you, I want to hear both sides, and I'll decide. Clear?"

"Clear," General Howe said.

"Yes, sir."

"General Howe wants to pick your brains, Captain McCoy," the President said. "I want you to tell him everything you know."

"Yes, sir," McCoy said.

"McCoy gave us a briefing tonight you might find fascinating yourself, Mr. President—"

"Us? Who's *us?*" The President interrupted sharply. "Who else have you let in on McCoy's assessment?"

"Sir, when you ordered my recall, General Cates assigned two officers to me, officers who had been with me in the OSS in War Two. Colonel Ed Banning and Marine Gunner Zimmerman."

"That was very obliging of the Commandant," the President said.

It was a question. Pickering decided he could let it pass, but decided not to.

Is that a courageous decision, or is the Famous Grouse talking?

"Mr. President, General Cates is afraid that when the Marine Corps can't perform the miracle everyone will expect it to, it will reflect badly on the Corps."

"What miracle won't it be able to perform? And how will the assignment of these two officers to you keep that from reflecting badly on the Marine Corps?"

"General Cates hopes that whenever I have the opportunity I will inject 'the First Marine Division is at half wartime strength.' "

"*Half* wartime strength?" General Howe asked incredulously.

"*Half* strength," Pickering repeated. "And in the entire Marine Corps, there are only about eighty thousand officers and men, plus twice that many in the reserve."

"God, I knew there had been reductions, but I didn't know it was that bad!" Howe said.

"It's that bad," Pickering said.

"It would appear General Cates got what he wanted, wouldn't it?" the President said. "I'll keep that unhappy statistic in mind, along with many others."

Neither Howe nor Pickering replied.

"McCoy gave a briefing to these two officers?" Truman asked.

"And to me, sir. I thought it was brilliant."

"I'd like to hear it," Howe said. "Can you do that for me, Captain?"

"Yes, sir," McCoy said.

"Not tonight," Truman said. "We have other things to talk about tonight, Ralph."

"Where can I find you in the morning, McCoy? Say about eight?" Howe asked.

"I'm here in the hotel, sir. But if you'll tell me where—"

"The hotel's fine. I'm staying here myself. Where are you? With General Pickering?"

"No, sir. I'm in the American Personal Pharmaceuticals suite."

"The American Personal Pharmaceuticals suite?" Howe asked, with a smile.

"He's like you, Ralph, he doesn't need the job, he just likes the uniform," Truman said, and immediately added: "I shouldn't have said that, I suppose. I meant it admiringly."

"I'll call you at eight, Captain," General Howe said.

"Aye, aye, sir."

"Ralph, why don't you walk down the corridor with General Pickering, and deliver a message from me to Mrs. Pickering?"

"What message, Harry?"

"His recall to active duty was my idea, not his."

"I'll be happy to."

"Thank you both," the President said. "I hope there will be a chance to see you both again before you go over there."

He went to the door and shook the hands of both men as they went through it.

VII

Brigadier General Clyde W. Dawkins, USMC, was annoyed—and his face showed it—when the telephone on his desk buzzed. He was in conference with Brigadier General Edward A. Craig, USMC, who until two days before had been Deputy Commanding General, 1st Marine Division, and was now Commanding General, 1st Marine Provisional Brigade, and he had, he thought, made it clear to Captain Arthur McGowan, USMC, his aide-de-camp, that he didn't want to be disturbed.

"Sorry," he said to Craig, a tall, lean officer beside him, a tanned man in his early fifties who wore his thick silver hair in a crew cut, and reached for the telephone.

"Sir, it's the Commandant," Captain McGowan announced.

"General Dawkins, sir."

"Dawkins," the Commandant of the U.S. Marine Corps said, without any preliminaries, "this is a heads-up on an Urgent TWX you're about to get from the JCS. In essence, it says by Direction of the President, Brigadier General Fleming Pickering, USMCR, will shortly be in San Diego. Give him whatever he wants, and tell him anything he wants to know."

"Yes, sir?" General Dawkins said.

"Do just that, Dawkins. Give him whatever he wants and tell him anything he wants to know."

"Aye, aye, sir."

General Dawkins waited for the Commandant to continue. And continued to wait until a dial tone told him that the Commandant, having said all he wished to say, had terminated the conversation.

Dawkins put the phone back in the cradle and mused, aloud, "I wonder what the hell that's all about?"

"What what's about?"

"That was the Commandant. I'm about to get an Urgent TWX from the JCS informing me that Brigadier General Fleming Pickering is coming here, and I am to give him whatever he asks for and tell him anything that he wants to know."

"Pickering?"

"He was on Guadalcanal, G-2 for a while when Goettge got killed . . ."

Craig nodded, indicating he knew who Dawkins was talking about.

"And the last I heard got out of the Corps the minute the war was over."

"What's he want here?"

"I have no idea. Whatever it is, it's Direction of the President," Dawkins said.

Craig pursed his lips thoughtfully, and then both men returned to the most pressing problems involved in forming, organizing, and equipping a provisional Marine brigade under orders to sail within ten days.

[TWO]
U.S. Navy / Marine Corps Reserve Training Center
St. Louis, Missouri
1920 5 July 1950

Captain George F. Hart pulled his nearly new unmarked blue Chevrolet into a parking slot behind the building, stopped, and reached for the microphone mounted under the dash.

"H-1," he said into it.

Hart was thirty-two years old, nearly bald, and built like a circus strong man.

"Captain?" Dispatch responded. H-1 was the private call sign of the Chief, Homicide Bureau, St. Louis Police Department. Dispatch knew who he was.

"At the Navy Reserve Training Center until further notice."

"Navy Reserve Training Center, got it."

"You have the number?"

"I think so."

" 'Think' don't count. Know. Check."

"Yes, sir," the dispatcher said, his tone suggesting he didn't like Captain Hart's tone.

"I have the number, Captain," the dispatcher said, and read it off.

"That's it," Hart said.

"Yes, sir," the dispatcher said.

Hart put the microphone back in its bracket, turned the engine off, got out of the car, went in the backseat and took from it a dry cleaner's bag on a hanger, locked the car, and then entered the building through a rear door to which he had a key.

He often thought the U.S. Navy / Marine Corps Reserve Training Center looked like a high school gymnasium without the high school.

The ground floor was essentially a large expanse of varnished wooden flooring large enough for two basketball courts, and there were in fact two basketball courts marked out on the floor, their baskets now retracted up to the roof. At one end of the floor was the entrance, and at the other rest rooms, and the stairway to the basement, which held lockers and the arms room.

On one side of the floor were the glass-walled offices of the Naval Reserve, and on the other, the glass-walled offices of the Marine Corps Reserve.

Hart unlocked the door with "COMMANDING OFFICER" lettered on the glass, then closed it, locked it, and checked to see that the venetian blinds were closed. One was not, and he adjusted it so that no one could see into his office.

His office was furnished with a desk, a desk chair, two straight-back chairs, two chrome armchairs, a matching couch, and a double clothing locker.

He unlocked the doors to both, then started getting undressed. First he took off his jacket, which revealed that he was wearing a shoulder holster. The holster itself held a Colt Model 1911 .45 ACP semiautomatic pistol under his left armpit. Under his right armpit, the harness held two spare seven-round clips for the pistol, and a pair of handcuffs.

So far as Captain Hart knew, he was the only white shirt in the department who elected to carry a .45. Only white shirts—lieutenants and higher; so called because their uniform shirts were white—were allowed to carry the weapon of their choice. Sergeants and below were required to carry the department issued handgun, either Smith & Wesson or Colt .38 Special five-inch-barrel revolvers. Plainclothes cops and detectives were required to carry two-inch-barrel .38 Special revolvers.

When Hart had come home from War II to become a detective again, he had ignored that regulation, and carried a .45. As a detective, he had shot two people with a .38 Special, neither of whom had died, and one of whom, despite being hit twice, had kept coming at him until he hit him in the head with the pistol butt. The people he had shot in the Corps with a .45 had gone down and stayed down, usually dead. He had decided that he would rather explain to an investigating board how come he had shot some scumbag with a .45 rather than the prescribed .38 Special than have a police department formal funeral ceremony and his picture hung on the wall in the lobby of police headquarters.

As it turned out, he had been a captain five months before he had to use the .45, and by then, of course, it was his business what he carried.

He put all of his civilian clothing on hangers and hung them, and the shoulder holster, in the left locker, then took a fresh Marine Corps khaki uniform from the dry cleaner's bag. He laid the shirt on his desk and pinned the insignia on carefully. His ribbons included the Bronze Star medal with V-device, and a cluster, indicating he had been decorated twice. He also had the Purple Heart medal, which signified he had been wounded. And he had, souvenirs of Parris Island, silver medals indicating he had shot Expert with the M-1 Garand Rifle, the U.S. Carbine Caliber .30, the M-1911A1 pistol, the Browning Automatic Rifle, and the Thompson machine gun.

He put on the fresh uniform and examined himself in the mirror mounted on the door of the left locker.

He looked, he thought, like a squared-away Marine captain, who had seen his share of war, and was perfectly qualified to be what he was, commanding officer of B Company, 55th Marines, USMC Reserve.

That was pretty far from the truth, he thought. Baker Company was an infantry company. Every Marine in Baker Company, from the newest seventeen-year-olds who had not even yet gone through boot camp at Parris Island through the non-coms, most of whom were really good Marines, many combat tested, to the other four officers, two of whom had seen combat—were absolutely delighted that the old man, the skipper, the company commander was a World War II veteran tested—and wounded, and decorated for valor—in combat.

The problem with that was that he wasn't an experienced, combat-tested, infantry officer. The first—and only—infantry unit in which he had ever served was Company B, 55th Marines, USMC Reserve. The only Table of Organization (TO&E) unit in which Captain Hart had ever served was USMC Special Detachment 16.

USMC Special Detachment 16 had been formed with the mission of supporting the Australian Coastwatchers, men left behind when the Japanese occupied islands in the Solomons, who at great risk to their lives had kept tabs on Japanese units and movements. He had been assigned to Detachment 16 because command of it had been given to Brigadier General Fleming Pickering, and then Sergeant Hart had been Pickering's bodyguard.

He'd won the Bronze Star and the Purple Heart fair and square with Detachment 16, going ashore on Japanese-held Buka Island, but that had been his last combat. Immediately after returning from Buka, he had been given a commission as a second lieutenant—not because he had done anything outstanding as a sergeant, but because his being an officer was more convenient for General Pickering.

The convenience had nothing to do with General Pickering's personal comfort, but rather with giving Hart access to one of the two most closely held secrets of World War II, MAGIC—the other was the development of the atomic bomb. Cryptographers in the United States and Hawaii had cracked many—by no means all—of the codes of the Imperial Japanese Army and Navy. Second Lieutenant Hart's name had appeared on a one-page typewritten list of those who held a MAGIC clearance.

The list was headed by the name of President Franklin Delano Roosevelt, followed by those of General Douglas MacArthur and Admiral Chester W. Nimitz, and worked its way down through the ranks past Brigadier General Pickering—who reported directly to Roosevelt—to those of the junior officers who had broken the code, and those—like Hart—who handled the actual decryption of MAGIC messages in Washington, Hawaii, and Brisbane.

Generals and admirals did not themselves sit down at the MAGIC machines and punch its typewriter-like keys. Second Lieutenant Hart, and a dozen others like him, did.

And, in a very real sense, Hart's MAGIC clearance had been his passport out of the fighting war. No one with a MAGIC clearance could be placed in any risk at all of being captured.

And then, in early February 1943, President Roosevelt had named General Pickering OSS Deputy Director for the Pacific. All of the members of USMC Special Detachment 16 had been *"detached from USMC to duty with the Office of Strategic Services (OSS), effective 8 August 1943"* and that remark had been entered into the service-record jackets.

That remark was still in Captain Hart's service records, and he knew that both his first sergeant and the gunnery sergeant had taken a look at his records, and suspected his officers had, too. In their shoes, he would have taken a look.

There were other remarks entered sequentially in his jacket, after the *"detached to OSS"* entry, that he knew his men had seen:

5 May 1944 Promoted Captain
4 October 1945 Relieved of Detachment to OSS
4 October 1945 Detached to USMC Inactive Reserve
18 April 1946 Detached to USMC Organized Reserve

18 April 1946 Attached Company B, 55th Marines, USMC Reserve, St. Louis, Mo., as Commanding Officer.

Hart knew that his service records jacket, combined with everyone's knowledge that he was the Chief of the St. Louis Homicide Bureau painted a picture of George Hart that was far more glamorous than the facts: a decorated, wounded Marine who had been an OSS agent in the War, had come home to the police force, and for patriotic reasons had joined the active reserve.

There had been questions, of course, about his wartime service, which he had declined to answer.

How could he have answered them?

I wasn't really an OSS agent, fellas. What I was was a bodyguard to a general who had a MAGIC clearance.

What's MAGIC?

He could not have answered that question. In 1946, anything connected to MAGIC was classified; as far as he knew, it still was.

It was far easier to say what he had said.

"I'd rather not talk about that, you understand."

They understood. They had all seen the movies about the OSS. OSS agents didn't talk about the OSS.

Until now, it hadn't made any difference. He had joined the Marine Corps Organized Reserve because the recruiter who had made the pitch had pointed out that he would draw a day's pay and allowances for one four-hour training session a week, plus two weeks in the summer, which wasn't bad money, especially since he had acquired a wife and ultimately three children to support on a police lieutenant's pay.

And if he put in a total of twenty years combined active duty and reserve service, there would be a pension when he turned sixty, something to consider, since police pensions were anything but generous.

On assuming command of Baker Company, he had had virtually no idea what a company commander was supposed to do, or how to do it. But he'd inherited a first sergeant who did have an idea, and who initially led him by the hand through the intricacies of commanding a company.

And he had taken correspondence courses in all kinds of military subjects from the Marine Corps Institute. And he asked questions of the regular Marine Corps officer assigned as instructor/inspector at the Navy/Marine Corps Reserve Training Center.

The I&I was an Annapolis graduate, but he had never been in a war, and he treated Captain Hart, who had, with respect and a presumption of knowledge on Captain Hart's part that Hart knew he really didn't deserve.

But with a lot of hard work, the I&I and Hart had turned Baker Company into a first-class reserve infantry company, at 94 percent of authorized strength, with everybody but the kids-yet-to-go-to-boot-camp trained in their specialty.

Which was not, Hart realized, the same thing as saying Baker Company was prepared to go to war under the command of Captain George S. Hart. It looked like that was going to happen.

Hart had just finished tucking his shirt into his trousers, and making sure the shirt placket was precisely aligned with his belt and fly, when there was a discreet knock on the glass pane of his door.

"Captain? You in there, sir?"

Hart recognized the I&I's voice.

"Come in, Peterson," Hart called.

"Good evening, sir," First Lieutenant Paul T. Peterson, USMC, USNA '46, a slim, good-looking twenty-five-year-old, said as he came through the door.

Hart could see that the platoon sergeants were forming the men on the glossy varnished floor.

"How goes it, Paul?" Hart asked.

"I don't know," Peterson said, turning from closing the door. "This Korea thing . . ."

"Yeah," Hart said.

"What do you think?" Peterson asked.

"I think we're going to get involved over there," Hart said.

"You hear anything, sir?"

Hart shook his head, "no."

But the White House—Jesus Christ, The White House!!!—*was looking for Killer McCoy, and the Killer hadn't come by St. Louis with his wife as he said he was going to.*

The Killer, the last I heard before he called and said he was coming to St. Louis, was stationed in Tokyo. As an intelligence officer.

And now the White House is looking for him!

Korea is right next door to Japan, and if anything is going to happen over there, the Killer will have a damned good idea of what and when. And probably why.

Hart was a cop, a good cop, a good detective, and he had heard from his father, also a cop, and now believed that good cops developed a special kind of intuition.

He *intuited* that there was going to be a war in Korea, despite what the President had said about it being a "police action," and that meant that Company B, 55th Marines, was going to be called to active duty.

"Neither have I," Peterson said. He looked at Hart. "Do you think there's anything we should be doing?"

Jesus Christ, you're supposed to be the professional Marine. Why ask me?

"I've been giving it some thought, Paul," Hart said. "Yeah, there is. And I'm not sure you're going to like what I've decided to do."

"Sir?" Peterson asked, at exactly the same moment as there was another knock on the glass of the door.

"We're ready, skipper," First Sergeant Andrew Mulligan called.

"Right," Hart called, and started toward the door.

The moment he came through the door, Mulligan bellowed, "Ten-hut on deck," and Company B, 55th Marines, lined up by platoons, popped to attention. Lieutenant Peterson stood in the open door.

Hart, trailed by Mulligan, marched across the varnished floor until he was in the center of the formation. He did a left face, so that he was facing the executive officer, First Lieutenant William J. Barnes, who had been a technical sergeant in World War II, and commissioned after he had joined the organized reserve.

Hart barked: "Report!"

Lieutenant Barnes did an about-face and barked, "Report!"

The platoon leaders, standing in front of their platoons, did an about-face and barked, "Report!"

The platoon sergeants saluted their platoon leaders, and reported, in unison, "All present or accounted for, sir!"

The platoon leaders did another about-face, saluted Lieutenant Barnes, and announced, in unison, "All present or accounted for, sir."

Lieutenant Barnes did an about-face and saluted Captain Hart.

"Sir, the company is formed. All present or accounted for, sir."

Hart returned the salute.

"Parade Rest!" he ordered.

The company assumed the position of Parade Rest, standing erectly, feet twelve inches apart, their hands folded stiffly in the small of their backs.

The entire little ballet, Captain Hart judged, had been performed perfectly, even by the kids who hadn't earned the right to wear the Marine Corps globe and anchor by going through boot camp.

Hart looked at his men, starting at the left and working his way slowly across the ranks and files.

Oh, to hell with it!

"Stand at ease," he ordered.

That was not the next step in the prescribed ballet, and he saw questioning looks on a lot of faces.

"You did that pretty well," he said. "Only two of you looked like cows on ice, and you know who you were."

Fifty men decided the skipper had detected a sloppy movement on their part, and vowed to do better the next time.

"There will be a change from the published training schedule," Hart announced. "Based on my belief that there are several things always true about the Marine Corps, first that there is always a change in the training schedule, usually unexplained."

He got the laughter he expected.

"The second truth is that every Marine is a rifleman."

His tone was serious, and he knew he had their attention.

"The third truth, and you may find this hard to believe, is that company commanders are sometimes wrong. I really hope I'm wrong now, and I want to tell you that I don't know a thing more about the possible mobilization of the Marine Reserve—of Baker Company—than you do."

There was absolute silence in the room as they waited for him to go on.

"But I have the feeling we're going to be called. I don't know where we'll go, or what we'll do, but we're the Marine Corps reserve, and the reserve gets called in time of war. I hope we're not in a war in Korea, but we may be, and it is clearly our duty to prepare for that."

He paused.

"Every Marine is a rifleman. My drill instructor taught me that when I went through boot camp at Parris Island. And during the war, I saw how right he was, how important it is to the Corps. So the one thing I know we can do to prepare for being mobilized is to make sure that every Marine in Baker Company is not only a rifleman, but the best rifleman he can be."

He paused again.

"The training schedule is therefore changed to rifle marksmanship. In the first hour of training tonight, you will draw your piece from the armory, clean it, inspect it, make sure it's as right as it can be. The following three hours will be devoted to dry firing, et cetera. I have arranged for us to use the St. Louis Police Department firing range. It's only a hundred yards, but it'll have to do. There will be a special drill next Saturday. You will report here, draw your weapons, and be taken by truck to the range. Those who will be working at your civilian jobs on Saturday, give your name to your platoon sergeant, and either your platoon leader will, or I will, call your employer and explain the importance of this."

He looked again at the faces of his men.

Well, I've done it. Peterson will shit a brick.

There will be no deviations from the prescribed training schedule without prior permission from battalion.

Special drill sessions will not be held without prior permission from battalion.

Ammunition will not be drawn from sealed armory stocks without prior permission from battalion.

The use of civilian and/or local governmental firing ranges is forbidden unless specifically directed by HQ USMC.

"Company, ten-hut!"

Baker Company snapped to attention.

"I will see the officers and senior noncoms in my office immediately following the formation," Captain Hart ordered his executive officer. "Dismiss the company for training."

"Aye, aye, sir," Lieutenant Barnes said, and saluted.

Captain Hart returned the salute, did an about-face movement, and marched across the varnished wood to his office.

Lieutenant Peterson was standing just inside the office.

"Questions, Lieutenant?"

"The colonel's going to shit a brick," Lieutenant Peterson said.

"I suppose he will," Captain Hart said. "Sometimes you have to do what you think is right even if it gives the entire Marine Corps diarrhea."

"Yes, sir," Lieutenant Peterson said. "Sir, permission to speak?"

"Granted."

"You didn't specify a time for the special drill on Saturday. May I suggest the company report at 0430? That will give us time to get to the range by first light."

"Make it so, Lieutenant."

"Aye, aye, sir."

[THREE]
Suite 401
The Coronado Beach Hotel
San Diego, California
1030 10 July 1950

Captain Kenneth R. McCoy sprang to his feet and opened the door of the suite.

"Good morning, gentlemen," he said to the two Marine brigadier generals and their aides-de-camp, both captains. "General Pickering expects you. Will you come in, please?"

"How are you, McCoy?" Brigadier General Clyde W. Dawkins said, extending his hand. "It's good to see you."

Captain McCoy had never seen either captain before, but Captain Arthur McGowan, Dawkins's aide, had heard about the legendary Captain "Killer" McCoy and looked at him curiously.

He doesn't look, McGowan thought, *like either a legend or somebody known as "the Killer."*

"Thank you, sir," McCoy said. "It's good to see you, sir."

Brigadier General Fleming Pickering, USMCR, came into the sitting room from the one of the bedrooms that offered a view of the Pacific and had long ago been converted to a bar, holding a mug of coffee in his hand.

"I was going to say, 'Christ, Dawk, you didn't have to come here,' " he said, "But I think I'd better make that, 'Good morning, gentlemen.' "

Dawkins chuckled.

He nodded at the officer beside him.

"I just now found out you two don't know each other; I thought you'd met on the 'Canal. General Fleming Pickering, General Edward A. Craig."

Craig offered his hand to Pickering.

"I think you left the 'Canal—" Craig began.

"Was ordered off," Pickering interjected.

"—before I got there," Craig finished. "But I know who you are, General, and I'm glad to finally get to meet you."

"General, I tried to tell General Dawkins that whenever he could find a few minutes for me, I would be in his office."

"Craig and I had to go to the Navy base, coming here was easier all around, and I don't think I could have given you an uninterrupted five minutes in my office," Dawkins said. "Things are a little hectic out there."

"I can imagine."

"Craig has been named CG of the 1st Provisional Marine Brigade," Dawkins said. "Which sails for Kobe, Japan, on the twelfth."

Colonel Edward J. Banning, USMC, and Marine Gunner Ernest W. Zimmerman came into the room.

"I didn't know you were here, too, Ed," Dawkins said.

"Good morning, General," Banning said. "It's good to see you."

"Ed Banning I know," Craig said. "Fourth Marines. Hello, Ed."

"Good morning, General," Banning replied, and added, "Mr. Zimmerman and Captain McCoy are old China Marines, too."

Craig shook Zimmerman's hand, then glanced at his watch.

"We are pressed for time," Craig said. "So if there's some place these fellows can wait. . . . ."

He nodded at McCoy, Zimmerman, and the aides-de-camp.

"Why don't you go in the bar?" Pickering said, nodding at the door to the room. "There's coffee. McCoy, you stay."

"Aye, aye, sir," McCoy said.

Captain McGowan and General Craig's aide were surprised, and possibly a little annoyed, that they were being excused, and Captain McCoy was not, but they and Zimmerman went into the bar and closed the door.

"I'm the self-invited guest, General," Craig said. "When Dawkins told me he was coming to see you, I invited myself."

"You're welcome, of course," Pickering said.

"I don't think I have to convince you of the value of intelligence, General," Craig said. "I have practically none about Korea. If the price of getting some is bad manners . . ."

"Ken's got some pretty detailed knowledge of the North Korean order of battle," Pickering said, nodding at McCoy. "With the caveat that you don't ask him where he got it, and if you can give him an hour between now and 1830, when we get on a plane for Tokyo, he could brief you."

"I'll find the hour," Craig said. "Thank you."

"You're going to Tokyo, General?" Dawkins asked.

His real question, Pickering understood, *is "What are you going to do in Tokyo?"* and after a moment, he decided to answer it.

"What you hear in this room stays in this room, OK?" he said.

"Agreed," Craig said.

"Yes, sir," Dawkins said.

"The President is unhappy that we were so badly surprised by what's happening over there," Pickering began. "And he's afraid that he's not going to get the whole picture from MacArthur. He called an old buddy of his, an Army National Guard major general, Ralph Howe, to active duty, to go over there and see for himself what's happened, and will happen. Then, because I'm acquainted with MacArthur, he did the same thing with me."

Craig nodded.

"May I ask what you're doing at Camp Pendleton?"

"That's Ed Banning's idea, and like most of his ideas, a good one. Howe and I will be reporting directly to the President. If we use the normal communication channels, the odds are that our messages would be in the hands of the brass at least half an hour before they were in the President's hands. If, on the other hand, we communicate with your comm center here, with Banning getting the messages, no one would see them but Banning. We haven't worked out the details yet, but I'm sure Ed can find a secure channel from here to Washington."

"That shouldn't be a problem," Dawkins said. "If necessary, we can set up a secure radio-teletype link between here and the White House Signal Agency."

"I have to say this, Dawk," Pickering said. "I don't want one of your commo sergeants making copies of our traffic for you."

"Yes, sir," Dawkins said.

"McCoy, Zimmerman, and I are going to Japan tonight," Pickering said. "I'm going to see General MacArthur. McCoy and Zimmerman are going to Korea."

"Why?" Craig asked McCoy.

"We want to interrogate prisoners, sir," McCoy said. "And see what else we can find out."

"What are you going to do about an interpreter?"

"Sir, I speak Korean, and Mr. Zimmerman speaks Chinese."

"At least two kinds of Chinese, General," Ed Banning said. "And Japanese. As does McCoy. McCoy also speaks Russian and—"

"I could really use officers with those skills," Craig said, and looked at Pickering. "I suppose that's out of the question?"

"I'm afraid so," Pickering said.

"How about access to what they learn?"

"With the caveat that it's not for—what do the newspaper people say, 'attribution'?—and doesn't go any further than you think it really has to, I can see no reason why Ed Banning can't filter out what he thinks would be useful to you from our traffic, and give it to you and Dawkins."

"Thank you," Craig said.

Dawkins looked at his wristwatch.

"Ed, it's that time. They expect us at the port."

Craig nodded.

"If you don't need Captain McCoy right now," Craig said. "He could ride along with us, and I could pick his brains in the car."

"Sure," Pickering said, and then saw the look on McCoy's face.

"Something I don't know about, Ken?" he asked.

"Sir, Zimmerman and I were going to go out to Pendleton and scrounge utilities, 782 gear,* and weapons," McCoy said.

"I think we can fix that," General Craig said.

He walked to the door of the bar and opened it.

"Charley," he said to his aide, "I can't imagine a Marine gunner needing help from a captain scrounging anything, but you never know. Get a car and take Mr. Zimmerman out to Pendleton and help him get whatever he thinks he needs."

"Aye, aye, sir," Craig's aide-de-camp said.

"And you better go with him," General Dawkins said to Captain McGowan. "We'll link up somewhere later."

Zimmerman looked at McCoy.

"Thompson?" he asked.

McCoy thought that over.

"I think I'd rather have a Garand," he said. "Maybe both? See if you can get a tanker's shoulder holster for me."

Zimmerman nodded.

McCoy turned to General Craig.

"Whenever you're ready, sir," he said.

[FOUR]
Office of the Chief of Staff
Headquarters, Supreme Commander, Allied Powers
The Dai Ichi Building
Tokyo, Japan
0830 14 July 1950

Major General Edward M. Almond was in his outer office talking to a tall, intense young lieutenant wearing the insignia of an aide-de-camp when Brigadier General Fleming Pickering, trailed by Captain Kenneth R. McCoy and Marine Gunner Ernest W. Zimmerman, walked in.

Almond broke off his conversation in midsentence and offered Pickering his hand.

---

*Field equipment—for example, web belts, harnesses, canteens, helmets, etc.

"We heard you were here," he said, "But Al"—he nodded at the lieutenant—"couldn't seem to find you."

It was a question, and Pickering answered it.

"We're in the Imperial," he said. "My wife's in the hotel business, and hotel people take care of each other. They call it 'comping,' and I take advantage of it whenever I can."

"I don't think Al thought of the Imperial," Almond said.

"No, sir, that's the one place I didn't look," the aide confirmed.

"Well, I guess I don't ask if you're comfortable," Almond said. "But I can offer you a cup of coffee. General MacArthur expects you at 0900."

"Thank you," Pickering said. "General, this is Captain McCoy and Mr. Zimmerman."

"You look familiar, Captain," Almond said, as he shook McCoy's hand.

"Captain McCoy was stationed in Japan," Pickering answered for him. "With Naval intelligence."

"I thought he looked familiar," Almond said. He turned to Zimmerman and smiled. "Is it true, Mr. Zimmerman, that Marine gunners can really chew railroad spikes and spit nails?"

"Carpet tacks, sir," Zimmerman replied.

"Would you rather we talked alone, General?" Almond asked. He nodded at his aide again. "Or . . ."

"I think it would be helpful if we all talked," Pickering said.

"Gentlemen, this is Lieutenant Al Haig, my junior aide," Almond said, "who will round up some coffee and then join us."

"I suppose the best way to do this is to show you my orders," Pickering said, taking two envelopes from his pocket and handing them to Almond.

Almond opened the smaller envelope and read it.

THE WHITE HOUSE

WASHINGTON, D.C.

JULY 8, 1950

TO WHOM IT MAY CONCERN:

BRIGADIER GENERAL FLEMING PICKERING, USMCR, IN CONNECTION WITH HIS MISSION FOR ME, WILL TRAVEL TO SUCH

PLACES AT SUCH TIMES AS HE FEELS APPROPRIATE, ACCOMPA-
NIED BY SUCH STAFF AS HE DESIRES.

GENERAL PICKERING IS GRANTED HEREWITH A TOP-
SECRET/WHITE HOUSE CLEARANCE, AND MAY, AT HIS OPTION,
GRANT SUCH CLEARANCE TO HIS STAFF.

U.S. MILITARY AND GOVERNMENTAL AGENCIES ARE DIRECTED
TO PROVIDE GENERAL PICKERING AND HIS STAFF WITH WHAT-
EVER SUPPORT THEY MAY REQUIRE.

Harry S Truman

HARRY S TRUMAN
PRESIDENT OF THE UNITED STATES

"Now, *that's* a blanket order," Almond said, and indicated Lieutenant Haig with a nod of his head. "May I?"

Pickering nodded, and Almond handed the order to his aide. Then he opened and read the orders in the second envelope.

S E C R E T

The Central Intelligence Agency
Washington, D.C.

Office of the Director

July 6, 1950

Mission Orders:

TO: Brigadier General Fleming Pickering, USMCR
Assistant Director of the CIA for Asia

By Direction of the President, and in compliance with
Mission Memorandum 23-1950, Classified TOP

SECRET/CIA/Director, with which you have been made
familiar, you and the following members of your staff,
all of whom have been granted TOP SECRET/CIA/Director
security clearances, will travel to Tokyo, Japan, and
such other places as you/they may feel necessary.
Travel may be accomplished by U.S. Government air, sea,
rail, or road transportation, for which Priority AAAAA
is assigned, or by any other means you/they determine
are necessary.

BANNING, Edward F., Colonel, USMC
McCOY, Kenneth R., Captain, USMC
ZIMMERMANN, Ernest W., Master Gunner, USMC

Roscoe M. Hillenkoetter
ROSCOE M. HILLENKOETTER
Rear Admiral, USN
Director

S   E   C   R   E   T

"Two questions," Almond said, as—after getting an approving nod from Pickering—he handed the second orders to Haig. "Colonel Banning? And why two sets of orders? The Presidential order would seem to cover everything."

"Colonel Banning, to answer that first, General, is at Camp Pendleton in California, setting up a communications link between there and the White House. I'm going to need such a link from here to Camp Pendleton, which is one of the reasons I asked to see you."

"Al, see that the General gets whatever he needs," Almond ordered.

"Yes, sir," Haig said.

"And so far as the orders are concerned," Pickering went on, "Captain McCoy thinks it would be a good idea to get a third set, issued by SCAP."

"Saying what, Captain?" Almond asked McCoy.

"Saying that Mr. Zimmerman and I are on a liaison mission—or something like that—from SCAP, sir," McCoy said. "Preferably signed by you, sir."

"Reason?" Almond asked.

"White House and CIA orders, sir, and orders signed by General MacArthur are likely to call more attention to us than we want."

"Point taken," Almond said. "When we finish here, Al, get with Captain McCoy and give him what he needs."

"Yes, sir," Haig said.

Almond looked at McCoy.

"I presume you're going to Korea?"

"Yes, sir."

"When?"

"As soon as we have the orders from here, sir."

"You're going to need some field equipment," Almond said. "And weapons. Things are pretty primitive over there. Lieutenant Haig can help you there."

"We have what we'll need, sir," McCoy said. "But thank you.

"I wish I had an interpreter to send with you. I don't."

"McCoy speaks Korean, General," Pickering said. "Reads and writes it, too."

"If I had known that, Captain, when you were here, I would have done my best to steal you from the Naval element. I'm surprised General Willoughby didn't," Almond said. Then he paused and looked at Pickering. "General Willoughby would of course be interested in whatever intelligence Captain McCoy turns up. It's an admission of failure on our part, obviously, but the truth is this Korean business caught us completely by surprise."

"I'm sure something can be worked out, General," Pickering said. "But I'm sure you'll understand that McCoy and Zimmerman have to do their job independently."

"Yes, of course," Almond said. He looked at his watch. "It might be a good idea if we walked down the corridor to the Supreme Commander's office. He doesn't mind if people are early. Late is an entirely different matter."

"Ken, don't leave until I see you," Pickering ordered, as he got to his feet.

"Aye, aye, sir."

[FIVE]

The Supreme Commander, Allied Powers, General of the Army Douglas MacArthur, rose from behind his desk and walked toward Brigadier General Fleming Pickering with his hand extended.

"My old friend is once again my comrade-in-arms, I see," he said, patting Fleming on the shoulder as he shook his hand.

"Good morning, General," Pickering said.

"Ned took good care of you on your arrival, I trust?" MacArthur said, nodding toward Major General Almond.

"General Almond has been very obliging, sir," Pickering said.

"Your quarters are all right? Everything you need?" MacArthur pursued.

"General Pickering took care of himself," Almond said. "He's at the Imperial."

"But you did meet the MATS flight?" MacArthur asked, a tone of annoyance in his voice. MATS was Military Air Transport Service.

"We came on Trans-Global," Pickering said, "It was faster, and I didn't want to take up space on an Air Force flight."

"And you knew that the Imperial would be a little nicer than the Menzies, right?" MacArthur said, chuckling.

"Yes, sir," Pickering said.

"Ned, in June of 1942, Supreme Headquarters, Southwest Pacific Command—all of it, including quarters for the senior officers—was in the Menzies Hotel in Melbourne," MacArthur explained. "The Menzies is not about to appear on a list of great hotels of the world."

Almond laughed dutifully.

"Those black days seem like a long time ago, don't they, Fleming?" MacArthur asked.

"Yes, sir, they do," Pickering agreed.

"Ned, if you'll excuse us, I'm sure General Fleming would like a little time in private with me."

"Yes, of course, sir," Almond said, smiled, nodded at Pickering and left the office.

If it bothers Almond—El Supremo's chief of staff—to be excluded from this conversation, it didn't show on his face.

MacArthur walked to his desk, picked up a humidor, and carried it to where Pickering stood. It held long, rather thin black cigars, which Pickering suspected were Philippine. He took one.

"Thank you," he said.

"Philippine," MacArthur confirmed. "I think they're better than the famed Havanas."

"They're good," Pickering said, as he took a clipper from the humidor. "I remember."

MacArthur returned the humidor to his desk, and returned with a silver Ronson table lighter. They finished the ritual of lighting the cigars.

"If I promise beforehand not to have the messenger executed," MacArthur said, with a smile, "perhaps you'll tell me what message you bear from the President."

"The only real message I have, sir, is that the President wants you to know he has full—absolute—confidence in you," Pickering said.

MacArthur nodded, as if he expected a statement like this.

"And his concerns?" he asked.

"He doesn't want Korea to start World War Three," Pickering said.

"There's not much chance of that," MacArthur said. "We have nuclear superiority."

"He was concerned that this has taken us completely by surprise," Pickering said.

"And it has," MacArthur said. "That's very probably a result of our underestimating North Korea's stupidity. There's no way they can ultimately succeed in this endeavor, and—stupidity on our part—we presumed they knew that, and that this sort of thing simply wouldn't happen."

"And their successes so far have been because of the surprise of the attack?"

"Yes, that's a fair description. Willoughby's best judgment, with which I concurred, was that the risk of something like this happening was minimal. Our mistake. But with nothing to suggest something like this was in the works . . ."

Nothing but a report from an intelligence officer that Willoughby not only didn't want to believe, ordered destroyed, and then tried to bureaucratically execute the messenger.

And if I had brought that report to you the last time I was in Tokyo, what would you have done? Put your faith in Willoughby, that's what you would have done.

"You've been traveling," MacArthur said. "Let me give you the current picture."

He gestured for Pickering to follow him to what looked like a large-scale map mounted on the wall. When he got close, Pickering saw that it was actually one of half a dozen maps, which could be slid out from the wall one at a time.

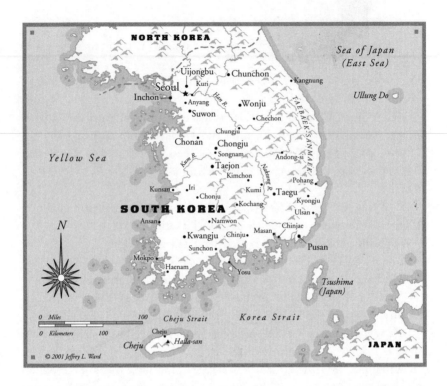

This map showed all of South Korea, and went as far north in North Korea—above the 38th parallel—to include the North Korean capitol of Pyongyang.

MacArthur took a two-foot-long pointer from a holder and held it between his hands like a riding crop. Pickering saw that the base of the varnished wood was a glistening .30-caliber rifle casing, and that the pointer was the bullet. The bullet was black-tipped—indicating armor piercing—and Pickering wondered if that was simply coincidental.

"This is the most recent intelligence we have," MacArthur began. "Early yesterday morning, the 24th Division withdrew to defensive positions along the south bank of the Kum River near Taejon."

He turned to the map and pointed to Taejon, which was roughly equidistant between Seoul—now in North Korean hands—and Pusan, a major port at the tip of the Korean peninsula, on the Straits of Korea.

"Engineers have blown all road and railroad bridges, and destroyed all ferries and flat-bottomed boats, and both the division commander and General Walker—who has established Eighth Army headquarters here at Taegu—feel these positions can be held, at least for the time being, and even that a counterattack may be possible."

That's why they retreated across the river, right, and blew the bridges? So they can counterattack?

"General Walker's front," MacArthur went on, using the pointer, "extends from Taejon northeast to Chongju, and across the Taebaek Mountains to Pyonghae-ri on the east coast. The 24th Reconnaissance Company is keeping their eye on the most likely river crossings west of Kongju, and the 34th Infantry Regiment is here at Kongju."

And what's the 24th Reconnaissance Company—no more than 200 men, and probably far less—going to do if the North Koreans start to cross the river?

"The 19th Infantry Regiment, which just arrived, is here at Taejon," MacArthur went on, "and the 21st Infantry is a blocking position here, southeast of Taejon. The 21st has been involved in some heavy fighting, and is down to about 1,100 men."

"They lost half their strength?" Pickering blurted incredulously. Just in time, he stopped himself from saying what came to his lips: *If they took those kind of losses, they're in no position to block anything.*

Keep your mouth shut, Pickering!

"A bit more than half," MacArthur replied matter of factly. "If memory serves, they lost a little over 1,400 men, KIA, WIA, and missing, in their first week of combat."

"General, I have to ask this question," Pickering said. "What's going to happen?"

"Well, what we're doing now is buying time until reinforcements can be brought in. Two days ago, the 2nd Infantry Division was ordered here from the West Coast, for example. The Marines are sending a brigade; it may already be at sea."

"It is," Pickering said. "Today's the fourteenth. They sailed from San Diego today for Kobe."

"You're sure?"

"I had a chance to meet with General Craig, the provisional brigade commander, in San Diego. That was his schedule."

"No wishful thinking involved?"

"No, sir. He said they would sail, not hoped to."

MacArthur nodded his head.

"Yesterday," he said, "the 24th Infantry—the third regiment of the 25th Division—debarked at Pusan, and at this moment are moving forward, which will bring the division to full strength."

If one of its regiments has lost more than half its men, then it won't be at full strength.

"Moreover, the 1st Cavalry Division is at this moment on the high seas, and the lead elements—the 5th and 8th Cavalry—are scheduled to debark here at Pohang-dong on the eighteenth."

He put the bullet-tip of his pointer on a small port on the west coast of the peninsula, and looked at Pickering to make sure that Pickering was following him.

"Delaying the enemy until we can achieve something like equal strength in the South is only part of the plan, Fleming," MacArthur said. "The other part, the part that will turn what some might consider a rout into a very bloody nose for the enemy, is not yet quite fixed in my mind, but essentially, what I plan to do—another of the reasons I asked for the Marines—is to strike somewhere far up the peninsula with an amphibious landing that will permit us to cut off the enemy's supply lines and then batter his forces to bits. They have to be made to pay for this invasion."

"Up the peninsula?" Pickering asked. "Where?"

"There are a number of possibilities," MacArthur said, using the pointer. "On the east coast of the peninsula we have suitable beaches in the Kunsan-Komie area, here. And farther north, at Taechon, Anhung, and Inchon."

Christ, Inchon is the port for Seoul. And I was in there only once, years ago, but I still have a memory of thirty-foot tides and mudflats. Inchon's not some gentle South Pacific beach, and the others are probably no better. Is he dreaming?

"Of all these," MacArthur went on, "I prefer Inchon, but I'm frankly a bit hesitant to say so. I don't want to be premature with this, as you can well understand."

What is he doing? Ever so subtly suggesting that I don't put this invade-behind-their-lines idea of his in my report to the President?

Of course, he is.

"And on the West Coast, working northward," MacArthur went on, using the pointer, "we have Yangdok, Kangwung, and ultimately Wonsan."

Wonsan is in North Korea!

"Wonsan—although it would be tactically ideal to cut the peninsula—is out of the question at this time, as I am under orders to push the enemy out of South Korea, not invade his homeland."

Is he reading my mind?

Both the Russians and the Chinese would take an American invasion of North Korea as an excuse to intervene in this war. Doesn't he know that?

Slow down, Pickering.

This is Douglas MacArthur talking, if not the greatest military mind of our era, then right at the top of that list.

*He not only knows as much about amphibious invasions as anyone else, proba-
bly more than anyone else, but is also probably as astute a judge of Soviet and Chinese intentions as anyone in the government.*

*Because we misjudged Russian ambitions, a quarter of Germany is a Russian
zone from which we are barred, and Berlin and Vienna are similarly divided. We
had to have the Berlin Airlift to keep the Russians from forcing us out.*

Because MacArthur knew what they were up to, he stood up to them.

There are no Russians in Japan, period.

"You seem lost in thought, Fleming," MacArthur said, smiling.

"This is a lot to take in at once," Pickering said.

"What we have to do is to strike decisively," MacArthur said. "Not to have
to fight our way inch by inch back up the peninsula. The question is where to
do so. At the least possible cost in American lives. As we're already learning, the
loss of life is not a high priority for the other side."

*That's another good side of him. He does try to keep losses at a minimum. I saw
that time and time again in World War II.*

"A moment ago, I might have seemed to be suggesting that you not get into
the details of my initial thinking when you report to the President," MacArthur
said. "I was."

Pickering looked at him but didn't reply.

"My thinking there, Fleming, is that there is certainly going to be a hunger
in Washington for any action which will turn the situation around. From my
standpoint, it would be better if one of my ideas were not seized upon—or the
flip side of the coin, strongly objected to—until I can firm up what I think
we should do, and then present a plan to the President for his approval. Or
disapproval. I am not asking you to do anything that would, in any way, violate your duty to report to the President anything you believe he should
hear."

*You're doing exactly that, of course. I was sent here to be a reporter, not a judge.
But you're right—as usual. There will be a frenzy in Washington to do something,
and there is a good chance they would hop on one idea that ultimately wouldn't
work, or reject another one that would.*

I can give him that much.

"I will report to the President that you have several plans under study,"
Pickering said, "and that I will furnish further details as they become available."

"If you think that's what you should do," MacArthur said. "One further
question: Can you tell me about General Howe?"

"I've only met with him briefly. Apparently, he and the President became friends after World War One, in the National Guard." Pickering paused and went off at a tangent. "Did you know the President is a retired National Guard colonel?"

"No. But I did know he served with distinction in France, as a captain of artillery."

"Well, sir, it appears Howe rose to major general, and commanded a division in Europe. He enjoys the President's confidence. From what I've seen of him, he's a good man."

"As you and I have both learned," MacArthur said with a smile, "it can be very useful for a field commander to have direct access to the commander-in-chief via a good man."

There comes the soft soap.

"Jeanne insists on having you for lunch," MacArthur went on. "If I sent a car for you at one, would that give you enough time to get settled?"

"Yes, thank you very much," Pickering said.

He was halfway down the corridor to General Almond's office before it occurred to him that (a) he had been dismissed; (b) the reason he had been dismissed was that El Supremo had something important to do; (c) which was most likely a conference about either the war at the moment, or his plans for the war in the future; and (d) that not only did he have every right to attend such a conference, but that's what he was supposed to be doing.

You got me that time, and good, Douglas MacArthur, but that will be the last time.

VIII

[ONE]
Headquarters
Eighth United States Army
Taegu, Korea
0530 15 July 1950

Captain Kenneth R. McCoy, who was wearing obviously brand new USMC utilities and 782 gear, and had an M-1 Garand rifle slung over his shoulder, saluted the U.S. Army transportation corps major in charge of the Headquarters, Eighth Army motor pool, and said, "Good morning, sir."

The major was a portly man in his mid-thirties, armed with a .45 ACP pistol. His fatigue jacket was sweat-stained under his armpits, and there were beads of sweat on his forehead. His eyes showed lack of sleep, and he needed a shave.

He returned McCoy's salute with a bored gesture.

"Yes?" he asked, impatiently.

"Sir, I'm going to need a Jeep, and a trailer and some gas in jerry cans."

"Out of the fucking question, Captain," the major said. Then he took a closer look at McCoy's utilities "Marine? I didn't know the Marines were here."

"So far, there's just two of us, sir," McCoy said, and handed the major what he thought of as "the Dai-Ichi orders"; they had come from SCAP headquarters in the Dai Ichi Building. "But we are going to need some wheels."

The major took the orders and read them.

SUPREME HEADQUARTERS

Allied Powers
Tokyo, Japan

14 July 1950

SUBJECT: Letter Orders

TO: MCCOY, K.R. Captain USMC
ZIMMERMAN, E.W. Master Gunner USMC

1. In connection with your mission, you are authorized and directed to proceed to such places in Japan and Korea at such times as may be necessary.

2. All U.S. Army, Air Force and Navy organizations under SCAP are directed to provide you with such logistical

---

```
      support as you may require. Priority AAAAA is
      assigned for travel.

FOR THE SUPREME COMMANDER:
```

                          Edward M. Almond

                              EDWARD M. ALMOND
                                Major General, USA
                                  Chief of Staff

```
EMA/ah
```

"So?" the major asked.

"Sir, the logistical support I need is a Jeep, trailer, and some gas in cans."

"Captain," the major said, "I don't give a good goddamn if you have orders signed by the President himself, I don't have Jeeps for bird colonels, so there's none for a captain. Now do us both a favor and get the fuck out of here!"

McCoy saluted—it was not returned—and did an about-face movement and marched out from under the canvas fly that presumably was intended to shield the motor pool officer's portable field desk from sun and rain.

Although General Pickering had told Captain McCoy that Eighth Army Headquarters had been "set up" in Taegu, when he and Zimmerman had arrived there after midnight—via the K-1 airfield at Pusan, and hitching a ride on a truck the rest of the way—it was immediately clear that "set up" was an intention rather than a *fait accompli.*

They had spent the night uncomfortably—it was hot, and muggy, and there were hordes of mosquitoes, flies, and other insects—in their clothing on mattressless folding canvas cots in a twelve-man squad tent. When they rose at first light, they saw the tent was one of a dozen that had been set up in what looked like the playground of a school building before which had been erected a plywood sign identifying it as Headquarters EUSAK.

McCoy had been surprised that someone had found the time and material to make the sign.

They had shaved with McCoy's electric razor, plugged into the 110-volt AC outlet of a gasoline generator whose primary outlet cable fed into the school building through an open window.

There was a great deal of activity, soldiers unloading from six-by-six trucks everything from folding field desks and file cabinets to Coca-Cola coolers and barracks bags, and either carrying them into the building or simply dumping them to the side of the door.

McCoy had entered the building, found the G-2 section, and—surprisingly to him, he was not challenged by anyone—took a look at the situation map. The action was around someplace called Taejon. McCoy made a compass with his fingers and determined that Taejon was about sixty miles—as the crow flies, probably considerably more on winding Korea National Highway One—from Taegu. They would need wheels to get there, and to move around once they did.

When he came out of the building, he found Master Gunner Ernest W. Zimmerman, USMC, waiting for him. Zimmerman had a Thompson .45-caliber submachine gun hanging from his shoulder. Two spare magazines for it were in one of the pockets on his utility jacket, and the other bulged with two, or possibly three, hand grenades.

"No wheels, Ernie," he said. "You have any luck with rations?"

"I took care of it," Zimmerman replied. "Let's get something to eat, and then get the hell out of here."

"Where's the rations?"

"I'll show you when we've had something to eat," Zimmerman said, and pointed to a line of people—officers and enlisted men—moving through a chow line.

Breakfast was powdered eggs, Spam, toast, and coffee served on a multi-compartment plastic tray in a canteen mess cup. At the end of the line, there was a stainless-steel tray filled with butter already liquefied by the heat.

When they had finished, Zimmerman led him outside the not-yet-completed ring of concertina barbed wire surrounding the headquarters compound and down a road to a field in which sat half a dozen communications vans, and finally behind the most distant van, where a Jeep sat.

It had a wooden sign reading PRESS WAR CORRESPONDENT in yellow letters mounted below the windshield. There were two cases of C-rations and two five-gallon jerry cans of gasoline in the backseat. A third jerry can was in its mount on the back of the Jeep.

Zimmerman went to the Jeep, put his Thompson on the seat, raised the hood, and then reached into one of the cavernous pockets of his utilities and took out a distributor cap, a distributor rotor, and the ignition wires.

He put them in place.

"Where did you get this?" McCoy asked.

"With respect, sir, the captain does not want to know," Zimmerman said, lowered the hood, fastened the hood retainers, and got behind the wheel. The engine started immediately.

"Let's get the hell out of here before the wrong guy wakes up," Zimmerman said.

McCoy jumped in the Jeep.

"Isn't that press sign going to make us conspicuous?" McCoy asked, as Zimmerman started to move.

"I thought about that," Zimmerman said. "Isn't that what we're doing? Sending reports from the war?"

Moments after they passed the entrance to the Eighth Army headquarters compound, a slight figure in an Army fatigue uniform leapt to his feet from the side of the road and jumped in front of them, angrily waving his arms.

"Guess who got up early?" McCoy said.

"That's my Jeep, you sonsofbitches!" the angry creature shouted in a high-pitched voice.

"He's a fucking fairy," Zimmerman said, as he slammed on the brakes.

"He's a she, Ernie," McCoy said, chuckling.

The creature, now recognizable as a female by the hair tucked under her fatigue camp, and a swelling in her fatigue jacket that was not hand grenades, stormed up to the Jeep.

"MP!" she screamed. "MP!"

McCoy looked over his shoulder back toward the MPs standing at the entrance to the Eighth Army Headquarters compound. She had attracted their attention.

He jumped out of the Jeep, went to the woman, wrapped his arms around her waist, pulled her to the Jeep, sat down—his legs outside the Jeep, and with the woman in his lap—and ordered, "Go, Ernie! Go!"

Zimmerman let the clutch out and the Jeep took off.

"If you keep struggling, we're both going to fall out," McCoy said to the woman.

"You're not going to get away with this, you bastard!" the woman said.

"When you get around the next bend, Ernie, stop," McCoy ordered.

"You're going to wind up in the stockade!" the woman said.

Zimmerman made the turn in the road, then pulled to the side and stopped.

"What are you going to do, dump her here?" Zimmerman asked.

"Only if Miss Priestly can't see the mutual benefit in the pooling of our assets," McCoy said.

"You know who I am!" Jeanette Priestly said. She was now standing by the side of the road, her hands on her hips, glowering at McCoy.

"Jeanette Priestly of the *Chicago Tribune*," McCoy said.

Slight recognition dawned.

"Do I know you?" she asked.

"We had dinner a couple of weeks ago in Tokyo," McCoy said.

"McCoy," she said. "The Marine."

"Right," McCoy said.

"Just what the fuck do you think you're doing?" she said. "You just can't steal my Jeep."

"Let me explain your options," McCoy said. "If we leave you here by the side of the road, you can run back to the MPs and tell them you just saw your Jeep driving off down the road—"

"My stolen Jeep!"

"—they will tell you they will do what they can, and you will go to the motor pool where—as I suspect you already know—that fat slob of a major will tell you he doesn't even have enough Jeeps for full colonels—"

"You son of a bitch!"

"Which will leave you where we found each other, you walking," McCoy continued. "I can't imagine how they would do it, but let's say they radio ahead of us, and we are stopped by some other MPs. . . ."

"That's exactly what's going to happen to you," she said. "And it's off to the stockade you go."

"First of all, I don't think they've had time to set up a stockade, but let's say we get stopped. At that point, we show them our orders, and say all we know . . ." He reached into his pocket and handed her the orders he had shown to the motor pool officer; she snatched them out of his hand and read them ". . . is that we went to the motor officer, showed him our orders, and he said we sure had a high priority and gave us the Jeep." He paused. "Who do you think will be believed?"

"You miserable son of a bitch!" Jeanette said after a moment.

"If you're going to be traveling with us, Miss Priestly, you're going to have to watch your mouth. Gunner Zimmerman is a very sensitive man. Say 'hello' to Miss Priestly, Ernie, and tell her you will forgive her for swearing like a Parris Island DI if she promises not to do that no more."

Zimmerman smiled but didn't say anything.

Although she really didn't want to, Jeanette Priestly was aware that she was smiling, too.

"Traveling with you?" she said. "Traveling where with you?"

"We're here to see how the war is going. According to the map in the G-2, that's up around Taejon."

"What's in it for you, if I go along?" she asked.

"You've been here before; we haven't. I think we can be very useful to each other."

She thought that over a minute.

"OK," she said. "I'll go."

"You have one more option," McCoy said. "You can ride along and wait until we get to the next MP checkpoint, and then scream that we've stolen your Jeep and kidnapped you. What would happen then, I think, is that we would all be held until a senior officer could be found to straighten things out. Which would mean that none of us would get to the war."

"You son of a bitch!" she said. There was an admiring tone in her voice.

"Are you coming, or not?"

She climbed into the backseat.

"OK, Ernie," McCoy ordered. "Let's go."

Five minutes later, Miss Jeanette Priestly, accredited war correspondent of the *Chicago Tribune,* leaned forward and asked, "What happened to the other fellow? The Trans-Global captain? Who set the speed record?"

"I expect about right now Major Malcolm S. Pickering, USMC Reserve, is trying to come up with a good excuse to get out of being mobilized," McCoy said.

Zimmerman laughed.

[TWO]
Headquarters, 34th Infantry Regiment
24th U.S. Infantry Division
Nonsan, South Korea
1530 15 July 1950

It had not proved hard to find the headquarters of the 34th Infantry Regiment, although the best location of it Captain McCoy had been able to extract from an S-3 sergeant at 24th Infantry Division headquarters had been rather vague:

"I think it's probably here, Captain," the sergeant had said, pointing to a map. "On Route One, a little village called Nonsan. That's where it's *supposed* to be."

Nonsan turned out to be a typical small Korean town, a collection of thatch-roofed stone buildings surrounding a short, sort of shopping strip of connected two-story, tin-roofed buildings, two of which, according to a plywood sign, had been taken over by "Hq 34th Inf Regt."

The officer standing outside one of the stores—probably the regimental commander; there was a white colonel's eagle painted on his helmet—looked, McCoy thought, a lot like the motor officer at Headquarters, Eighth Army.

Not only was he a portly man armed with a .45 ACP pistol, his fatigue jacket sweat-stained under his armpits, and with a sweaty forehead, as the major had been, but from the moment he had seen the Jeep, it was clear he was not at all pleased at what he saw.

McCoy pulled the Jeep in beside two other Jeeps and a three-quarter ton truck, and got out.

"Stay in the Jeep," he ordered, then walked up to the colonel and saluted.

The colonel returned the salute.

"Who's the woman?" the colonel asked.

"Miss Jeanette Priestly, of the *Chicago Tribune,* sir," McCoy replied.

The colonel motioned for McCoy to precede him into the building, and when they were both inside, asked, disgustedly, "What's she doing here?"

"She's an accredited war correspondent, sir, with orders permitting her to go wherever she wants to go."

"Jesus H. Christ!" the colonel said. "With two bodyguards, right?"

"Not exactly, sir," McCoy said. "May I show you my orders?"

The colonel gestured impatiently for McCoy to hand them over. McCoy gave him the Dai-Ichi orders. The colonel read them and handed them back.

"Marines, huh? I thought your fatigues were a little odd."

"Yes, sir."

"OK, Captain McCoy of the Marine Corps, what exactly is your mission, except for escorting a female—who has absolutely no business being here—around?"

"We've been sent here, sir, to see what's going on."

"By who? General Almond himself?"

McCoy didn't reply.

"That was a question, Captain," the colonel said, sharply.

"Sir, we work for General Pickering."

Almost visibly, the colonel searched his memory for that name, and failed.

"He's in the Dai Ichi Building?"

"Yes, sir."

"So what is your connection with the lady?"

"When Eighth Army couldn't give us a Jeep, sir, I commandeered hers."

"And brought her along with you?"

"Yes, sir."

"Well, Captain, she's your responsibility. I don't want to be responsible for her safety. Not that I could if I wanted to."

"Yes, sir."

"You want to 'see what's going on'? Presumably you somehow intend to relay what you see to your boss—General *Pickering*, you said?"

"Yes, sir."

"I don't have any communications that will permit you to do that, and I would be surprised if division does."

"Yes, sir."

"But it has just occurred to me," the colonel said, somewhat bitterly, "presuming you can find somewhat to communicate with the Dai Ichi Building, that it might be a very good thing for our senior officers to learn '*what's going on*' here. Come with me, Captain, and I'll tell you what I know about '*what's going on.*'"

"Yes, sir. Thank you, sir."

The colonel turned and walked farther into the long and narrow building, which, judging from the shelves on both walls, had been a store of some kind or another.

There were the usual officers and enlisted men, and their equipment, of a regimental headquarters crowding the room, and the colonel had apparently elected to put his field desk at the far end, where there was another door.

As McCoy followed the colonel between the desks and around the field telephone switchboard and radio sets, he glanced into a side room.

In it were three North Korean soldiers, wearing insignia that identified them as a sergeant, a corporal, and a private. They were seated with their backs against a wall. A sergeant with an M1 carbine sat on a folding chair, guarding them.

"Colonel," McCoy called. "Excuse me, Colonel."

The colonel looked impatiently over his shoulder. By then, McCoy had gone into the room.

"God damn!" the colonel said, and went after him.

The sergeant looked at McCoy curiously.

"Get to your feet when an officer enters a room, Sergeant!" McCoy snapped unpleasantly.

The sergeant did so with very little enthusiasm.

The colonel appeared at the door, his mouth open to speak.

McCoy spoke first. He pointed at the North Korean private.

"That applies to you, too," he said, nastily, in Korean.

The private looked for a moment as if he was going to stand, but then relaxed against the wall.

"On your feet, all of you," McCoy barked, in Korean.

They all stood up.

"Have you eaten?" McCoy asked. "Do you need water?"

The North Korean sergeant said "water" in Korean.

The private glowered at him.

"Colonel," McCoy said, "the private of the 83rd Motorcycle Regiment, the one with the good leather boots, is almost certainly an officer, and very probably speaks English. Most of the officers of the 83rd do. I will speak with him, with all of them, after your sergeant gets them water, rations, and some cigarettes."

The colonel looked at McCoy for a long moment, then turned to the sergeant.

"You heard the captain," he said. "Get a canteen and a box of C-rations in here."

McCoy took the sergeant's carbine from him and held it on his hip, like a hunter, until the sergeant returned with two canteens and a box of C-rations.

He set the box on the floor, and tried to hand one of the canteens to the North Korean sergeant. He shook his head, "no."

"Take the water," McCoy ordered in Korean. "You are all prisoners. I give the orders here, not your officer."

The sergeant looked at the private, then took the canteen.

"Bingo," McCoy said, very softly, to the colonel, handed the American sergeant his carbine, and walked out of the room.

He walked out of earshot of the room, then stopped.

"You speak Korean. I'm impressed," the colonel said.

"Are they your prisoners, sir? Or did you inherit them?"

"My third battalion captured them," the colonel said. "Division was supposed to send for them—take them for interrogation. . . ."

"They're from the 83rd Motorcycle Regiment," McCoy said. "They're pretty good. The regimental commander is—the last I heard, a Colonel Pak Sun Hae, who used to be a lieutenant in the Soviet Army. They're well trained, and well-equipped."

"Which is, sadly, more than I can say about the 34th Infantry," the colonel said.

"Colonel, for my purposes—it would make them even more uncomfortable than they are—I'd like Miss Priestly to take their picture. Would that be all right?"

The colonel thought that over.

"Why not?" he said, after a minute, and turned to a master sergeant standing nearby. "There's a lady and a Marine in a Jeep outside, Sergeant. Would you ask them to come in, please?"

"Tell her to bring her camera, Sergeant," McCoy ordered.

As Jeanette Priestly followed Zimmerman and the sergeant through the narrow building, there were looks of disbelief on the faces of the regimental officers and soldiers.

"With the caveat that I don't think you should be here," the colonel said. "welcome to the 34th Infantry, Miss Priestly."

"Thank you," she said, and looked at McCoy. "What's up?"

"There're three North Korean prisoners in there," McCoy said, pointing. "I want you to take their picture. Plural. Pictures."

"And then you take my film, right?"

"No. I don't want your film. When you have it processed in Tokyo, I'm sure they'll make prints for G-2. Ernie, you go in there and see if you think any of them speak Chinese. The little guy in the good boots is, I suspect, an officer. He's not going to say much, but if you think one of the others speaks Chinese, take him someplace and see what he knows. They're from the 83rd Motorcycle Regiment."

Zimmerman nodded. "Aye, aye, sir."

"I would like to use the ladies' room," Jeanette announced.

"I'm afraid we can't offer you much, Miss Priestly," the colonel said.

"I didn't expect that you could," she said, and smiled dazzlingly at him. "Why don't you call me 'Jennie,' Colonel. We're friends, right?"

"Sergeant, escort Miss Priestly to the latrine, and stand guard," the colonel ordered. Then he turned to McCoy. "Would you like to have a look at the map, Captain?"

"Yes, sir. Thank you."

The map, covered with transparent celluloid, was mounted on a sheet of plywood against the wall behind the colonel's desk.

"Here we are now, the regiment—and the division—strung out along the Kum River." He pointed.

"Yesterday morning, Item Company of my 3rd Battalion, here, on the south bank of the Kum, was brought under tank fire at about 0600—first light. No real damage was done, but the artillery forward observer couldn't come up with the coordinates of the tanks, so we couldn't hurt them either.

"About the same time, an outpost of Love Company—here on the far left flank—reported seeing two barges ferrying North Koreans across the river two miles to their west. Accidentally, or intentionally, they were out of range of any of our artillery.

"By 0930, they had five hundred men across the river. The North Korean artillery was working, and they brought Love Company under fire, at about the same time as did the mortars of the North Koreans who had crossed the river: 0935 to 0940."

The colonel stopped and looked at McCoy.

"Have you ever been under mortar and artillery fire, Captain? Or have you spent your entire career in intelligence?"

"I've been under fire, sir."

"More than once?"

"Yes, sir."

"Do you remember the first time?"

"Yes, sir."

"Where was that?"

"In the Philippines, sir. The Japanese used naval gunfire before landing."

"Were you afraid?"

"Very much, sir."

"Did you 'withdraw'?"

"Sir?"

"Did you 'withdraw'—the new word for that is 'bug out'?"

"No, sir."

"Do you remember why not?"

"No, sir," McCoy said. "We were there to try to repel the landing barges."

"My first time was in Italy," the colonel said. "I shat my pants. But I didn't bug out."

"Sir?"

"The company commander of Love Company, Captain, within minutes of coming under fire, 'withdrew.' Not only personally, but ordered his soldiers to do likewise."

McCoy did not reply.

"As it turned out," the colonel went on, "it wasn't as bad as it could have been. The artillery fire on Love Company was apparently a diversionary attack to conceal their real intention, which was to move to the south in this direction—he pointed—and sever the road here. If they had attacked the deserted positions of Love Company . . ."

"I think I get the picture, sir," McCoy said.

"I relieved the officer in question, of course, as soon as what he had done came to my attention, but I didn't come into that information until some time after it happened. By that time—several hours, later, whatever time it took them to move three miles against virtually no opposition—approximately three hundred North Korean infantry were here, on this road, near the village of Samyo.

"So was the 63rd Field Artillery Battalion, 105-mm howitzers. They had been providing much of my artillery support. The North Koreans launched an immediate attack against them. Tell me, Captain, how are Marine cannoneers armed?"

"Sir?"

"Are they armed with carbines?"

"I'm not sure. It's my understanding that the officers, and some senior non-coms, can elect to carry carbines . . ."

"But the junior NCOs and privates have M1 Garands, and are trained in their use?"

"Sir, every Marine is a rifleman."

"There were very few Garands in the 63rd Field Artillery," the colonel said, matter of factly, "which is the explanation offered for the failure of the 63rd to adequately defend itself by an officer who managed to escape the debacle there."

"Sir?"

"Wouldn't you agree that roughly two hundred men—which was the strength of the 63rd—should be able to hold out longer than two hours against three hundred infantry, not supported by artillery?"

"Yes, sir, I would."

"The enemy attacked the 63rd at approximately 1330. By 1530, the enemy had killed or captured all but a lucky few officers and men who managed to escape, and captured all of the 63rd Field's vehicles, cannon, and a considerable supply of ammunition."

"They got all the guns?" McCoy asked, incredulously.

"All of them. And before the 63rd was able to spike them," the colonel said, confirmed.

"Jesus!" McCoy said.

"At about this time," the colonel went on. "Item Company learned for the first time that Love Company had bugged out, and that the enemy was astride its road to the rear. The company commander asked for permission to withdraw, and 3rd battalion commander recommended that it be granted; he said that he didn't think the re-formed Love Company—he described them as 'demoralized'—could be trusted to counterattack and reopen the road behind Love Company. I gave permission for the withdrawal."

The colonel let that sink in and then went on.

"It was necessary for them to 'withdraw' over the mountains—the roads were in enemy hands—and they eventually made it here. Without a substantial percentage of their crew-served weapons, which simply could not be carried over the mountains."

The colonel gave McCoy time to absorb that, and then went on:

"I have no reason, Captain, to believe that the 19th Infantry will fare any better than the 34th has, for the same reasons. One of the reasons I believe that to be true is that the division's third regiment, the 21st Infantry, in three days of fighting, has lost about half its officers and men."

"Half?"

"Half," the colonel confirmed. "What was left of the 21st was gathered near Taejon, and reorganized. Reorganized, rather than reconstituted, which implies bringing a unit up to strength. There is no replacement system in place from which replacements for losses can be drawn. What happened to the 21st is that an attempt has been made to form companies and battalions from its remnants.

"What that means, of course, is that when the 21st goes back into combat, very few, if any, of the men will have served—much less trained—together. Moreover, because many officers are among the dead and missing, many companies—perhaps most—will be commanded by lieutenants who were platoon leaders four days ago, and many platoons will be led by sergeants. In some cases, corporals.

"Early this morning, the 21st was trucked from Taejon to Okchon, here." He pointed on the map. "That's about ten miles east of Taejon. They have been ordered to set up positions here, on the Seoul-Pusan highway, about halfway between Okchon and Taegu. If the enemy elects to attack down the highway—or to take the high ground on either side of the highway—resistance to those sort of moves will obviously be hindered by the lack of artillery. In fact, I suspect that when the North Koreans attack, their assigned artillery will be augmented by the 105-mm tubes the 63rd Field lost."

Again, the colonel paused to give McCoy time to absorb what he had told him.

"And there will, of course, be another attack. If not this afternoon, then during the night, or at the very latest, very early in the morning. The only question is where." He paused. "That, Captain, is 'what's going on.' I really hope you can find communications somewhere and get through to the Dai Ichi Building. Somehow, I suspect that they don't know what's going on.'"

"Colonel, your prisoners are from the 83rd Motorcycle Regiment. It's one of their best—sort of an elite regimental combat team—normally attached to their 6th Division. Maybe if I—"

"If you know that, Captain, I have to presume that's common knowledge around the Dai Ichi Building. I wonder why they didn't think we would be interested to know that."

"I'm not sure how common that information is around SCAP, sir."

"So you—whatever organization you work for—had that information, but didn't pass it on?"

There was a perceptible pause before McCoy replied.

"Colonel, I'm only a captain. I gather intelligence, not disseminate it. I can't answer your question."

"You were saying, about the prisoners?"

"Maybe I can learn something from them, sir, about their intentions. Because it's highly mobile, I suspect that its officers have to be told more about the overall picture than officers are in standard units."

"That would be helpful," the colonel said. "Providing you do it quickly. I want you—especially the woman—out of here as soon as possible. I'm going to have enough on my platter without having to worry about her. Or you."

"Sir, with respect. I have no authority over Miss Priestly. Even if I returned her Jeep to her, there's no way I can make her leave, go back to Eighth Army. And I need that Jeep."

"And if I order you to get in your Jeep and, taking Miss Priestly with you, to get the hell out of here?"

"Sir, with respect, I'm not subject to your orders."

The colonel looked at him intently for a long moment.

"You intend to stay, then?"

"Yes, sir, for the time being. I really would like to talk to some more prisoners."

"It's occurred to you, I presume, that if you stay, you're likely to become a prisoner yourself?"

"Yes, sir, it has."

After a moment, the colonel nodded.

"OK. I gave it my best shot. Will you need me, or any of my men, to deal with the prisoners?"

"No, thank you, sir."

[THREE]

"The corporal speaks Cantonese," Zimmerman reported outside the room where the prisoners had been held. "He was willing to talk, but he didn't know much. But you're right, they are from the 83rd Motorcycle Regiment, and the little guy is an officer."

"Who speaks English?"

"And Russian."

"That's interesting," McCoy said. "What's his rank?"

Zimmerman nodded, in agreement with "interesting," and then shrugged.

"The corporal didn't know. He said when he got drafted to do a little reconnaissance—there were originally five of them, two of them got killed when they ran into one of our patrols, where they got caught—the little guy was already wearing the private's jacket. But one of the others, one who got blown away, called him 'sir,' and he was obviously in charge."

"What else did the corporal have to say?"

"He said that after they took Seoul, the regiment was taken out of action, and sent down the peninsula right behind the units on the line. Now they're getting ready to go back into action. Soon."

"No specifics?"

"No, but it can't be far off, Ken. It looks to me as if this guy, the officer, is an intel officer. Maybe not even from the 83rd. He wanted a closeup of where they were going, and got himself bagged."

"Did the 6th Division come up?"

"They're here. The corporal didn't know if the 83rd was attached to them or not."

"How's your Russian these days, Ernie?"

"Not bad. Milla Banning and Mae-Su decided the kids should know how to speak it, and then Banning got in the act. We have Russian suppers, talk only Russian. I'm all right with it."

"Let's go talk to the officer," McCoy said. "Where's the corporal?"

"I had him put in another room, to get him away from the officer."

"You go in there, tell the guard to put the sergeant with the corporal, make a show of chambering your Thompson, and in a couple of minutes, I'll come in. You pop to, when I do."

"Got it," Zimmerman said.

"Where's Priestly?"

Zimmerman pointed out the door, to where Jeanette Priestly was talking to several GIs, who were beaming at her.

McCoy nodded and motioned for Zimmerman to enter the room where the prisoners were being held. A minute later, the American sergeant came out, holding his carbine in one hand, and with his other on the North Korean sergeant's shoulder.

McCoy looked at his watch, then helped himself to a cup of coffee from an electric pot next to one of the radios—and thus a source of 110 volts AC—and exactly five minutes later, put the mess kit coffee cup down and walked into the room where the North Korean officer was being held.

Zimmerman, who had been sitting on a folding chair, popped to rigid attention. McCoy made an impatient gesture with his hand, and Zimmerman relaxed slightly.

"My friend," McCoy said, conversationally, in Russian, "I'm a little pressed for time, so I suggest it would be to your advantage to make the most of what time I can give you."

There was a flicker of surprise on the North Korean officer's face, immediately replaced by one intended to show that he didn't understand a word.

"All right, we'll do it in Korean," McCoy said, switching to that language, "although my Korean is not as good as my Russian." He switched to English: "Or perhaps you would prefer English?"

The officer looked at him in what was supposed to convey a complete lack of comprehension.

McCoy went back to Russian:

"The fortunes of war have gone against you, Major," he said.

There was another flicker of surprise in the North Korean's eyes, and McCoy thought it was reasonable to presume that his guess that the man was a major was right on the money.

"With a little luck, Major, at this very minute, you could be sitting in a POW enclosure, as a simple private, biding your time until the forces of international socialism overwhelmed the capitalist imperialists and you were liberated. But that didn't happen. What happened is that I happened to come by here. We are not soldiers. We are Marines. Moreover, we are more or less—probably more than less—in the same line of work."

"He understood that, Captain," Zimmerman said, in English. "I could tell by his eyes. But I also saw in his eyes that he won't be useful, so may I suggest, considering the time, that—"

"I would rather not dispose of him," McCoy said, and chuckled. "Professional courtesy, Ernest. You and I could easily find ourselves in his position."

"Sir, with respect, I suggest we have him shot, and be on our way."

"Kim Si Yong," the North Korean said, in English. "Seven-five-eight-eight-nine."

"Ah," McCoy said, now in English, "the major is partially familiar with the Geneva Convention."

"Partially?" Zimmerman asked.

"The Convention requires that prisoners of war furnish their captors with their name, rank, and service number. I did not hear a rank, did you?"

"No, sir," Zimmerman said.

"He has therefore not complied with the Geneva Convention," McCoy explained. "Not that it matters anyway, for under Paragraph Seventeen, Subsection B, since he is an officer, wearing a private soldier's uniform, it may be presumed that he is not a combatant, entitled to the protection of the convention, but instead a spy, who may be legally executed."

"Under those circumstances, may I respectfully suggest we have him shot, and be on our way?"

McCoy looked at the North Korean officer, then shrugged, and appeared to be on the verge of leaving the room.

"Kim Si Yong," the North Korean said, in English. "Major, seven-five-eight-eight-nine. I claim the protection of the Geneva Convention."

McCoy switched to Russian.

"Major Kim," he said. "There's one small problem with that. Your government is not a signatory to the Geneva Convention. That means that it is at the option of your captors—and that means me—whether or not to apply it to prisoners. The other problem you have is your confession that you are an officer masquerading as a private soldier, which changes your position from prisoner of war to spy."

"Sir, with all respect," Zimmerman said, in Russian. "He probably doesn't know anything we don't already know. Sir, we're already going to be very late—"

McCoy held up his hand to silence him.

"Major, as a professional courtesy between fellow intelligence officers, let me explain your options," McCoy said. "They do not include being returned to your side anytime soon, so put that out of your mind. They do include being shot in the next few minutes as a spy. Keep that in your mind. Now we know that the 83rd Motorcycle Regiment, which has been kept out of the fighting since Seoul, will lead the attack of the 6th Division. We don't know when that attack will take place. If you tell us when that attack will take place, you will not be shot immediately. You will be kept here until the time you tell us the attack will take place. If it occurs when you say it will, I will personally deliver you to Eighth Army Headquarters, and guarantee that you are treated as an officer prisoner under the Geneva Convention. If it does not take place when you tell us it will, you will be shot at that time. I will give you as long as it takes me to go to the latrine to make up your mind."

McCoy walked out of the room, looked at his watch, picked up the mess kit coffee cup where he had laid it down, finished drinking it, and precisely five minutes after he had left the room, walked back into it.

Five minutes after that, he walked back out of the room, found the colonel, and told him what he had learned.

"You believe this officer, Captain?"

"Sir, I believe he thought I was prepared to have him shot. What he may have done is tell me that attack will be at 0300, because he knows it will be earlier; if it's earlier, and we're overrun, then he might be freed. I don't think it will be after 0300, because he thinks he'll be shot if it doesn't happen then."

"They don't usually start anything in the middle of the night," the colonel said, thoughtfully. "But they're on a roll, and it would give them the advantage of surprise."

McCoy didn't reply. The colonel paused again, obviously in thought, and then said, "I'll pass this on to division. And order a fifty-percent alert from nightfall. You're still determined to stay here?"

"Yes, sir."

"And Miss Priestly?"

"If Zimmerman and I stay, sir, I don't think there's much chance of getting her to leave."

"Then I suggest you find someplace where you'll have protection from incoming," the colonel said. "They're certainly going to fire their tubes—and probably the 105s they took from the 63rd Field Artillery—as a prelude to the attack, whenever they decide to make it."

"Yes, sir," McCoy said. "Sir, I'd like to go see the 19th Infantry. Would you have objection to my taking the major with me?"

"What are you going to do, put him in the back of Miss Priestly's Jeep with Miss Priestly?"

"Actually, sir, I thought I'd put him in the front seat with Gunner Zimmerman and Miss Priestly, and I would ride in the back."

What could have been a smile appeared momentarily on the colonel's lips.

"Just make sure she's in the Jeep, Captain," he said.

"Aye, aye, sir."

"Here, I'll show you on the map where I think the 19th CP is," the colonel said.

[FOUR]
Headquarters 19th Infantry Regiment
24th Infantry Division
Kongju, South Korea
1805 15 July 1950

"Jesus H. Christ!" the Garand-armed corporal standing to one side of the sandbagged door of the command post exclaimed when he saw the Jeep with a Korean in the front seat and the American woman in the back.

He walked over to the Jeep.

After apparently thinking it over first, he saluted.

"Yes, sir? Can I help you?"

"You can keep an eye on this enemy officer while we go inside," McCoy said.

"Enemy officer" caught the ear of a major who had been standing talking to a sergeant on the other side of the sandbagged entrance. He walked over to the Jeep.

McCoy saluted.

"Enemy officer?" the major asked, then "Marines?" and finally, "War correspondent?"

"Yes, sir, three times," McCoy said.

"The only thing I can do for you is advise you to get back to Division," the major said. "We've just been advised to expect an attack anytime from darkness—which means just about now—'til 0300."

"Yes, sir, we know," McCoy said.

"This is no place for you, ma'am," the major said to Jeanette.

"Jeanette Priestly, *Chicago Tribune,*" she said, with a dazzling smile, and offered the major her hand.

"We have a Korean sergeant who speaks some English," the major said to McCoy. "I'd like him to talk to your prisoner." Then he had a second thought: "Public relations? What are you doing with a prisoner?"

Here we go again.

"Sir, Gunner Zimmerman and I are not public relations," he said, and handed the major the "Dai Ichi" orders. "I found it necessary to commandeer her Jeep when Eighth Army didn't have one for us."

The major read the orders, his eyebrows rising as he did.

"I think we'd better go see the regimental commander, Captain," he said.

The regimental colonel was a slight man with a mustache. Somehow he had managed to remain dapper despite the heat, the dust and everything else.

"I don't want to seem inhospitable, Captain," he said, looking up at McCoy after he'd read the orders. "But we're a little busy here. Can we cut to the chase? What are two Marine officers doing here with a female war correspondent?"

He, too, had a second thought.

"Fred, ask the lady and the other officer to come in here," he said to the major. "And bring the prisoner." He looked at McCoy. "We're expecting an attack at any time; there will certainly be artillery."

"Yes, sir," the major said, and went out of the sandbagged CP.

"That information came from the prisoner, sir," McCoy said.

The colonel looked at him, waiting for him to go on.

"He's a major attached to the 83rd Motorcycle Regiment—probably their G-2. He was making a reconnaissance when he was captured by a squad from the 34th Infantry doing the same thing."

"How do you know this?"

"He told me."

"You speak Korean?"

"Yes, sir."

The colonel's eyebrows rose.

"How'd you get him to talk?"

"I told him that since he was an officer wearing a private's uniform, he was subject to being shot as a spy."

"I'm starting to like you, Captain," the colonel said. "What else did he have to say?"

"He said the attack will start at 0300, with the 83rd Motorcycle Regiment and the 6th Division."

"And you believe him?"

"I told him if it doesn't happen at 0300, I'll have him shot. If it does, I'll take him to the 24th Division Headquarters and see that he's treated as an officer prisoner."

"So you're not a two-man Marine bodyguard for a female war correspondent?" the colonel asked, smiling.

"No, sir."

"With those orders, you could be anything. What *is* your 'mission'? Your orders are a little vague about that."

"To see what's going on here, sir."

"For General Almond himself?"

"Actually for General Pickering, sir."

The colonel, as the 34th Regiment's commander had done, searched his memory back for "Pickering" and came up blank.

"In the Dai Ichi Building?" he asked.

"Yes, sir."

"Where does the lady fit in?"

"Eighth Army didn't have wheels for us, sir. So I commandeered hers."

"And brought her along?"

"Yes, sir."

"OK. I'll tell you 'what's going on,' " he said. "Apparently largely based on your intelligence, we expect an attack sometime between right now and 0300. The only signs we've had of anything are reports—half a dozen reports—of small groups of North Koreans trying to wade across the Kum River"—he turned to his map and pointed—"in this area."

He turned back to face McCoy.

"Small groups," he said. "I think they know we're short on artillery. You heard about the 63rd Field Artillery getting overrun? . . ."

McCoy nodded.

". . . and are reluctant to fire what little we have on groups of five or six men. And they're also aware of the location of our positions. As a ballpark figure, my regiment is holding three times as much line as I was taught was the absolute maximum at Leavenworth,* and there are holes in it. The North Koreans are wading across where, in many cases, it is impossible for us to bring small-arms fire to bear."

"Can you give us a guide to some of these positions?"

"Why?"

"I'd like to try to get another prisoner or two, sir."

"I'd like another one, too," the colonel said. "Particularly since you speak Korean. I can send you up here"—he pointed at the map again—"with Major Allman, my G-3, and one of his sergeants. It'll be really dark in an hour . . ."

"Thank you, sir."

---

*Graduation from the U.S. Army Command & General Staff College is a prerequisite for promotion to colonel and being given command of a regiment.

". . . which means that you and the lady will have to remain here for the night. Which means that you had better hope we can hold out until first light, because you won't be able to get out of here before then."

"I understand, sir."

[FIVE]

Five minutes after Major Allman, Captain McCoy, and Master Gunner Zimmerman had started out from the regimental command post for the outpost positions of Baker Company, 1st Battalion, 19th Infantry, a female voice called out, "Hey, guys, wait for me!"

"Miss Priestly," Major Allman said, dryly, "has apparently chosen to ignore the colonel's suggestion to remain in the CP."

"Escaped from the CP is more like it," Captain McCoy said.

"Fuck her," Master Gunner Zimmerman said.

"That thought has occurred to me," Major Allman said. "But this isn't the time nor place. The question is what do we do about her, here and now?"

"The light's failing," McCoy said. "We don't have time to take her back."

"Your call, Captain," Allman said.

"I don't see where we have a choice," McCoy said.

He started walking again.

Three minutes later, the war correspondent of the *Chicago Tribune* caught up with them. She had a Leica III-c 35-mm camera hanging around her neck, and was carrying a .30-caliber carbine in her hand.

"You're supposed to be a noncombatant," McCoy said.

"I should use it on you, you son of a bitch," Jeanette said, conversationally, "for leaving me back there."

Five minutes later, they reached the Baker Company CP—which was nothing more than a sandbag reinforced shelter on the military crest* of a small hill overlooking the river.

The company commander was not there; the first sergeant said he was out checking positions. He showed them—on a hand-drawn map—where they were, on the other side of the hill, overlooking the river, and thus visible to the enemy.

"This is as far as you go, Jeanette," McCoy said. "If necessary, I'll have you tied up."

"Where are you going?" she demanded.

---

*The military crest of a hill is just below the actual crest, and therefore is not under enemy observation.

"Zimmerman and I are going to go down to the positions, the foxholes. We're going to try to get a prisoner. Maybe two."

"And I don't get to watch?" she asked, angry and disappointed.

"There's an FO OP right up there," the first sergeant offered helpfully, pointing. A forward observer's observation post. "It's sandbagged. She could watch from there. They've got binoculars."

"And you'd go with her, right?" Major Allman asked, smiling.

"Yes, sir."

"I don't think so, Jeanette," McCoy said. "How do I know you'd stay in the OP?"

"I'll stay there," she said.

"I'll make sure she doesn't leave the OP," Major Allman said, and added: "Unless you'd rather have me go to the outposts with you."

"I don't think that would be necessary, sir," McCoy said. "Thank you."

It took McCoy and Zimmerman another five minutes to climb past the military crest of the hill, and then to run, zigzagging, down the other side until they reached an obviously freshly dug, sandbag-reinforced two-man foxhole.

It held two men, manning an air-cooled Browning .30-caliber machine gun on a tripod. There were half a dozen cans of ammunition in the hole, and half a dozen hand grenades—with their pins in, and the tape still holding the safety lever in place—were laid out neatly on the sandbags.

The sergeant and the PFC manning the gun were surprised when two officers suddenly joined them, and even more surprised when they saw the Marine Corps emblem painted on Zimmerman's utilities jacket.

McCoy looked back up the hill for the forward observer's position, and easily found it—its brown sandbag reinforcement stood out from the vegetation—which meant the enemy could also see it.

He turned to the sergeant, who so far had neither said a word nor saluted.

"Sergeant, they tell me there's North Koreans trying to wade across the river," he said.

The sergeant pointed over Zimmerman's shoulder. McCoy and Zimmerman looked where he pointed. Zimmerman reached into one of the cavernous pockets of his utilities and came out with a pair of binoculars.

At what McCoy estimated to be from 450 to 500 yards, half a dozen men were wading across the Kum River. When Zimmerman had his look through his binoculars and handed them to him, McCoy saw that the North Koreans were holding their weapons and packs over their heads.

He handed the binoculars back to Zimmerman.

"Sergeant, have you been ordered not to fire?" McCoy asked.

"We're not that heavy on ammo," the sergeant said, pointing at the ammunition cans. "I decided we better save that for later."

"And your rifle?" McCoy asked, pointing to an M-1 Garand resting against the sandbags beside a .30-caliber carbine.

"You can't hit them with a rifle at that range, sir," the sergeant said.

Zimmerman looked at the sergeant incredulously, and opened his mouth. McCoy held up a hand to silence him.

"Sergeant," McCoy said, not unkindly, "when I had an air-cooled thirty-caliber Browning machine-gun section, we were taught that if you could hit something with a machine gun, you could hit it with a rifle. It's the same cartridge."

The sergeant shrugged.

Zimmerman made a *give it to me* gesture toward McCoy's Garand, and McCoy handed it to him.

The sergeant and the PFC were now fascinated.

"Where's the zero?" Zimmerman asked.

"Two hundred," McCoy said.

"You're sure? I really hate to fuck with the sights."

"Give it back, Ernie," McCoy ordered. "You spot for me."

Zimmerman shrugged, and handed the Garand back.

McCoy moved up to the sandbags, tried the sitting position, found that it placed him too low to fire, and assumed the kneeling position.

Then he reached up and moved two of the grenades out of the way.

"Sergeant," he said. "If you think you might need those grenades in a hurry, it might be a good idea to take the tape off now."

The sergeant looked at him a moment, and then offered a noncommittal "Yes, sir."

McCoy pounded the sandbag with the fore end of the Garand until the groove in the sandbag provided what he thought was adequate support. Then, with quick sure movements born of long practice, he unlooped the leather sling of the Garand from the stock, adjusted the brass hooks, and arranged it around his arm.

The sergeant and the PFC looked at him in fascination.

McCoy took a sight, then looked up at Zimmerman, who nodded and put the binoculars to his eyes.

McCoy took another sight and squeezed one off, then—very much as if they were on a known-distance rifle range firing at bull's-eye targets—looked up at Zimmerman—the coach—to see how he was doing.

"You got the one closest to this bank," Zimmerman reported.

"I held a foot over his head," McCoy said, and then reached into his utilities jacket pocket for an eight-round Garand clip. He laid it on the sandbags beside the hand grenades and resumed his shooting position.

In the next sixty seconds, he fired the remaining seven cartridges in the Garand. The empty clip flew out of the open breech in an arc. Before it hit the ground, he reached for the spare clip and a moment later thumbed it into the Garand, and slammed the operating rod with the heel of his hand, ensuring that the fresh cartridge would be fully chambered. Then he quickly got in firing position again.

"They're gone, Ken," Zimmerman said. "*Their* side of the river. You got three of them, maybe four."

"Jesus Christ!" the sergeant said.

"And in the Marine Corps, the captain's considered only a so-so shot," Zimmerman said, oozing sincerity.

"And in the Marine Corps, Master Gunner Zimmerman has a reputation for being as good a man as they come with the Garand," McCoy, "and *that's* not bullshit."

He pointed at the PFC's Garand.

"Is that zeroed?"

"We got a chance to fire a couple of clips before we left Japan, sir."

"What Mr. Zimmerman's going to do now, Sergeant, is have a look at that Garand, and then—if the light doesn't go—help you zero it at two hundred yards."

"Jesus," the PFC said. "Thank you."

"And then, when it's dark, you and I, Ernie, are going to go down to the bank and see if we can't grab a prisoner."

Zimmerman nodded.

[SIX]
Headquarters 19th Infantry Regiment
24th Infantry Division
Kongju, South Korea
0300 16 July 1950

"Incoming!" one of the sergeants in the G-3 section called out excitedly.

Quite unnecessarily, for everyone present had heard the sound an artillery shell makes in flight.

The impact came a moment later, a hundred yards away.

"It looks like you're going to live, Major," Zimmerman said to their North Korean prisoner. "I was beginning to wonder."

"There will be more, much more," the major said.

McCoy wondered: *Was that a gratis offer of more information, or is he hoping that when they fire for effect, it will be right on our heads?*

And then he wondered: *Would I have caved in the way he did? Or Zimmerman? There's two sides to that tell-the-enemy-nothing business. What's the point of dying if it's not going to change things?*

His reverie was interrupted by more incoming.

Lots of incoming: Between the sound of the exploding incoming rounds, there could be heard the rumble of artillery—a lot of artillery—firing.

Very little seems to be directed at us, here at regimental headquarters, which probably means that it's being directed at positions on the line.

They know where the positions are. They've been infiltrating men across the river all night. And some certainly infiltrated back, carrying maps on which are marked the position of every last goddamn foxhole and machine-gun position.

And some stayed, and hidden by the darkness are calling in the shots: Right 200, up 50, fire for effect.

And if there is counterfire, I don't hear it.

The 19th is not going to be able to do much about turning this attack, if that sergeant and PFC are typical of the kind of people they've got. They don't know what the hell they're supposed to do, and if you don't know what to do, or what's going to happen, you're liable to panic.

The real question for us is how soon is it going to happen? It would be suicide to try to drive away from here now. Maybe at first light, it will be different. Maybe at first light, they'll make the major assault, and that means they're likely to lift the artillery barrage. That would give us a chance.

He looked at Miss Jeanette Priestly of the *Chicago Tribune*, who was sitting beside Major Allman on the floor, against the wall.

So if we can't get out of here, what do I do with you?

Tough broad. If she's about to become hysterical—which is always what I feel like doing when they're firing artillery at me—it sure doesn't show on her face.

If we're overrun, do I place my faith in the humanity of the Army of the People's Democratic Republic of North Korea, and let her get captured?

It's possible that an officer might recognize the propaganda value of capturing a female—the only female—American war correspondent, and she would be treated well, so they could put her on display.

It's more likely that she would be raped on the spot by the squad that comes in here, and if she lives through that, taken to maybe a battalion, where she would be raped all over again.

Maybe, she might get lucky and get killed before the troops actually arrive.

And if that doesn't happen, do I do the kind thing?

When the Apaches attacked the wagon trains and settlers, they always saved the last couple of rounds to do the kind thing for the women.

And that's about what we have here, the Apaches attacking the outnumbered good guys. And the 7th Cavalry isn't going to suddenly appear at the gallop with the flags flying and the bugles sounding "charge" to save our ass.

Oh, shit!

What you should have done, McCoy, is dump her at the side of the road, as Zimmerman suggested. Why the hell didn't you?

Unkind thought: If I didn't have to play sir Galahad with you, Ernie and I could make it out of here on foot.

He searched in his pack and came out with one of his last four cigars.

Zimmerman looked at him but didn't say anything.

McCoy reached up his left sleeve and came out with a dagger.

Jeanette Priestly saw that, and her attention drew that of Major Allman to McCoy and his dagger.

McCoy carefully laid the cigar against the plywood top of a folding desk, and chopped at it with the dagger. One half fell to the floor.

He tossed it to Zimmerman.

"Next time, bring your own," he said.

"Aye, aye, sir."

McCoy returned the dagger to its sheath, pulled his utility jacket sleeve down over it, produced a wooden match, and carefully started to light his cigar.

"What's with the knife?" Jeanette Priestly asked.

McCoy ignored her.

"I don't think I've ever seen one like that before," Jeanette Priestly said.

"It's not a knife, it's a dagger," Zimmerman furnished helpfully. "That's a Fairbairn."

"I don't know what that means, either," she said, flashing Zimmerman a dazzling smile.

"It was invented by an Englishman named Fairbairn," Zimmerman went on. "When he ran the police in Shanghai. Hell of a knife fighter."

What the hell turned his mouth on?

Oh. He likes her.

Likes her, as opposed to having the hots for her. She's tough.

"But it's so small," Jeanette pursued. "Is it really . . . what . . . a *lethal* weapon?"

"Huh!" Zimmerman snorted. "Yeah, it's lethal. Three Eye-talian Marines jumped him one time in Shanghai. He took two of them out with that dagger. That's how come they call him 'Killer.' "

"Shut your goddamn mouth, Zimmerman," McCoy said, his voice icily furious.

Zimmerman, as if he suddenly realized what he had done, looked stricken.

"They call him 'Killer'?" Jeanette relentlessly pursued.

"And you, too, goddamn you!" McCoy said. "Just shut the hell up!"

Her eyebrows went up, but she didn't say anything else.

The artillery and mortar barrage lasted about an hour, but even before it did, there were reports from the outposts of large numbers of North Koreans coming across the Kum River.

When the artillery barrage lifted, and Major Allman and others tried to call the battalion and company CPs, in many cases there was no response.

Major Allman, sensing McCoy's eyes on him when he failed to make three connections in a row, said, "I guess the artillery cut a lot of wire."

"Yes, sir," McCoy said.

Or the outposts, the platoons, and maybe even the companies have been overrun.

McCoy went outside the command post. It was black dark. There was the sound of small-arms fire.

He went back into the command post.

"Let's go," he ordered.

"I thought you said we couldn't leave until light," Jeanette said.

"If you want to stay, stay," McCoy said, and turned to the North Korean major.

"Let's go, Major," he said, in Russian.

The major got to his feet.

"If you try to run, you will die," McCoy added. "They're not here yet."

It took them forty-five minutes, running with the Jeep's blackout lights, to reach 24th Division Headquarters, and when McCoy asked where the provost marshal was, so that he could not only turn the prisoner over to military police but make sure that he was treated as an officer, he was told that the provost marshal had been pressed into service with the 21st Infantry, and the MPs had been fed into the 21st as replacement riflemen.

Taking the major with them, McCoy drove back to Eighth Army Headquarters in Taegu. There was a POW compound there, and McCoy was able to get rid of the prisoner.

They exchanged salutes. The major then offered his hand. After a moment's hesitation, McCoy took it and wished him good luck.

But despite the "Dai Ichi" orders, he got no further with the Eighth Army signal officer than he had with the Eighth Army headquarters motor officer when he'd arrived in Korea.

"Captain, I don't care if you have orders from General MacArthur himself, I've got Operational Immediate messages in there that should have been sent hours ago, and I will not delay them further so that you can send your report."

And once again he got back into the Jeep.

"Pusan," he said to Zimmerman. "K-1. Their commo is tied up."

"I have dispatches to send," Jeanette protested indignantly.

"I should probably encourage you to wait until the commo has cleared," McCoy said. "But, from the way the signal officer talked, that's not going to happen anytime soon. If you're in a rush to get something out . . ."

" 'Rush' is a massive understatement," Jeanette said,

". . . then I suggest you come back to Tokyo with us."

Jeanette thought that over for a full two seconds.

"OK," she said. "Tokyo it is. I really need a good hot bath anyway."

They departed K-1, outside Pusan, at one o'clock the next morning, aboard an Air Force Douglas C-54.

After they broke ground, McCoy took out his notebook and wrote down the time.

Then he did the arithmetic in his head.

He and Zimmerman had landed in Korea just after midnight on the fifteenth, and they were leaving forty-eight hours later.

But two days was enough. I saw enough to know that the Eighth United States Army really has its ass in a crack, and unless something happens soon, they'll get pushed into the sea at Pusan.

IX

[ONE]
U.S. Navy / Marine Corps Reserve Training Center
St. Louis, Mo.
1025 21 July 1950

Captain George F. Hart, USMCR, commanding Company B, 55th Marines, USMC Reserve, was more or less hiding in his office when First Lieutenant Paul T. Peterson, USMC, Baker Company's inspector/instructor, came in with a copy of the *St. Louis Post-Dispatch* in his hand.

"There's a story in here I thought you would like to see, sir," he said. "Apparently things are pretty bad over there."

"Thank you," Hart said.

By "over there," Peterson obviously meant Korea.

It seemed self-evident that "apparently things are pretty bad over there"; otherwise Company B 55th Marines would not have been called to active duty for "an indefinite period."

The official call had come forty-eight hours, more or less, before.

The Marine Corps had found Captain Hart, USMCR, in the office of the second deputy commissioner of the St. Louis Police Department, discussing a particularly unpleasant murder, that of a teenaged prostitute whose obscenely mutilated body had been found floating in the river.

The deputy commissioner had taken the call, then handed Hart the telephone: "For you, George."

Hart had taken the phone and answered it with the announcement "This had better be pretty goddamned important!"

His caller had chuckled.

"Well, the Marine Corps thinks it is, Captain," he said. "This is Colonel Bartlett, G-1 Section, Headquarters, Marine Corps."

"Yes, sir?"

The second deputy commissioner looked at Hart with unabashed curiosity.

"This is your official notification, Captain," Colonel Bartlett said, "Baker

Company, 55th Marines, USMC Reserve, is called to active duty, for an indefinite period of service, as of 0001 hours today. You and your men are ordered to report to your reserve training station within twenty-four hours prepared for active service. Any questions?"

"No, sir."

"I have a few for you. Unofficially. What would be your estimate of the percentage of your officers and men who will actually report within twenty-four hours?"

"All my officers, sir, and probably ninety-five percent or better of the men."

"And the percentage, officers first, prepared to perform in the jobs?"

"All of them, sir."

"And the men?"

"I have fourteen kids who have yet to go through boot camp, sir. With that exception . . ."

"And your equipment?"

"Well, sir, we have some things that need replacement, but generally, we're in pretty good shape."

"Including weapons?"

"Individual and crew-served weapons are up to snuff, sir. We ran everybody—including the kids who haven't been to boot camp—through the annual qualifying course. Finished last week."

"Really?" Colonel Bartlett asked, obviously surprised. "I didn't know you had a range."

"The police loaned us theirs, sir."

"Then you're really ready to go, aren't you?" Colonel Bartlett asked, rhetorically, as if surprised, or pleased, or both.

"Yes, sir."

"If it were necessary, how soon could you depart your reserve training station?"

"I'd like to have seventy-two hours, sir, but we could leave in forty-eight."

"You're sure?"

"Yes, sir. Sir, may I ask where we're going?"

"That hasn't been decided yet, Captain, but I feel sure you'll be ordered to either Camp Lejeune or Camp Pendleton. There will be official confirmation of your mobilization, by Western Union. And as soon as it is decided where you will go, you will be notified by telephone, with Western Union confirmation to follow. Any other questions?"

"No, sir."

"Good morning, Captain Hart."

"Good morning, sir."

Hart put the telephone down and looked at the second deputy commissioner.

"You've been mobilized?" the commissioner asked.

"As of midnight last night," Hart replied. "It looks as if I'm back in the Marine Corps."

"You have to leave right away? What do you suggest we do about this?" He pointed at the case file.

Hart shrugged.

"I'm in the Marine Corps now, Commissioner," he said. "Right away means I go from here to the Reserve Center."

"I thought they'd give you a couple of weeks to settle your affairs," the commissioner said.

"I didn't," Hart said. "I thought if they called us at all, they would want us as of the day before."

He looked down at the case file, at the gruesome photograph of the victim's body. He tapped the photo.

"Gut feeling: A sicko did this, not a pimp. If he's getting his rocks off this way, he's going to do it again. I was going to suggest setting up a team, under me, of vice guys. Look for the sicko. If I'm not here, that means setting it up under Fred Mayer, because he's a captain, and Teddy, who I presume will take my job, is only a lieutenant. But Fred's a vice cop. . . ."

"I'll set it up under Teddy," the commissioner said. "Mayer will understand."

The hell he will. He'll be pissed and fight Teddy every step of the way, and then when Teddy bags this scumbag, he'll try to take the credit.

But it's really none of my business anymore, not "for an indefinite period."

"That's what I would recommend, Commissioner," Hart said.

The commissioner stood up, holding out his hand.

"Jesus, we can't even throw you a 'goodbye and good luck' party, can we, George?"

"It doesn't look that way, Commissioner."

"Well, Jesus, George! Take care of yourself. Don't do anything heroic!"

"I won't," Hart said.

Company B had a telephone tree call system. When a message had to be delivered as quickly as possible, it began at the top. Hart would call three of his officers. They in turn would call three other people, who would call three other people, until the system had worked its way down through the ranks to the privates.

The system was copied from that used by the St. Louis Police Department, to notify off-duty officers in case of emergency.

When Hart parked his unmarked car behind the Reserve Training Center and went inside wondering when he would return the car to the police garage, Lieutenant Peterson had already "lit the tree" and was making a list of those who hadn't answered their telephone.

Hart changed into utilities, then called Mrs. Louise Schwartz Hart and told her the company had been mobilized, and he didn't know when he could get home, certainly not in the next couple of hours.

"Oh, my God, honey!" Louise said.

"We knew it was coming, baby."

"I was praying it wouldn't," Louise said.

Hart knew she meant just that. She had been on her knees, asking God not to send her husband to war. She did the same thing every time he left the house to go on duty. *Dear God, please send George home alive.*

He called her four hours later and asked her to meet him downtown; he had to turn the car in, and he might as well do it now as later.

By that time, a lot of people had already shown up at the training center.

Peterson told him he had made arrangements with Kramer's Kafeteria, across from the training center, to feed the men, and asked if he should order the breaking out of cots for the men. Hart told him no.

"I don't think we'll get orders to move out tonight, and even if we do, there will be time to light the tree and get people back. Have the first sergeant run a check of their 782 gear, then send them home with orders to be here at six in the morning."

"Oh six hundred, aye, aye, sir."

And then Peterson told him that he had called the *Post-Dispatch* and told them Baker Company had been mobilized, and the *Post-Dispatch* wanted to know when would be a convenient time for them to send a reporter and a photographer to take some pictures.

"Tomorrow morning at nine."

"Oh nine hundred, aye, aye, sir."

When Louise met him in the Dodge at the police garage downtown, she was all dressed up and making a real effort to be cheerful, which made it worse.

"Can you have supper with us?"

"Sure," he said. "But I'll have to spend the night at the training center."

Over supper with Louise and the kids—she made roast pork with oven-roasted potatoes, which she knew he liked—he decided to hell with spending the night at the training center. He would spent his last night in his own bed with his wife; if something came up, they could call him.

Peterson called him at two in the morning to report they'd just had a call.

Five cars had been added to "the Texan," which ran between Chicago and Dallas, and would arrive in St. Louis at 1725 that afternoon. One of the cars was a baggage car. Two were sleepers, and the other two coaches. It might, or might not, be possible that an additional two sleeping cars would be found in Dallas, where all the cars would be attached to a train to Camp Joseph Pendleton. Freight cars not being available at this time, Company B's Jeeps and trucks would have to be left behind.

Furthermore, since it wasn't sure if the dining car on the train could accommodate an unexpected 233 additional passengers, Company B was to be prepared to feed the men C- and/or 10-in-1 rations.

"Orders, sir?"

"First thing in the morning, we'll truck the gear to the station," Hart ordered. "Check with the motor sergeant and see if he can get at least one Jeep—the more the better—in the baggage car."

"I don't believe that's authorized, sir."

"And then ask Karl Kramer what he can do about putting dinner and breakfast together so that we can take that with us, too."

"Sir," Lieutenant Peterson said, "they said confirmation of our orders would follow by Western Union. They're quite specific about feeding C-rations, and leaving the vehicles behind."

"Somehow, I think that telegram is going to get lost in the shuffle," Hart said. "You've been to Pendleton. You want to take long hikes around it?"

"No, sir."

"Light the tree at 0430. I want everybody at the center by 0600."

"Aye, aye, sir."

"I'll be there about five," Hart said.

"Yes, sir."

"You can relax, Paul," Hart said. "I'll take the heat for the Jeeps and the picnic lunches."

He hung the phone up and looked at Louise.

"Honey," he said. "I'd rather say so long here, than have you at the center. I'll be pretty busy. There's really, come to think of it, no point in you driving me there, either. I'll call dispatch and have a black-and-white pick me up and take me."

She nodded, but didn't say anything.

When he arrived at the Navy / Marine Corps Reserve Training Center at 0505, he was surprised to see a Navy staff car parked outside and a Marine major he'd never seen before, wearing a dress blue uniform, waiting for him inside. The major was accompanied by two photographers, one a Marine, the other a sailor.

The major said they had driven down overnight from Chicago, where the major was in charge of Marine Corps recruiting for "the five-state area."

Hart had no idea what that meant.

The major said they were going both to assist the press in their coverage of the departure of Company B for active service, and to cover it for recruiting purposes as well. He had, the major said, already arranged with the mayor and other local dignitaries to be at Union Station when Company B marched up there to board the train.

Hart said nothing, because he didn't trust himself to speak.

His immediate reaction had been that the whole public relations business was bullshit, and he didn't have time to fool with it.

But he was a captain, and captains do what majors want.

After he had had his breakfast, he had accustomed himself to the picture-taking and the parade to the railroad station. The men seemed to like the attention, and it really didn't do any harm.

When he came back from Kramer's Kafeteria, he saw—because he had failed to officially "discourage" it, that the men—and three of his officers—had arrived with wives, mothers, children, cousins, and four rather spectacular girlfriends.

There were a number of things wrong with that, starting with the presence of the civilians interfering with what they had to do before they left, and that most of the wives, mothers, children, and cousins and two of the four spectacular girlfriends had wanted to meet "the skipper."

Plus, of course, he had made Louise stay at home. And she was sure to hear that the families had been at the center. If by no other way than on the pages of the *St. Louis Post-Dispatch,* whose photographers had shown a good deal of interest in the spectacular girlfriends.

He had finally decided to hell with it, he'd call Louise and tell her to come to the Center, and while she was at it, to get the kids out of school, and bring them, too.

"Oh, all right," Louise said. "But I'll have to call Teddy back and tell him not to pick us up here."

Lieutenant Theodosus Korakulous, now Acting Chief, Homicide Bureau, had called Louise and offered to take her and the kids to Union Station.

"If you're with me," Teddy had told Louise, "we can get through the barriers. Traffic told me it looks like a lot of people are going to be there."

He had not wanted to go back into the main room to try to smile confidently at one more wife/mother/spectacular girlfriend and assure her he would take good care of the Family Marine now going off to war.

He wasn't at all sure that he could do that. He was a Marine captain, he had thought at least a dozen times that morning, but he really knew zero, zip, zilch about being a Marine Infantry company commander.

So he'd been more or less hiding in his office when Lieutenant Paul Peterson had come in to show him a story in the *Post-Dispatch* he "thought he'd like to see."

THE MARINES ARE COMING!!!
BUT IN TIME??

By Jeanette Priestly
Chicago Tribune War Correspondent
With the 24th Infantry Division in Korea

Taejon, Korea—July 16—(DELAYED) The Eighth United States Army provided a Jeep for this correspondent to cover the war. Two Marines, saying they needed it more than I did, stole it from me. Within hours, on the front lines of the 34th and 19th Infantry Regiments of the battered and retreating 24th Division, I was glad they had.

When Marine captain Kenneth R. McCoy and Marine Master Gunner Ernest W. Zimmerman commandeered my Jeep, they told me bluntly that this was no place for a woman, and only with great reluctance agreed to take me with them wherever they were going. Their only other option was to leave me on the side of the road. The Marine Corps code of never abandoning their dead or wounded was extended in this case to include a female war correspondent.

Where they were going was the front lines of this war, sent to see how the Eighth U.S. Army and particularly the 24th Division was handling the North Korean invasion.

The Marine Corps sent two experts to investigate. Both McCoy, a lithe, good-looking officer in his late twenties, who is known as "the Killer" in the Marine Corps, and Master Gunner Ernest W. Zimmerman, a stocky, muscular man a few years older—served with the legendary Marine Raiders in World War II.

What they—and this correspondent—saw was not encouraging. Within minutes of arriving at the command post of the 34th Infantry, we learned that in the previous 48 hours, the 21st Infantry, one of the two other regiments making up, with supporting units, the 24th Division, had lost over half its strength in combat.

Worse, their breakup and retreat in the face of the North Korean onslaught had been so quick and complete that the enemy had been able to overrun the 65th Field Artillery Battalion, which had been in their support. Almost a thousand officers and men, and their intact cannon and a large supply of ammunition, fell into the hands of the North Koreans.

There were three North Korean prisoners at the 34th Infantry Command Post. An American patrol had captured them on a reconnaissance mission. They had not been interrogated, as no one in the 34th Infantry spoke Korean, and calls to division headquarters to pick up the prisoners had gone unanswered.

McCoy and Zimmerman—both speak Korean—not only uncovered that one of them, who was wearing a private's uniform, was an officer, but got from him the enemy's intentions for the rest of the day, including the units that would make the attack.

Taking the officer with us, we moved to the 19th Infantry command post, where the attack was supposed to take place at three the next morning. McCoy and Zimmerman went to the regiments' most forward outposts to see if they could take another prisoner.

This correspondent was taken to an artillery forward

observer post by a major, who promised to have me tied up if I tried to go further forward. From there I could see Zimmerman and McCoy making their way to a machine-gun outpost, beyond which was only the enemy.

Through powerful, tripod-mounted binoculars, I could clearly see a half-dozen North Korean soldiers wading across the Kum River. When I asked why the enemy was not being fired upon, the major explained that it apparently had been decided to conserve artillery and machine-gun ammunition for the expected attack.

"And they're out of rifle range," the major added.

At that moment, through my binoculars, I could see McCoy unlimbering the .30-caliber Garand rifle he carried slung from his shoulder. Most Army officers arm themselves with the .45 Colt pistol or the .30-caliber carbine.

"He's wasting his time," the major said.

McCoy opened fire, dropping three, possibly four, of the North Koreans in less than a minute, and sending the survivors scurrying for safety on the far bank of the river.

Darkness fell then, and the major insisted we go back to the regimental CP. Two hours later, when McCoy and Zimmerman hadn't shown up, I grew concerned. The major, without much conviction, told me he was sure they would be all right.

An hour after that, they appeared, calmly leading two North Korean prisoners.

At three in the morning, the North Korean artillery barrage—the terrifying prelude to the attack to follow—began. We were all then sitting on the floor of the command post. McCoy calmly took a long black cigar from his pack. Zimmerman looked at it hungrily. McCoy took a lethal-looking dagger from its sheath, strapped it to his left arm, calmly cut the cigar in half, and gave half to Zimmerman.

The artillery and mortar barrage lasted an hour. The only thing McCoy had to say, a professional judgment, was that some of "the incoming sounds like 105," which meant the North Koreans were using the 105-mm howitzers captured from the 65th Field Artillery against the 19th Infantry.

Shortly afterward, McCoy went outside the CP, listened in the darkness to the sounds of the battle developing, and returned to announce that it was time for us to go.

Taking the North Korean officer prisoner with us, we drove—using blackout lights only—back to the 24th Division headquarters. McCoy learned that he could not turn the prisoner over to the POW compound there because there was none. The military police who would normally run the compound had been pressed into service as replacement rifleman. The provost marshal himself had been pressed into service as an infantry officer.

We then drove back to Eighth Army headquarters in Taegu, where McCoy was finally able to turn the North Korean officer over to the military police. They exchanged salutes and shook hands.

Communications at Eighth Army headquarters were overwhelmed by high-priority messages reporting to Tokyo the disaster that was taking place all over the peninsula. McCoy realized that he could deliver his report to his superiors in Tokyo quicker if he went to

Japan, rather than waiting for Eighth Army to find time to transmit it, and announced he was going to Pusan to see if he could find a plane.

There was zero chance that this reporter's dispatches could be transmitted from Taejon, so I went with him. We drove to Pusan and flew out for Tachikawa Air Base, outside Tokyo, just after midnight on an Air Force C-54.

In Tokyo, we learned not only that the 19th and 34th Infantry Regiments had been forced to "withdraw" to new positions farther south, but that the 24th division commander, Major General William F. Dean, had not been seen since he had personally gone out with a bazooka to use against North Korean tanks, and it was feared that he had been captured or killed.

McCoy and Zimmerman are by nature taciturn men, and they certainly were not about to offer their opinion of what they saw to a war correspondent. But it wasn't at all hard, during the time we spent together, to read their faces. And what their faces said—the individual courage of the officers and men aside—was that the

> Eighth United States Army was not prepared for this war, is taking a terrible beating, and may not be able to halt the North Koreans.
>
> The Marines are coming. The question is, will they get here in time? And will they be able to do a better job than the Eighth Army has so far?

"What do you think, sir?" Lieutenant Peterson asked when Hart had finished reading the article.

"I know the two Marines she was with," Hart replied, thinking out loud. Then he looked at Peterson. "I don't know what to think, Paul."

"You know them, sir?"

"In the last war, they called people like that 'the Old Breed,' " Hart said. "I wonder what they call them now."

[TWO]
Office of the Senior Inspector/Instructor
El Toro Marine Corps Air Station, California
1025 21 July 1950

Brigadier General Lawrence C. Taylor, USMC, whose promotion to flag officer rank had occurred shortly before his graduation from the U.S. Army War College on 30 May, had elected to take thirty days' leave before reporting for duty at Headquarters, USMC.

For one thing, the year had been a rough one, and there hadn't been much time to spend with his family. For another, unless he took some leave, he was going to lose it, as regulations dictated the forfeiture of leave in excess of sixty days. Finally, he suspected that as a brand-new one-star, there would not be an opportunity to take much—if any—leave in the next year.

Both he and Margaret, his wife, had Scottish roots, and had always wanted to see Scotland, so they talked it over, decided that they could afford it, and that it was really now or never, and went.

It was not as easy for him as he first thought it would be. It was necessary for him, as a serving officer, to get permission to leave the country. There were forms to fill out, listing where he wanted to go and why, and permission didn't come when he expected it to, and he had to spend time on the phone to Eighth & Eye to make sure he would have permission in time to leave.

Permission came seventy-two hours before they were scheduled to leave. That just about gave them enough time to leave the kids with Margaret's mother in upstate New York and get to New York for the TWA flight to Scotland. They flew on a Trans-Global Airways Lockheed Constellation, which was really very nice, and on the way decided all the paperwork was worthwhile. It was going to be sort of like a second honeymoon.

On 28 June, when he learned of the North Korean invasion in the Glasgow newspaper, he had—with more than a little difficulty—managed to get through on the telephone to Eighth & Eye and asked if he should report for duty. He was told that would not be necessary.

And when he reported for duty, they didn't seem to know what to do with him, except to suggest that it might not be wise "in the present circumstances" to plan on spending two years at Eighth & Eye, which was the original plan.

General Taylor was thus able to consider the possibility—slight but real—that, should there be a war and an expansion of the Marine Corps, he might find himself serving with a Marine division in the field, or in command of a base—Parris Island, for example, while the incumbent there went off to a field command—instead of shuffling paper at Eighth & Eye.

That fascinating prospect was shattered when General Cates, on 13 July, summoned him to his office and told him (a) that on the fourteenth he was going to issue a confidential order to the Corps to prepare for mobilization and (b) that he thought General Taylor could be of most use to the Corps by going to the West Coast and doing what he could to facilitate the mobilization of the Marine Corps Reserve.

General Taylor took a plane that night for Camp Pendleton, with Margaret and the kids to follow by auto. The West Coast assignment was temporary duty, which meant that their furniture would be stored, rather than shipped to California.

At Camp Pendleton, Brigadier General Clyde W. Dawkins, the deputy commanding general, told General Taylor he was glad he was there, as he expected there would be "administrative problems" in the mobilization of Marine Reserve Aviation, and anything that Taylor could do to "sort things out" would be a real contribution.

General Taylor had not met General Dawkins previously, which he supposed was because Dawkins was wearing the golden wings of a Marine aviator, and Taylor had come up through artillery. He also wondered privately why Dawkins, an aviator, was deputy commander of Pendleton, which was not a Marine aviation facility. Logic would seem to dictate that a Marine aviator would be more suited to "sort out" the "administrative problems" involved in mobilizing Marine aviation, and someone such as himself, an experienced ground officer, would be better suited to be the deputy commander of Camp Pendleton.

General Dawkins said that it would probably be best that General Taylor "pitch his tent" at the El Toro Marine Corps Air Station, not far from Pendleton, rather than on the Pendleton Reservation.

"Pendleton is going to be one huge Chinese fire drill when the mobilization starts," Dawkins said. "You'll be more productive there than here. There's a light colonel there—John X. O'Halloran, good man—as inspector/instructor. You can use his office and people."

At El Toro, General Taylor was given quarters in a small building set aside for visiting senior officers. As soon as he unpacked, he went into the small town of El Toro itself to find someplace for Margaret and the kids. He quickly learned that there was the opposite of an abundance of furnished rental houses or apartments in the area, and what was available was priced accordingly.

In desperation, he rented a small, unattractive apartment that cost 125 percent of his housing allowance, and one which he knew would disappoint Margaret and the kids. They'd had really nice quarters at the War College, and the apartment was a real comedown.

And then he went to work at El Toro to prepare for the mobilization, which was almost certain to happen.

Lieutenant Colonel O'Halloran, USMC, the inspector/instructor, was a muscular, red-haired Irishman. He wore an Annapolis ring, which immediately made General Taylor feel confident in him, even if he was also wearing the gold wings of a Marine aviator. Five minutes into their first conversation, they were agreed that calling an immediate meeting of the commanding officers of the three reserve squadrons on the West Coast to bring them up to speed on what was very likely going to happen was the first thing to do.

Two of the three squadron commanders showed up as ordered at 0800 19 July. The third—the commanding officer of VMF-243—did not. His name was Major Malcolm S. Pickering.

Lieutenant Colonel O'Halloran was not at the meeting either. He sent word—which was not the same thing as requesting permission to do so—that he was going to spend the morning checking on enlisted housing for the flood of reservists soon to arrive at El Toro.

Since he could not ask O'Halloran what he recommended should be done about the officer who had not, in Marine parlance, "been at the prescribed place at the prescribed time in the properly appointed uniform" and was thus technically absent without leave, General Taylor inquired of Technical Sergeant Saul Cohen, the senior staff NCO of the I & I staff, if he had been able to contact Major Pickering.

"Not exactly, sir. I left word at his office to tell him as soon as he got back."

"Back from where?"

"No telling, sir. Major Pickering travels a lot."

"And the executive officer of VMF-243? Did you contact him?"

"Same story, sir. As I understand it, he's with Major Pickering. Permission to speak out of school, sir?"

"Go ahead."

"VMF-243's the best of our squadrons. They just about aced the annual inspection. And I'm sure Major Pickering will be here when he's really needed."

"Just to remove any possible misunderstanding, Sergeant," General Taylor said, "I have the authority to determine when the major's presence is really needed."

"Yes, sir."

The meeting with the other two squadron commanders did not go well. Neither of them made much of an effort to conceal their opinion that they had developed a good working relationship with the inspector/instructor and the last thing they needed when they were about to get called back to the Corps was to have to answer dumb questions posed by some strange brigadier who wasn't even an aviator.

General Taylor told Technical Sergeant Cohen to make sure there was a note in Major Pickering's box at the Bachelor Officer's Quarters instructing him to report to him, no matter what the hour, as soon as he got to El Toro.

"Sir, Major Pickering doesn't use the BOQ. But I'll try to get word to him at the Coronado Beach."

"The Coronado Beach? The hotel?"

"Yes, sir. VFM-243—the officers and the staff non-coms—stay there when they're on El Toro for training. Buck sergeants and under stay on El Toro in the barracks."

"Let me be sure I understand you, Sergeant. You're telling me that the officers and staff noncommissioned officers of VMF-243 have been staying in a hotel when they're on active duty for training?"

"Yes, sir."

"How can they afford that?"

"I think the hotel gives them a special rate, sir."

At this point, General Taylor told Sergeant Cohen to bring him the records of both Major Pickering and Captain Stuart W. James, the executive officer of VFM-243.

It didn't take him long to learn that neither officer had come into the Marine Corps—as he had—from the United States Naval Academy. Major Pickering had graduated from Harvard, and gone through Officer Candidate School. Captain James had gone through the Navy V-12 program at Yale, which earned him a commission on his graduation.

Both had good records in World War II. Major Pickering had become an ace on Guadalcanal, and one more downing of an enemy aircraft would have made Captain Stuart an ace. James had not been on Guadalcanal, but flipping between the records, General Taylor learned that both had been assigned to the same squadron later in the war, during the last campaigns, including the invasion of Okinawa.

Both had had some problems living up the standards expected of officers and gentlemen. Pickering's record included three letters of official reprimand for conduct unbecoming an officer and a gentleman, and Stuart's record had two such letters. One of them made reference to joint action. They both had been reprimanded for using provoking language to a shore patrol officer then acting in his official capacity.

When he saw that, since their release from active duty after World War II, both officers had been employed by Trans-Global Airways, and that both had been in VMF-243 since its organization as a reserve component of the Corps, it was not hard for General Taylor to form an initial opinion of the two:

Hotshot, Ivy League–educated, Marine fighter pilots, wartime buddies who had probably joined the Marine Corps reserve because it gave them the opportunity simultaneously to continue flying high performance aircraft and get paid for doing so. They had apparently not been able to secure civilian employment as pilots. Trans-Global Airways was employing both as "flight coordinators." General Taylor wasn't sure what a "flight coordinator" was, but it didn't seem to imply that either officer was involved in actual flight.

At 1015, Sergeant Cohen knocked at the door of General Taylor's—until recently, Lt. Col. John X. O'Halloran's—office, was granted permission to enter, entered, and reported that both Major Pickering and Captain Stuart were in the office.

They were supposed to be here forty-eight—no, fifty—hours ago.

"Sergeant, will you please find Colonel O'Halloran and ask him to drop whatever he's doing and come here?"

"Aye, aye, sir."

When Sergeant Cohen left, General Taylor got a quick look through the door and saw Major Pickering and Captain Stuart. They were in flight clothing, that is to say, brownish, multipocketed coveralls and fur-collared leather jackets. So far as General Taylor knew, the wearing of flight clothing was proscribed when not actually engaged in flight operations.

Both officers were bent over a newspaper, spread out on Technical Sergeant Cohen's desk.

There was also reverse observation. One of them looked through the open door, saw General Taylor, elbowed the other, who then had a moment's glance at General Taylor before Sergeant Cohen closed the door.

Lieutenant Colonel O'Halloran came into his old office by a side door three minutes later.

"I'm sorry if I interrupted something, Colonel, but I thought you should be here for this," General Taylor said.

"No problem, sir. For what, sir?"

General Taylor pressed the lever on his intercom box.

"Sergeant Cohen, would you ask Major Pickering and Captain Stuart to come in, please?"

After a polite knock at the door, the two officers entered. The taller of them had the newspaper tucked under his arm, where his cover would normally be. His cover, if any, was not in sight.

"Good morning, sir," he said to General Taylor, adding, "How goes it, Red?" to Lieutenant Colonel O'Halloran.

"You are?" General Taylor inquired, somewhat icily.

"General Taylor," O'Halloran said. "This is Major Malcolm S. Pickering."

Major Pickering offered General Taylor his hand.

"How do you do, sir?" he asked, adding, "My friends call me 'Pick.' "

General Taylor was about to comment that he had virtually no interest in what Major Pickering's friends called him, when Pickering went on:

"You've seen the paper, Red?"

O'Halloran shook his head, "no."

"Guess who's already in Korea?" Pickering said.

O'Halloran indicated by gesture and shrug that he had no idea.

"The Killer," Major Pickering said. "The story's on page one."

"No kidding?" O'Halloran said, as he reached for the newspaper. He then remembered General Taylor, and added: "Major Pickering is referring to a mutual friend, sir. A Marine officer."

"Is that so?"

"Killer McCoy, sir," O'Halloran said.

"What I really would like to know, Colonel, as I'm sure you would, is why Major Pickering is some fifty hours late in reporting as ordered."

"I'm sorry about that, sir," Major Pickering said. "When I got the word, I came—Stu and I came—as quickly as we could."

"And that took fifty hours?"

"Actually, sir—I figured it out just a couple of minutes ago—from the time we got the word, it took us thirty-one hours."

"Where were you? In Siberia?"

"Scotland, sir."

"Scotland?"

"Prestwick, Scotland, sir."

"I reviewed your records a day or so ago, Major. I found nothing indicating that you had permission to leave the continental United States."

"We don't need permission, sir," Pickering said. "We've got a waiver."

"That's the case, General," Colonel O'Halloran said.

"I'm fascinated," General Taylor said. "Who granted a waiver? Why?"

"Eighth and Eye, sir. They chose to interpret the regulation as not applying to us. As much time as we spend out of the country, it would be a real pain in the ass for them, as well as for us, to have to fill out those permission requests, and go through the routine, every time we left."

"I see. Colonel O'Halloran, I assume you're familiar with this?"

"Yes, sir, I am."

"Why didn't you inform me?"

"Sir, the subject never came up."

"Why, Major, do you spend as much time as you tell me you do out of the country?"

It was obvious from the look in Major Pickering's eyes that he was surprised at the question.

"Sir, we're in the airline business," Pickering said.

"And your duties as 'flight coordinator' require extensive travel outside the country? What exactly is a flight coordinator?"

For the first time, there was a crack in what General Taylor thought of as an offensive degree of self-confidence in Major Pickering's demeanor.

Major Pickering looked nervously at Lieutenant Colonel O'Halloran.

"In the case of Captain James and myself, General," he said, carefully, "it means that we sort of supervise the flight activities of Trans-Global Airways."

"Sort of?"

"Sir," Colonel O'Halloran said, "Major Pickering is president of Trans-Global airways and chief pilot. And you're what, Stu?"

"Standardization pilot," James replied.

President and chief pilot? Standardization pilot? That's not what it says in their records.

"Major, I'm a little curious. Why does it say 'flight coordinator' on your records?"

"A year or so ago, sir, there was concern that, in the event of mobilization, some pilots would try to get out of it by saying that they were essential to an essential industry. The phrase 'airline pilot' raised a red flag at Eighth and Eye. So we got around that by changing our job titles."

"You didn't consider that deceptive? Perhaps even knowingly causing a false statement or document to be issued?"

"Well, sir, since it was not my intention—or Captain James's—to try to get out of being mobilized, we didn't think it mattered."

"And your employer went along with this deception?"

"Sir, I figured I could call myself a stewardess if I wanted, and it got the chair-warmers at Eighth and Eye off my back."

Prior to his attendance at the War College, General Taylor had spent a three-year tour in administrative duties at Eighth and Eye.

It is beyond comprehension that an Annapolis man, even a Marine aviator, would have knowledge of something like this, and not only do nothing about it, but, by not doing anything about it, lend it respectability.

"Colonel O'Halloran," General Taylor said. "I will wish to discuss this with you at some length."

"Aye, aye, sir."

"Major Pickering, it is my belief that your squadron will shortly be called to active duty. . . ."

"As of 23 July, sir. And I wanted to talk to you about that."

"The twenty-third?" Colonel O'Halloran asked. "You're sure about that, Pick?"

Pickering nodded.

"I'm sure, Red."

Majors do not call lieutenant colonels by their nicknames, certainly not in the presence of a flag officer he has never seen before. O'Halloran should have called him on that. But flag officers do not question, much less reprimand, lieutenant colonels in the presence of majors. I will deal with that later.

"You seem to be privy to information Headquarters, USMC has not yet seen fit to share with me, Major," General Taylor said.

"Yes, sir, I probably am. The warning order will be issued tomorrow, with the order itself coming the next day."

"How do you know that, Major?"

"I'm not at liberty to tell you that, sir. But I'm sure General Dawkins will confirm the mobilization dates."

"General Dawkins told you, is that what you're saying?"

"No, sir. I happened to be with General Dawkins when we both learned about the dates."

"From whom?" General Taylor snapped.

He heard the tone of his voice and was thus aware that he was a hairbreadth from losing his temper.

"Sir, that's what I'm not at liberty to tell you."

"Can you tell me what you were doing with General Dawkins?"

"Yes, sir. I knew the mobilization was coming, and I wanted to ask General Dawkins about getting a week, ten days' delay for Captain James and myself before reporting."

"And General Dawkins's reaction to this request?"

"He said it made sense to him, and you would be the man to see, sir."

"You have to fly off to Scotland again," General Taylor heard himself saying, "and reporting for active duty in two days would be inconvenient. Is that what you're saying, Major?"

Again there was a visible crack in Major Pickering's composure.

"Sir, what I told The Dawk was—"

" 'The Dawk'? 'The Dawk'?" General Taylor exploded. "Do I have to remind you, Major, that you're speaking of a general officer?"

"Sorry, sir. That slipped out," Pickering said. "General, I'm not trying to get out of mobilization. . . ."

"You just told me you wanted a delay!"

General Taylor was aware he was almost shouting, which meant that he was losing/had lost his temper, and this made him even more angry.

"General," Colonel O'Halloran said. "I'm sure Major Pickering intended no disrespect to General Dawkins, sir. Sir, both Major Pickering and I flew for General Dawkins out of Fighter One on Guadalcanal . . ."

"Is that so?"

". . . and everyone there referred to then Lieutenant Colonel Dawkins as "The Dawk" in much the same respectful way one refers to the commanding officer as 'the old man' or 'the skipper,' sir."

Taylor glowered at O'Halloran, but didn't reply directly.

"Tell me, Major Pickering," General Taylor said, "why you think it would be to the advantage of the Marine Corps to delay for a week or ten days your recall to active duty? And that of Captain James?"

"Sir, with your permission, Captain James and I will catch the 0800 Trans-Global flight to Tokyo tomorrow morning. There's a lot we can do if we get over there now, before the squadron. . . ."

"What makes you think your squadron will be sent to Korea? More information to which I'm not privy?"

"No, sir, but VMF-243 is the best prepared squadron on the West Coast. We're ready to go, sir. I think Colonel O'Halloran will confirm that."

"Yes, sir, VFF-243 can be ready to fly onto a carrier twenty-four hours after mobilization," O'Halloran said.

"And if James and I can get over there now, there's all sorts of things we can do for the squadron. Or squadrons, if they decide to send more than one right away. And then we would just go on active duty to coincide with the arrival of the carrier in Kobe."

"Sir, with respect," O'Halloran said. "What Major Pickering suggests makes a good deal of sense. There are a large number of things—"

General Taylor silenced Colonel O'Halloran by raising his hand.

He did not trust himself to speak. No officer, much less a flag officer, should lose his temper in the presence of subordinates.

After a moment, he decided he had his temper sufficiently under control.

"Major," he said, as calmly as he could manage, "would you and Captain James please step outside for a minute? I'd like a word with Colonel O'Halloran."

"Yes, sir," Major Pickering said, and nodded his head to Captain James to precede him out of the room.

General Taylor waited until the door had closed behind them, then looked at Colonel O'Halloran, who was smiling at him.

"Major Pickering is an interesting officer, isn't he, General?"

" 'Interesting' is an interesting choice of word, Colonel," General Taylor said. "Let me ask you—"

The telephone on what had been Lieutenant Colonel O'Halloran's desk rang. O'Halloran picked it up.

"Colonel O'Halloran," he said, and then: "Yes, sir. He's right here."

He handed the telephone to General Taylor.

"It's General Dawkins for you, sir," he said.

General Taylor took the telephone.

"Good morning, General," he said.

"You getting settled in all right over there?" Dawkins asked.

"I'm working on that, General."

"Did Pick Pickering—Major Pickering—show up there yet?"

"Yes, he did. As a matter of fact, General, he was fifty hours late in reporting."

"He said he was in Scotland," Dawkins said. "He was just in here, suggesting that his recall be delayed for a week or ten days so he could go to Japan and set things up before his squadron gets there."

"He so informed me."

"I told him that you were the person to see about that, but after he left, I gave it a second thought."

"I see," General Taylor said. "Colonel O'Halloran and I were just about to discuss that—"

"I decided I could probably handle it easier than you could," Dawkins interrupted. "I just got off the horn with Eighth and Eye. When the mobilization order comes down, it will state that Pickering and his exec, Captain James, will enter upon active duty effective on the arrival in the Far East of VMF-243, or on 21 August, whichever occurs first."

"I see," General Taylor said. "Isn't that a little unusual, General?"

"These are unusual times, Taylor, and Pickering is an unusual man."

"I'm sure you gave the matter thought, General," Taylor said.

"Actually, it didn't require much thought," Dawkins said. "The question was the best way to do it. I have to run, Taylor. Let's see if we can find time to have lunch."

The line went dead.

Taylor put the telephone in its cradle and looked at O'Halloran.

"General Dawkins," he reported evenly, "has arranged for Major Pickering and Captain James to enter upon active duty on the arrival of VMF-243 in the Far East, or on 21 August, whichever occurs first."

"Yes, sir?"

"In these circumstances, I suggest that we call him back in here and so inform him. Wouldn't you agree?"

"Yes, sir."

"Tell me, Colonel, is that the way things are normally done in Marine aviation?"

"Well, sometimes, sir, we bend the regulations a little to get the job done."

"So I am learning," General Taylor said.

[THREE]
The Supreme Commander's Conference Room
Headquarters, Supreme Commander, Allied Powers
The Dai Ichi. Building
Tokyo, Japan
1035 25 July 1950

The briefer, a natty, crew-cutted major, turned from the map on which he had just located the positions of the North Korean forces advancing on Pusan, came almost to attention with his pointer held along his trouser leg, and, addressing Major General Charles A. Willoughby, who sat at the end of the table closest to the maps, said, "That's all I have, sir."

"Do you have any questions, sir?" Willoughby asked.

General of the Army Douglas MacArthur, the Supreme Commander, who was sitting at the far end of the long, highly polished table, took a long pull at a thin black cigar and after a moment, shook his head, "no."

"Anyone else?" Willoughby asked. He looked at Major General Edward M. Almond, the SCAP chief of staff who was at the left side of the table next to MacArthur. "General Almond?"

Almond shook his head, "no."

"General Stratemeyer?"

Lieutenant General George E. Stratemeyer, the senior Air Force officer on the SCAP staff, who was sitting next to Almond, shook his head, "no."

"Admiral Joy?"

Rear Admiral C. Turner Joy, the senior Naval officer on the SCAP staff, who was sitting across the table from Willoughby's own empty chair, shook his head, "no."

"General Whitney?"

Major General Courtney Whitney, the SCAP G-3, who was sitting next to Stratemeyer, shook his head, "no."

Willoughby looked at Brigadier General Fleming Pickering, who was sitting next to Stratemeyer and across from Almond.

"Thank you, Major," Willoughby said. "That will be all." Then he added, "Leave the map," and took his seat.

"Yes, sir," the major said, and walked out of the room.

General Almond got to his feet and walked to the end of the table, so that he was standing in front of the map.

"Sir?" he asked MacArthur.

"General Pickering," MacArthur asked, "have you anything to add?"

Brigadier General Fleming Pickering rose.

"No, sir," he said.

Was that simply courtesy on El Supremo's part? Or was he letting Willoughby know he shouldn't ignore me?

"Then I believe our business is concluded," MacArthur intoned, getting to his feet. "Thank you, gentlemen."

The dozen officers at the table, all general or flag officers, rose to their feet as MacArthur walked to the door that led to his office and passed through it.

General Almond pushed the map back into its storage space.

The other senior officers began to stuff the documents they had brought to the briefing back into their briefcases.

Almond sensed Pickering's eyes on him and walked to him.

"You look as if you have something on your mind, General," he said.

Pickering met Almond's eyes.

"I didn't think the briefing was the place to bring this up . . ."

"But?" Almond asked.

"I had people on the wharf in Pusan yesterday when the 29th Infantry debarked from Okinawa," Pickering said. "They told me the regiment has only two battalions . . ."

"Peacetime TO and E," Almond said. "You told me the 1st Marine Division's regiments were similarly understrength."

"Yes, sir," Pickering said. "General, my people . . ."

"You're speaking of . . . your aide-de-camp?" Almond asked, a slight smile on his face.

Pickering nodded. "Yes, I am."

Almond had been present at a luncheon meeting when MacArthur had announced that Pickering was going to have to do something about an aide-de-camp.

"I have one, sir," Pickering said. "Captain McCoy."

That had not been the truth, the whole truth, and nothing but the truth. Pickering did not have an aide-de-camp. He didn't think he needed one. But he knew MacArthur well enough to know that if MacArthur thought he needed an aide-de-camp, and there was no suitable young Marine officer available, he would give him a suitable young Army officer "for the present."

There were a number of things wrong with that, starting with the fact that any bright young officer assigned to SCAP would naturally feel his loyalties lay with SCAP—either *the* SCAP, MacArthur, or SCAP generally, which would include Almond, the SCAP chief of staff, and Willoughby, the SCAP G-2, rather than solely to Brigadier General Fleming Pickering.

That was understandable. The Supreme Commander was the Supreme Commander. Supreme Commanders were in command of everything, especially including all one-star generals.

And MacArthur and Willoughby—and possibly Almond, although Pickering wasn't sure about Almond—had done a number of things, possibly simply courtesy, to make Pickering seem like, feel like, a member of the SCAP staff.

He had been given an Army staff car (a Buick, normally reserved for major generals or better, rather than a Ford or Chevrolet) and a driver, for one thing. He had been given an office, staffed by a master sergeant and two other enlisted men, in the Dai Ichi Building, "on the SCAP's floor."

A seat had been reserved for him at the daily briefings/staff conference. He had been offered quarters, in sort of a compound set aside for senior officers, and two orderlies to staff it.

This would have been very nice if Pickering had been assigned to the SCAP staff, but that wasn't the case. Officially, he was the Assistant Director of the Central Intelligence Agency for Asia. The CIA was not under MacArthur's command, although the CIA station chief in Tokyo was under mandate to "coordinate with SCAP."

More than that, Pickering was under orders from the President of the United States to report directly to him his assessment of all things in the Far East, including General of the Army Douglas MacArthur.

Pickering had quickly learned that the CIA Tokyo station chief (whose cover was senior economic advisor to SCAP) had quarters in the VIP compound, a staff car, and considered himself a member of the SCAP staff.

If he could have, Pickering would have relieved the station chief on the spot for permitting himself to be sucked into the MacArthur magnetic field. The CIA was not supposed to be subordinate to the local military commander or his staff. But he realized that would have been counterproductive. For one thing, it would have waved a red flag in MacArthur's face. For another, he didn't know who he could get to replace him.

Pickering had declined the VIP quarters, saying that he was more comfortable in the Imperial Hotel. When Willoughby heard about that, he replaced the driver of Pickering's staff car with an agent of the Counterintelligence Corps wearing a sergeant's uniform, and assigned other CIC agents, in civilian clothing, to provide around-the-clock security for Pickering in the Imperial Hotel.

Willoughby's rationale for that was that the Assistant Director of the CIA for Asia obviously needed to be protected. That was possibly true, but it also meant that CIC agents, who reported to Willoughby, had Pickering under observation around the clock.

Pickering typed out his own reports to President Truman, personally encrypted them, and personally took them to the communications center in the Dai Ichi Building, waited until their receipt had been acknowledged by Colonel Ed Banning at Camp Pendleton, and then personally burned them.

When Pickering told MacArthur that he already had an aide, Captain McCoy, General Willoughby had been visibly startled to hear the name, and Almond had picked up on that, too.

"The same McCoy?" MacArthur had inquired.

"Yes, sir."

"Ned," MacArthur said to Almond, "during the war, when we were setting up our guerrilla operations in the Philippines, Pickering set up an operation to establish contact with Americans who had refused to surrender. He sent a young Marine officer—this Captain McCoy—into Mindanao by submarine. Outstanding young officer. I personally decorated him with the Silver Star for that."

That was even less the truth, the whole truth, and nothing but the truth. MacArthur had originally flatly stated that guerrilla operations in the Philippines were impossible.

President Roosevelt had learned there had been radio contact with a reserve officer named Fertig on Mindanao. Fertig, a lieutenant colonel, had promoted himself to brigadier general and named himself commanding general of U.S. forces in the Philippines. MacArthur and Willoughby had let it be known they believed the poor fellow had lost his senses, and repeated their firm belief that guerrilla action in the Philippine Islands was, regrettably, impossible.

Roosevelt had personally ordered Pickering to send someone onto the Japanese-occupied island of Mindanao to get the facts. Lieutenant Kenneth R. McCoy, Gunnery Sergeant Ernest Zimmerman, and twenty-year-old Staff Sergeant Stephen M. Koffler, a radio operator, had infiltrated Mindanao by submarine and found Fertig.

McCoy's report that Fertig was not only sane (he had promoted himself to brigadier general on the reasonable assumption that few, if any, American or Philippine soldiers who had escaped Japanese capture would rush to place themselves under the command of a reserve lieutenant colonel) but prepared, if supplied, to do the Japanese considerable harm. Roosevelt had ordered that Fertig be supplied. At that point, MacArthur had begun to call Fertig and his U.S. forces in the Philippines "my guerrillas in the Philippines."

When the U.S. Army stormed ashore later in the war on Mindanao, Fertig was waiting for them with than 30,000 armed, uniformed, and trained guerrillas. USFIP even had a band. In very real terms, except for artillery and tanks, USFIP was an American Army Corps. Army Corps are commanded by lieutenant generals. MacArthur continued to refer to Fertig as "that reserve lieutenant colonel."

In the face of that gross distortion of the facts, Pickering had felt considerably less guilty about saying McCoy was his aide.

"And what did your 'aide-de-camp' have to say about what he saw on the wharf at Pusan?" Almond asked, smiling.

"General, this was an observation by an experienced officer, not, per se, a criticism," Pickering said.

Almond nodded his understanding.

"McCoy said that most of the enlisted men are fresh from basic training, and that the officers and noncoms are also mostly replacements. There has been no opportunity for them to train together, nor has there been an opportunity for them to fire or zero their weapons."

Almond looked pained.

"Zimmerman checked their crew-served weapons," Pickering went on. "He knows about weapons. The 29th has been issued new .50-caliber Browning machine guns; they were still in cosmoline when they were off-loaded from the ships in Pusan. None of their mortars have been test-fired."

"God!" Almond said.

"The 29th was ordered to move immediately to Chinju, where it will be attached to the 19th Infantry of the 24th Division. The 19th has taken a shellacking in the last couple of days—you heard the G-3 briefing just now. In these circumstances, McCoy doesn't think that either unit is going to be able to offer much real resistance to the North Koreans."

Almond was silent a moment.

"I agree. That information would not have contributed anything to the staff conference, in the sense that anything could be done about it by anybody at that table. But I thank you for it."

"I thought you should know, sir."

"What Walker is doing is trying to buy enough time to set up a perimeter around Pusan, and hold that until we can augment our forces."

"I understand, sir," Pickering said.

"Between you and me, Pickering, that's all that can be done at the moment.

The arrival of the Marine Brigade will strengthen the perimeter, of course, and the 27th Infantry is about to arrive. I understand they're better prepared to fight than, for example, the 29th is."

Pickering didn't reply.

"Maybe we'll get lucky," Almond said, as if to himself. And then he added, "Your 'aide.' Is he still in Korea?"

"No, sir. He came in early this morning."

"I'd like to talk to him," Almond said. "Would that be possible?"

"Yes, sir. Of course. You tell me where and when."

"Would it be an imposition if I came by the Imperial?"

"No, sir. Of course not."

"I have to see General MacArthur," Almond said. "He normally sends for me fifteen, twenty minutes after the staff meeting. And there's no telling how long that will take; he's doing the preliminary planning for the amphibious operation up the peninsula. But when that's over, I think I'll be free. If I'm not, I'll call. That OK with you?"

"That's fine with me, sir. McCoy will be waiting for you."

"I don't want to make talking to him official," Almond said. "You understand?"

"Yes, sir."

"Then I'll see you in an hour or two," Almond said, offered his hand, and left the conference room.

[ONE]
The Dewey Suite
The Imperial Hotel
Tokyo, Japan
1105 25 July 1950

When Captain Malcolm S. Pickering of Trans-Global Airways started to walk down the corridor toward the Dewey Suite, he was mildly curious to see an American in a business suit—a young one, not more than twenty-one, he thought—sitting in an armchair in the corridor reading the *Stars & Stripes*.

He had apparently been there some time, for on a table beside him was a coffee thermos and the remains of breakfast pastries.

Pick just had time to guess, *some kind of guard,* when there was proof. The young man stood up and blocked his way.

"May I help you, sir?" he asked.

"I'm going in there," Pick said, pointing at the next door down the corridor.

"May I ask why, sir?"

"I'm here to see General Pickering."

"Are you expected, sir?"

"No, I'm not."

"Sir, I'm sorry. . . ."

"Knock on the door and tell General Pickering that Captain Pickering requests an audience," Pick ordered, sounding more like a Marine officer than an airline pilot. He heard himself, and added, "I'm his son. It'll be all right."

After a moment's indecision, the young man went to the door to the Dewey Suite and knocked.

Captain Kenneth R. McCoy, in khakis, tieless, opened the door, then made a gesture to the young man to permit Pick to pass.

He entered the room. His father, dressed like McCoy, was looking at a map spread out on a table in the middle of the sitting room. He smiled when he saw his son.

"When did you get in?" he asked.

"A couple of hours ago. I dropped Stu James off at the Hokkaido and then came here. What's with the guard?"

"That's General Willoughby's idea," Fleming Pickering said.

"Oh?"

"He said it was his responsibility to see that 'someone like me' was 'secure.'"

"Secure from what?"

"Captain McCoy," Pickering said, wryly, "who some people suspect is a cynic, suggests that General Willoughby wants to keep an eye on me for *his* security. Anyway, when I declined to move into some officers' compound where he could keep an eye on me, he sent me a guard here for the same purpose. Guards, plural. There's some young man sitting out there around the clock."

"I thought maybe he was there to protect our well publicized hero—Dead-Eye McCoy—from a horde of adoring fans."

General Pickering chuckled.

"You saw the story, I gather?"

"The whole world has seen the story," Pick said. "I understand the recruiters have long lines of eager young men wanting to emulate him."

"I knew that fucking woman was trouble the first time I saw her," McCoy said.

"Speaking of women, Dead-Eye," Pick said, "you better clean up your language and send the native girls back to the village. Your wife's about to arrive."

"I hope you're kidding," General Pickering said.

"Uh-uh," Pick said. "Expect her in seventy-two hours, more or less."

"Jesus, couldn't you talk her out of it?" McCoy asked.

"Your wife took lessons in determination from his wife," Pick said, nodding at his father. "I tried, honest to God."

"I won't be here," McCoy said.

"Ken's been sort of commuting to Korea," General Pickering said. "It's the only way I can get accurate information in less than a week."

"And how are things in the 'Land of the Morning Calm'?"

"Not good, Pick," General Pickering said.

"Well, fear not, the Marines are coming," Pick said. "You know there's a provisional brigade on the high seas, for Kobe, I suppose?"

"They're being diverted to Pusan," General Pickering said. "We found out yesterday."

"If we still hold Pusan when they get there," McCoy said.

"Are things that bad?" Pick asked.

"Yeah, they are," McCoy said, matter-of-factly.

"What shape is the provisional brigade in?" General Pickering asked.

"I saw General Dawkins at Pendleton," Pick said. "Ed Banning was there. They knew I was coming here, and asked me to relay this to you."

"Relay what?" McCoy asked.

"Okay. The 1st Marine Division at Pendleton was not, apparently, a division as we remember. Way understrength. And that got practically stripped to form the provisional brigade. So the way the Corps decided to deal with that was to transfer people from the 2nd Marine Division at Camp Lejeune to Pendleton to fill out the 1st Marine Division, bring it to wartime strength. Since there weren't enough people to strip from the 2nd Division to do this, they also ordered to Pendleton whatever Marines they could find anywhere—Marine Barracks at Charleston, recruiting offices, et cetera, et cetera. No sooner had they started this than the word came to bring the 2nd Division to wartime strength. The only way to do that was mobilize the entire reserve!"

"Including you?" General Pickering asked.

"VMF-243 was mobilized two days ago," Pick said.

"So what are you doing here?" McCoy asked.

"I got a delay for Stu James and me, so that we could come here and get the lay of the land," Pick said. "We go on active duty when the squadron gets here." He paused and looked at McCoy. "I don't suppose you're brimming with information about airfields, et cetera, in Korea?"

"Not much," McCoy said. "The ones we still hold are full of Air Force planes."

"I really want to take a look at what's there," Pick said. "Dad, can you get me an airplane?"

"Get you an airplane?" General Pickering asked, incredulously.

"I'm not talking about a fighter. What I'd really like to have is a Piper Cub, something like that."

"I don't know, Pick," General Pickering said, dubiously.

"There's a Marine Corps air station at Iwakuni," Pick said. "I don't know what's there. That's one of the things I want to find out."

"Where's that?" McCoy asked.

"Not far from Hiroshima, east," Pick said.

McCoy bent over the map, found what he was looking for, and laid a plastic ruler on the map.

"It's almost exactly two hundred miles from Iwakuni to Pusan," McCoy announced. "Most of it over the East China Sea. Can you fly that far in a Piper Cub?"

"If I wind the rubber bands *real* tight," Pick said. "From the coast, it's just a little over a hundred miles. You can make that in a Cub. Step one, get a Cub. Step two, fly to Iwakuni. See if there isn't a small field on the coast somewhere where I could take on fuel. . . ."

"Pick, that sounds—"

"General," McCoy interrupted, "if Pick had a Cub in Korea, it would make things a lot easier for Zimmerman and me."

"What about this Marine Corps air station?" General Pickering asked. "Couldn't you borrow a plane there? Or—with Ken and Zimmerman in the picture—borrow one from the Army, or the Air Force, there?"

"General," McCoy said. "I have to steal Jeeps in Korea. What light airplanes Eighth Army has they are not about to willingly loan to anybody. And I would really hate to make them loan us one; they need what they have."

"What makes you think there's an airplane here they don't need and would willingly lend us?"

McCoy and Pick smiled at each other.

"With all possible respect, General, sir," Pick said, smiling. "We lower grade officers sometimes suspect that senior officers sometimes have more logistical support than they actually need."

"In other words, if I decide you really need an airplane, better that I take one away from the brass?"

"Very well put, sir, if I may say so, with all due respect, General, sir," Pick said.

Pickering shook his head.

"Did you bring a Marine uniform with you?" General Pickering asked.

Pick nodded.

"We brought all our gear in footlockers," he said. "They wouldn't fit in a cab, but they're going to bring them into town in a pickup. Mine should be here any minute. I told them to take Stu James's to the Hokkaido."

"Well, as soon as it gets here, put a uniform on. General Almond—El Supremo's chief of staff—is coming here. You can tell him yourself what junior officers think about excess logistics for senior officers."

McCoy smiled at Pick's discomfiture. Pickering saw it.

"Your smile is premature, Captain McCoy," he said. "General Almond is coming here to see you."

"What for?"

"He didn't say, but he made it pretty clear that he'd rather Willoughby didn't know about it," Pickering said. He turned to Pick and went on: "If you can convince General Almond that getting you an airplane makes sense, it would solve a lot of problems. He can order it. If I ask anyone else, there will be fifty reasons offered why one can't be spared."

"I'll give it a good shot," Pick said. "I really would like to see the airfields, get a feel for the place, before the squadron gets here."

"Almond's a reasonable man," General Pickering said. "When General Cushman was here, trying to talk MacArthur out of putting all Marine aviation under the Air Force—"

"Jesus Christ!" Pick exploded. "What's that all about?"

"The phrase General Stratemeyer—the Air Force three-star who's the SCAP Air Force commander—used was 'optimum usage of available aviation assets,'" Pickering said. The phrase General Cushman used was 'reduction by ninety percent of the combat efficiency of the 1st Marine Brigade if they lost control of their aviation.'"

"You were there?" Pick asked. His father nodded.

"I'm afraid to ask who won," Pick said. "Christ, I've been on maneuvers with the Army and the Air Force. The Air Force just doesn't understand close air support."

"So General Cushman said," Pickering said. "He phrased it a little more delicately. What Almond said, very respectfully, was 'General, I would suggest we defer to the feelings of the Marine Corps.' El Supremo gave him a long, cold, look, and then said, "I don't think we are in any position to risk lowering Marine combat efficiency in any degree. Subject to later review, the Marine Corps may retain control of their aviation.' It was close, Pick. I think if Almond hadn't said what he did, you'd be under Air Force control."

"I think I'm starting to like this guy," Pick said.

"I don't think he's been co-opted by the Bataan Gang," Pickering said.

Pick's footlocker appeared five minutes later, and he had just enough time to shower and shave and put a uniform on before there was a knock at the door, and without waiting for a response, the CIC guard in the corridor opened it and Major General Almond entered the room.

"You wanted to see me, General?" Almond asked.

That question was asked for the benefit of the CIC guy, Pickering realized. *Almond knows that Willoughby—and possibly MacArthur, too—gets a report on everything that happens here.*

"Yes, sir, I did. Thank you for coming."

The CIC agent closed the door.

"General, this is my son, Major Malcolm Pickering," Pickering said. "I wanted you to meet him. He has something to ask you."

Almond met Pickering's eyes for a moment before offering his hand to Pick.

We have just agreed on our story. "Pickering wanted me to meet his son."

God, poor Almond. He has to spend his life walking the razor's edge between disloyalty to his general and keeping his integrity.

"How do you do, Major?" Almond said. "You're here with General Cushman?"

"In a sense, sir. My squadron, VMF-243, was mobilized on the twenty-third. When the squadron gets here, we'll be under General Cushman's command."

"And when do you think that will be?"

"Sir, they should sail within a day or two. They may already have."

"That sounds a little improbable, Major," Almond challenged.

"Sir, we trained to be able to fly aboard a carrier within forty-eight hours."

"And you won't need any additional training, equipping, filling out the ranks, that sort of thing, before you go aboard an aircraft carrier for active service?"

"We're a little better than ninety percent on our enlisted men, sir. And we have one hundred percent of our officers. The squadron's ready to go, sir."

"You're here," Almond said, making it a question.

"Yes, sir. My exec and I flew in this morning, commercial, as sort of the advance party."

"Sort of?"

"Well, sir, we won't go on active duty until the squadron gets here."

"You're in uniform."

"Sir, the CO of VMF-243 has the authority to call up people for seventy-two hours for special training. I called myself and my exec up."

Almond smiled. "That sounds highly practical and very irregular."

Pick shrugged.

"What do you know about the 1st Provisional Marine Brigade?" Almond asked.

"Sir, I'm not sure I understand the question."

Almond turned to McCoy.

"You're Captain McCoy, right?"

"Yes, sir."

"You look familiar, Captain," Almond said, as he shook McCoy's hand. "Do we know each other?"

"No, sir."

"Captain McCoy was stationed here recently, General," General Pickering said. "With the Naval Element, SCAP."

"I thought I'd seen the face," Almond said.

Either he's got one hell of a poker face, or he doesn't know a thing about McCoy's analysis, or that Willoughby buried a knife in McCoy's back.

"Major," Almond went on, "your father's aide-de-camp reported to your father, who relayed the information to me, that when a regiment arrived for Korean duty yesterday in Pusan, the ranks were filled with recent basic training graduates; there had been no opportunity for the unit to train together; no opportunity for the men to zero their individual weapons; and that their crew-served weapons, heavy machine guns and mortars were still packed in cosmoline." He paused and looked at McCoy. "That is the essence of what you said?"

"Yes, sir, it is."

"So my question to you, Major, is what is the 1st Provisional Marine Brigade like, in that context?"

"I think it will be in much better shape than that, sir," Pick said.

"Is that Marine Corps pride speaking, or do you know?"

"Sir, I know a lot of the officers who are with the brigade. They tell me that most of the officers, and noncoms are War Two veterans, and most of the Marines have been with the 1st Marine Division for some time. When they formed the brigade, they didn't just send in bodies, but intact squads, platoons, companies from the division, with their officers and noncoms. Men who have trained together, sir." He chuckled. "Sir, these are Marines. I can't believe they haven't zeroed their rifles. Or that their machine guns are packed in cosmoline. They'll get off their ships ready to fight."

"How is it that you, an aviator, know the officers of a division?"

"Sir, we train together. When we get a call from the ground to hit something, we usually recognize the voice asking for the strike."

"How far down does that go? Battalion? Company?"

"Sometimes to platoon, sir."

"Well, I'm impressed," Almond said. "And frankly a little relieved. Generals Cushman and Craig told me essentially what you've been telling me, but I like to get confirmation from the people actually doing things. Senior officers can only hope the junior officers are doing what they're supposed to do."

"Yes, sir," Pick said.

"General," General Pickering said, "Pick made an interesting observation a little while ago, just before you came. He said that most senior officers have more logistical support than they actually need."

"Interesting," Almond said. "Tell me, General, why I am I getting the feeling I am about to be ambushed by Marines?"

"I have no idea, General," Pickering said.

"And that there's a hook in the phrase 'more logistical support than they actually need'?"

"Now that you mention it, General . . ." Pickering said.

"What, Pickering?" Almond said, smiling.

"Pick wants to borrow a light aircraft, and make a personal survey of airfields in Korea," Pickering said. "And my 'aide-de-camp' tells me that having access to a light airplane in Korea would make his work there considerably easier."

Almond looked at Pickering for a long moment.

"Is that an official request from the Assistant Director of the CIA for Asia?"

"Yes, sir, it is."

"There are very few light aircraft left in Japan," Almond said. "I ordered almost all of them sent to Korea."

Disappointment showed on Pick's face.

"I was afraid that might be the case, sir. But I had to ask."

"There are four at SCAP," Almond went on. "Two L-19s, one L-4—that's a Piper Cub—and one L-17, that's a four-seater North American Navion."

"Sir, if I could have the Cub for a couple of days . . ."

"You can't," Almond said. "That's mine. I call it *The Blue Goose.'*"

"I understand, sir," Pick said.

Curiosity overwhelmed General Pickering.

"Why the *'Blue Goose?'*" he asked. "Goose suggests . . . the index finger raised in a vulgar manner."

"Somehow that lettering appeared on the nacelle shortly after every other general officer on the SCAP staff got a new L-19 but me," Almond said. "You are the first senior officer to ask me what it means."

Pickering chuckled.

"The L-19s are out, too," Almond went on. "One belongs to General Willoughby, and the other to the G-3, who really needs it. That leaves General MacArthur's Navion. He rarely uses it. General Willoughby uses it rather often. So what I'm going to do is go back to the Dai Ichi Building and inform the Supreme Commander that General Pickering asked to see me here to meet his son, and to ask for the use of a light aircraft. I'm going to tell the Supreme Commander that I told you, General Pickering, that I would bring your request to his attention, and that, barring objections from him, I would see if I could find one for you. I don't think the Supreme Commander will object. Then I'm going to send Al Haig, my aide, out to Haneda to inform the people there that with the permission of the Supreme Commander, the L-17 will be picked up by General Pickering's pilot for purposes not known to me."

"Thank you, sir," Pick said.

"It might be wise to get the aircraft out of Tokyo as soon as possible," Almond said.

"Yes, sir," Pick said.

"There's always tit-for-tat," Almond said to Pickering. "OK?"

"What can I do for you, General?" Pickering replied.

"I'd like to see McCoy's—and, come to think of it, Major Pickering's—reports on what they find. Unofficially. I sometimes wonder if the reports we're getting at the daily briefings are designed to spare General MacArthur unnecessary concern."

In other words, you suspect—with damned good reason—that Willoughby isn't reporting anything to MacArthur he doesn't think he should know.

"I'll see you get them," Pickering said.

Almond nodded.

"Major," he said to Pick, "it might be a good idea if you happened to be around the SCAP hangar at Haneda, in case Captain Haig might show up there."

"Yes, sir, I'll be there," Pick said.

Almond walked to the door and opened it. Then he turned, and in a voice loud enough to ensure the CIC could hear it, said, "I'll take your request to the Supreme Commander as soon as I can."

"Thank you, sir," Pickering said.

They smiled at each other, and then Almond went through the door.

[TWO]
The Press Club
Tokyo, Japan
1530 28 July 1950

It was alleged by many of Miss Jeanette Priestly's associates in the SCAP (and now UN Command) press corps—all of whom were male—that the *Chicago Tribune's* war correspondent had a Jesuit-like attitude regarding the development of her sources. That, in other words, the end justified the means.

While it was obviously not true that Miss Priestly would fuck a gorilla to get a story—as was sometimes alleged around the press club bar—it was on the other hand true that Miss Priestly was not above looking soulfully into the eyes of some virile major—or general or, for that matter, PFC—simultaneously allowing him to glimpse down her blouse at her bosom, onto which she often sprayed Chanel number 5, and perhaps even laying a soft hand on his, if she thought the individual concerned was possessed of knowledge that would give her a story. Or, more recently, in Korea, if he had access to a Jeep, or space on an airplane.

But she did not take these sources of news or air passage space to bed in payment for their cooperation. While it had been some time since she had lost the moral right to virginal white, the facts were that the urge and the opportunity had not coincided for quite some time.

Jeanette was honest enough to admit to herself that she had been strongly drawn to Captain Kenneth R. McCoy, USMC, probably because he had seemed like the only man in Korea who knew what he was doing. And he *was* cute. But he hadn't made a pass at her, and if he had, where could they have gone to share carnal bliss?

The green rice fields of Korea in the summer are fertilized with human feces, the smell from which tends to dampen romantic ardor.

And since they had been together in Korea, she had never seen McCoy again, so he was added in her mind to her long list of missed opportunities.

And sometimes, when everything else was right, something in her psyche made her back off. There was no denying that the Trans-Global Airways pilot, the one who had set the speed record, and whose father was a buddy of MacArthur, Pickering, was the legendary answer to a maiden's prayer. Tall, good-looking, wicked eyes, and with an undeniable charm. And rich.

Pickering had obviously been smitten with her. If he'd been a horse, he would have been neighing and tearing up the carpet with his hooves. And, if she had been willing to drop her almost maidenly reticence, there would have been a soft bed in the Imperial Hotel, with room service champagne. And she had heard somewhere that airline pilots could provide free tickets, which was something to think about, too.

But there was something about Captain Pickering of Trans-Global Airways that turned on her alarm system. She had not become a foreign—now war—correspondent for the *Tribune* by making herself vulnerable. As the boys in the press club bar would phrase it, she knew how to keep her ass covered, literally *and* figuratively.

She could have made an ass of herself over Pickering, and she rarely put herself in that position. And anyway, he was gone. Since it was unlikely that she would ever see him again, she put him out of her mind.

Jeanette had learned that her best sources of information came from men who both lusted after her and were pissed off about something, who wanted to tell her something that she would write about, and put somebody else's ass in a crack.

When she saw Major Lem T. Scott, Signal Corps, U.S. Army, smile at her as she walked into the press club bar, she *knew* that in addition to whatever lustful fantasies might be running through his head, he was really there to tell her something.

Major Scott was a tall, rather good-looking man in his early thirties. He was an Army aviator, which gained him sort of unofficial membership in the press club. No journalist was going to kick an Army aviator out of the press club. Sooner or later, every journalist had to beg a ride in one of the Army's fleet of light aircraft. In the sure and certain knowledge that some journalist would stand drinks for them on the expense account, Army aviators often went to the press club bar.

It took Jeanette about thirty minutes to get from Major Scott what he had obviously come to the press club bar to tell her, "accidentally; in conversation."

Major Scott was attached to the Flight Section, Headquarters, SCAP. Most of the light Army aircraft, and their pilots, had been sent to Korea by General Almond. General MacArthur's personal light aircraft, a North American L-17 Navion, had not, and consequently neither had Major Scott, who was MacArthur's Navion pilot.

Possibly, Jeanette thought somewhat unkindly, because he had not been there, Major Scott wanted to be in action in Korea. It wouldn't be so bad, he said, if he was actually flying the Supreme Commander around, but he wasn't even doing that. The Supreme Commander had loaned his Navion to the CIA, and he had absolutely nothing to do, except once in a while fly one of the two L-19s that were left at the SCAP flight section.

Jeanette had long ago learned that letting a source think you know more than you actually do was a way to put them at ease. All she knew about the CIA in Japan was that it was rumored that MacArthur's economic advisor, Jonathan Loomis, was the CIA Tokyo station chief.

"What do you suppose Jonathan Loomis is doing with the general's Navion?"

"It's not Loomis," Scott said. "It's his boss, a Marine general named Pickering. He lives in the Imperial Hotel."

This was the first Miss Pickering had heard that General Fleming Pickering had any connection with the CIA at all. He'd even denied *being* a general.

The sonofabitch!

"Well, what do you suppose that General Pickering's doing with the Supreme Commander's Navion?"

"I don't know. He's got some Marine major flying it. He brings it back to Haneda for service. I know he's been in Korea. And all over Japan. I don't know who, if anybody, he's had with him. . . . The CIA doesn't say much."

"Huh," Jeanette said, thoughtfully.

"Just before I came here this afternoon," Scott added. "I found out this major is flying the Navion to Kobe first thing in the morning."

That was interesting. Another source had told her that the aviation elements of the First Provisional Marine Brigade would arrive at Kobe two days from now. She had already made reservations to take the train to Kobe to meet them.

"Anyone going with him?"

"I don't know, but if you're thinking of trying to catch a ride with him, forget it. Whatever they're doing, they don't want anyone to know about it."

In another five minutes, Jeanette was sure that she had extracted from Major Scott all that interested her, and, trying to sound as sincere as possible, told him she was really sorry she couldn't have dinner with him. Another time.

It wasn't a long walk from the press club to the Imperial Hotel, but it was hotter than she thought it was, and she arrived at the Imperial sweaty.

When she tried to call General Pickering on the house phone, the operator politely denied having a guest by that name. Jeanette took the elevator to the floor on which the Dewey Suite was located and started down the corridor.

She was stopped by a young American in civilian clothing who politely asked what she wanted. She took her press credentials from her purse, and while the young man—obviously a guard—was examining them, said that she was there to interview General Pickering.

"Ma'am, this is a restricted area. I'll have to ask you to leave."

"I want to see General Pickering."

"Ma'am, this is a restricted area. I'll have to ask you to leave."

With ten minutes to spare, Jeanette managed to make the train to Kobe. She arrived there after midnight, and took a cab to the U.S. Naval Base, Kobe.

Lieutenant Commander Gregory F. Porter, USN, the public affairs officer was disturbed and annoyed that she had heard that Marine aviation would be arriving in the very near future, and was afraid she would break the story—"Marine Aviation to Debark at Kobe"—before it happened. There was no censorship, he told her, but he really hoped she could see her way clear to embargo the story until the Marines actually got there. The other way might really give aid and comfort to the enemy. If she would embargo the story, the Navy information officer would do everything he could to help her get the story once the Marines were actually there.

Jeanette told him she understood completely, and would happily hold the story until told its publication would in no way give aid and comfort to the enemy. Lieutenant Commander Porter was grateful, and said that he would be honored to buy her breakfast in the morning, at which time he might have some other news for her that she might find of interest.

The dining room of the Kobe U.S. Naval Base Officer's Mess provided a good view of the airfield, and at 0815 the next morning, while she was eating a surprisingly good grapefruit, Miss Priestly saw a North American Navion touch down smoothly on the runway.

"Oh, I didn't know the Army used this field," she said to Lieutenant Commander Porter. "General MacArthur has an airplane just like that."

"Actually, Jeanette," the commander said. "That's his. But he's not in it."

"Who is?" she asked, sweetly.

"Right now, that's classified," Commander Porter said. "But if you'll give me another couple of hours, I'll tell you all about it. And I'll even get you some exclusive pictures of something I think you'll agree is one hell of a story."

Jeanette had already decided that Commander Porter was no dope, and that he had told her all she was going to hear until he decided to tell her more, so she smiled sweetly at him, laid her hand on his and said, "Thank you."

She looked to see if she could see who was in the Navion, but it taxied out of sight.

At 1015, Commander Porter found Jeanette in the lounge of the Officers' Club and led her back to the table at which they had breakfast.

"In a very few minutes, you're going to see something very interesting—perhaps even historic—out there. I'm not at liberty to tell you what now, but you have my word I will at the proper time, and I'll have those exclusive pictures I promised you."

He's talking, probably, about the first Marine planes which will land here. But if I get the pictures first, and exclusively . . .

"You're very kind, Greg," she said, softly, and touched his hand with hers.

"I'll see you shortly," he said.

At 1025, two Chance-Vought F4U Corsairs dropped out of the sky and landed. The word *Marines* was lettered large on their fuselages.

"The Marines have landed," Jeanette said, out loud, and just slightly sarcastically, although there was no one in the dining room to hear her.

The Corsairs parked on the tarmac and shut down. Ground crewmen approached them as a fuel truck drove up. First two Navy photographers, carrying Speed-Graphic press cameras, and then Lieutenant Commander Porter and another man, wearing those overalls pilot's wear, walked up to the airplanes as their pilots got out.

I'll be damned, if I didn't know better, that pilot looks just like Captain Pickering of Trans-Global Airways.

The pilot of the first Corsair saluted the pilot who looked just like Captain Pickering of Trans-Global Airways and Commander Porter.

Then Pick Pickering's *doppelgänger* walked up to the pilot of the second Corsair and saluted him, then wrapped his arms around him, picked him off the ground, and kissed him on the forehead.

The ground crewmen swarmed around the aircraft, refueling them, circling them, examining them.

The pilot of the second Corsair and—*Damn it, that is him*—Pick Pickering were herded reluctantly to the nacelle of one of the Corsairs and the Navy photographer took their picture.

Then the pilot of the second Corsair climbed back into his aircraft, and Pickering climbed into the other one.

What the hell is he doing?

He looked down from the cockpit to make sure there was a fire extinguisher in place, then made a *I'm-gonna-wind-it-up* motion with his hand, and then the propeller began to turn slowly and a moment later, in a cloud of blue smoke, the engine caught.

My God, he's going to fly that thing!

A moment after that, with Pickering's Corsair leading, both aircraft taxied toward the runway.

The Navy photographers trotted toward the runway so they would be in position to photograph the takeoff. Commander Porter and the pilot who was now without an airplane walked toward the officers mess.

Jeanette could quite clearly see the takeoff of the two aircraft—including the pilot of the first aircraft, who had earphones cocked jauntily on his head, and was without any possibility of mistake whatever, Captain Pick Pickering of Trans-Global Airways.

Commander Porter and the pilot came into the dining room.

"What you have just seen, Jeanette," Commander Porter announced somewhat dramatically, "what you will within thirty minutes have the first, and exclusive, photos of, was the takeoff of the first Marine aviation combat sortie to Korea."

"Who was flying . . . who was the pilot who took his airplane?" Jeanette demanded.

"Major Malcolm S. Pickering, ma'am," the pilot said.

"The other pilot was Lieutenant Colonel William C. Dunn," Commander Porter said.

"Why did you give him your airplane?"

"Pick's the skipper, ma'am," the pilot said. "Of VMF 243. He didn't ask me. Skipper's order, ma'am, they don't ask."

"What happened, Jeanette," Commander Porter said, "was that Major Pickering came to the Far East before his squadron. And flew orientation missions to Korea. . . ."

"In MacArthur's Navion?" she asked, incredulously.

"Yes, ma'am."

"And then Colonel Dunn and . . . excuse me, Jeanette, may I present Captain David Freewall of USMC Reserve Fighter Squadron 243? Freewall, this is Miss Jeanette Priestly of the *Chicago Tribune.*"

"I know," Captain Freewall said.

"You do?"

"Yes, ma'am," Captain Freewall said, smiling at her. "The last thing Ol' Pick said to me before he climbed in the airplane was that the penalty for treading on his turf was two broken legs."

Jeanette looked at him wordlessly for a long moment.

"Treading on his turf"? Does that arrogant sonofabitch actually think I'm his turf?

She turned to Commander Porter.

"You were saying, Commander?"

"Well, when the *Badoeng Strait*—the aircraft carrier, Jeanette, that brought Marine Air Group 33 from San Diego—got close enough to fly Corsairs off her to here, Major Pickering communicated with Colonel Dunn . . ."

"They're ol' pals, Miss Priestly," Captain Freewall said. "They go back to Guadalcanal. And for a regular, Colonel Billy's a pretty good ol' boy."

"Colonel Billy, is that what they call him?" Jeanette asked.

". . . offering *Colonel William C.* Dunn," Commander Porter went on, "the opportunity, if he so desired, of making an orientation flight/*cum* sortie, of Korea three days before he would have otherwise have had the opportunity to do so. And *Colonel* Dunn—his first name is William; middle initial C, and that's Dee You En En—accepted."

"I see."

"And very shortly, other aircraft from the *Badoeng Strait* and *Sicily,* the other aircraft carrier in the task force, will begin to land here to prepare for Korean service. But you saw, and will have exclusive photos of, the takeoff of the first combat sortie."

"What kind of 'combat sortie'?" Jeanette said.

"In this case, it will be what they call targets of opportunity," Captain Freewall said. "Which means they'll take on anything that looks like the enemy."

"I was under the impression that Major Pickering was an airline pilot—"

"Captain," Captain Freewall corrected her. "Ol' Pick's an airlines *captain.*"

"And is he qualified to go out and 'take on anything that looks like the enemy'?"

"I think you could say he is, ma'am," Freewall said. "Ol' Pick's capable of just about anything."

Including, the arrogant bastard, of considering me his turf.

"The other aircraft from the *Sicily* and the *Badoeng Strait* will shortly be arriving, Jeanette," Commander Porter said. "Perhaps you'd like to watch that from the control tower?"

"Yes, I would, thank you very much," Jeanette said. "When did you say you thought Colonel Dunn and Major Pickering will be getting back?"

"Two, two and a half hours," Commander Porter said.

[THREE]
K-1 USAF Air Field
Pusan, Korea
1137 29 July 1950

Lieutenant Colonel William C. Dunn could see the Korean landmass approaching, was aware that Pick had had them in a gentle descent from 10,000 feet for the last couple of minutes, and knew that something was up.

It was about 375 miles from Kobe to Pusan, which Pick had said was their "first destination in the Picturesque Land of the Morning Calm."

They had been wheels-up at Kobe at 1040, and they had been indicating a little better than 400 miles per hour. That meant they would reach Pusan in a little under an hour, and just about an hour had passed.

"K-1, Marine Four One One," Pick's voice came over the air-to-ground.

"Four One One, K-1."

"K-1, Marine Four One One, a two-plane F4-U flight, at five thousand, about five minutes east. Request permission for a low-speed, low-level pass of your airfield."

My God, what's he want to do that for?

And they're not going to let him.

He said it was the only decent airfield in Korea. Therefore it will be crowded. Therefore they won't want two fighters buzzing the place.

"Say again, One One?" the K-1 tower operator asked, incredulously.

"Request a low-speed, low-level pass over your field in about three and a half minutes."

"One One, be advised there is heavy traffic in the area. State purpose of low level pass."

"K-1, One One. Two purposes. Purpose one, visual observation of possible emergency landing field. Purpose two, to confirm the rumors that the Marines are about to get in your little war."

"One One, permission denied."

"K-1, your other option is to let us land, following which we will want to taxi all over the field to have a look from the ground. If you grant permission for a low-level pass, we will be out of your hair in less than sixty seconds. Your call, K-1."

"Stand by, Marine One One."

"One One standing by. We are now at three thousand feet, and have the field in sight."

There was a sixty-second delay, during which the two Corsairs dropped below two thousand feet.

"Attention all aircraft in the vicinity of K-1. Be on the lookout for two Marine Corsair aircraft approaching from the east at low level. They will make a low-level low-speed pass over this field. Marine One One, you are cleared for one low-level low-speed pass, east to west."

"Thank you ever so much," Pick's voice said. Then, over the air-to-air radio: "Billy, you get that?"

"Affirmative," Lieutenant Colonel Dunn said into his microphone.

"Low and slow, Billy," Pick ordered. "Here we go."

Dunn saw Pick put the nose of his Corsair down, and followed him. Pick dropped to about a thousand feet over the water, and lower than that once they crossed the shoreline.

"Flaps and wheels, Colonel, sir," Pick's voice said.

The airport was dead ahead.

Dunn's Corsair slowed as he lowered the gear and applied flaps. The airspeed indicator, after a moment, showed that he was close to stalling speed. The airfield was dead ahead; Dunn saw a Navy R5D transport turning off the runway.

Well, he apparently meant low and slow. Why did I think we were going to buzz the place at 400 knots?

Why do I always suspect that Pick will do something crazy?

What he's doing here makes sense. I can see all I really need to know about this airfield making a low and slow. You can't see much from the cockpit of a Corsair on the ground.

This made sense.

They flew straight down the main runway. They were almost at the end of it and Dunn had reached the gear control when Pick's Corsair, its wheels and flaps going up, raised the nose and gained speed.

"Thank you, K-1," Pick's voice came over the air-to-ground. "You may now tell all your friends that the Marines are here and almost landed."

That's why. He didn't have to get on the air like that.

There's something about Pick that makes him show his ass.

"Having seen just about all the Pusan offers," Pick's voice came over the air-to-air, "we will take a quick look at picturesque Chinhae, not far from here, which will take Piper Cubs and those helicopters, but where landing a Corsair would be a little hairy."

Chinhae was maybe thirty miles from Pusan, and Pick—with Dunn copying him—lowered his flaps and gear and flew over it. There was a single runway, with a half dozen Army light aircraft parked on the west side of it.

Dunn saw enough of it to be able to report to General Cushman that it would be usable by the Piper Cubs and helicopters of the brigade's observation squadron when they arrived.

"And now to Taegu," Pick's voice came over the air. "The second-largest city in unoccupied South Korea."

It was a flight of just a few minutes. Pick had climbed to 3,500 feet, and Dunn could see from the exposed, raw earth where trenches and other positions had been built southeast of the city, as if in anticipation that the enemy would take Taegu.

"And the war, Billy, begins just a little farther north." He switched to the air-to-ground.

"Marine Four One One. Any air controller in the area."

There was no reply, and Pick repeated the call. And again there was no reply.

"Aw, come on, fellas, any air controller in the area. We have two Marine F4-U's up here ready, willing, and able to shoot up anything you think deserves a shot."

And again, there was no reply.

Pick switched to the air-to-air frequency.

"Can you believe that, Billy? You think they're asleep? Maybe too proud to call on the Marines?"

"There has to be a reason," Dunn replied.

When he'd heard Pick calling, Dunn had thought there would be far more calls from the ground than they could possibly respond to.

"To hell with it," Pick said. "Let's go shoot up a choo-choo."

A "choo-choo"? Now, what the hell?

"Say again?"

"You never saw those wing camera shots of the Air Corps shooting up trains in Europe? I always wanted to try that, but I never saw one damned choo-choo in all of War Two."

"There was one on the 'Canal," Dunn said, with a clear memory of an ancient, tiny, shot-to-pieces steam locomotive in his mind's eye, "but somebody shot it up before I had a chance. Is there a rail line around here?"

"I found a couple in my trusty Navion," Pick reported. "Let's hope we get lucky."

Ten minutes later, they got lucky.

"Nine o'clock, Billy," Pick's voice came over the air-to-air.

Dunn looked.

A train, a long train—mixed boxcars, flatcars, and tank cars—powered by two steam locomotives, was snaking along a river.

"I'm going to break left and get pretty close to the deck, and then turn back," Pick said. "I've got dibs on the locomotive. In the unlikely event I miss, you can try on a second pass."

"*Dibs on the locomotive*"? *Are you never going to grow up? Good God, you're a Marine field-grade officer!*

"I'll be on your tail, Pick," Dunn said over the air-to-air.

And then Pick surprised him again, by rapidly picking up speed, as soon as he had broken to the left.

You can hit a lot more if your throttles aren't at the firewall. You know that. What the hell is the matter with you?

Pick completed his turn, and not more than 500 feet above the undulating terrain, turned back toward the train—

—from three or four cars of which came lines of tracer shells.

My God! Why didn't I think about antiaircraft fire?

You make a much harder target if you're flying as fast as it will go.

You knew there would be counterfire.

How?

My God, Pick, did you do a dry run in that little Navion?

You did. You crazy sonofabitch, that's exactly what you did!

Streams of tracers erupted from Pick's Corsair's wing mounted .50-caliber Brownings.

Dunn saw them walking across the rice paddies and the river toward the locomotives. Steam began to come from the rearward locomotive's boiler. He moved the nose of his Corsair to the rear of the train and pressed the firing button on the stick. The Corsair shuddered with the recoil.

Just as he picked up his nose, the locomotive exploded.

"Goddamn, Billy! Look at that!" Pick's delighted voice came over the air-to-air.

A second later, there was an orange glow from one of the tank cars, and a split second after that, an enormous explosion.

Dunn flew for half a second through the fireball, and then was on the other side.

He saw Pick's Corsair climbing steeply and got on his tail again.

"Did you see that sonofabitch blow up?" Pick's voice asked, excitedly.

"I saw it. We also got what had to be a gasoline tank car."

"*You* got the tank car," Pick said. "*I* got the choo-choo."

"Whatever you say," Dunn replied.

"Your ADF working?" Pick asked.

Dunn checked.

"Affirmative," he said.

"Mine isn't," Pick replied matter-of-factly. "I guess I lost that antenna."

"Any other damage?"

"The gauges are all in the green," Pick said. "There's some openings in the wing I don't remember seeing before, but I don't see any gas leaking. Do you think you can find Kobe, Colonel?"

"Get on my wing, Pick," Dunn ordered

He advanced his throttle and pulled his Corsair beside Pick's.

Pick's canopy was open. He had a long cigar in his mouth, and was using the cockpit lighter to fire it up. The lighter was technically called "the spot heater," because smoking was supposed to be forbidden in the cockpit. Ignoring all that, Pick had the cigar going, then he raised his eyes to Dunn and waved cheerfully.

Dunn shook his head and moved ahead of him, on a course for Kobe.

[FOUR]

In her capacity as a journalist, Miss Priestly decided it was her duty to meet the two Corsairs when they returned from the first Marine aviation combat sortie in Korea.

The first thing she thought was that she was really going to pay the arrogant sonofabitch back for that "his turf" crack.

The second thing she thought was *My God, he looks tired.*

The third thing she thought was *My God, there's holes all over the fuselage. He was hit. He could have been shot down!*

Major Pickering jumped off the wing root of the Corsair.

"Well, what an unexpected pleasure. How are you, Miss Priestly?"

"You knew I was here," she snapped. And then was surprised to hear herself ask, "Pick, are you all right?"

"Couldn't be better, except after when I have a double scotch, when I'll really be in good shape."

"There's bullet holes in your airplane!"

"No. I don't think so. I think that's part of a locomotive."

"A locomotive?"

"I got one. Billy got a gasoline tank car," he said.

"A locomotive?"

"Yeah. And there's an old Marine Corps custom about that. Every pilot who gets a locomotive gets to kiss the first pretty girl he sees."

"Good luck," she said. "I hope you find one."

And then he put his hand on her cheek and shrugged.

"What the hell," he said. "It might have worked. And I really wanted to kiss you."

He dropped his hand and started to turn from her.

She caught the sleeve of his flight suit. It was damp with sweat.

He probably smells like a horse.

Then she raised her face and kissed him, and it lasted much longer than she intended, and while she was kissing him, she realized that there probably wouldn't be a double bed and room-service champagne, but this was going to be one of those rare times when the urge and the opportunity had really come together.

[FIVE]
Replacement Battalion (Provisional)
Camp Pendleton, California
0705 29 July 1950

At the time it had been asked for and promised, Marine Corps assistance in the production of the motion picture film *Halls of Montezuma,* which would star John Wayne, had seemed like a splendid idea.

The script had been reviewed, and while there was a certain melodramatic aspect to it, there was nothing in it that would in any way reflect adversely on the United States Marine Corps. To the contrary, John Wayne's character manifested traits of selfless heroism in keeping with the highest traditions of the Marine Corps.

And it was to be a major film, which would appear on the screens of at least half the motion picture theaters in the United States.

As one senior officer put it privately to Marine Corps Commandant Cates, "What we get, for loaning them a couple of companies of infantry, the use of the boondocks at Pendleton, and letting them take pictures of amphibious landings under close air support—which we're going to run anyway—is really a two-hour recruiting film. I think it's a win-win situation for the Corps, and I recommend we do it."

That was then, nine months before the Army of the People's Democratic Republic of North Korea had crossed the 38th Parallel and started for Pusan.

Now was now. The last thing the United States Marine Corps needed at Camp Pendleton now was a civilian army of motion picture production people running around the reservation, and expecting—demanding—what they had been promised, "full cooperation."

One of the problems that crossed the desk of Brigadier General Clyde W. Dawkins shortly after it had been made clear the Corps was going to war again was in the form of a succinct note from the sergeant major.

General:

The Hollywood Marines are starting to arrive.
Maj L. K. Winslow (Pub Info) has been assigned
to 1st Prov Brigade.

Sgt Major Neely.

Major L. K. Winslow, who had been on the staff of the G-3, had been detailed to the Public Information Office to deal with the *Halls of Montezuma* motion picture production company. He was a good officer. When Brigadier General Craig had begun to staff the 1st Provisional Marine Brigade, one of the first officers he'd asked for was Major L. K. Winslow.

That meant there was no officer now charged with dealing with the movie people.

General Dawkins had summoned Sergeant Major Neely to his office.

"What do we do about this?"

"Sir, we have a major who is now spending most of his time inventorying supply rooms."

"A major doing what?" Dawkins had blurted, then remembered hearing that

Major Macklin—having somehow irked the G-1—had been sent to contemplate his sins while he inventoried supply rooms. "You mean Major Macklin?"

Sergeant Major Neely nodded.

"I don't know . . ."

"The PIO is up to his ass in alligators," Neely said. "Somebody has to deal with the Hollywood Marines."

There is no reason, Dawkins decided at the moment, *that Macklin can't contemplate his sins, whatever they were, while dealing with the Hollywood Marines.*

"Send for Major Macklin, please, Sergeant Major," Dawkins ordered.

"Aye, aye, sir."

In the forty-five minutes it took to notify Major Macklin that the deputy commanding general wished to speak to him personally, and for Macklin to reach Dawkins's office, Dawkins had a little—very little—time to ruminate on his decision.

He was aware that he was not one of those who thought the John Wayne cinematic opus was a great thing for the Marine Corps. He was further aware that he had heard somewhere that this Macklin character was a three-star asshole. He was forced to draw the conclusion that he had allowed his personal feelings to color his decision; that he had sent an asshole to deal with the Hollywood assholes.

That was not the thing to do. The Marine Corps had decided the movie was in the best interests of the Marine Corps, and that being the case, it behooved him to support the movie as best he could, which obviously meant he shouldn't send this asshole major to deal with the Hollywood assholes.

He would have to find some really competent officer, on a par with Major L. K. Winslow, to assist the Hollywood people in their production.

Just about at the time he had reached this conclusion, Sergeant Major Neely stuck his head in the door and reported that Major Robert B. Macklin, USMC, had arrived.

"Send him in, please," Dawkins had ordered. Since he had summoned him, courtesy required that he at least talk to him.

Major Macklin—who was, Dawkins was somewhat surprised to see, a good-looking, trim, shipshape Marine officer—entered the office, walked to precisely eighteen inches from General Dawkins's desk, and came to attention.

"Major Macklin, Robert B., reporting as ordered, sir."

"At ease, Major," Dawkins said.

Macklin stood at ease.

"This may sound like a strange question, Macklin, but do you have any public relations experience?"

"Yes, sir, I do."

That's not what I expected to hear.

"In the Corps?"

"Yes, sir."

"Tell me about it," Dawkins ordered.

"Sir, when I returned from the 'Canal—"

"You were on Guadalcanal?" Dawkins asked.

I'll be damned.

"Actually, sir, I was on Gavutu."

"Then why did you say 'Guadalcanal'?"

"I've found, sir, that it's easier to say Guadalcanal than have to explain that Gavutu was a nearby island."

That's true. Gavutu is not well-known.

"What were you doing on Gavutu?"

"Actually, sir, I didn't get a chance to do much on Gavutu. I went in with the ParaMarines and took a hit before I reached the beach."

The ParaMarines were decimated—literally, they lost ten percent of their men— landing on Gavutu.

"I see," Dawkins said. "And?"

"I was on limited duty, sir, and the Corps assigned me to a war bond tour. It had several aces from Guadalcanal."

"Oddly enough, I'm familiar with that tour. Several of those aces were mine. And you were the public relations guy for that tour?"

"Yes, sir, and—I was still on limited duty, sir—for others that followed."

"And that's how you spent the war? On public relations duties?"

"No, sir. When it became obvious that I wasn't going to be able anytime soon to pass the full duty physical, I volunteered for the OSS. I was sent on to Mindanao, which the Japs then held—"

Goddamn it! I don't need a spy. I need somebody to deal with the Hollywood Marines and John Wayne.

Well, at least he has some public relations experience.

"Major" Dawkins interrupted, "the Marine Corps is cooperating with a Hollywood motion picture company. They're making a movie to be called *Halls of Montezuma*, which will star John Wayne."

"Yes, sir?"

"The coordinating officer was assigned to the 1st Marine Provisional Brigade, and I have to find someone to take his place, and do so right now— the Hollywood people have already begun to arrive here. Do you think you could handle something like that?"

"Sir, if I have a choice between going to Korea or this, I really would prefer going to Korea."

"Most of us would prefer to be going to Korea, Major," Dawkins said. "My question was do you think you could handle something like that?"

"I'm sure I could, sir, if that's what the Corps wants me to do."

"Okay. Just as soon as you can wind up whatever you're doing now, report to Colonel Severance in public relations."

"Aye, aye, sir."

"That will be all, Major. Good luck."

"Yes, sir. Thank you, sir."

Before Major Macklin was out of the building, General Dawkins got Colonel Severance on the horn and told him that he was sending him an experienced public relations officer to take the place of Major Winslow.

He also told Colonel Severance that he wanted "the Hollywood project" to go smoothly; that the Corps had promised "full cooperation," and full cooperation was what they were going to get.

"Unless it actually interferes with our movements to Korea, see that they get everything they want."

Colonel Severance said, "Aye, aye, sir," and General Dawkins put the Hollywood Marines out of his mind.

Major Macklin was delighted with his new assignment. He would have gone willingly to Korea, of course, and still would. But the facts were that his previous service had denied him the privilege of command. He had never been a company commander, and service as a company commander as a captain was at least an unofficial prerequisite to serving as a battalion executive officer as a major.

Neither had his intelligence service prepared him for duty with a brigade as an intelligence officer. He had spent most of his OSS service on the Japanese-occupied island of Mindanao. That was certainly valuable service—and certainly dangerous service—but it wasn't the sort of thing that had given him the experience to assume duties as a regimental intelligence officer.

So the situation was that even if he was ordered to Korea with the brigade—or later, with the 1st Marine Division—he more than likely would have been given duties in personnel or supply. That was certainly important work, but looking at the big picture, he could make a far larger contribution to the Marine Corps by doing an outstanding job supporting the filming of *Halls of Montezuma*.

And his work would certainly be noticed by senior officers, which was important, if he looked down the road to selection time for promotion to lieutenant colonel.

When he reported to Colonel Severance, Severance repeated to him what General Dawkins had said about the importance of the project, and told himself to guide himself accordingly. He also told him that the "senior members" of the production company were putting up at the Coronado Beach Hotel, and that he should establish contact with the producers and the director there.

He was given a copy of the "shooting script" and a long list of things, from Jeeps and trucks to telephone service, the production company would require. He was also asked to escort the "location manager" around the Camp Pendleton reservation to find suitable sites for various "scenes" and "shots" in the film.

He got right on that, and returned the same evening to the Coronado Beach to report his progress to the director and producers. While he was at Camp Pendleton, he suggested to Colonel Severance that since he was going to have to be on twenty-four-hour call to take care of the requests of "the company," he thought it would be a good idea if he took a room at the hotel. That would mean that he would have to be put on temporary duty, so that he could draw per diem and quarters pay. Colonel Severance said he would take care of it.

Two things happened the very first day. When he told the producer that he had arranged to stay in the hotel so that he would be available around the clock, the director said the least the company could do in return was pick up the hotel bill.

That meant that he would be drawing quarters pay but would not have to spend it.

The second thing that happened the very first day was that he got to meet the star, Mr. John Wayne. Wayne had, of course, a suite in the Coronado Beach, but he had come to San Diego on his yacht, which was a converted Navy PT-Boat.

They met on the yacht. Mr. Wayne was more than charming, and told him that he would be sleeping on the yacht, rather than in the hotel, and that Macklin should feel free to come aboard whenever he pleased.

"We party a little out here," Wayne said. "On the boat, nobody notices."

That was certainly an interesting prospect, and over the next ten days, Major Macklin learned that many—perhaps most—of the beautiful women associated with a motion picture company were not actresses, but technicians and assistants of one kind or another. And many of these, he quickly learned, were drawn to a real-life Marine major, who had been wounded on a real battlefield, and then been an real OSS agent doing his fighting behind enemy lines.

In order to carry out his duties, he requested first—and got—a staff car. After two days, he decided that what he really needed was a station wagon, and a driver, and Colonel Severance got that for him, too.

On 28 July, the production company's extras casting director came to Major Macklin, and said that as of six-thirty in the morning, 30 July, the company was going to shoot some "filler shots" of utilities-clad Marines crawling through the terrain, and he thought he could get by with forty or fifty people, although more would be better.

"You just tell me how many Marines you need," Major Macklin said, in the spirit of full cooperation.

"What I really would like to do is see if I can't come up with some interesting faces."

"How can I help you with that?"

"Do you suppose you could line up a bunch—say, a hundred or so—of your guys, and let me pick the ones I think would fit with the concept we're trying for?"

"No problem at all. I'll get right on it, and get right back to you."

Major Macklin then called the commanding officer of the provisional replacement battalion he knew had been formed to deal with the inflow of Marines to Camp Pendleton. He explained to him what he wanted.

"There's hardly anybody here," he said. "The casuals we had, the regular Marines sent here to fill out the 1st Division, are just about gone, and there's only one reserve company here . . . they weren't expected until August first, but they got in this morning."

"How many men are we talking about?"

"A little over two hundred, plus five officers."

"Have them standing by at 0700 tomorrow. A casting director will select from them the fifty or so men he needs for the *Halls of Montezuma* project."

"What exactly does that mean?"

"It means for two days—possibly three, whatever it takes—the men selected will be used as extras in the motion picture."

"Christ, Macklin, I don't know. For one thing, there's in-processing to be done, you know, for reclassification and assignment. And then their company commander has reserved the known distance range so they can zero their individual weapons. . . ."

"That will have to be put on hold, I'm afraid, until after the filming is completed."

"By whose authority?"

"General Dawkins has said this project has the highest priority. Are you willing to accept that, or should I call General Dawkins and tell him you're telling me we can't provide the full cooperation Headquarters Marine Corps has promised these Hollywood people?"

The provisional reception battalion commander did not want to discuss anything with the assistant commanding general.

"They'll be standing by at 0700, Macklin," he said.

"Thank you," Major Macklin said, and then went to find the production company's extras casting director to tell him what had been arranged.

When Captain George F. Hart was informed that the 29 July breakfast meal would be served to his company at 0430, as at 0700, he was to have his company formed in front of battalion headquarters, in field gear, and carrying their assigned weapons, he perhaps naturally assumed that battalion headquarters was where the trucks would pick up Baker Company to transport them to one of the known distance firing ranges.

Company B, 55th Marines, was formed at 0655. At that point, the commanding officer of the Replacement Battalion (Provisional) appeared at the door to his headquarters, and when he had caught Captain Hart's attention, signaled him to join him.

Hart turned his company over to his exec and walked to the battalion headquarters. Since they were both out of doors and under arms, Hart saluted.

"Good morning, sir," he said.

"Good morning, Captain," the battalion commander said. "You and your officers aren't going to be needed for this little exercise. Turn the company over to the first sergeant."

"Excuse me, sir?"

"Turn your company over to your first sergeant, Captain, and dismiss your officers from the formation."

"Aye, aye, sir," Captain Hart said. He complied with his orders and then returned to the Replacement Battalion (Provisional) commanding officer.

"Sir, may I ask what's going on?"

"Fifty of your men are going to be in the movies, Captain. A talent scout will shortly appear to determine which ones."

"Sir, I don't understand. . . ."

"That must be them now," the battalion commander said, nodding with his head toward a Plymouth station wagon coming down the street.

The station wagon was driven by a sergeant. In the rear seat were two men, a Marine officer and a plump, wavy-haired blond man the far side of forty. The sergeant opened the door and the two men got out.

"Jesus Christ," Captain Hart said. "Macklin!"

"Are you acquainted with Major Macklin, Captain?"

"Yes, sir, I am."

The last time I saw that cowardly sonofabitch was when we loaded the bastard on the sub, Sunfish to go to Mindanao. Killer McCoy had authority to blow the bastard away if he interfered with anything, and I was actually disappointed when the Killer came out and told me Macklin was still alive; that he'd decided the best way to deal with the sonofabitch was just leave him on Mindanao and hope the Japs caught him.

"Major Macklin is the action officer for the *Halls of Montezuma* movie project," the Replacement Battalion (Provisional) commander said.

"With respect, sir," Captain Hart said, "I don't really give much of a damn about Major Macklin or his movie project. Sir, my company was scheduled to go to the known distance range . . ."

"I'm sorry to have to tell you this, in this way, Captain," the replacement battalion commander said, "but you no longer have a company."

"Sir?"

"As of 0001 this morning, Company B, 55th Marines was disbanded, and its officers and men transferred to the Replacement Battalion (Provisional) for reassignment. They—and you—will be reassigned within the Marine Corps—mostly likely as replacements to the 1st Marine Division—where they are needed."

"I'm not sure I understand," Hart said.

"Company B, 55th Marines no longer exists. It was disbanded as of 0001 this morning. Its personnel—including you—are now assigned to the Replacement Battalion. You will be reassigned where the Marine Corps thinks you will be of the greatest value to the Marine Corps."

"That's absolutely fucking outrageous!" Hart exploded.

"Watch your mouth, Captain," the major said.

"Goddamn it!" Hart went on. "I trained those men. I'm responsible for them. I promised their families I would look out for them!"

"Be that as it may—"

"I'll be a sonofabitch if I'll put up with this!"

"All right, Captain, that's quite enough. You will go to your room, and you will stay there until I send for you. That's an order."

Hart glowered at him for fifteen seconds, which seemed much longer.

"I request permission to see the Inspector General, sir," he said.

"You will go to your room and stay there until I send for you. When I do, I will consider your request to see the Inspector General."

"Sir, I believe it is my right to see the Inspector General with or without your permission."

At this point, the commanding officer of the Replacement Battalion (Provisional) lost his temper.

"All right, goddamn it, go to the IG. And when the IG throws you out on your ass, you will then report to me, and I'll deal with your insubordinate behavior. Just get the hell out of my sight!"

Hart walked away from the major, took a final look at Major Robert B. Macklin, USMC, who was walking slowly down the lines of Baker Company following the civilian, and writing down the names of those members of his company of which the civilian apparently approved on a clipboard.

Then he walked angrily away.

He walked for three blocks without any real idea of where he was going.

Then he stopped a passing corporal and asked him where the office of the Inspector General was.

"On the main post, sir," the corporal said. "In the headquarters building."

"How do I get to the main post?"

"It's down this road, sir," the corporal said. "Too far to walk."

"Thank you," Hart said, and went to the side of the road, and when the first vehicle approached, held up his thumb to hitchhike a ride.

The captain in the office of the Inspector General wasn't much more help than the commanding officer of the Replacement Battalion (Provisional) had been.

"Captain, that decision has been made. The men of your reserve unit will be assigned where they will be of most use to the Marine Corps."

"I can swallow that, I suppose," Hart said, his voice rising. "I don't like it, but I can swallow it. But they should be getting ready to go to war, not fucking around with some bullshit movie!"

"Calm down, before you get yourself in trouble," the captain said.

"Where's the commanding general's office? On this floor?"

"You really don't want to go there, Captain."

"The hell I don't! Where's his fucking office?"

The captain did not reply.

Hart glowered at him, then stormed out of his office.

There was a sign in the lobby of the building. The offices of the commanding general and the deputy commanding general were on the second floor.

Hart took the stairs to the second floor two at a time.

There were three people in the outer office: Sergeant Major Neely, Corporal Delbert Wise, and Colonel Edward Banning.

"Well, I'll be damned!" Colonel Banning exclaimed. "How are you, George?"

"Pretty goddamned pissed off is how I am!"

"About what?"

"They took my company away from me, and that miserable sonofabitch Macklin is using them as extras in some bullshit movie!"

"George, calm down," Banning said.

Banning looked at Sergeant Major Neely and Corporal Wise, and indicated with a nod of his head that they should make themselves absent. When they had left the office, he turned to Hart.

"Okay. Now start at the beginning, George."

Seven minutes later, Brigadier General Clyde W. Dawkins entered the outer office, a look of annoyance on his face that neither his sergeant major nor the clerk-typist had answered his two pushes of the intercom button, signaling that the deputy commanding general wished coffee.

The look of annoyance on his face changed to one of curiosity when he saw Colonel Banning and Captain Hart.

"What's going on, Colonel?"

"May I see the general a moment, sir?" Banning asked.

Dawkins considered that a moment, then signaled Banning to follow him into his office. Banning did so, closing the door after him.

"Okay, now what's going on, Ed?" Dawkins asked.

"General, you have one highly pissed off captain out there," Banning said.

"Pissed off about what?"

"He had a reserve infantry company in St. Louis, which they just took away from him and turned over to Major Macklin to make a John Wayne movie."

Speaking very rapidly, General Dawkins replied: "One, breaking up the units was a tough decision. It was the right one. Two. Eighth and Eye ordered that we support that movie. Understand?"

"General, unless some action is taken, there will be a headline in tomorrow's *St. Louis Post-Dispatch* reading, 'Over Bitter Objections of Commanding Officer, St. Louis Marine Reserve Company Broken Up; Men Scattered Through Marine Corps'. Or words to that effect."

"Oh, Christ! Is that guy some kind of nut? Doesn't he know how to take orders?"

"I don't think that he would obey an order not to talk to the press. It's the only option he sees to right what he really considers a wrong."

"Jesus!"

"Will you trust me on this, General?"

"Okay. Why not?"

"May I use your phone, sir?"

Dawkins waved at the telephone on his desk.

Banning dialed the operator.

"Get me the Commandant in Washington, please. Colonel Edward Banning is calling."

"Jesus Christ!" Dawkins exclaimed.

Someone in Washington answered the telephone.

"No, Major, I don't wish to tell you what I wish to speak to the Commandant about. Please tell him I'm calling in a matter connected with General Pickering."

There was another pause.

"Sir, I wouldn't bother you with this personally, except that I feel it's necessary."

Pause.

"Sir, Captain George F. Hart, who was General Pickering's aide-de-camp— actually bodyguard—in the last war has just reported on active duty. I can think of nowhere else in the Corps where he would be of more use than serving with General Pickering again, and I'd like to get him over there as soon as possible."

Pause.

"Yes, sir, there is. I'm in General Dawkins's office. Hold one, sir."

He handed the telephone to Dawkins.

"General Dawkins, sir."

Pause.

"Aye, aye, sir. Do you wish to speak to Colonel Banning again, sir?"

The Commandant of the Marine Corps apparently had nothing else to say to Colonel Banning, for General Dawkins put the telephone back in its cradle.

He looked at Banning, and then went to his office door and issued an order.

"Come in here, please, Sergeant Major," he said. "You, too, Wise. Bring your pad." He paused and added. "You, too, Captain. You might as well hear this."

The three trooped into the office.

"Wise, take a memorandum, record of telecon."

"Aye, aye, sir."

"This date, this hour, between the Commandant of the Marine Corps and the Deputy Commanding General, Camp Pendleton. The Commandant desires . . ." He paused. "What does the Commandant desire, Colonel Banning?"

"That appropriate orders be issued immediately detaching Captain George F. Hart from Replacement Battalion (Provisional) Camp Pendleton and attaching subject officer to the Central Intelligence Agency, Washington, D.C., with further detachment to the staff of the Assistant Director of the CIA for Asia, and directing subject officer to proceed by the first available air transportation to Tokyo, Japan. You get all that, Corporal?"

"Yes, sir."

"Any questions, Captain Hart?" Banning asked.

"Who is the . . . What did you say, Assistant Director of the CIA? What am I going do there?"

"That will be up to General Pickering, Captain. I'm sure that he can find something useful for you to do."

"I'd like to say goodbye to my men," Hart said.

"That can be arranged," Banning said.

"You go with him, Sergeant Major," General Dawkins ordered. "See if you do a better job of explaining why the Corps has been forced to disband the reserve units than anybody else over there has."

"Aye, aye, sir."

"I'll go, too," Banning said.

"I wish I had the time," General Dawkins said. "But . . ." He put out his hand to Hart. "My compliments to General Pickering, Hart. And good luck."

XI

[ONE]
Communications Center
Eighth United States Army (Rear)
Pusan, Korea
0730 2 August 1950

Master Sergeant Paul T. Keller, twenty-nine years old, had been drafted into the U.S. Army almost immediately upon graduation from high school in June of 1942. After basic training, he had been trained as a high-speed radio operator, and had been assigned to Major General I. D. White's 2nd Armored "Hell on Wheels" Division, ending up the war as a technical sergeant on the banks of the Elbe.

A recruiter had argued that if he went home now—as his points entitled him to—and got out, he was going to find himself just one more ex-GI looking for a job. On the other hand, if he reenlisted, he would immediately be promoted to master sergeant. Moreover, he could go home by air—instead of on a troop ship—and go on a sixty-day reenlistment leave. After that, he could have his choice of both any course he wanted to attend at the Army Signal School at Fort Monmouth, and any post, camp, or station in the United States or around the world.

Midway through his leave, Master Sergeant Keller elected to attend the Cryptographic School. He didn't know the first thing about cryptography, except what he'd seen in the movies, and had never heard of the Army Security Agency, but it sounded interesting—even exciting—and he'd had enough of supervising a room full of radio operators sitting at typewriters with cans on their ears. And he suspected that Germany was going to be a good place to be stationed, now that the war was over.

Orders came assigning him to the Army Security Agency, and his parents and brother told him the FBI had been asking questions of everybody about him, "in connection with a high-level security clearance."

The clearance—Top Secret, Cryptographic I—came through when he was at Fort Monmouth taking Phase I of the course. By then he'd learned once you were in the ASA, had been granted the clearance, you stayed in the ASA. That meant that although he would be in Germany, he wouldn't be assigned there. He would be assigned to the ASA Headquarters, in Vint Hill Farms Station, Virginia, outside Washington, with "duty station wherever."

It turned out that he had a flair for cryptography. After being the honor graduate of Phase II of the course, at Vint Hill Farms, he was sent to work at Headquarters, U.S. Forces, European Theater, in the Farben Building in Frankfurt, Germany. After two months there, the ASA changed his "duty assignment" to "Crypto NCO for the U.S. Element, Allied Commandatura, Berlin."

That was really good duty. He had his own apartment, and there were none of the annoying details usually associated with Army life, standing formations, pulling staff duty NCO, that sort of thing. All he had to do was let them know where he was twenty-four hours a day in case something hot had to go out, or came in.

And the Berlin girls were beautiful. So beautiful that he really had to take care not to fall for one of them. The CIC kept a close eye on everybody in the ASA and especially on crypto people. Keller didn't know if it was true, but the CIC thought the Russians were using good-looking fräuleins to put ASA/Crypto people in compromising positions. If it looked to the CIC that you were getting too close to a fräulein, you got your security clearance jerked—by then his clearance was Top Secret/Crypto IV, which meant he was cleared to en- and decrypt anything—and losing that meant it would be back to some radio room.

The ASA assigned him temporary duty stations all over Europe—Vienna, Budapest, Moscow—filling in for other crypto people on leave or sick or whatever.

He was really unhappy when in late 1949, the ASA called him back to Vint Hill Farms to be an instructor. But even that proved to be very good duty. It was a good place to be stationed, near Washington, and he could go home to Philadelphia just about whenever he wanted.

Two weeks before, the First Soldier had called him in. With a five-day delay-en-route leave, he was to report to the transportation officer, Fort Lewis, Washington, for further shipment by air to Headquarters, Eighth United States Army, which had an urgent priority for crypto people.

This was not like Frankfurt or Berlin. They took him from the airport outside Tokyo, to Camp Drake, where they took his personal possessions from him for storage, and issued him two sets of fatigues, field gear, combat boots, and an M1 Garand, the first one he'd held in his hands since 1943. And then put him on another airplane the same day and flew him to K-1, the airport outside Pusan.

He quickly learned the Eighth Army (Rear) really did have "an urgent need" for crypto people. Things were fucked up beyond description. When he got there, he saw that Operational Immediate messages, which were supposed to get encrypted and transmitted *right then,* took hours—even days—to get out.

It would take him a couple of days to straighten things out, but he knew he could do it.

It was going to be a lousy assignment, living in a goddamn tent, sleeping on a no-mattress cot, eating off stainless-steel trays, taking a crap in a wooden-holer GI outhouse, but that's the way it was. It was payback, he decided philosophically, for all the good times.

The first thing he did was get rid of the Garand. Crypto centers needed to be protected, sure, but not by the NCOIC carrying a Garand. There were guards on the door, armed with Thompson submachine guns. Keller got a Thompson for himself, plus a .45 pistol.

The second thing he did to speed things up was to get the signal officer to agree that since Operational Immediates—and for that matter, Urgents—

should really get immediate encryption and transmission, the authority to clas-
sify messages should be restricted to officers senior enough to know what an Operational Immediate really was. Henceforth, the signal officer agreed,
Operational Immediates would require the signature of a full bull colonel, or
better, and Urgents, the signature of at least a light colonel.

Within twenty-four hours—once the backlog had been cleared—Operational Immediates and Urgents were going out in minutes. Which meant that
before senior officers had started to sign off on them, most of the messages with
that priority really shouldn't have been Operational Immediate and Urgent.

Master Sergeant Keller was surprised when the door opened and two
Marines came in. After a moment, he saw that one of them had captain's bars
painted in black on the collar points of his fatigue jacket. He remembered that
the Marines called fatigues "utilities." The other one had metal warrant officer's
bars pinned on his collar points.

Keller knew the 1st Provisional Marine Brigade was coming to Pusan—he
had personally decrypted the Top Secret Urgent from the convoy commander,
saying when they would arrive, and the reply from the Marine general saying
they should be prepared to get off the ships ready to fight—but they'd been
scheduled to arrive in thirty minutes.

And these two looked like they'd been in Korea for weeks, and up with the
infantry, not as if they'd just gotten off a ship. They were sweat-soaked, looked
tired, and the captain had a Garand slung from his shoulder, with two spare clips
clipped on the strap. Grenades bulged in the warrant officer's pockets.

*Whenever they'd gotten here, they should not be in here. What the hell's the mat-
ter with the guards?*

"Good morning, Sergeant," the captain said.

"Good morning, sir," Master Sergeant Keller replied. "Sir, you really
shouldn't be in here. How'd you get in?"

"Through the door," the captain replied, somewhat sarcastically. "I just
want to use the landline."

There was a secure landline, connected to the Communications Center in
the Dai Ichi Building in Tokyo. But it wasn't really secure, and it was intended primarily to keep the technicians in Pusan in touch with the technicians in Tokyo.

"Sir, there's no landline available," Keller said. "And, sir, I'm going to have
to insist that you leave. This is a restricted area."

"Yeah, I know," the captain said. "Maybe you better call your officer,
Sergeant."

Master Sergeant Keller went into the encryption room itself, and signaled the duty officer, Captain R. C. "Pete" Peters, SigC, USA, that he needed a word with him.

The captain went into the outer room.

"Hey, McCoy," Captain Peters greeted the two Marines with a smile. "What can we do for the Marines this morning?"

"You might want to thank God, Pete," the captain said. "The Marines are about to land."

"That's not funny, McCoy," Captain Peters said. "I hope to Christ they got here in time. What can I do for you?"

"I need to make a quick call on your landline," Captain Kenneth R. McCoy.

"Help yourself," Captain Peters said, and then saw the look on Master Sergeant Keller's face. "It's okay, Keller," he said. "He and Master Gunner Zimmerman are cleared for whatever they ask for."

"Yes, sir," Keller said.

Captain McCoy picked up the telephone. It was a direct line, and when the receiver was lifted, the communications switchboard operator in Tokyo answered.

"Patch me through to the Hotel Imperial, please," McCoy said. A moment later, he added, "Captain McCoy for General Pickering."

And a moment after that, he repeated those exact words, then: "When will he be back, do you know?" Another pause, then: "No. No message, thank you."

He turned to the other Marine.

"Not there, and no ETA."

"OpImmediate him," the Marine warrant officer suggested.

"Yeah," McCoy said, and picked up a lined pad, wrote quickly on it, and handed it to Master Sergeant Keller.

Operational Immediate
Unclassified
Hq SCAP
Eyes only Brig General Pickering, USMC

Telephoning failed 0730 2 Aug.
   Going to pier to meet 1st Provisional Marine
Brigade. Request permission for Zimmerman

> *and me to temporarily attach ourselves to Gen Craig to make ourselves useful. Will continue to report.*
>
> *McCoy, Capt, USMCR*

"You want this to go Operational Immediate?" Master Sergeant Keller asked, a little dubiously.

"He has the authority," Captain Peters said. "I guess I should have said there's an exception to the colonel's rule. Captain McCoy."

"And Mr. Zimmerman," McCoy said.

"And Mr. Zimmerman," Captain Peters echoed.

"I'll get this right out," Keller said, and went into the radio room. When he came out, the two Marines were gone.

"What's with those two?" Keller asked.

"CIA," Captain Peters said.

He was not really surprised. He'd handled a lot of traffic for CIA agents when he was in Europe, especially in Berlin.

"They're not Marines?"

"They're Marines, *and* they're CIA. If you really want to know what's going on here, you ought to encrypt their reports yourself."

"Interesting."

Keller decided he would do just that.

[TWO]
Pier Three
Pusan, Korea
0805 2 August 1950

Captain McCoy found Brigadier General Edward A. Craig, USMC—in utilities, sitting in a U.S. Army Jeep that he was apparently driving himself—on the wharf, looking more than a little unhappy as he watched the USS *George Clymer* (APA-27) being tied up, her rails lined with utilities-clad Marines acting for all the world as if they were being docked at a liberty port.

McCoy and Zimmerman got out of their "borrowed" U.S. Army Jeep—the lettering on the bumpers of which identified it as belonging to Fox Company, 21st Infantry—and approached Craig's Jeep. Craig heard them coming and looked over his shoulder.

McCoy and Zimmerman saluted.

"Good morning, sir," McCoy said.

Craig returned the salute.

"You two look like you need a bath," he said.

"We were up at Taejon, sir," McCoy said. "We wanted to see this," he gestured at the *Clymer* and the USS *Pickaway* (APA-222), another attack transport, which was tying up farther down the pier, "and there's something else. . . ."

"Take a good look at those happy tourists, McCoy," General Craig said, a little bitterly. "Would you suspect that I sent them a radio ordering that ammo be issued and they debark prepared to fight?"

McCoy was trying to frame a reply to that when Zimmerman laughed, and said, "Jesus, will you look at that!"

A military unit was marching down the pier, between the warehouses and the ships. There was a color guard, in mussed and baggy khakis, carrying the flags of the United States, Korea, and the United Nations. Marching behind them, in U.S. Army fatigues, was a Korean Army military band, playing what could have been—and then, on the other hand, might not have been—the Marine Hymn.

General Craig smiled.

"In the interests of international cooperation, Mr. Zimmerman," he said. "I think we should commend those splendid musicians for at least trying."

"Yes, sir," Zimmerman said.

They could hear guffaws and laughter from the Marines hanging over the rails of the decks and gun positions of the *Clymer*.

"You said there was something else, McCoy?" General Craig asked.

"Yes, sir," McCoy said. "Sir, I just asked General Pickering for permission for Zimmerman and myself to attach ourselves temporarily to the brigade. I thought we could be useful. If nothing else, as interpreters."

"And General Pickering's reply?"

"I couldn't get through to him, sir. But I can't think of any reason he'd object. I told him we'd continue to report."

"Subject to General Pickering's approval, I accept," General Craig said. "For the time being, consider yourselves attached to me."

"Aye, aye, sir. Thank you," McCoy said, and went on: "We were at Headquarters Eighth Army last night, sir. They hadn't decided where the brigade will be sent."

It was a statement that was also a question.

"They still haven't," Craig said. "What do you know about Masan, McCoy?"

"It looks to me like the next North Korean objective, sir," McCoy said. "And a couple of prisoners Zimmerman and I talked to last night were the 6th NK Division. So far the 6th has done very well. One of them had this in his pocket."

He handed General Craig a small sheet of flimsy paper, crudely printed.

"What's it say?"

McCoy translated it in a matter-of-fact voice.

"Comrades, the enemy is demoralized. The task given us is the liberation of Masan and Chinju . . ."

"That sort of spells it out, doesn't it?" Craig said.

"There's more, sir. Shall I—"

Craig signaled him to go ahead.

". . . the liberation of Masan and Chinju and the annihilation of the remnants of the enemy. The liberation of Chinju and Masan means the final battle to cut off the windpipe of the enemy. Comrades, this glorious task has fallen to our division!"

He raised his eyes to Craig to show that he had finished.

Craig looked at McCoy for a moment. After a moment, Craig said:

"I decided late last night that in the absence of orders from General Walker to the contrary, I'm going to move the brigade by truck and train up toward Masan. I borrowed two companies of six-by-six trucks from the Army Transportation Corps. If I can break up the parties on the attack transports, and get those ships unloaded today and tonight, we'll move out in the morning."

"The 6th Division has T-34 tanks, sir."

"Just before we left Pendleton, we drew new M-26s," Craig said. "'Pattons.' I suppose we are about to learn if they're as good as Fort Knox thinks they are."

"Sir, the T-34 looks as if it's vulnerable to the 3.5-inch bazooka. The 27th Infantry managed to stop a column—"

Craig held up his hand to silence him, then pointed to the *Pickaway*. A ship's ladder had been put over the side, and a dozen Marines were hurrying down it.

"Save it, McCoy," General Craig said. "I'm going to gather the officers in the mess. I was going to brief them on enemy intentions and capabilities. I just decided you're better qualified to do that than I am."

"Aye, aye, sir."

Craig got out of his Jeep, motioned for McCoy and Zimmerman to follow him, and walked down the pier, toward the officers now approaching him.

Salutes were exchanged, then handshakes.

"Has ammunition been issued?" General Craig asked.

"No, sir."

"I sent a message to do so," Craig said. "Apparently it went astray."

The officers looked uncomfortable.

Craig turned to one of the enlisted Marines—a young PFC, obviously a runner.

"Son, have you ammunition for that piece?"

"Yes, sir," the Marine said, and patted his cartridge belt.

"Well, then, here's your first lesson in how things are in Korea. Load and lock, son. And then guard those two Jeeps down the pier. Unguarded Jeeps get stolen here. Isn't that right, Captain McCoy?"

"Yes, sir."

"Assign one lieutenant per company to supervise the issue of basic ammunition loads," Craig ordered. "*All* other officers will assemble *now* in the mess of the *Clymer* for a briefing by Captain McCoy on enemy locations, intentions, and capabilities. After that, we will begin to unload the ships. We move to the lines in the morning."

The ship's ladder of the *Clymer* was dropped to the dock. Marines started to climb down it.

Craig went to the foot of the ladder and held up his hand to stop them, then started up the ladder.

"As pissed as he was," Zimmerman said softly to McCoy, "about them not being ready to fight, I expected to see some brass getting a *real* ass-chewing."

McCoy chuckled.

"Ernie, General Craig can chew ass better with a raised eyebrow and a little disappointment in his voice than you and I can shouting ourselves hoarse."

Zimmerman shrugged. There was immediate confirmation of McCoy's theory.

"Anytime you're ready, Captain McCoy," General Craig called politely from near the top of the ship's ladder.

"Coming, sir," McCoy said. "Sorry, sir," and trotted toward the ladder.

[THREE]
Communications Center
Eighth United States Army (Rear)
Pusan, Korea
0730 2 August 1950

The secure landline telephone between the communications center of Eighth
United States Army (Rear) in Pusan and the communications center of Headquarters, Supreme Commander Allied Powers and United Nations Command
was intended solely to provide communications between the technicians in the
two commo centers.

So when Master Sergeant Paul T. Keller, heard it buzz, he answered it cryp-
tically before it could buzz again, wondering what the hell else somebody in
Tokyo was going to announce was wrong with the crypto machines, the radio
or radio-teletype circuits, or all three, what would have to be fixed, how much
would have to be retransmitted.

On another telephone line, he would have said "Eighth Army Rear Com-
Center, Sergeant Keller, sir." Now he just said, "Keller."

"Who's speaking, please?" the caller asked.

"Master Sergeant Keller. Who's this?"

"Sergeant, my name is Pickering. Brigadier General, Marine Corps."

*The addressee of that OpImmediate that Marine captain sent. How did he get
access to this line?*

"Yes, sir?"

"A short time ago, there was a message, an Operational Immediate, sent
from Pusan by Captain K. R. McCoy. A Marine officer."

"Yes, sir, I'm familiar with it."

"Is he still there, anywhere near, by any chance?"

"No, sir."

"Have you any idea where he went?"

"Sir, I believe he's going to the pier."

"I have to get a message to him. To him and Brigadier General Craig, the
commanding general of the 1st Provisional Marine Brigade. How can I do that?"

"General Craig'll be no problem, sir. They're setting up a commo center for
the Marines right now."

"Right now is when I need to send this message. It may be necessary to send
someone to hand-deliver it. Can you do that, or would you rather I spoke with
an officer?"

"I can arrange that, sir," Keller said. "What's the message?"

"Permission denied. Repeat denied. Return immediately. Repeat immediately. Signature Pickering Brigadier General. Got that?"

"Yes, sir."

"And I'll want you to message me, either by telephone—they'll patch you through to me at the Imperial Hotel—or by Operational Immediate that the message has been delivered."

"Yes, sir."

"You're very obliging, Sergeant, and I realize this will foul up your schedule. But if it wasn't important, I wouldn't ask you to do it."

"No problem, sir."

"I'll be waiting to hear from you. Thank you again."

"Yes, sir."

Master Sergeant Keller stuck his head in the radio room and caught Captain Peter's eye.

"Captain, I've got an errand to run. I'll be back as soon as I can."

Captain Peters nodded, and Keller pulled his head back out of the door before Peters could ask him, "What kind of an errand?"

He picked up his Thompson and went outside the building and commandeered one of the message center Jeeps and told the driver to take him to the pier.

"You can't get on the piers, Sergeant. The Marines are getting off their boats, and they put up a guard."

"Just take me there," Keller said.

On the way through Pusan's narrow, filthy streets, crowded with military vehicles too large to pass side by side, Keller wondered why he had been so obliging.

Because the caller was a general, and generals—even Marine Corps generals—get what they ask sergeants to do for them?

Because, in addition to being a general, this guy had obviously had access to the SCAP/UN commo center and the landline?

Or maybe because Peters had told him the captain was CIA?

And Captain Peters, who's a good guy, is obviously going to be pissed because I didn't tell him what was going on.

There was a guard post at the entrance to the wharf area, and three Marines, a sergeant, and two PFCs, all of them in field gear, one of them with a Browning automatic rifle hanging from his shoulder.

The sergeant stepped into the road and held up his hand in a casual, but very firm, gesture meaning "stop."

"Off-limits, Sergeant," he said. "Sorry."

"I'm from the Eighth Army ComCenter," Keller said. "I have a message for General Craig."

"Let's have it. I'll see it gets to him."

"It's an oral message, Sergeant?" Keller said.

"An *oral* message?" the Marine sergeant asked, dubiously.

"Is there an officer of the guard?" Keller asked.

"Of course there's an officer of the guard," the Marine sergeant said.

"Send for him," Keller said.

"What?"

"Send for him."

"Why should I do that?"

"Because I have six stripes and you have three, and that's what they call an order."

The Marine sergeant looked at Keller for a long moment, then gestured to one of the PFCs, who started off at a trot down the dock.

Two minutes later, a Marine captain walked up, trailed by the PFC.

Keller and the Marine sergeant saluted him.

"What's up?" the captain asked.

"Sir, I've got a message for General Craig," Keller said.

"An *oral* message," the Marine sergeant said.

"What is it, Sergeant?" the captain said. "I'll get it to him."

"Sir, it is oral, and I was ordered to deliver it personally," Keller said.

"By who?" the captain said.

"Brigadier General Pickering, sir," Keller said, then added: "U.S. Marine Corps."

"Never heard of him," the captain said, matter-of-factly. "But I can't imagine why a master sergeant would . . . Come with me, Sergeant."

The captain started walking down the wharf, and Keller started to get back in the message center Jeep.

"The Jeep stays," the Marine sergeant said.

"Wait for me," Keller said to the driver, who nodded.

The reason the captain was walking and the Jeep denied access to the wharf became immediately clear.

The wharf was jammed with men, equipment, and supplies. Lines of Marines—their rifles stacked using the stacking swivels near the muzzles, something Keller hadn't seen since Germany—waited for cargo nets jammed with supplies being lowered from the two ships to touch the dock, then began to carry the individual cartons and crates to waiting U.S. Army GMC 6 × 6 trucks.

Other booms lowered Marine 6 × 6s, and trailers for them, many of them stacked high with supplies, to the dock. The trucks were joined with their trailers, and then quickly driven off to make room for other trucks, trailers, and other piles of supplies dumped from cargo nets.

The closest ship was the USS *Clymer.* The captain started up her ladder. There was a Navy officer and a sailor in a steel helmet at the top of the ladder. As the captain was explaining to the Navy officer who Keller was, Keller could see, farther down the wharf, the USS *Pickaway,* and past her—too far away for him to read her name—some kind of a Navy freighter unloading artillery pieces and M-26 "Patton" tanks.

"This way, please, Sergeant," the captain said, and Keller followed him onto the deck of the *Clymer* and then down a passageway and a narrow stairway and then another passageway until they reached a door guarded by two Marines. A sign read "Mess & Wardroom II."

"Wait here, Sergeant," the captain said, and went through the door.

A moment later, a tall, silver-haired man in Marine fatigues came through the door.

"My name is Craig," he said. "You have a message for me?"

"Yes, sir," Keller said. "General Pickering called from Tokyo and first asked if Captain McCoy was available. When I told him I believed Captain McCoy was on the pier, he gave me a message for you and Captain McCoy, and asked if I could deliver it personally."

He paused. Craig waited for him to go on.

"The message is 'Permission denied. Repeat denied. Return immediately. Repeat immediately. Signature, Pickering, Brigadier General, USMC'."

"I'll see that he gets the message, Sergeant. Thank you."

"Sir, General Pickering asked me to confirm that the message was delivered. To call him, sir."

Craig looked at him for a moment, then went into the mess.

"Gentlemen," Keller heard him say, loudly enough to be heard, "Captain McCoy will take one more question. We have to get on with the off-loading. Please join me, Captain McCoy, after the next question."

Then he came back into the passageway.

"He will be here shortly, Sergeant," he said. "How is it you—a master sergeant—are doing this personally?"

"I told General Pickering I would, sir."

A minute later, he heard someone in the mess call "At-ten-hut," and there was the sound of scraping chair legs.

Then McCoy, followed by Zimmerman, came into the corridor.

Craig steered him to the right of the door.

"The sergeant has a message for you, McCoy," Craig said. "For us. Go ahead, Sergeant."

"Permission denied. Repeat denied. Return immediately. Repeat immediately. Signature, Pickering, Brigadier General, USMC."

McCoy's face showed surprise, then regret.

"I'm sorry, sir," he said to General Craig.

"Never be sorry when you've tried to do a good thing, Captain," Craig said. "At least we got a splendid briefing out of you before other duty called."

"Thank you, sir," McCoy said.

"I presume General Pickering's order includes Mister Zimmerman?"

"I believe it does, sir."

"How will you get to Tokyo? You have orders?"

"Yes, sir, we do. We'll catch a ride out to K-1. . . ."

"You have a Jeep."

"Sir, I'd just have to leave it at K-1 for somebody to steal, and I wouldn't be surprised if that Jeep was already wearing some kind of Marine insignia."

"I'll get you a ride out to K-1," Craig said.

"Captain," Master Sergeant Keller said. "I've got a Jeep. I'll run you out to K-1."

"By your leave, sir?" McCoy said, coming to attention.

"Carry on, Mister McCoy," General Craig said.

[FOUR]

"I'll drive," Master Sergeant Keller said to the driver of the message center Jeep.

"Sergeant, I don't think you're supposed to do that."

"What I know you're supposed to do is what I tell you," Keller said. "Get in the back."

Keller got behind the wheel. McCoy got in beside him, and Zimmerman clambered over the back to sit beside the driver.

"Captain, before we go out there," Keller asked, "what are you going to do with that rifle, and Mr. Zimmerman's Thompson, when we get to K-1?"

"I don't understand the question," McCoy said.

"The Air Force . . . K-1 is now a MATS terminal," Keller said. "They won't let you get on a plane with a weapon."

"Jesus!" Zimmerman said, disgustedly.

With our orders, McCoy thought, *I could load a 105-mm howitzer on the plane. But that would mean using the CIA orders, and I don't really want to do that.*

"What do you suggest, Sergeant?" McCoy asked.

"Well, if you're coming back, sir, I could keep them for you."

"What's in it for you?"

"You might not come back . . .," Keller said.

"In which case, you end up owning a first-rate Thompson and a National Match M-1?"*

"Yes, sir. It looks to me like your choice is maybe getting your weapons back from me, or for sure losing them to the Air Force," Keller said.

"Ernie, we're going to leave the Thompson and the Garand with this doggie," McCoy said. There was a tone of approval in McCoy's voice. "How come a smart guy like you didn't join the Marines?" he asked.

"I couldn't, sir. I didn't qualify. My parents were married, sir," Keller said.

McCoy's eyebrows went up. Zimmerman guffawed, then laughed out loud.

"You're okay, Keller," Zimmerman said. "For a goddamn doggie."

"Thank you very much, sir," Keller said, straightfaced.

This time McCoy laughed.

"Keep your pistol, Ernie," McCoy ordered.

The pistols Master Gunner Zimmerman had drawn for them from a fellow master gunner at Camp Pendleton were also National Match, far more accurate and reliable than a standard-issue Pistol, 1911A1, Caliber .45 ACP. They were worth trying to sneak past the Air Force.

As they approached the base operations building at K-1, there was a new sign, neatly painted on a four-by-eight sheet of plywood.

UNITED STATES AIR FORCE
MILITARY AIR TRANSPORT SERVICE
U.S. AIR FORCE STATION K-1
PUSAN, KOREA

There was an Air Force C-54, a four-engine Douglas transport, sitting in front of the building, with a ladder leading up into it.

"Looks like you got here just in time," Keller said.

---

*Standard M-1 rifles that demonstrated especial accuracy, and were fine-tuned by master gunsmiths, were set aside for use in the annual National Matches rifle competition.

"When we come back, Keller," Zimmerman said, "and there's rust on my Thompson, I will turn you into a soprano."

They shrugged out of their field gear and put their National Match .45's in the small of their backs, under their utilities jackets, which they wore outside their trousers.

"In case you do wind up owning that Garand, Keller," McCoy said. "Take care of it. And thank you for everything."

"Forget it, Captain."

"Forget what? The thanks or the M-1?"

"Maybe both, sir," Keller said. "I'll wait until you're airborne, then call General Pickering and tell him you're on the way."

"Thank you, Number Two," McCoy said.

Keller saluted. McCoy and Zimmerman returned it, and went into the terminal building, where there was an Air Force staff sergeant behind a counter.

"Can I help you, Captain?"

"If that C-54's headed for Tokyo, we need to be on it."

"Not a chance, sir. It's full. There may be another flight late this afternoon, but I think you'd better find a bed in the BOQ. I know I can get you on the flight first thing tomorrow."

"We need to be on that one," McCoy said, and took the Dai Ichi orders from his pocket and handed them to the sergeant.

"Sorry, Captain," the sergeant said. "Just about everybody on that airplane has SCAP orders, and a priority, like yours. And the junior one is a major—"

"How about these orders?" McCoy said, and handed him the CIA orders.

The sergeant's eyes went up.

"I'll have to show these to the duty officer," he said, and turned from the counter.

"I don't let those orders out of my sight, Sergeant. Why don't you go fetch the duty officer?"

The sergeant shrugged, handed McCoy the CIA orders, and went to an office at the end of the room. An Air Force major came out and went to the counter.

"Sir, we need to be on that airplane," McCoy said. "Here's the authority."

The major read the orders. His eyebrows went up.

"You have the manifest, Sergeant?" he asked.

The sergeant handed him a clipboard, on which had been typed the names of the passengers.

He went down the list with a finger.

"There's a bird colonel on here with a Triple A," he said, "Minor, George P.

And the junior officer with a Quadruple A is apparently Major Finney, Howard T. Go out there, Sergeant, and tell them they've been bumped. They are not going to like it."

"Yes, sir," the sergeant said.

"As soon as they get off," the major went on, "you two get on. While they're in here, raising hell with me, I'll have the pilot close the door and taxi away from here until he gets his takeoff clearance."

"Thank you, sir."

"I never saw orders like that before," the major said.

Three minutes later, Colonel Minor and Major Finney, in khaki uniforms, came down the ladder from the C-54, saw the two Marine officers in sweat- and dirt-stained utilities waiting at the foot of the ladder, returned the Marines' salutes, and walked toward the passenger terminal.

Colonel Minor looked over his shoulder as he entered the building and saw McCoy and Zimmerman climbing the stairs. Then he hurried into the building.

[FIVE]
Haneda Airfield
Tokyo, Japan
1305 2 August 1950

As the MATS C-54 taxied toward the terminal, McCoy and Zimmerman seen a long line of staff cars and several small buses obviously waiting to transport the passengers from the airfield into Tokyo.

"The question now is how we get into Tokyo," McCoy said.

"My question is what the hell is going on?" Zimmerman said. " 'Immediately. Repeat immediately.' What the hell is that all about?"

McCoy shrugged.

"I have no idea," he confessed.

When they finally reached the door of the aircraft and stepped out onto the platform at the head of the stairway, Zimmerman said, "Hey, there's a Marine officer."

McCoy looked where Zimmerman was pointing, and saw the Marine officer just as Zimmerman added, "Jesus, that's George Hart, or his twin goddamn brother!"

"I'll be damned," McCoy said, and waited impatiently for the SCAP brass to get off the stairway.

Captain George F. Hart, USMCR, or his *doppelgänger,* in a crisp uniform, pushed himself off the front fender of a 1950 Chevrolet U.S. Army staff car and walked to the stairway.

He saluted.

"Hello, Ken," he said. "Ernie."

"Jesus, George, I thought you'd be running around the hills of Pendleton," McCoy said, reaching for Hart's hand.

"So did I," Hart said. "Delicate subject. I'll tell you later."

"You're here to meet us?" McCoy asked.

Hart nodded. "Old times, huh?" he said. He gestured toward the staff car, and they started walking to it.

"What's going on, George?" Zimmerman asked. "What's this 'return immediately, repeat immediately' all about?"

"I don't know much," Hart said, interrupting himself to ask, "You have luggage, gear?"

McCoy and Zimmerman shook their heads, "no."

"I don't know much about what's going on," Hart repeated. "It's got something to do with an Army two-star, a guy named Howe."

"General Howe is here?" McCoy asked.

Hart nodded. "We got in yesterday afternoon—"

" '*We*?'" McCoy interrupted.

"Same plane," Hart said. "I think it was a coincidence, but with Colonel Banning involved, you're never sure."

They reached the car. The driver, an Army sergeant, got from behind the wheel and opened the rear door on the driver's side.

"I'll get in front," Hart said, and got in beside the driver. McCoy and Zimmerman got in the back.

The driver got behind the wheel.

"Take us to Captain McCoy's quarters, please," Hart said.

"Yes, sir," the sergeant said.

"My quarters?" McCoy asked, confused.

Hart turned on the seat, held his right hand in front of his face, nodded toward the driver, and put his left index finger on his lips.

"Your orders, gentlemen," Hart said, "are to shower, shave, put on uniforms, and join General Pickering as soon as possible. You, Captain, under the circumstances, may have thirty minutes of personal time—no more; the general was quite specific about that—with Mrs. McCoy."

McCoy didn't speak, but asked with his eyes and eyebrows if he had heard correctly. Hart nodded.

"My uniforms are in the Imperial Hotel," Zimmerman said.

"Not any longer, Mr. Zimmerman," Hart said.

Zimmerman opened his mouth to speak, and McCoy laid a hand on his leg to silence him.

They rode the rest of the way to Denenchofu in silence.

[SIX]
No. 7 Saku-Tun
Denenchofu, Tokyo, Japan
1420 2 August 1950

The wooden sign reading "Capt K. R. McCoy USMCR" that had hung on the stone wall was gone, but what he could see of the house through the gate—*Why is the gate open?*—looked very much the same as it had when it had been home to Ken and Ernie. That surprised McCoy, until he realized that it had been only two months—*exactly* two months—since he had left here more or less in disgrace, about to be booted out of the Marine Corps.

It seems like a hell of a lot longer.

"Wait for us," Hart ordered the driver. "We won't be very long."

McCoy had a lot of questions to ask, but Hart had made it clear that they shouldn't be asked in the hearing of the CIC agent/staff car driver Willoughby had assigned to "ensure General Pickering's security."

He got out of the car and walked through the gate toward the house.

The door to the house slid open. A female that Captain Kenneth R. McCoy sincerely believed was the most beautiful woman in the world came out.

Maybe you can't gild a lily, but Jesus, Ernie never looked that good before!

Mrs. Ernestine McCoy was wearing an ankle-length elaborately embroidered black silk kimono.

She bowed, in the Japanese manner.

"Welcome home, most honorable husband," she said.

I am so goddamned dirty it would be obscene to get close to, much less hug, something that beautiful.

"Hey, baby," he said. His voice sounded strange.

Ernie turned and reached through the open door and came back with what looked very much as if it was a double scotch.

"I hope my humble offering of something to drink pleases my honorable husband," Ernie said, and bowing again, handed him the drink.

"What's with the Japanese-woman routine?" McCoy asked, taking the drink.

"I hoped that my honorable husband would be pleased," Ernie said.

"Your honorable husband is delighted," McCoy said. "Have you got one of those for Zimmerman?"

"For Zimmerman-san and Hart-san, honorable husband," Ernie said, and signaled through the door.

A Japanese woman came out with two drinks on a tray. Ernie took them one at a time, and bowing to Zimmerman and Hart, gave them to them.

"Hey, Ernie," Zimmerman said. "Could you get Mae-Su to think along these lines?"

"You'll have to do that yourself, Honorable Zimmerman-san," Ernie said.

"Baby, I really need a bath," McCoy said. "You don't want to know where Ernie and I have been."

"I can make a good guess from the way you smell, honorable husband," Ernie said.

"The only difference between a Korean outhouse and a Korean rice field," Zimmerman said, "is that some of the outhouses have roofs."

Ernestine Sage McCoy, still playing the Japanese wife, put her hands in front of her chest, palms together, stood to one side, bowed, and indicated that her husband was supposed to go into the house.

The living room, too, was unchanged from the last time he'd been in the house. McCoy had presumed their furniture was in a shipping crate somewhere, but he didn't know. Ernie took care of the house and everything connected with it.

He walked through the living room into the bedroom, also unchanged. The sheets on the bed were even turned down. He stuck his head in the bathroom, saw towels on the racks, and went inside and started to undress. He really wanted to put his arms around Ernie, and he couldn't do that reeking of the mud of human feces–fertilized Korean rice fields.

When he was naked, he turned the shower on, stepped into the glass walled stall, and let the water run over him for a full minute before even trying to soap himself.

He closed his eyes when he soaped his head and hair and was startled after a moment when he felt Ernie's arms around him, her breasts pressing against his back.

He raised his face to the showerhead, and after a moment opened his eyes and turned in his wife's arms and held her to him. She raised her face to his, and they kissed.

She caught his hand and directed it to her stomach.

"It's starting to show," she said, softly. He caressed her stomach for a moment, and then, with a groan, picked her up and carried her out of the shower to the bed.

"You want to tell me what's going on?" Ken McCoy asked.

Ernie was lying with her head on his chest, her legs thrown over his.

"Going on about what?"

"About everything," he said. "The house, the Japanese-wife routine. Everything."

"Well, they're sort of tied together," Ernie said.

"Start with the house," he said. "How did we get it back? General Pickering?"

"Actually, it's ours," Ernie said.

"What do you mean, 'ours'?"

"We own it," she said.

"How come we own it?"

"Well, when I went to the housing office when we first came to Japan, what they were going to give us was a captain's apartment—a captain/no children's apartment. They give out quarters on the size of the family. A captain/no children, gets one bedroom and a bedroom/study. I didn't like what they showed me, and I knew you wouldn't, so I went house-hunting. . . ."

"And bought this, and didn't tell me?"

"I didn't tell you because you thought our having money was going to hurt your Marine Corps career," she said. "I was willing to go along with that, but the quarters were different. I didn't want to live in that lousy little apartment. You really want to hear all of this?"

"All of it," he said.

"Okay. If you don't like what they offer you, you can 'go on the economy,' and if you can find something to rent that your housing allowance will pay for, they'll rent it for you."

"You said you bought it?"

"What you can rent on a captain's housing allowance is just about what they have, a dinky little apartment. So I made a deal with the Japanese real estate guy. I would buy this place. He would say he was renting it to me. They would send him a check for your housing allowance, which he would turn over to me."

"Jesus!"

"Then, when they sent us home, I figured it would sell better with furniture in it . . . No, that's not true. I wanted to sell the furniture, except for a few really personal things—that Ming vase we bought in Taipei, for example. When we started our new, out-of-the-Marine-Corps life, I didn't want you to remember, every time you sat on the couch or something, how they had crapped all over you."

McCoy said nothing.

"So it didn't sell while we were in the States," she said. "So when you and Uncle Flem came back, I called the real estate guy and told him to take it off the market. Then I decided, what the hell, since we have a house in Tokyo, there's no point in me staying in the States all by my fucking lonesome." She paused. "Are you really pissed, honey?"

"I'm shocked, is what I am," he said. " 'Fucking lonesome'? 'Crapped all over you'? 'Pissed'? What happened to that innocent lady I married?"

"She married a Marine, and she now knows all the dirty words," she said. "Answer the question."

He exhaled audibly.

"No," he said. "I can never be . . . pissed at you."

"Good, because there's more," Ernie said. "Now that we know how the Marine Corps paid you back for all your loyal service, I don't care if the goddamn Commandant himself knows we're well off—"

" *You're* well off," McCoy interrupted.

"—*we're* well off," Ernie repeated, firmly, even angrily. "Don't start that crap again, Ken. I've had enough of it."

"Yes, ma'am," he said.

"And we're going to live like it," Ernie said, firmly.

"Okay," he said.

"Okay?" she asked, as if she had expected an argument.

"Okay," he repeated.

"Starting tonight with dinner in the best restaurant in Tokyo," she said.

"Fine," he said.

"Well, with that out of the way," Ernie asked, "whatever shall we do now?" Her hand moved sensually down from his neck over his chest and stomach.

"Hart said Pickering said I get thirty minutes, no more, 'personal time' with my wife."

"Fuck him," Ernie said. "He can wait a couple of minutes. The whole fucking world can wait a couple of minutes."

"My thoughts exactly," McCoy said.

[SEVEN]

Captain Kenneth R. McCoy, USMC, came out of his bedroom in a crisp uniform fresh from the dry-cleaning plant of the Imperial Hotel.

He was just a little light-headed. It was probably due, he thought, to the sudden change of uniform, from foul utilities to clean greens, from foul and heavy boondockers to highly shined low-quarter shoes, which felt amazingly light on his feet, and he was, of course, freshly bathed and shaved.

And freshly laid, he thought somewhat crudely. *Freshly laid twice. It'll be a long goddamn time before those guys on the* Clymer *and* Pickaway *get to share any connubial bless again. If they ever do.*

Master Gunner Ernest W. Zimmerman, USMC, similarly attired, was sitting in one of the armchairs in the living room with Captain George F. Hart. They both had a drink dark with scotch in one hand, and a bacon wrapped oyster on a toothpick in the other.

"Do I live here now, or what?" Zimmerman asked. "From the way the room I took a shower in looks, it looks that way."

"There's plenty of room," McCoy said. "You, too, George."

"The boss wants me in the hotel, but thanks."

That's the difference between a reservist and a regular. I never think of General Pickering as anything but "the general," and neither does Zimmerman. George thinks of him as "the boss." And George is perfectly comfortable with that drink in his hand at three o'clock in the afternoon, and I was just about to jump Ernie's ass about it.

Fuck it. We're entitled to a drink.

He walked to the bar and made himself a drink.

"How come we never came here before?" Zimmerman asked.

"I didn't know until fifteen minutes ago that Ernie owns this place," McCoy said. "Until then, I thought it was GI quarters; that we'd given them up when they sent me to the States."

"Ernie bought this?" Hart asked.

"Ernie didn't like the GI quarters," McCoy said.

"Good for her," Zimmerman said. "Mae-Su got us out of officer's housing at Parris Island just as soon as she could get a house built in Beaufort."

"Duty calls," McCoy said. "Should I gulp this down, or trust that CIC spook to drive slowly?"

"Gulp it down," Zimmerman said, stood up, finished his drink, burped, and walked toward the door.

As he did, the doorbell—actually, a nine-inch brass bell hung on the wall just inside the gate—rang.

"Our driver getting impatient?" McCoy asked. "Who else knows we're here?"

"Maybe something for Ernie?" Zimmerman asked.

McCoy shook his head, "no"—there was a rear entrance to the property, with its own bell; tradesmen used that—and went to the front door, carrying his glass with him.

Brigadier General Fleming Pickering, USMCR, was halfway between the gate in the wall and the house. On his heels was Major General Ralph Howe, U.S. Army, and a large, muscular man in civilian clothing. He was carrying a briefcase. There was something about him that made McCoy suspect he was a soldier, a noncom, or maybe a warrant officer.

There being nothing else to do with it, McCoy shifted what was left of his double Famous Grouse on the rocks to his left hand, and saluted with his right.

Pickering and Howe returned the salute.

"You look pretty natty for someone fresh from the rice paddies of Korea, Captain," General Howe said. "Please forgive the intrusion. General Pickering said you wouldn't mind."

"We were just about to go to the Imperial, sir."

"Who's here, Ken?" Pickering asked.

"Hart, Zimmerman, and Ernie, sir," McCoy said. "And—I guess—the housekeeper and a maid."

"Well, if you don't mind, Captain, after you fix us all one of those, why don't you send them shopping?" Howe said.

"Yes, sir."

"Just the Japanese," Howe said. "Mrs. McCoy's going to have to be brought in on this. Your home just became what I understand you CIA people call a 'safe house.' "

"Yes, sir," McCoy said.

"Charley," General Howe said to the muscular man in civilian clothing. "This is the legendary Killer McCoy—"

"Who really doesn't like to be called that, Ralph," Pickering said.

He's calling him "Ralph"?

"Sorry," Howe said. "Captain McCoy, Master Sergeant Charley Rogers."

Master Sergeant Rogers wordlessly shook McCoy's hand.

Hart and Zimmerman came more or less to attention as everybody entered the living room.

Howe made a gesture indicating they should relax. He went to Zimmerman.

"You look like what a Marine gunner should look like," he said. "Zimmerman, right?"

"Yes, sir," Zimmerman said.

"My name is Howe. This is Master Sergeant Charley Rogers. We go back to his being my first soldier when I was a company commander."

The two shook hands wordlessly.

Ernie McCoy, in the kimono she had worn earlier, came into the room.

"Nice to see you again, Mrs. McCoy," Howe said. "Sorry to barge in you like this. We just couldn't take a chance that the ears in the walls in the Imperial might be active."

"Excuse me?" Ernie said.

"Charley found three microphones in General Pickering's suite. They might be Kempe Tai leftovers, and then again they might not be."

"Oooh," Ernie said, then: "Welcome to our home, General."

"Ernie, send the help shopping for a couple of hours," Pickering ordered.

"Just the servants?"

"I think you're going to have to be in on this, Mrs. McCoy," Howe said.

Ernie nodded and headed for the kitchen.

"McCoy, if you'll point out the booze to Charley?" Howe said.

"I'm the aide," Hart said. "I'll make the drinks. What will you have, sir?"

"What's that in your glass? Pickering's brand of scotch?"

"Yes, sir. Famous Grouse."

"Sergeant?" Hart asked.

Master Sergeant Rogers nodded his head.

Ernie McCoy came back into the room two minutes later.

"I told them to buy enough pressed duck to feed us all for dinner," she said. "Not to come back for two hours—and to ring the bell when they came in."

Howe looked at her a little surprised.

"This is not the first time I've sent the help shopping, General," Ernie said.

"I'm not surprised," Howe said. "And I think you'll understand what it means when I tell you that you're about to be made privy to some national security information that it is not to leave this room."

"I understand," Ernie said.

"Can we talk here?" Howe asked.

"There's the dining room," Ernie said. "In case anyone wants to write, or take notes."

"The dining room, please, then," Howe said.

Ernie led them into the dining room, and indicated that Howe should take a seat at the end of the table.

"This is your house, Mrs. McCoy," Howe said. "That's your husband's chair. I'll sit here."

He pulled out the first chair next to the head of the table, and gestured for McCoy to sit at the head. Master Sergeant Rogers took the chair across from General Howe, and set his briefcase on the floor. He reached into it and came out with three pencils and a pad of yellow lined paper. McCoy saw that the briefcase also held a 1911A1 Colt and what looked like the straps of a GI tanker's shoulder holster.

Pickering sat down beside McCoy; Zimmerman beside Rogers, and Hart beside him.

"I had the maid start coffee," Ernie McCoy said. "It'll be ready in a minute."

"That's very kind," Howe said. "But I'm doing fine with this."

He raised his whiskey glass.

Ernie sat down beside Pickering.

"Okay," Howe said. "Where to begin?"

He thought about that for a moment.

"At the beginning is always a good place. Harry S Truman. Our President and the Commander-in-Chief of the Armed Forces of the United States. I work for him, and so does everybody else in uniform, but sometimes people have trouble really understanding that.

"He's a very good man. If he had his druthers, when War Two started he would have gone on active duty as a colonel—we both made colonel on the same National Guard promotion list—and probably would have made two stars, as I did. But he was in the Senate, doing important work, and they talked him into not going on active duty, and retired him as a colonel.

"That's important to keep in mind. You don't get to be a colonel unless you know something about soldiering, more important, soldiers, and more important than that, officers.

"If I forget, and refer to our commander-in-chief as 'Harry,' no disrespect is intended. I have picked up a lot of respect for him since the time we were both captains. He was a good captain, and he was a good colonel, and he was a damned good senator. He wasn't vice president long enough to make any judgments about that, but since he's been President, he's done a good job, and I wouldn't be surprised if a hundred years from now, he's regarded by the historians as being in the same league as Washington and Lincoln.

"Having said that, Harry S Truman is no saint. He's got a temper, and he holds a grudge, and once he makes up his mind, he finds it hard to admit his original decision was wrong. I honest to God don't know what he's got against the Marine Corps, but it's pretty obvious he really doesn't like it.

"He's got a lot against the professional officer corps generally. Probably some of that goes back to our National Guard days, when the regular army used to rub their superiority in our faces. And some of it, I'm sure, goes back to when he had the Truman Committee in the Senate, and a lot of brass thought they could get away with lying to him.

"The President told me that right now there are two general officers—two only—he trusts completely. Both of them are at this table. And he told me why: He knows I don't have a personal agenda, and he doesn't think General Pickering does, either.

"The truth seems to be that the military services are loaded with prima donnas, and I'm not only talking about General MacArthur, although he can certainly give lessons to the others in that regard.

"Okay. All of this is to explain what I'm doing here, and what you all have to do with it. The day after tomorrow, Ambassador W. Averell Harriman and General Matthew B. Ridgway are going to get on a plane and come here. Item one on Harriman's agenda is to tell MacArthur that he is absolutely not, not, going to use any of Chiang Kai-shek's troops, and item two is Inchon. That has to be resolved—"

"My feelings won't be hurt," Ernestine McCoy interrupted.

Howe looked at her in surprise.

"—if you tell me I'm not supposed to ask questions. But I don't understand . . ."

Captain Kenneth R. McCoy looked at his wife in disbelief. General Howe's eyebrows went up. General Pickering smiled tolerantly, and waited for General Howe to more or less politely put her in her place.

"Ask away, Mrs. McCoy," Howe said, surprising everybody. "I meant it when I said I think you have to be involved in this, and the more you understand, the better."

"Well, I know who Ambassador Harriman is," she said. "I *know* Ambassador Harriman. He and my father are friends. My father told me he's President Truman's ambassador-at-large. But who's General Ridgway? And what's Inchon?"

"Harriman is also the President's national security advisor," Howe said. " 'Ambassador-at-large' is a personal rank; when Harriman goes someplace, it means he speaks for the President.

"MacArthur really wears two hats. The senior American someplace is the U.S. ambassador. There's no U.S. ambassador here; MacArthur fills that role. The decision about using Chiang Kai-shek's soldiers in this war is a diplomatic decision, so Harriman will give him his orders about that.

"But MacArthur is also the senior military officer in the Pacific. Wearing that hat, he takes—at least in theory—his orders from the Chairman of the Joint Chiefs of Staff, General—General of the Army, five stars, like MacArthur—Omar Bradley. MacArthur is not only senior to Bradley—time in grade—but outranks the Army chief of staff, General 'Lightning Joe' Collins, who has only four stars. So Collins has to 'confer' with MacArthur, since he can't tell him what to do. Matt Ridgway is another four-star general. He's the deputy chief of staff for administration, number two to Collins, and his likely successor as chief of staff, unless Truman decides to fire MacArthur, when he would be candidate number one to replace him."

"Fire General MacArthur?' Hart blurted.

"We're back to what I said before: What's said here stays in this room," General Howe said. "Truman doesn't want to fire MacArthur, for several reasons, including the fact that he's a military genius and a military hero and the political repercussions would be enormous. But if MacArthur keeps ignoring him, firing him's a genuine possibility."

"I didn't know about Chiang Kai-shek," Ernie said.

"He offered us thirty thousand troops," Howe said. "On the advice of General Bradley, Truman decided they would be more trouble than they would be worth, both because they would have to be trained and equipped, and because it would cause serious problems with the mainland—communist—Chinese. We don't want them in this war. Collins sent MacArthur a message ordering him not to take them. MacArthur acknowledged the message, and then—the next day—flew to Taipei to 'confer' with Chiang Kai-shek. I was there when Truman found that out. He was furious. Bradley wanted him fired. Harry decided to send Harriman to bring him into line. Understand?"

Ernie nodded.

"Inchon?" she asked.

"It's the port for Seoul," Howe said.

"Ken and I have been there," Ernie said.

"Okay. What happened is that when General Collins, and General Vandenburg—the Air Force chief of staff—were here . . . July seventeenth, right, Charley?"

Master Sergeant Rogers nodded.

"July seventeenth. Three weeks after we got in this mess," Howe went on. "MacArthur told them he'd 'come up with a plan' to stage an amphibious operation at Inchon, which would cut the North Korean line of supply. When I got here, General Pickering told me that MacArthur had told him the idea had occurred to him earlier than that, that when he went to Suwon a couple of days after the North Koreans invaded, he had thought about an amphibious invasion at Inchon, and had directed Almond to start the initial planning.

"Collins, to put it mildly, was not enthusiastic about an amphibious invasion at Inchon, and neither was the Navy. It's not like landing on some Pacific Island, or, for that matter, Normandy. There's a long channel the invasion fleet would have to pass through to get to the beach, and it's not far from North Korea, which could quickly send reinforcements. But the question became moot after we lost Taejon. All the troops that MacArthur wanted to use for the invasion had to be sent to Pusan, or we were going to be forced off the Korean Peninsula.

"Everybody in the Pentagon sighed in relief when the invasion was called off, but now MacArthur's brought it up again.—using the words '*when I* land at Inchon,' not '*if we decide to* land at Inchon.' So Ridgway is going to 'confer' with him about Inchon. If we can get away with it, General Pickering and I are going to invite ourselves to that meeting; I don't think we can crash the one between Harriman and MacArthur.

"What the President sent me here to do is to find out what I can about Inchon and report to him directly what I think. That poses two problems. First, I don't know anything about Inchon except what General Pickering has told me—"

"Based on damned little," Pickering interjected, "except my memory of taking a P & FE freighter in there before the war—and aground on the mudflats."

"Sir, there's a guy," McCoy said. "A Navy officer—I talked to him a couple of times—who was in there a lot on an LST," McCoy said. "He knows all about Inchon, and the channel islands."

"You have his name?' Howe asked. "Where is he?"

"Taylor," McCoy said. "David R. Taylor, Lieutenant, USNR. I don't know where he is. Naval Element, SCAP would probably know." He paused and added, "He's a Mustang."

"A what?" Howe asked.

"He was an enlisted man, sir," McCoy said.

"Yeah, that's right, isn't it? That's what the Navy and the Marines call somebody who's come out of the ranks. 'Mustang' seems to suggest they're not as well-bred as somebody from the Naval Academy, a little wild, maybe uncontrollable, likely to cause trouble to the established order of things."

McCoy and Hart looked uncomfortable. General Pickering was about to reply when General Howe went on: "Well, then, he'll be right at home with this bunch, won't he? Unless I'm wrong, we all belong to that exclusive club."

He turned to Master Sergeant Rogers.

"Charley, call SCAP Naval Element and have this guy placed on TDY to us as soon as possible. Like as of eight o'clock tomorrow morning. Have him report to the hotel. He doesn't need to know about this place."

Master Sergeant Rogers nodded, and wrote on his lined pad.

General Howe saw the look on McCoy's face.

"Yeah, I can do that, McCoy," he said. "Before I came here, Admiral Sherman—the chief of naval operations—sent a commander to see the admiral, to tell him that by direction of the President, I'm to get whatever I ask for from the Navy, and that SCAP is not to be told what I asked for."

"Yes, sir," McCoy said.

"What's left?" Howe asked. "Oh, yeah. Communications. The problem with cryptography, sending encoded messages, Mrs. McCoy, is that the technicians who do the encoding obviously get to read the message. General Pickering tells me that during War Two, when he was dealing with the MAGIC business, he had his own cryptographers."

"Including George," McCoy said, nodding at Hart.

"We talked about that," Howe said. "The equipment Hart used is no longer in service. And I'm concerned that anything we send through the SCAP crypto room will be read by people who'll pass it on to people here. I may be wrong, but I can't take that chance. Charley called the Army Security Agency, and they're going to send us a cryptographer, one we know won't share what he's read with anybody. But I don't know how long that will take—if he can get here before we start to need him. Suggestions?"

"Ken," Zimmerman said. "Keller?"

"Who's Keller?" General Pickering asked.

"The crypto guy in Pusan," McCoy said. "Eighth Army Rear. Master Sergeant. The one you talked to . . . the 'return immediately, repeat immediately' message?"

"Very obliging," Pickering said. "What about him?"

"General, he just got to Pusan," Zimmerman said. "He's new, not part of the SCAP setup."

"Good man, I think," McCoy said.

"Why do you say that?" Howe asked.

"He talked me out of my National Match Garand," McCoy said, smiling. "And when I asked him why somebody as smart as he was wasn't a Marine, he said he didn't qualify for the Corps; his parents were married."

Howe laughed.

"That's terrible," Mrs. McCoy said, smiling.

"Charley?" Howe asked.

"He'd have the right clearances, General," Master Sergeant Rogers said. His voice was very deep and resonant. "And I could have a word with him about keeping his mouth shut."

That's the first time he's said a word, McCoy realized.

"You have the number of the SCAP Army Security Agency guy?" Howe asked.

Rogers nodded.

"Call him and have him send this fellow here on the next plane," Howe ordered.

Rogers nodded, and wrote on his lined pad.

"Have the message say, 'Bring Marine weapons,'" Zimmerman said.

"Weapons? More than one?" Rogers asked.

"He's got my Thompson, too," Zimmerman said.

"This has to be one hell of a man," Pickering said, "to talk these two out of their weapons."

Howe chuckled.

XII

[ONE]
The Dewey Suite
The Imperial Hotel
Tokyo, Japan
0755 3 August 1950

Lieutenant David R. Taylor, USNR, a stocky, ruddy-faced thirty-two-year-old, walked down the corridor of the hotel and raised his eyebrows in a not entirely friendly manner when the young American in a business suit rose from a chair in the corridor and blocked his way.

"May I help you, sir?"

"If you can show me where the Dewey Suite is, that'd help."

"And you are, sir?"

"Who're you?"

The CIC agent produced his credentials, a thin folding wallet, with a badge pinned to one half and a photo ID card on the other.

Taylor was not surprised. He had spent the last four days in the Dai Ichi Building, working on the plans to stage an amphibious landing at Inchon. The corridor outside the G-3 section had half a dozen young men like this one in it around the clock.

"My name is Taylor," he said.

"May I see some identification, sir?"

Taylor produced his Department of the Navy officer's identification card.

The CIC agent examined it.

"They're expecting you, Lieutenant," he said. "Second door on the left."

Taylor walked down the corridor, and knocked at the door.

Brigadier General Fleming Pickering, USMCR, who was in a crisp, tieless shirt, with the silver star of his rank on both sides of the collar.

I would have sworn they said Major General.

"My name is Taylor, sir," he said. "I was ordered to report to Major General Howe."

"We've been expecting you, Lieutenant," Pickering said. "Come on in. General Howe's taking a shave." He pointed into the room, where Howe, draped in a white sheet, was being shaved by a Japanese barber, a woman. "My name is Pickering."

Pickering offered Taylor his hand, and was pleased but not surprised at the firmness of his grip. He had decided the moment he'd seen Taylor at the door that he was probably going to like him.

Taylor's khaki uniform was clean but rumpled. The gold strap and the insignia on his brimmed cap was anything but new. It looked, Pickering decided, one sailor judging another, that Taylor would be far more comfortable on the bridge of a ship than he would be sitting at a desk, and certainly more comfortable on a bridge than reporting—reason unstated—to an Army major general in one of the most luxurious suites in the Imperial Hotel.

"Be with you in a minute," Howe called from his chair. "Have you had breakfast?"

"Yes, sir."

"Well, there's coffee, and if you change your mind, there's stuff on a steam table in the dining room."

Pickering smiled at Taylor, and motioned for him to follow him.

"You're the first to show up," Pickering said. "The others will be here soon."

Pickering went to a silver coffee service, poured two cups of coffee, and handed one to Taylor.

"Black, okay?"

"I'm a sailor, sir. Sailors get used to black coffee."

"I know," Pickering said. "Once upon a time, I was an honest sailor-man myself."

What the hell does that mean?

"Yes, sir," Taylor said.

The first of "the others" to arrive was a Marine captain, who walked into the dining room and headed straight for the coffee.

"You got him, George?" Pickering asked when he had finished pouring coffee.

"Sergeant Rogers is having a word with him," the Marine captain said.

Lieutenant Taylor was surprised that the captain had not said, "Sir," and even more surprised when he took off his tunic and pulled down his tie, and then still more when he saw that the captain had a .45 ACP pistol in a skeleton holster in the small of his back.

General Howe came into the dining room.

"Did you get him, George?" he asked.

"Yes, sir. Charley's having a word with him," Hart replied.

"McCoy and Zimmerman?" Howe asked.

"They should be here now, Ralph," Pickering said.

"Should I call?" the captain asked.

"What Ernie's going to say," Pickering replied, "is that they're on the way, and should be here now."

The captain went to a telephone—one of four—on the sideboard and dialed a number.

"Could you get him out of bed, Ernie?" he said when someone answered. Howe chuckled.

"Okay, sorry to bother you," the captain said, and hung up.

"And?" Pickering asked.

"They left early because of the traffic and should be here any minute," Hart reported.

Pickering spread his hands in a *what did I tell you?* gesture.

Howe chuckled again.

"We'll wait," he said. "Then we'll only have to do the welcoming ceremony once."

"I thought that's what Charley was doing to Keller," Hart said.

"No, what Charley is doing to Sergeant Keller is impressing upon him the wisdom of paying close attention to the welcoming ceremony," Howe said. He looked at Taylor and walked over to him. "My name is Howe, Lieutenant."

"Yes, sir."

A barrel-chested Marine master gunner with a chest full of ribbons came into the dining room.

"We got stuck in traffic," he announced. "Sorry."

"No problem, you're here," Howe said. "Zimmerman, this is Lieutenant Taylor."

Zimmerman wordlessly shook Taylor's hand.

Now this is the kind of jarhead with whom a wise sailor does not get into a bar-room argument. And this kind of jarhead is the last kind of jarhead you expect to find in a room in the Imperial Hotel with two generals.

Another Marine captain came in the room.

Christ, I know who he is. He's the guy—McCoy is his name—who asked me, two, three, times—once in Taipei, another time in Hong Kong, and some other place, places, I forget, the sonofabitch was all over the Far East—always the same question, Had I seen any unusual activity in North Korea, or along the China Coast?

And I told him yeah, I had. Why not? He had an ID card that said he was with Naval Element, SCAP.

But then there was some scuttlebutt that they gave some Marine captain in Naval Element SCAP the shitty end of the stick when he tried to tell them this god-damn war was coming, and I figured it had to be the guy asking the questions. The scuttlebutt was that he pissed off, big time, some big brass, and they sent him home; kicked him out of the Marine Corps. So what the hell is he doing here with an Army general? What the hell is going on here?

"Sorry, sir," McCoy said. "The traffic—"

Howe gestured that it was not important.

"Hart, go get Charley and the sergeant," he ordered.

"Hello, Taylor, how are you?" McCoy said.

"McCoy," Taylor replied.

McCoy had just enough time to pour himself a cup of coffee before the other Marine captain returned with two Army master sergeants in tow.

The one in the Class A uniform looks old enough to have been at Valley Forge; the one in fatigues doesn't look old enough to be a master sergeant. And fatigues in a fancy suite in the Imperial?

"My name is Pickering, Sergeant Keller," the Marine one-star said. "We've talked on the telephone. This is General Howe, and I think you know everybody else but Lieutenant Taylor."

Everybody shook hands.

"You have the weapons, Keller, right?" McCoy said. "You can look forward to spending the rest of your life singing baritone?"

"I've got them, sir," the young master sergeant said.

Everybody but Taylor—who had no idea why this was funny—chuckled.

"Okay," General Howe said. "Let's get this started. Sergeant Keller, did Sergeant Rogers clue you in on what's going on here?"

"Yes, sir," Keller said.

"Did he show you our orders?"

"No, sir," Keller said.

Howe reached into his shirt pocket and came out with a squarish white envelope. He handed it to Keller.

"When you're through, show that to Lieutenant Taylor," Howe said.

"Yes, sir."

There was a knock at the door.

"Jesus, now what?" Howe asked, in great annoyance.

Hart went to the door.

The CIC agent was standing there with an Army signal corps captain.

"This officer has an Urgent for General Pickering," the CIC agent said.

Pickering motioned for the captain to enter the room. He entered, saluted, and handed Pickering a sealed eight-by-ten-inch manila envelope, on which SE-CRET was stamped, top and bottom, in red ink.

Pickering tore the envelope open, took the carbon of a radio teletype message from it, read it, and then slipped it back in the envelope.

"Anything important, Fleming?" Howe asked.

"No, sir. It will wait," Pickering said. Then he added, to the Signal Corps officer, "Answer is, Thank you. Pickering, Brigadier General, USMCR."

"Yes, sir, I'll get that right out," the Signal Corps captain said. He saluted and left the room.

"Lieutenant?" Master Sergeant Keller said, and when he had his attention, handed him the squarish envelope.

Taylor took it and read it.

THE WHITE HOUSE

WASHINGTON, D.C.

JULY 8, 1950

TO WHOM IT MAY CONCERN:

MAJOR GENERAL RALPH HOWE, USAR, IN CONNECTION WITH HIS MISSION FOR ME, WILL TRAVEL TO SUCH PLACES AT SUCH TIMES AS HE FEELS APPROPRIATE, ACCOMPANIED BY SUCH STAFF AS HE DESIRES.

GENERAL HOWE IS GRANTED HEREWITH A TOP SECRET/WHITE HOUSE CLEARANCE, AND MAY, AT HIS OPTION, GRANT SUCH CLEARANCE TO HIS STAFF.

U.S. MILITARY AND GOVERNMENTAL AGENCIES ARE DIRECTED TO PROVIDE GENERAL HOWE AND HIS STAFF WITH WHATEVER SUP- PORT THEY MAY REQUIRE.

Harry S Truman

HARRY S TRUMAN
PRESIDENT OF THE UNITED STATES

"Jesus Christ!" Taylor blurted.

Howe said, "General Pickering has identical orders, with only the name changed."

"Yes, sir," Taylor said, and handed the orders back.

"As far as Sergeant Keller is concerned," Howe said, "he's on indefinite temporary duty to us. 'Us' is defined as whatever General Pickering and I decide that it means. You're also on indefinite temporary duty to us, Lieutenant, but right now I don't know for how long that may be. But so far as both of you are concerned, so long as you are assigned to us, that means your chain of command is directly through either General Pickering or myself, and then the President of the United States. You are not subordinate to the orders of anyone but General Pickering and myself. Anyone else includes General MacArthur and any and all members of the SCAP headquarters and subordinate units. Is that clear?"

Master Sergeant Keller said, "Yes, sir."

Howe looked at Taylor, who said, "I understand, sir."

"You will consider anything you hear or see in connection with your duties here to be classified Top Secret/White House, and you will not share that information with anyone, repeat anyone, who doesn't have a Top Secret/White House clearance, and I have been informed that no one in SCAP, including the Supreme Commander, has such a clearance. Is that clear?"

This time the two said "Yes, sir" almost in unison.

"Okay. Early tomorrow morning, Ambassador W. Averell Harriman and General Matthew B. Ridgway are going to get on an airplane in Washington to fly here. Ambassador Harriman is going to inform General MacArthur, in his role as Supreme Allied Powers—and now UN Command—Commander that the President does not wish General MacArthur to employ in any shape or manner Chiang Kai-shek's Nationalist Chinese troops. Ambassador Harriman will report to the President his assessment of how General MacArthur receives this order, and probably what he thinks MacArthur will do. I think it highly probable that after receiving the Ambassador's report, the President will wish to comment on it, and perhaps give the Ambassador supplemental orders.

"Obviously, neither the President nor Ambassador Harriman wants anyone to be privy to this interchange of information. If the customary cryptographic channels were used, SCAP cryptographers would have to read the exchange. The possibility of a leak is there. That's where you come in, Sergeant Keller. In Sergeant Rogers's briefcase, there is a special code which will be used solely for the communications between the Ambassador and the President. Getting the picture?"

"Yes, sir," Keller said. "There's a story going around that the President used a system like this at Potsdam, sir."

"You crypto people gossip, do you?"

"Only about techniques, sir, not message content."

"I'll give you the benefit of a large doubt on that, Keller. But no, the President did not use this system at Potsdam. I was there with him. He started using it *after* Potsdam, when he suspected that his 'eyes only' messages to and from Potsdam had been read by a large number of senior military and State Department officers who knew how to cajole—or intimidate—crypto people into sharing information with them."

"You were at Potsdam, Ralph?" Pickering asked.

"Lovely place," Howe said. "Even right after the war. It's now in the Russian zone."

He turned to Keller.

"This one you don't gossip about, clear?"

"Yes, sir."

"General Ridgway is going to confer with General MacArthur about Inchon," Howe went on. "That's where you come in, Lieutenant Taylor. Both General Pickering and I have been charged by the President to come up with opinions—independent opinions—of whether MacArthur—who is now using the phrase '*when* I land at Inchon'—can really carry that off."

"That's what I've doing at SCAP, General," Taylor said. "Working on that plan. They pulled me off my LST right after this war started, and put me to work on that."

"Gut feeling, Mr. Taylor? Is it possible?" Pickering asked.

"Gut feeling, sir: It's a hell of a gamble."

"I'd never even heard of the place a month ago," Howe said, "and aside from what General Pickering has told me, I still know virtually nothing about it."

General Pickering told you? What the hell does a Marine general know about Inchon? was written all over Taylor's face, and both Howe and Pickering saw his confusion.

"I was a sailor, a long time ago," Pickering said. "I told you." He chuckled, and added: "Who once ran the *Pacific Wanderer* aground at Inchon."

Pacific Wanderer? That's a P&FE freighter. This general was master of a P&FE freighter?

Oh, Jesus Christ. This guy's name is Pickering. P&FE is owned by the Pickering family. There has to be a connection. So what's he doing in a Marine general's uniform?

"You look as if you have a question, Mr. Taylor," Pickering said.

"Ran aground, sir? Or got caught by the tides?" Taylor asked.

"Caught by the tides," Pickering said. "The effect is the same. The question is, how is MacArthur's invasion fleet going to deal with Inchon's infamous tidal mudflats?"

"Let's start with that," Howe said. "What mudflats? What are we talking about? Show me. Charley, have we got that map?"

Master Sergeant Rogers took a map from his briefcase and laid it on the table.

"You tell us, Taylor," Howe ordered. "Remembering that you and General Pickering are the only sailors in the room. Keep it simple."

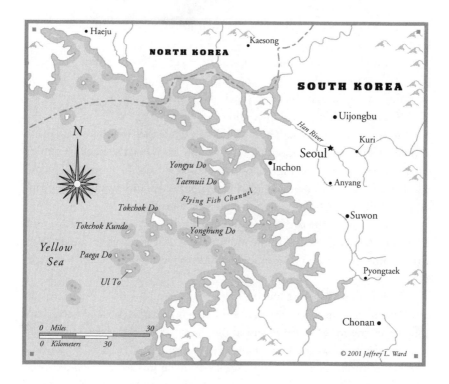

"Yes, sir," Taylor said.

He took a lead pencil from his pocket and used it as a pointer.

"Here's Seoul," he said. "And here's Inchon. This is the Yellow Sea. The channel into Inchon from the Yellow Sea—it's called 'The Flying Fish Channel'—starts here, about thirty air miles from Inchon, at this group of little islands, called the Tokchok. There's a lighthouse there on a little island called Samni.

"Flying Fish meanders along through here. The distance by water is about forty-five nautical miles from the lighthouse to Inchon."

"And that's the only way you can get into Inchon?" Howe asked.

"Yes, sir. That's one of the problems the invasion fleet is going to face, moving forty-five miles, and moving slow—the channel twists and turns, and in some parts you have to move at steerage speed—"

"Which is?" Howe asked.

"The slowest speed at which you have steering ability," Pickering answered for him. "And the channel is not very wide; it'll mean moving the ships most of the way in a column."

"And that means, sir," Taylor said, "the chances of surprising anyone at Inchon are pretty slim."

"Just for openers, it seems like a lousy place to stage an amphibious invasion," Howe said.

"And we haven't even touched on the tides yet," Pickering said.

"Tell me about tides," Howe ordered, "in very simple terms."

"You know, sir, that tides are cyclic?" Taylor asked.

"Not enough. Tell me," Howe said.

"In the Atlantic Ocean, there're two tides a day—they call that semidiurnal. A tidal day is twenty-four hours and fifty minutes. When the tides are semidiurnal, that means you get high tide at, say, six o'clock in the morning, low tide a little after noon, and another high tide at about six-twenty-five that night, and another low tide six hours and twelve minutes after that.

"In the Pacific, there're both semidiurnal tides and diurnal, which means that you get high tide at six in the morning, low tide twelve hours and twenty five minutes after that, and another high tide the next morning at ten minutes to seven."

"And that's what it is at Inchon?"

"Not exactly, sir. What they have at Inchon is *mixed* tides, which means that sometimes the moon and the sun are both acting on the water at the same time. And what that means that the tides are huge. At Inchon, high tide is sometimes thirty feet above normal sea level, and at low six feet below normal. That means a difference of thirty-six feet. That's at the high end of the cycle."

"What does *that* mean?" Howe asked. "High end of the cycle?"

"There's a monthly cycle to tides, twenty-eight days, like the lunar cycle," Taylor explained. "At the high end of the cycle, at Inchon, high tide is sometimes thirty feet above sea level, and low, six feet below. At the low end of the cycle, high tide is maybe twenty feet above normal, and maybe four feet above at low tide." Taylor paused. "This is twice a day, you understand?"

"You may have to explain it all over again, but go on, what does this mean?"

"Sir, it means that at low tide, all these areas here, from the mainland shore, and around the islands, don't have any water over them. . . ."

"Mudflats, Ralph, miles and miles of mud," Pickering said.

"Which means," Taylor explained, "that the invasion would have to take place at high tide at the high end of the monthly cycle. Maybe a day, either way, but no more than a day."

"I don't understand that," Howe said.

"You need the highest tide you can get, to get the ships through the channel into Inchon, and then get them out again," Pickering said. "And you have the highest tides only on one day a month."

"Jesus!" Howe said.

"Even then, there's no way that I can see that they can get every vessel in and out, sir," Taylor said. "Maybe they can get one or two attack transports in there, unload them, and get them out on one tide, but there're going to be LSTs and everything else stuck in the mud."

"I agree," Pickering said. "Stuck until the tide comes in again and refloats them."

"When do we get a high tide? Is that the correct term?" Howe asked.

"August eighteen is the next one, sir, and the one after that is 15 September. That's what they're shooting for, 15 September."

Howe looked at Pickering.

"So when 'I will land' at Inchon is September fifteenth?"

"It would appear to be," Pickering said.

"Is there more bad news, Mr. Taylor, about this brilliant invasion idea? Or have I heard it all?"

"Not quite, sir," Taylor said.

"Jesus! What else can go wrong?"

"Sir, if you look here," Taylor said, pointing at the map. "You see this little island here, Paega-do? It's about five miles off the mainland. The water between it and the mainland is fifteen, sometimes twenty, feet deep at high tide. At low tide, it's a mudflat. From the west side of Paega-do, it's about five miles to Yonghung Do. The Flying Fish Channel, half a mile wide, runs north-south through there, mostly right in the middle. That's the only place where, at high tide, the channel, is deep enough for the attack transports."

"Okay," Howe said after he'd studied the map a moment.

"The channel there is within artillery range of guns on either island," Taylor finished.

"Which means they'd have to be taken out before the attack transports—or anything else—could use the channel?" Pickering asked, but it was really a statement rather than a question.

"And taking them out would be a pretty good signal of our intentions, wouldn't it?" Howe said, thoughtfully.

"Yonghung-do, Paega-do, and all these islands east of there are held by the North Koreans," Taylor said, pointing.

"And west of there?" McCoy asked. It was the first question he had asked.

"The South Korean national police holds them," Taylor said. "I don't mean . . ."

"You said 'police'?" General Howe asked.

"Yes, sir. They hold the major islands, sir, is what I mean. They don't have people on every island."

"The front, the battle line, is way down the peninsula, almost to Pusan," Howe said. "Why don't the North Koreans at least try to run the South Koreans off those islands?"

"I can only guess, sir, that they don't consider them a major threat; that they're waiting until they take Pusan. Once that happens, they'll have the means to clean up—"

"Hey," McCoy said. "They're not going to take Pusan."

"They're not?" Taylor asked, dubiously.

"The Marines have landed, haven't you heard?"

"You really think the Marines can hold Pusan, McCoy?" General Howe asked. "Or are you just parroting the official Marine Corps line?"

"Not by themselves, sir, I didn't mean to suggest that. But if they can help the Army hold on to it a little longer, until the Army can get some more troops in there . . . The last prisoners Ernie and I talked to not only looked beat, but admitted they were running out of food, ammunition—everything. That's a long supply line they're running."

"Why should the Marines do any better than the Army has? It looks to me like the more men the Army sends to Korea, the further Eighth Army has to retreat."

"Sir, most of the Provisional Brigade officers and noncoms have combat experience in the Second War. And—at least down to company level—they've trained together."

"How do you know that?"

"General Craig told me, sir."

"The Provisional Brigade commander?"

"Yes, sir."

"You two had a little chat? In my experience—and remember, Captain, I used to be Captain Howe—generals don't have many conversations with captains."

"You're having one right now, General," General Pickering said.

"Point taken," Howe said, with a smile.

"I spoke with General Craig in San Diego, sir," McCoy said. "When the brigade was getting on the transports, and yesterday . . ." he paused. "Yeah, that was only yesterday. It seems a lot longer. I saw General Craig and the brigade debarking in Pusan."

Howe looked at him.

"You were about to say something else," he said. "Say it."

"The Marines in the Brigade looked like . . . Marines, sir."

"You mean they looked to you as if they could fight?"

"Yes, sir," McCoy said.

"Well, let's hope you're right, McCoy," General Howe said. "Now, where were we?"

"You were talking about the islands from which artillery could be brought to bear on the invasion fleet," General Pickering said.

"Right," Howe said. "So what does General MacArthur plan to do about them?"

"I believe the current plan is to take them on D Minus One, sir," Lieutenant Taylor said.

"You mean twenty-four hours before the actual landing at Inchon?"

"Yes, sir."

"Which would certainly tell the North Koreans we were going to land at Inchon, and give them twenty-four hours to bring up reinforcements, right?"

"Yes, sir," Taylor said.

"Nobody had a better idea than that?" Howe asked.

"Sir," Taylor said, and stopped.

"Go on," Howe ordered.

"Sir, I've given that some thought—"

"You have an idea, ideas?"

"Yes, sir," Taylor said. "I think it would be possible—"

Howe stopped him by holding up his hand.

"Not now," he said. "Later."

"Yes, sir."

"No, I *mean* later. I want to hear them. But right now, I have to send the President what I have so far about MacArthur's idea to land two divisions of men he doesn't have some place where an invasion can be held on only one or two days a month, and where the tides are thirty feet. Let's go, Charley, and you, too, Keller."

He got to his feet, gestured for the others to keep their seats, and walked out of the room, with Master Sergeants Rogers and Keller on his heels.

"Taylor," General Pickering asked, "these ideas of yours, have you put them on paper?"

"No, sir."

"I'm sure General Howe meant it when he said he wanted to hear them. Step one to do that is get them on paper—just the rough idea, or ideas."

"Yes, sir. How much time do I have?"

"See how much you can get down by seventeen hundred," Pickering said.

"General Howe and I are going to be at SCAP most of the afternoon. Have you got someplace to work?"

"Only at SCAP, sir, or in my BOQ."

"George, get him a typewriter and a desk, and put him in one of the rooms here."

"Aye, aye, sir," Hart said.

Pickering looked at McCoy and motioned for him to follow him into his bedroom. McCoy motioned for Zimmerman to wait.

Pickering closed the bedroom door after McCoy entered.

"Sir?" McCoy said.

Pickering handed him the large envelope marked "Secret" the signal corps had given him, then went to his window and looked out of it, his back to McCoy. McCoy looked at him curiously for a moment and then went into the envelope and took out the carbon copy of the radio teletype message.

```
SECRET
URGENT
1650 2 AUGUST 1950


FROM: ASST COMMANDER
      1ST AIRCRAFT WING
TO: EYES ONLY BRIG GEN FLEMING PICKERING USMC
      HQ SUPREME COMMANDER, ALLIED POWERS


1. DEEPLY REGRET TO INFORM YOU THAT AT SHORTLY AFTER
1220 THIS DATE MAJOR MALCOLM S. PICKERING, USMCR, WAS
FORCED TO MAKE AN EMERGENCY LANDING IN HIS F4-U
AIRCRAFT BEHIND ENEMY LINES IN THE VICINITY OF TAEJON
SOUTH KOREA AND HIS WHEREABOUTS AND CONDITION ARE
PRESENTLY UNKNOWN.


2. AT APPROXIMATELY 1220 HOURS THIS DATE, MAJOR
PICKERING, WHO WAS FLYING ALONE ON A RECONNAISSANCE
MISSION OFF USS BADOENG STRAIT, MADE A MAYDAY RADIO
CALL STATING HE WAS APPROXIMATELY FIFTEEN MILES NORTH
NORTHEAST OF TAEJON, AND THAT HE HAD BEEN STRUCK BY
ANTI-AIRCRAFT FIRE, HAD LOST HYDRAULIC PRESSURE, HAD AN
ENGINE FIRE AND WAS GOING TO DITCH.
```

3. LT COL WILLIAM C. DUNN, USMC, WHO WAS LEADING A
THREE F4-U AIRCRAFT FLIGHT FROM THE USS BADOENG STRAIT
IN THE VICINITY, HEARD THE MAYDAY AND IMMEDIATELY WENT
TO THE AREA. LT COL DUNN FIRST SPOTTED A HEAVY COLUMN
OF SMOKE COMING FROM A DESTROYED BUT STILL BURNING
ENEMY RAILROAD TRAIN AND THEN APPROXIMATELY THREE MILES
NORTH OF THE TRAIN A COLUMN OF SMOKE FROM A BURNING
F4-U AIRCRAFT. IN THREE LOW LEVEL PASSES OVER THE
DOWNED AND BURNING AIRCRAFT LT COL DUNN WAS ABLE TO
DETERMINE THE COCKPIT WAS EMPTY. THERE WAS NO SIGN OF
MAJOR PICKERING, AND LT COL DID NOT SEE A DEPLOYED
PARACHUTE.

4. LT COL DUNN BELIEVES THAT MAJOR PICKERING WAS
ENGAGING THE ENEMY RAILROAD TRAIN AS TARGET OF
OPPORTUNITY AND THAT HIS AIRCRAFT WAS STRUCK BY.50 AND
20-MM ANTIAIRCRAFT FIRE FROM THE TRAIN AND/OR DEBRIS
CAUSED BY THE DETONATION OF EXPLOSIVE AND/OR
COMBUSTIBLE MATERIALS ABOARD THE TRAIN.

5. FIXED AND ROTARY WING AIRCRAFT OF 1ST MAW WERE
IMMEDIATELY DIRECTED TO THE CRASH SITE, ARRIVING THERE
AT APPROXIMATE 1335. THEY REPORTED THAT MAJOR
PICKERING'S AIRCRAFT HAD BEEN CONSUMED BY FIRE AND
THERE WAS NO SIGN OF MAJOR PICKERING.

6. IN CONSIDERATION OF THE ABOVE, MAJOR PICKERING IS
NOW CLASSIFIED AS MISSING IN ACTION. HQ USMC HAS BEEN
NOTIFIED. FURTHER INFORMATION WILL BE FURNISHED AS
DEVELOPED.

THOMAS J. CUSHMAN
BRIG GEN, USMC

SECRET

"Goddamn it!" McCoy said, and then raised his eyes to look at General Pickering. Pickering had turned from the window and was leaning against the windowsill, facing McCoy.

"God damn this war," Pickering said, almost conversationally. "God damn wars in general."

"Nothing was said about spotting a body," McCoy said.

"I'm going to have to call his mother," Pickering said, "and now. Before some unctuous chaplain gets to her with the usual nonsense about God's mysterious ways."

"Nothing was said about spotting a body," McCoy repeated. "Billy Dunn said the aircraft was on fire and the cockpit empty. It obviously burned up later. Pick had time to get out of it."

Pickering didn't reply.

"This was not Pick's first emergency landing," McCoy said. "He's a hell of a pilot, and you know it. And this would not be the first time he's run around behind the lines."

Pickering looked into McCoy's eyes for a long moment.

"You tell me what you think happened, Ken."

"He got out of the airplane and got away from it."

"Or he got out of the airplane and the NK's got him. And shot him."

"More likely, they would have taken him prisoner," McCoy said.

Pickering looked at McCoy for another long moment.

"If you're going to call Mrs. Pickering," McCoy said, "why don't we go out to my place?"

Pickering considered that for a long moment.

"One of the reasons I was less than overjoyed when Ernie came over here was because I knew that if you didn't come back from one of your Korean commutes, I knew I was going to have to be the one to tell her," Pickering said. "Now you're going to have to tell her about Pick."

"Come out to the house anyway," McCoy said.

"Thank you, but I don't have the time right now. Later, maybe."

"Sir?"

"General Howe and I are going to meet with MacArthur; he's going to tell us all about his Inchon landing. I don't want to miss that."

McCoy nodded but didn't reply.

"Best possible pissing-in-the-wind scenario," Pickering went on. "Phase one: Pick survived the crash in reasonably good shape . . ."

"And we will shortly hear that he's been spotted by the Air Force, or one of the Marine helicopters . . ."

"More likely he was captured. With a little luck, the North Koreans decide to keep him alive—he's a Marine major, and I'm sure they would like to learn as much about the Marines and Marine aviation as they can. Any officer would know that and keep him alive."

McCoy nodded his agreement.

"Phase two of the pissing-in-the-wind scenario," Pickering went on. "MacArthur's generally believed-to-be-insane notion of a Corps-strength amphibious landing at Inchon goes off without a hitch. We cut the peninsula in half and—the word is 'envelop'—*envelop* North Korean forces in the south, including their POW enclosures. In one of which we find Pick."

"Is that what you think, sir? Inchon's an 'insane notion'?"

"No. I just asked myself that question. And I was aware that my emotions would probably cloud my judgment. But no, I don't think it's insane. Whatever else can be said about Douglas MacArthur, he is a military genius. I've seen him in action, Ken. When ordinary mortals look at a projected military operation, it's like—trying to shave in a steam-clouded mirror. For him, there's no steam on the glass. He sees things, things the rest of us can't see, and he sees them clearly. He proved that time and again in War Two. If he thinks Inchon's the answer, I'll go with him."

"Is that what you're going to tell the President?"

"Yes, that's what I'm going to tell the President."

"And what's General Howe going to tell him?"

"In the message he's writing right now, I'm sure he's going to use a phrase like 'insane notion.' But he's never had a personal meeting like this with MacArthur. MacArthur can sell iceboxes to Eskimos. I think that will happen this afternoon. I hope it does."

"And if it doesn't?"

"If, as a result of what Howe tells the President, or for any other reason, MacArthur is forbidden to do the Pusan operation, there's a good chance he'll quit."

"Quit?" McCoy asked, more than a little surprised. "What the hell would he do if he wasn't El Supremo?"

"Run for commander-in-chief," Pickering said.

"Jesus! You really think so?"

"This goes no further, Ken," Pickering said. "Not even to Ernie."

McCoy nodded his agreement.

"Senator Fowler tells me either Eisenhower or MacArthur can have the Republican nomination if they want it."

"Not both," McCoy thought aloud.

"No. Whoever acts first. Try this on. Truman kills the Inchon landing. MacArthur resigns, very publicly, saying he cannot in good conscience serve under a president who is soft on communism, and doesn't recognize the threat it poses. He'd probably believe that, too."

"Truman's not soft on communism," McCoy argued. "He sent the Army to Greece, and now this. . . ."

"I agree, but the Republicans keep accusing him of it. Anyway, MacArthur knows that unless he acts to get the nomination, it will go to Eisenhower. El Supremo has described Eisenhower as the best clerk he ever had. In his mind, it would be his duty to become President, to get Truman out of office, and to keep Eisenhower from getting it."

"Jesus!"

"I think he really believes the Inchon landing will end this war. The flip side of that is that if there is no Inchon landing, there *will* be a long war to take South Korea back. MacArthur believes that, and so do I, as a matter of fact.

"So the election is held, and we're still fighting here, and MacArthur will make it clear that if Truman had had the good sense to let him—the experienced general who won World War Two in the Pacific—invade Inchon, it would be over. And as soon as he's President, he will end the war. Who do you think would win?"

"I don't like the idea of him being President," McCoy thought aloud.

"Neither do I," Pickering said. "But it could happen."

McCoy could think of nothing to say.

"So that's why I can't go to your house, Ken, as much as I would really would like to. What I'm going to do this afternoon is what I can to convince Howe that MacArthur is right about Inchon, and everybody else wrong. The trouble with doing that is Howe is likely to decide that I'm just one more MacArthur worshiper, and so inform the President."

"Are you going to let me know what happens?"

"I won't know," Pickering said. "This is hold your breath and cross your fingers time."

He pushed himself off the windowsill, walked to McCoy, and touched his shoulder.

"One bit of advice before you go to tell Ernie," he said.

"Yes, sir?"

"From you, Ken."

"Sir?"

"Do I tell Howe about Pick?"

McCoy thought that over for a full fifteen seconds.

"If you don't, and he finds out, and he *will* find out, he'll wonder what else you haven't told him."

"That's what I've been thinking. I'll tell him now, and then I'll call my wife. Get out of here, Ken."

[TWO]
No. 7 Saku-Tun
Denenchofu, Tokyo, Japan
1330 3 August 1950

"Aunt Patricia," Mrs. Ernestine McCoy said, "Now, I want you to listen to me. . . ."

She was on the telephone, standing by the couch's end table in the living room. Tears were running down her cheeks.

Captain Kenneth R. McCoy, in his shirtsleeves, was sitting on the couch, leaning over the coffee table, idly stirring a large ice cube in his drink with his finger, and looking at his wife.

She loved him, McCoy thought. *Christ, I loved him. Goddamn it. Present tense. She loves him. I love him. We don't know he's dead.*

"The only thing you would accomplish by coming here would be getting in the way," Ernie went on. "If there's anything that can be done, Uncle Flem and Ken will do it."

The doorbell rang.

"Who the fuck is that?" McCoy exploded.

"Watch your mouth," Ernie said, and then, a moment later, into the telephone: "Ken spilled his drink."

"Shit!" McCoy said, softly.

The truth is, it doesn't matter who rang the goddamn bell. Kon San was told "no visitors, nobody."

He picked up his drink and took a healthy swallow.

The truth is, I don't want this goddamn drink.

He heard the door open and close.

Kon San will now come in here and tell us it was the goddamned butcher or somebody, and she sent him away, and is there anything else we need?

The couch on which he was sitting faced away from the sliding door giving access to the foyer. He turned on it, so that when Kon San slid it open, he could signal her not to say anything and to go away.

Smile when you do that. She's trying to be helpful.

The sliding door—of translucent parchment—slid open.

Kon San was standing there, a look of discomfort on her face. And so were Captain George F. Hart, USMCR, Master Gunner Ernest Zimmerman, USMC, and Lieutenant David R. Taylor, USNR.

Goddamn it, they didn't take their shoes off! Ernie will blow a gasket!

And what the fuck are they doing here? Hart and Zimmerman want to help. But Taylor?

He got quickly to his feet, nodded at Ernie, put his finger over his lips to signal silence, and went to the door.

He grabbed Zimmerman by the arm and led him down the corridors to the foyer.

"Take off your goddamn shoes," McCoy ordered, not pleasantly. "What the hell's the matter with you? You know better!"

"Ken . . ." Zimmerman started.

McCoy cut him off with an angry finger in front of his lips.

The three removed their shoes and slipped their feet into slippers.

McCoy gestured for them to follow him, and led them through corridors to the kitchen.

"Ernie's on the phone with Pick's mother," he said.

"I'm sorry about Pick, Ken," Hart said.

"You could have told me that on the phone," McCoy said. "Ernie's pretty upset. They're like brother and sister."

"Yeah, I know," Hart said. "I wouldn't have come, but I thought this was important."

"Taylor, a friend of ours is MIA."

"General Pickering told me," Taylor said. "Sorry."

Then what the fuck are you doing here? What the fuck is wrong with Hart and Zimmerman, bringing you here?

"What's important, George?" McCoy asked.

"He asked me," Zimmerman said. "Hart did. We thought we should come."

"To do what?"

Watch your goddamn temper. They're just trying to be helpful.

"Lieutenant Taylor has some ideas about the islands in the Flying Fish Channel," Hart said.

"Right now, I don't give a rat's ass about the islands in the Flying Fish Channel," McCoy said.

"You better hear him out, Ken," Zimmerman said.

McCoy, just in time, bit off what came to his lips—"Go fuck yourself"— and said nothing.

Instead, he opened one cabinet after another until he found the liquor supply, found a bottle of Famous Grouse—

"You drink scotch, Taylor? There's everything."

"Scotch is fine," Taylor said.

—set it on the butcher's block, and then went back to cabinets to find glasses. He put the glasses on the butcher's block, poured Famous Grouse an inch deep in each, and wordlessly passed them out.

"To Pick, wherever he is," he said.

The others raised their glasses. Zimmerman and Hart said, "Pick."

"The general said he's probably a prisoner," Zimmerman said.

"That's good news?"

"Considering the alternatives," Zimmerman said, "yeah."

"So what's so important?" McCoy said.

"If you want to be pissed at somebody, be pissed at me," Hart said. "This was my idea."

"*What* was your idea, goddamn it, George?"

"I asked Taylor what sort of a plan he had, and he said it was sort of like a Marine Raider operation in War Two," Hart said. "So I told him he ought to talk to Zimmerman and you; you were in the Raiders."

"For a cop, George, you have a big mouth," McCoy said.

"So I got Zimmerman in the room, and Taylor told him what he was thinking, and Zimmerman said, 'We got to show this to the Kil—McCoy.'"

"Why?" McCoy asked.

"Because Taylor has to show it to the boss and that Army general, and probably by seventeen hundred," Zimmerman said. "And the first thing the boss is going to do—and you know it, Killer—is ask you what you think."

"I think the idea will work . . . ," Taylor said.

"So do I," Zimmerman interjected.

"You do, huh?" McCoy said.

" . . . and I don't want the idea shot down just because some Army colonel, or Annapolis captain didn't think of it first, or it's not according to the book," Taylor finished.

Mrs. Ernestine McCoy came into the kitchen. There was no sign of the tears that had run down her cheeks, but her mascara and eye shadow were mussed, and her eyes were red.

"Hey, Ernie," Zimmerman said. "Sorry about Pick."

He went to her and with surprising delicacy, put his arms around her and kissed her on the cheek.

"I heard someone come in," she said. "I didn't know who it was." She put her hand out to Lieutenant Taylor. "I'm Ernie McCoy."

"Sorry to barge in like this, Mrs. McCoy. I'm David Taylor."

"Hello, George," Ernie said. "Rotten news, huh?"

"What am I, the only one in the room who hasn't given up on him? Christ, he walks through raindrops. He always has. You know that."

"I haven't given up on him, goddamn it," McCoy said.

"None of us, have, George," Ernie McCoy said. "I just talked to his mother. She wanted to come over here."

"Did you manage to talk her out of it?" McCoy asked.

"Yes, I did. I told her she'd only be in the way; that you and Uncle Flem . . . General Pickering . . . were already working on the problem. Is that—I hope— what this is?"

"Not exactly," McCoy said. "Taylor has an idea about a major problem with the Inchon landing, and these two think I should have a look at it." He saw the look of surprise on Taylor's face, and added: "General Howe has granted my wife a Top Secret/White House, Mr. Taylor."

"Probably because he knows you can't keep a secret from a woman," Zimmerman said.

"Screw you, Zimmerman," Ernie McCoy said, conversationally. "I think I'll have one of those," she added, and reached for the bottle of Famous Grouse. "And then, if you don't think I should know about this, I'll fold my tent and silently steal away."

Fuck it, why not? If she walks out of here, she'll go to the bedroom and start crying again. I can't stand to hear her cry.

"OK, Taylor, let's hear the idea," McCoy said. "Honey, will you take notes?"

"You want to do it in here, or in the dining room?" Ernie asked.

"The dining room," McCoy said.

"I'll send Kon San and the others shopping," Ernie said. "And get a pad and pencil. If you're going to drink in there, you bring the bottle and glasses."

[THREE]

"Let's start from scratch," Taylor said, pointing with a pencil at a map laid out on the dining room table. "Here's Taemuui-do island and here's Yonghung-do

Island, both of which have to be taken before the invasion fleet can make it into Inchon.

"If they're taken on D Minus One, as the brass wants to do, that means the North Koreans will know about the invasion twenty-four hours before it happens, and damned sure will be waiting for the invasion. So the thing to do, it seems to me, is take them just as soon as we can."

"Wouldn't that give the North Koreans even more notice of the invasion?" Ernie McCoy asked.

It was evident on Taylor's face that he was not accustomed to having a woman—even an officer's wife—just join in a discussion of a military operation.

"It would, Mrs. McCoy—"

"Please call me 'Ernie,' " she interrupted.

"Okay. It would, *Ernie*, if the Army did it. Or the Marines. But if they thought it was a South Korean operation, they might—probably would—think it was just that. And if their intelligence didn't come up with any unusual Naval activity in the next week, ten days, they'd probably relax again."

"I see a couple of problems with that," McCoy said, "starting with the fact that the South Koreans don't have any forces to spare, and if they did, they wouldn't know to attack an island."

"I'm not thinking of the South Korean Army, McCoy," Taylor said. "I want to do this with irregulars, guerrillas, militia, whatever the right word is."

"Where are they going to come from?" McCoy said.

"We recruit them, train them . . ."

"Who's we?" McCoy asked. "You and me?"

"Give me a chance with this, will you, McCoy?" Taylor said.

"Go ahead," McCoy said. "Convince me."

"There are hardly any troops on these islands. Maybe a platoon, maybe a reinforced platoon on Taemuui-do, and even fewer men on Yonghung-do. And they're not first-class troops, either. Some of them are North Korean national police."

"How do you know that?"

"I know," Taylor said.

"As of when?"

"As of ten days ago," Taylor said.

"That's what's known as old intelligence," McCoy said. "A lot can happen in ten days."

"Mr. Taylor, he's always doing that," Zimmerman said. "Looking for the worst thing. Trust me, he's good at this sort of sh—operation."

"But keep in mind, Taylor," Hart said, "that his bite is really worse than his bark."

There were chuckles.

"On the Tokchok-kundo islands . . . ," Taylor said, pointing at the map again, "here, in addition to the natives, there're a lot of refugees from the mainland. And fishermen from Inchon, and up and down the coast, are always going there. Going off at a tangent, the fisherman should be put to work keeping us aware of what's going on in the area; they're always going in and out of Inchon, and the North Koreans leave them alone, by and large."

"Are you talking about recruiting the natives and the refugees?" McCoy asked.

"Something wrong with that? Those people don't want the North Koreans to win. They know what will happen to them."

"I didn't say there was anything wrong with it," McCoy said.

"Ken, you and I could go have a look," Zimmerman said.

"Yeah," McCoy said, thoughtfully.

"If we could recruit these people, quietly," Taylor urged, "arm them, train them, and maybe get a destroyer to provide some naval gunfire—it wouldn't take much—we could—they could—take both Taemuui-do and Yonghung-do, and the North Koreans would think the *South Koreans* were doing it because they thought they could get away with it."

"And not as step one in an amphibious invasion of Inchon," Ernie McCoy said, agreeing with him. "Ken?"

"I could probably talk General Craig out of enough Marines to train these people. . . . You're talking about training them right on those islands, right?"

"Right."

"Killer, there're South Korean marines," Zimmerman said.

"Yeah, we saw them on the pier in Pusan, right?" McCoy replied. His tone made it clear that he didn't want to employ South Korean marines in this operation.

"They wouldn't need anything heavy," Taylor said. "Carbines and .30-caliber air-cooled machine guns. Maybe a couple of mortars."

"The problem is going to be getting this past Whitney and the other clowns on the SCAP staff. From painful personal experience, I know they don't think much of operations like this."

"But you think it would work?" Taylor asked.

"Well, hell, it's worth a shot. But Ernie—the Ernie with the beard—is right. We'll have to take a look at these islands ourselves."

"The question, Killer, is what are you going to say when the boss asks you what you think of the idea?" Zimmerman said.

"It makes sense," McCoy said. "It's worth a shot. Anything that will change the odds at Inchon in our favor is worth a shot."

"How are you going to get to those islands?" Ernie McCoy asked.

"I don't know yet. We must have some Navy vessels operating in that area that could sneak us in at night."

"They don't have PT boats anymore, do they?" Zimmerman asked.

"No. They'd be ideal, too," McCoy said. "There must be something."

"There's some junks around with diesel engines in them," Taylor said.

"That would do it," McCoy said. "How do we get one?"

"Have the South Korean Navy commandeer one," Hart suggested.

"No. That would attract too much attention. Maybe we could buy one."

"Buy one?" Taylor asked.

"Now, that opens a whole new line of interesting thoughts," McCoy said. "If the boss would go along, we could run this as a CIA operation, and we wouldn't have to ask SCAP's permission. Just, when the time is right, hand them the islands."

"I'm new to all this," Taylor said. "Would there be money for something like this?"

"Oh, yeah. The one thing the CIA doesn't have to worry about is money. I'm going to go to the boss and see if he can't give me some money to buy information about Pick. Money is not a problem."

"He won't want special treatment for Pick, honey," Ernie said.

"I'm going to tell him he doesn't have any choice," McCoy said. "I'd like to get Pick back before the North Koreans find out his father is the Assistant Director for Asia of the CIA."

"I didn't think about that," Ernie said.

"You sound as if you're pretty sure he's alive," Taylor said.

"Yeah. Probably because I do," McCoy said. "Okay. If we have to show this to the boss and General Howe by seventeen hundred, we're going to have to get off the dime. There's a typewriter here, honey, right?"

"Yes," Ernie said, simply.

"You make coffee, and I'll type, okay?"

"You think Pick's alive?" she asked.

He met her eyes and nodded.

"George," she said, "I'm a delicate woman. You can carry the typewriter."

[FOUR]
The Dewey Suite
The Imperial Hotel
Tokyo, Japan
1905 3 August 1950

"I'd like a word with General Pickering," Howe said.

Captains McCoy and Hart, Master Gunner Zimmerman, Lieutenant Taylor and Mrs. Kenneth McCoy started to get up from their chairs at the table of the dining room.

"Keep your seats," General Howe said. "This won't take long. Can we use your bedroom, General?"

"Of course," Pickering said, got up, and led the way out of the dining room.

Howe closed the door of Pickering's bedroom behind them, walked to the desk against the wall, and leaned on it.

"There wasn't much—damned near nothing—in the CIA reports I read in Washington about these islands," he said. "Is there any more that you know of?"

Pickering shook his head, "no."

"I've been going damned near blind since I got here, reading the files," he said. "I didn't see anything. It looks like all we know about them is what Taylor is telling us."

"We can't go on that alone, Fleming," Howe said.

"I don't know what you mean by 'go,' Ralph," Pickering said.

"Earlier today, I messaged the President that I thought the Inchon invasion was idiotic," Howe said. "The phrase I used was 'from my understanding of its feasibility, the risks involved would seem to make the invasion inadvisable.' If I had had him on the phone, I would have said, 'It looks like a dumb idea to me, Harry.' "

Pickering didn't reply.

"And then we had our afternoon with General MacArthur," Howe said. "After which I tried to call the President. He was not available. So I left a message with his secretary. 'Last judgment Inchon premature. Sorry. More follows soonest.' "

"MacArthur changed your mind?" Pickering said.

"He should have been a door-to-door salesman," Howe said. "He could have made a fortune selling Bibles to atheists."

Pickering chuckled.

"When he's in good form, he's really something."

"If you don't want to answer this, don't," Howe said. "What did you message the President?"

" 'I have concluded that despite the obvious problems, the Inchon invasion is possible, and the benefits therefrom outweigh the risks.' " Pickering said. It was obvious he was quoting himself verbatim.

"You think he can carry it off?"

"I've seen him in action, Ralph. That military genius business is not hyperbole."

"What do you think of Taylor's idea?"

"I think the bunch around MacArthur—and maybe MacArthur himself, if it ever got that high—would reject it out of hand—"

"Maybe not 'out of hand,' " Howe interrupted.

Pickering looked at him a moment.

"You're right," he said. "They would 'carefully consider' the proposal, such careful consideration lasting until it would be too late to put it into execution."

"As I understand the role of the CIA, Fleming," Howe said, "it is an intelligence-gathering operation."

"So I understand."

"Taylor suggested that the people on the islands are possessed of knowledge of intelligence value . . ."

"He did say that, didn't he?"

"And unless I'm mistaken, the Assistant Director of the CIA for Asia doesn't need MacArthur's approval to conduct what could be considered a routine intelligence-gathering operation. . . ."

"As a matter of fact, I don't even have to tell El Supremo what I'm doing," Pickering said. "Or have done."

"How annoyed do you suppose he'd be if—when—he found out later?" Howe asked.

"If we can take those bottleneck islands quietly, with McCoy and a dozen or so Marines in the next couple of weeks, MacArthur will thereafter refer to it as 'my clandestine operation.' If this blows up in our faces—which would, obviously, signal the North Koreans that we plan to land at Inchon—Whitney and Willoughby would recommend public castration, prior to my being hung by the neck until dead, and he'd probably go along."

"You don't sound particularly worried."

"I have the gut feeling that Taylor knows what he's talking about, and I know McCoy is just the man who could organize and execute an operation like this."

Howe met Pickering's eyes for a moment, then nodded.

"Okay," he said. "How about this? 'Have just learned Pickering is conducting a clandestine operation which if successful will remove my primary objection to an invasion at Inchon. I believe the operation will be successful. More follows.' "

"That's what you're going to send?"

"I'm afraid if I call again, he'll take my call," Howe said.

"And if President Truman calls you?"

"By then, I suspect, Captain McCoy and Lieutenant Taylor and Mr. Zimmerman . . . is Zimmerman going?"

"They're a team," Pickering said.

". . . will be en route to the Flying Fish Channel islands, and, since we have no means of communicating with them, until they reach the islands—and maybe not then—it will be too late to call the operation off."

XIII

[ONE]
Headquarters, 1st Marine Brigade (Provisional)
Near Chindong-Ni, South Korea
1505 4 August 1950

The helicopter pad at Brigade Headquarters consisted of a flat area more or less paved with bricks, brick-size stones and gravel, and a windsock mounted on what looked like two tent poles lashed together.

Ten Marines, five enlisted men—a sergeant major and four Jeep drivers, ranging from private to buck sergeant—and five officers—a lieutenant colonel, a major, two captains, and one master gunner—stood to one side and watched as the HO3S-1 helicopter made its approach and fluttered to the ground.

U.S. Marine Corps HO3S-1, tail number 142, was one of four Sikorsky helicopters that had been quickly detached from HMX-1* at Quantico, Virginia, and assigned to the 1st Marine Brigade's observation squadron, VMO-6, when the brigade was ordered to Korea. VMO-6 had four other aircraft, Piper Cub–type fixed-wing aircraft called OY-2 by the Marine Corps, and L-4 by the Army.

---

*H for Helicopter; X for Experimental.

The HO3S-1 was manufactured by the Sikorsky Aircraft Corporation, and had in fact been designed by Igor Sikorsky, a Russian refugee from communism himself. Sikorsky had also earlier designed the—then huge—Sikorsky Flying Boats, which had permitted the first intercontinental passenger travel.

The HO3s-1 was powered by a nine-cylinder, 450-horsepower radial Pratt & Whitney engine. It had a three-blade main rotor, which turned in a 48-foot arc. It could lift just over 1,500 pounds (fuel, cargo, and up to three passengers, plus pilot, in any combination) and fly that much weight at up to 102 miles per hour in ideal conditions for about 250 miles.

For the first time, commanders had a means to move literally anywhere on the battlefield at 100 miles per hour. Brigadier General Edward A. Craig, who had begun to use the helicopters the moment they had arrived in Korea, later said that without the helicopters he doubted they "would have had the success we did" in Korea.

Three of the five officers awaiting the helicopter were members of General Edward A. Craig's staff. The lieutenant colonel was his G-3, the major his G-2, and one of the captains, his aide-de-camp. The second captain and the master gunner were not.

Aside from the briefing Captain McCoy had given the assembled officers on the attack transport the day they arrived in Pusan, the S-3 had never seen him before, and frankly doubted the sergeant major's belief that the clean-cut young officer was the legendary "Killer" McCoy who had single-handedly stabbed twenty Japanese to death in Shanghai, or some such bullshit. For one thing, he didn't look old enough, and for another, he didn't believe the story about twenty stabbed-to-death Japanese.

What he thought was that McCoy was an intelligence officer with an exaggerated opinion of his own importance and his role in the Marine Corps scheme of things.

Marine captains customarily answer any question lieutenant colonels put to them. When he had asked Captain McCoy why he wished to see the general, McCoy had—politely, to be sure—told him that he was not at liberty to discuss that.

The S-3, the aide-de-camp, and the sergeant major, all of whom considered it part of their duties to protect the general from wasting his time dealing with people who could have their problems solved by somebody else, were all privately hoping that General Craig would emerge from his helicopter, learn that Captain McCoy had demanded to know when he would return to the CP, and eat him a new asshole.

Everyone more or less came to attention when the door of the helicopter opened and General Craig got out. The G-3 and Captain McCoy saluted.

"Reporting for duty, McCoy?" Craig asked, as he returned the salute.

"No, sir. I need a few minutes of your time."

"I have very little of that," Craig said. "What do you need?"

"Sir, I have to speak to you privately."

"OK, let's go to the CP," he said.

"Sir," the S-3 said, "there're several things. . . ."

"First, McCoy gets three minutes, OK?"

"Aye, aye, sir."

The Jeeps made a little convoy as they drove to the command post, a rather spartan sandbag reinforced collection of tents set up against a steep incline. Bringing up the rear was a Jeep whose bumper markings identified it as belonging to the signal company of the Army's 24th Division. It held Captain McCoy and Master Gunner Zimmerman, who was driving.

General Craig's "office" was a chair and a desk, on which sat two field telephones in the interior of one of the tents. With his sergeant major, the G-3, the G-2, his aide, his sergeant major and McCoy and Zimmerman on his heels, he walked to it.

General Craig mimed wanting coffee to one the of the clerks, who said, "Aye, Aye, Sir," and went to the stainless-steel pitcher sitting on an electric burner on the dirt floor.

"OK, McCoy," General Craig said. "I interpret 'a few minutes' to mean no more than three. Then you can get yourself a cup of coffee."

"Sir, I must speak to you privately."

"Captain, Colonel Fuster is my G-3. He has all the security clearances he needs."

"With respect, sir, he doesn't," McCoy said.

Craig looked at him coldly for a moment.

"This had better be important, Captain," Craig said, then, to the G-3, "Give us three minutes, please, Colonel."

Lieutenant Colonel Fuster said, "Aye, aye, sir," and gestured to the G-2, the aide, and the sergeant major to leave the general's "office."

"OK," Craig said. "What's on your mind?"

"Sir, I need a dozen men, noncoms, staff sergeants, and weapons and ammunition. Zimmerman has a list."

"Not that I have either men, weapons, or ammo to spare, but what for?"

"A clandestine operation, sir."

"Simple answer, no," Craig said. "Sorry."

"Sir, I was instructed to show you this, by General Pickering, as his authority to conduct the operation."

He took the White House orders from his utilities pocket and handed them to General Craig.

Craig read them and handed them back.

"Am I permitted to know the nature of this clandestine operation?"

"Yes, sir. But General Pickering directed me to tell you, sir, that this is classified Top Secret/White House, and is not to be divulged to anyone."

"Understood," Craig said.

"There are two NK-occupied islands in the Flying Fish Channel leading to Inchon, sir, from which artillery could be brought to bear on vessels attempting to reach Inchon. We intend to occupy them now, using South Korean national police."

"I thought they called that invasion operation off—Operation Bluehearts was what they called it—when we lost Taejon," Craig said. "Now it's back on?"

"I don't know if that operation is back on, sir, but General Pickering thinks there will be an amphibious operation at Inchon."

"And you and a dozen noncoms are going to—*invade* is the wrong word; a dozen men can't *invade* anything—*infiltrate* these islands and secure them?"

"Yes, sir."

"Won't that tip the North Koreans that we're going to land at Inchon?"

"We hope they will believe it is a South Korean national police operation, sir. What I'm going to do with the noncoms is train and arm South Koreans—"

"South Koreans already on the islands?"

"Yes, sir. And I understand there's a lot of refugees from the mainland on the islands, too."

"What makes you think they'll volunteer?"

"When the North Koreans took Seoul and Inchon, they shot a lot of people they thought might cause trouble. The refugees want to pay them back."

"OK," Craig said.

"South Koreans, recruited into the South Korean national police, will be the bulk of the landing force. The Marines will wear South Korean national police uniforms. . . ."

"I suppose wearing the uniform of a cobelligerent is permitted under the rules of land warfare, but I wonder what would happen to a Marine who was caught on these islands dressed as a Korean national policeman."

"Realistically, sir, they'd shoot him."

"I can't order Marines to do something like this, McCoy. They'll have to be volunteers, and they'll have to know what they're getting themselves into. How do you plan to handle that?"

"Sir, I don't know, but I'll bet there's some old Raiders in the brigade," Zimmerman said. "They'd volunteer, I'm sure, for something like this, and they'd be ideal."

"There'd be no way to find them without going through all the records," General Craig said.

"Sir, what about passing the word that all former Marine Raiders are to report here now?" McCoy asked.

"I said they would have to volunteer, McCoy," Craig said.

"I will ask whatever old Raiders who show up to volunteer—"

" 'For a classified mission, unspecified, involving great personal risk to life?' "

"Yes, sir."

"And if you don't get a dozen volunteers, then what?"

"We'll get some, sir, I'm sure," Zimmerman said.

"Why are you sure?"

"If I'd been a Raider, and somebody gave me a choice between doing a small-unit operation, and what I was going to have to do here . . ."

"Meaning what, Mr. Zimmerman?"

"Saving the Army's ass, sir," Zimmerman said, a little uncomfortably. "That's liable to be really dangerous."

General Craig seemed about to reply, but didn't.

After a moment, Zimmerman went on:

"And say I come up with four ex-Raiders who are willing to go—"

"You're going to be the recruiting officer for this, I gather?" Craig interrupted.

"Yes, sir. Captain McCoy's got other things to do. So if I get four ex-Raiders, I'll ask them who else they know who would like to go along. What might be a problem is getting their commanding officers to let them go."

"You get the volunteers, Mr. Zimmerman. I'll deal with their commanding officers."

"Aye, aye, sir. Thank you."

Craig looked at McCoy.

"The idea, then, is to seize this island and make it look as if the South Korean national police did it on their own? Is that about it, McCoy?"

"Yes, sir. And if we do it now, and an invasion doesn't immediately follow, we think they'll relax."

"That's a long shot, isn't it?"

"Sir, the alternative is taking the islands on D Minus One. That would really tip them off than an invasion was coming."

Craig nodded his agreement, then raised his voice: "Sergeant Major!"

The sergeant major walked very quickly down the tent to them.

"Sir?"

"Get on the horn right now. Call the battalions—make sure they know the order came from me—and have them send anybody who was once a Marine Raider here, and right now."

"Aye, aye, sir."

"We've been levied for twelve noncoms," General Craig said. "Ex–Marine Raiders would be ideal, according to Mr. Zimmerman. If he can't turn up a dozen of them, we'll have to look elsewhere. He's also going to need some weapons and ammunition. He'll tell you what."

"Aye, aye, sir. Can I ask what he needs them for? For how long?"

"I'm sorry, but that's classified," General Craig said. "It's important, Sergeant Major. I can tell you that much. Some very senior Marines think so, and so do I."

"Yes, sir."

"Mr. Zimmerman is concerned that their commanders won't want to give up the kind of really good Marines he has to have."

"I can deal with that, sir," the sergeant major said.

"Let's see how many Raiders we come up with, and play it by ear from there," General Craig said. "Captain McCoy and Mr. Zimmerman get anything they ask for. Clear?"

"Aye, aye, sir," the sergeant major said.

"Anything else, McCoy?"

"That's about it, sir. Thank you, very much."

"Good luck, McCoy," General Craig said. "You, too, Zimmerman."

General Craig raised his voice again.

"Colonel Fuster, you wanted to see me?"

Colonel Fuster came down the tent as McCoy, Zimmerman, and the sergeant major went the other way.

The sound reflecting characteristics of the tent were such that all three heard General Craig say, "Don't ask me what that was all about, Fuster. I can't tell you."

[TWO]
USAF Airfield K-1
Pusan, Korea
1635 4 August 1950

K-1 was a busy airport.

Lieutenant Commander Andrew McDavit, USNR, in his TBM-3G Avenger* was third in the landing pattern behind a C-54 of the Air Force air transport command, and an R5D of the Naval air transport command. Behind him was a Marine F4-U from the *Sicily,* then a two-plane flight of USAF P-51 Mustangs, and, he thought, maybe half a dozen other aircraft.

"K-1, Marine Double Zero Four," the pilot of the F4-U called.

"Double Zero Four, go ahead."

"I have a fuel warning light blinking at me. Could you get those elephants to let me in ahead of them?"

"Double Zero Four, are you declaring an emergency?"

"Negative at this time. Ask me again in sixty seconds."

"Air Force Four Oh Nine, you are clear to land on One Six," the K-1 tower operator ordered. "Navy Six Six Six, you are number two after the C-54. Acknowledge."

"Four Oh Nine, understand Number One. Turning on final at this time."

"Six Sixty-six understands Number Two behind the Air Force."

"Navy Five Niner Four."

"Niner Four."

"Five Niner Four, turn ninety degrees right, climb to five thousand, and reenter the landing pattern after an Air Force C-47. I have a Marine F4-U with low fuel. Acknowledge."

"Shit," Lieutenant Commander McDavit said, then pushed the button on his microphone. "Niner Four making a right ninety-degree at this time. Un-

---

*The Grumman TBF- and TBM-series aircraft (most of which were actually built by the Eastern aircraft division of General Motors) were single-engine torpedo bombers with a three-man crew. Powered by a 1,900-horsepower Wright engine, it had a top speed of 275 mph, and could carry 2,000 pounds of bombs or torpedoes, etc. It served in that role throughout World War II. Some Avengers were COD (*Carrier On Board Delivery*) modified to serve as small transport aircraft able to operate from aircraft carriers, by the addition of seats in the torpedo/bomb bay.

During World War II, the youngest aviator in the U.S. Navy was forced to crash-land his combat-damaged Avenger in the sea. Rescued almost immediately by a submarine improbably in the area, Ensign George Herbert Walker Bush, USNR, survived to become the forty-first President of the United States and father of the forty-third.

derstand climb to five thousand to reenter pattern after an Air Force Gooney-Bird."

"Marine Double Zero Four, you are number three on One Six after the two transports."

"Thank you kindly, K-1. And sorry about this, Navy Niner Four."

"Fuck you, jarhead," Lieutenant Commander McDavit said, without pressing his microphone button.

Goddamn hotshot jarheads do this all the goddamn time—linger so long looking for something to shoot at that they don't have the fuel to make it back to the carrier.

It was another fifteen minutes before Lieutenant Commander McDavit was able to land.

Which will make me fifteen fucking minutes late getting back to the Badoeng Strait. *Which means that I will probably get back to her just in time to have the sun right in my fucking eyes when I line up on final.*

Ground control directed Navy Five Niner Four to the tarmac in front of Base Operations.

Lieutenant Commander McDavit shut the aircraft down and then he and Aviation Motor Machinist's Mate 2nd Class Richard Orwell climbed down to the ground.

"You start unloading the mail," Commander McDavit ordered. "And I'll see about getting us a Jeep or something."

"Right," Orwell said.

The proper response to an order was "Aye, aye, sir," but Orwell was a good kid, and meant no disrespect, so McDavit decided to let it pass.

Somewhere on K-1 was a small Navy detachment charged with dealing with the mail. It came from San Diego—sometimes San Francisco—on a Navy R5D. R5Ds could not land on "Jeep" carriers such as the *Sicily* and the *Badoeng Strait*, so a COD Avenger had to fly to K-1 and pick it up.

Commander McDavit was directed to the fleet post office detachment, told "sorry, no Jeep," and walked to it, wondering how the hell he was supposed to get the *Badoeng Strait's* outgoing mailbags from the Avenger to the FPO, and the incoming mailbags from the FPO to the Avenger, without a Jeep.

There was a Marine captain, in utilities, leaning on an Army Jeep in front of the FPO. A Garand rifle was hanging from its strap, hooked on the corner of the windshield.

The Marine captain stood straight and saluted.

"You're the COD from the *Badoeng Strait?*" the Marine captain asked.

"Right."

"I need a ride out to her, Commander," the Marine said.

"You're reporting aboard?"

"Not exactly," the Marine captain said, and showed McDavit a set of orders from SCAP, signed by some Army three-star general, saying he was authorized to go just about any place he wanted to go.

"I'll tell you what I'll do, Captain," McDavit said. "You help me get the mailbags I brought from the *Badoeng Strait* here, and the mailbags that are going to the *Badoeng Strait* out to my airplane, and if I have the weight left, I'll take you out."

"I'll help you with the mail," the Marine captain said, as he produced another set of orders, this one—*Jesus Christ!*—signed by the Commander-in-Chief himself, "but if it's a question of me or the mail going, the mail will have to wait."

[THREE]
The USS *Badoeng Strait*
35 Degrees 60 Minutes North Latitude, 130 Degrees 52
**   Minutes East Longitude**
The Sea of Japan
1945 4 August 1950

"*Badoeng, Badoeng,* Niner Four at 5,000, five miles east. I have *Badoeng* in sight."

"Niner Four, Recovery operations under way. You are number two to land after an F4-U on final approach."

"Roger, I have him in sight. *Badoeng,* be advised I have aboard a passenger traveling on Presidential orders."

"Say again, Niner Four?"

"Be advised I have aboard a passenger traveling on Presidential orders."

Commander McDavit set his *Avenger* down on *Badoeng Strait*'s deck more or less smoothly, and the hook caught the second cable, which caused the aircraft to decelerate very rapidly.

Which caused Captain Kenneth R. McCoy, USMCR, to utter a vulgarity instantly followed by an obscenity, and then a blasphemy.

There were no windows in the passenger/cargo area of the Avenger, and very little light. The seat faced the rear, which had produced a certain feeling of un-

ease in Captain McCoy, especially during the last few moments of Commander McDavit's landing approach, during which he had abruptly moved the aircraft to the right, and then even more abruptly to the left, and then raised the
nose sharply in the second before he touched down.

Captain McCoy was recovering from this traumatic experience when the
hatch in the fuselage suddenly opened, filling the interior with brilliant light
from the setting sun. It took Captain McCoy's eyes a long moment to adjust to
the change in light intensity, but when they had, he saw a Marine corporal, in
dress blue trousers, khaki shirt, and brimmed cap with white cover, standing at
attention by the door, his right arm raised in a rigid salute.

Captain McCoy unstrapped his harness and started to go through the hatch,
then remembered the National Match Garand and backed into the passen-
ger/cargo compartment to unstrap it.

When he finally passed through the door and stood in the bright sunlight
of the deck, he saw that he was being met by a welcoming party. There was a
Navy lieutenant, in the prescribed regalia identifying him as the officer of the
deck. There was also a commander, a lieutenant commander, a Marine lieutenant colonel—wearing aviator's wings—and a Marine staff sergeant.

What's going on? Who the hell are all these people?

The *Badoeng Strait*'s captain, having been advised that an officer traveling
on Presidential orders was about to come aboard, and not knowing that it was
a lowly jarhead captain, had ordered that the distinguished guest be greeted with
appropriate ceremony, and sent the *Badoeng Strait*'s executive officer, the senior
Marine officer aboard, and the two Marine orderlies on duty to do so.

Captain McCoy remembered the protocol.

He saluted the officer of the deck.

"Permission to come aboard, sir?"

"Granted."

McCoy faced aft and saluted the national colors, then faced left and saluted
the Navy commander and the Marine lieutenant colonel, who returned his salute.

"Welcome aboard, sir," the officer of the deck declared. "May I ask to see
the captain's orders, sir?"

This time, McCoy decided, *the White House orders first.*

He handed them to the officer of the deck, who read them, then handed
them to the executive officer, who read them, handed them to the Marine lieutenant colonel, who read them and handed them back.

"The captain's compliments, Captain," the executive officer said. "The captain asks that you join him on the bridge."

"Aye, aye, sir," McCoy said.

A little parade was formed and marched to the island, entered it, and then wended its way up several ladders to the bridge.

The *Badoeng Strait*'s captain rose from his swivel chair when he saw the little parade file onto the bridge.

"Captain McCoy, Captain," the executive officer said, "who is traveling under authority of the President."

The captain looked amused.

"Welcome aboard, Captain," he said. "What can we do for you?" and then, before McCoy could reply, he added: "I've never seen Presidential orders."

McCoy handed him the White House orders.

"Very interesting," he said. "How can we help you, Captain?"

"Sir, I'm going to need some aerial photos of the Inchon area," McCoy said. "Updated every day or two."

"I'm sure Colonel Unger can handle that," the captain said, nodding at the Marine lieutenant colonel.

"Just tell me what you need," Lieutenant Colonel Unger said, and stepped to McCoy and offered his hand.

"Anything else?" the captain asked.

"I'd like a few minutes with Lieutenant Colonel Dunn, sir," McCoy said.

The captain turned to the Marine corporal.

"My compliments to Colonel Dunn," he said. "Would he please join me immediately in my sea cabin?"

"Aye, aye, sir," the Marine corporal said, and marched off the bridge.

"You have the conn, sir," the captain said to the officer of the deck, then turned to McCoy. "Why don't we go to my cabin, Captain? You look as if you could use a cup of coffee and somewhere to sit down."

"Thank you, sir."

"And since I doubt if you'll need it in my cabin, may I suggest you give the sergeant your rifle for the time being?"

"Aye, aye, sir," McCoy said, and handed it over. Then he had another thought. "You better unload it, Sergeant," he said.

Lieutenant Colonel William C. Dunn, USMC, stood at the open door of the *Badoeng Strait*'s captain's sea cabin until the captain saw him, and motioned him inside.

"You wanted to see me, Captain?"

"This officer wants to see you," the captain said, nodding at McCoy. "Captain McCoy, this is Colonel Dunn."

"I know the captain, sir. How are you, Ken?"

"Colonel," McCoy said, taking Dunn's proffered hand.

"Captain McCoy needs some photographs of islands in the Flying Fish Channel off Inchon," the captain said. "And he has a very interesting authority directing us to make them for him—the Commander-in-Chief."

"Sir, McCoy and I go back a long way," Dunn said. "To Guadalcanal. Nothing he does surprises me."

There were some chuckles at that.

"And before that, I just remembered," Dunn said, "he was in Major Pickering's OCS class."

"Oh, really?" the captain said. "You've heard, McCoy, that Major Pickering went down?"

"Yes, sir, I have."

"We all feel badly about that," the captain said.

He shook his head, then went on: "It would probably be useful, Captain, if we knew why you wanted the photographs," the captain said.

"Sir," McCoy said. "The problem there is that I can't take the risk of another aviator going down with that knowledge."

"Obviously, it has to do with an amphibious operation in the Pusan area," the captain said. "On our way here—before the First Marine Brigade was diverted to Pusan—I was given a preliminary alert that such an operation—"

"Operation Blueberry," his executive order furnished.

The captain flashed him a displeased look and then went on: "—was being planned. And then it was called off. Since you come here asking for photographs of the Flying Fish Channel islands, it would then seem logical to me that the operation is back on, or another operation with the same purpose is being planned. My point, Captain, is that if I can figure that out, so can the enemy."

This guy doesn't like getting his marching orders from a lowly captain. If I were the captain of an aircraft carrier, I wouldn't either.

McCoy didn't respond directly. Instead, he dipped into the cavernous pockets of his utilities, came out with a map, and laid it on the captain's chart table.

"My superiors feel, sir," he said, "that during routine reconnaissance flights—or flights seeking to engage targets of opportunity—along the coastline here, photographs could be taken of the Flying Fish Channel, and the islands along it, without unduly raising the enemy's suspicions."

"Captain, as you're doubtless aware, the First Marine Brigade is already engaged in the Pusan area," the captain said. "The aircraft aboard the *Badoeng Strait* are changed with close air support of the brigade. What if there is a conflict between what the brigade needs and your photographic mission?"

"Sir, I would hope that this requirement would not conflict with the re-quirements of the brigade—"

"But if it does?" the captain asked, not very pleasantly.

"This mission, sir, requires photographs as I have described at least once in every twenty-four-hour period until further notice," McCoy said.

"Even if that means the brigade doesn't get what it asks for?"

"Yes, sir."

"How am I to explain that to General Craig?"

"General Craig is aware of this operation, sir."

"In detail?"

"Yes, sir."

"And, if I understand you correctly, Captain, I am not to be made 'aware' of the details of this operation?"

"Yes, sir."

"Those are your orders? Not to tell me?"

"Sir, I was told that only General Craig was to be informed of the details."

"Captain, I'll be very frank. If those orders you have just shown me were not signed by the Commander-in-Chief, I'd tell you to go to hell," the captain said. He turned to his executive officer: "See that it's done, Mr. Grobbley."

"Aye, aye, sir."

The captain started to walk out of his sea cabin. The others watched him un-comfortably until someone on the bridge called out, "Captain on the bridge!" then Lieutenant Colonels Unger and Dunn—the two Marine aviators—bent over the map McCoy had spread on the captain's chart table.

"Charley," Dunn said. "We'll just have to squeeze this into the schedule. It can be done."

Lieutenant Colonel Unger snorted.

Dunn raised his eyes to McCoy.

"How do we get the pictures to you, McCoy?"

"The first ones, sir, on the COD flights to K-1. In a sealed envelope, clas-sified Top Secret, to be delivered to the Marine liaison officer at K-1. He'll be expecting them, and I'll get them, somehow, from him."

Dunn nodded.

"In a week, sir," McCoy went on, walking to the chart table, then pointing, "maybe less, they'll have to be airdropped onto one of the Tokchok-kundo is-lands, here. I'll get the signal panel display to you. And there will be ground-to-air radios."

"You're going to be on those islands, are you?" Dunn asked.

McCoy didn't reply.

"The colonel asked you a question, Captain," Lieutenant Colonel Unger said, unpleasantly.

"Which question, obviously," Dunn said, "Captain McCoy is not at liberty to answer. Easy, Charley."

"I don't like diverting aircraft from the brigade for any purpose," Unger said.

"And I know Captain McCoy doesn't like it any more than you do," Dunn said. "You said you wanted to see me privately, McCoy?"

"Yes, sir, I do."

"Why don't we go to my cabin?" Dunn suggested. "And get out of the captain's sea cabin?"

He gestured for McCoy to precede him into a passageway.

The *Badoeng Strait*—and the *Sicily*—on which the Marine air wing had been transported from the United States and from which the wing was now operating, were officially "escort carriers," often called "Jeep carriers." They were smaller than "a real carrier," and everybody believed they were in service because they were far cheaper to operate than "real" carriers.

While they were perfectly capable of doing what they were doing now, they were smaller all over, which also meant "the creature comforts," such as officers' staterooms, were fewer in number and less spacious than those on a "real carrier."

Even senior officers often had to share their staterooms with another officer. There was a cardboard sign in a slot on the door of the stateroom to which Dunn led McCoy, white letters stamped on a blue background. It read:

LtCol W.C. Dunn, USMC
Maj M.S. Pickering, USMCR

Dunn pushed the door open and motioned for McCoy to precede him inside, then gestured for him to sit in one of the two chairs in the stateroom. He closed the door and leaned against it.

"Taking care of his gear is another little task Pick left behind for me to take care of," Dunn said, pointing to a packed canvas bag sitting on one of the bunks.

McCoy didn't reply.

"It has been decided that Major Pickering will become a Marine legend," Dunn said. "An ace, a hero of Guadalcanal and other places, a reservist who rushed to the sound of the guns when they blew the trumpet, who flew the first Marine combat sortie of this war, and died nobly in the glorious traditions of the Corps while engaging a target of opportunity. The sonofabitch should have been court-martialed for disobeying a direct order, and I'm the sonofabitch who should have court-martialed him."

McCoy looked up at him.

Tears were running unashamedly down Lieutenant Colonel Dunn's cheeks.

"What happened?" McCoy asked.

Dunn went to the desk and took from it an envelope and handed it to McCoy. There were three eight-by-ten-inch color photographs in it. At first glance, McCoy thought they were three copies of the same photograph, but then he saw there were differences. In each, Pick, smiling broadly, was pointing up at the cockpit of his Corsair. But Pick was dressed differently in each photo. In one of the photos, he was wearing a .45 in a shoulder holster; in the others he was not. And he was wearing different flight suits. Then McCoy saw what he was pointing at.

Below the cockpit canopy track there was the legend "Major M.S. Pickering, USMCR," and below that, nine "meat balls," representations of the Japanese battle flag, each signifying a downed Japanese aircraft.

And then, on one photograph, below the meatballs, there was a rather clever painting of a railroad locomotive blowing up.

There were two blowing-up locomotives painted on the fuselage in the second picture, and three in the third.

"The sonofabitch told me he was going to be the first 'locomotive ace' in the history of Marine aviation," Dunn said. "He even wrote a letter to the Air Force asking if they had kept a record of who had blown up how many locomotives in the Second War."

"Jesus Christ!" McCoy said.

"He was like a fourteen-year-old with a five-inch firecracker on the Fourth of July after he got the first one," Dunn said. "The first time, debris got his ADF, and there were holes all over his wings. That should have taught him something. It didn't."

"That's what he was doing when he got shot down?"

"In direct disobedience of my order not to go locomotive hunting. Said direct order issued after he got his second locomotive, the debris from which took out the hydraulics to his left landing gear, which made it necessary for him to crash-land on the deck. I ordered him (a) not to go locomotive-hunting—"

"You don't consider them important targets?" McCoy asked.

"There's plenty to shoot at out there. The idea, McCoy, is to fly over the area, and establish contact with the ground controller. He knows what needs to be hit. If he doesn't have an immediate target you wait—they call it 'loiter'—

until he has a mission. If the controller didn't have a mission, Pick then went locomotive-hunting."

McCoy didn't reply.

"Sure, locomotives, trains, are legitimate targets. We regularly schedule three-plane flights to see what's on the railway. When three planes attack a train, their antiaircraft fire, ergo sum, is divided between the three airplanes. A single plane gets all the antiaircraft, which multiplies the chances of getting hit by three. Pick knew all this, and . . ." He stopped. "I (a) ordered him not to go locomotive hunting; (b) if he happened on a train, he was not to attack it without permission, and not try himself. The train's not going to go anywhere in the time it would take to have a couple of Corsairs join up. . . ."

"I get the picture," McCoy said. "It sounds like Pick."

"My God, Ken, he's not twenty-one years old anymore, fresh from Pensacola, thinking he can win the war all by himself. He was a goddamn major, a squadron commander, supposed to set an example for the kids. He set an example, all right. When he didn't come back, the pilots in his squadron were ready to take off right then and shoot up every locomotive between Pusan and Seoul. Remember that football movie? Ronald Reagan? 'Get one for the Gipper!' Now they want to 'Bust one for the skipper!' "

Dunn exhaled audibly.

"I don't know how the hell I'm going to stop that," he went on. "What we are supposed to do here is provide close air support, on demand, for the brigade. Not indulge some childish whim to see a locomotive explode, as if Korea is a shooting gallery set up for our personal pleasure."

"You said 'was,' Billy," McCoy said. "You think he's dead?"

Dunn shrugged.

"I don't know," he said. "As he himself frequently announced, 'God takes care of fools and drunks, and I qualify on both counts.' " He paused again. "I think he probably survived the crash. When I thought about it, that was the seventh Corsair he's dumped. What happened afterward, I don't know. The North Koreans obviously went looking for him. If they found him . . ."

"If he survived, and was captured alive, they might want to see what they can find out about Marine aviation from a Marine major," McCoy said. "What worries me is that they might make the connection between Major Pickering and Brigadier General Pickering. . ."

"I didn't think about that," Dunn said.

". . . who is the Assistant Director of the CIA for Asia," McCoy went on. "I don't think there are many North Korean agents reading *The Washington Post* for their order of battle, but the Russians certainly do. That information was in

Moscow within twenty-four hours of the time that story was printed. Did the Russians already pass it on to the North Koreans? I don't know."

"Is there some way you can find out? If he's a prisoner, I mean. An extra effort?"

"When I get back to Pusan, and when I get to Tokchok-kundo, I'll see what I can do."

"Two questions," Dunn said. "If you can't answer them, fine. You're going to . . . What was it you said?"

"The Tokchok-kundo Islands," McCoy furnished. "Yeah, but keep that to yourself."

"How can you find out?"

"I have some sources, maybe," McCoy said. "Money—gold—talks, and I have some gold. All I can do is play it by ear."

"How's the general taking this?"

"Like a Marine," McCoy said.

"What does that mean? This Marine wept like a baby when Hotshot Charlie went down."

"He got the message, and stuck it in his pocket, and we finished the business at hand—setting up this operation—and then he took me into his bedroom and showed me the message."

"Tell him I'm sorry, Ken. Really sorry. It's my fault."

"No, it isn't, Billy. It's nobody's fault except maybe Pick's. And if he got the train, then maybe there was ammo on it that won't be shot at the brigade."

Dunn met his eyes, but didn't say anything for a long moment.

"What happens now? You, I mean?"

"I don't suppose there's some other way except that Avenger to get back to Pusan?"

"You didn't find that fun?"

"It scared hell out of me," McCoy said.

Dunn picked up the telephone on his desk and dialed a one-digit number.

"Colonel Dunn for the captain, please," he said to whoever answered, then: "Captain, Dunn. I'd like permission to take Captain McCoy back to Pusan to set up the photo delivery procedure." He paused. "Aye, aye, sir," he said, and broke the connection with his finger.

"That was quick," he said. "What the captain said was 'Get that sonofabitch off my ship; I don't care how'."

He dialed another number.

"Colonel Dunn. Get a COD Avenger ready for immediate takeoff. I will fly."

He hung up.

He turned to McCoy.

"There's an enlisted crew chief," he said. "He rides in the aft position in the cockpit. I can't order him out of there, but I can suggest if he lets you ride upstairs, he probably won't have to clean puke out of the cargo hold."

[FOUR]
USAF Airfield K-1
Pusan, Korea
2155 4 August 1950

The runway lights went off even before Lieutenant Colonel Dunn turned the Avenger onto a taxiway. There really wasn't much chance of a North Korean attack on K-1, but on the other hand, the possibility existed, and runway lights would be as useful to an attacking aircraft as they would be to one landing.

A Jeep, painted in a checkerboard pattern, and with a FOLLOW ME sign and a large checkerboard flag mounted on its rear, came out and led the Avenger to Base Operations. Dunn parked the airplane and shut it down, and he and McCoy climbed down from the cockpit.

The crew chief, a slim, nineteen-year-old, blond crew-cutted aviation motor machinist's mate, came through the small door in the fuselage.

"Thanks for letting me ride on top," McCoy said.

"Anytime, Captain," the Navy crew chief said.

"Thank you, sir, for the ride," McCoy said.

"I'll go see the Marine liaison officer with you," Dunn said.

"I've already spoken with him, sir," McCoy said. "But thank you."

"But you're a captain, and I'm a lieutenant colonel," Dunn said. "It has been my experience that Marine captains pay more attention to lieutenant colonels than they do to other captains. Wouldn't you agree?"

"Yes, sir. I suppose that's true. Thank you, sir."

"This won't take long," Dunn said to the crew chief. "Why don't you see if anything important fell off, or is about to."

"Aye, aye, sir," the crew chief said, smiling.

As Dunn and McCoy walked to the Base Operations building, a Marine with a Thompson submachine gun stepped out of the shadows and walked up to them and saluted.

"Good evening, sirs," he said. "Captain McCoy, sir?"

McCoy returned the salute.

"I'm McCoy."

"Technical Sergeant Jennings, sir. Mr. Zimmerman sent me to meet you."

"Where is he?"

"In a warehouse on the pier, sir. With the others."

"You've got wheels?" McCoy asked.

"Yes, sir."

"I'll be with you in a minute," McCoy said.

There was someone else waiting for McCoy. When they entered the tiny room assigned to the Marine liaison officer, there was a plump army transportation corps major sitting backwards in a folding metal chair talking across a small wooden desk to the Marine liaison officer, whose folding chair was tilted back against the wall.

Both got up when McCoy and Dunn entered the room.

"Captain McCoy?" the Army major said.

"Yes, sir."

"I'm Captain Overton, sir," the Marine officer said to Dunn.

Dunn nodded at him and looked curiously at the Army major.

"My name is Dunston, McCoy," the major said, and first handed McCoy a sheet of radio teletypewriter paper, and then before McCoy could unfold it to read it, extended a small, folding leather wallet, holding it so he could read it. It was the credentials of a CIA agent.

McCoy nodded, then said, "You better show that to Colonel Dunn."

Somewhat reluctantly, the major did so, while McCoy read the sheet of paper.

```
URGENT
SECRET
4 AUGUST 1950


FROM STATION CHIEF, TOKYO
MESSAGE TOKYO 4AUG50 05
TO STATION CHIEF, PUSAN


CAPTAIN K.R. MCCOY, USMCR AND MASTER GUNNER E.
ZIMMERMAN, USMC, OF THE PERSONAL STAFF OF THE CIA
ASSISTANT DIRECTOR FOR ASIA ARE IN KOREA IN CONNECTION
WITH A CLASSIFIED MISSION.
```

```
BY AUTHORITY OF BRIG GEN FLEMING PICKERING, USMCR, CIA
ASST DIR ASIA, SHOULD EITHER OF THESE OFFICERS CONTACT
YOU FOR ANY ASSISTANCE IN CONNECTION WITH THEIR
MISSION, YOU WILL FURNISH THEM WITH WHATEVER THEY ASK
FOR FROM ASSETS UNDER YOUR CONTROL.


IF YOU ARE UNABLE TO PROVIDE WHAT THEY REQUEST, STATION
CHIEF TOKYO WILL BE ADVISED BY URGENT RADIOTELETYPE,
CLASSIFIED TOP SECRET, OF WHAT YOU ARE UNABLE TO
PROVIDE, WHY, AND WHAT YOU HAVE DONE AND ARE DOING TO
ACQUIRE THE UNAVAILABLE REQUESTED SUPPORT.


ACKNOWLEDGEMENT OF RECEIPT OF THIS MESSAGE WILL BE MADE
TO STACHIEF TOKYO BY RADIO TRANSMISSION OF THE WORD
SHOPKEEPER REPEAT SHOPKEEPER.


LOWELL C. HAYNES
STACHIEF TOKYO


SECRET
```

McCoy handed the radio teletype to Dunn, then noticed that the major didn't seem to like this.

"Colonel Dunn is cleared for this operation," McCoy said.

"I don't even know what this operation is all about," the major said.

"Major, it looks to me that if you had the need to know, that would have been spelled out in that," McCoy said, nodding at the teletype message.

The major visibly didn't like that.

Dunn handed the major the teletype message.

"Have you seen that, Captain?" McCoy asked the Marine liaison officer.

Marine captains are not required by protocol to use the term "Sir" when speaking with other Marine captains. But there was a certain tone of command in McCoy's voice that triggered a Pavlovian response in the liaison officer.

"Yes, sir," he said.

"Forget you ever saw it," McCoy ordered.

"Yes, sir," the liaison officer repeated.

"McCoy," Major Dunston said, "he wouldn't admit ever having heard your name until I showed him my credentials."

"What made you think he would know my name?" McCoy asked.

"This is what I do for a living, Captain," the major said. "Figure things out. I figured you would be using K-1, and probably be dealing with the Marine liaison officer here."

"Captain," Billy Dunn said. "Let me explain your role in this."

"Yes, sir?"

"Tomorrow, probably before eleven hundred, a COD Avenger will land here. The pilot will hand you a sealed envelope. You will treat that envelope as if it contains Top Secret material, and secure it appropriately until either Captain McCoy or Master Gunner Zimmerman, only, repeat only, either of those two officers relieves you of it. You will not, repeat not, log the envelope—or any message from McCoy going out to me on the *Badoeng Strait*—in your classified-documents log."

"Aye, aye, sir."

"If I have to say this, you will not comment on the mysterious envelopes from and to the *Badoeng Strait* to anyone. Clear?"

"Aye, aye, sir."

"The idea is the fewer people who know about this, the better. Clear?"

"Understood, sir."

"That about take care of it, Captain McCoy?" Dunn asked.

"Yes, sir."

"Then I'd better be getting back to the *Badoeng Strait,*" Dunn said.

"I'll walk you out to the plane, sir," McCoy said. "I'll be with you shortly, Major."

"Thank you, Billy," McCoy said when they were standing at the wing root of the Avenger, outside Base Operations, where he was sure no one could hear them. "That helped, and I appreciate it. I really need those pictures. I don't want to paddle up to those islands and find half the North Korean army waiting for us. But I really didn't want to have to show that captain the White House orders."

"I think he was sufficiently dazzled by that CIA fellow's badge," Dunn said. "And the message from Pickering."

"More by Colonel Dunn," McCoy said.

"Ken, what if there are more North Koreans on those islands than you think there are there? Then what?" Dunn asked.

"I guess we'll have to play that by ear. With a little luck, your pictures will let us know, one way or the other."

"Ken, we have some pretty good photo interpreters on the *Badoeng Strait*. Maybe they'd be better at looking at the photos than you are."

"Maybe, hell," McCoy said. "But they'd have to be told what we're looking at, and for."

Dunn nodded. "I understand. I noticed you didn't tell that CIA guy much. What's his role in this?"

"I don't know. I wish the general hadn't done that. I know his intentions were good. . . ."

"But?"

"I'm afraid he's clever and will be able to figure things out from what I ask him to get for me. And I'm afraid of who he will tell what's he's thinking."

"But, Christ, he's a CIA agent—an intelligence officer. He's not liable to talk too much, is he?"

"From the tone of the radio teletype, he's obviously subordinate to the Tokyo station chief, which means he would like to prove how clever he is to his boss."

Dunn considered that for a moment, then touched McCoy's shoulder.

"Take care of yourself, Ken," Dunn said. "If you hear anything . . . you'll let me know?"

"Absolutely," McCoy said.

"Get the bastard back for me," Dunn said. "I really want to burn him a new anal orifice."

"I'm sure as hell going to try," McCoy said, and then: "I'm glad you brought that up. I can turn the CIA guy onto that, and maybe away from what we're going to be doing."

Dunn squeezed McCoy's shoulder with his fingers, and then hoisted himself onto the Avenger's wing root.

McCoy waited until Dunn had started the Avenger's engine and was taxiing after the FOLLOW ME Jeep to the runway, then started back toward Base Operations, looking for the sergeant Zimmerman had sent to meet him. . . .

Technical Sergeant Jennings found him first. He pulled a Jeep behind McCoy and flashed the headlights on and off to get his attention. McCoy got in beside him.

"Where did you say Mr. Zimmerman was?" McCoy asked.

"In a warehouse on the pier, sir."

"What's he doing there?"

"I really don't know, sir," Sergeant Jennings said, his tone telling McCoy that he knew what Zimmerman was doing but was a wise enough noncom not to be the one who told the new commanding officer.

"Where are we headed, sir?"

"Stop right here and turn the headlights off," McCoy said. "Before we go to the pier, I need some answers."

"Yes, sir?"

"You're going to be part of this operation?" McCoy said.

"Whatever it is, yes, sir."

"Welcome aboard," McCoy said. "Did Mr. Zimmerman tell you what we're going to do?"

"He said you'd get into that, sir."

"Is there a Navy officer with Mr. Zimmerman? Lieutenant Taylor?"

"Yes, sir."

"What else is there?"

"There's a dozen of us, sir."

"Mr. Zimmerman was trying to recruit ex–Marine Raiders," McCoy said, but it was a question.

"I was a Raider, sir."

"And that's why you volunteered for this?"

"Yes, sir," Sergeant Jennings said, then added, "Raiders are something special, sir."

"Yes, we are, aren't we? Women find us irresistible, and movie stars ask for our autographs."

Sergeant Jennings chuckled.

"You were a Raider, sir?"

"A long time ago. At the beginning. I was just out of OCS, a really bushy-tailed second lieutenant."

"There was a Lieutenant McCoy on the Makin Island raid. . . ."

"I was at Makin," McCoy said.

"I thought . . . ," Jennings said, and stopped.

"You thought what?"

"That you might be Killer McCoy, sir."

"Pass the word, Sergeant Jennings, that your new skipper has the nasty habit of castrating, with a dull knife, people who call him that."

"Aye, aye, sir," Sergeant Jennings said. "But I have to say this. Knowing that makes me feel a lot better about volunteering for this . . . whatever it is."

"What we're going to try to do is, dressed up in Korean national police uniforms, take a couple of small islands off Inchon with as little fuss as possible. They're supposed to be lightly defended by second-class troops."

Sergeant Jennings considered that, but said nothing for several minutes.

"There's an army transportation corps major waiting for me in Base Operations," McCoy said. "He's actually a CIA agent, actually the CIA's station chief here. He's been ordered to give us what support he can. But, I decided in the last couple of minutes, I want him to know as little as possible about what we're doing. Make sure that word gets passed."

"Aye, aye, sir." Jennings said, then went on, somewhat hesitantly: "Mr. Zimmerman said you and he have been in Korea for a while, sir?"

"For a while."

"Why is the Army so fucked up, sir?"

"They didn't train," McCoy said. "It's as simple as that. And they're not all fucked up. There's one regiment—the 27th, they call themselves the 'Wolfhounds'—that's first class. And there are others. But what it looks like to me is the brass just didn't expect a war, and just weren't prepared for this."

"Nobody thought this was coming?"

As a matter of fact, Sergeant, I told them it was coming. And they tried to get me kicked out of the Marine Corps because they didn't want to hear it.

"Apparently not," McCoy said. "OK, turn the lights on and drive me to Base Operations. Maybe this guy can get us someplace more comfortable to set up shop than a warehouse on the pier."

[FIVE]

Major Dunston was waiting for McCoy in a Jeep parked beside the base operations building.

McCoy got out of Jenning's Jeep and walked up to Dunston's Jeep.

"I have to go to the pier in Pusan," he announced. "We have to talk, obviously. Talking in the Jeep OK with you?"

"Fine, get in," Dunston added. "I know where you're going on the pier."

"You've got people on the pier?" McCoy asked.

Dunston nodded, started the Jeep, and drove off. McCoy made a *follow me* gesture with his arm, and Sergeant Jennings pulled his Jeep behind Dunston's.

"First things first, I suppose," McCoy said. "Are you a major?"

"I'm a civilian with the assimilated rank of major," Dunston said. "In War Two, I was an OSS captain in Europe. 'Major' Dunston is a convenient cover."

"I'm a Marine captain who was a Marine major in the OSS during War Two," McCoy said. "In the Pacific."

"I know who you are, McCoy," Dunston said. "What do they say? 'Your rep-utation precedes you.' I'm really looking forward to working with you."

What is that, soft soap?

What reputation precedes me? The Killer McCoy business? Or that I was sent home from Tokyo and almost booted out of the Corps?

"One of Colonel Dunn's Corsair pilots was shot down yesterday morning near Taejon, while shooting up a North Korean railroad train. Colonel Dunn flew over the crash site almost immediately afterward. He believes the pilot walked away from the crash."

"And?"

"Extraordinary measures are called for to get him back," McCoy said. "Or to determine beyond any doubt that he's KIA."

"Who is he, some congressman's son?"

"General Pickering's son," McCoy said.

"Jesus Christ!" Dunston exclaimed, genuinely surprised. "And the Marine Corps let him fly combat sorties?"

"Why not?" McCoy said. "Joseph Stalin's son was not only in the front lines as an infantry officer but was captured by the Germans."

"I heard that," Dunston said. "He committed suicide in a POW camp by walking past the Dead Line. I also heard the Germans shot the two Germans on the Dead Line machine gun for gross stupidity."

"It would be gross stupidity on our part if we let the NKs know who they may have taken prisoner."

"Yeah."

"You have some reliable agents the other side of the line?"

"Some. A lot of them were caught up in the NKs shoot-anybody-who-even-might-be-dangerous occupation policy."

"Gold talks," McCoy said. "You believe that?"

"Absolutely. What are you going to try to buy?"

"What do you think of putting a price on Pickering?"

"For what?"

"So much for locating him, so much more for hiding him from the North Koreans, so much more—a lot more—for getting him back."

"Let me think about that," Dunston said.

"Sure. But we don't have much time. In the meantime, I'm setting up a small unit to go after him, if he can be found. . . ."

"That's the Marines on the pier?" Dunston asked.

"Right," McCoy said. "And I'm going to need a junk, a junk with a good engine."

"I have one," Dunston said, and added, somewhat smugly, "with a two hundred–horse Caterpillar diesel."

"No kidding?"

"It was used by smugglers," Dunston said. "The national police caught them—before the war started—and confiscated it, and I swapped them a stock of Japanese small arms for it. Luckily, it was here when the war started—normally I kept it up north, on the East Coast."

This guy seems like he's pretty competent. Which makes him all the more dangerous. If he puts together what we're really doing here, he'll sure as hell tell the station agent in Tokyo, who'll fall all over himself rushing to let Willoughby know.

"Two other things," McCoy said.

"Name them."

"I'm going to have to find someplace to keep my team. I don't want to operate out of a warehouse on the pier."

"And?"

"I need a senior national police officer, a senior one, major or lieutenant colonel, one who can be trusted."

"Kim Pak Su," Dunston said, immediately. "Major. Very bright."

"Can he be trusted?"

"He got out of Seoul by the skin of his teeth. His wife and kids didn't. They shot his wife, and he doesn't know what happened to the kids."

"The NKs might have gotten word to him that they have the kids, and will shoot them if he doesn't turn. And by shooting his wife, they've made the point they mean it."

"I considered that," Dunston said. "And fed him some almost good intel to see if it turned up on the other side. It didn't."

Jesus, he is good!

"When can I see him?"

"Tonight, if you want. Tomorrow would be better."

"I'll also need a dozen national policemen for guards."

"No problem."

"And someplace to set up shop?"

"There's a place in Tongnae you could use," Dunston said.

"Where's Tongnae?"

"About twenty miles out of town," Dunston said. "On the water. It's where the junk is tied up, as a matter of fact."

"What's there?"

"It used to be a Japanese officer's brothel," Dunston said. "When our wives were here, we didn't tell them that. We said it used to be a Japanese officer's leave hotel."

"Are the NKs watching it?"

"I don't think so. If they are, they haven't seen anything. I haven't had a hell of a lot of time free lately. I would guess, if they are watching it, they think we're just sitting on it."

"Sounds good."

"If you use it, and like Major Kim, he could increase the security."

"Who's there now?"

"Kim and maybe three other national police officers."

"I thought you said it would be better to see Kim tomorrow?"

"That was before I thought about turning the place over to you. You want to go out there tonight?"

"Let's see what's going on at the pier," McCoy said.

This guy is good. He knew about the Marines at the pier. So he probably has had this ex-officer's whorehouse in mind all along. And Major Kim is his buddy, who therefore can be counted on to tell him what we're doing.

"OK," Dunston said. "You married, McCoy?"

"Yeah."

"Your wife know what you do for a living?"

"Yes, she does."

"Don't misunderstand me, I love my wife. But she's a little flighty. Until twenty minutes before I didn't get on the plane with her when they flew the embassy people out of Suwon, she really thought I was a financial analyst in the office of the business attaché in the embassy in Seoul."

"Where's she now?"

"In Chevy Chase, Maryland, with her folks."

"Mine is in Tokyo," McCoy said. "Which is what they call a mixed blessing."

Dunston braked the Jeep abruptly, almost losing control, to avoid hitting an elderly white-bearded Korean in a white smocklike garment who came out of nowhere and ran, on stilted shoes, in front of them. Sergeant Jennings, behind them, almost ran into them.

"Goddamned poppa-sans," Dunston said. "They do that—"

"So the evil spirits chasing them," McCoy said, in Korean, "will get run over."

"I heard that, too," Dunston replied, in perfect Korean, "That your Korean is five-five."

"What the hell does five-five mean?" McCoy asked, switching to English.

"If you're a civilian spook, and speak and read and write the indigenous tongue of the country in which you are working five-five—with absolute fluency—you get another hundred a month. When I came here, I was two-one, which means barely qualified, and you don't get no bonus pay."

McCoy chuckled.

"There is no such provision in Marine regulations," he said.

I like this guy. Which makes him twice as dangerous.

[SIX]

McCoy recognized the pier as the one at which the Attack Transports *Clymer* and *Pickaway* had been tied up to debark the First Marine Brigade (Provisional), but those vessels were gone. Three civilian merchantmen—one of them with the insignia of Pacific & Far East shipping on her smokestack—were tied up where transports had been.

Long lines of Korean longshoremen were manhandling cargo from all three.

Dunston drove the Jeep away from the quai side, and down a road before a second row of warehouses. A Marine staff sergeant, armed with a Thompson, was sitting on a stool in front of one of the sliding doors. He got to his feet when he saw the Jeeps stopping, and looked curiously at McCoy and Dunston.

"My name is McCoy, Sergeant," McCoy said.

The sergeant saluted.

"Good evening, sir," he said. "I was told to expect you. But this other officer? I was told to let only you pass."

"Major Dunston's with me," McCoy said. "He's with the army transportation corps."

That announcement seemed to make the sergeant even more nervous.

"Yes, sir. Would the captain wait a minute, please?" he said.

He went to the sliding door and beat three time on it with his fist.

"Mr. Zimmerman!" he called. "Special visitors!"

There had been a crack of light at the side of the sliding door. The light went out, after a minute, and then the door slowly slid open just wide enough for Master Gunner Zimmerman's bulk.

He saluted McCoy.

"Good evening, sir," he said.

"Can we come in, Mr. Zimmerman?" McCoy asked.

"I'm not sure bringing that doggie officer in here is a good idea," Zimmerman said, quickly, softly, and in Korean. Then he raised his voice and switched to English. "May I speak to the captain privately, sir?"

"This doggie officer," Dunston said, in Korean, "not only knows what you're doing in there, Mr. Zimmerman, but hopes that by now he has convinced Captain McCoy that he's one of the good guys."

"He's OK, Ernie," McCoy said.

"If you say so," Zimmerman said, dubiously. "Open the door."

The sergeant slid the door fully open. It was pitch dark inside the warehouse. McCoy, Dunston, and Sergeant Jennings followed Zimmerman inside. Zimmerman then carefully closed the door.

"Lights!" he ordered.

Ceiling mounted lights came on.

There were a dozen Marines in the room, plus a Dodge three-quarter-ton weapons carrier, two Jeeps, and trailers for all three vehicles. Lieutenant David R. Taylor, USNR, was sitting on a tarpaulin covering a five-foot-high stack of crates.

All three vehicles bore a fresh coat of Marine green paint.

Zimmerman looked at McCoy expectantly.

"Major Dunston, may I present Lieutenant Taylor, of the Navy, and Master Gunner Zimmerman?"

Taylor and Zimmerman wordlessly shook Dunston's hand.

"May I suggest, Mr. Zimmerman," McCoy said, formally, "that you turn the lights off again, so that Sergeant Jennings can bring his Jeep in here for a little freshening up?"

"Lights!" Zimmerman ordered again. The lights went out, the door was opened, and a moment later, Jennings drove his Jeep into the warehouse. The door was then closed.

"Lights!" Zimmerman ordered. The lights came back on, and then there was the sound of an air-compressor starting. Two Marines went to the Jeep and started removing the top, seats, and spare tire. A third Marine appeared with a paint spray gun in his hand and started to expertly over-paint the hood.

"How soon can we use any of these?" McCoy asked.

"We got the weapons carrier first," Zimmerman said. "It's had a couple of hours to dry. Besides, if it looks a little dirty—"

"It would probably look a little less suspicious than a fresh paint job," Dunston said, in Korean. "You seem to be everything I've heard about you, Mr. Zimmerman. That you are very good at what you do."

McCoy chuckled.

Zimmerman looked confused.

"May I see you a moment, gentlemen?" McCoy ordered, gesturing toward a far corner of the warehouse, as he started walking to it.

Zimmerman and Taylor followed him.

"Who is that guy?" Zimmerman asked.

"The Pusan CIA station chief," McCoy said. "I sort of like him, but I don't want him to know about the Channel Islands. He thinks we're here to see if we can get Pick back."

Zimmerman nodded.

"You went to him?" Taylor asked.

"The general sent him a TWX telling him to give us anything we need. He went looking for me."

"How did he find you?" Zimmerman asked.

"He not only found me, he knew where to find you," McCoy said, chuckling. "I guess you could say he's very good at what he does."

"OK."

"How much did you tell these guys?"

"I was waiting for you to do that."

"What's with Sergeant Jennings? Why did you send him to K-1?"

"I knew him at Parris Island," Zimmerman said. "Good man."

"Can he keep his mouth shut? My brain was out of gear when I landed at K-1 and I told him what we're really going to do."

"Yeah," Zimmerman said. "He can. I'll tell him right now."

"Dunston's going to be useful. He's got a place we can use outside of town, and a junk with a two hundred–horsepower Caterpillar, and a national police major he says can be trusted."

"Well, the junk will come in handy," Taylor said.

"Maybe he trusts this Korean to report on everything we do?" Zimmerman asked.

"Probably. So the thing we do is make the we're-going-to-try-to-rescue-Pickering story credible."

Zimmerman nodded.

"So what do we do now?"

McCoy pointed across the room, where a canvas tarpaulin shrouded a five-foot-high stack of crates.

"What's in those?"

"Rations, some Japanese Arisaka rifles, ammo for them, beer, and a brand-new SCR-300 transceiver."

"Well, start loading that stuff in the weapons carrier and a trailer, and we'll go look at our new home. We can take Jennings with us, so he knows how to find this place. I want to get out of here before we all wind up in an Army stockade."

There was little sign of life in the village of Tongnae except for a Korean national policeman standing in the center of the major intersection. He had a Japanese Arisaka rifle hanging from his shoulder, and was wearing what McCoy recognized as a Japanese army cartridge belt. He was wearing rubber sandals, and he didn't move as Dunston's Jeep and then the weapons carrier drove past him.

"What's that awful stink?" Jennings asked from the backseat, where he was sitting with Taylor.

"Korea, the land of the morning calm and many awful stinks," Taylor said. "What we're smelling now is drying fish. They put their catches on racks on roofs and dry them. They don't rot, for some reason. I've wondered how they do that."

Dunston drove down deserted streets and finally stopped before a double door in a stone wall. He blew the horn, and after a moment the doors were opened by a national police sergeant who didn't look old enough to be wearing a uniform, or large enough to be able to fire the Garand he held in his hands.

He took his right hand from the Garand and saluted awkwardly as Dunston drove the Jeep past him.

Inside the wall was a rambling one-story wooden building with a wide verandah. As McCoy looked at it, a door slid open and a Korean appeared. He was slight, bare-chested, wearing only U.S. Army fatigue trousers and rubber sandals. He held a Thompson submachine gun in his hand. He saluted.

There was something about him that told McCoy he was looking at Major Kim Pak Su.

Dunston got out of the Jeep and walked to Major Kim.

"Who's here tonight besides you?" he asked, in Korean.

"No one's here but me," Kim said. "Who are these people?"

"They're working with me, or more accurately, I'm working with them," Dunston said, and switched to English. "Captain McCoy, this is Major Kim."

"How do you do?" Kim said, in British accented English.

"Very well, thank you," McCoy said, in Korean. "This is my deputy, Master Gunner Zimmerman, and Lieutenant Taylor, of the Navy."

Major Kim was visibly surprised that Taylor and Zimmerman also said the equivalent of "How do you do?" in Korean.

"Have you got somebody to help unload our gear?" Zimmerman asked, indicating the weapons carrier and its trailer.

"More important, someone reliable to guard it?"

"I have national policemen over there," Kim said, pointing to an outbuilding. Then, surprising everybody, he put his fingers in his mouth and whistled shrilly.

A moment later, a young Korean wearing only his underwear and sandals, and carrying a Garand, came trotting up to them.

"Unload the truck and trailer, put it in the garage, and put a guard on it," Major Kim said.

"Yes, sir," the Korean said.

"Why don't we go inside?" Major Kim asked. "I'm afraid there's not much I can offer you in the way of food or drink. . . ."

Zimmerman put his fingers in his mouth and whistled shrilly.

The Korean in his underwear returned.

"There are six cases of beer in the truck," Zimmerman announced. "Bring five in the hotel. The other is for you and your men. There are ten cases of rations. Take two for your and your men."

The Korean looked to Major Kim for guidance.

"You heard the officer," Kim said.

The Korean scurried off.

"Major, is there someone here who can cook?" Zimmerman asked.

"Yes, there is."

"Wash clothes?"

"Yes."

"And is there a bath, with showers?"

"Yes. This was a Japanese officer's rest hotel. . . ."

"You mean whorehouse?" Zimmerman asked.

"Yes."

"Then what I suggest we do, Captain McCoy, sir," Zimmerman said, "is go inside, have a shower, a couple of beers, something to eat, and call it a day. This has been a long day."

"Make it so, Mr. Zimmerman," Captain McCoy ordered.

XIV

[ONE]
The Dewey Suite
The Imperial Hotel
Tokyo, Japan
2200 4 August 1950

Brigadier General Fleming Pickering fully understood that drinking alone was not wise, but that's what he was doing—but slowly, he hoped—when the door chime to the Dewey Suite sounded.

Pickering was alone because General Howe had sensed he wanted to be alone, and had taken Master Sergeant Rogers out for dinner. Then, after Howe and Rogers had left, Hart had hung around, looking both morose and sympathetic, which Pickering had decided was the last thing he needed, so he had sent Hart to the movies.

He smiled at that memory as he walked to the door to answer it. It had been the only cause to smile all day.

He thought he had found a tactful way to get rid of George when he read in *Stars & Stripes* that a John Huston film, *The Asphalt Jungle,* starring Sterling Hayden and Louis Calhern, was playing at the Ernie Pyle Theater.

"George, why don't you go? Get out of here for a couple of hours?"

"Sir, I think I'll pass," George said. "*The Asphalt Jungle* sounds like a stupid movie."

"Captain Hart, when one of our own makes a movie, stupid or not, it behooves us to go see it, and whistle, cheer, and applaud loudly whenever he has a line."

"One of our own?" George had asked, baffled.

"Sterling Hayden is not only a Marine, but like yourself, a former agent of the Office of Strategic Services," Pickering had said.

"No shit?" Hart had asked, genuinely surprised.

"No shit. Go see the stupid movie. It's your duty."

"What about you, General? You were an OSS agent, too. We'll both go."

"No, I was an OSS executive, not a lowly agent, and besides I'm a general, and we get to make our own rules. Go on, George, I really would like to be alone."

"Aye, aye, sir," George had said, reluctantly.

Drink in hand, his tie pulled down, Pickering pulled the door open.

Colonel Sidney L. Huff, a tall, rather handsome officer, was standing there. The aiguillette of an aide-de-camp hung from the epaulette of his splendidly tailored tropical-worsted uniform, and on its lapels was a small shield with a circle of five stars.

Huff saluted.

"The Supreme Commander's compliments, General Pickering," Huff said. "The Supreme Commander desires that you attend him at your earliest convenience."

Pickering returned the salute a little uncomfortably. For one thing, Marines don't salute indoors, and for another, he was aware that he was standing there a little smashed with a drink in his hand.

"Come on in, Sid," he said. "I'll have to get my tunic."

"Yes, sir."

"I don't suppose you can tell me what's going on?" Pickering asked.

"Sir, the Supreme Commander sent me to present his compliments, that's all I know."

Pickering felt his chin.

"Fix yourself a drink, Sid," Pickering said. "I'll need a quick shave and a clean shirt."

"Thank you, sir, but no, thank you, General."

"I'll be right with you," Pickering said, and went into his bedroom.

The Supreme Commander's black 1941 Cadillac limousine was parked in the circular drive of the hotel. The red flag with five stars in a circle that normally flew from the left fender was now shrouded, but the small American flag on the right hung limply from its chrome pole. The chauffeur, a master sergeant in crisp khakis, stood by the rear door.

It was enough to attract a crowd of the curious—even reverent—who stood under the marquee and along the drive hoping to catch a glimpse of MacArthur.

The master sergeant saluted as Pickering and Huff entered the limousine, then walked around to the front of the car and slipped a red flag with one star—the flag to which Pickering was entitled—over the shrouded flag. Then he got behind the wheel and started down the drive.

"I think we have some disappointed people standing there, Sid," Pickering said.

"The Supreme Commander's car always attracts that kind of attention, sir," Huff said. "The Japanese people revere him."

"They really do, don't they?" Pickering agreed, thoughtfully.

Huff led Pickering into what had been the U.S. Embassy and was now The Residence—and so called—of the Supreme Commander, Allied Powers, and now Supreme Commander, UN Forces, and to the MacArthur apartment.

He knocked at a double door, but did not wait for a response before pulling it open and announcing, "Brigadier General Pickering, United States Marine Corps."

General of the Army Douglas MacArthur carefully laid a long, thin black cigar into the ashtray and then rose from a red leather armchair. He was wearing his usual washed-soft khakis.

He started toward Pickering, but before he reached him, Mrs. Jean MacArthur, in a simple black dress with a single strand of pearls, walked to Pickering, took his hand in both of hers, and said,

"Oh, Fleming, we're so sorry."

She then stood on tiptoes and kissed his cheek.

Pickering could smell her perfume.

I wonder if she can smell the scotch; I should have used Sen-Sen or something.

MacArthur came up and laid a hand on Pickering's shoulder.

"I got the word only now, just before I sent Sid to the hotel," he said. "I'm so very sorry, Fleming."

"Thank you," he said.

"You should have told us," Jean MacArthur said.

"Yes," her husband agreed.

What the hell was I supposed to do? Call up and say, "General, I thought you would like to know my son has just been shot down"?

Pickering didn't reply.

MacArthur looked in his eyes, then patted his shoulder and turned and walked to a sideboard.

"I think a little of this is in order," he said, picking up a bottle of Famous Grouse by the neck.

"Thank you, sir," Pickering said.

Jesus, what's wrong with me? The last thing I need is another drink. Not here.

MacArthur poured an inch of scotch in a glass, walked to Pickering, handed it to him, and then returned to the sideboard, where he poured white wine in a glass, walked to his wife and handed it to her, then returned to the sideboard a final time to pour scotch in a glass and then returned.

He solemnly touched his glass to Pickering's. His wife touched her glass to Pickering's.

"Major Pickering," MacArthur said, solemnly.

They all sipped at their glasses.

Not that I really give a damn, but how did he find out? He's not on a next-of-kin list—anything like that—and I can't believe he reads a report with the names of everybody who's KIA or MIA on it.

"General Cushman was at the Dai Ichi Building . . . ," MacArthur said.

My God, is he reading my mind?

". . . briefing General Almond and myself on the splendid—absolutely splendid!—job Marine aviation is doing in the Pusan area. He concluded his briefing by saying that 'sadly, our operations have not been without a price' and then told us what has happened to Major Pickering."

"General Cushman was kind enough to message me with the details," Pickering said, and took a pull at his drink.

"General Cushman also told me that Major Pickering flew the Marine's first combat sortie of this war, during which he destroyed an enemy train . . ."

"I understand that's the case, sir."

". . . and is in complete agreement with me that Major Pickering's flying skill and valor entitle him without question to the Distinguished Flying Cross. The citation at this moment is being prepared."

What am I supposed to do, say "Thank you"?

"Thank you."

"Thanks are not in order, Fleming. Your son upheld the finest traditions of the Marine Corps."

"Pick was a fine Marine officer," Pickering said.

"Indeed, he was."

"I don't know why I said that, past tense," Pickering heard himself say. "Colonel Billy Dunn flew over the site where Pick crashed his Corsair and said the cockpit was empty. It's entirely possible that he's alive. That was not the first Corsair he was shot down in."

You know better than that: "Never end a sentence with a preposition."

You're pissing in the wind, and you know it.

If he didn't get killed in the crash landing, the odds are that he was shot by the North Koreans.

MacArthur looked at him intently for a moment.

"Jean, darling," he said. "Would you give Fleming and me a moment alone?"

Jesus, what's this? Does he know something I don't? Did Cushman find Pick's body?

He imagined the exchange:

Does Pickering know that they found the body?

No, sir. I'd planned to go to the Imperial from here to tell him myself.

That will not be necessary. I will tell him. We are old friends.

"Of course," Mrs. MacArthur said, softly, touched Pickering's arm for a moment, and then walked out of the room.

"Let us speak as soldiers," MacArthur said.

Pickering waited for him to go. He was aware that his stomach ached.

"General Willoughby believes there is more than a seventy-thirty probability that Major Pickering survived the crash," MacArthur said.

"He does?"

"And, if that is the case, that there is an eighty-twenty probability that Major Pickering is now a prisoner of the enemy."

Pickering didn't reply.

"I know you're as aware as I am, Fleming, that the enemy has been executing prisoners out of hand," MacArthur went on, "but—and this is Willoughby's professional judgment, not a clutching at straws—in this case, because (a) your son is an officer; and (b) a Marine aviator, about whom the enemy knows very little, it would be in the enemy's interests to keep him alive."

"I see," Pickering said.

"As one soldier to another, Fleming, there is something that might happen to turn this situation."

"Sir?"

"As we speak, Ambassador Averell Harriman and General Matt Ridgway are somewhere between San Francisco and Hawaii, en route here."

"General Howe told me, sir," Pickering said.

"Did he tell you why?"

"In general terms, sir."

"Harriman is coming because the President didn't quite understand my going to Taipei to meet with Chiang Kai-shek," MacArthur said. "I had no intention of asking for Chinese Nationalist troops for the war in Korea, and not only because all he would have to offer is poorly trained and poorly equipped troops. What I feared at the time was that the Chinese might see our difficulties in Korea as an opportunity for them to invade Formosa. I wanted to disabuse them of the notion that the United States would permit them to do so without instant retaliation. My presence there made that point. I was prepared to send several fighter squadrons to Formosa, but intelligence developed by Willoughby has convinced me that will not be necessary. The Chinese Communists are not preparing to attack Formosa. They do not wish to go to war with us."

"I see."

"The President, as I say, apparently didn't quite understand my motives. When I meet with Harriman, I will be able to put any misunderstanding to rest once and for all."

"And General Ridgway?"

"General Ridgway is coming for two reasons, I believe. He is the prime candidate to become chief of staff. I think he wants to see for himself what's going on in Korea. There is—again, a question of not having firsthand knowledge of the situation—some concern with the manner in which General Walker is waging that war. There is also, in the Pentagon, far from the scene of action, a good deal of uneasiness about my plan to invade the west coast of Korea, at Inchon, at the earliest possible date."

"You have decided to make the Inchon invasion?"

"I hope to convince General Ridgway, and through him the Joint Chiefs of Staff and the President, that not only would such an action bring this war to a satisfactory conclusion very quickly, but also that it is the *only* way to avoid a lengthy and bloody conflict to drive the enemy from the Korean peninsula. The President committed the United States to the defense of South Korea, which means the defeat, total defeat, of North Korea's army. There is no substitute for victory, Fleming, as you are well aware."

"And you think that Ridgway is the key to JCS approval of Inchon?"

"Yes. And I don't see that as a problem. When I lay the operation on the table, he can't help but see—he has the reputation of being not only a fighter, but one of the finest brains in the Army—how it would cut the enemy's supply lines, leaving the troops now in South Korea unable to wage war, in a position where they can be annihilated."

"General, I'm way over my head here, but I understand there are problems involved in bringing an invasion fleet to Inchon."

"Ned Almond and I have considered them carefully," MacArthur said. "They can be overcome."

"Yes, sir," Pickering said.

"All of this is to bring a ray of hope—faint but real—into your painful situation," MacArthur said. "The situation as I see it is this: The North Koreans have failed to sweep us into the sea at Pusan. Walker's Eighth Army grows stronger by the day, and the enemy weaker. Willoughby believes, and I concur, that they are growing desperate. They will make every effort to continue their attack, and every day Walker will be better prepared to turn the attack. In that circumstance, the movement of prisoners of war to North Korea—if indeed they ever intended to do so—has a low priority.

"If Ned Almond can land with a two-division force at Inchon and cut the head of the dragon from its body—and I believe he can—then it is entirely possible that rapidly moving armored columns can sweep through the territory now held by the enemy and liberate our men from their prison compounds. In much the same way the First Cavalry operated—you were there, you remember—when I returned to the Philippines."

"I remember," Pickering said.

That's more pissing in the wind. But right now, pissing in the wind is all I have.

"Your glass is empty, Fleming. Another?"

"Thank you, sir, but no."

"One more, Fleming, and then you can go. It will help you to sleep."

"All right," Pickering said. "Thank you."

[TWO]

Master Sergeant Charley Rogers was sitting in one of the armchairs in the lobby of the Imperial Hotel when Pickering walked into it. He was in civilian clothing, and there was a copy of *Life* magazine in his lap. He rose quickly and intercepted Pickering.

"Hello, Charley," Pickering said. "What's up?"

"General Howe thought maybe you'd feel up to a nightcap, General," Rogers said. "But he said it was a suggestion, not an order."

Howe has heard about MacArthur's limousine hauling me off.

"Sure," Pickering said. "Why not? How was dinner?"

"We went to a place that serves Kobe beef," Rogers said. "What that means is they massage the cattle to make it tender. The steaks were beautiful, cost an arm and a leg, and tasted like bread dough."

Pickering chuckled.

"I had ham and eggs for breakfast years ago in a hotel in—here, come to think of it, Yokohama—and it looked like a magazine advertisement. Just beautiful. But it was ice cold. They'd made it the night before and put it in the refrigerator."

Rogers smiled. "The CIA guy was here. Hart wasn't here, so I took the message. The CIA guy in Pusan got your message about McCoy."

"Thank you."

"How are you doing, General?"

Pickering shrugged.

"First, I feel sorry for my wife, then for me, and finally I get around to feeling sorry for my son. I think my priorities are screwed up."

"I lost a boy in War Two," Rogers said, and left it at that.

"Thank you for coming, Fleming," General Howe said. "Bullshit aside, I wondered what the Viceroy had to say." He turned to Rogers and signaled that he was to make Pickering a drink.

"He was very gracious about my son," Pickering said, "and I wondered how he found out. And then I got—now that I think about it—a very skillful pitch that I should do what I could to convince General Ridgway that Inchon makes sense."

"I got a message he and Harriman are in—I suppose *were* in—Hawaii. It was just a fuel stop," Howe said, and then asked, "What did he say about his going to see Chiang Kai-shek?"

"That the President misunderstood his intentions. He said he never wanted Chinese Nationalist troops because they'd have to be trained and equipped, and he went there solely to impress on the Communists that we were behind Chiang and wouldn't permit an invasion of Formosa."

"You believe him?"

Pickering nodded.

Master Sergeant Rogers handed him a drink. Pickering noticed that he'd made himself one.

Rogers is far more to Howe than an errand boy. What is that line, "Command is a lonely thing"? I guess the next step is "Even generals need friends."

I'll bet that when I get to my room, George Hart will be sitting there, waiting for me, wondering, worrying, where the hell I am.

"You mind if I message the President, and tell that to Harriman when he gets here?" Howe asked.

"No, of course not. I should have thought of messaging President Truman myself."

"You heard that, Charley," Howe said. "Find Sergeant Keller and have him get that off right now."

Rogers nodded.

"If you see Captain Hart, Charley," Pickering said. "He doesn't know where I went. Tell him I'm here."

"Ask him if he wants a drink, Charley," Howe ordered.

Rogers wordlessly left the room.

"You think he can carry it off, don't you?" Howe asked.

"The Inchon invasion?"

Howe nodded.

"Yes, I do," Pickering said.

"Right now, it's the Viceroy, that gang of sycophants around him, and you, versus the collective wisdom of the Joint Chiefs of Staff," Howe said.

"I thought the Bible salesman had made a convert of you," Pickering said.

"I've been thinking about that," Howe said. "I started thinking about McCoy and Taylor. What that is, really, Fleming, is two junior officers, a squad of Marines, and maybe two squads of Korean policemen taking two small islands. The invasion can't succeed unless they succeed. On solemn reflection, that seems to be a lousy way to stage an invasion."

"What makes it worse," Pickering agreed, "is that Taylor's idea makes a hell of a lot more sense than what the Dai Ichi planners want to do, take the islands on D Minus One."

Howe looked at him intently for a moment.

"Having granted my point, you still think it will work?"

"Yeah, I do."

"Is that what they call 'faith'? As in 'faith in God' or 'faith in the Viceroy'?" Howe challenged, pleasantly.

Or maybe I think it will work because I desperately want it to work, so that one of El Supremo's armored flying columns can liberate Pick from a POW camp?

No. That's not it. I think it will work because MacArthur says it will. I thought that before tonight, even before Pick got shot down.

"I'd like to think it's a calm, professional judgment, but since I'm not really a professional, and with my son missing, I don't suppose I'm thinking very calmly—clearly—either."

Howe opened his mouth to reply, but stopped when the door opened and George Hart came in.

"That was quick, George," Pickering said.

"Something was said about a drink," Hart said, and then blurted, "When I came back from the movie, and you weren't in the suite . . ."

My God, he was really worried about me!

"You must be the only man in the hotel who didn't know that Colonel Huff carried me off to meet with MacArthur," Pickering said.

"That miserable sonofabitch!" Hart said, furiously.

"Captain," General Howe said, amused, "you are referring to the very senior aide-de-camp to the Supreme Commander of all he surveys. A little respect might be in order."

"Very little," Pickering said.

Christ, that was a dumb thing to say. You must be more than a little plastered, Fleming Pickering.

"I'm talking about that CIC clown in the hall. I asked him if he had seen you, and he said he had no idea where you were."

"So you went looking for me?" Pickering asked, softly.

"Yes, sir. I thought maybe you took a walk, or something."

"Or was having a belt or two in the hotel bar? You looked for me there?"

"Yes, sir. I was about to go to General Howe—I didn't know what the hell to do—when Charley . . . Sergeant Rogers . . . came in the suite."

"I'm all right, George. MacArthur heard about Pick and wanted to express his concern."

"Yes, sir."

"Make yourself a drink, George," Howe said.

He looked at Pickering as he spoke.

My God, he's thinking the same thing I am. George was really concerned, really worried. More than that, he saw that George's concern went far beyond that of an aide-de-camp/bodyguard for his general. It was—what?—loving concern? Well, maybe not loving concern, more like the concern of a son for his father. But isn't that, by definition, loving concern?

"No, thank you, sir," Hart said. "I'll just stick around until the boss decides to go to bed."

"The boss has just decided to do just that," Pickering said, and drained his glass. He looked at Howe. "By your leave, sir?"

"That sounded very military, Flem," Howe said. "Very professional, if you take my meaning. And just to keep things straight between us: I don't think you're capable of not thinking clearly. Goodnight, my friend."

When Pickering got out of the shower and went into his bedroom, a crack of light under the door to the sitting room made him suspect that George was still in there.

"Go to bed, Captain Hart!" he called.

"Aye, aye, sir," Hart called back. "In just a minute."

Pickering got in bed and turned out the light.

It was three full minutes before the crack of light under the door went out.

Well, if I think about it, it's not so strange that George thinks of me as a son thinks of a father. From the time the Killer recruited him from Parris Island, from the first day, he's been taking care of me. When I was sick in Washington. All through the war. After. I was his best man when he got married, because he'd lost his own father. His second son is Fleming Pickering Hart. And not to kiss my ass. On half a dozen occasions, I made it as clear as I could that I would be delighted to help—loan him money, give him money—and he always turned me down.

And he was really uncomfortable when Patricia and I set up the trust funds for his kids.

What does that mean?

It means that while I may have—probably have—lost one son, I still have another. Named George.

Jesus! Not one. Two! The Killer.

The three of them were like brothers.

Patricia was really upset when Ernie married the Killer and not Pick. I wasn't. As far as I was concerned, the Killer was family, and it didn't really matter whether Ernie married Pick or Ken McCoy.

My God! The Pickering line ends here. And the Foster line.

Now, obviously there is very little chance that there will ever be a squalling infant named either Malcolm S. Pickering, Jr., or Fleming Pickering II. Or Foster Pickering. Anything like that.

Does that matter to me?

Pick being gone matters a hell of a lot. I really would have liked to see the family continue. Patricia will never be a grandmother of a child carrying her father's name.

And that thought opens the door to another problem I never considered before: What happens to P&FE and Foster Hotels, now that Pick won't be around to inherit them, the way that Patricia and I did?

Jesus H. Christ, all the time and money we spent on lawyers to make sure that when Patricia and I were gone, Pick would get P&FE, and Foster Hotels, Inc., and not the goddamn government.

That's all down the tube.

What does it matter?

Who cares?

Something will have to be done.

I will be goddamned if the government gets P&FE and Foster. Or one of those goddamned charities of Greater San Francisco United Charities, Inc.!!!

Leave it to George and the Killer?

Suddenly dumping enormous sums of money on someone whose previous experience with money is worrying about how to make the mortgage and the car payments is a sure blueprint for disaster.

If we split it between George and the Killer, Ernie could handle the Killer's share, but George?

That will require some thought. Just as soon as this mess is over—hell, before it's over—I'm going to have to get with the goddamn lawyers. . . .

Jesus Christ, Pickering, you are drunk!

You don't even know that Pick is dead, and you're worrying about what's going to happen to his inheritance.

Oh, Pick, goddamn it!

Why you and not me? My life's about over, and yours was just starting!

He felt a sudden pain in his stomach, and he was having trouble breathing, and his throat convulsed, and his eyes watered.

Jesus Christ, I'm crying!

Dear God, please let Pick be alive!

[THREE]
Evening Star Hotel
Tongnae, South Korea
0605 5 August 1950

Captain Kenneth R. McCoy went from sleep to full wakefulness in no more than five seconds. It had nothing to do with where he was, or any subconscious perception of danger. That was just the way he woke. Sometimes it annoyed his wife, who took anywhere from three to thirty minutes to be fully awake, and was not prepared to report, for example, what the guy at the garage had said about the condition of the brakes on the car, the moment she opened her eyes.

Without moving his head, McCoy looked around the room, establishing where he was. Next he looked at his wristwatch, establishing the time, and a moment later, kicked off the sheet covering him and swung his legs out of the bed.

He had slept naked, anticipating a hot and humid night. That hadn't happened. The hotel was not only close enough to the water to get a breeze from it, but some clever Oriental—he wondered if it was a clever Japanese or a clever Korean; but whoever had built the "rest house" for the officers of the Emperor's army—had rigged some sort of power-less device that directed the breeze into the rooms.

He was in one of the better rooms—perhaps the best—in the hotel. It had its own bathroom, toilet, washbasin, and tub and shower, as opposed to most of the others, which had only toilets and washbasins, according to Major Kim Pak Su while conducting a tour of the place the night before.

McCoy tested the water, and after a moment it turned hot. He got a safety razor from his duffle bag and shaved while showering. When he returned to the bedroom, the bed had been stripped, and a freshly pressed set of utilities had been laid on it. And a freshly pressed T-shirt and drawers.

He wondered how many Marines in the 1st Brigade would wear freshly washed—much less pressed—utilities and underwear today.

And he was just a little uncomfortable with the knowledge that someone in the hotel was watching him closely enough to know when he'd gotten out of bed, and that he hadn't heard anyone enter the room while he was showering.

He put on the underwear, then strapped his Fairbairn to his lower left arm, put on the utilities, and slipped his bare feet into rubber sandals. Then he went looking for the dining room.

There were five oblong, six-place tables in the room. Major Kim, Lieutenant Taylor, and Master Gunner Zimmerman were sitting at one of them. The chair at the head of the table was empty. McCoy wondered if that was a coincidence or if it had been left empty for him, as recognition that he was in charge. The Marines recruited from the 1st Brigade were spread among the other tables.

They were, McCoy noticed, all wearing freshly laundered utilities.

Zimmerman rose as McCoy approached the table. After a moment, Major Kim got up, and finally Taylor.

"Good morning, sir," Zimmerman said.

That explained the empty chair at the head of the table. It was Zimmerman's method of making the pecking order clear to all hands.

"Good morning, gentlemen," McCoy replied, as he sat down at the head of the table. "Please take your seats."

A young Korean woman in a white ankle-length dress and white apron immediately appeared with a pitcher of coffee. She was no beauty, but she was female and young, and McCoy made a mental note to pass the word to the Marines that the help was off-limits.

Breakfast was in keeping with what were apparently the standards of life in the hotel; it was not at all like what the rest of the Marines in Korea were getting. They were eating powdered eggs with chopped Spam off stainless-steel trays and drinking black coffee from canteen cups. McCoy was served two fried eggs and two slices of Spam on a china plate. Another plate held toast. There was both orange marmalade and butter.

It was too much for McCoy to let pass without comment.

"I'm delighted the Navy has taken over the mess, Mr. Taylor," he said. "We Marines are not used to living like this."

"But you can get used to it in a hurry, right?" Taylor said. "Actually, you have Major Kim to thank."

"Then thank you, Major Kim," McCoy said, in Korean.

Kim shrugged to suggest thanks were not necessary.

"Major Dunston said whatever I could do to . . ."

"Did he get into what we're supposed to do here?"

"No, sir."

"A Marine pilot has been shot down," McCoy said. "Near Taejon. There is reason to believe he survived the crash and may still be alive. For reasons I can't get into, it is important that we get him back. Or have proof that he's dead."

"If he has been taken prisoner," Kim said, immediately. "We can probably find that out, and also, probably, where he is being held. But . . . the Communists often do not take prisoners. . . ."

"And they don't keep records of which prisoners were shot and where," McCoy finished for him.

Kim nodded.

"Right after breakfast," McCoy said, "you and I are going into Pusan. Major Dunston's been working on this overnight, and maybe you'll be able to help," McCoy said.

"Yes, sir."

I think he swallowed that.

"If we can locate him," McCoy went on. "My men here are trained to operate behind the enemy's lines. We may try to go get him."

Major Kim said nothing.

He thinks that's a stupid idea. But I think he believes me, which is important.

"The junk here, if we decide to go after this pilot, would be useful in infiltrating the team," McCoy said. "So while we are in Pusan, Lieutenant Taylor is going to see what shape it's in. If there's something wrong with it, it will have to be repaired. If it's seaworthy, we'll take it out for a dry run as soon as we can. Maybe as soon as this afternoon. Time is important."

Major Kim nodded.

"On the dry run—the practice run, the rehearsal run—we'll take half of the Marines and eight or ten of your men with us," McCoy said.

"May I ask why?"

"In the Marine Corps, we try to make a dry run as much like the real thing as we can," McCoy said.

"I will tell my lieutenant to prepare the men," Kim said.

And he swallowed that, too. So far, so good.

"I don't know how much, if any, fuel is aboard the junk," Taylor said. "Or available here."

"Give that problem to Sergeant Jennings, Mr. Zimmerman," McCoy said. "Have it solved by the time we get back from Pusan."

"Aye, aye, sir," Zimmerman said.

McCoy looked down at his plate and was surprised to see he had finished eating.

He stood up.

"Let's get this show on the road," he said.

[FOUR]
Marine Liaison Office
USAF Airfield K-1
Pusan, Korea
1105 5 August 1950

"The *Badoeng Strait*'s COD isn't here yet, McCoy," Captain Kenneth Overton said when McCoy and Zimmerman walked into his office.

"Colonel Dunn said 'by twelve hundred,' " McCoy replied.

"But you have *an* envelope," Overton said, smiling somewhat smugly, and handed McCoy a business-size envelope, with "Capt K. McCoy, USMC" written on it in pencil.

McCoy took it and opened it. There was a note, written in pencil.

> *K-1, 0800 5 Aug*
>
> *McCoy:*
>
> *I want to know what's happened to Pick Pickering.*
>
> *I know what his father really does for a living.*
>
> *The PIO at Eighth Army will know where I am.*
>
> *If I don't hear from you, I will write my story on what I do know.*
>
> *Jeanette Priestly*
> *Chicago Tribune*

"Shit," McCoy said, and handed the note to Zimmerman.

"Oh, Jesus!" Zimmerman said.

"When was she here?" McCoy asked of Captain Overton.

"She was here twice. Last night, right after you were. And again this morning. She was asking about a Major Pickering."

"What was she asking about Pickering?"

"If I'd heard anything about him."

"And had you?"

"Isn't he the guy who's been busting all the locomotives?"

"That's all you know about him?"

"I had the feeling the lady has the hots for him. She said he was aboard the *Badoeng Strait,* and she wanted a ride out to her."

"And?"

"Last night, I told her there wouldn't be a COD until first thing this morning. She was back here at oh seven hundred. A COD from the *Sicily* landed at oh seven thirty and she leaned hard on the pilot to take her out to the *Badoeng Strait.*"

"And?"

"She's a persuasive lady. Good-looking lady, too. The *Sicily* pilot caved in enough to get the Air Force to radio for permission. It was denied. Then she asked if I ever saw you around here."

"And you told her 'yeah'?" McCoy asked, icily.

"I told her you'd been here."

"And that I would be back before noon?"

"No. Just that you came by sometimes. And then she wrote that note and told me to give it to you."

"What are you going to do, Ken?" Zimmerman asked.

"I know what I'd like to do to her," McCoy replied.

"You and every other Marine in Korea," Captain Overton said.

"I'm not talking about nailing her," McCoy said.

He pointed to the telephone on Overton's desk.

"Can I get the Eighth Army PIO on that?"

"You can try," Overton said.

"Ernie, go to Eighth Army. Get her. Take her out to the Evening Star."

"What if she doesn't want to come?"

"Take her out to the Evening Star," McCoy repeated. "I don't care how you do it."

"How are you going to get back there?"

"Dunston said he would send Major Kim out there in a Jeep. I'll have Kim pick me up here. And I'll call Eighth Army—if I can get through—and get word to Miss Priestly that you're on the way."

"You want her to see the Evening Star?"

"I don't want her to write a story based on what she thinks she knows."

"And if she asks about Pick?"

"Tell her I'll tell her everything she wants to know," McCoy said.

Captain Overton touched McCoy's arm and pointed out the window. An Avenger had taxied up in front of the Base Operations building.

"There's your *Badoeng Strait* COD," Overton said.

"Get going, Ernie," McCoy said.

[FIVE]
Evening Star Hotel
Tongnae, South Korea
1215 5 August 1950

When McCoy and Major Kim drove around the hotel to the pier, there was a U.S. Army water trailer backed up to the shore end of the pier behind one of the freshly painted USMC Jeeps. A white legend on it read "Potable Water ONLY!!!" But what was coming out of the faucet and being fed into five-gallon jerry cans was obviously not water.

As soon as one of the jerry cans was full, one of the South Korean national policemen carried it onto the pier, to the side of the junk, and hoisted it high enough so that another Korean on the junk could reach it and haul it aboard. Then an obviously empty jerry can was lowered over the side to the man on the pier, who carried it back to the "water trailer" and took up his position in line.

There were four men engaged in filling the jerry cans and carrying them to the junk, and they wasted little effort. Still, the trailer held five hundred gallons, which meant the procedure would have to be repeated one hundred times. McCoy wondered how long they had been at it.

"They brought the diesel about twenty minutes ago," Lieutenant Taylor called out, as if he had been reading McCoy's mind.

McCoy looked up and saw Taylor leaning on the rail of the high stern.

"This is going to take a little time," Taylor added, and pointed to a wood-stepped rope ladder on the side of the junk forward of the stern.

McCoy got out of the Jeep and went to the ladder. He was hoping Major Kim would wait for an invitation to join him—he needed to talk to Taylor privately—but Kim followed him to the ladder.

What the hell, he's just trying to make himself useful.

McCoy climbed the ladder to the deck. There were three hatches, and all were open. He walked down the deck and looked into each. The farthest aft hold was just about empty. The center hold held a Caterpillar diesel engine and its fuel tanks, one on each side. They each looked larger than the water trailer on shore, which translated to mean the fuel capacity was over one thousand gallons, information which was useless unless one knew how much fuel the Cat diesel burned in an hour, and how far the junk would travel in that hour.

The forward hold was half full. There were a dozen wooden crates with rope handles, all marked as property of the Japanese Imperial Army. Three of them had legends saying they held ten Arisaka rifles; the others held ammunition for them.

McCoy pushed open a door in the forecastle and saw that it was combination bunking space and a "kitchen." There were crude bunks, eight in all, mounted on the bulkheads. Against the forward bulkhead was a table. In the center of the space was a square brick stove, on which sat three large, round-bottomed cooking pans.

Woks, McCoy thought. *I wonder who invented that pan? The Chinese? The Japs? The Koreans? They're all over the Orient.*

Under one of the bunks he saw a wicker basket full of charcoal.

He walked aft, and pushed open a hatch leading to space under the high stern. There were three doors off a center corridor, and crude sets of stairs leading down and up to the open area where he had seen Taylor. He started up those, aware that Major Kim was still on his heels.

Taylor, who was still leaning on the rail, looked over his shoulder as McCoy came onto the deck.

McCoy saluted him.

"Permission to come aboard, sir?" he said.

"Granted," Taylor said, returned the salute, and then asked, "Is that what they call McCoy humor?"

"No," McCoy said. "I wanted to make the point that knowing a hell of a lot less than a Marine officer should know about things that float, you're in charge, Captain."

"This your first time on a junk?" Taylor said, smiling.

"No, but this is the first time I didn't pretend that I knew all about junks and wasn't particularly impressed with what I was seeing."

Taylor chuckled and smiled.

"You want a quick familiarization lecture?"

"Please."

"OK. This one, according to her stern board, was christened—maybe Confucius-ed?—the *'Wind of Good Fortune.'* She's about ten years old, I would guess, and I suspect she was made somewhere in China. Good craftsmanship, good wood. You don't often find that in Korean junks. The Caterpillar, I'll bet, was installed in Macao. I found some papers in Portuguese, and the Macao shipbuilders have been catering to the smuggler trade since Christ was a corporal. Nice installation. It cost the former owners a fortune. I suspect she'll make maybe thirteen, fourteen knots."

"And we have enough fuel to go how far?"

"I'll guess that Cat will burn ten, twelve gallons an hour. Say twelve. Hell, say fifteen—her hull may be six inches deep in barnacles. I figure we have twelve hundred gallons in those two tanks. Twelve hundred gallons divided by fifteen is eighty hours' running time at a reasonable cruising speed—say, twelve knots. Eighty hours—provided the winds and tides are not really against us— at twelve knots is 960 miles."

"Major Kim, will you please excuse us for a minute?" McCoy said, as politely as he could. "I need a word with Lieutenant Taylor."

"Yes, of course," Kim replied, smiling. He came to attention for a brief moment, then went down the stairs.

McCoy waited until he appeared on the deck.

"In other words, we have enough fuel to reach the Tokchok-kundo islands?"

"Easily, even running at full bore," Taylor replied.

"At regular cruising speed, how long will that take us?"

"It's about four hundred miles from here. At twelve knots—I think we can do that without sweat, but I won't know until we're actually at sea—that's four hundred divided by twelve: thirty-three point forever. Call it thirty-four hours."

"And at fourteen knots?"

"Call it thirty," Taylor said. "But I'd rather not push her unless I have to."

"What I want to do as soon as we can is get to Tokchok-kundo, get ashore, have a look around, and get the SCR-300 up and operating."

Taylor nodded his understanding.

"Are you planning on staying?"

"I'm going to leave Zimmerman there, and Major Kim. If Kim's there, he can't tell Dunston what we have in mind."

"Did the Marines come through with aerial photographs?" Taylor asked.

"Lots of them," McCoy said. "But until I can compare them against maps, I don't know what I'm looking at."

"*Charts,* Captain McCoy, *charts.*"

"I beg the captain's pardon," McCoy said, smiling.

"You'll have thirty-four hours to do that," Taylor said. "We can shove off in about an hour. That soon enough?"

"We have to wait for a passenger," McCoy said.

"Am I allowed to ask who?"

McCoy reached into his pocket for Jeanette Priestly's note, and handed it to Taylor.

"Jesus!" Taylor said when he read it. "This is that female war correspondent who wrote that piece about you and Zimmerman?"

"Yeah."

"What's her connection with Pickering's son?"

"She knows him. The guy at K-1 thinks she has the hots for him. I don't know how she found out what the general does for a living."

"Do I understand this? You want to take her along?"

McCoy nodded.

"Can I ask why?"

"Because I can't think of anything else to do with her," McCoy said. "I can't let her write a story saying who Pickering's father is."

"What makes you think she'll be willing to go?"

"She'll be on board when we sail, Captain."

Taylor looked at him a long moment, but said nothing.

"Captain," Major Kim called, and both Taylor and McCoy walked to the railing and looked down at him.

"Captain, my sergeant reports the fuel tanks are full."

"Tell him thank you, please," Taylor called back, and then looked at McCoy.

McCoy turned from the railing and spoke softly, in English.

"He was talking to you. He picked up on me making it clear you're the captain."

"Good man, I think," Taylor said.

"The trouble with good men is that they tend to be pissed when they find out you've been lying to them," McCoy said.

"Your orders, Captain?" Major Kim called.

"Tell him to wait a minute," McCoy said.

"Stand by, please, Major," Taylor called, in Korean.

"We'll be taking Major Kim, and a dozen of his people, and their equipment," McCoy said. "Plus eight of the Marines and Zimmerman. And their equipment."

"Plus the lady war correspondent," Taylor interjected.

"Where do we put them all?"

"There's three cabins below," Taylor said. "One is the mess and kitchen for the officers. There's a captain's cabin, more or less—we can put the lady in there—and another cabin for you, me, Zimmerman, and Major Kim. The weather's nice. If it stays that way, we can sleep on deck. The officers up here, the men on the main deck."

"And if the weather is foul?"

"As soon as it starts to turn nasty, the men are going to have to go in the holds, with the hatch covers battened."

"That's not going to be much fun."

"It'll be more fun than capsizing," Taylor said.

"What are you going to do for a crew?" McCoy asked.

"Three of Kim's men were sailors. They can show the others what to do. There's not much to know about the rigging on a junk. The sails are square— OK, oblong—and they're stiffened with bamboo. They're like Venetian blinds, you open—raise—them by pulling on a rope. There's no wheel, just this thing . . ."

He pointed to a six-inch-square handle, lashed to the stern.

". . . the rudder. The rudder is huge; it also serves as the centerboard when you're under sail. Sometimes—to turn sharply—you need more than one man on it. Same thing when you're under way with the engine. There's one propeller, mounted forward of the rudder. All the power of the engine is directed at the rudder. If you can hold the rudder, you can make really sharp turns."

"I don't see any engine controls, or a compass," McCoy said.

Taylor walked to the forward rail and pulled backward on what McCoy had thought was a sturdy support for the railing. Inside was a control panel for the Caterpillar diesel engine, and a compass. They were chrome-plated, and completely out of place on the junk.

"Like I said, McCoy, Macao shipbuilders know what they're doing," Taylor said.

He reached down into the small compartment and threw several switches. The compass and the engine instrument dials lit up and became active. There was a red light—obviously a warning light of some kind.

McCoy was about to ask what it was when it went out. Taylor reached into the compartment again and pressed a button. There was a rumble, and then the diesel engine started.

"I'll be damned," McCoy said. "Very nice."

Taylor shut the engine off again.

"You're confident we can use this to make the landings?" he asked.

"Hell no, I'm not," Taylor replied, shaking his head. "I don't know much about the waters off Yonghung-do and Taemuui-do, but I've never seen a junk tied up at a pier either place. That makes me think the adjacent waters are too shallow, even at high tide, to take a junk's rudder. We're going to have to get boats somewhere."

"Jesus!"

"I was thinking we could get some from the Navy," Taylor said. "A couple of shore leave boats would be perfect."

"And asking for them would make the Navy very curious about what we planned to do with them. . . ."

"And we'd have to tow them from Kobe or Yokohama or someplace."

"We have to think about that," McCoy said. "Goddamn it!"

Taylor shrugged.

"I'm going ashore to see if I can find out where Zimmerman and that goddamned woman are," McCoy said. "And we better start loading everything we're taking with us. You tell Kim."

Taylor gave a thumbs-up sign, and McCoy started down the ladder to the main deck.

[SIX]
Evening Star Hotel
Tongnae, South Korea
1625 5 August 1950

Master Gunner Zimmerman drove right to the pier, followed by a Jeep with a "War Correspondent" sign mounted below the glass of its windshield. Zimmerman got out of his Jeep, and collected his Thompson and a canvas musette bag from the Jeep.

Miss Jeanette Priestly of the *Chicago Tribune*, who was dressed in U.S. Army fatigues much too large for her, and had her hair tucked up inside her fatigue cap, got out of her Jeep, then leaned over the rear seat and took a notebook and a Leica camera from a canvas bag and walked toward McCoy, who was leaning on a pier piling.

"What's going on, McCoy?" she greeted him, stopped, opened the Leica's leather case, and raised the camera to take a picture of him with the *Wind of Good Fortune* in the background.

McCoy put one hand, fingers extended, in front of his face, then extended the fingers of the other hand in an obscene gesture.

"You sonofabitch!" she said. There was a tone of admiration in her voice, then, smiling, she asked: "How long are you going to stand there with your hand in front of your face?"

"Until you put the camera away," he said.

After a moment, she closed the Leica's case and he took his hand from his face.

"Tell me about Pick Pickering," she said.

"If you take that camera out of the case again without permission, I'll take it away from you," he said.

"Jesus Christ!"

"Having said that, I think I can guarantee you some pictures for your newspaper," he said.

"Are you going to tell me about Pickering, or not?"

"Once we get under way," he said. "Get on the junk."

"The hell I will!"

"Suit yourself," he said, and started to walk down the pier.

After a moment, she went back to her Jeep, took a carbine and a musette bag from it, and trotted after him. When she caught up with him, he mockingly bowed, and gestured that she should climb the ladder ahead of him.

When she had started up the ladder, McCoy signaled for Zimmerman to get the rest of her things from her Jeep.

The Marines lining the rail of the *Wind of Good Fortune* watched the female war correspondent climbing the ladder with great interest.

When—not without effort; she had the carbine, the Leica, and her musette bag all hanging around her neck—she finally made it to the deck, she found herself facing Lieutenant David R. Taylor, USNR.

She flashed him a dazzling smile.

"I'm Jeanette Priestly of the *Chicago Tribune,*" she said.

"Welcome aboard," he said.

Jeanette smiled and waved at the Marines.

McCoy came over the rail.

"Permission to get under way, sir?" Taylor asked.

"Granted," McCoy said.

Taylor walked aft and went up the exterior ladder to the junk's stern. Jeanette followed him. She did not see Zimmerman come aboard carrying the rest of her things.

Taylor began to issue orders in Korean.

McCoy came up the ladder.

"Permission to come on the bridge, sir?" he asked.

"Granted," Taylor said.

Taylor opened the cover of the control panel and started the engine, which fascinated Miss Priestly.

Korean sailors, assisted by Marines, hauled on ropes, and three sails rose up their masts like so many venetian blinds.

Taylor unlashed the rudder, then engaged the engine. The *Wind of Good Fortune* moved almost sidewards away from the pier.

"What's going on?" Jeanette asked, in her most charming voice.

No one replied.

Taylor got the *Wind of Good Fortune* headed out to deep water, then shut down the engine.

The *Wind of Good Fortune's* sails filled with wind, and she began to act like a sailing vessel.

"Ah, come on, McCoy, tell me what's going on," Jeanette asked, entreatingly.

"In just a minute," McCoy said. "I've got to have a word with Major Kim first. Enjoy the sights."

He went down the ladder to the main deck and walked forward to Major Kim, who was standing midway between the stern and the forecastle. McCoy had given a lot of thought about how he was going to deal with Major Kim, and had finally decided that the old saw, "When in doubt, tell the truth," seemed to be not only the best, but really the only, solution.

When he reached Kim, the Korean national police officer looked at him expectantly.

"Major, we're headed for Tokchok-kundo," McCoy said.

Kim nodded, and waited for him to go on.

"There is a strong possibility that General MacArthur will make an amphibious invasion at Inchon," McCoy said. "There are two islands in the Flying Fish Channel, now occupied by the enemy, from which the ships of the invasion fleet could be brought under artillery fire—"

"Yonghung-do and Taemuui-do," Kim interrupted, nodding.

McCoy was surprised, even startled, that Kim knew of the islands.

"—and should be taken as quickly and as quietly as possible," McCoy went on, hoping that his surprise had not been evident on his face or in his voice.

It apparently had been.

"Major Dunston," Kim said, sensing an explanation was in order. "When there was talk of Operation Bluehearts—"

McCoy was again surprised. This time he blurted: "You knew about Operation Bluehearts?"

Kim nodded. "When that looked possible—not likely, but possible—Major Dunston had me look into the Flying Fish Channel. We saw the danger Yonghung-do and Taemuui-do posed."

"How do you mean, 'saw'?"

"I went there on a fishing boat, Captain McCoy," Kim said, "to both Yonghung-do and Taemuui-do, and looked around."

"I didn't know that," McCoy said.

What the hell, McCoy, you decided this was "when all else fails, tell the truth" time.

"If Major Dunston filed an intel report . . ."

"He did," Major Kim said.

"I didn't see it. I got my—more importantly, my superiors got their—Yonghung-do and Taemuui-do intelligence from Lieutenant Taylor. I'm positive that General Pickering never saw Dunston's report."

"That's curious," Kim said.

"Dunston's report was filed before General Pickering took over as CIA Assistant Director for Asia," McCoy said, thinking aloud.

"Yes," Kim agreed.

"General Pickering has ordered me to take Yonghung-do and Taemuui-do as quickly and as quietly as possible," McCoy said.

Kim nodded.

"I decided," McCoy went on, "that Major Dunston didn't have the need to know about this operation, and I didn't tell him about it. And I kept you in the dark, Major Kim, because I knew you worked for Major Dunston, and might feel duty-bound to tell him what we're up to."

Kim nodded.

"When he hears that the *Wind of Good Fortune* has sailed with you and your Marines and me and my men . . ."

"He will probably make a very good guess about what we're doing," McCoy said. "I'm sorry about that. But the fewer people who know about this operation, the lesser the chance that the North Koreans will hear about it."

Kim nodded, but said nothing.

"I had to keep the Marines in the dark, too," McCoy said.

"Sir?"

"Major, I'm a captain. I don't think you should call me 'Sir'—the other way around."

"You are in command," Kim argued. "Under that circumstance, I suggest we address one another as 'Captain' and 'Major.' "

"In front of the men," McCoy said. "Between us, I would be pleased if you call me 'Ken.' "

Kim looked into McCoy's eyes for a moment.

"My given names are Pak Su. My friends call me 'Su.' I would be pleased if, between us, you called me 'Su.' "

He put out his hand.

One of the first things I learned in Shanghai was that when an Oriental smiles and offers you his hand, you should quickly put the other hand on your wallet.

I don't think that applies here. I think this guy is an honorable man, an honorable officer, who has just come on board.

"Thank you, Su," McCoy said.

"You were saying something about the Corps of Marines?" Su said.

It took McCoy a moment to remember what he had said.

"Oh, yeah," he said. "The Marine aircraft aboard our aircraft carriers are going to provide us, once a day, with aerial photographs of the islands in the Flying Fish Channel. I didn't want to run the risk of a Marine pilot being captured and knowing that we were interested in any particular island. So I didn't tell them about Yonghung-do and Taemuui-do."

"When will you get the first photographs?"

"We already have the first photographs," McCoy said, and gestured toward the stern.

"I think it would be useful if I saw them," Su said.

"I know it would be useful if you could point out to me which of the islands are Yonghung-do and Taemuui-do," McCoy said, and waved his hand as a signal for the South Korean officer to follow him to the stern.

Jeanette Priestly was waiting for McCoy at the head of the ladder.

"Now?" she asked.

"In just a minute," McCoy said.

Visibly annoyed, she followed him as he went to his musette bag and took from it the envelope of photographs flown to Pusan on the *Sicily*'s COD Avenger.

"What's that?" she asked.

"Lieutenant Taylor was going to turn the captain's cabin over to you," McCoy said. "I've just decided we need it more than you do."

"What am I going to need a cabin for?"

"Because it will be four—maybe five—days before we get back to Pusan," McCoy said.

"What?" she asked, incredulously.

"Captain," McCoy said to Taylor, "I suggest we turn your cabin into the operations room, and give Miss Priestly one of the other cabins."

"Permission granted," Taylor said, smiling.

"If you think I'm going to spend the night on this thing . . ."

"You're a pretty good swimmer, are you?" McCoy asked, and waved his hand at the now far-off shore.

Zimmerman chuckled. Jeanette glared at him.

"Ernie, take Major Kim to the captain's cabin and have him explain these photographs to you," McCoy ordered.

"Aye, aye, sir," Zimmerman said.

McCoy turned to Jeanette.

"Okay," he said. "Now's now. Would you rather talk here, or in your cabin?"

"What you're going to do, McCoy, is tell this man to turn this thing around and let me off of it."

"No, what I'm going to do now is go down and have a look at your cabin. If you want to come there to talk, fine. If you don't, enjoy the view."

Zimmerman chuckled again, and Jeanette glared at him again.

McCoy reached into his musette bag again and came out with a bottle of Famous Grouse wrapped in a clean T-shirt.

"What's that for?" Jeanette asked.

"It's 1700," McCoy said. "The cocktail hour. Once a day on this voyage, we get one drink. I'm going to have mine now. You can have yours now, or you can stay up here and enjoy the view."

Carrying the bottle, he went down the interior ladder and walked into the smallest of the three cabins.

A minute later, Jeanette walked into it after him.

He stepped around her and closed the door. She looked at him with her eyebrows raised.

"Zimmerman—no, Sergeant Jennings—got some air mattresses from the Army," McCoy said. "This shouldn't be too uncomfortable."

She looked at him with mixed incredulity and anger.

He handed her the bottle of Famous Grouse.

"I don't want a goddamn drink, goddamn you!"

"You may need one," McCoy said. "Pick's been shot down, behind North Korean lines, near Taegu. We don't know whether he's still alive."

She looked at him for a long moment, then reached for the whiskey. She unscrewed the cap, took a pull, and handed it back to him.

"What happened?" she asked, levelly.

"He was shooting up locomotives. Best guess is he got hit by either antiaircraft or by pieces of the locomotive. Colonel Dunn flew over the site right afterward. It was on fire, but the cockpit was empty. We think he was probably in one piece when he put it down."

"And is now a prisoner?" she asked, calmly.

"The odds are . . . ," McCoy began, and stopped when she took the whiskey bottle from his hand again. He didn't say anything when she took another pull and handed the bottle back again.

"That's my drink for tomorrow, OK?" she said. "You were saying?"

"The odds are that the North Koreans would like to have a Marine aviator, a major, to interrogate."

"Especially if they knew his father was the CIA guy for Asia," she agreed.

"We don't think they know that," McCoy said. "And obviously, I could not permit you to write a story telling them."

"What are you going to do, keep me a prisoner until the end of the war?" He didn't reply.

"Goddamn you, McCoy," she went on. "All you had to do was tell me."

"I couldn't take that chance," he said.

"And what is this, some kind of rescue operation?"

"There are two islands in the Flying Fish Channel leading to Inchon from which the North Koreans could bring artillery fire to bear on the invasion fleet headed for Inchon. What we're going to try to do is take them now, very quietly, using South Korean national police, in such a way that they won't guess it's a prelude to an amphibious invasion."

She took a moment to consider that.

"That would be a good story," Jeanette said. "And, under these circumstances, it would be an exclusive, wouldn't it?"

He nodded.

"Not as good a story—not one that would get as much front-page play as 'CIA Chief's Marine Hero Son Shot Down in Korea,' of course—but a pretty good little story."

McCoy didn't reply.

"But, obviously, I couldn't write about Pick, could I?"

"Why 'obviously'?"

"You dumb sonofabitch, you don't understand, do you?"

"Understand what?"

"I'm in love with the sonofabitch!"

After a moment, McCoy asked: "When did that happen?"

"It probably happened in the hotel, the night I met him," she said. "Or maybe when he came back from that first sortie, kissed me, and I practically dragged him to bed."

"I didn't know," McCoy said. "I'm sorry."

"But I didn't *know* until just now," she said. "When you told me."

McCoy said nothing.

"Oh, Jesus, McCoy!" she said.

He reached out to touch her shoulder. He felt her shudder, and the next thing either of them knew, she was sobbing shamelessly in his arms, and he was patting her comfortingly.

XV

[ONE]
Aboard *Wind of Good Fortune*
34 Degrees 18 Minutes North Latitude, 126 Degrees 30
  Minutes East
Longitude
The Yellow Sea
0445 6 August 1950

They had not wanted to attract attention to themselves by leaving Pusan Harbor under power—McCoy guessed there were probably a hundred North Korean agents in Pusan—so they had sailed out into deep water. Once out of sight of Pusan, they'd lowered the sails, started the diesel, and "steamed"—Lieutenant Taylor's term—as fast as Taylor thought prudent, through the night.

McCoy volunteered to relieve Taylor at the tiller for however long he wanted, but Taylor said he'd catch up on his sleep when they reached Tokchok-kundo, and suggested that McCoy get as much sleep as he could.

When wakened by the first light that came through the small window—he couldn't think of it as a port, since it was wooden, thin-glassed, and even had a small curtain—McCoy went to the bridge and found both Zimmerman and Jeanette Priestly were already there.

A shoreline was just visible to starboard. He guessed the distance to be four miles. He thought he could smell bacon frying.

"Well, Captain Kidd has finally woken," Jeanette greeted him.

"I prefer to think of myself as Jean Lafitte," McCoy replied. "He was one of the *good* pirates, we won that war, and he was pardoned for his crimes, and lived happily ever after. They hung Captain Kidd."

Taylor chuckled.

"Is that bacon I smell?" McCoy asked. "And who do you have to know to get coffee?"

"Me," Zimmerman said, and pointed to the deck where an olive-drab thermos chest on which was stenciled "D Co. 24th Inf" was lashed to the railing.

McCoy went to it and opened it. It held two canteens, presumably full of coffee, and a stack of aluminum canteen cups. He helped himself, then offered the canteen cup to Taylor, who nodded and smiled.

"Breakfast will be served shortly," Zimmerman said. "Bacon-and-egg sandwiches."

"All the comforts of home," McCoy said. "What else could anyone ask for?"

"A flush toilet would be nice," Jeanette said.

"Where are we?" McCoy asked, handing Taylor the coffee.

"Well, if we are where I hope we are, we made it through the Cheju Strait, and are now in the Yellow Sea, heading north, and it's decision time."

"Let me get myself a cup of coffee before I start making decisions," McCoy said, and went back to the thermos chest. Then he went and stood by Taylor.

"I meant it, you know, when I said you were the captain," McCoy said.

Taylor didn't reply directly.

"It's getting light," he said. "I don't know if we're going to meet anybody out here—and there would be less chance we would if we went another couple of miles offshore—but if we did meet somebody, using the diesel, questions would be asked. Our speed will be cut in half if we raise the sails. Decision time."

"We have to get to Tokchok-kundo as soon as we can," McCoy thought aloud. "Operative words: 'have to get to' and 'as soon as we can.' The options conflict."

"Your decision, McCoy."

"I think 'as soon as we can' justifies a certain risk."

"In other words, keep the diesel running?"

"If we run into a navy vessel, ours, British, or South Korean," McCoy said, "they'd probably fire a shot across our bow and stop us. We could talk our way out of that."

"All these waters are closed to all but local fishermen," Taylor said. "If we get spotted by a reconnaissance airplane, all they're going to see is a junk under power. Local fisherman don't have powered junks. If I were a pilot, I'd think North Koreans."

"Why?"

"Because I would have been told if a friendly vessel was going to be in the area."

"Well, let's hope if we get spotted by one of our guys, he'll make a low and slow pass before blowing us out of the water. I don't see how we can justify moving at six knots when he can make twelve."

"What about her?" Taylor asked.

"She's a war correspondent, right? They get in the line of fire."

"I like her," Taylor said. "As a person, I mean."

"Yeah, me too," McCoy said, without thinking.

I'll be damned. I mean that.

McCoy saw that Taylor, with an effort, was making a major course change with the tiller, heading away from the coastline.

Ten minutes later, the *Wind of Good Fortune* made another course correction, and McCoy saw they were now headed north. He looked at the landmass.

"Mr. McCoy!" Taylor called, trying to sound like Charles Laughton in *Mutiny on the Bounty.*

McCoy turned and then walked to him.

"You called, Captain?"

"You have the conn, sir," Taylor said.

"You better tell me what to do with it, Captain."

"Steer the course we're on," Taylor said, pointing to the compass.

"Aye, aye, sir," McCoy replied, and put his hand on the smooth wood of the tiller.

Taylor went below and immediately returned with an air mattress and two sleeping bags, with which he quickly made himself a bed on the deck and lay down on it.

And then he went to sleep, without even waiting for their egg-sandwich breakfast.

When, a few minutes later, breakfast arrived, Jeanette took an egg sandwich from another Army thermos chest and handed it to McCoy.

"Thank you."

"When are we going to get wherever we're going?" she asked.

He did the arithmetic in his head—so many miles to go at so many knots—and concluded that the voyage would take just about twenty-four hours.

"We're going—I thought I told you—to an island called Tokchok-kundo, and the way I figure it, we should get there between four and five tomorrow morning."

She nodded.

McCoy had another thought, and repeated it aloud.

"It'll still be dark at 0400, and I don't think Taylor will want to dock this thing in the dark, so it will probably be later, maybe a couple of hours later."

"And when we get off the *Queen Mary,* then what?"

"The first thing we do is get the SCR-300 up and running," McCoy said. "Kim says there is a diesel generator on the island, but probably little—or no—fuel. We brought fuel, and also a small, gas-powered generator that'll work—if we're lucky—for a couple of hours, if we have to use it."

"What does SCR stand for?"

"Signal Corps Radio," McCoy said.

Jeanette took a notebook from her pocket and wrote that down.

"And once it's up and running, then what?"

"We radio Tokyo and let them know we're here, and see if they have anything for us."

"Like maybe word about Pick?" she asked.

"If there's word about Pick, General Pickering will pass it on," McCoy said.

"And then?"

"We're going to unload the stuff we brought with us, take an inventory of what's on Tokchok-kundo that we can use, and start planning to take Taemuui-do and Yonghung-do."

"Those are the islands in the Flying Fish Channel," Jeanette asked.

McCoy nodded.

"You know how to spell them?" she asked, taking out her notebook again.

"The more information you have, the more I'm tempted to leave you on Tokchok-kundo until this operation is over."

She met his eyes.

"And you'd do just that, wouldn't you?" she asked. "How did a nice girl like Ernestine Sage get involved with a ruthless bastard like you?"

"She was lucky, I guess," McCoy said.

"I thought I had made it plain that I now have a personal interest in this war," Jeanette said.

"I don't know how far I can trust you," McCoy said. "If at all."

"OK. Leave me on the fucking island if you think you have to. But spell the fucking islands for me now."

"When it gets light, Taylor has charts with the islands identified. I'm not sure of the spelling."

"You're going to invade islands you can't even spell?" she asked.

"We're Marines—we can do anything," McCoy said.

"The sad thing is you really believe that," she said. "And after you get the *Queen Mary* unloaded, and make your plans to invade the unspellable islands, then what?"

"Taylor and I go back to Pusan with a couple of Koreans for crew. Everybody else—probably including you—stays on the island, and starts training the Koreans for the operation. Taylor and I've got a lot to do in Pusan, and maybe in Tokyo, too."

"For instance?"

"Well . . . Jeanette, you understand I'm serious about leaving you on Tokchok-kundo? And the more you know. . . ."

"I'd stay on that fucking island forever if I thought it would help Pick," she said. "OK?"

"OK. That's settled. We're going to need boats to make the assault," McCoy said, "which means (a) we have to find boats, and (b) find some way to get them to Tokchok-kundo."

"What kind of boats? How many?" she asked.

What the hell, as long as I'm physically sitting on her, and she has no access to communications, it doesn't matter how much she knows. And talking an operation like this through is always a good idea. You almost always come up something you didn't think of.

So he told her what kind of boats, and how many of them, they were going to need. And everything else she asked him.

[TWO]
The Dewey Suite
The Imperial Hotel
Tokyo, Japan
1730 6 August 1950

When the knock at the door came, Captain George F. Hart, USMCR, was sprawled on a couch in the sitting room, reading a paperback copy of Mickey Spillane's *My Gun Is Quick*.

He went quickly to the door and pulled it open.

Major General Ralph Howe was in the corridor, dressed as Hart was, in a tieless uniform shirt and trousers.

"Professional reading, George?" Howe asked.

"I can't believe this thing," Hart said.

"Maybe that's why they call it fiction," Howe said. "Where's your boss?"

Hart pointed to the bedroom.

"I hope he's asleep," Hart said, and added: "The drinks I fed him at the cocktail hour were stiff ones."

Howe's eyebrows rose.

"Not drunk," Hart said. "I've never seen him drunk."

"I have to talk to him, George," Howe said.

"Yes, sir," Hart said, tossed *My Gun Is Quick* onto the couch, and went to Pickering's door. He knocked twice and then went in without waiting.

Pickering—also dressed in only a uniform shirt and trousers—was lying on his bed.

"Sorry to disturb you, boss," Hart said.

"No problem," Pickering said. "I've already counted the kimono-ed ladies on the wallpaper twice. What's up?"

"General Howe, sir."

Pickering swung his feet out of bed and walked into the sitting room in his stocking feet.

"Sorry to wake you, Flem," Howe said.

"I was awake," Pickering said. "Would you like a drink?"

"I'd love one, but this may not be the time," Howe said. "I had a telephone call from Harriman. They just landed at Haneda, and they're coming here to see us. They want to see us both, and separately."

"They meaning Harriman and Ridgway?" Pickering asked.

Howe nodded.

"Get us some coffee, George, while I put my shoes on," Pickering ordered.

"Aye, aye, sir."

"You all right, Flem?" Howe asked.

"Meaning am I plastered? No. I gave getting plastered some serious thought and decided it wasn't the smart thing to do."

Howe followed Pickering and leaned on the bedroom door as Pickering put his shoes on.

"The other day, McCoy's wife said she knew Harriman. Do you?"

Pickering nodded.

"That's probably why he said he wants to see you, first," Howe said.

"We're not pals," Pickering said. "I've met him, oh, a bunch of times over the years. My wife knows him better than I do. And can't stand him."

"What's he like?"

"You never met him?"

"Only briefly. Truman is impressed with him."

"Interesting man. His father died when he was eighteen, leaving him the Union Pacific Railroad. *And* the Southern Pacific. He was our ambassador to Russia during the Second War. I always thought that was Roosevelt playing Machiavelli again, sending one of the richest men in America to be ambassador to the Communists."

"I got the feeling that he was one of the first—and very few—of that bunch around Roosevelt to warn Truman that Uncle Joe 'The Friendly Bear' Stalin was a real sonofabitch," Howe said.

"Could be," Pickering said, grunting as he tied his shoelaces. "He's working for Truman. Most of the rest of that bunch, thank God, is gone."

He stood up and walked into the bathroom.

"Five o'clock shadow," he said. "I don't know if Ernie Sage thought that line up, but it's made him a hell of a lot of money."

"Ernie Sage?" Howe asked, walking across the bedroom to stand in the bathroom door.

"McCoy's father-in-law," Pickering said. "First, American Personal Pharmaceuticals—that was actually Ernie's father—made men ashamed of having beards, and then started selling them safety razors and shaving cream. You ever think about how stupid shaving is?"

Howe chuckled.

"You ever have a beard?" he asked.

"I had a beard from the time I got out of the Corps after the First War until the day I got married. Literally, the day I got married. Patricia said she wouldn't marry me with 'that fur on your face,' and I believed her. I should have held my ground."

"From what I've seen of her, she's a formidable lady," Howe said. "You said before she doesn't like Harriman?"

"Can't stand him."

"Why?"

"Patricia has always had the odd notion that men should not have carnal knowledge of ladies to whom they are not joined in holy matrimony," Pickering said, as he lathered his face.

"I wonder where they get that silly idea," Howe said.

"And the sin is compounded when the chap boffing the lady to whom he is not married is himself married."

"Of course," Howe said. "You're talking around Harriman? He looks—and acts—like the Chairman of the Vestry."

"And he probably is," Pickering said.

"But?"

"During the war, Patricia was in London a good deal—she was on the War Shipping Board. She kept an apartment in Claridge's Hotel. Claridge's was where Ambassador Harriman stayed when he flew in from Moscow to confer with Eisenhower and, incidentally, to boff Pamela Churchill."

"*Pamela* Churchill?"

"Winston's daughter-in-law," Pickering said. "His son Randolph's wife."

"I never heard this before," Howe said.

"Well, it was hardly a secret," Pickering said. "I heard about it over here, in one of Wild Bill Donovan's Top Secret monthly reports on Important World

Events, before Patricia told me. And if Wild Bill knew about Harriman and his girlfriend, then Roosevelt did. You were in Europe during the war Ralph. You ever hear about Eisenhower's 'driver,' the English girl he had commissioned into the U.S. Army as a captain?"

Howe nodded.

"My God, I am running off at the mouth, aren't I?" Pickering said. "Maybe George's drinks were stronger than I thought."

"Indelicate question," Howe said. "You ever hear anything about the Viceroy?"

"Not a word. And I would have. Of course, it's a lot easier to be faithful to your wife if she's with you. What did Oscar Wilde say, 'Celibacy is the most unusual of all the perversions'?"

"If you don't ask me about my fidelity while overseas defending God, Mother, and Apple Pie," Howe said, "I won't ask you about yours."

Pickering chuckled.

"I think what really annoyed Patricia was that Harriman apparently didn't give a damn who knew about the Churchill woman, which had to be very embarrassing for Mrs. Harriman."

"What does it say in the Good Book, Flem? 'Judge not, lest ye be judged'?"

"I've never met a woman who got that far in reading the Bible," Pickering said.

He splashed water on his face, wiped it with a towel, and then splashed on after-shave.

"Well, there we go. My shameful five o'clock shadow having been shorn, and smelling like a French whore, I am now prepared to meet with the ambassador. And Ken McCoy's father-in-law is just a little bit richer."

"When do you expect to hear from McCoy?" Howe asked.

"When he has something to tell me," Pickering said. "He's very good at what he does, Ralph. My father taught me to get out of the way of people who know what they're doing, and let them do it."

Howe nodded.

"I'd better put a tie and my tunic on," Pickering said.

"I've been thinking about that," Howe said. "I didn't particularly like Harriman's tone of voice."

"What?"

"He was giving orders," Howe said. "As if he had that right."

"Doesn't he?"

"And if he walks in here and finds us all dressed up in our general's suits," Howe said, "shoes shined, et cetera—and one of us freshly shaved and smelling like a French whore—he will have established the pecking order as he wants it.

Harriman will be the exalted ambassador dealing with a couple of unimportant lower-ranking generals who may have some information he may find useful."

"Isn't that what we are?"

"Flem, what it says on our orders—which are signed by Harry Truman—is that we are on a mission for him. I don't know about you, but I haven't had word from the President that I'm supposed to place myself at the disposal of this guy, just that he's coming."

Pickering didn't reply.

"What about you?" Howe pursued.

Pickering shook his head, "no."

"Harry Truman sent me here to do a job for him—this isn't Ralph Howe's ego in high gear—and I don't think I can do that job if Harriman thinks I am— we are—just a couple of guys whose function is to assist him in his mission. More important, that he can listen to what we have to say, and ignore it if it's not what he wants to hear."

"Yeah," Pickering said, thoughtfully.

"I think the word is 'agenda,' " Howe said. "And I don't think ours is necessarily locked in step with his."

Pickering nodded.

"You know him well enough to call him by his first name?" Howe asked.

Pickering considered that a moment.

"Why not?"

"Do you ever call the Viceroy 'Douglas'?"

"Not often," Pickering said. "Sometimes, on private occasions, when no one, not even his wife, is there, I do. I call her Jean, which greatly annoys the Palace Guard."

"When you mention the Viceroy in conversation tonight, refer to him as 'Douglas,' " Howe said. "Are we agreed on this, Flem?"

Pickering nodded again.

Howe smiled.

"And I will manage at least several times to forget my status in life and refer to our President and Commander-in-Chief as 'Harry,' " Howe said.

[THREE]

When Master Sergeant Charley Rogers, wearing khakis, and with his tie pulled down, answered the knock at the door, Major General Ralph Howe, USAR, Brigadier General Fleming Pickering, USMCR, and Captain George F. Hart, all in their shirtsleeves, all looked toward it from the table at which they were sitting, playing poker.

"Gentlemen," Colonel Sidney Huff announced, "Ambassador Harriman and General Ridgway."

"Come on in, Averell," Pickering called. "How was the flight?"

Harriman came into the room, and Pickering remembered what Howe had said about Harriman looking like the Chairman of the Vestry: He was a tall, slim, balding man with sharp features. His eyebrows were full and almost startlingly black.

He walked toward the table, and Pickering and Howe rose to their feet.

"Good to see you, Fleming," Harriman said, offering his hand. "When we can have a moment alone, I have a message and a small package from Patricia."

"You know Ralph, don't you, Averell?" Pickering asked.

"Yes, of course," Harriman said. "How are you, General?"

General Matthew B. Ridgway was now in the room, walking toward the table. He was a large and muscular man, and when Pickering met his bright and intelligent eyes, he remembered what MacArthur had said about Ridgway being "one of the finest brains in the Army."

Colonel Sidney Huff and a lieutenant colonel carrying a briefcase and wearing the aiguillette of an aide-de-camp came in and stood by the door.

"It's good to see you again, sir," Howe said, offering his hand to Ridgway.

"How are you, Ralph?" Ridgway said.

"You don't know Pickering, do you?" Howe said.

"No, I don't," Ridgway said, offering Pickering his hand. "How do you do, General?"

"How do you do, sir?" Pickering said, and then turned to Harriman: "Are you hungry, Averell? Did they feed you on the plane? A drink, perhaps?"

"I could use a little taste," Harriman said.

"General?" Pickering asked Ridgway.

"Please," Ridgway said. "I don't know what time it is according to my body clock, but it's obviously 1700 somewhere."

"Charley," Howe ordered. "Fix drinks, please."

"George, call downstairs and have them send up a large order of hors d'oeuvres," Pickering ordered. "We'll decide about dinner later." He turned to Huff. "Come on in, Sid," he said.

"Excuse me, gentlemen," Ridgway said. "This is Colonel James, my aide."

"We're trying to come up with a term to describe Charley and George," Howe said. "Charley was my first sergeant when I was commanding a company, and George—who is a captain of homicide when he's not a Marine—was with

Flem all through the second war. He was with Flem on the first plane to land in Japan after the Emperor decided to surrender."

"With your permission, sir, I will leave now, and report to the Supreme Commander that you have been safely delivered here."

Ridgway made a gesture with his hand signifying he could leave.

"You have my number, Colonel, in case you need anything at all. And the car will be here from 0800," Huff added, to Ridgway's aide.

"Yes, sir. Thank you," Colonel James said.

Huff left.

"Sid's been Douglas's chief dog-robber forever," Pickering said. "No offense, Colonel."

"None taken, sir," James said, smiling. "I'm familiar with the term."

"Gentlemen . . ." Charley Rogers said, and they looked at him. He was at a sideboard loaded with whiskey bottles.

"Scotch for me, please," Harriman said.

"I'm a bourbon drinker," Ridgway said.

"Colonel?" Rogers asked James, who looked at Ridgway for guidance.

"Jack usually drinks scotch," Ridgway said.

"Scotch it is," Rogers said.

"You were on the first plane, were you, Captain?" Ridgway asked Hart.

"Yes, sir."

"That must have been interesting," Ridgway said.

"The streets from the airport were lined with Japanese—soldiers, sailors, and civilians standing side by side. They bowed as the car drove us here," Hart said. "Very interesting."

"I presume both you and Master Sergeant Rogers have all the security clearances required?" Ridgway asked.

"Top Secret/White House," Howe answered for him. "And we have our own communications with the White House."

"You understand, I had to ask," Ridgway said. "Well, that means we can get right down to business, doesn't it?"

"Give me a moment alone with General Pickering first, please," Harriman said.

"Certainly," Ridgway said.

"We can use my bedroom," Pickering said, and pointed to that door.

Harriman opened the door and went through it, and Pickering followed him.

"I saw Patricia in the Foster Lafayette literally on my way to the airport," Harriman said. "She asked me to give you her love—and this."

He handed a small jewelry box to Pickering, who opened it.

The box had been designed for a ring. In it, stuck into the small slot designed to hold a ring, was a small silver object on a thin silver chain. There was also a sheet of jeweler's tissue.

"My God, I thought this thing was long lost," Pickering said, taking the object in his hands. "It's an Episcopal serviceman's cross. Patricia gave it to me when I went off to World War Two."

"There's two more in the tissue," Harriman said. "I am under orders to tell you they are to be delivered to your son and a Captain McCoy."

"That may prove a little difficult," Pickering said.

"Excuse me?"

"Captain McCoy is now somewhere behind enemy lines," McCoy said. "And my son—*our* son—was shot down just after noon August second."

"Good God! My dear fellow, I didn't know!"

"There is some hope, some faint hope, that he is still alive. He went down behind the enemy's lines near Taegu. Another Marine flew over the site shortly afterward, and reported the cockpit was empty."

"You think he may have been captured?"

Pickering shrugged.

"Capture is better than the alternative," Pickering said. "The enemy has shot a lot of American prisoners—at least a thousand, almost certainly more—out of hand."

"If he is a prisoner . . . will that compromise you, Pickering?"

Pickering didn't reply.

"Forgive me, I should not have asked that."

"No, Averell, you shouldn't have asked that," Pickering said. "Thank you for bringing this to me."

He held up the serviceman's cross, then draped it around his neck. He closed the jewelry box and slipped it into his pocket, and then he walked back into the sitting room.

Harriman followed him a moment later.

"It has always been my experience when faced with a difficult situation to deal with it as quickly as possible," Harriman said.

Everyone looked at him curiously.

"General Ridgway," Harriman said. "General Pickering has just told me his son is missing in action."

"Oh, God!" Ridgway said. "General, I'm so sorry."

"Thank you," Pickering said.

"The President, in my judgment, under the circumstances, will have to be informed," Harriman said.

"The President knows," Howe said.

"Indeed?" Harriman asked. "You're sure of that?"

"I called him myself and told him," Howe said.

"And his reaction?"

"He asked me how General Pickering was taking it, and I told him, and he said to use my judgment whether or not to express his deep personal regret. I decided that General Pickering didn't need any more expressions of sympathy."

"That's all?" Harriman asked.

"What Harry said to me, Mr. Ambassador," Howe said, coldly, "was use your judgment, Ralph. If telling him I'm really goddamn sorry will help, tell him. If not, don't.' That's practically verbatim. And that's all he had to say. Is that clear enough?"

"Yes, of course," Harriman said. "I meant no offense."

There was a moment's awkward silence, and then General Ridgway said, "The ambassador and I will be meeting with General MacArthur in the morning. There are some things that I think you should know, and may not, and there are some things I know you know that we don't know, and should, before that meeting. May I suggest we get on with this?"

There was a knock at the door. Hart opened it, and a waiter rolled in a cart on which an enormous display of hors d'oeuvres was arranged.

"Is this place secure?" Ridgway asked.

"Charley found some microphones," Howe said. "They may have been Japanese leftovers, or not. Anyway, both Charley and Sergeant Keller, our cryptographer, have gone over it—and keep going over it, and Charley's and my suite—and as far as we know, it's secure."

" 'Or not'?" Ridgway quoted.

"I don't think the KGB has bugged this place, General," Howe said. "And I also don't think the KGB would be the only people interested in what might be said in this room."

"You don't have a safe house, Fleming?" Harriman asked.

"There doesn't seem to be any way to say this delicately," Pickering said. "So: The station chief here thinks of himself as a member of MacArthur's staff. I think anything said in the CIA safe house would be in the Dai Ichi Building within an hour."

"And there's no other place?"

"Ernie McCoy—Ernie Sage McCoy—has a place here," Pickering said. "Ralph and I have been using that."

"That's Ernest's daughter, right? She's married to a Marine?"

Pickering nodded.

"And she's cleared for Top Secret/White House," Howe said. "I cleared her."

"And we could go there?" Harriman asked.

"George, call Ernie and tell her to expect guests," Pickering ordered. "And tell her not to worry about hors d'oeuvres. We'll be bringing our own."

"They'll know we went there, Flem," Howe said.

"Perhaps the ambassador can casually mention he went to see the daughter of an old friend when he's with MacArthur," Pickering said.

[FOUR]
No. 7 Saku-Tun
Denenchofu, Tokyo, Japan
1905 6 August 1950

"I thought it might be you, Mr. Ambassador," Ernie Sage said when they walked up to her door. "It's nice to see you again, sir."

"Forgive the intrusion, Ernestine," Harriman said. "But we needed someplace to talk, and General Pickering suggested your home."

"There's coffee in the dining room, and I understand you've brought hors d'oeuvres? . . ."

"George is getting them out of the trunk," Pickering said.

". . . and I sent the help out. And now I'll get out of your way."

"You're very gracious, Ernestine," Harriman said.

"My name is Ridgway, Mrs. McCoy," Ridgway said. "Thank you for letting us intrude."

"No intrusion at all," she said. "My husband is—what should I say, 'Out of town on business'?—and it's good to have something to do."

She led them into the dining room, then left them alone. Hart and Rogers carried in the hors d'ouevres, and looked at Pickering and Howe for directions.

"Go keep Ernie company, George," Pickering ordered.

"Take some of the hors d'oeuvres with you, Charley," Howe ordered.

When they had left, Harriman picked up a shrimp, took a bite, and then said: "That's what the President was worried about—that you two would get along too well, and that therefore it might be best to talk to you separately. He said you were two of a kind."

"We haven't had anything to disagree about," Howe said. "We see the same things—from our different perspectives—the same way. But we can make ourselves available to be interrogated separately, can't we, Flem?"

"Interrogation is not the word, General," Harriman said.

"That's what it sounded like you had in mind on the telephone," Howe said, bluntly.

"From my perspective," Ridgway said, quickly, as if to keep the exchange from getting more unpleasant, "given that both General Howe and General Pickering enjoy the confidence of the President, we could save a lot of time by just sitting down at the table and talking this out together."

"That's fine with me," Harriman said, sat down, and reached across the table for another shrimp.

The others sat down.

"This place is secure?" Ridgway asked.

"More so than the Imperial," Howe said.

"I defer to you, Mr. Ambassador," Ridgway said.

Harriman nodded, and touched his lips with a napkin.

"Marvelous shrimp," he said, and then went on, seriously: "The President is concerned—as something of an understatement—about several recent actions of General MacArthur. Let's deal with his trip to Formosa first. Two questions in that regard. One, does General MacArthur understand that the President does not wish to have the Nationalist Chinese involved in Korea? Two, what was he doing in Formosa? General Howe?"

"I'll defer to General Pickering," Howe said. "MacArthur has not discussed that with me."

"And he has with you, Fleming?"

"I was at the Residence," Pickering replied. "General and Mrs. MacArthur had heard about my son, and wished to express their concern. The subject came up. He understands how the President feels about using Nationalist troops, and didn't want them in the first place because they would have to be trained and equipped. He went to Taipei, he told me, as a symbol that the United States would not stand idly by if the Communists used the mess in Korea as an invitation to invade the island."

"And you believe him?"

"Yes, I do," Pickering said.

"And you think, when I broach the subject to him, that's what he will say?"

"I'm sure he will."

"When the President heard that General MacArthur had gone to see Chiang Kai-shek," Harriman said, "he was furious. Several members of his cabinet, and others, made it clear that, in their opinions, it was sufficient justification to relieve General MacArthur."

Neither Pickering nor Howe responded.

"The question of relieving General MacArthur came up again with regard to his message to the Veterans of Foreign Wars, the VFW," Harriman said. "You're familiar with that?"

Pickering shook his head, no, and looked at Howe, who shrugged his shoulders, indicating he had no idea what Harriman was talking about.

"Neither of you is familiar with the message?" Harriman asked.

"No," Pickering said. "What was in the message?"

"A disinterested observer would think that General MacArthur was not in agreement with the foreign policy of the United States," Harriman said, sarcastically. "A cynic might interpret it to be the first plank in the platform of presidential candidate Douglas MacArthur."

"There was nothing about a VFW message in the *Stars & Stripes,*" Howe said.

"The message was 'withdrawn' at the President's order," Harriman said.

"Then what's the reason for the pressure on the President to relieve him?" Howe asked.

"There are those, I surmise," Harriman said, "who do not share General MacArthur's opinion of himself."

"You know what Frank Lloyd Wright said, Averell," Pickering said. "Something about it being rather difficult to be humble if you're a genius."

"But Wright *is* a genius," Harriman said.

"So is MacArthur," Pickering said. "He's flawed, certainly. We all are. But he's a military genius, and that should not be forgotten."

"There are those who blame him for this mess we find ourselves in, in Korea," Harriman said.

"How about Acheson's speech?" Pickering said. "I took the trouble to read it. He made it pretty clear—maybe by accident—that Korea was not in our zone of interest. It was almost an invitation for North Korea to move south."

"MacArthur has been in command of any army here that is—as has been demonstrated—incapable of fighting a war," Harriman argued.

"I've talked to a lot of officers here since I got here," Pickering said. "They place the blame on Louis Johnson. Johnson's 'defensive economies' went far beyond eliminating fat—they cut to the bone and scraped it. The First Marine Division was at half—*half*, Averell, *half*—wartime strength. And there's been almost no money for the Army. When there's no money, there's no training, and without training, armies cannot prepare to fight."

"By inference—Louis Johnson serves as Secretary of Defense at the President's pleasure—you're saying the officers you spoke with, and perhaps you yourself, place the blame for this mess on the President."

"The last time I was in the Oval Office," Howe said, "there was a sign on Harry's desk that said 'The Buck Stops Here.' "

" 'Harry's desk', General?" Harriman asked. "General, you're referring to the President of the United States."

Howe looked uncomfortable.

Pickering laughed. Everybody looked at him in surprise.

"I just figured out what you're doing, Harriman," he said. "I'm an amateur playing your game. It took me a little while."

"I have no idea what you're talking about, General," Harriman said, smoothly.

"You're collecting damaging quotes from me—and from Ralph—that you can use as aces in the hole with Harry Truman if we don't go along with what you have already decided he should hear."

"Now see here, Pickering. . . ."

"Let me save some time for you," Pickering said. "I think Douglas MacArthur is a military genius; I've seen him at work. He's a soldier who fully understands how to obey an order, especially one that comes from the Commander-in-Chief. He thinks an invasion at Inchon is the best—and probably the only—way to avoid a very bloody and lengthy battle back up the Korean peninsula. I agree with him. If there are those who don't agree with him, in my opinion, they're wrong.

"What the President is going to have to do is decide who is best qualified to run this war: MacArthur, or someone half a world away in the Pentagon. That's obviously his right. But until he decides the brass in the Pentagon is right and MacArthur is wrong, what he should do is get out of the way—and keep his people out of the way—of MacArthur, and let him fight this war. Relieving him, or sending Pentagon brass here to look over his shoulder, nitpicking his plans, would be almost criminally stupid."

Harriman's face tightened.

"Do you include General Ridgway in your definition of Pentagon brass, Pickering?" Harriman asked.

"I wish, Mr. Ambassador," Howe said, icily, "to associate myself completely with General Pickering's comments. I shall so inform the President of the United States."

Harriman looked at him with cold disdain.

"Nothing personal, certainly, General Ridgway," Pickering said. "But the number-two man in the Army is by my definition 'Pentagon brass.' "

"I never considered 'Pentagon brass' to be a pejorative term," Ridgway said, smiling. "Becoming Pentagon brass is every second lieutenant's ambition. And I agree that General MacArthur is a military genius."

That earned Ridgway a look of disdain from Harriman.

"Thank you," Pickering said.

"On the other hand," Ridgway said, "there are certain members of the Pentagon brass—General Collins and myself among them—who are yet to be convinced than an amphibious landing at Inchon is either the best tactical move to make, or, indeed, that it's even possible. That's not saying we're against it. Just that right now we don't have sufficient information to take a pro or con position. I intend to ask General MacArthur to tell me in detail what he plans to do. I don't know if that could be deemed 'nit-picking.' "

"He's prepared to tell you anything you want to know," Pickering said. "And he'll probably do it from memory."

"My mission here is to gather information for General Collins," Ridgway said. "And to solicit opinions, specifically from General Howe and yourself, about General MacArthur and the situation here, not limited to the invasion at Inchon."

"I just thought of something, General Ridgway," Howe said. "If Truman fires MacArthur, you'd be the likely choice to take his place, wouldn't you?"

"I hope it doesn't come to that," Ridgway said. "Are you asking if that doesn't pose a conflict of interest for me?"

"That thought ran through my mind, frankly," Howe said.

"I'd like to think that I'm a soldier, obeying his orders," Ridgway said. "You'll have to take my word I didn't come here looking for MacArthur's job."

"Your word is good enough for me," Howe said.

"Thank you," Ridgway said.

"What other opinions of ours are you after?" Howe asked.

"There are those who wonder if General Walker is up to the challenge."

"Relieving General Walker would have enormous political implications," Harriman blurted.

Howe and Pickering looked at him.

Well, that's the first Harriman's heard of that, Howe thought.

I thought diplomats were supposed to have poker faces, Pickering thought.

"Like most Americans, Averell," Pickering said, "I like to think our senior officers consider political implications as little as possible when making military decisions."

"Frankly, Pickering, that's a little naive."

Pickering shrugged, contemptuously.

"If you're asking whether I think he's 'up to the challenge,' " Howe said, "I wouldn't presume to make a judgment like that."

"Neither would I," Pickering said.

"The question in General Collins's mind—and mind—given that General MacArthur has never been reluctant in the past to relieve underperforming officers is why he hasn't relieved General Walker. Is it because he's satisfied with his performance? Or because he feels the same loyalty to him he shows to those who were with him in the Philippines? Or because he doesn't want to be accused of looking for a scapegoat? Or because if he relieves him, he's likely to get a replacement not of his choosing?"

"Walker is not a member of the Bataan Gang," Pickering said. "I don't think MacArthur even likes him. MacArthur's not going to criticize a senior officer like Walker to a lowly part-time brigadier, but, having said that, I think I would have picked up on unspoken criticism, and there's never been even a suggestion of that."

"MacArthur's been trying very hard to get General Almond promoted."

"I'm not surprised. It would be well-deserved," Pickering said.

"I agree. Almond strikes me as a very competent officer," Howe said. "I've wondered why he's only a two-star."

"General Collins does not share those opinions of General Almond," Ridgway said. "I don't know why. How does Almond get along with Walker?"

"They don't like each other," Pickering said. "But I don't know why."

"General Collins is particularly upset by General MacArthur's plans to have Almond command X Corps. . . ."

"Why?" Howe said. "Isn't picking his subordinate commanders MacArthur's prerogative?" Howe asked.

"And by MacArthur's frankly odd decision to have him command it as an additional duty," Ridgway went on without replying. "Without relieving him of his post as chief of staff, which is what normally would happen."

"He hasn't discussed that with me, either," Pickering said. "But that could damned well be because he doesn't want Almond replaced by someone he didn't choose."

"And X Corps will be established as a separate corps, not as part of Eighth Army," Ridgway said. "Not under General Walker's command. That also raises questions in General Collins's mind—and mine."

"There could be a number of reasons for that," Pickering said. "The first that comes to me is that Almond has been in on the Inchon invasion from the beginning, and Walker hasn't. Neither Walker nor Almond has amphibious invasion experience. I get the feeling that MacArthur, who has enormous experience, plans to command the invasion itself, and that would be awkward if X Corps were under Eighth Army."

Ridgway nodded.

"If the Inchon invasion goes forward," Harriman said, "and fails—"

"I don't think it will fail," Pickering said.

"But if it does, it would be a monumental disaster, wouldn't you agree?"

"For which Douglas MacArthur would take full responsibility," Pickering said. "I think he would resign if it did. And that's another reason I think he wants to command it himself, so it will not fail."

"General, you've been asking all the questions," Howe said. "I'd like to ask one. What's the problem between Collins and MacArthur?"

Ridgway hesitated a moment before deciding to answer the question.

"Quick answer: I don't think General Collins thinks General MacArthur pays him, or the office he holds, the respect he and it deserve."

"Blunt response," Pickering said. "MacArthur respects the office of chief of staff—and understands its problems—because he served as chief of staff. He has five stars—he had them when General Collins had two. During World War Two, when Collins was a corps commander, MacArthur was a theater commander. He had more men under his command then—and I don't think anyone faults his command of them—than are now in the entire U.S. Army. Under those circumstances, I think it's understandable that MacArthur is not as awed by the chief of staff as the chief of staff might prefer."

"But he's subordinate to the chief of staff," Harriman said.

"And he has been taking, and will take, his orders from the chief of staff," Pickering said. "That does not mean he has to be very impressed with the officeholder personally. So far as MacArthur is concerned, the officeholder is just one more general, junior to him in rank and experience."

"Is that how he will think of me?" Ridgway said.

"This may be violating a confidence, General: I hope not," Pickering said. "MacArthur referred to you admiringly as about the best brain in the Army, or words to that effect."

"I've never met him," Ridgway said.

"Then it will be an interesting experience for you," Howe said. "You're tempted to back out of his presence with your head bowed."

Pickering laughed.

"I have one more question for you, General Pickering," Ridgway said.

"Shoot," Pickering said.

"There has been some talk that Admiral Hillenkoetter will resign . . ."

"Voluntarily?" Howe asked.

Ridgway didn't reply.

". . . and that you will be offered the position."

"I'm wholly unqualified to be Director of the CIA," Pickering said. "If I was offered the job, I wouldn't take it."

"That will disappoint the President," Howe said. "The last time I talked to him, he asked if I had come to know you well enough to have an opinion about you taking over the CIA. I told him I thought you'd do just fine."

"Then, obviously, you don't know me well enough," Pickering said.

"Gentlemen," Harriman said. "Doesn't this about conclude our business?"

I think the sonofabitch has decided that since he can't control the meeting— meaning me, Howe, and Ridgway—there's no point to it.

They looked at each other, and Howe, Pickering, and Ridgway each shrugged or made other gestures indicating that he had nothing else to say or ask.

Harriman stood up.

"I'm going to stick around a little longer," Pickering said. "I want to spend a little time with Ernie McCoy."

"Me, too," Howe said.

"Shall we send the car back for you?" Ridgway asked.

"Please," Pickering said.

"Would you please tell Ernestine we very much appreciate her hospitality?" Harriman asked.

Pickering nodded.

"I'll walk you to the door," he said.

"Fleming," Harriman said. "I regret the . . . tone . . . this sometimes reached."

"Me, too," Pickering said.

"You're not going with us to meet General MacArthur tomorrow?" Ridgway asked.

"Pickering and I have heard the Viceroy's opinions," Howe said.

" 'The Viceroy's'?" Harriman asked.

"There you go again, Averell," Pickering said. "Collecting quotes."

Howe chuckled.

Pickering gestured for Harriman and Ridgway to go ahead of him through the dining room door.

Surprising him, Howe followed them all out to the street, and watched as Ridgway and Harriman got in the staff car and drove off.

Pickering started to go back through the passage in the wall. Howe stopped him by touching his arm.

"That was interesting, wasn't it?" Howe said. "You made it pretty plain what you think of Harriman. What did you think of Ridgway?"

"Good man," Pickering replied instantly.

"Could he take over for the Viceroy?" Howe asked. "The President's going to want to know what we think about that."

"No man is indispensable," Pickering said, thoughtfully. "I learned that when my father—whom I regarded much as I regard MacArthur—suddenly checked out and left me in change of P & FE. But I repeat what I said before: Relieving MacArthur would be criminally stupid."

"Harriman was right about one thing, Flem. You are naive. At this level, political considerations do matter to military brass."

"I had the feeling in there, again, Ralph, that I was out of my league," Pickering said.

"I was a buck general, a division artillery commander, when the division commander had a heart attack. My corps commander named me commander over two other guys, regular army guys, who I thought were far better qualified than me—not modesty, Flem. I had spent my life learning how to run a company that makes machines for the shoe industry, with a little time out to be a captain in War One, and to be a weekend warrior between wars—I *knew* I was out of my league as a division commander. I took that division from the Rhine to the Elbe, and they gave me a second star and a medal. When, two days after Roosevelt died, Harry Truman told me he knew he was out of his league being President, I knew just how he felt."

Pickering looked at him, but didn't reply.

"The President sent the both of us over here to do a job for him," Howe went on. "I'm not sure how I did in that meeting, but you damned sure did what the President hoped you would."

"Thank you," Pickering said.

"Now let's go inside and have a drink," Howe said. "Or two drinks."

[FIVE]
USS *Badoeng Strait*
35 Degrees 42 Minutes North Latitude, 130 Degrees 48
Minutes East
Longitude
The Sea of Japan
1105 7 August 1950

There were large sweat stains on the flight suit of Lieutenant Colonel William C. Dunn, USMC, under his arms, down his back, and on his seat. When he opened the door to the photo lab, he almost instantly felt a chill as the air-conditioned air blew on him.

He had been flying all morning, and he had flown all day the day before. The fatigue was evident on his face.

Reinforcements had begun to flood into Pusan, enough for General Walker's Eighth Army to begin more serious counterattacks than had been possible a short time before. That was the official line. In Dunn's judgment, counterattacks with only a slight chance of success were a better alternative than allowing the North Koreans to push Eighth Army into the sea.

The proof of that seemed to be that the First Marine Brigade (Provisional) was being used as Eighth Army's fire brigade, putting out the fires either when American counterattacks failed, or the North Koreans broke through American lines anywhere along the still-shrinking perimeter.

The day before, for example, Walker had ordered counterattacks by the Army's 19th Infantry Regiment on North Korean positions on terrain south of a village called Soesil. Because of its shape, the area was known as "Cloverleaf Hill." The attack was to begin at first light.

The attack didn't begin on time, and when it finally began, just before noon, the 19th learned that during the previous night, the North Koreans had moved a battalion of troops across the Naktong River, and that this reinforcement of their positions—plus, Dunn believed, the delay in making the attack, which had given the enemy time to prepare their positions—was enough to defeat the counterattack.

To the south, an attack by the Army's 35th Infantry was at least partially successful. It started when planned, but three miles from the departure line, ran into a tank-supported North Korean position that took five hours to overwhelm.

Lieutenant Colonel Dunn, who had flown three strikes against the tanks, privately thought, *Better late than never.*

Even farther south, a counterattack by the Army's 24th Infantry against enemy positions in the Sobuk mountains simply failed.

And farther south than that, an attack by the Army's 5th Regimental Combat Team and a large portion of the 1st Marine Brigade had turned out to be, in Colonel Dunn's opinion, even more of a Chinese fire drill.

The 5th RCT, which was supposed to move west on the Chinju road, came to a road junction and took the wrong fork, down which the Marines had already passed. By noon, they were in positions on hills three miles south of the road fork, instead of on the hill where they were supposed to be, northwest of the fork.

The North Koreans promptly moved onto the unoccupied hill, and in the confusion, Fox Company of the 5th RCT found itself surrounded by the enemy on yet another hilltop, which was now dubbed "Fox Hill."

While this was going on, the enemy, with other troops, also managed to block the MSR (main supply route) from Masan.

All of this forced Eighth Army to order the Marines to halt, turn around—which meant abandoning the terrain they'd just taken—and go to work trying to put these fires out.

The 2nd Battalion of the brigade tried, and failed, to get through to the surrounded men of Fox Company of the 5th, and the 3rd Battalion of the brigade, together with some troops from the 2nd Battalion of the Army's 24th Infantry, tried—and failed—to destroy the enemy's roadblock of the MSR.

At dawn this morning—with Marine Corsairs lending support—the 2nd Battalion of the brigade had broken through to—*a more honest phrase, Dunn thought, would be "saved the ass of"*—Fox Company, but another try at breaking the roadblock of the MSR by the 3rd Battalion—with Marine Corsairs lending support—had failed again.

But the 3rd Battalion would try again to open the roadblock just as soon as Dunn's Corsairs had been refueled and rearmed and were back overhead.

On the flight deck, after landing just now, Dunn had told Captain Dave Freewall—now commanding USMC Reserve Fighter Squadron 243, following the loss of its commander—to ask the steward to make him some fried-egg sandwiches and put them in a bag. He was going to have to see the air commander, Dunn said, and go by the photo lab, and it was either fried-egg sandwiches in the cockpit, or no lunch.

Reporting to the air commander hadn't taken as much time as he thought it would, and unless there was a problem in the photo lab, he would be out of there in two minutes, so he probably could have had a sit-down lunch, even if a quick one.

The photo lab had what could have been a personnel problem. There was a Navy chief photographer's mate in nominal charge, but under orders to make his facilities available to the Marines, which in fact meant to Master Sergeant P. P. McGrory, USMCR, who was not known for his charm.

Surprising Dunn, the two had apparently gotten along from the moment they'd met. Dunn, however, always waited to see if the other shoe had fallen every time he went into the photo lab.

He raised his hand in a gesture indicating they didn't have to come to attention.

"And how are things in your air-conditioned little heaven?" he asked.

"Morning, Colonel," they said, in unison.

"The pictures from up north?"

"They went to Pusan on the COD at 1020, sir," Sergeant McCrory said.

"Good, thank you very much. And now I will see if I can get something to eat before I go back to work."

"Chief Young's got something I thought you ought to have a look at, Colonel," McGrory said.

I should have known lunch would be egg sandwiches.

"What's that?"

McGrory went to a cabinet and came back with a stack of eight-by-ten-inch prints.

"There was a photo mission this morning—Air Commander's request—for pictures of a railroad bridge near Tageu," McGrory said. "Near where that goddamn fool Pickering went down."

Dunn knew no disrespect was intended. In civilian life, McGrory was a member of the ASC and a bachelor. The American Society of Cinematographers are those people engaged in the filming of motion pictures who have proved worthy of membership by their experience and skill. McGrory's skill was in making beautiful women seem even more so on the silver screen. He was well paid for the practice of his profession, and maintained a beachfront home in Malibu, in which there often could be found an array of astonishingly beautiful women. And Captain Malcolm S. Pickering of Trans-Global Airways, who shared McGrory's interest in really good-looking women.

McGrory handed Dunn the aerial photographs.

"Young saw this when he was processing the film, and made extra copies," McGrory said.

"What am I looking at, Mac?" he asked.

McGrory pointed.

Dunn looked again, and shook his head.

"In the rice field, Colonel," Chief Young said. "It looks like it was drained. They bombed the hell out of that bridge, and it looks like they broke the dam, or whatever keeps the water in."

Dunn looked again.

"Have we got a magnifying glass, or whatever?"

Chief Young picked the picture up, took it to a desk, laid it down, and set up over it a device on thin metal legs.

"That's stereo," he said. "But it helps even when it's an ordinary picture."

Dunn bent over it. With some difficulty, he managed to get the picture in focus.

"I'll be damned," he said.

"Yeah," McGrory said. "That's no accident. Somebody stamped that out in the mud with his feet."

Dunn bent over the viewing device again.

And then he put his hand out to steady himself. The *Badoeng Strait* was turning sharply. She was turning into the wind.

"All hands, prepare to commence launching operations," the loudspeaker blared. "Pilots, man your aircraft. All hands, prepare to commence launching operations. Pilots, man your aircraft."

"Has anyone seen this?" Dunn asked.

"No, sir."

"Let's sit on it until I get back," Dunn said, and then asked a sudden question. "Which way is south on this?"

McGrory pointed.

"He's going the wrong way," Dunn said.

"It looks that way," McGrory agreed.

"You haven't told anybody about this?"

"No, sir. I figure if the word got out, everybody in VMF-243 would be out there looking for him."

"Keep it that way, please, Mac. Until I get back."

McGrory nodded, then appeared to be waiting for additional orders.

And if you don't come back, Colonel?

"I should be back about 1500. If I'm delayed, give this to Captain Freewall."

"Aye, aye, sir," McGrory said. "I'll see you about 1500, then, sir."

"Right."

"How's things over there?"

"Would you believe a doggie regiment took the wrong fork on a road and wound up holding the wrong hill?"

"Jesus H. Christ!"

Dunn left the photo lab and rapidly climbed what seemed like endless steep ladders, ultimately reaching the level of the flight deck. He went, already starting to sweat a little, onto the flight deck itself, and saw that his Corsair, the engine running, was first in line to take off.

He stood at the wing root as his airplane captain told him about the airplane, and simultaneously helped him properly fasten the personal gear—the Mae West inflatable life preserver, the survival gear pack, and a .45 ACP pistol—he had unfastened when he landed.

He climbed up onto the wing, then into the cockpit. The airplane commander strapped him into his parachute, gave him a thumbs-up, handed him a small brown paper bag, and then got off the airplane.

Then Dunn waited to take off.

But he wasn't thinking about flying the aircraft.

It has to be Pick, he thought. *Who the hell else would stamp out "PP" and an arrow in the mud of a ruptured Korean rice field?*

And who else but that dumb sonofabitch would be headed away from our lines?

Not quite forty-five seconds later, he was airborne.

XVI

[ONE]
Aboard *Wind of Good Fortune*
37 Degrees 44 Minutes North Latitude, 126 Degrees 59
 Minutes East Longitude
The Yellow Sea
1155 7 August 1950

"That looks like a lighthouse," Captain Kenneth R. McCoy, USMCR, said to Lieutenant David R. Taylor, USNR.

"God, you're a clever chap, Mr. McCoy," Taylor replied, in his best Charles Laughton *Mutiny on the Bounty* accent. "That, indeed is a lighthouse, marking the entrance to the Flying Fish Channel."

Jeanette Priestly laughed.

"That makes it three for Captain Bligh and two for Jean Lafitte," she said.

"A question, Captain, sir," McCoy said. "May I dare to hope that we will soon be at our destination?"

"I would estimate, Mr. McCoy, that we should be there within the hour, perhaps a little less."

The preceding twenty-four hours had passed slowly and uneventfully. The landmass of South Korea had always been in sight to starboard, but Taylor's course was far enough out to see so the *Wind of Good Fortune* would be practically invisible to anyone on the shore.

The flip side was that the people on the *Wind of Good Fortune* couldn't see anything on the shore. It was quiet and peaceful, and Jeanette Priestly had observed that it was hard to believe a war was going on.

They had seen a dozen small ships—probably fishing boats—but they had been far away, just visible on the horizon, and none had come close. They had seen no larger vessels, and if the naval forces of the United Nations Command were patrolling the Yellow Sea, there had been no sight of them, except possibly for four aircraft—flying, McCoy had guessed, at about 10,000 feet, too high to identify their types—none of which seemed to have noticed the *Wind of Good Fortune.*

During the day, Taylor had wakened every hour to take a quick look around. Once satisfied with what he had seen, he'd gone back to sleep. McCoy had been so intrigued with Taylor's ability to so easily and regularly stir himself that he asked him how he did it. Taylor had somewhat smugly held up his wristwatch and said, "Ding-a-ling." His wristwatch was also a miniature alarm clock.

Using food from the cases of 10-in-1 rations Sergeant Jennings had stolen from the Army warehouses on the pier in Pusan, and chickens, fish, eggs, pork loins, and vegetables Major Kim's national policemen had bought in Tongnae, two of the Marines and two national policemen had prepared a surprisingly tasty lunch, an even better dinner, and an evening snack on the charcoal-fired brick stove in the forecastle. It had to be eaten from mess kits, of course, and after Zimmerman reminded the Marines how the vegetables had been fertilized, they lost their appeal, but aside from that, there was nothing whatever to complain about.

Jeanette had spent most of her time with the Marines, shooting several rolls of film in the process. The Marines thought she was a willing passenger, along to chronicle their mission for her newspaper, and they were flattered by the attention of the press.

Once darkness had fallen, there hadn't been much to do except post lookouts fore and aft and sleep, and by 1900 there were sleeping Marines and national policemen stretched out wherever they could find room on the deck.

Taylor took over the helm at nightfall, and shortly after 2000, McCoy had gone below to sleep.

When McCoy woke, his watch told him it was 0600 and the rolling of the *Wind of Good Fortune* told him they were still at sea. He went on deck, expecting to find they were approaching whatever kind of a port Tokchok-kundo had to offer.

He found instead that the South Korean landmass was now to port, and that the *Wind of Good Fortune's* sails had been raised.

"I thought Tokchok-kundo was that way?" McCoy said, pointing over the *Wind of Good Fortune's* stern.

"It is," Taylor replied. "What I'm doing now is trying to figure out the tides. They're not doing what the book says they should be doing. And running aground on the mudflats would be awkward."

"By when do you think you'll be able to have the tides figured out?"

"Never," Taylor had said, seriously. "But today, with the relatively shallow draft of this vessel, I think I can try to get into port about eleven."

"If we can see the lighthouse, they can see us," McCoy said.

"Another astute observation," Taylor said, still playing Charles Laughton, "I am amazed at your perspicacity, Mr. McCoy."

McCoy was forced to smile.

"You don't think the lighthouse keeper might report that a strange junk loaded with more people than usual, some of whom don't look very Oriental, just sailed past?"

"That would be a real possibility if (a) there was a lighthouse keeper at the lighthouse, and (b) he had a generator to power a radio to communicate with somebody," Taylor said. "But you may relax, Mr. McCoy. I have it from a reliable source that there is neither."

"What reliable source?"

"Our own esteemed Major Kim," Taylor said, pointing to Kim, who was leaning against the stern railing.

Kim was wearing a baggy black cotton shirt and trousers. The last time McCoy had seen him, he had been in neatly pressed American khakis.

"When I was last on Tokchok-kundo," Major Kim said. "The lighthouse keeper was hiding out there," Major Kim said. "He told me that he had removed the important parts of the generator and the radio and took off when he saw the North Koreans were in Inchon."

"You don't think the North Koreans would try to get it up and running? What are they doing without a lighthouse? Taking their chances?"

"The enemy isn't running any deep-draft vessels into Inchon, Captain McCoy," Kim said. "They are using their own ports, which are protected by antiaircraft weapons. They'll wait until they have taken the Pusan perimeter to clean up this area. They have more important things to do than fix a lighthouse which right now would do nothing more than help guide South Korean fishermen home."

"But won't our invasion fleet need it?" McCoy asked.

"If they start down the Flying Fish at night, they will," Taylor said. "And they're going to have to do just that."

"So we have to think about getting it up and running ourselves?"

"In the Dai Ichi Building, the brass's idea was, when they sent you Marines to take Taemuui-do and Yonghung-do on D Minus One, the landing boats would drop half a dozen men off at the lighthouse with either a generator or enough gas and oil to make a fire."

"So that's why you didn't say anything?"

"I figured I'd wait to see if we got away with taking Taemuui-do and Yonghung-do," Taylor said. "If we do get away with that, and if they don't send people to take them back, there'll be plenty of time to think about what we want to do with the lighthouse."

" 'If'?" Jeanette quoted. " *'If'?* What do they call that, 'confidence'?"

"Facing facts," Taylor said. Then he pointed. "There it is. To port?"

McCoy saw a rocky island, with what looked like thatch-roofed stone houses at the water's edge.

"Where's Taemuui-do and Yonghung-do?" McCoy asked.

"You can't see them from here; you can, just barely, from the other side of Tokchok-kundo. But from here in, I think we'd better get everybody below. That includes you, Jeanette. If you're going to stay up here, McCoy, put on a Korean shirt."

He pointed to Major Kim's floppy black cotton clothing.

"My Korean stuff is below. I'll go get it," McCoy said.

Major Kim touched his arm, and when McCoy turned to look at him, handed him a black cotton shirt and trousers.

"Thank you," McCoy said.

"With your permission, Captain," Kim said, addressing Taylor, "I will have my men prepared to deal with whatever we find when we tie up."

"Like what, for example?" Jeanette asked.

"We have had no communication with Tokchok-kundo Island, Miss Priestly," Kim said. "The North Koreans may have decided to occupy it."

"Have at it, Major," Taylor ordered.

"And if they have, then what?" Jeanette pursued.

"Then we hope we have more men than they do," Taylor said. "Please get below, Miss Priestly."

[TWO]

The landing plan was simple. Taylor would sail the *Wind of Good Fortune* into Tokchok-kundo's harbor—actually nothing much more than an indentation in the shoreline with a crude stone wharf jutting out into it—and "see what happens."

In case "what happened" was a detachment of North Korean soldiers, he would have the diesel engine running, so if McCoy decided retreat was the smart thing to do, they could move quickly.

There was a strong possibility, however—depending on McCoy's assessment of the strength of the enemy force, if there was one—that the smart thing to do would be to take the detachment out before retreating.

If there was a North Korean detachment on the island, they would probably have a radio, with which they could call the mainland and report that an attempt by white men (read: Americans) was trying to take the island. That might send North Korean patrol vessels after them, and it would certainly tip the North Koreans that the Americans were showing an unusual interest in Tokchok-kundo.

Taking the detachment out would prevent that. If there were prisoners, they could be taken to Pusan. Any bodies could be buried at sea. By the time someone investigated why Tokchok-kundo hadn't been heard from lately, the *Wind of Good Fortune* would be far at sea.

And the plan for taking out the North Korean detachment—if there was one—was also simple. Major Kim, hoping to look like a sailor, was to stand on the deck to starboard just aft of the forecastle. His national policemen would be in the forecastle itself, ready to move onto the deck on his signal.

Captain McCoy would be aft on the deck to starboard, sitting on the deck, where he hoped the solid railing would keep him from being seen by anyone on the shore. He didn't look much like a Korean sailor.

Neither did Lieutenant Taylor, even though he was now also wearing a black cotton shirt and trousers, and had his hair and forehead wrapped in black cotton. He was in the best position to see what was on the wharf and shore, and was also in the worst position to try to pass himself off as a Korean sailor.

The Marines were to be in the passage below the bridge on the stern, ready to move at McCoy's order.

That order would come when either Major Kim or Lieutenant Taylor decided that it no longer mattered if someone on shore could see that McCoy was not a Korean seaman and would call his name.

McCoy would then stand up, have a look himself, and decide what was the smart thing to do.

A flash of reflected light struck the solid railing behind which McCoy was concealing himself. He looked and saw Jeanette Priestly, on her hands and knees, crawling toward him from the door to the passageway under the stern. Her Leica, its case open, hung from her neck and dragged along the deck.

"OK?" she asked when she reached him, and was sitting on the deck, her back against the stern bulkhead.

"Fine. With a little luck, when the shooting starts, you'll catch a bullet."

"You don't mean that," she said.

"Don't I?"

"No," she said, and put the Leica up and took his picture.

"I told you the next time you took my picture without asking, I'd throw your camera over the side."

"You didn't mean that either," she said. "And anyway, you can't do that now. Anyone on shore would see it."

He shook his head.

"You looked very thoughtful, just now, before you saw me," Jeanette said. "Penny for your thoughts, Captain McCoy."

"Jesus Christ!" he said, but he realized he was smiling.

"Well?"

"When I was a kid," he said. "My grandmother had a big plate—from China, I guess—in her dining room. It was painted with pictures of pagodas, and there was a junk, and trees—"

"Willows," she interrupted. "They were willow trees. They call those dishes 'Blue Willow,' I think."

"If you say so," he went on. "And I used to look at the damn thing all the time. It fascinated me. Little did that little boy know that one day he would get to ride on a real junk in the Yellow Sea—"

"Maybe you are human after all," she said.

"—with a crazy lady who's likely to get herself killed, like the cat, from curiosity."

"I'm just trying to do my job," she said.

"Your job is interfering with me doing mine," he said. "When I stand up in a couple of minutes, you stay where you are until I tell you you can move. If you stand up, I'm going to knock you down. Got it?"

"That, I think you mean," she said. "OK."

A minute later, McCoy gingerly raised his head alongside a stanchion, took a quick look, and dropped quickly back down.

"Remember the cat," Jeanette said. "What did you see?"

"We're fifty yards, maybe a little more, from the wharf. Aside from a couple of hungry-looking dogs on shore, I didn't see any sign of life at all."

Korean seamen lowered all but one sail.

McCoy waited for Taylor to start the engine, in case they had to make a quick exit.

And waited.

And waited.

"What?" Jeanette asked.

"Taylor said he was going to start the engine," McCoy said.

He looked down the deck to Major Kim, who met his glance, then shrugged and held both hands, palms up and out. The message was clear: *I don't see anything.*

McCoy stood up, as the *Wind of Good Fortune* scraped against the stone wharf.

Aside from the dogs, who had come from the shore out onto the wharf in curiosity, there was still no sign of life.

"Kim, get your men over the side, get us tied up," McCoy ordered in Korean, and then switched to English. "Ernie, send four men down the wharf to see what they can see in the village."

Zimmerman came out of the passageway under the stern in a crouch, carrying his Thompson. He laid it on the deck and tossed a rope ladder over the side. By the time he had done that, two Marines, one armed with a Browning automatic rifle, the other with a Garand, came out of the passageway and knelt behind the rail, training their weapons on the wharf.

Zimmerman, his Thompson slung over his back, started down the ladder and passed from sight. Sergeant Jennings, also with a Thompson, came out of the passageway and immediately went down the ladder. The Marine with the M-1 then slung it over his back and went over the side. He was followed by the Marine with the BAR, who chose to toss his weapon over the side to one of the Marines on the wharf before getting on the ladder.

McCoy was pleased with the way that had gone. Not only did the Marines who had been recruited from the brigade seem to know what they were doing, but they were halfway down the wharf before Kim's national policemen managed to get the *Wind of Good Fortune* tied up to the pier.

"Can I stand up now?" Jeanette asked.

"In a minute," McCoy answered.

An elderly Korean man came out of one of the thatch-roofed stone houses as the Marines reached the shore. Zimmerman motioned for two of the Marines following him to go around him and into the houses nearest to the wharf.

Moments later, they came out of the houses, one of them making a thumbs-up gesture.

"OK, you can stand up," McCoy said, slung his Garand over his back, and started down the ladder.

When he was on the wharf, and had turned toward the houses, he saw Major Kim, armed with a carbine, trotting down it, almost at the shore. One of his national policemen was right behind him, and as McCoy trotted toward shore, another ran past him.

Kim introduced the old man to McCoy as the village chief, and McCoy as the officer commanding. The old man didn't seem at all surprised that McCoy spoke Korean.

The old man told them that no North Koreans had been to Tokchok-kundo since Kim had last been there, and that he had seen no indication that the small garrisons on Taemuui-do and Yonghung-do had been reinforced with either men or heavier weapons.

"OK, Ernie," McCoy ordered, "let's get the stuff off the boat."

The old man turned suddenly and walked, or trotted, as fast as he could on his stilted shoes toward the houses, and went inside first one of them, and then two others. Immediately, people, men, women and children came out of the house, and started down the wharf toward the *Wind of Good Fortune,* obviously to help carry whatever the *Wind of Good Fortune* held ashore. Then he came back to McCoy, Kim, and Zimmerman.

"Do you speak English?" McCoy asked, surprised.

The old man looked at him without comprehension.

"You were speaking Korean," Major Kim said, with a smile.

McCoy saw Jeanette kneeling on the wharf, taking pictures of the Koreans.

I didn't tell her she could come ashore, just that she could stand up. But I should have known what she would do.

"First priority, Ernie, is to get the SCR-300 on the air."

Major Kim asked the old man if the generator was running, and where it was.

The generator was running, or would be, if there was fuel. And he pointed to a small stone, thatch-roofed building. McCoy saw that there was a small electrical network coming out of it, with one wire leading to several of the houses and another leading out to the wharf.

McCoy walked to the building and went inside, with Kim following him. There was a small, diesel-powered generator. McCoy saw that it had been made in Germany. And there was room to set up the SCR-300, and he said so.

"I'll have them bring it here," Kim said.

"And then I think we should see if the mayor can see anything on the aerial photos we may have missed," McCoy said. "And see about finding someplace my people can stay. I don't like the idea of them being at the water's edge—too easy to see if somebody comes calling."

"There's several houses up the hill," Kim said.

"Let's have a look at those. We can have the mayor look at the photos there."

The houses on the hill had two advantages. They were within range of the Marines' weapons should the North Koreans decide to have a look at Tokchok-kundo, but they were far enough away so that Marines wearing Korean clothing could probably pass for Koreans.

And one disadvantage. They had been placed where they were to facilitate the drying of fish on racks fastened to their thatched roofs.

What the hell, after a day, they'll probably not even notice the smell.

The houses were made of stone, basically round structures, with small rooms with straight walls leading off them. In the center structure were platforms apparently used as beds against the outer wall. There was a place for a fire in the middle, apparently used both for cooking and to heat the floors and the platforms in winter. They were at once simple and sophisticated.

McCoy had been in similar huts on the mainland during the winter, and had never been able to figure out how the heating system worked.

A bare lightbulb—one of three strung over the platforms—glowed red for a moment and then shone brightly, signaling that the generator was now up and running. McCoy laid out the aerial photographs on the platform, and told the old man he would be grateful if he would look at them.

Surprising McCoy not at all, the war correspondent of the *Chicago Tribune* came into the house as the old man was looking at the aerial photographs.

"Is this where I get to stay?" she asked.

"Probably," McCoy said. "Every maiden's prayer—the only girl sharing a seaside cottage with four handsome and virile Marines."

"What are you doing?" she asked, annoyed.

"These are aerial pictures of Taemuui-do and Yonghung-do," he said. "The islands we're going to have to take."

As she bent over them for a look, Zimmerman, Taylor, and Staff Sergeant Worley, the radio operator, a small, slim man in his late thirties, came into the house. All three were sweating.

They ran up the hill, McCoy decided. *But they look more disgusted than angry or alarmed. Now what?*

"Look at this goddamn thing," Zimmerman said, pointing to a nearly square—about five inches on a side—olive-drab tin can in Worley's hand.

"What is it?"

"It's from the SCR-300. . . ."

"It's a transformer, sir," Sergeant Worley said.

"Without which the SCR-300 won't work?"

Oh, shit!

"When we took it out of the crate, sir, I noticed oil," Worley said. "It came from here, I found out."

He pointed to a corner of the transformer, where the soldered joint had separated.

"The question was, the radio won't work without it?"

"No, sir."

"You can't fix it? Replace the oil, whatever?"

"I could maybe have done something," Worley said, embarrassed. "But I burned the sonofabitch up when I fired up the transformer." He met McCoy's eyes. "Captain, I never had one of these fail on me before. But it's my fault, I should have checked."

Yeah, you should have. But there's no point in eating you out now. What's done is done.

"I told you getting that thing up was the first priority," McCoy said. "So you hurried. It's as much my fault as yours."

"No, sir, it's not," Worley said.

"So what do we do now?"

"I'll try to rig something, Captain, but I can't promise. . . ."

"How long will that take?" McCoy asked.

"Longer than we have," Taylor said. "Unless you want to spend another twelve—maybe twenty-four—hours here."

"Those fucking tides?" McCoy asked angrily.

"Those . . . expletive deleted . . . tides," Taylor replied.

"Sorry, Jeanette," McCoy said. "That slipped out."

"I told you," Taylor said. "The data in the tide book is wrong."

"Is that the same tide book they're using in the Dai Ichi Building?"

"That's where I got this one."

"And it's wrong?"

"I told you, this place has mixed tides. And this must be, for here, the worst part of the monthly cycle. This area was not supposed to be as low as it is. Or going out as fast as it is."

"And what about an invasion fleet?"

"We better have that radio up and running by the time they decide to try to come down the Flying Fish," Taylor said. "Or there's liable to be ships stuck in the mud from here to Inchon."

"How soon do we have to leave?"

"Now," Taylor said. "The sooner the better."

"OK," McCoy said. "Worley, I'll get a transformer to you as quick as I can. How delicate are they?"

"They're usually built . . . hell, sir, look at it. What happened to this one probably won't happen again for years."

"If we wrapped one up well, cushioned it good, could it be dropped from an airplane?"

"Yeah, but dropping it with a chute would probably be better, sir."

"Zimmerman, I'm going to take Jennings back with me. He's a world-class scrounger. And we have to do some fast and fancy scrounging."

Zimmerman nodded his understanding.

"I suggest you set up in these houses. Make firing positions in case you need them. When you put out panels, put them between the houses. Start training the natives," McCoy said. "And make sure the bad guys don't learn you're on the island."

Zimmerman touched his forehead in a gesture only vaguely resembling a salute. But that's what it was.

"You're going to drop supplies on here from an airplane?" Jeanette asked.

"If I can," he said.

"And you're going to Tokyo?"

"Right."

"I need to talk to you a minute," she said.

"You heard what Taylor said. We have to get out of here now."

"It's important to me," she said.

"OK," he said, gesturing to one of the small rooms opening off the center of the house.

He followed her into the room.

"Make it quick," he said when she didn't immediately start to talk.

"I don't know why the hell I'm so embarrassed," she said. "You're a married man, right? And you had those 'personal hygiene' classes in high school, right?"

"What the hell are you talking about?"

"Would you please ask your wife to go to the PX and get me sanitary napkins and tampons? And then drop them in here with that transformer for the radio?"

He didn't reply for a moment.

"Don't be clever about this, McCoy," she said. "I hadn't planned to make this trip."

"You really thought I was going to leave you here?"

She didn't reply.

"Jeanette, my Marines need all the strength they can conserve," he said. "I can't have you doing to them what Delilah did to Sampson. Get your ass on the *Wind of Good Fortune.*"

"You sonofabitch!" she said.

The water level had dropped so far at the wharf that the deck of the *Wind of Good Fortune* was only four or five feet above it.

And, McCoy thought, *she's riding high because just about everything we had aboard has been taken off.*

Taylor clambered aboard and immediately started the engine, as Major Kim and two of his men untied the lines. The bottom of the *Wind of Good Fortune* noisily scraped the bottom twice as Taylor backed away from the wharf, and twice again as he turned her around and as they moved toward and then into the Flying Fish Channel.

[THREE]
Pilot's Ready Room
The USS *Badoeng Strait*
39 Degrees 06 Minutes North Latitude, 129 Degrees 44
   Minutes East Longitude
The Sea of Japan
0955 8 August 1950

When Lieutenant Colonel William C. Dunn walked up to him in the ready room, Lieutenant Commander Andrew McDavit, USNR, prepared for flight, was sitting in the rearmost of the rows of leather-upholstered chairs with a cigarette in one hand and an ice-cream cone in the other.

He started to push himself out of the chair, and Dunn gestured, telling him not to bother.

"Good morning, Colonel," McDavit said. He wasn't overly fond of most of the jarhead birdmen aboard *Badoeng Strait,* but he liked Dunn. "You're already back?"

"We took off at oh dark hundred," Dunn said. "The North Koreans tried to send a division—the Third, I think—across the Naktong starting at 0300."

" 'Tried'? Don't tell me the Army held them?"

"The 5th Cavalry chewed them up pretty bad," Dunn said. "They had pre-registered artillery, a lot of it. And pretty good fields of fire for their automatic weapons. Part of one NK regiment got across, but the other two took a pretty good licking from the air and went back to their side of the Naktong."

"Marine and Navy Air, you mean?"

Dunn nodded. "The brigade wasn't going to need us until this afternoon, so they released us to the Army."

"What happens this afternoon?"

"The 3rd Battalion of the brigade's going to attack up towards Chindong-Ni. They'll need us then."

"For my part, I can look forward to another exciting flight, dodging Air Force transports at K-1," McDavit said. "Did I ever tell you that I once was an honest Wildcat pilot?"

"Flying the Avenger is a dirty job, right, but someone has to do it?" Dunn said, sympathetically. "And you're wondering why you?"

"Even the name is obsolete," McDavit said. "That war's long over. We *already* avenged Pearl Harbor."

"Actually, that's what I wanted to talk to you about."

"Pearl Harbor?" McDavit joked, then: "What can this old sailor do for you, Colonel?"

"You're about ready to go to Pusan?"

"Just as soon as I get some sort of mysterious envelope for the Marine liaison at K-1, I am."

Dunn pulled the zipper of his flight suit down and indicated that he had the mysterious envelope.

"There's a fellow I really want to see in Pusan," he said. "And they're replacing some hydraulics on my Corsair, which means I have the time to go."

"There's plenty of weight on the way in," McDavit said, "and you're sure welcome to it. But I have no idea what I'll have to haul back. Maybe a couple of mailbags, maybe the Golden Gate Bridge in pieces. You're liable to get stuck there overnight."

"I'm checked out in the Avenger," Dunn said, simply. "I flew one as recently as last week."

McDavit met his eyes.

"I'd need the skipper's permission," he said.

"I've already asked. He said it's up to you."

"You must want to see this guy pretty bad. When the word gets out that you've been flying the truck, everyone will wonder how *you* fucked up."

"I do," Dunn said, simply.

"Sure, Colonel," McDavit said. "But please don't bend my bird. I'm not sure they even make parts for it anymore."

Lieutenant Colonel William C. "Billy" Dunn regarded being devious as about as unacceptable—even despicable a behavior for a Marine officer as bold-faced lying. He was being devious now, and it made him very uncomfortable, but he didn't know how else he could handle the situation.

It had started when he told Master Sergeant Mac McGrory to sit on the aerials of the rice field where someone had stamped "PP" and an arrow into the mud.

He just hadn't had time to think about it then—the loudspeakers had blared "Pilots, man your aircraft" while he was still looking at the aerials—but that didn't justify his subsequent behavior. Which, on sober analysis, had been both unprofessional and devious.

On that first mission, right after seeing the aerials, he had diverted from the mission plan, dropped down to the ground, and flown over the wreckage of Pick's Corsair. He knew where that was, but he didn't know where the muddy rice paddy was. The only thing McGrory had said was that it was "near" where Pickering had gone down, and he hadn't asked "how near?" or "in which direction?"

He thought that he could possibly find it because it was a muddy—as opposed to water-filled—rice paddy, and there probably wouldn't be too many of those.

There were. The bombing, and probably artillery as well, had ruptured the dirt walls of more than a dozen paddies near the wreckage of Pick's Corsair and let the water escape. And during his one pass at 200 knots—he could not fly over the area more than once—it had been impossible to look for "PP" and an arrow in all of them.

He hadn't found the one he was looking for, but he had seen Korean farmers hard at work restoring the mud walls of several of the paddies.

When he overflew the location the next day, now armed by Chief Young with a more precise location of what he had come to think of as "Pick's rice paddy," he found proof of the industry of Korean paddy rice farmers, even in the middle of war: there was water in all the paddy fields. *The bastards must have worked all night!*

The only proof that someone had stamped out "PP" and an arrow was in the aerial photos.

The Marines have a long-standing tradition of not leaving their dead and wounded on a battlefield. It is almost holy writ.

There were several problems with that near-sacred tradition in this circumstance.

The first was that Dunn didn't *know* that Major Malcolm S. Pickering, USMCR, had done the stamping.

And even if he had, the odds were that he had done so immediately after getting shot down. In the opinion of an expert in the field of operations behind the enemy's lines—Captain Kenneth R. McCoy—the odds were that Pick was now either a prisoner, or the North Koreans had shot him. It was unlikely that he was hiding out in the area, waiting to be rescued. For one thing, there didn't seem to be any place for him to hide.

If he took the photographs to General Cushman, he was sure that Cushman—probably after asking some very pointed questions about why Dunn hadn't brought the photographs to him immediately, and not taken two days to do it, obviously lowering the chances of a successful rescue—would order an immediate rescue attempt.

Dunn doubted that Cushman would risk sending one of the four Sikorsky helicopters to look for Major Malcolm S. Pickering. There were only four of them—not enough—and when they weren't flying General Craig around the battlefield, they were transporting wounded Marines to medical facilities.

Pick Pickering would not want to be responsible for putting helicopters—and their pilots—at risk looking for him when they could be more gainfully employed carrying some shot-up Marine, who otherwise might die, to a hospital.

That left the Piper Cubs. There were more of those, but not enough, either. Dunn couldn't fly helicopters, but he could fly a Cub. He was also a lieutenant colonel, and he knew that General Cushman was going to decide that while there were a number of lieutenants and captains who could fly Cubs, there were very few lieutenant colonels around commanding fighter squadrons. Dunn knew he would not be allowed to go looking for Pick in a Cub. General Cushman would look askance at him for even asking if he could.

But the lieutenants and the captains would go flying low behind enemy lines, because the Corps didn't leave its dead and wounded on the battlefield. And very likely, at least one of them would get shot down.

It had to be considered, too, that Major Malcolm S. Pickering, USMCR, would not be where he was—if indeed he was there—if he hadn't been trying to be the First Locomotive-Busting Ace in the history of Marine aviation.

And Brigadier General Fleming Pickering, USMCR, had to be considered, too. Dunn really admired General Pickering and thought he knew him well enough to know that he had accepted the loss of his son and gone on doing his duty. Pick's father would be the first to agree that using the helicopters to carry the wounded and the Cubs to direct artillery fire, or otherwise make themselves useful to the First Marine Brigade (Provisional), had a higher priority than being put at risk to *maybe* be able to rescue one officer.

And if he heard about the stamped-out PP and arrow, he would naturally want to believe it was Pick, and that would tear the scab off his wounded heart.

The flip side of all this, of course, was that Pick may have stamped out his initials and an arrow to show his planned course—or maybe that was disinformation; he knew where the American lines were—and might be hiding out somewhere, maybe literally up to his ears in a feces-fertilized rice paddy, and by now getting pretty hungry and discouraged.

And if one of Pick's pilots was down, and needed to be looked for with a Cub, Pick would be out there flying it, and worrying about what General Cushman would say about a squadron commander taking a risk like that later, not about the risk to his own skin.

I just can't leave the sonofabitch out there. Even if he deserves it. He wouldn't leave me out there, and I can't leave him.

Dunn had always heard there was no such thing as a hopeless situation. Until now, he had never believed it.

There was only one thing he could think of to do, and that was find Killer McCoy and dump the situation in his lap.

[FOUR]
K-1 USAF Air Field
Pusan, Korea
1105 8 August 1950

Captain James Overton, the Marine liaison officer at K-1, was surprised when Lieutenant Colonel William C. Dunn climbed down from the cockpit of the Avenger. But not too surprised to forget to take his shoes off his desk, stand up, and come to attention as Dunn came into his office.

"As you were," Dunn said, smiling, putting him at ease.

"Good morning, sir," Overton said. "Didn't expect to see you flying the COD."

"Well, Overton, life is full of little surprises, I've found," Dunn said.

He took the envelope of photos from inside his flight suit.

"You know what this is," Dunn said.

"Yes, sir."

"What time does Captain McCoy usually come by to pick it up?"

"Sir, a sergeant comes by and picks it up," Overton said, looked at his watch, and added, "Usually between 1230 and 1300."

"I have to see Captain McCoy," Dunn said. "You think the sergeant would know where he is? Is there a phone where we can reach him?"

"I don't think so, sir," Overton said. "I get the feeling, sir, that they're out of town someplace."

"You mean out of town, as in away, or out of Pusan?"

"Out of Pusan, sir. But I don't know where."

"Damn it, it's really important that I get to see Captain McCoy. Do you have any idea who would know where he is, or how I can get in touch with him?"

Captain Overton lowered his voice.

"That CIA agent, Major Dunston, would probably know, sir."

"And how would I get in touch with Major Dunston?"

"I don't know, sir. Maybe the Army's G-2 would know. But they might not tell you if they did know."

"The G-2 would be the Eighth Army G-2, right?"

"Yes, sir."

"You have a Jeep. How long would it take me to drive there?"

"An hour, sir. Maybe a little longer."

And that means an hour and a half. Twice an hour and a half. I'd have to come back. And Overton is right. They might know where the CIA guy is—they might even know where McCoy is—but they probably wouldn't tell me. I don't have the need to know.

"Then I don't seem to have much choice, do I, except to wait here for McCoy's sergeant to show up."

"It doesn't look that way, sir," Overton said.

Thirty minutes later, the Avenger's crew chief came in and reported that since there "wasn't hardly nothing for the *Badoeng Strait,*" they could take off whenever the colonel was ready.

Dunn decided to wait another thirty minutes for McCoy's sergeant, and when that passed, decided to wait another thirty minutes.

Twenty-five minutes into the second thirty minutes, he took Captain Overton's arm and led him outside.

"Overton, I don't care how you do it, you *discreetly*—this is an intelligence situation—get word to Major Dunston, asking him to tell Captain McCoy to get in touch with me as soon as he can. It's very important. And call the sergeant major at the brigade, same message. Or anyone else you can think of to ask. Discreetly."

"Aye, aye, sir."

Then Dunn went out and got into the Avenger and fired it up and flew back to the *Badoeng Strait.*

[FIVE]
K-1 USAF Air Field
Pusan, Korea
0905 9 August 1950

"Good morning, keep your seat," Major William Dunston, TC, USA, said to Captain James Overton, USMC, as he walked into Overton's tiny office. "Word is you've been looking for me?"

"Yes, sir. I have been. I called every place in Pusan I could think of."

Dunston made a joking gesture with his hands, signifying, *Here I am.*

"What's on your mind?"

"Sir, do you know how I can get in touch with Captain McCoy?"

Dunston shook his head, "no."

"Do you know where he is, sir?"

Dunston shook his head again.

"What's your interest in Captain McCoy?"

"Colonel Dunn . . ." Overton paused until Dunston nodded, signifying he knew who he meant. ". . . was in here yesterday, sir, from the *Badoeng Strait.* He said it's really important that he talk to Captain McCoy, and told me to find you, and ask you to tell him."

"Are you going to be in touch with Colonel Dunn?"

"I can get a message to him, sir. The *Badoeng Strait*'s COD will be here in a couple of hours. I don't know if the colonel will be flying it again today—"

"Dunn was flying the Avenger?" Dunston asked, surprised.

"Yes, sir."

"Then he must be as anxious for a word with McCoy as I am," Dunston said. "Got a piece of paper and an envelope?"

"Yes, sir," Overton said, handed it over, and then motioned for Dunston to take his seat so he would have a place to write.

Dunston wrote a short message on a sheet of lined paper, put it in an eight-by-ten-inch envelope—all Overton could offer—wrote Dunn's name on it, and then handed it to Overton.

"If Colonel Dunn is flying, tell him I don't know where McCoy is. I would tell him if I knew. And I would really be grateful if he finds McCoy before I do, if he would tell him to get in touch with me."

"Aye, aye, sir."

"Oh, you salty Marines," Dunston said. "That's what the note says. If Dunn comes here, burn the note. Otherwise, give it to the pilot of the COD and tell him to personally put it in Dunn's hand."

"Yes, sir."

"And if you see McCoy . . ."

"Have him get in touch with you. Yes, sir."

"I sort of like that 'aye, aye' business," Dunston said. "And I just remembered what it means: 'Order understood and will be carried out.' Right?"

"Yes, sir."

" 'Yes, sir,' on the other hand means, "I heard what you said, and I will consider doing it.' "

Overton laughed.

"How about an 'aye, aye, sir'?" Dunston asked. "This is really important, Overton."

"Aye, aye, sir."

[SIX]
Communications Center
Eighth United States Army (Rear)
Pusan, Korea
0120 10 August 1950

Captain R. C. "Pete" Peters, Signal Corps, USA, was taking a nap, lying on the counter of the outer room, when Captain Kenneth R. McCoy, USMCR, and Technical Sergeant J. M. Jennings, USMC, entered. It was the first sleep he'd had in twenty-four hours, but he woke immediately nevertheless when he heard the squeak of the door. And was momentarily startled, even a little frightened, when he saw the two Marines.

They were wearing black cotton shirts and trousers. The shirts were too small for them, and therefore unbuttoned, leaving their chests exposed. McCoy had a Garand hanging from his shoulder and Jennings was armed with a carbine. There were two eight-round clips on the strap of McCoy's rifle, and Jennings's carbine had two fifteen-round magazines in the action, taped together, upside down, so that when one was emptied, the other could quickly be inserted.

"Jesus Christ, McCoy! What are you dressed up for?"

"Don't you ever go to spy movies? All we secret agents go around in disguise."

"Do you know that everybody and his brother is looking for you?" Peters asked, as he got off the counter.

"Does everybody and his brother have names?"

"Starting with your general," Peters said. "He calls—or his aide does—every four hours or so to remind me that I am to tell you, the minute I lay eyes on you, to call him."

"Anybody else?"

"Major Dunston of the Transportation Corps," Peters said, his tone of voice putting that name and identification in quotes. "And Captain Overton, of the Marines."

"Who's he?"

"The liaison officer at K-1," Peters said.

"Oh, yeah," McCoy said, remembering. "Did he say what he wanted?"

"You're supposed to get in touch with a Colonel Dunn at your earliest convenience."

"OK, I'm going out there from here," McCoy said.

"What happened to your uniform? Am I allowed to ask?"

"Would you believe they got swept over the side while they were being washed? Or, actually, being dried? One moment, they were on the deck of our luxury liner, drying in the sun, and the next minute a wave came out of nowhere, and so long utilities."

"I don't think you're kidding," Peters said. "What were you doing on a boat?"

"That you're not allowed to ask," McCoy said.

"I am under the personal orders of a Marine brigadier general to get you on the horn to him thirty seconds after I lay eyes on you. That time is up."

"Before I call him, maybe you can help."

"What?"

"I need a part for an SCR-300," McCoy said.

"What part?"

"The oil-filled transformer," McCoy said.

"There are three oil-filled transformers in an SCR-300," Peters said. "Which one?"

"The one that looks like a square tin can."

"They all look like square tin cans," Peters said.

"Marvelous!" Jennings said.

"Then we'll have to have three of each."

"You don't happen to have the one that's broke?" Peters asked.

"No."

"When do you need them?"

"Now."

"I've got two SCR-300s here, about to go back to Japan for depot-level maintenance. I can take the transformers out of them, if that would help?"

"How would we know if they're any good?"

"We don't," Peters said. "But as a general rule of thumb, if they haven't lost their oil, they run forever."

"That's what Sergeant Worley said, Captain," Jennings said. "He said it was the last thing he expected to fail."

"Are they hard to get out?"

"Unfasten a couple of screws, unsolder a couple of connections. . . ."

"Give Sergeant Jennings a soldering iron and a screwdriver, and he can get started while I report in."

"If you'd like, I've got a pretty good sergeant who could take these out and put them in yours," Peters said.

"Mine is a long way away," McCoy said. "But thanks anyway."

"You know what you're looking for, Sergeant?"

"Yes, sir."

"They're out in back, I'll show you."

[SEVEN]
K-1 USAF Air Field
Pusan, Korea
0325 10 August 1950

The Transient Officers' Quarters at K-1 was a dirt-floored U.S. Army squad tent. The tent was furnished with six folding wooden cots and one lightbulb.

Lieutenant (j.g.) Preston Haywood, USNR, hadn't planned to spend the night in Pusan, but he'd had a couple of red lights on the panel of his Avenger and by the time he'd gotten the Air Force mechanics to clear them, it had been too late to take the COD aircraft back to the USS *Sicily*.

Night landings on aircraft carriers are understandably more dangerous than daylight landings, and unless there was a good reason to make them, they were discouraged. In Lieutenant Haywood's judgment—discretion being the better part of valor—carrying half a dozen mail bags out to the *Sicily* was not a good enough reason to make a night landing on her.

After making sure that Aviation Motor Machinist's Mate 3rd Class José Garcia, his crew chief, would have a place to sleep and be able to get something to eat, Haywood had taken advantage of the situation and gone to the K-1 O Club, thinking, if nothing else, he could probably have a beer there. There was, of course, no beer, or any other kind of alcohol, aboard the *Sicily.*

He had four bottles of Asahi beer in the K-1 O Club. And he had occasion to muse again that the Air Force didn't feed as well as the Navy. Supper had been two tough pork chops, mashed potatoes, and mushy green beans.

There being absolutely nothing else to do at K-1, when he'd finished his fourth beer, he'd gone to bed, which is to say he'd gone to the tent, stripped to his underwear, and lay down on the folding wooden cot, sharing it—there being nothing else he could find to do with his khakis and flight suit.

Haywood sat up abruptly when the bare lightbulb suddenly turned on.

Two men had entered the Transient Officers Quarters. One he recognized as the Marine liaison officer. The other was a strange apparition, a white man wearing what looked like black pajamas, and with a Garand rifle slung from his shoulder. He was carrying, as was the Marine liaison officer, a cardboard carton.

"Haywood, right?" the Marine liaison officer asked.

"Yes, sir."

"Haywood, this is Captain McCoy," the Marine liaison officer said.

"Yes, sir?" Haywood asked, wondering if he should try to get dressed.

"I need a ride out to the *Badoeng Strait,*" the white man in the black pajamas said. "As soon as possible."

"Sir, I'm from the *Sicily.*"

"Captain Overton told me," McCoy said. "I want to get there before the Marines fly their first flight of the morning."

"Sir, I'm not sure I can do that," Haywood said. "For one thing . . ."

"You can do it," McCoy said. He handed Haywood a sheet of paper. "There's my authority."

Lieutenant Haywood's only previous experience with the Central Intelligence Agency had been watching it portrayed in a movie, but he realized he was holding in his hand an order issued by the Director of the CIA—who was a rear admiral, USN. He knew there were no flag officers aboard *Sicily,* and he was almost positive there weren't any aboard *Badoeng Strait* either.

"Yes, sir," Lieutenant Haywood said. "Sir, I'll have to ask permission to land on *Badoeng Strait.*"

"Hypothetically speaking, Mr. Haywood," McCoy said. "What would happen if you called *Badoeng Strait* and said you had an emergency and needed to land?"

"They'd give me permission, of course, sir."

"OK, that's what we'll do."

"You don't want me to ask permission, sir?"

"They're liable to say 'no,' " McCoy said. "Get dressed, Mr. Haywood, please."

[EIGHT]
The USS *Badoeng Strait*
35 Degrees 24 Minutes North Latitude, 129 Degrees 65 Minutes East Longitude
The Sea of Japan
0420 10 August 1950

Lieutenant Haywood was wrong about there being no flag officers aboard *Badoeng Strait.* The *Badoeng Strait* was flying the red, single-starred flag of a Marine brigadier general.

Brigadier General Thomas A. Cushman, Assistant Commander, First Marine Air Wing, had flown aboard late the previous afternoon, piloting himself in an Avenger he'd borrowed from USN Base Kobe.

General Cushman wanted to be with his men. The previous evening, he had dined in the chief petty officer's mess, which also served the Marine master sergeants aboard. He had taken dessert in the enlisted mess, and finally, he'd had coffee with the Marine officers in the Pilots' Ready Room and in the wardroom.

He had spent the night—although he had at first declined the offer—in the cabin of the *Badoeng Strait*'s captain. The captain, who had known General Cushman over the years, told him he preferred to use his sea cabin—a small cabin right off the bridge—anyway, and Cushman had accepted the offer.

Cushman had set his traveling alarm clock for 0400, The first Corsairs would be taking off at 0445, and he wanted to attend the briefing, and then see them off.

All the intelligence General Cushman had seen indicated that the North Koreans were aware that the longer they didn't succeed in pushing Eighth Army into the sea, the less the chance—American strength in the Pusan perimeter grew daily—that they would ever be able to do so.

Consequently, while perhaps not in desperation, but something close to it, they were attacking all the time, and on all fronts. The Marine Corsairs would have a busy day.

Cushman was surprised and pleased when he turned the lights on to see that someone had very quietly entered the cabin and left a silver coffee set on the captain's desk. He poured half a cup, then had a quick shower and shave, and wearing a freshly laundered and starched khaki uniform—courtesy of the captain's steward—left the captain's cabin and made his way to the bridge.

"Permission to come on the bridge, Captain?"

"Granted. Get a good night's sleep, General?"

"Very nice, and thank you for the coffee and your steward's attention."

"My pleasure, sir. More coffee, sir?"

"Thank you," Cushman said, and one of the white caps on the bridge quickly handed him a china mug.

"Bridge, Air Ops," the loudspeaker blared.

"Go."

"We have a call from an Avenger declaring an emergency, and requesting immediate permission to land."

The captain and General Cushman looked at each other. The general's lower lip came out, expressing interest and surprise.

The captain pressed the lever on the communications device next to his chair.

"Inform the Avenger we are turning into the wind now," the captain said. Then he pushed the lever one stop further, so that his voice would carry all over the ship.

"This is the captain speaking. Make all preparations to recover an Avenger who has declared an emergency," he said. He let the lever go.

"Turn us into the wind," he ordered.

"Turning into the wind, aye, aye, sir," the helmsman replied.

The *Badoeng Strait* began a sharp turn.

The captain steadied himself, then gestured courteously to General Cushman to precede him to an area aft of the bridge, from which they could see the approach and landing of the Avenger.

By the time the *Badoeng Strait* had turned into the wind and was sailing in a straight line, frantic activity on the flight deck had prepared the ship to recover an aircraft under emergency conditions.

General Cushman turned to the officer actually in charge of the recovery operation, saw that he wasn't at that moment busy, and asked, "Did he say what's wrong with him?"

"No, sir, and I asked him three times."

"There he is," the captain said.

General Cushman looked aft and saw an Avenger making what looked like a perfectly normal approach to the carrier.

A minute later, having made a nice, clean landing—his hook caught the first cable—the Avenger was aboard the *Badoeng Strait* surrounded by firefighters in aluminum heat-resistant suits, other specialists, and even a tractor prepared to push the aircraft over the side if that became necessary.

The door in the fuselage opened, and someone dressed in what looked like black pajamas backed out of it.

"What the hell is that?" General Cushman asked.

"If it's who I think it is, it's someone who's going to spend the next twenty years in Portsmouth Naval Prison," the captain said.

The character in black pajamas reached into the fuselage and took one cardboard carton, and then another, and finally a U.S. Rifle, Caliber .30 M1, to the strap of which were attached two eight-round ammunition clips.

"Excuse me, General," the captain said. "I'll deal with this. I was going to have him brought here, but I don't want that sonofa—character to foul my bridge."

The captain started down a ladder toward the flight deck. General Cushman looked at the character in the black pajamas long enough to confirm his first identification of him, then started down the ladder.

As he reached the flight deck, General Cushman almost literally bumped into Lieutenant Colonel William C. Dunn, USMCR, who was suited up for the morning's first sortie.

"Good morning, sir," Colonel Dunn said.

"Billy, is that your friend, Captain McCoy?"

"Yes, sir, it is."

"What's going on?" Cushman asked.

"I have no idea, sir," Dunn said.

"Let's go find out," Cushman said. "The captain's talking about twenty years in Portsmouth for him."

Captain Kenneth R. McCoy was standing at attention before the captain of the USS *Badoeng Strait*—who had his balled fists resting on his hips and was speaking in a rather loud tone of voice—when General Cushman and Lieutenant Colonel Dunn walked up.

On seeing General Cushman, the captain broke off whatever he was saying in midsentence.

"Captain, may I suggest that we get off the flight deck?" General Cushman said, politely.

The captain looked at him for a long moment, then finally found his voice.

"Yes, sir," he said. "I agree. If you'll follow me, please?"

The captain, the general, and the lieutenant colonel started to march off the deck. The lieutenant colonel, sensing that the captain was not in the parade, looked over his shoulder.

McCoy had picked up one of the cardboard cartons.

"Colonel, I can't carry both of these myself," McCoy said, indicating the second carton.

Lieutenant Colonel Dunn walked quickly back to McCoy, picked up the second carton, and joined the parade.

The captain led the way up interior ladders to his cabin. The others followed him inside. The captain closed the door. McCoy and Dunn put the cartons on the deck.

"Captain," General Cushman said. "May I suggest that since we all are anxious to ask Captain McCoy about a number of things, we probably would be better off to hold our questions until Captain McCoy explains his presence aboard *Badoeng Strait?*"

"Yes, sir. That would probably be best."

"All right, McCoy," General Cushman said.

"Sir, I felt it necessary to get here before Colonel Dunn took off on the morning's missions," McCoy said. "The only way I could see to do that was to commandeer that Avenger."

" 'Commandeer that Avenger'?" the captain parroted. "Who the hell are you to commander anything? Who gave you that authority?"

"I thought we'd agreed to hold our questions," General Cushman said, courteously. "But I think we all would like to hear that one answered."

McCoy handed General Cushman what he thought of as the White House orders.

Cushman read them, raised his eyebrow, and handed them to the captain.

"I've seen them, sir," the captain said.

"Well, that would seem to give you the authority, McCoy," General Cushman said. "But it doesn't answer why you felt you had to come aboard the *Badoeng Strait,* and why you felt declaring an emergency when there was none was justified."

"Sir, I was afraid we would be denied permission to land."

"And your purpose? What's so important?"

"Those cartons, sir, contain parts for an SCR-300 radio. I have to get them to . . . where the radio is as soon as possible. I was going to have Colonel Dunn deliver them, sir."

"Deliver them where?"

"Sir," McCoy said, uncomfortably, "with all possible respect, I must inform you and the captain that what I am about to tell you is classified Top Secret/White House and cannot be divulged to anyone else without General Pickering's specific permission."

"Not even to General Craig?" Cushman asked.

"General Craig is in on this, sir," McCoy said. "But he's one of the very few."

"But the very few include Colonel Dunn?"

"The colonel knows some of this, sir."

"But not, presumably, General of the Army Douglas MacArthur?" the captain asked, coldly sarcastic. "The Supreme Commander?"

"As far as I know, no, sir," McCoy said.

The captain opened his mouth, but Cushman spoke before he could.

"I acknowledge the classification," Cushman said. "Go on."

"Sir, there are islands in the Flying Fish Channel leading to Pusan . . . ," McCoy began.

"Let me get this straight," Cushman said. "You have installed a handful of Marines on this island— What's the name?"

"Tokchok-kundo, sir."

"And from which you intend to launch an operation to take . . ."

"Taemuui-do and Yonghung-do, sir."

"And General MacArthur is unaware of this operation?" the captain asked, incredulously.

"I don't believe he is aware, sir."

"Who besides the people you've mentioned knows about this?" Cushman said.

"Just General Howe, sir."

"Who is he?" the captain demanded.

"An Army two-star, sir. He's on the same sort of mission for the President as General Pickering."

"To your knowledge, is the President aware of this operation?" Cushman asked.

"To my knowledge, no, sir. But I'd bet he is."

"Why do you say that?" Cushman asked.

"Because both General Pickering and General Howe are on orders to tell the President anything they think he might like to know, sir."

"We've gone off at a tangent," Cushman said. "Picking up my original question where I think I left it: You have installed your Marines on Tokchok-kundo—"

"And the South Korean national policemen, sir."

"And the South Korean national policemen, and after you got there, your radio was inoperable?"

"Yes, sir."

"And you want Colonel Dunn to airdrop whatever those things are in the cartons to your people?"

"Yes, sir."

"Can you do it, Billy?" Cushman asked.

"If I can find the island, yes, sir."

"I can show you the island on the aerials, Colonel," McCoy said. "The word I left for Zimmerman is that when a Corsair flies over, he will spread a yellow panel between two houses on a hillside."

"I'd have to make three passes, then? One, fly over; two, spot the panel; three, drop your stuff. Won't that attract attention to the island?"

"I thought, sir, if you flew out of sight each time, for, say, five minutes . . ."

"I can do it, sir," Dunn said.

Cushman looked very thoughtful for a long moment.

"It looks to me that what we have here is a presidentially sanctioned covert mission that we are obliged to support," he said, finally. "Wouldn't you agree, Captain?"

It took the captain even longer to consider his reply.

"Yes, sir, I would agree," he said, finally.

"OK, Billy, that's it. Good luck," Cushman said.

"Aye, aye, sir. Thank you, sir," Dunn said.

"One other question, McCoy," Cushman said. "No, two. Where do you go from here? And what's with the black pajamas? Where's your uniform?"

"The last time I saw it, it was sinking into the Yellow Sea, sir," McCoy said. "It was washed overboard on the way back from Tokchok-kundo."

"I'm sure the captain can find some khakis for you," Cushman said. "And then?"

"Back to Pusan, sir."

"And?"

"Catch a ride to Tokyo. I've got to report to General Pickering."

"I'll take you to Tokyo," Cushman said. "I'd like to see General Pickering myself."

"Yes, sir. Thank you, sir."

"You can use my cabin to take a shower and shave," Dunn said. "I'll show you the way."

When they reached Lieutenant Colonel Dunn's cabin, McCoy saw that the name of Major Malcolm S. Pickering had been removed from the sign outside.

Dunn went immediately to the cabin safe and took an envelope from it.

"Nobody but the two photo lab guys have seen this," Dunn said. "And they won't say anything to anybody."

McCoy opened the envelope and saw the picture of the muddy rice paddy in which someone had stamped out "PP" and an arrow.

"That was taken the day after Pick went down," he said. "The time and map coordinates are on the back."

McCoy looked at him in genuine surprise.

"You think he's still alive and running around loose up there?"

"You tell me, Killer. You're the expert."

"Jesus Christ!" McCoy said.

"Yeah," Dunn said, then patted McCoy on the arm and left his cabin.

XVII

[ONE]
Haneda Airfield
Tokyo, Japan
0805 10 August 1950

The Marine liaison officer at Haneda, having been advised by approach control that an Avenger with a Code Seven aboard who did not wish honors but did require ground transportation was fifteen minutes out, had time to procure a staff car with a one-star plate from the Army, and see to it that the Marines who would meet the aircraft were shipshape and were standing at almost parade rest when the Avenger taxied up to the Navy hangar and stopped.

If the Marine liaison officer thought there was something slightly odd about the man in the backseat of the Avenger who climbed down to the ground—that he was carrying an M-1 rifle, for instance, and that when he took off his flight suit, he was wearing what looked like Navy khakis fresh from the clothing sales store, with no insignia of any kind—he asked no questions.

The Code Seven was Brigadier General Thomas A. Cushman, assistant commander of First Marine Air Wing. The Marine liaison officer recognized him.

Marine first lieutenants presume that Marine general officers know what they are doing at all times, and that the latter will offer an explanation if they feel an explanation is required.

Cushman said he needed the aircraft topped off, that he would return in an hour or two, and that something would be needed to "cover the Garand." A U.S. Army rubberized raincoat was quickly found, and General Cushman and the man with the Garand got in it and drove off.

[TWO]
The Imperial Hotel
Tokyo, Japan
0905 10 August 1950

The CIC agent in the corridor of the Imperial Hotel had seen General Cushman in the Dai Ichi Building and recognized him. And he recognized McCoy. He didn't even challenge them as they walked past him and McCoy raised the knocker on the door to the Dewey Suite.

But—he was a very thorough special agent of the Counter Intelligence Corps—he did make note in his report that Captain McCoy was wearing an insignia-less uniform and carrying a rifle, probably an M-1 Garand, not very well concealed in a raincoat.

"Jesus Christ!" Captain George Hart exclaimed when he opened the door, and then he saw General Cushman. "Good morning, sir."

McCoy thought: *At least he's in a pressed uniform with his tie pulled up.*

Brigadier General Fleming Pickering, also in a freshly pressed uniform with his tie in place, appeared at Hart's shoulder.

"I didn't expect to see Captain McCoy until much later today," Pickering said. "And I didn't expect to see you at all, General."

"Catch you on the way out, Pickering?"

"Surprising the hell out of me, General MacArthur sent word that he would be pleased if I attended the meeting he's having with General Collins and Admiral Sherman," Pickering said.

"Can I have a few minutes?" Cushman asked, as he and Pickering shook hands. "Maybe ride over to the Dai Ichi Building with you? I have a car."

"Come on in," Pickering said. "Truth to tell, when the chime went off, I was thinking it might be a good idea if I was a little late for the meeting."

"Excuse me?"

"Something I learned from General Howe when Averell Harriman and General Ridgway were here," Pickering said. "If I'm on hand, all shined up like some corporal waiting for the first sergeant's morning inspection, when the distinguished visiting officers show up, they're going to take a quick look at my shined shoes—and my one lonely star—and logically conclude that I'm a minor glow in the galaxy surrounding the Supreme Commander, and therefore to be ignored."

Cushman, warmly shaking Pickering's hand, chuckled.

"You like the prestige that goes with being the CIA's man for Asia? That's a little out of character for a spymaster, isn't it?"

"That's not all I'm doing over here, Tom," Pickering said, then turned to Hart. "Get us some coffee, George, please."

"McCoy mentioned something about that," Cushman said.

"Well, if he did, that's really out of character for him."

"He didn't want to, Fleming. The circumstances demanded it."

"Did he also tell you what he was up to in Korea?"

Cushman nodded. "And that the operation is classified as Top Secret/White House."

"OK," Pickering said. "Since the cow is out of the barn: Ken, an hour ago, we heard from Zimmerman."

"I guess those transformers got there, McCoy," Cushman said.

Pickering looked at him, but didn't say anything.

"What did he say, sir?" McCoy asked.

"The entire message was 'standing by,'" Pickering said. "How did he get his radio fixed so quickly? When I talked to you last night, you said you were going to have to figure out some way to get the parts to him."

"Sir, Colonel Dunn dropped the replacement transformers to them first thing this morning."

"How did Billy Dunn get involved?"

Cushman chuckled.

"At 0400, as *Badoeng Strait* was getting ready to launch aircraft for the first sorties of the day," he said, smiling, "an Avenger declared an emergency. All emergency procedures were put into operation. The Avenger came in, made a perfect landing, and McCoy, wearing black pajamas, and needing a bath and a shave, got out, carrying what looked like a half a dozen square tin cans."

"I thought you said the *Avenger* had declared an emergency," Pickering said.

"McCoy had commandeered the Avenger in Pusan. It belongs to the *Sicily,*" Cushman said, "and to avoid the possibility that *Badoeng Strait* would refuse permission for it to land, had the pilot declare an emergency. *Badoeng Strait*'s captain, as you can probably understand, was apoplectic."

"That was necessary, Ken?" Pickering asked, shaking his head.

"I wanted to get the transformers to Colonel Dunn before he took off for the first sorties."

"And those were the circumstances under which Captain McCoy felt obliged to let me know what he was up to," Cushman said.

"What is it the Jesuits say? 'The end justifies the means'?" Pickering asked.

"I hope this end does," Cushman said.

"In this case, I believe it does," Pickering said.

"McCoy said General MacArthur is not privy to his—I suppose your—clandestine operation, but he believes the President is?"

"He is. General Howe told him."

"That was the first I'd heard of General Howe," Cushman said.

"A very good officer," Pickering said.

"Do I get to meet him?"

Hart handed Pickering and Cushman cups of coffee, then handed one to McCoy and took one himself.

"Certainly. When he comes back from Korea," Pickering said.

"General Howe is in Korea?" McCoy asked, surprised.

"He'll be back, he said, either tonight or tomorrow," Pickering said. He turned to Cushman and went on. "He went there to see General Walker. General Collins, and some others, think Walker should be removed. The President wants Howe's opinion."

"Not yours?"

"I'm not qualified—or about to—voice an opinion of an Army commander's performance."

"And this General Howe is?"

"He commanded a division in Europe. He's far better qualified than I am, but he's damned uncomfortable with Truman's order. And since one of us had to stay here in Tokyo to keep an eye on Sherman and Collins, here I am."

"You think the Inchon invasion is a sure thing?"

"That's why I ordered this operation," Pickering said.

"And MacArthur doesn't know you're doing this?"

"As the Deputy Director of the CIA for Asia, I don't have to tell MacArthur of every small clandestine operation I'm running."

"And what's going to happen when he finds out?"

"That's one of those bridges somewhere down the road," Pickering said.

"You're walking pretty close to the edge of a cliff, I guess you know."

"If I told him I thought these islands should be in our hands as soon as possible, I would be challenging the collective wisdom of his staff. Most of them were with him in the Philippines."

"And he would back them, of course."

Pickering nodded.

"Is there anything I can do to help?" Cushman asked.

"You already have. And since you are now in on this, I won't be reluctant now to ask for any help I think we need."

Pickering looked at his watch.

"Now we have to leave, George," he said. He turned to McCoy. "Go home, Ken. Get a little rest. Whatever you think you have to do will wait until I get back from the Dai Ichi Building. Come back about 1300. Bring Ernie, if you like. We can have a room-service lunch and talk here."

"Aye, aye, sir."

"What's Taylor up to?" Pickering asked.

"He's sitting on Jeanette Priestly for me."

"I beg your pardon?"

"Until I talked to her, she was going to write a story about Pick getting shot down," McCoy said.

"And you were able to talk her out of it?" Pickering asked, surprised.

"I took her with us to Tokchok-kundo," McCoy said. "It was the only thing I could think of to do with her."

"So now she's in on everything?" Pickering said, coldly.

McCoy met Pickering's eyes.

"I don't think we have to worry about her. I put her on the junk before I knew that she thinks she's in love with Pick," he said. And then he blurted, "Fuck it."

"Excuse me?" Pickering said, partly a question, mostly a reprove.

McCoy took a manila envelope from inside his shirt and handed it to Pickering.

"Billy gave me these just before he took off from the *Badoeng Strait,*" McCoy said. "Nobody knows about these pictures but two guys in the photo lab on the *Badoeng Strait,* Dunn, me, and now you."

"What am I looking at?"

"These pictures were taken the day after Pick went down, near the spot. Somebody stamped 'PP' and an arrow in a ruptured rice paddy."

"My God," Pickering said. "He's alive."

He handed the photographs to Cushman.

"Why weren't these photographs . . . ," Cushman began. "Pickering, you have my word that every effort will be made—"

"Sir, with respect," McCoy said. "Colonel Dunn knew that if these pictures got out, a lot of people and, as important, the helicopters would be put at risk to try to get him."

"You're a Marine, Captain. You know our tradition. . . ."

"Colonel Dunn knows the only way to look for Major Pickering, to get him out, would be with helicopters, and the only helicopters we have are carrying the wounded. Colonel Dunn knows, and I know, that Major Pickering wouldn't want that."

"And neither do I," General Pickering said. "I don't want helicopters put at risk looking for my son, General Cushman. We'll think of something else."

"That's really not your decision to make, is it, Fleming?" Cushman argued.

"I think it is," Pickering said. "I would deeply appreciate your respecting my wishes in this matter."

Cushman met Pickering's eyes.

After a long moment, he said, "Of course."

"I've got a couple of ideas," McCoy said.

"And so far as *you're* concerned, Ken, the priority is the taking of Taemuui-do and Yonghung-do," Pickering said.

"Aye, aye, sir," McCoy said.

[THREE]
The Dewey Suite
The Imperial Hotel
Tokyo, Japan
1425 10 August 1950

Mrs. Ernestine McCoy was helping herself to another piece of pastry when the door chime went off, so she answered it.

It was Brigadier General Pickering, trailed by Captain Hart. Pickering kissed her on the cheek, looked around the room, and said, "You've eaten, good. The Grand Encounter lasted longer than it was supposed to."

"Ken wanted to wait," Ernie said.

"And you didn't," Pickering said. "Proving what I've suspected all along, that you're the smarter of the two."

He went to the room-service cart, opened silver covers until he found a bowl of salad, and popped a radish into his mouth. Then he turned to Hart.

"In this order, George, order us some lunch. A small steak, a tomato, more salad for me, hold the dressing. And coffee, of course. Then show McCoy where we've moved the typewriter. And then run down Sergeant Keller, and have him standing by here, and have a car standing by downstairs to carry him to the Dai Ichi Building."

"Aye, aye, sir."

"Ken, you feel up to a little fast typing?"

"Yes, sir."

"OK, let's get started. I want what happened at that meeting to be in the President's hands as soon as possible."

General Pickering had just finished his small steak when McCoy came back in the room with several sheets of typewriter paper in his hands. Pickering took them and read them.

"You're a great typist, McCoy," Pickering said, cheerfully. "If you ever need work, we can always use a good typist at P & FE."

"I think I'd rather sell deodorant for American Personal Pharmaceuticals, but thanks just the same," McCoy replied.

"Uncle Flem," Ernie McCoy flared. "My God!"

"Sometimes my mouth runs away with itself," Pickering said. "Ken, I'm sorry. You know that was a bad shot at trying to be funny."

"It's OK?" McCoy asked, indicating the material he'd typed.

"It's perfect," Pickering said, handing it back. "If you'd have made a couple of typos, I wouldn't have . . ."

McCoy took the sheets of paper from Pickering and handed them to Master Sergeant Keller.

"Take a look, Keller," McCoy ordered, "then stick them in an envelope and get them going."

Keller read them.

```
TOP SECRET/WHITE HOUSE
DUPLICATION FORBIDDEN ONE (1) COPY ONLY
DESTROY AFTER TRANSMISSION


TOKYO, JAPAN 0625 GREENWICH 10 AUGUST 1950
VIA SPECIAL CHANNEL
EYES ONLY THE PRESIDENT OF THE UNITED STATES


DEAR MR. PRESIDENT:


IT IS NOW ABOUT 3 PM TOKYO TIME. I HAVE JUST COME FROM
THE DAI ICHI BUILDING WHERE I ATTENDED THE MEETING
BETWEEN GENERAL OF THE ARMY DOUGLAS MACARTHUR, GENERAL
JOSEPH C. COLLINS, USA, AND ADMIRAL FORREST SHERMAN,
USN, AND OTHER SENIOR MEMBERS OF THEIR RESPECTIVE
STAFFS. GENERAL HOWE IS IN KOREA, BUT I FEEL SURE, HAD
HE BEEN PRESENT, HE WOULD CONCUR WITH THE CONCLUSIONS
DRAWN HEREIN.


THE BASIC PURPOSE OF THE MEETING WAS TO GIVE GENERAL
MACARTHUR THE OPPORTUNITY TO EXPLAIN HIS PLAN TO MAKE
THE AMPHIBIOUS LANDING AT PUSAN, SCHEDULED AT THE
MOMENT FOR 15 SEPTEMBER 1950.


I HAD THE FEELING THAT BOTH COLLINS AND SHERMAN ENTERED
THE MEETING STRONGLY OPPOSED ESPECIALLY TO THE INCHON
LANDING (THE TIDES ARGUMENT, WITH WHICH YOU ARE
```

FAMILIAR), AND GENERALLY OPPOSED TO ANY AMPHIBIOUS
OPERATION UNTIL THE SITUATION IN THE PUSAN PERIMETER IS
STABILIZED, PRIMARILY BECAUSE THE INCHON INVASION WILL
REQUIRE THE USE OF THE MARINES NOW FIGHTING IN THE
PUSAN PERIMETER.

I ALSO FELT THAT WHILE COLLINS LEFT THE MEETING
UNSWAYED BY MACARTHUR'S—IN MY OPINION—COGENT AND
BRILLIANT EXPLANATION OF WHY INCHON WAS THE RIGHT THING
TO DO, SHERMAN HAD COME AROUND TO AT LEAST PARTIAL
APPROVAL OF THE INCHON OPERATION. HE SAID NOTHING TO
THIS EFFECT, BUT THE QUESTIONS HE ASKED OF MACARTHUR
INDICATED HE DID NOT THINK INCHON IS AS HAREBRAINED AS
COLLINS MADE CLEAR HE THINKS IT IS.

COLLINS VERY SKILLFULLY GAVE MACARTHUR THE OPPORTUNITY
TO LAY THE BLAME FOR OUR INITIAL REVERSES ON GENERAL
WALKER. MACARTHUR STATED VERY CLEARLY THAT HE BELIEVED
WALKER "HAD DONE AND IS DOING A REMARKABLE JOB, GIVEN
WHAT HE HAS BEEN FACING AND WHAT HE HAS TO FACE IT
WITH."

IF IT WAS COLLINS'S INTENTION TO HAVE MACARTHUR
ACQUIESCE IN THE RELIEF OF WALKER, EITHER BECAUSE HE
BELIEVES THAT WALKER HASN'T MEASURED UP, OR BECAUSE HIS
RELIEF WOULD ALLOW HIM TO GIVE RIDGWAY, OR SOMEONE ELSE
OF HIS LIKING, THE JOB, HE FAILED.

VERY EARLY THIS MORNING, GENERAL HOWE CALLED ME FROM
KOREA ON A LINE WHICH WE SUSPECTED WAS NOT AS SECURE AS
WE WOULD HAVE LIKED. HE SAID THAT HE WOULD COMMUNICATE
HIS THOUGHTS ON HIS MISSION THERE TO YOU AS SOON AS
POSSIBLE, BUT THAT, IF I SHOULD COMMUNICATE WITH YOU
BEFORE HE WAS ABLE TO, I SHOULD GIVE YOU THE FOLLOWING
MESSAGE:

"FROM WHAT I SEE, A CHANGE OF LEADERSHIP AT THIS TIME
WOULD BE UNJUSTIFIED AND ILL-ADVISED."

IT IS MY OPINION, MR. PRESIDENT, THAT, ABSENT SPECIFIC
ORDERS NOT TO DO SO FROM YOURSELF AND/OR THE JOINT
CHIEFS OF STAFF, MACARTHUR WILL PROCEED WITH HIS
INTENTION TO LAND WITH TWO DIVISIONS AT INCHON ON 15
SEPTEMBER. IT IS ALSO MY OPINION THAT COLLINS WILL MAKE
A STRONG CASE BEFORE THE JCS, AND PERHAPS TO YOU
PERSONALLY, TO FORBID INCHON, BUT THAT HE WILL NOT HAVE
AS STRONG AN ALLY IN THIS IN SHERMAN AS HE PROBABLY
HOPED HE WOULD.

CAPTAIN MCCOY AND LIEUTENANT TAYLOR RETURNED FROM THE
ISLAND WE HOLD IN THE FLYING FISH CHANNEL THIS MORNING.
HE WILL RETURN THERE SHORTLY, AND IS PREPARED TO LAUNCH
HIS OPERATION WITHIN A WEEK. CIRCUMSTANCES REQUIRED THAT
BRIG GEN THOMAS CUSHMAN, USMC, ASSISTANT COMMANDER, 1ST
MARINE AIR WING, BE INFORMED OF THAT MISSION, AND OF THE
MISSIONS OF GENERAL HOWE AND MYSELF.

RESPECTFULLY SUBMITTED,

F. PICKERING, BRIGGEN USMCR

TOP SECRET/WHITE HOUSE

"This looks fine to me, Captain," Keller said.

"Go with him, George, will you?" McCoy ordered. "Now I'm going to have my coffee." He handed him more typewriter paper, torn in half. "This gets burned and shredded with the clean copy."

"What is it?"

"It's the version with the typos, before I retyped it," McCoy said. He sat down at the table and reached for the coffeepot.

"Ernie," a female voice cried, "did that husband of yours tell you what he did to me?"

His head snapped to the door.

Miss Jeanette Priestly of the *Chicago Tribune* was coming through the door, trailed by Lieutenant (j.g.) David Taylor, USNR.

"Well, Jeanette," Ernie said, rising to the occasion. "How nice to see you again."

"I didn't expect you'd beat us here," Taylor said to McCoy.

"Long story. I'll tell you later."

"What's this all about?"

"*This* would have been here sooner," Jeanette said, flashing McCoy a dazzling smile. "But *this* had to freshen up a little. And *this* must say that you look a lot better than the last time *this* saw you."

McCoy realized he was smiling.

The last time he had seen her, just before midnight at the Evening Star Hotel in Tongnae, she had been wearing U.S. Army fatigues and combat boots. She hadn't been near soap or running water for a week, and had spent all but an hour of the previous two and a half days on a junk running through some often rough water in the Yellow Sea. There had been a visible layer of dried salt-water spray all over her face, hands, and hair.

She was now clean, wearing makeup, an elegantly simple black dress, high heels, and enough perfume so that McCoy could smell it across the room.

The only thing that was the same about her was the Leica camera in its battered case hanging around her neck.

"She insisted on coming here," Taylor said. "I didn't know what to do...."

Taylor was wearing one of his well-worn, but clean, khaki uniforms.

"It's all right," General Pickering said. McCoy looked at him and saw he was smiling. "Hello, Miss Priestly."

He got a dazzling smile.

"How nice to see *you* again, General," she said.

"Zimmerman's on the air," McCoy said.

"That was quick," Taylor said, surprised. "That's damned good news."

"I'll want to know, in detail, exactly how you managed that," Jeanette said.

"Later," McCoy said.

"What can we do for you, Miss Priestly?" Pickering asked.

"Didn't Captain McCoy tell you?" she asked. "In exchange for me not writing one story, he promised he would give me an exclusive story about something else I'm afraid to mention, not knowing how many secrets McCoy shares with his wife. No offense, Ernie."

General Pickering chuckled.

"I don't think Captain McCoy has any secrets from his wife," he said. "How was the cruise, Miss Priestly?"

"It was absolutely awful, frankly," she said. "Anyway, until what happens happens, I'm going to stick to these two"—she indicated McCoy and Taylor—"like glue."

"Fair enough," Pickering said.

"And I also thought that if there was any news about Pick?"

Pickering signaled McCoy with his eyes not to mention the photographs McCoy had gotten from Dunn.

"Unfortunately, no," Pickering said.

"Damn," she said.

"Where's the film you shot on the *Wind of Good Fortune?*" McCoy asked.

"In here," she said, tapping her purse.

"I forgot to impound it," McCoy said. "Or to tell Taylor to. May I have it, please?"

"You still don't trust me?"

"Let's say I'm cautious by nature," McCoy said.

"Give them to me, please, Miss Priestly," Pickering said. "You have my word you'll get them back."

She shrugged, opened her purse, and took from it a rubberized bag and handed it to Pickering.

"Thank you," he said.

"Is it really all right to talk?" she asked.

Pickering nodded.

"How are you coming with the boats?" she asked McCoy.

"What boats?" Pickering asked.

"Do you suppose I could have that roll?" Jeanette asked, pointing at one on Pickering's bread plate. "I'm really starved."

"Of course," Pickering said.

"You didn't eat?" McCoy said.

"We had some powdered eggs at K-1 about 0500," Taylor said.

"Nothing here?" McCoy asked.

"I told you," Jeanette said. "*This* couldn't come here looking like *this* did when *this* got off the *Queen Mary.* That took a little time."

"You didn't eat either?" McCoy asked Taylor, smiling.

"You told me to sit on her," Taylor said, not amused. "I sat on her. I sat in her room in the Press Club while she had a bath, and the rest of it, and then I took her to my room while I had a quick shower. No, I didn't eat either."

"We can fix that," Ernie McCoy said, and walked to the telephone, picked it up, and, in Japanese, asked for room service.

"What boats?" General Pickering asked again.

"Didn't Ken tell you? Jeanette said. "We're going to need a couple of boats to move the men from Tokchok-kundo to Taemuui-do and Yonghung-do. We can't use the *Wind of Good Fortune*. Not only can't we count on having enough water under the rudder, but a junk makes a lousy landing craft."

" '*We're* going to need a couple of boats'?" Pickering parroted.

"You weren't listening, General, when I said I wasn't going to let Captain Bligh and Jean Lafitte out of my sight until this operation is over. That means when they go to Taemuui-do and Yonghung-do, the *Chicago Tribune* is going to be there."

"Which one is Captain Bligh?" Pickering asked, smiling.

She pointed at Taylor.

"And it fits, too," she said. "Taylor told me Bligh was really the good guy, and Fletcher Christian a mutineer who should have been hung."

Pickering chuckled.

"That's true," he said. "Bligh was also a hell of a sailor. He sailed the long-boat from the *Bounty* a hell of a long way, after they put him over the side. OK, Captain Bligh, tell me about the boats."

"She said it, sir," Taylor said. "We're going to need a couple of boats. Maybe small lifeboats. Just large enough to carry eight, ten, men and their equipment. It would be better if they had small engines, maybe even outboards—it's a long row from Tokchok-kundo to either Taemuui-do or Yonghung-do. But in a pinch we can make do with just oars."

"The first thing I thought was 'no problem,' " Pickering said. "We'll see if P & FE here can't come up with a couple of boats. But that doesn't answer the question of how to get them to Tokchok-kundo, and quickly and quietly, does it?"

"No, sir," McCoy said. "And if we go to the Navy, they'd want to know what we want them for."

"And even if we could talk our way around that, we still would have to get them to Tokchok-kundo," Pickering said.

"Yes, sir."

"I just thought of a long shot," Pickering said. "Taylor, do you know who Admiral Matthews is?"

"The Englishman?"

Pickering nodded.

"Yes, sir."

"Is there anybody you could call at the Dai Ichi Building and get his number, without it getting around that you asked for it?"

"Is he in town, sir?"

"He was at the meeting this morning," Pickering said.

"Who is he?" McCoy asked.

"He commands the UN fleet blockading the west coast of Korea," Pickering said.

Five minutes later, Taylor had the telephone number of Admiral William G. Matthews, and three minutes after that, the Admiral came on the line.

"Yes, of course, I remember you, Pickering. You were one of the very few people in that room this morning who seemed to understand that tides rise as well as fall."

"Admiral, could I have a few minutes of your time?"

"I was about to leave for Sasebo, but yes, certainly, if you could come here right away. You know where I am?"

"Yes, sir. And I will leave right away."

"I'll even buy you a drink. God knows we earned one in that bloody roomful of fools this morning."

"Thank you, sir," Pickering said, and hung up.

He turned to the others.

"We may just have gotten lucky," he said. "And no, Miss Priestly, you may not go. But you have my word that I will bring Captain Bligh and . . . who was it, Bluebeard the Pirate? . . . back to you."

"Jean Lafitte, sir," McCoy said.

[FOUR]
The Office of the Naval Attaché
HM Delegation to the Supreme Command, Allied Powers,
   in Japan
Tokyo, Japan
1605 10 August 1950

"Ah, Pickering!" Admiral Sir William G. Matthews, RN, said, getting to his feet as Pickering was shown in. Then he saw Taylor and McCoy, and added: "I didn't know you were bringing these gentlemen with you. Now I will have to mind my manners. And my mouth."

"I apologize, sir."

"It doesn't matter," Matthews said. "I am so glad to be out of that bloody room that I'll give them a drink, too."

"Very kind of you, sir," Pickering said. "And please feel free to say anything you like. Both Captain McCoy and Lieutenant Taylor know how I feel about that bloody meeting, too."

Matthews growled.

A Japanese in a white coat appeared and took drink orders. Matthews waited until he had finished, then ordered another double for himself.

"I was just telling Fitzwater here," he said, pointing to a very slim, very tall Royal Navy captain, "that I'd finally found a Marine who'd actually been to sea. God, I had trouble keeping my temper when that Army general started lecturing me on the hazards of tides."

"Actually, sir," Pickering said. "I'm more of a seaman than a Marine."

"How's that?"

"I was about to tell Sir William, sir," Captain Fitzwater said, "that unless I was mistaken, you are connected with Pacific and Far East Shipping. Was I correct?"

"So far as I know," Pickering said, "I am the only PF and E master who has run his vessel aground on the Pusan mudflats."

"Really?" Admiral Matthews said. "How did that happen?"

"I was a little younger at the time," Pickering said. "And thus far more impressed with myself as a mariner than the facts warranted."

"So what the hell were you doing dressed up in a Marine's uniform in that bloody room?"

"Admiral, I'm the Assistant Director of the CIA for Asia," Pickering said.

"Ah!!" the admiral said.

"I was hoping you would offer that information, General," Captain Fitzwater said. "Otherwise, I would have had to whisper it in Sir William's ear."

"And are these two spies as well?" the admiral asked. "That one looks like a sailor."

"Lieutenant Taylor, sir," Taylor said.

"Actually, he's a hell of a sailor," Pickering said. "He just returned from sailing a junk in the Yellow Sea."

"Really? What was that about? A *junk*, you say?"

"I'd love to tell you, Sir William," Pickering said, stopping when the steward handed him his drink.

"Cheers!" Admiral Matthews said when he had raised his fresh drink. "And you would love to tell me, but?"

"I would hate to have it get back to anyone in that bloody room. For that matter, to leave *this* room."

"Ah, the plot darkens," the admiral said, and thought over what Pickering was clearly asking. "You have my word, sir."

"Would you prefer that I . . ." Captain Fitzwater asked.

"No," Pickering said, "but if you could give me your word?"

"Of course," Fitzwater said.

Pickering had decided it made more sense to have Fitzwater on his honor not to repeat what he heard than to really arouse his curiosity by asking him to leave. Pickering thought he was obviously some sort of intelligence officer—he had known about P&FE and the CIA—and he would go snooping, with no restrictions on disseminating what he found out. And Pickering was pleased when he saw approval on McCoy's face.

"Lieutenant Taylor just sailed the junk *Wind of Good Fortune* to Tokchok-kundo Island," Pickering said. "Aboard were four Marines, in addition to Captain McCoy, and eight South Korean national policemen."

"How interesting," the admiral said.

"With which Captain McCoy and Lieutenant Taylor plan, just as soon as they can, to occupy Taemuui-do and Yonghung-do Islands, and thus deny the North Koreans a platform from which to fire upon vessels navigating the Flying Fish Channel."

"You know the plan calls for the neutralization of those islands on D Minus One?"

"Yes, I do."

"You got them to change their minds about that?"

"No, sir. They do not know about this operation."

"Ah!" Admiral Sir William Matthews said.

"And what about the lighthouse?" Captain Fitzwater asked.

"On the night of 13–14 September," Taylor said. "Presuming we can take Taemuui-do and Yonghung-do without attracting too much North Korean attention, we'll take that, too."

"And why is it, if I may ask, you don't want this operation of yours to come to the attention of the fools in the Dai Ichi Building?"

"Because I know they would object to it," Pickering said. "Probably forbid me to go on with it."

"They almost certainly would object, and object rather strenuously, for the very good reason that it makes a bloody hell of a lot more sense than what they're proposing. Your intention is to present them with a *fait accompli?*"

"Yes, it is."

"How can I help without—how do I phrase this delicately?—without exposing my scrotum to the butcher's ax on the chopping block to the degree you are?"

"Taylor," Pickering said. "Tell the admiral what you need."

"Two small boats, sir, lifeboats would do. Capable of carrying eight or ten men and their equipment. Preferably with an auxiliary engine—"

"No problem," the admiral interrupted.

"—delivered as soon as possible as near as possible to Tokchok-kundo," Taylor finished.

"Ah!" the admiral said.

He looked around for his drink, found it, took a sip, and then frowned.

"Fitz, when is *Charity* due to leave Sasebo?" he asked, finally.

"At first light on the sixteenth, sir."

"Round figures, she should be able to make twenty knots easily; it's about five hundred miles to Inchon. That would put her off the Flying Fish Channel lighthouse twenty-four hours later. At first light, and I don't think Mr. Taylor wants to do this in the daylight."

The admiral paused, and everyone waited for him to go on.

"Signal the yardmaster at Sasebo that (one) I should be seriously distressed to hear *Charity* didn't make that at-first-light departure schedule, and (two) before she sails, he is to mount on her two ten-man open boats with functioning auxiliary engines—emphasize functioning—in such a manner that they may be launched quickly on the high seas."

"Yes, sir."

"And when he inquires, as he doubtless will, what in the hell is going on, as politely as you can, hint that I have been at the gin again, and you haven't an idea what it's all about."

"Yes, sir."

The admiral turned to Taylor.

"HMS *Charity* is a destroyer. Before she leaves Sasebo to return to her blockade duty in the Yellow Sea, I will have a private word with her captain—or Fitz will, he's his brother-in-law and that might attract less attention—telling him, (one) that two Americans will board her as supercargo on the night of August fifteenth, for a purpose to be revealed to no one but him until after she is under way, and (two) that he is to authorized to make whatever speed is necessary to put *Charity* three miles off the Flying Fish Channel lighthouse not later than 0300 17 August, where he will put the boats and the Americans over the side."

He paused again.

"This all presumes that nothing will go awry," he went on, "as it almost certainly will. But it is the best I can do under the circumstances. Will that be satisfactory?"

"I don't know how to thank you, Admiral," Pickering said.

"One way would be to make sure that when *Charity* starts down the Flying Fish Channel on fifteen September, the lighthouse will be operating, and she will not come under artillery fire."

XVIII

[ONE]
Haneda Airfield
Tokyo, Japan
1530 15 August 1950

There were seven officers—the senior of them a captain—and eleven enlisted men—ranging in rank from technical sergeant to corporal—in USMC Platoon Aug9-2 (Provisional). The platoon was the second of two that had been organized at the Replacement Battalion (Provisional) at Camp Joseph J. Pendleton, California, six days before, on August 9. All of the members of Aug9-2 were Marine reservists, involuntarily called to active duty by order of the President of the United States for the duration of the present conflict, plus six months, unless sooner released for the convenience of the government.

Both platoons had the same purpose, to get replacements to the First Marine Brigade (Provisional) in Pusan, South Korea, as expeditiously as possible. The size of Aug9-2 had been determined by the number of seats available on Trans-Global Airways Flight 1440, San Francisco to Tokyo, with intermediate stops at Honolulu, Hawaii, and Wake Island.

Platoon Aug9-2 had been formed at 0715 in the morning, and had departed Camp Pendleton by Greyhound Bus for San Francisco at 0755. Travel was in utilities. The trip took a little more than ten hours, including a thirty-minute stop for a hamburger-and-Coke lunch outside Los Angeles.

There was just time enough at the airfield in San Francisco for the members of Aug9-2 to make a brief telephone call to their families. Most of them did so, and although each member of Aug9-2 had been admonished not to inform their family members of their destination until they reached it, with the exception of one officer, a second lieutenant, all of them told their family members they were in San Francisco about to get on an airplane for Tokyo and eventually South Korea.

Why the hell not? Who did the goddamn Crotch think it was fooling? What was the big goddamn secret? Where else would the goddamn Crotch be sending people except to goddamn Korea?

The flight aboard Trans-Global Airways Flight 1440 was a pleasant surprise. It was a glistening—apparently not long from the assembly line—Lockheed Constellation. There was a plaque mounted on the bulkhead just inside the door, stating that on June 1, 1950, the *City of Los Angeles* had set the record for the fastest flight time between San Francisco and Tokyo.

The seats were comfortable, the stewardesses good-looking and charming. Almost as soon as they were in the air, the stewardesses came by asking for drink orders. Drinks were complimentary.

One of the staff sergeants of Aug9-2, who three weeks before had been a maritime insurance adjuster in Seattle, and often flew to Honolulu on Trans-Global and other airlines, was surprised that Trans-Global was passing out free booze in tourist class, and asked about it.

"I don't really know," she said. "I heard something that the president of the company was a Marine, or something. All I know is that all our military passengers get complimentary refreshments."

The military passengers in tourist class also got the same meal—filet mignon, baked potato, and a choice of wine—that was being served in first class. The civilians in the back got a chicken leg and no wine.

Still, with the fuel stops in Hawaii and Wake Island, it was a hell of a long flight to Tokyo, and all of Aug9-2 got off the plane at Haneda on 12 August tired, needing a bath and a shave, and in many cases, more than a little hungover.

They were taken by U.S. Army bus to Camp Drake, outside Tokyo, for processing, which included a review of the inoculation records; their service record; an opportunity for those who didn't have it to take out an insurance policy that would pay their survivors $10,000 in the case of their death; zeroing their individual weapons; issuance of 762 gear and a basic load of ammunition; and two hour-long lectures.

One of the lectures, by an Army captain, told them what they could expect to find, in a military sense, once they got to Korea. It surprised none of them, for they had all read the newspapers.

The goddamned Army was getting the shit kicked out of it, and—what else?—had turned to the goddamn U.S. Marine Crotch to save its ass.

The second lecture, by a Navy chaplain, told them what they could expect to find in Korea in a sexually-transmitted-diseases sense. It included a twenty-minute color motion picture of individuals in the terminal stages of syphilis, and of other individuals whose genitalia were covered with suppurating scabs.

At 1200 15 August 1950, Marine Corps Platoon Aug9-2 (Provisional) was fed a steak-and-eggs luncheon, causing many of its members to quip cleverly that the condemned men were getting the traditional hearty last meal.

Then they were loaded on an Army bus that took them back to the Haneda Airfield. There, they were told, they would board a Naval Air Transport Command Douglas R5D, which would depart at 1400, and after several intermediate stops—Osaka, Kobe, and Sasebo—would deposit them at K-1 Airfield, Pusan, South Korea, where they would be met by a Marine liaison officer who would get them to the First Marine Brigade (Provisional), where Aug9-2 would be disestablished, and they would be assigned billets in the brigade according to the needs of the brigade at the moment.

Shortly after boarding the aircraft—half of the fuselage was devoted to cargo—they were told there was an unexpected delay in the departure time, they were going to have to wait for some big shot, and since it was going to get hot as hell in the aircraft, those who wished could get off and wait in the shade offered by a hangar.

The lieutenant (j.g.) who gave them this word also reminded them that anyone who missed the departure of the aircraft would be subject to far more severe penalty under the Uniform Code of Military Justice, 1948, than provided for simple absence without leave. Missing this flight would be construed as absence without leave to avoid hazardous service.

All of Aug9-2 got off the airplane and sat down in the shade on the concrete before the doors of an enormous hangar.

At 1525, the big shot they were holding the flight for showed up in a two-US-Army-staff-car convoy. The first of the two glistening olive-drab 1949 Chevrolet staff cars had the single-starred flag of a brigadier general flying from a short staff mounted to the fender.

An Army sergeant jumped out and opened the door. A Marine brigadier general got out, and then a Marine captain, and then a Navy lieutenant. The sergeant opened the trunk, and the Navy officer took a suitcase from it.

A Marine captain—wearing, like the other Marine officers, a crisply pressed uniform—got out of the second staff car and went to the trunk. Then a—*Jesus*

H. Christ, will you look at that?—well-dressed, quite beautiful American woman got out of the car and watched the captain take a suitcase from the trunk.

She walked with him as he walked to the brigadier general. They exchanged salutes. The general shook hands with the captain and the Naval officer. The captain touched the cheek of the *goddamn* beautiful woman, and then she threw herself into his arms, and he held her for a moment.

Then he and the naval officer walked to the airplane and went up the ladder. The general put his arm around the beautiful woman in a fatherly, comforting manner.

The Navy officer who'd told them they could wait in the shade appeared at the door of the airplane and waved at USMC Platoon Aug9-2 (Provisional), signaling them that it was now time for them to reboard the aircraft.

They did so.

McCoy leaned across Taylor and waved at Ernie, although he was reasonably sure that she couldn't see him.

"That's tough on you, isn't it, Ken?" Taylor asked, thoughtfully. "Having her here, and you commuting to the war?"

"What about the Air Force guys?" McCoy responded. "They do it every day: 'How was your day, honey?' 'Oh, I bombed a couple of bridges, shot up a convoy, took a little antiaircraft in my landing gear, and had to land wheels-up. Nothing special. How about you?' 'My day was just awful. Ellsworth, Junior, kicked Marybelle Smith, Colonel Smith's little girl, and you have to call Mrs. Smith and apologize. The battery's dead in the car, and the PX doesn't know when they're going to get the right one. They want you on the PTA committee, and I didn't know how to tell them no—' "

He was interrupted by the roar of the engines as the pilot set the throttles to takeoff power, but Taylor had heard enough to laugh.

The R5D began its takeoff roll.

When McCoy decided that the roar of the engine had gone down enough for Taylor to hear him, McCoy said:

"All we have to worry about now is (one) whether Jennings and the other guys and the stuff from Pusan made it to Sasebo, and (two) whether we'll be allowed to take them and it with us on the destroyer. I wish the general had been able to come to Sasebo. People usually find it hard to say 'no' to generals."

"I wonder what the hell Howe's doing for so long in Korea?" Taylor asked. Howe being in Korea was the reason Pickering had to stay in Tokyo.

McCoy shrugged.

"I don't know. But whatever it is, he thinks it's important. He's a good man."

"I think Jennings will be waiting for us at Sasebo," Taylor said. "The Marine guy at K-1 . . . ?"

"Captain Overton," McCoy furnished.

Taylor nodded and went on: ". . . told me that a lot, probably most, of the Air Force and Navy transports that land at K-1 don't fuel up there. They head for Sasebo, which is both the closest field for large aircraft, and has a pretty good off-the-tanker-and-into-the-airplanes fueling setup. K-1, you saw that, doesn't. They don't even have a decent tank farm for avgas. . . ."

"You are a fountain of information I really don't give a damn about, aren't you, Mr. Taylor?"

"You care about this, Mr. McCoy, because the aircraft that fly from K-1 to Sasebo to take on fuel are very often empty. That means Jennings will be able to find space for himself, the other jarheads, the camouflage nets, the rations, the medical supplies, and whatever else he stole from the Army aboard one of these empty airplanes headed for Sasebo."

"I stand corrected, sir," McCoy said.

"And I don't think Her Majesty's Navy's going to give us any trouble about taking Jennings, et cetera, aboard the *Charity* with us," Taylor said. "But let's say they do. . . ."

"In which case we're fucked. The Brits are going to give us lifeboats. You can't hide a lifeboat on Tokchok-kundo. And that means the North Koreans will learn sooner or later, probably sooner, that there're two lifeboats on Tokchok-kundo and start wondering why."

"In which case—I admit this is a desperate measure—we get General Pickering to get us an airplane to fly the stuff back to Pusan, and ship it to Tokchok-kundo on the *Wind of Good Fortune.*"

"I thought about that. There's a few little things wrong with it. If Pickering asks for an airplane, they'll want to know what for, and this is supposed to be a secret operation. And who would sail it?"

"Her. Sail *her.* Either of those two Koreans we had aboard is capable of sailing her to Tokchok-kundo."

"OK. Let's say we did that, and it worked. The *Wind of Good Fortune* couldn't make it to Tokchok-kundo until we'd been there—which means the lifeboats would have been there, exposed to the curious eyes of every sono-fabitch in the Flying Fish Channel—three or four, maybe five days—"

"Hi," someone said. "I'm Howard Dunwood."

McCoy turned and found himself looking at the smiling face of one of the Marine officers he'd seen waiting in the shade of the hangar at Haneda.

Three weeks before, Howard Dunwood had had a reserved parking spot for his top-of-the-line DeSoto automobile—identified as being reserved for "Salesman of the Month"—at Mike O'Brien's DeSoto-Plymouth in East Orange, New Jersey.

He had been just about to leave the dealership for an early-afternoon drink at the Brick Church Lounge & Grill—he was actually outside the showroom, about to get in his car—when there came a person-to-person long-distance telephone call for him.

A week after that, Captain Howard Dunwood, USMCR, had reported to the Replacement Battalion (Provisional) at Camp Joseph J. Pendleton, California. On 9 August, Dunwood had been given command of USMC Platoon Aug9-2.

High above the Pacific Ocean seventy-four hours later, as Trans-Global Airways Flight 1440 was nearing the end of its journey to Tokyo, Captain Dunwood had had the foresight aboard to slip into his utilities jacket pockets eight miniature bottles of Jack Daniels' sour mash bourbon.

You never know, he had reasoned, *when a little belt would be nice.*

He had consumed four of the miniatures at Camp Drake, two of them in the darkened auditorium during the motion picture portion of the chaplain's presentation. He had consumed two on the bus to Haneda, and the last two while in the shade of the hangar, waiting for the big shots to come so they could take off.

What the hell, the veteran of four World War II amphibious invasions—including Tawara and Iwo Jima—had reasoned, *why not? I suspect they're going to be shooting at me in Korea, and you don't want to be half-shitfaced when people are shooting at you.*

There were, of course, no refreshments of any kind aboard NATS Flight 2022, except for a water thermos mounted on the wall. But there was an illuminated "Fasten Seat Belts" sign, and when, several minutes into the flight, he had seen the light go off, Captain Howard C. Dunwood, USMCR, the commanding officer of USMC Platoon Aug9-2 (Provisional), had unfastened his seat belt and walked down the short aisle to the seats in which the two candy-asses in their neatly pressed uniforms were sitting.

He squatted in the aisle, smiled, and put out his hand.

"Hi," he said. "I'm Howard Dunwood."

"How are you?" McCoy said.

"You don't look like you're going to Korea."

"No, we're not," McCoy said.

"I sort of didn't think so," Dunwood said. "No weapons, and the wrong kind of uniform."

McCoy didn't reply.

"Stationed in Japan, are you? I couldn't help but notice the lady. Your wife, was she? Maybe the general's daughter?"

"What's on your mind, Captain?" McCoy asked.

"I'm just a little curious about you," Dunwood said. "We're both Marine officers, right?"

"OK, we're both Marine officers."

"Well, I was just wondering what the hell you're doing in Japan that's so important they hold up a plane taking Marines to Korea for more than an hour to wait for you."

"Captain, you've had a couple of drinks," McCoy said. "Why don't you go back to your seat and sleep them off before you get to Korea?"

"And why should I do that, you candy-ass sonofabitch?"

And then Captain Dunwood yelped in pain, and exclaimed, "God damn you!"

Taylor, who had been studiously ignoring the exchange between the two Marine officers—by looking out the window, from which he could see Mount Fuji—now snapped his head toward the aisle, and saw that McCoy had grabbed the index finger of the captain who had been squatting in the aisle looking for a fight, moved it behind his back, and forced him from his squatting position to his knees.

"OK. I'm a candy-ass and you're drunk," McCoy said. "Agreed?"

"Fuck you, candy-ass!"

Captain Dunwood then yelped in pain again, almost a shriek.

"Agreed?" McCoy asked.

"Agreed, OK. Agreed. Let go of my finger!"

Two other officers of Aug9-2 came down the aisle.

"What the hell?" one of them—a large lieutenant, who looked like a foot-ball tackle—asked.

McCoy let go of Dunwood's finger. Dunwood looked at the finger McCoy had held, then moved it, then yelped, not so loud this time, in pain.

"Take the captain back to his seat and make sure he stays there," McCoy ordered.

"What the hell happened?"

"Nothing happened. Just put him back in his seat before something does."

"Well, OK," the large lieutenant answered, a little reluctantly.

" 'Well, OK'? Is that the way you acknowledge an order?" McCoy snapped.

"No, sir. Aye, aye, sir."

The two lieutenants helped Dunwood to his feet—he was still staring at his hand in disbelief—and started him down the aisle.

"Jesus Christ," Taylor asked. "What the hell was that all about?"

"Nobody likes a candy-ass," McCoy said. "And you and I, to a bunch of Marines headed for Korea, look like candy-asses."

"Did you really break his finger?"

"I started to disjoint it," McCoy said, matter-of-factly. "It'll probably go back in by itself. If it doesn't, any corpsman can put it back in place."

"Jesus," Taylor said, chuckling.

"We were talking about how to hide the lifeboats, I think," McCoy said.

[TWO]
U.S. Navy Base Sasebo
Sasebo, Kyushu, Japan
1740 15 August 1950

Lieutenant Commander Darwin Jones-Fortin, RN, who was well over six feet tall, obviously weighed no more than 145 pounds, and was wearing a white open-collared shirt, white shorts, and white knee-high stockings, was standing outside the passenger terminal when McCoy and Taylor came down the ladder.

"I think that's our captain," Taylor said softly, as he started down the stairs.

"Let's hope my friend doesn't see him," McCoy said.

"If he's commanding a destroyer, he's no candy-ass," Taylor said.

"Appearances are often deceiving," McCoy said. "Didn't you ever hear that?"

When he saw Taylor and McCoy come down the ladder, Captain Darwin-Jones walked toward them from the passenger terminal and met them halfway.

"I suspect you two gentlemen are my supercargo," he said. "My name is Jones-Fortin."

"My name is Taylor, Captain," Taylor said, returning the salute and putting out his hand. "And this is Captain McCoy."

"Delighted to meet you both," Jones-Fortin said. "Captain, there's a Marine sergeant in there . . ."

Jones-Fortin nodded toward the terminal building.

". . . who asked if I was from *Charity.* I thought it a bit odd."

"Captain McCoy and I were just discussing the best way to bring this up to you, Captain." Taylor said.

"Let me make a stab in the dark," Jones-Fortin said. "You would like to bring him and that mountain of whatever that is."—he nodded his head toward a stack of crates and a camouflage net sitting next to the small passenger terminal—"wherever you're going."

McCoy smiled.

"You don't know where we're going, Captain?" he asked.

"I was under the impression that it was a military secret," Jones-Fortin said.

"Yes, we really would, sir," Taylor said. "Will that be possible?"

"I've had a chance to think about that," Jones-Fortin said. "I believe it falls within my orders from Admiral Matthews to make *Charity* as useful as possible."

"Thank you, Captain," Taylor said. "That's a large weight off our shoulders."

"I made discreet inquiries," Jones-Fortin said. "There are apparently three Marines in addition to the one I spoke with."

"Let me see what's going on, sir," McCoy said, and started toward the terminal.

As he did, Technical Sergeant J. M. Jennings, USMC, came out and saluted.

"Well, I see you made it here," McCoy said.

"It was easy, Captain," Jennings replied. "There's a lot of transports leaving K-1 empty that come here. . . ."

"I know," McCoy said, smiling. "How'd you know about the *Charity?*"

"I went out to the wharfs," Jennings said. "And there was this Limey destroyer, and swabbies lashing a couple of lifeboats to her."

"You are a clever man, Sergeant Jennings," McCoy said. "And where're the other guys?"

"In the Metropole Hotel, sir. I thought it better to get them off the base."

"How'd you know about the hotel?"

"I was here before, sir, in '48. I was the gunny of the Marines on board the *Midway.*"

"OK. Come with me, I'll introduce you to the captain of the *Charity.* And don't use the word 'Limey.' "

"Aye, aye, sir."

"Ah, yes," Lieutenant Commander Jones-Fortin said, "the Hotel Metropole. If I may make a suggestion, gentlemen?"

"Of course, sir," Taylor said.

"Your people here were kind enough to provide me with a lorry. A weapons carrier, I believe you call them?"

"Yes, sir."

"I propose that we load your matériel onto the lorry. I think it will hold it all. Then we will drop you gentlemen and the sergeant off at the Metropole. Then I will have the matériel loaded aboard *Charity*. When it is dark, I will have you picked up at the Metropole. I would be pleased if you were to join me for dinner at the Officers' Club, and after that, we can board *Charity.*"

"That's fine, Captain, except that we insist you be our guest at dinner," Taylor said.

"We can argue that later," Jones-Fortin said. "Shall we deal with whatever it is?"

[THREE]

There was a neatly lettered sign mounted on the wall next to the reception desk in the Hotel Metropole.

> # IMPORTANT NOTICE !!!
>
> ### ALL LADIES USED IN THE HOTEL
> ## MUST BE
> ### PROVIDED BY THE MANAGEMENT!!!
>
> ## NO EXCEPTIONS
> #### THANK YOU.
> #### THE MANAGEMENT

Technical Sergeant J. M. Jennings, USMC, opened the door to Room 215 and bellowed, *"Ah-ten-hut on deck"* just before Captain McCoy and Lieutenant Taylor marched in.

There is something essentially ludicrous in the sight of three naked men standing rigidly at attention, especially when two of the three have naked Japanese women hanging from their necks, and Captain McCoy was not able to resist the temptation to smile.

"As you were," he managed to say, which caused the two Marines with the ladies dangling from their necks to disengage themselves and all three Marines to quickly attempt to cover their genital areas with their hands.

Captain McCoy found it necessary to cough; Lieutenant Taylor found it necessary to turn and look through the door.

"Lieutenant Taylor and I are pleased to see that you've taken advantage of your spare time to sample the cultural delights of Sasebo," McCoy said. "But all good things must come to an end."

The three Marines looked at him, stone-faced.

"Shortly after dark, a weapons carrier will be here to take—"

"I like the Marine," one of the ladies said to one of her sisters, speaking, of course, in Japanese."

"Thank you very much," McCoy replied, in Japanese. "And I like you, too, but I am a married man."

All three ladies tittered behind their hands.

"So what?" the first lady asked.

"My wife is much stronger and larger than I am, and when she is angry she beats me severely," McCoy said.

All three ladies tittered delightedly again, and Taylor laughed. The three Marines looked baffled and very curious.

". . . as I was saying before the lady asked me if all Marines have dongs the size of their little fingers, or whether you three were just shortchanged—"

"She didn't ask that," one of the Marines challenged, seriously. "Did she, sir?"

"You don't think I made that up, do you, Sergeant?"

After a long moment, the sergeant said, "No, sir, I guess not."

He looked at his lady, then dropped his eyes to his genitals.

"As I was saying," McCoy went on, "a weapons carrier will be here shortly after dark to take us where we are going. I don't think the chow there will be as good as the chow Sergeant Jennings tells me you can get here. Your choice. But you're finished with the booze, and in an hour, you will be all dressed and sober and with all the bills paid. Are there any questions?"

All three said, "No, sir."

"You have anything, Mr. Taylor?"

"I think you covered everything," Taylor said.

"Sergeant Jennings?"

"No, sir."

"In that case, men, carry on," McCoy said. "I will see you in an hour."

He did an about-face and marched out of the room, with Taylor and Jennings marching after him.

[FOUR]
Aboard HMS *Charity*
33 Degrees 10 Minutes North Latitude, 129 Degrees 63
Minutes East Longitude
(The East China Sea)
0635 16 August 1950

Lieutenant Commander Darwin Jones-Fortin, RN, saw the face of Lieutenant David R. Taylor, USNR, peering through the round window in the interior bulkhead. He waved at him, then pointed first at the door in the bulkhead—Taylor nodded his understanding—and then at the sailor standing behind the helmsman, indicating that he should go to the door and help undog it.

Undogged and unlatched, the heavy steel door swung open as *Charity* buried her bow in the sea, and it was all the sailor could do to hold it. Taylor came onto the bridge and leaned against the bulkhead, then was followed by McCoy.

"Permission to come on the bridge, sir?" Taylor called out.

"Permission granted," Jones-Fortin said. "Both of you."

Taylor waited until the moment was right, then came quickly across the deck to where Jones-Fortin sat in his captain's chair. McCoy followed him. The ship moved, and McCoy half slid, half fell across the deck, ending up crashing into Taylor.

"Smooth as a millpond, what?" Jones-Fortin said. "Seriously, is this weather going to be a problem? I'm afraid we're in for a bit of it. Possibly, very possibly, worse than what we're getting now."

"Are we?" Taylor said.

"And *Charity* is of course a destroyer," Jones-Fortin added. "She doesn't ride as well as the *Queen Mary,* or, come to think of it, better than any other man-of-war that comes to mind."

"Try a destroyer escort sometime, Captain," Taylor said. "Or even better, an LST. Although calling an LST a man-of-war is stretching the term considerably."

"Is that the voice of experience speaking?"

"I had a DE during the war," Taylor said. "And LSTs since."

"I was the first lieutenant on a DE some time ago. I've always thought the RN assigned to DEs people they hoped would get washed over the side. I've never been aboard an LST in weather."

"Truth being stranger than fiction, when I was sailing LSTs through these waters after the war," Taylor said, "I used to think back fondly on the smooth sailing characteristics in rough seas of the *Joseph J. Isaacs,* DE-403. In weather like this, the movement of an LST has to be experienced to be believed."

"I wonder how my men took to waking up in a storm like this," McCoy said. "They were still feeling pretty good when we came aboard."

"Didn't someone once say, 'the wages of sin are death'?" Jones-Fortin said. "I suspect that a number of my crew are in the same shape."

McCoy chuckled.

"But I'm afraid, McCoy," Jones-Fortin went on, "that I have to correct you. This isn't the storm. This is what they call 'the edges' of the storm. The storm itself is further north, coming down from China into the Yellow Sea."

"Right on our course to Inchon, right?" Taylor said.

"I'm afraid so," Jones-Fortin said. "There's an overlay of the latest weather projection on the chart. Perhaps you'd like to have a look. We have a decision to make."

He indicated the chart room, aft of the wheel.

"Thank you, sir," Taylor said, and went for a look.

"Did you see what I saw?" Jones-Fortin asked when Taylor returned.

"I think so, sir," Taylor said, and turned to McCoy: "Ken, the way the storm is moving—and as the captain said, it's a bad one—I don't think we can put the boats over the side tomorrow morning. And maybe not even the morning after that."

"You mean it would be risky, or we just can't do it?"

"Tomorrow, we just can't do it. Period. The morning after that, maybe, with more of a chance of something going wrong than I like."

"So what do we do?" McCoy asked.

"That's up to Captain Jones-Fortin," Taylor said.

"It's a bit over six hundred miles," Jones-Fortin said. "I think *Charity* can make fifteen knots, even through the storm. A little less when it gets as bad as I suspect it's going to get, a bit more when there are periods of relative calm. That would put us off the Flying Fish Channel lighthouse in forty hours— sometime before midnight on 18 August. As Mr. Taylor saw, the storm will still be in the area at that time. Whether or not it will have subsided enough for us to safely put the boats over the side—or for you to be able to safely make Tokchok-kundo in them—by 0300 of the nineteenth is something we won't know until then."

"And if it doesn't clear, sir, then what?" McCoy asked.

"Then we shall have to spend the daylight hours of the nineteenth steaming in wide circles offshore. Or, for that matter, we could steam farther south, to the northern edge of the storm, and follow its movement southward and see where we are, and when."

"You mean we would move at the speed of the storm, sir?" McCoy asked.

"It's moving now," Taylor said, "somewhere between fifteen and twenty miles an hour."

"As we followed it, we'd be out of it?" McCoy asked.

"That would depend, Ken," Taylor said, tolerantly, as if explaining something to a backward child, "on how close we were to it as we followed it."

"I will, of course, defer to the judgment of Captain Jones-Fortin," McCoy said. "And even to yours, Mr. Taylor. But if there were some way we could get out of the storm, that would be this landlubber's choice."

"Well, Mr. Taylor," Captain Jones-Fortin said, "another option would be to steam on a east-northeasterly course, hoping to find calmer waters on the storm's eastern edge."

"Your decision, of course, Captain," Taylor said, but his tone of voice made it clear what he hoped Jones-Fortin's decision would be.

"Then that's what we'll do," Jones-Fortin said.

"What that means, Ken," Taylor said, "is that it probably won't get much worse than it is now."

"Wonderful," McCoy said.

[FIVE]
Aboard HMS *Charity*
39 Degrees 06 Minutes North Latitude, 123 Degrees 25
  Minutes East Longitude
(The Yellow Sea)
0405 19 August 1950

"Have a look at that, Mr. McCoy," Captain Jones-Fortin said, pointing out the spray-soaked window of the bridge. "What is it they say, 'all good things come to those who wait'?"

There was a bright glow of light coming through the cloud cover.

"Is that the northern edge of the storm?" McCoy said.

"Not exactly," Jones-Fortin said. "We are *in* the northern edge of the storm—I'm sure you will not be much surprised to learn that the weather people have finally decided what we have been steaming through is a hurricane—and that light you see is dawn coming up over what I devoutly hope will be calm waters."

"Me, too."

The *Charity* didn't seem to be tossing as much as she had been for the past forty hours, but McCoy wasn't sure if this was the case, or wishful thinking.

Ten minutes later, Jones-Fortin turned to McCoy again.

"Master mariner that I am, Mr. McCoy, it is my professional judgment that in, say, ten minutes, it will be safe to step into my shower and have a wash and a shave. If you feel a similar need, may I suggest you go to your cabin, and then join me for breakfast in the wardroom in twenty minutes?"

"Thank you, sir."

"If you'd be so kind, ask Mr. Taylor to join us."

"Yes, sir, of course."

Jones-Fortin raised his voice. "Number One, you have the conn. I will be in my cabin."

"Aye, aye, sir."

"If, in your judgment, the situation continues to improve, in ten minutes order the mess to prepare the breakfast meal."

"Aye, aye, sir."

Twenty minutes later, McCoy and Taylor walked into the wardroom. Jones-Fortin was already there, wearing a fresh, crisply starched uniform of open-collared white shirt, shorts, and knee-length white socks. Taylor was in his usual washed soft khakis, and McCoy in Marine Corps utilities.

A white-jacketed steward handed them a neatly typed breakfast menu the moment they sat down, and poured tea from a silver pitcher for them.

A moment later, another steward delivered what McCoy at first thought was breakfast for all of them. But he set the entire contents of his tray—toast, six fried eggs on one plate, and a ten-inch-wide, quarter-inch-thick slice of ham on another—before the captain, then turned to McCoy and Taylor.

"And what can I have Cooky prepare for you, gentlemen?"

They gave him their order.

"Shortly after joining His Majesty's Navy," Jones-Fortin said, as he stuffed a yolk-soaked piece of toast into his mouth, "I learned that the hoary adage, 'If you keep your stomach full, you do not suffer from mal de mer,' did not apply at all to Midshipman the Honorable Darwin Jones-Fortin. Quite the contrary. If I eat so much as a piece of dry toast in weather such as we have just experienced, I turn green and am out of the game. I trust you will forgive this display of gluttony. I haven't had a thing to eat since we left Sasebo."

"I haven't been exactly hungry myself, sir," McCoy said.

"On the subject of food," Jones-Fortin said. "Is there anything we can give you from *Charity's* stores to better the fare on Tokchok-kundo?"

"You're very kind, Captain," Taylor said.

"Bread, sir," McCoy said. "The one thing I really miss when I'm . . . I really miss fresh bread."

"I'll see to it."

"When do you think we'll be getting to the Flying Fish, sir?" Taylor asked.

"It's about two hundred twenty miles. The storm is moving southward at about fifteen knots. That should put us off the lighthouse somewhere around 2100. It'll be dark then, and I think the seas will have subsided."

"But how would we find Tokchok-kundo in the dark?" McCoy asked. "The original idea was to head for shore in the dark, but to arrive there as it was getting light."

"And I think we had best stick to that, too," Taylor said. "I don't want to try running in the channel in the dark."

"Then that means we'll have to arrange things to arrive at the original hour."

"Three days late," McCoy said.

"Unfortunately," Jones-Fortin agreed.

"They'll be worried about us," McCoy said. "On Tokchok-kundo and in Tokyo."

"They'll know, of course, about the storm," Jones-Fortin said. "Tokchok-kundo's been in it."

"And General Pickering will be worried about that, too," McCoy said.

"He does have quite a bit on his plate, doesn't he?" Jones-Fortin said.

There was something in his voice that made McCoy look at him.

"It came out somehow," Jones-Fortin said. "Fitz—Tony Fitzwater, my brother-in-law—said that Sir William had heard that General Pickering's son had gone down."

"That's right," McCoy said.

"That's rotten luck," Jones-Fortin said. "It must be really tough for a senior officer to lose a son. I mean, more so than for someone not in the service."

"There's a chance that Pick—Major Malcolm Pickering, who's my best friend—"

"Oh, God, I am treading on glass, aren't I?" Jones-Fortin interrupted.

"—may walk through raindrops again," McCoy finished.

"Oh?"

"There's some reason to believe he survived the crash," McCoy said. "I think he has. He's done that before. And is running around behind the enemy's lines waiting for someone to come get him before the North Koreans capture him."

"And they really can't go looking for him, can they?" Jones-Fortin said, sympathetically.

"If I wasn't on my way to Tokchok-kundo, I'd be looking for him," McCoy said.

"I thought, when we were in Pusan, that you told Dunston to ratchet up the search operation?" Taylor said. "You don't think that's going to work?"

"That was a tough call," McCoy said. "I don't know who Dunston's agents are, or who they're working for. Agents have been known to change sides. Ratcheting up the search also ratcheted up the risk that the North Koreans will learn we're looking for someone, and they would know we would only be running an operation like this for someone important. All I may have done is ratchet up the search for him by the North Koreans, if they even had one going. Or, if they've already caught him, it would let them know they have an important prisoner."

"And yet you ordered this . . . search?" Jones-Fortin asked.

McCoy nodded.

"I decided if I was in his shoes . . ."

"Tough call, Ken," Taylor said. "But I'd have made the same one."

"I rather think that I would have, too," Jones-Fortin said. "Thank God, I didn't have to."

[SIX]
Aboard HMS
37 Degrees 41 Minutes North Latitude, 126 Degrees 58
Minutes East Longitude
(The Yellow Sea)
0405 20 August 1950

HSM *Charity* was dead in the water.

Captain the Honorable Darwin Jones-Fortin, RN, in starched and immaculate white uniform, Lieutenant (j.g) David R. Taylor, USNR, and Captain K. R. McCoy, USMCR—both in Marine utilities—were on her flying bridge, looking down to the main deck where, in the glare of floodlights, a work gang was loading the supplies into the two lifeboats bobbing alongside.

The work was being supervised by a wiry chief petty officer, also in immaculate whites, who stood no taller than five feet three and weighed no more than 120 pounds, but whose bull-like "instructions" to his work detail could be easily heard on the flying bridge.

"I've always felt," Captain Jones-Fortin said, "that this sort of thing is best handled by a competent petty officer; that the only thing an officer attempting to supervise the accomplishment of something about which he knows very little does is to create confusion."

"How about 'chaos,' sir?" McCoy replied.

"The voice of experience, Captain?" Jones-Fortin asked, dryly.

"Unfortunately," McCoy said. "I can still remember some spectacular examples from my days as a corporal."

The chief jumped nimbly into one of the lifeboats, started its engine, motioned for two of the Marines standing on the deck to get into the boat, waited until they were in it, sitting where he thought they should be sitting, and then he nimbly moved to the second boat and—this time with some difficulty—got the engine started.

He motioned for the other two Marines on deck to get into the boat, seated them, then looked up toward the flying bridge.

"We seem to be ready for the officers, Captain," he called, in a deep voice that did not need the amplification of a bullhorn.

"They will be down directly," Jones-Fortin called. "Good show, Chief!"

Jones-Fortin offered his hand first to Taylor and then to McCoy.

"Best of luck," he said. "We'll see you soon again."

The chief watched from the deck as Taylor—nimbly—and McCoy—very carefully—both got into one boat.

Taylor checked McCoy out on the engine controls again, then signaled to the chief to let loose the lines. Then, very carefully, he took the tiller and moved the boat alongside the second.

"Just follow me, Ken," he said. "You steered the *Wind of Good Fortune*—you can steer this."

McCoy nodded and took the tiller.

Taylor jumped into the second boat, signaled for its lines to be let loose, and then shoved it away from *Charity*'s hull with a shove with his foot. Then he took the tiller, advanced the throttle, and moved away from *Charity*.

McCoy waited until ten feet separated the boats, then advanced his throttle.

The floodlights went out a moment later. It took McCoy's eyes what seemed like a very long time to adjust to the darkness. When they had, he saw that Taylor's boat was getting farther away.

He eased the throttle forward a hair.

Moments after that, Jones-Fortin's amplified voice called, "Godspeed, gentlemen!" across the darkness.

When McCoy looked over his shoulder, he could barely see HMS *Charity*.

Thirty minutes later, a bump on the just barely visible horizon changed slowly into the lighthouse at the entrance to the Flying Fish Channel.

And thirty minutes after that—by then it was light—the houses on the shore of Tokchok-kundo came into view. As they came closer, the damage the storm had caused became visible.

The roofs of two of the houses were gone, and the doors and windows of most of them.

They were almost at the wharf before anyone appeared, and then it was Master Gunner Ernest W. Zimmerman, USMC.

He stood on the wharf and saluted as Lieutenant Taylor skillfully brought his lifeboat up it, and managed to keep a straight face when the boat conned by Captain McCoy rammed into Taylor's boat, knocking Taylor off his feet.

XIX

The two-starred red flag of a major general flew from a small staff on the right front fender of the glistening olive-drab Buick staff car. Even before it stopped before the main entrance of the Dai Ichi Building, a captain of what was usually referred to as the Honor Guard—or, less respectfully, as the Palace Guard, and, even less respectfully, as the "Chrome Domes"—sent two members of the guard trotting quickly down the stairs so they would be in position to open the staff car's doors when it stopped.

The "Chrome Domes" appellation made reference to the chrome-plated steel helmets worn by the troops who guarded the headquarters of the Supreme Commander, and the Supreme Commander himself. The rest of their uniforms were equally splendiferous. They wore infantry blue silk scarves in the open necks of their form-fitting and stiffly starched khaki shirts. Their razor-creased khaki trousers were "bloused" neatly into the tops of glistening parachutist's boots. This was accomplished by using the weight of a coiled spring inside the leg to hold the trousers in place.

Not all of the Chrome Domes were parachutists entitled to wear Corcoran "jump" boots. The basic criteria for their selection was that they be between five feet eleven and six feet one in height, between 165 and 190 pounds in weight, and possessed of what the selection officers deemed to be a military carriage and demeanor.

The standard-issue boot for nonparachutists was known as the "combat boot." It consisted of a rough-side-out ankle-high shoe, to which was sewn a smooth-side-out upper with two buckles.

The combat boot was practical, of course, but the rough-side-out boot was difficult to shine, and it was not really suited to be part of the uniform of the elite troops selected to guard the Supreme Commander and his headquarters, and jump boots were selected to replace them.

The brown laces of the Corcoran boots were also replaced, with white nylon cord salvaged from parachutes no longer considered safe to use. The "laces" were worn in an elaborate crossed pattern.

Officers of the Palace Guard wore Sam Browne leather belts, which had gone out of use in the U.S. Army in the early days of World War II. Enlisted members of the Chrome Domes wore standard pistol belts, but they were painted white, as were the accoutrements thereof—the leather pistol holster, and two pouches for spare pistol magazines.

The Buick stopped. The doors were opened, and three men got out. One of them was Colonel Sidney Huff, senior aide to General Douglas MacArthur. He was in his usual splendidly tailored tropical worsted tunic and blouse, from which hung all the especial insignia decreed for the uniform of an aide-de-camp to a five-star general. Colonel Huff was not armed.

The second man out of the Buick was wearing somewhat soiled fatigues and mud-splattered combat boots, into which the hem of his trousers had not been stuffed. The chevrons of a master sergeant were sewn to his sleeves. He was armed with a Model 1928 Thompson .45 ACP Caliber submachine gun and a Model 1911A1 Pistol, Caliber .45 ACP, worn in a shoulder holster. The pockets of his fatigue jacket bulged with spare magazines for both weapons.

The third man was dressed identically to the master sergeant—including jacket pockets bulging with spare magazines—with these exceptions: He was carrying a Submachine Gun, M3, Caliber .45 ACP, instead of a Thompson. The M3, developed in World War II, was built cheaply of mostly stamped parts, and was known as a "grease gun" because it looked like a grease gun. And instead of chevrons indicating enlisted rank, there were two silver stars on each of his fatigue jacket collar points.

Major General Ralph Howe, NGUS, returned the salute of the Chrome Dome holding open his door and started to follow Colonel Huff up the stairs and into the Dai Ichi Building. Master Sergeant Charley Rogers brought up the rear.

Standing just outside the door itself were six more Chrome Domes and the Chrome Dome officer, already saluting, and two more were holding the door itself open.

"Perhaps," Colonel Huff said, in the Supreme Commander's outer office, "it would be best if you left your weapons with your sergeant."

"Colonel, I really hadn't planned to shoot General MacArthur," Howe said. He handed Rogers the grease gun, but made no move with regard to his pistol.

"Colonel, how about seeing if you can have someone send something up here for Charley to eat? Neither one of us could handle the powdered eggs they were feeding at K-1."

Huff's face tightened.

"Yes, sir," he said, then went to the right of the double doors, knocked twice, and pushed it open before Howe heard a reply.

"General, Major General Howe," Huff announced.

He indicated that Howe should enter the office.

MacArthur, who was behind his desk in his washed-soft khaki, tieless uniform, rose as Howe entered the room. Howe saluted. MacArthur returned it, then came around the desk and offered Howe his hand.

"Thank you for coming so soon, General," MacArthur said. "I didn't think, frankly, it would be *this* soon."

"I came right from the airport, sir. Your colonel, at Haneda, said you wanted to see me 'at my earliest convenience.' Coming from you, I interpreted that you meant you wanted to see me immediately."

"I would have understood certainly that you might have taken time to freshen yourself," MacArthur said.

"If I had known that, sir, I would have stopped for breakfast," Howe said.

"Can I get you something here?" MacArthur asked.

"General, I would just about kill for a fried-egg sandwich, a glass of milk, and a cup of coffee."

Howe saw the look of surprise that flashed across MacArthur's face.

I was supposed to say, "No thank you, sir, but thank you just the same." Right? You're not supposed to order a snack in El Supremo's office, right?

MacArthur turned and pushed a button on the desk.

Colonel Huff appeared immediately.

"Huff, have the mess send a fried-egg sandwich—make that two; no, make it three, I'm suddenly hungry myself—a glass of milk, and coffee up, will you, please?"

Colonel Huff wasn't entirely able to keep his face from registering surprise.

"Right away, General," he said.

"It should be here shortly," MacArthur said. "Is it too early in the morning for you, General, for a cigar?"

"It's never too early or too late for a good cigar or a good woman, sir," Howe said.

MacArthur laughed, then turned to his desk again, picked up a small humidor, and offered it to Howe. Howe took one of the long, black, thin cigars, sniffed it, then rolled it between his fingers.

"Philippine," MacArthur said. "I smoked them all through the war, courtesy of our friend Pickering."

"How's that, sir?"

"The *Pacific Princess* brought one of the first troop shipments to Australia shortly after we arrived there. Fleming, in his role as commodore of the P & FE Fleet, emptied her humidor of cigars and enough of that scotch he drinks . . ."

"Famous Grouse, sir," Howe furnished.

". . . and I now do . . . to carry the both of us for the rest of the war."

He's going out of his way to make the point that he and Pickering are pals. I wonder where that's leading?

MacArthur handed him first a cutter, then a lighter.

"Very nice," Howe said after taking his first puff. "Thank you."

MacArthur made a deprecating gesture.

"I had occasion several times while you were in Korea—about every time that Colonel Huff stuck his head in the door to tell me you were still there—to reflect on those times, and the role of the aide-de-camp in the army."

Howe looked at him and waited for him to go on.

"This is in no way a reflection on Colonel Huff—I don't know what I'd do without him—but I thought that his role as my aide-de-camp represents a considerable change from the role of aides-de-camp in the past, and from your, and Fleming Pickering's, roles here. And during World War Two."

"How is that, sir?"

Here it comes, but what the hell is it?

"Think about it, Howe. Napoleon's aides-de-camp—for that matter, probably those of Hannibal, marching with his elephants into the Pyrenees in 218—were far more than officers who saw to their general's comfort. They were his eyes and his ears, and when they were in the field, they spoke with his authority."

"Neither General Pickering nor I have any authority, General, to issue orders to anyone," Howe argued.

"The difference there is that when one of Hannibal's aides was in the field, he was not in communication with Hannibal. You are in communication with our Commander-in-Chief. Pickering was in private communication with President Roosevelt all through the war until Roosevelt died. If he then, or you now, told me it was the President's desire that I do, or not do, thus and so, I would consider it an order."

Where the hell is he going?

"I can't imagine that happening, General," Howe said.

"Neither can I," MacArthur said. "The other difference being that if the commander-in-chief wishes to issue an order to me, or anyone else, directly, he now has the means to do so. But that wasn't really the point of this."

OK. Finally, here it comes.

"Oh?"

"I was leading up to the other function of aides-de-camp: being the commander's eyes and ears. Has it occurred to you that that's what you're doing? You and Pickering?"

"Yes, sir. It has. Our mission is to report to the President anything he tells us to look into, or what we see and hear that we feel would interest him."

"Of course, Fleming Picking has the additional duty—or maybe it's his primary duty; it doesn't matter here for the moment—of running the CIA and its covert intelligence, and other operations."

"That's true, sir," Howe said.

OK. Now we have a direction. I think.

There was a knock at the door, and a white-jacketed Japanese entered bearing a tray on which was a silver coffee set and a plate covered with a silver dome.

"Our egg sandwiches, I believe," MacArthur said. "Just set that on the table please."

"That was quick," Howe said.

"It's nice to be the Emperor," MacArthur said, straight-faced, and then when he saw the look on Howe's face, suddenly shifting into a broad smile, showing he had made a little joke.

"I suppose it is, sir."

"I am a soldier, nothing more," MacArthur said. "And I really have done my best to discourage people from thinking I am anything more, and more important, that I think I am."

I don't know whether to believe that or not. But I guess I do.

MacArthur lifted the dome over the plate.

"Help yourself," he said. "They are much better when hot."

"Thank you, sir."

"They take me back to West Point," MacArthur said. "My mother had the idea I wasn't being properly nourished in the cadet mess, and when I went to see her at night in the Hotel Thayer, she would have egg sandwiches sent up."

Howe remembered hearing that MacArthur's mother had lived in the Hotel Thayer at West Point during all of his four years there. He had a sudden mental image of a photograph he had once seen of Douglas MacArthur as a cadet.

He looked like an arrogant sonofabitch then, too. And a little phony. How many other cadets were coddled by their mothers, and fed fried-egg sandwiches at night?

And why did he tell me that?

Ralph, you're out of your league with this man. Watch yourself!

The Supreme Commander Allied Powers in Japan and United Nations Command thrust most of a triangular piece of fried-egg sandwich into a wide-open mouth, chewed appreciatively, and announced.

"Very nice. I'm glad you thought of this, Howe."

"I learned to really loathe powdered eggs during the war," Howe said. "That was the menu at K-1."

"Not a criticism of you, of course, Howe, but whenever I am served something I don't like, I remember when we were down to a three-eighths ration on Bataan and Corregidor, and suddenly I am not so displeased."

Was that simply an observation, or is he reminding me that I am eating a fried-egg sandwich in the presence of the Hero of Bataan and Corregidor?

"Powdered eggs aside, I ate better in Korea just now than I often ate in Italy," Howe said.

"That's good to hear, Howe, and it actually brings us to the point of this somewhat rambling conversation we've been having."

Is this it, finally?

"What occurred to me, Howe," MacArthur went on, "is that Hannibal, Napoleon, and Roosevelt had—and President Truman now has—something I don't, and, I am now convinced, I really should have."

"What's that, sir?"

"And, come to think of it, that General Montgomery was wise enough to have during his campaigns in the Second War: experienced, trusted officers—aides-de-camp in the historical sense of the term—who moved around the battlefield as his eyes and ears, and reported to him what they thought he should know, as differentiated from telling him what they think he would like to hear."

"Yes, sir, I suppose that's true."

"I don't know where I am going to find such officers to fulfill that role for me—it will have to be someone who is not presently on my staff—but I will. And just as soon as I can."

Here it comes.

But what did that "it will have to be someone who is not presently on my staff" crack mean?

"I'm sure that you would that useful, sir."

"In the meantime, Howe, with the understanding that I am fully aware that your reports to President Truman enjoy the highest possible level of confidentiality, and that I would not ask you to violate that confidence in any way, I sent Colonel Huff to Haneda to ask you to come to see me in the hope that you would be able to share with me what you saw, and felt, in Korea."

The sonofabitch wants me to tell him what I'm reporting to Truman. Jesus Christ!

"I can see on your face that the idea makes you uncomfortable, Howe, and I completely understand that. Let me bring you up-to-date on what has happened since you've been in Korea, to give you an idea what I'm interested in, and then I will ask you some questions. If you feel free to answer them, fine. If you don't, I will understand."

"Yes, sir," Howe said.

"I don't think I managed to convince General Collins that the Inchon invasion is the wisest course of action to take—" MacArthur interrupted himself, went to his desk and pulled open a drawer, took out a radio teletype message, and then walked around the desk and handed it to Howe. "Read this, Howe."

It was an eight-paragraph Top Secret "Eyes Only MacArthur" message from the Joint Chiefs of Staff. MacArthur waited patiently until Howe had read it.

"Stripped of the diplomatic language, I think you will agree, Howe," MacArthur said, "that what that *doesn't* say is that the JCS approves of Inchon. That they agree with Collins that the invasion—and they don't even call it an 'invasion' but rather a 'turning operation'—should take place somewhere, preferably at Kunsan, but anywhere but Inchon."

"That's what it sounds like to me, sir," Howe agreed.

"But what it also *doesn't* say," MacArthur went on, "is that I am being denied permission to make the Inchon landing. That suggests to me, frankly, that someone in Washington is reluctant to challenge my judgment about Inchon— and that someone is the President himself. Who else could challenge the judgment of the Joint Chiefs of Staff but the President? And why would the President, absent advice he's getting from person or persons he trusts that I'm right about Inchon and General Collins is wrong, challenge the judgment of the JCS?"

I'll be damned. He knows—doesn't know, but has figured out—that Pickering and I both messaged Truman that we think the Inchon invasion makes sense.

"I don't expect a reply to that, Howe," MacArthur said. "But let's say this: Absent orders to the contrary from the Commander-in-Chief, I will put ashore a two-division force at Inchon 15 September."

Howe looked at him, but didn't respond.

He must know that I'll message Truman that he said that. But Harry's no dummy. He knows that already.

"There are several interrelated problems connected with that," MacArthur said. "If you feel free to comment on them, I would welcome your observations. If you feel it would be inappropriate for you to do so, I will understand."

"Yes, sir?"

"The first deals with General Walker. I am sometimes, perhaps justifiably, accused of being too loyal to my subordinates. There has been some suggestion that otherwise I would have relieved General Walker."

"General, I'm not qualified to comment on the performance of an Army commander."

"All right, I understand your position. But I hope you can answer this one for me. General Almond, for whom I have great respect, feels he needs the First Marine Division to lead the invasion. That means taking the 1st Marine Brigade—which is, as you know, essentially the Fifth Marine Regiment, Reinforced—from Pusan, and assigning it—reassigning it—to the First Marine Division. General Walker, for whose judgment I have equal respect, states flatly that he cannot guarantee the integrity of his Pusan positions if he loses the 1st Marine Brigade to the invasion force—which has now been designated as X Corps, by the way. That problem is compounded by the fact that Generals Walker and Almond are not mutual admirers."

Howe looked at MacArthur without speaking.

"No comment again?" MacArthur asked.

"General, you're certainly not asking me for advice?"

"I suppose what I'm asking—the decision has been made, by the way—is what, if you were in my shoes, you would have done."

"I can only offer what any smart second lieutenant could suggest, General, that you had to make a decision between which was more important, a greater risk to the Pusan perimeter by pulling the Marines out of there, or a greater risk to the Inchon invasion because the Marines were short a regiment."

"And what do you think your hypothetical second lieutenant would decide?"

Howe met MacArthur's eyes for a moment before replying.

"To send the Marines to Inchon, sir."

"And Major General Howe, after seeing what he saw in the Pusan perimeter?"

"To send the Marines to Inchon, sir," Howe said.

"History will tell us, I suppose, whether the hypothetical second lieutenant, the aide-de-camp to the Commander-in-Chief, and the commander forced to make the decision were right, won't it? X Corps will land at Inchon with the full-strength First Marine Division as the vanguard."

MacArthur picked up the coffee pitcher and added some to Howe's cup, then refreshed his own.

"There's one more delicate question, Howe, that you may not wish to answer."

"Yes, sir?"

"It has come to the attention of my staff that our friend Fleming Pickering has mounted one of his clandestine operations. I don't know how reliable the information my staff has is, but there is some concern that it might in some way impact on Inchon."

In other words, Charley Willoughby's snoops have heard something—how much?—about the Flying Fish Channel operation. Why should that be a surprise? They've been following us around the way the KGB followed me around at Potsdam.

"I thought perhaps this operation might be connected with Pickering's son," MacArthur went on. "Who is not just a Marine aviator, but the son of the CIA's Director of Asian Operations."

So why don't you ask Pickering yourself?

"General Pickering doesn't tell me much about his CIA covert operations, General," Howe said. "But I'm sure there's more than one of them, any—or all—of which might have an impact on Inchon. If any of them did, I'm sure he would tell you."

"Well, perhaps after you tell him—you will tell him?—that the Inchon invasion is on, he'll come to me. If he has something to come to me with."

"I will tell him, General," Howe said.

MacArthur put his coffee cup down.

"Thank you for coming to see me, and with such alacrity," MacArthur said.

Well, I have just been dismissed.

How much did I give him that I should not have?

"I hope it was worth your time, General," Howe said.

MacArthur put his hand on Howe's shoulder and guided him to the door.

"Thank you again," he said, and offered him his hand.

Major General Charles A. Willoughby was in the outer office waiting to see MacArthur.

And probably to find out what MacArthur got from me.

"Come on, Charley," Howe said, looking at Willoughby, and waiting until Master Sergeant Charley Rogers had gotten quickly from his seat and handed him his grease gun before adding, "Good morning, General Willoughby."

[TWO]
Command Post
Company C, 2nd Battalion, 5th Marines
First Marine Brigade (Provisional)
Obong-Ni, The Naktong Bulge, South Korea
1155 20 August 1950

The battalion exec found Charley Company's commander lying in the shade of a piece of tenting half supported by poles and half by the wall of a badly shot-up stone Korean farmhouse.

The company commander's uniform was streaked with dried mud, and he was unshaven and looked like hell, which was, of course, to be expected under the circumstances. But nevertheless, when the company commander saw the battalion exec, he started to get up.

The exec gestured for him to stay where he was, dropped to his knees, and crawled under the canvas with him.

The company commander saluted, lying down, and the exec returned it.

"You look beat, Captain," the exec said.

"I guess I'm not used to this heat, sir."

"I don't think anybody is," the exec said. "It was a little cooler during the storm—"

He broke off when the captain's eyes told him he was monumentally uninterested in small talk.

"How badly were you hurt?" the exec asked, meaning the company, not the company commander personally.

"I lost a little more than half of my men, and two of my officers. Fourteen enlisted and one officer KIA. Some of those who went down went down with heat exhaustion."

The exec nodded.

At 0800, 2nd Battalion, 5th Marines had attacked North Korean positions on Obong-ni Ridge. There had been a preliminary 105-mm howitzer barrage, and a mortar barrage, on the enemy positions, after which the 5th had attacked across a rice paddy and then up the steep slopes of the ridge. In that attack, Company A had been in the van, with B Company following and C Company in reserve.

The colonel had thought that order of battle best, primarily because the Charley Company commander had been on the job only a couple of days.

The colonel had found it necessary to employ his reserve, for by the time

Able Company reached the crest of the ridge, more than half its men were down, either from enemy fire or heat exhaustion, and by the time Baker Company got there, they had lost a fifth of their men, mostly to exhaustion, and what was left was put to work carrying the dead and wounded off the slopes of the ridge, with Charley Company now needed to protect them.

And then the colonel had ordered everybody off Obong-ni Ridge when it was apparent to him that the men holding the crest were not going to be able to repel a North Korean counterattack.

Once everyone was back, reasonably safe, in the positions they had left to begin the attack, the artillery was called in again, and the mortars, and the North Korean positions on Obong-Ni Ridge again came under fire.

Following which, the 2nd Battalion attacked again, this time with what was left of Able and Baker Companies in the van, and with Charley Company following, and with Headquarters & Service Company in reserve.

By the time the 1st Marines again gained the crest of the hill, their strength had been reduced by forty percent, and Charley Company had lost almost that many, but there was enough of them left, in the colonel's judgment, so they stood a reasonable chance of turning the North Korean counterattack when it inevitably came, and he had ordered the Charley Company commander to take command of the Marines on the crest and defend it to the best of his ability.

Thirty minutes after the North Korean counterattack began, the colonel began receiving reports of the casualties suffered and of the ammunition running low. The colonel knew he didn't have the manpower to get ammunition in the quantities requested up the crest of Obong-ni Ridge.

He called Brigade and explained the situation. Brigade said the 1st Battalion would be immediately sent to the area, and as soon as they arrived, he had permission to order his Marines back off the hill. And ordered him to make every effort to see they brought their dead and wounded back with them.

Once back, they would reform. There were some replacements, not as many as he would like, but that was all there was, and they would be sent as soon as possible.

"Trucks are coming," the exec said. "They're having a hell of a time getting through the mud, but they'll be here shortly."

The company commander did not reply.

"They're bringing the noon meal, and some replacements," the exec said. "And following an artillery softening-up, 2nd Battalion will attack through the 1st at 1600. Charley Company will lead."

"Major, I have, counting me, two officers and a platoon and a half of men."

"You'll have some of the people who went down with the heat back by then, and as I say, some replacements."

"Aye, aye, sir," the company commander said.

"And the softening barrage may be more effective this time. We've been promised a bunch—including some 155-mm—from the Army, and half the ammunition will be fused for airburst, which should do a better job on the far slopes. And it will be TOT*."

"I wondered if anyone here had ever heard of airbursts, or thought about TOT," the company commander said.

"We're hurting them, too, Captain," the exec said.

"Yes, sir, but there seems to be a lot more of them than us," the company commander said.

"I'll be back before you move out. The 1st is up there. I don't think the NKs will try to come this way. Get the men as much rest as you can."

"Aye, aye, sir."

"You hurt your hand, Captain? You seem to be favoring it."

"My finger was hurt on the airplane on the way over here, sir. Little sore, nothing serious."

But if I ever see that candy-ass captain who did this to me again, I'm going to pull his arm off and shove it up his ass.

I wonder what that cocksucker's doing right now. Probably playing tennis with his wife, the general's daughter.

Goddamn the U.S. Marine Corps!

[THREE]
Tokchok-kundo Island
1215 20 August 1950

"A little problem, Mr. Zimmerman?" Captain McCoy asked, surveying what was left of the small stone, thatch-roofed building that had housed the small German diesel generator and, the last time McCoy had been there, the SCR-300 radio. "I would say we have a world-class, A Number One fucking problem."

There was nothing left of the building but three walls, one of them on the

---

*Time On Target. All artillery pieces fire their tubes at the same predetermined instant. Among other things, this takes the enemy by surprise, and keeps him from seeking shelter before more shells land. It also has an often terrifying psychological effect.

edge of falling over, and the generator, which now lay on its side. The floor of the building—and the generator—was covered with a six-inch-thick layer of foul-smelling mud.

"When the storm really started getting bad, we moved the SCR-300 up the hill," Zimmerman. "We didn't have the muscle to move the generator. By then, anyway, there was three feet of water in here. I mean all the time. When the waves hit, it was deeper; you had a hard time standing up."

Ernie means "I had a hard time standing up," McCoy decided. *I left him in charge, and he met that responsibility as best he could.*

He had a mental picture of the barrel-chested Marine gunner standing in water up to his waist trying to salvage something, anything, in the generator building from the fury of the storm.

"I guess the diesel fuel's gone, too? Even if we can get that generator running again."

Zimmerman nodded.

"Everything that wasn't up the hill got washed away," he said. "Including most of the ammo for the Jap weapons."

"What about food?"

"We moved the rations up the hill, including the rice the Koreans had. And a couple of their boats are left. They were starting to try to get them back in the water when we saw you. Major Kim says he thinks they can catch enough fish to feed them and us."

"Anybody get hurt?"

Zimmerman shook his head, "no."

"I was thinking that maybe if we hit one of their islands—Taemuui-do is closest—maybe they'd have some diesel fuel," Zimmerman said.

If they had diesel fuel in the first place, what makes you think they'd still have it? Taemuui-do and Yonghung-do got hit by the storm as hard as Tokchok-kundo did. And if we hit Taemuui-do now, and didn't hit Yonghung-do immediately afterward, when we finally did hit it, they'd be expecting an attack, and certainly would have reported that right after the storm somebody took Taemuui-do. They'd be curious as hell about that.

Dumb idea, Ernie.

"Do you think that diesel's going to run after being under water for hours?"

"We'll have to take it apart and make sure there's no water in the cylinders. And then who knows?"

"Let's hold off on getting diesel for a diesel engine we're not sure can be fixed," McCoy said.

Zimmerman nodded.

"There are engines in the lifeboats," McCoy said. "Can we use those to power the SCR-300?"

"Wrong voltage, I'll bet," Zimmerman said. "But maybe we can rig something."

"OK. First things first," McCoy ordered. "Put people to work helping Taylor unload the lifeboats, and then drag them on shore and get them covered. Then get the Korean fisherman's boats in the water. Send Major Kim with one of them. Maybe he see what the storm did to Taemuui-do and Yonghung-do."

"And then what?"

"Ernie, I don't have the faintest fucking idea," McCoy said. "Right now, it looks like we're stranded on this beautiful tropical island."

[FOUR]
The Dewey Suite
The Imperial Hotel
Tokyo, Japan
1315 20 August 1950

Major General Ralph Howe, NGUS, was sitting in one of the green leather armchairs in the sitting room when the door opened and Brigadier General Fleming Pickering walked in, trailed by Captain George F. Hart.

"I let myself in, Flem," Howe said. "I hope that's all right?"

"Don't be silly," Pickering said. "When did you get back?" He waved at Master Sergeant Rogers. "Hello, Charley."

"After hanging around K-1 most of last night waiting for a break in the storm, we finally got off, and landed at Haneda a little after eight," Howe said, and added, "where Colonel Sidney Huff was waiting for me, to tell me El Supremo would be pleased if I would join him at my earliest opportunity."

Pickering's lower lip came out momentarily.

"What was that all about?"

"I'm not sure I know," Howe said, "and I have been thinking about it ever since I was dismissed from the throne room. About the only thing I am sure about is that Willoughby is onto your Flying Fish Channel operation."

"I suppose that was inevitable. Is that what he called you in for, to ask you what you knew about that?"

"I don't know, Flem. Let me tell you what happened, and you tell me."

"Will it wait until I have my twelve hundred snort?" Pickering asked. He walked to the sideboard and picked up a bottle of Famous Grouse. "Would you like one?"

"Why not?" Howe said. "God knows I deserve one." Then he asked, " 'twelve hundred snort'?"

"I found that unless I went on a schedule, I was prone to keep nipping all day," Pickering said. "I think with a little effort, I could easily become an alcoholic."

"I don't believe that for a minute," Howe said. "You've had a lot on your mind, Flem."

"I have one at twelve," Pickering said, ignoring him, "another at five, a brandy after dinner, and sometimes a nightcap. That way, I can go to sleep reasonably sure of what my name is and where I am. Tell me about your session with El Supremo."

"Well," Howe said, and chuckled. "It began, if you can believe this, with a fried-egg sandwich, just like Mommy used to make for him when he was at West Point, and Hannibal's elephants . . ."

"I don't know either," Pickering said when Howe had finished. "It's entirely possible he wanted to hear what you might have to say about Korea. But more likely—now that I've had a minute to think about it—it was his back-channel response to the JCS message he showed you. I think it's significant that he showed it to you. He knows you report to the President, which means you'd report what he said, and what he said was that unless he is expressly forbidden to do so, he's going to ignore what Collins and the JCS think, and send two divisions ashore at Inchon on 15 September. He got his message to the President without sending the President a message through channels."

Howe grunted.

"That's what Charley thinks, too," he said, and added: "You've heard me observe that the true test of another man's intelligence is the degree to which he agrees with you? I seem to be surrounded by geniuses."

Pickering and Rogers chuckled.

"You don't think—maybe in addition to the above—that he wanted to send you an ever-so-subtle warning that he was onto your Flying Fish Channel operation? He said he was concerned about its possible 'impact' on Inchon. Maybe it's time for you to tell him about it?"

"I don't think the Flying Fish operation is going to have any impact on the Inchon invasion at all," Pickering said.

"I don't like what I think I'm hearing," Howe said.

"We have not heard from Zimmerman for four days," Pickering said. "Since his 0730 call on the sixteenth. You know how that works?"

Howe shook his head, "no."

"We transmit a code phrase at a predetermined time. Zimmerman's radioman, who is monitoring the frequency, responds with a two-word code phrase, repeated twice. The idea is to reduce the chance of the North Koreans hearing a radio transmission at all, and if they should get lucky and hear it, not to give them time to locate the transmitter by triangulation."

Howe nodded his understanding.

"There has been no response from Tokchok-kundo since 0730 on the sixteenth," Pickering went on. "This morning, we got the code word message 'Egg Laid 0430' from HMS *Charity*. At the time we coined the code word, we thought it was rather clever for the meaning: 'McCoy, Taylor and all hands have been successfully put over the side at half past four.' It should have taken them no more than an hour to make Tokchok-kundo. On their arrival, Zimmerman was to transmit a code phrase meaning they had arrived. There has been no such transmission."

"The storm could have knocked out their radio," Howe suggested.

"That's a possibility. The other possibility that has to be considered is that the North Koreans discovered our people on Tokchok-kundo, took the island, and McCoy and Taylor sailed into the North Korean's lap."

"You don't know that, Fleming," Howe said.

"We set up another message, an emergency message, a phrase meaning change your frequency to another and be prepared to communicate. George and I just came from the commo center, where we watched Sergeant Keller send that code phrase every ten minutes for an hour and a half. There was no response."

"Which proves, I suggest, *only* that Zimmerman's radio is out again. There was trouble with it before, wasn't there?"

"You always look for a silver lining in situations like this," Pickering said. "What I'm hoping now is that if the North Koreans went to Tokchok-kundo and discovered our people there, they will think that it was nothing more than an intelligence-gathering outpost, and won't make a connection with the invasion of Inchon."

The first thing Howe thought was that Pickering was being unduly pessimistic, but then he remembered that this wasn't the first covert operation Pickering had run, and that his pessimism was based on experience.

"Goddamn it," Howe said, and then asked, "What are you going to do?"

"For the next twenty-four hours, I'm going to hope—pray—that you—and George—are right, and that the only problem is Zimmerman's radio."

"And then?"

"I'm going to Pusan to see what my station chief there thinks about sending the *Wind of Good Fortune* back up there."

[FIVE]
Evening Star Hotel
Tongnae, South Korea
2105 23 August 1950

"Oh, shit!" Captain George F. Hart said, as the headlights of the Jeep swept across the courtyard of the hotel.

"Oh, shit what, George?" Brigadier General Fleming Pickering asked.

"Pick's . . ." Hart said, and stopped.

"Pick's what?" Pickering said.

"I was about to say Pick's girlfriend is here," Hart said. "Or maybe it's somebody else with a war correspondent's Jeep. At the corner?"

"I don't need her right now," Pickering said. "But I'm afraid you're right."

"Maybe Major Whatsisname . . ."

"Dunston," Pickering furnished.

". . . *Dunston*'s got a Jeep like that," Hart said, as he pulled the nose of the Jeep, which had been more or less cheerfully furnished to them—along with directions to the hotel—by Captain James Overton, the Marine liaison officer at K-1.

"Could be," Pickering said. "I really hope it's not her."

"She was a little excited the last time we saw her, wasn't she, boss?" Hart asked.

"It has been some time since I have been called 'a treacherous sonofabitch,' " Pickering said. "Especially with such sincerity."

"I think her exact words were *'you miserable,* treacherous *sonsofbitches,* plural,' " Hart said. "She seemed to be a little annoyed with me, too."

"Well, I couldn't let her go back to Tokchok-kundo, even if the English would have let her get on the destroyer."

"No, you couldn't," Hart said, seriously, as he pulled the nose of the Jeep up to the wall of the hotel. "And I don't think you could have explained that to her."

Before they reached the door, other headlights announced the arrival of another Jeep at the hotel.

"That must be him," Hart said. "The Killer said he looked like an Army Transportation Corps major."

"Ken also said he struck him as very bright," Pickering said. "Keep that in mind."

"Major" William Dunston walked up to them.

"General, I'm Bill Dunston, your station chief here. I'm sorry you got here before I did, and delighted that you could find the place at all."

"George is a cop when he's not working for me," Pickering said. "He's good at finding things."

"Bill Dunston, Captain," Dunston said, offering Hart his hand. "I understand you've been with the general a long time."

"Yeah, we go back a ways," Hart said. "How are you? Who's the war correspondent?"

"Jeanette Priestly," Dunston said.

"What's she doing here?" Pickering asked.

"The bottom line is that I didn't know to keep her away," Dunston said. "What she asked for was if she could stay here rather than in the press center. What she's doing, obviously, is hanging around here as probably the best place to learn what's going on in the Flying Fish Channel. She said that you wouldn't let her go back up there."

"I don't think she put it that diplomatically, did she?" Pickering asked.

"The words 'betrayed' and 'broken promises' did enter our conversation," Dunston said. He hesitated, then went on: "One of the reasons I wasn't here at 8:30, as you requested in your message, was that I was hoping to have word of Major Pickering. I had some agents come back across the line at nightfall. . . ."

"And?"

"The good news is that there's no intel that the NKs have a Marine pilot in their POW lockups," Dunston said. "The bad news is that's all the intel. I'm sorry, sir. I think everything that can be done is being done."

"I'm sure it is," Pickering said. "Thank you."

"How good are your sources?" Hart asked.

"I own an NK field police major," Dunston said. "If there was a Marine pilot POW, he'd know."

"And he'd tell you?" Hart pursued, more than a little sarcastically.

"Hey, George," Pickering cautioned.

"It's all right, sir," Dunston said. "Yeah, he'd tell me. I have his father."

"Captain McCoy said you were very good at what you do," Pickering said.

"I seem to be laying one egg after another about Major Pickering, sir."

"Well, keep working on it, please," Pickering said.

"General, how much can I tell Miss Priestly about Major Pickering?"

"How much have you told her so far?"

"Only that we're looking for him."

"Tell her what you find out," Pickering ordered.

"In all circumstances, sir?"

"If we're both thinking the same thing, tell me before you tell her. If at all possible, I'd like to . . . break the news of that circumstance to her personally."

"Yes, sir."

"Am I allowed to ask what's going on in the Flying Fish Channel?"

"That's why I'm here," Pickering said. "There's a very good chance that the operation is blown. We haven't heard from Zimmerman in seven days. McCoy and Taylor were put off a British destroyer at 0430 on the twentieth and should have reached Tokchok-kundo an hour later. There has been no word of them, either."

"The storm may have knocked out their radio," Dunston said. "Or it simply failed again."

"We're working on that slim possibility. I wanted to . . ."

There was a flash of light as the hotel door opened.

Jeanette Priestly, in Army fatigues, was standing in the door, holding a carbine in one hand.

"Well, look who's here," she said.

"Hello, Jeanette," Pickering said.

"I'd ask what's going on, except I know that I couldn't believe a goddamn word any of you said."

"I really like a woman who can hold a grudge," Hart said.

"Shut up, George," Pickering said. "I'll tell you what's going on, Jeanette, and you can make up your mind whether to believe me or not."

She turned and went inside the hotel. The men followed her inside.

"Oh, Jesus," Jeanette said. "Everything is really fucked up, isn't it?"

"We don't know that," Dunston said. "I keep getting back to the idea that their radio is out."

"Again, admitting that slim possibility," Pickering said, "then the solution is to get them another radio. There are problems with that. I am unable to get my hands on a radio right now that is (a) suitable to be dropped onto Tokchok-kundo from a Marine aircraft, and is (b) powerful enough to communicate with either Pusan or Korea. All that's available that can be dropped with a reasonable chance of it landing intact are the standard emergency ground-to-air radios carried in airplanes. They have the power to communicate only with another airplane operating in the area. If we have aircraft orbiting over Tokchok-kundo, the NKs are going to know it and wonder why. So that's out.

"The Army has some experimental radios that may work, operative words, 'may work,' and they're being air-shipped to Tokyo. But the shortest time in which it is reasonable to expect them is six days from yesterday. Sometime tonight—it may already be here—the Yokohama signal depot is shipping another SCR-300 and a gasoline generator to power it to K-1. Our thought was that if we could get that loaded aboard the junk tonight, and the junk could sail in the morning, it could make Tokchok-kundo in thirty-odd hours."

"If the *Wind of Good Fortune* goes, I go," Jeanette announced.

"No, you don't," Pickering said. "The last thing we want to do is give the NKs the war correspondent of the *Chicago Tribune.*"

"I'm willing to take my chances on that," Jeanette said.

"I'm not," Pickering said. "The NKs would wonder what was so important about Tokchok-kundo that a war correspondent had ridden a junk up there. That's not open for discussion, Jeanette. The next time you see Tokchok-kundo will be from the deck of the *Mount McKinley* on fifteen September."

"What's the *Mount McKinley?*" Dunston asked.

"The command ship for the Inchon invasion."

"The Palace Guard will make sure I don't get a press space for that," Jeanette said.

"You'll have a CIA space," Pickering said. "Sid Huff called me and said El Supremo told him to ask me how many cabins I would require on the *Mount McKinley.* I told him I would have two people with me and would need two cabins. You're one of the two people. Trust me, Jeanette, it will take a direct order from MacArthur to keep you off the *Mount McKinley.*"

She looked at him closely for a moment and then said, "Well, maybe you're not such an *unmitigated* sonofabitch after all."

"So the invasion is definitely on for the fifteenth?" Dunston asked.

"And so, unless we can grab those islands beforehand, is the planned attack on them on D Minus One," Pickering said. "Which brings us back to the people we may have on Tokchok-kundo without a radio. What George and I came up with is to have only one American—to operate the radio—aboard. He will go on the air to report that they're about to reach the island. Then he will make himself as invisible as possible while your South Korean crew sails her into Tokchok-kundo. If our people are there, we're home free."

"And if they're not?" Jeanette said.

"With a little luck, the junk simply goes back to sea," Pickering said.

"And if Lady Luck is looking the other way," Jeanette said, "everybody on the *Wind of Good Fortune* gets bagged, and after interrogation, gets shot as spies."

"She's right, boss," Hart said.

Pickering started to say something in reply, and then didn't. He turned instead to Dunston.

"Do you think the idea has merit, Dunston?"

"Yes, sir, it does," Dunston said.

"And would you be willing to take the junk there?"

"Yes, sir, of course."

"That would be stupid," Hart announced.

"Excuse me?"

"For one thing, it would be foolish to risk his getting bagged. The NKs must know who he is. For another, you need him here. I'll ride the goddamn boat."

"That's out of the question," Pickering said, without thinking.

"Why? Who else have you got?" Hart said. "I can be spared, and I can do it. That looks pretty simple to me."

"I guess you're not, either," Jeanette said.

"Either what?"

"An *unmitigated* sonofabitch," Jeanette said.

"Are you sure, George?" Pickering asked.

"I'm sure, boss," Hart said.

[ONE]
Tokchok-kundo Island
0605 24 August 1950

Major Kim Pak Su, Korean national police, Captain Kenneth R. McCoy, USMCR, Lieutenant David Taylor, USNR, and Master Gunner Ernest W. Zimmerman, USMC, all attired in black cotton shirts and trousers, stood looking down at the two panels laid on the ground between the two houses on the hill.

On one panel was written the letters R, A, and D, and on the other the letters I and O. The letters were written large, from the tops of the eight-by-ten-foot panels to their bottoms. They were written in mud, of which there was an abundant supply, and was the only thing they had.

Master Gunner Zimmerman was embarrassed that he hadn't thought of using the panels to make a message board as soon—twenty-four hours before McCoy and Taylor had arrived—as the storm had taken out the generator, but McCoy pointed out that the rain had stopped only hours before his arrival, and that the rain would have washed the letters away as soon as they could be written.

"Anyway, Ernie, it's a hell of a long shot," McCoy said. "We don't know when there will be another flyover, or whether he will be taking aerials, or whether he . . ."

There was the sound of aircraft engines.

The three officers moved to the side of the area between the houses and started to scan the sky.

Not quite two minutes later, two Corsairs suddenly appeared, flying down the Flying Fish Channel from the lighthouse at five hundred feet, making maybe 250 knots. Not flat out, in other words, but slower than they would have been flying had they not been interested in the islands around the Flying Fish Channel, and still fast enough so that if anyone on the North Korean–held shore happened to see them, it would not appear they were having a really good, close look at the Channel Islands and wonder why.

They didn't divert from their course, and thirty seconds after they appeared, they disappeared in the direction of Inchon.

They would, McCoy suspected, engage targets of opportunity in Inchon before either flying a little farther north, or returning directly to their carrier, once they had, so to speak, justified their presence in the area to the enemy.

"You were saying, Mr. McCoy?" Taylor said.

"We don't know if those guys either (a) saw the panels, or if they did, could make sense of them, or (b) were taking pictures," McCoy said. "Or, (c) if they were taking pictures, that they got a shot of the panels clear enough to be read by the photo interpreters, or (d) if they saw them, and could read them, that the pictures'd wind up in the hands of someone who can do us any good. As I just observed to Mr. Zimmerman, Mr. Taylor, it's a long shot, a very long shot."

"What the hell, Killer, we gave it a shot," Zimmerman said. "We'll just have to wait and see."

"I don't like the idea of just sitting here waiting for the other shoe to drop," McCoy said.

"Meaning what, Ken?" Taylor asked.

"Correct me if I'm wrong, Major Kim, but your best guess of the North Korean strength on Taemuui-do is thirty people, under a sergeant, with their heaviest weapons a couple of machine guns?"

"That's my best information," Major Kim said.

"And on Yonghung-do?"

"There were a total of twenty-six men, including the lieutenant in charge and his sergeant. But we also learned that they've put people on Taebu-do—"

"Which is the little island to the south?" McCoy interrupted.

"From here, moving north, the nearest island is Taemuui-do, then Taebu-do, and then Yonghung-do. I would guess—if I were the lieutenant, it's what I would do—that he probably sent six, seven, eight men, under his sergeant, to the smaller island. That would leave him sixteen men, plus himself. And he's got two machine guns—"

"He probably sent one of them to the little island," Zimmerman chimed in.

"That's a total of fifty-six NK soldiers, give or take, right?" Taylor said. "We have ten Marines, counting you two, and fifteen national policemen, including the major . . ."

"And, of course, you," McCoy replied. "And the local militia. . . ."

"Cut to the chase," Taylor said. "What are you thinking, McCoy?"

"That if the NKs have a radio, or had one, it—and the generator for it, and fuel for the generator—would probably be with the lieutenant," McCoy said.

"And if they lost theirs, too, in the storm?" Taylor asked.

"Then we're no worse off than we are now," McCoy said.

"Let me make sure I understand you," Taylor said. "What you're suggesting is that—"

"We get off the dime," McCoy interrupted. "And it's not a suggestion, Dave."

Taylor ignored that, and continued:

"—we load our twenty-six people in the lifeboats, and try to take Yonghung-do—the most distant island—first—"

"Because that's where their CP and their radio, if they have one, is."

Taylor ignored that, too, and went on:

"—to do that, our little invasion fleet would have to sneak past both Taemuui-do and Taebu-do, which means we'd have to do that in the dark because if we did it in the daylight, two lifeboats and three fishing boats under sail—"

"I guess you weren't listening when I said this is not a suggestion, Dave," McCoy said.

"It's not?"

"No, it's not," McCoy said, evenly, but there was a steely *I will be obeyed* tone of command in his voice.

Taylor met his eyes for a long moment.

"Can I ask why Yonghung-do first?" he asked, finally.

"If we took Taemuui-do first, the lieutenant on Yonghung-do would know it. If nothing else, he would hear the gunfire. And we'll probably have to use grenades if they put up much of a scrap. If he has a radio, he'd report that to the mainland. And then would probably try to send help to Taemuui-do, whether or not he got orders from the mainland. This way, we'll knock out the radio, if there is one, and the lieutenant, too. And from what I've seen of the North Koreans, the sergeants on the other islands aren't going to do anything without orders."

"Moving the Koreans over there without getting spotted is going to be tough, Killer," Zimmerman said. "Taylor's right. You can see a sail a long way off, and if they see two sailboats headed even for Taemuui-do, they're going to know something's up."

"Your militia's our second wave, Ernie," McCoy said. "They won't even put out from here until daylight. By then we should have taken Yonghung-do. They go ashore there and garrison it, and we head back this way, bypassing the little island, and take Taemuui-do. Then the Koreans garrison that, and finally we take the little island."

"We leave just the Koreans on the islands?" Taylor asked.

"I think what Captain McCoy has in mind," Major Kim said, "is that if the North Koreans counterattack from the mainland, and do so successfully, they would not find any Americans."

McCoy nodded.

"When do we go, Killer?" Zimmerman asked.

"You got heavy plans for 0400 tomorrow that you can't break?"

[TWO]
Photographic Laboratory
USS
35 Degrees 48 Minutes North Latitude, 129 Degrees 91
  Minutes East Longitude
The Sea of Japan
1105 24 August 1950

"Hey, Mac," Chief Photographer's Mate Young called to Master Sergeant P. P. McGrory. "Have a look at this."

"What am I looking for?"

Chief Young pointed.

"R A D on one panel, I O on the other," he said. "See it?"

"Yeah. Radio."

"That's the guys on that island Colonel Dunn dropped the radio parts to," Chief Young said. "They probably broke their radio again."

"He'll want to see this," McGrory said. "Right away."

"They're about to launch aircraft," Young said.

McGrory grabbed the print from the table and left the photo lab on the run. He was winded when he reached the flight deck.

"Where's Colonel Billy?" he shouted, over the roar of starting aircraft engines.

The mechanic pointed.

Dunn was standing at the wing root of his Corsair, being helped into his flight gear.

"This just out of the soup, Colonel," McGrory said, handing it to him.

Dunn took one look at the picture.

"Stick this in an envelope, give it to the COD driver, and tell him to get it to the Marine liaison officer as soon as possible. On the envelope, write Major William Dunston, Army Transportation Corps."

"Aye, aye, sir," McGrory said.

Dunn saw the look on his face.

"No, Mac," he said. "Sorry, you can't ask what that's all about."

[THREE]
The Dewey Suite
The Imperial Hotel
Tokyo, Japan
1525 24 August 1950

"I didn't expect to see you back so soon," Major General Ralph Howe said when Brigadier General Fleming Pickering knocked at his door. He was sitting in an armchair, feet on a bolster, reading the *Stars & Stripes.* "Come on in. Tell me what's going on."

"I didn't want to come back at all," Pickering said.

"Then why did you?"

"I've been asked to supper at the Residence," Pickering said.

"You are already famous as the only man in Japan who dares tell El Supremo 'Sorry, I have a previous engagement,'" Howe said. It was an unspoken question.

"Two reasons, Ralph," Pickering said. "I didn't want him wondering what my previous engagement was, and second, I was following my father's—now my own—advice about getting out of the way of the competent people who work for you, and let them do their job."

"Have you had your twelve o'clock snort already? And if so, is half past three too early for your five o'clock?"

"No, and no," Pickering said. "Keep your seat, Ralph, I'll make them."

"Where's our usual bartender?"

"Somewhere in the East China Sea. I hope to know precisely where in the East China Sea shortly after nine tonight," Pickering said.

"What have you got him doing there?" Howe asked.

"Right now, he's on the junk, headed for Tokchok-kundo," Pickering said. "It was the only thing we could think to do to find out what's happened on the island, and, presuming McCoy and company are there, and the problem is a malfunctioning radio, to get another to them."

"Why Hart?"

"Because he made the point that he could be better spared—we both knew he meant 'is more expendable'—than Dunston, my station chief in Pusan," Pickering said, as he made their drinks. "Dunston was willing to go. George, with somewhat less than overwhelming tact for a captain speaking to his general, correctly pointed out that sending Dunston would be stupid."

He handed Howe his drink, and they touched glasses.

"What are you going to do if El Supremo asks you flat-out about this operation tonight? I suspect he's going to do just that."

"I've been thinking about that," Pickering said. "I guess—"

The door opened, and Master Sergeant Charley Rogers came in.

"I didn't know you were back, General. There's a Major Dunston on that back-channel telephone line from Pusan. When they couldn't find you or Hart, he asked to speak to General Howe."

"Can I take it in here?"

"I don't think it makes much difference," Rogers said, more than a little bitterly. "There's a tap on all our lines."

He walked to the telephone, picked it up, said, "Put my call in here, please," and held the telephone out to Pickering.

"Dunston," Pickering said to the telephone, "I don't think this is a secure line."

"Yes, sir," Dunston said. "General, I'm looking at an aerial our friend Dunn sent us. It was taken early this morning. Can you guess where?"

"I've got a pretty good idea," Pickering said.

"The shot shows a panel on which someone has written 'Radio,' " Dunston said. "It also shows, faintly, what looks like a man in black pajamas."

"Interesting," Pickering said.

"I thought you'd want to know, General."

"Thank you. Everything is ready on your end for 2100 tonight?"

"Yes, sir."

"Let me know as soon as you know anything, will you?"

"Yes, sir, of course."

"Thank you, Bill."

"Yes, sir," Dunston said, and the connection broke.

"Charley, is Sergeant Keller handy?"

"I'll get him, General," Rogers said, and left the room.

"Good news?" Howe asked.

"Very good," Pickering said.

"About your son?" Howe asked.

"No. The best news I have about Pick is that Dunston says he's pretty sure Pick is not a POW."

"What was that call?"

Master Sergeant Keller came into the room.

"Yes, sir?"

"I need a message to go—it doesn't have to be classified, but send it Urgent,

Immediate Personal Attention of Lieutenant Colonel William Dunn, aboard the *Badoeng Strait.*"

"Yes, sir?"

"Message is, quote, Many thanks. Radio is on the way. Signature, Pickering, Brigadier General, USMC, unquote. Got it?"

"I'll get it right out, sir," Keller said.

Pickering turned to Howe.

"One of the aerials Colonel Dunn took this morning of Tokchok-kundo shows a panel on which the word 'radio' is written," Pickering said.

"Then maybe—presuming Charley is right, and I'm afraid he is, and someone was listening to your phone conversation—El Supremo will think it had to do with looking for your son."

"Oh, to hell with it, Ralph. If he asks me, I'm going to tell him," Pickering said.

[FOUR]
Aboard *Wind of Good Fortune*
34 Degrees 20 Minutes North Latitude, 126 Degrees 29
Minutes East Longitude
The Yellow Sea
2050 24 August 1950

Captain George F. Hart, USMCR, who was leaning on the railing on the aft of the high stern of the *Wind of Good Fortune,* next to the Korean sailor on the tiller, became aware that he could now see the light illuminating the compass in the small control compartment on the forward edge of the stern's deck.

He looked at his watch, then pushed himself off the railing and walked across the deck to the captain, whose name was Kim, as were the names of two of the four Korean seamen aboard. The fourth seaman, the cook, was named Lee.

He touched Captain Kim on the shoulder and mimed—first by pointing at his watch, then pointing below, and finally by holding a make-believe microphone in front of his face—that it was time for him to report their position to their higher headquarters.

Captain Kim nodded, and either cleared his throat or grunted.

Hart took a chart from the pocket of his tunic. Surprising him, after a long, hot humid day, it had actually gotten chilly on the stern about half past five, and he had gone below to his cabin to get the tunic.

He held the chart out to Captain Kim, who studied it a moment, and then pointed out their position with a surprisingly delicate finger. They were slightly southwest of the extreme tip of the Korean peninsula. They had, in other words, just begun to sail northward up the Korean Peninsula, far enough out to sea so it was unlikely that anyone on the shore could see the *Wind of Good Fortune.*

They weren't, technically, sailing. The sails had been lowered as soon as they were out of sight of Pusan, and they had moved under diesel power since.

Hart went to his—the captain's—cabin, closed the door and turned on the light. The SCR-300, still on a shipping pallet, was lashed to the deck. On top of it was a non-GI Hallicrafters communications receiver, also carefully lashed in place.

The radios had been installed in the wee hours of the morning personally by Captain R. C. "Pete" Peters, Signal Corps, USA, of the 8th Army (Rear) Communications Center. And he had personally supervised the installation of the antennae at first light in the morning. Then he had established radio contact with his radio room.

The radios had worked then, which did not mean, Hart thought, that they would work now, either because something was wrong with them, or more likely because he didn't really have a clue how to work the sonofabitch, despite Captain Peters's instructions, each step of which Hart had carefully written down in a notebook.

Hart laid the chart on top of the radio, then took a large sheet of translucent paper from his tunic pocket and carefully laid this on top of the chart. It was an overlay. The night before, "Major" Dunston had spent two hours carefully preparing overlays. There were two sets of them, one set for the waters offshore the Korean peninsula, and the other set for the islands in the Flying Fish Channel. The overlays in each set were identical. On each were drawn a number of boxes, each one labeled with number. The numbers were—intentionally—in no way sequential. "063," for example, was surrounded by "109," "040," "101," and "171."

When he placed the overlay on the chart, Hart saw that the position Captain Kim had pointed out to him was inside the box numbered "091." Hart wrote the number in his notebook, then carefully folded the chart and the overlay and put them back in his tunic pocket, with the aerial photo of the Flying Fish Channel islands and its overlay.

Then, carefully studying the first of the notes he had made during Captain Peters's very patient orientation, he threw BOTTOM LEFT-HAND SWITCH on the Hallicrafter and was relieved and pleasantly surprised when the dials immediately lit up.

Three minutes later, all the dials and gauges on both the transmitter and the receiver were lit up, and indicating what Hart's notes said they should.

He put on his earphones, and heard a hiss.

He picked up the microphone, pressed the PRESS TO TALK switch, and said, "Dispatch, Dispatch, H-1, H-1."

H-1 was the radio call sign assigned to the chief of the homicide bureau of the St. Louis police department. When the question of radio call signs for the good ship *Wind of Good Fortune* had come up about 0300 that morning, H-1 had seemed be as good a call sign as any of the others suggested, and a lot better than some. And, Hart knew, he was unlikely to forget it.

He thought about this now, and of St. Louis, and its police department, and asked aloud, "What the fuck am I doing here?"

The hiss in his earphone vanished suddenly, and a voice so loud it actually hurt his ears said, "Dispatch. Go ahead."

"Zero Niner One," Hart said into the microphone, and then repeated it.

"Dispatch understands Zero Niner One, Confirm," the too loud, very clear voice said in Hart's earphones.

"Confirm, confirm," Hart said into the microphone.

"Dispatch clear," the too loud voice said, and the hiss came back to Hart's earphones.

Hart put the microphone on top of the SCR-300, then carefully studied the front of the Hallicrafters, finally settling on a round knob. He moved it very carefully. The hiss in his earphones diminished. He started to leave the knob where it was, but on reflection—*If I turn it too far down, I might not be able to hear him the next time*—turned it back up.

Then, consulting his notes, he began to shut the radio down.

[FIVE]
Tokchok-kundo Island
0405 25 August 1950

They had spent most of the previous day rehearsing how to gets the boats into the water, and their equipment into the boats, and what ran through Captain Kenneth R. McCoy's mind as he jumped from the wharf into Boat Two was that at least the boat part of the operation wasn't going to cause any problems.

He pushed the starter button on the control panel, and the lifeboat's engine, after a few anemic gasps, came to life.

The rehearsals for getting the boats into the water had been sort of fun, although smiling at the men's activities would have been inappropriate.

He had begun the exercise by explaining that they weren't actually going to remove the camouflage netting over the boats—because the boats might then be seen—they were going to mimic uncovering them, and getting them into the water, and getting the equipment into them once they were in the water.

Everyone seemed to agree that was a logical approach to the problem.

As the boats when they were *really* put into the water would have to be carried there, they started with that. They were heavy, and would require eight men on each side to carry them.

The men were assigned numbers, Left One through Left Eight, Right One through Right Eight.

After Boat One was in the water, Boat Two would be uncovered and put in the water. Whereupon Left #7 and Left #8 would remain in Boat Two, Right #7 and Right #8 would move to Boat One, and everybody else would form a line to the now-roofless house where their weapons, ammunition, and everything else they were taking with them had been laid out in a precise pattern. Then, first each individual weapon would be passed from man to man down and into the boats, and then each man's equipment.

Setting the system up and running through it, even in mine, had taken all morning, and through the lunch break, and then they had rehearsed how they would assault Yonghung-do.

About 1700, McCoy had gathered everybody together and gone through what Major Kim had learned of the disposition of the physical characteristics of the island, the location of the North Korean troops on the island, and the plan:

Yonghung-do was about three miles long, north to south, and shaped something like an hourglass. Each end of the island was about a mile wide, and each had a 250- to 300-foot hill in its center. About in its middle, the island narrowed to a few hundred feet.

"That's where we'll land," McCoy said, pointing to a drawing he'd made of the island in the now-dried mud. "They won't expect us, and we can land there without being seen. We'll leave a four-man team there—the .30 Browning machine-gun team plus one BAR and one rifleman—plus eight of Major Kim's men, under Mr. Taylor. Their job will be to keep the NKs in the village at the north end of the island, Nae-ri, from coming to help the NKs in the village, Oe-Ri, on the south end of the island.

"With a little bit of luck, the people we leave on the beach won't have anything to do. If we can move that mile over the hill quietly—no one fires a round by mistake, or Mr. Zimmerman doesn't fart—"

He got the expected laughter, waited for it to subside, and then went on:

"They won't expect us, and we can take them without firing a shot. 'Them' is their lieutenant, one of their machine guns, probably the ammo supply for all the islands, and their radio, with maybe a generator we can use to power ours. We're not going into that village shooting. If there's a radio, or diesel fuel, I don't want it full of bullet holes. There's also about two hundred civilians. I will really have the ass of anyone who pops a civilian.

"OK, once we have secured the southern village, we leave Major Kim's people there, go back to the landing beach, pick up everybody except the machine-gun team and Mr. Taylor, head north, go over the other hill, and secure the other village, Nae-ri. Once we do that, a volunteer will run happily back over the hill to the beach and tell Mr. Taylor, who will then bring the boats to Nae-ri, and haul us—less Major Kim and his policemen, who will be staying until we can get the militia in there—out. Any questions?"

There had been no questions.

"Well, in that case, before it gets really dark, I think we ought to have one more—maybe even two more—dry runs of the boat launching," McCoy said.

There were groans. Once the system had been set up and tried and it worked once, and then twice, and then three times, it had become a flaming, stupid, pain-in-the-ass chickenshit exercise.

He waited until they had subsided.

"On the other hand," McCoy went on, straight-faced, "maybe it would just be easier to put the boats in the water now, load the gear in them, put the camo nets over them, and then all we'd have to do in the morning would be get in them, take off the nets, and take off."

There was a moment's shocked silence, and then murmurs.

McCoy pointed his finger at one of the Marines, a technical sergeant who had been a Marine Raider.

"What did you say, Sergeant?"

"I didn't say anything, sir."

"That's odd," McCoy said. "I could have sworn I heard you say, 'Oh, what a pity our beloved and brilliant commander didn't think of that earlier!' Or words to that effect."

"Yes, sir, words to that effect."

"What happens now is that you, Sergeant, will run out to the end of the wharf, taking these with you . . ."

He tossed him his binoculars.

". . . through which you will scan the sea. When you are absolutely sure there is nothing out there, you will make an appropriate signal . . ."

McCoy had put his arms over his heads and waved them.

". . . whereupon the rest of this magnificent Marine expeditionary force, having assembled by Boat One, will get the camo off and get it into the water as soon as they can, load the gear in it, put the camo back on, and then look at you again. If you are not making some sort of signal suggesting that there's a boat out there, they will then repeat the operation with Boat Two.

"If you see a boat while they're doing their thing, you will signal, but they will finish loading the boat and covering it with the camo net before getting out of sight. Any questions?"

"No, sir," the sergeant said.

"Let's do it," McCoy said.

The sergeant took off in a fast trot for the wharf, and then down it.

Twenty minutes later, both boats were in the water, loaded, and covered with camouflaged netting.

McCoy signaled for the sergeant at the end of the wharf to come back.

"To answer the questions you're afraid to ask," McCoy said. "You went through that mimicry business so that it would be second nature when you actually did it. And we didn't do the real thing until now. It's almost dark. Even if a boat did show up, I don't think they could see the lifeboats at the wharf unless they came into the harbor. Any questions?"

There had been no questions.

"Are you ready, Captain McCoy?" Lieutenant Taylor called.

"Ready."

The sound of the engine in Taylor's boat changed as he put it in gear.

McCoy saw that the two Marines holding the lines holding the boat to the wharf were looking at him.

"Let loose the lines," McCoy called. "Shove us off."

Both Marines pushed the boat away with the wharf with their feet.

McCoy pulled the transmission lever away from him, into forward.

There was immediately the screech of tortured metal.

He had no idea what it was, but it was obviously time to put the transmission in neutral. He pushed it forward, and the screaming stopped.

"What the fuck was that?" someone in the boat said.

Taylor made a tight circle with his lifeboat, pulled up beside McCoy's boat, and nimbly jumped into it.

"I don't know what the hell . . . ," McCoy said.

Taylor moved the transmission control into forward, and then immediately back out as the screeching started again.

"You got the shaft, I think," Taylor said. "I hope that's all that's wrong."

"Is it serious?"

"It means we're not going anywhere this morning," Taylor said. "I can't even look at it until it's out of the water and there's light."

[SIX]
Tokchok-kundo Island
0725 25 August 1950

Boat Two was now on the shore, upside down, with the camouflage net suspended over it from the wall of the generator building.

Boat One was still in the water, loaded and under a camouflage net. It had been a gamble lost. McCoy—and Taylor, too, although he kept it to himself—desperately had hoped that whatever was wrong with the boat would be able to be fixed quickly, so the operation could go on. That seemed to justify the risk of leaving Boat One in the water, where it might—almost certainly would—look very suspicious to anyone coming close to Tokchok-kundo.

By the time they had gotten Boat Two unloaded, so that it could be brought ashore, the predawn darkness had given way to dawn, and that meant the operation had to be scratched. There was no way to sneak past Taemuui-do and Taebu-do in daylight.

Neither was the damage to Boat Two something that could quickly be repaired, if it could be repaired at all. The shaft, coming through the hull to the propeller, had somehow been bent.

To repair it would mean removing it from the boat, heating it, beating it with hammers until it was straight again, and then putting it back in the boat. Taylor was not at all sure it could be done, and told McCoy so.

"We can't tow this with the other boat?" McCoy asked.

Taylor shook his head, "no."

"Maybe in the open sea," he said. "But not with the tides in the Channel."

"Then I guess we'll have to fix this one," McCoy said.

When they heard the sound of aircraft engines, they had gotten as far as removing the bent shaft from the boat, and building a makeshift forge and anvil, both from rocks. The shaft would have to be heated first until it was glowing red before an attempt could be made to straighten it.

There was considerable doubt that the shaft could be heated hot enough on the wood fire, and neither Taylor nor the Korean, who had some experience with rudimentary metalworking, could even make a guess as to how often the heating/hammering process would have to be repeated, if, indeed, the heating could be done at all.

Two Corsairs appeared where the Corsairs had appeared the day before, coming down the Flying Fish Channel from the lighthouse. But today one of them was much lower, not more than 300 feet off the water, and with his landing gear down.

"Jesus," McCoy said, softly, to Taylor and Zimmerman, "do you think he's going to drop us a radio?"

"He's going to drop something," Zimmerman said.

McCoy stared intently at the approaching airplane, but could see nothing but ordnance hanging from the hard-points under its wings.

And then something did come off the aircraft, something small, at the end of what looked like a ribbon.

The moment the object started to fall, the landing gear of the Corsair started to retract into the wings, and the aircraft banked to the left to avoid the hill and began to pick up altitude.

The object dropped from the Corsair lost its forward velocity and then dropped straight down, landing ten yards from the wharf and twenty yards from the shore. The ribbon, or whatever it was, now lay on the surface of the mud left by the receding tide. Whatever it was attached to was buried in the mud.

McCoy turned to look at Zimmerman. He was sitting on the ground, pulling his boondockers and socks off. Then he stripped out of the black pajama shirt and trousers and then his underpants.

Zimmerman started wading out through the mud toward the ribbon. He sank over his ankles in the mud, and once, for a moment, it looked as if he was stuck in the mud and about to fall. But he regained his balance, and finally had his hand on the white ribbon. He started to pull on it, and then met more resistance than he thought he would. So he waded farther out, to where the ribbon's end entered the mud. He carefully began to haul upward on the ribbon. Thirty seconds later, he was holding something in his hand.

"It's a fucking flashlight!" he called in disgust.

"Bring it ashore," McCoy called, and Zimmerman started to wade back toward the shore, winding the ribbon around the "flashlight" as he moved.

He finally came ashore, puffing from the exertion.

"How'm I going to get this stinking fucking muck off my legs?" he asked, and tossed the "flashlight" and the muddy ribbon around it to McCoy.

The ribbon, McCoy immediately saw, was parachute silk. He unwound it from around the "flashlight," and saw that it was indeed a flashlight, a big four-battery-size one from some mechanic's tool kit. The twenty-foot-long strip of parachute silk had been attached to the flashlight's cylinder with heavy tape.

He moved the switch. There was no light.

He unscrewed the head and saw that one of the batteries had been removed, and that there was a piece of folded paper where it had been. He carefully removed it and unfolded it. It was a message written in grease pencil:

> *From Pickering*
> *" Radio on the way. "*
> *Hang In There.*
> *Semper Fi*
> *Dunn*

Lieutenant Taylor, Major Kim, and Master Gunner Zimmerman—who was still naked, and had both hands covered with the mud he had tried unsuccessfully to wipe from his legs—walked up to McCoy.

"What the hell is it?" Taylor asked.

McCoy handed the note to him. Taylor read it and started to hand it to Zimmerman, changed his mind, and held it in front of Zimmerman's face so that he could read it.

"Mr. Zimmerman, if you don't mind my saying so," McCoy said. "You smell of dead fish and other rotten things I don't even want to think about."

"Fuck you, Killer," Zimmerman said, but he had to smile.

Taylor handed the note to Major Kim.

" 'On the way' doesn't tell us when," Taylor said. "Or how."

"If General Pickering says a radio is on the way, a radio is on the way," McCoy said. "That's good news."

"And what do we do until the good news arrives?" Zimmerman asked.

"You, Mr. Zimmerman, will make every effort to make yourself presentable," McCoy said. "The rest of us will try to fix the boat, meanwhile hoping that nobody goes sailing by and wonders what the hell the natives here have concealed under that camouflage net by the wharf."

"With the tide out like this," Taylor thought aloud, "we can't get it ashore, either."

"Let's get started on the boat," McCoy said. "Major Kim, would you put a couple of people out on the wharf to give us warning if we're going to have visitors?"

[SEVEN]
Aboard *Wind of Good Fortune*
37 Degrees 38 Minutes North Latitude, 126 Degrees 57 Minutes East Longitude
The Yellow Sea
1500 25 August 1950

Captain George F. Hart, USMCR, now attired in black cotton pajamas, with a band of the same material around his forehead, nodded when Captain Kim pointed at a landmass on the horizon.

Then he mimed making his radio report by holding an imaginary microphone in front of his mouth. Captain Kim nodded, and either cleared his throat or grunted.

Hart went down the ladder to his cabin, turned on the light, took out his notebook, and went through each step necessary to turn the radio on. Then he put on the headset and picked up the microphone.

"Dispatch, Dispatch, H-1, H-1," he said.

There was an immediate response, which this time—Hart having acquired faith in his ability to control the volume in his headset—did not hurt his ears.

"H-1, Dispatch, go."

"One Seven Three," Hart said into the microphone. "I say again, One Seven Three."

"Dispatch understands One Seven Three, confirm," the voice in Hart's earphones said.

"Confirm, confirm," Hart said into the microphone.

"H-1, Dispatch. Stand by to copy."

That was the first time he'd heard that order, and he had absolutely no idea how he was supposed to reply.

"OK, Dispatch," he said into the microphone.

"Message begins, Proceed your discretion with great caution. Report immediately. Godspeed. The Boss, Message ends. Acknowledge."

"Acknowledged," Hart said, without really thinking about it.

"Dispatch clear."

The hiss came back to Hart's earphones.

Hart laid the microphone down, took off the headset, and then shut the radio down.

He went back on deck.

Captain Kim looked at him with a question in his eyes.

He wants to know if I've finished.

Hart nodded.

The question on Captain Kim's face was still there.

Hart made a cutting motion across his throat, which he hoped Captain Kim would interpret to mean that he had finished making his report.

Captain Kim began to shout.

What the hell is that all about?

One of the other Kims, and Lee, the cook, suddenly appeared in the forecastle door, and looked up at Captain Kim for orders. He shouted something, and they immediately went to the forward mast and started to raise the venetian blind—like sail.

Captain Kim reached into the control compartment and shut down the diesel engine.

Within minutes, all the sails were up, and the *Wind of Good Fortune* was moving toward the landmass under sail.

Three minutes later, Hart was able to pick out the lighthouse that marked the entrance to the Flying Fish Channel.

He went over the message from General Pickering in his mind.

He didn't have to tell me to proceed at my discretion and with great caution. I don't have any "discretion." I told him I would sail into Tokchok-kundo on this thing and get the SCR to McCoy, presuming he and the others are still there, which means I have to do it, and there's no discretion involved.

Great caution? I'm not, and he knows I'm not, John Wayne. Of course I'm going to be careful.

Report immediately? He should have known I'd do that, anyway. The only reason I'm bringing the goddamn radio is so that he'll have contact with McCoy, and McCoy—presuming he's there—wouldn't wait until Thursday of next week to get in contact.

What's the variable meaning? What am I missing?

OK. McCoy is not there. He and Taylor never made it to the island from the de-

stroyer, or they made it and were grabbed by the North Koreans. If that's the case, Zimmerman and the others have also been grabbed by the NKs.

Wishful thinking aside, that's the most likely situation.

So we sail in there, fat, dumb, and happy, and we get grabbed. And get shot as spies, especially me in these goddamn pajamas.

Oh, shit! Report immediately *means that if he doesn't hear from me, immediately, I will have been grabbed—which would mean that everybody else has been grabbed, too—and* that *would mean this whole operation has gone down the toilet.*

Of course, he'd want to know that immediately. Maybe there would be time to try something else, maybe not, but he would want to know right away.

So what's the point of the great caution?

If the NKs are holding Tokchok-kundo, is there any chance I could see them before they see me and get out of there with my ass intact?

About as much chance as there is of me being taken bodily into heaven.

So what this really boils down to is we go in there and (a) McCoy greets me with a brass band and asks me what took me so long, or (b) we go in there and half the North Korean army greets me with a couple of machine guns.

And after a suitable interrogation, shoots me—which they have every right to do, with me in my spy pajamas.

I don't want to be interrogated; somehow I suspect I won't be able to claim my constitutional right to refuse to answer any questions on the grounds they may tend to incriminate me.

So what else is there I can do?

I can get out of these fucking pajamas, is what I can do. And if I am going to get blown away, maybe I can take some of them with me before I go. And get buried in a Marine uniform.

Ten minutes later, Captain George F. Hart came on the stern again. He was now in the prescribed semi-dress uniform for the summer months of the year for officers of the U.S. Marine Corps, including a field scarf. The uniform had lost its press and was not very clean. A Thompson Submachine Gun Model 1928 Caliber .45 ACP was hanging from his shoulder on a web strap.

When he looked around, the Flying Fish Channel lighthouse was behind him to his left.

There was a nautical way to say that, but he couldn't think what it was.

[EIGHT]
Tokchok-kundo Island
1535 25 August 1950

One of the two national policemen Major Kim had stationed on the end of wharf came running down the wharf to where Kim was watching another of his men hammering at the dull red—not heated quite enough—shaft of Boat Two.

He reported that a junk was on the horizon, coming down the Flying Fish Channel, but that it was too early to tell whether it was headed for Tokchok-kundo.

Major Kim started to make the translation, then stopped when McCoy held up his hand.

"Thank you," McCoy said, in Korean, to the national policeman. "I would be grateful if you would return to your post and perhaps climb down from the wharf itself, so that anyone looking might not see you. And please tell us what else you see."

The national policeman saluted and ran back out onto the wharf.

"So what do we do," Zimmerman said, "if it comes here, or even close enough to get a look?"

"Dave, could you climb onto that junk from the lifeboat if it was, say, fifty yards offshore?"

"I could if there weren't people on the deck shooting at me," Taylor replied.

"Zimmerman and I will try to make sure there's nobody on the deck alive," McCoy said. "We'll go halfway up the hill, Ernie, so we'll have a good shot at the deck. . . ."

"We could do sort of a TOT on it," Zimmerman suggested. "We have enough firepower to really sweep it clean."

"There's probably no more than four or five people on it," McCoy said. "I'll start at the stern, you start at the bow."

Zimmerman nodded his acceptance.

"I don't want a sudden burst of small-arms fire to attract anybody else's attention," McCoy said, then turned to Major Kim: "Major Kim, see how well you can hide this"—he gestured at the upside-down lifeboat and the makeshift forge—"and then make sure everybody's out of sight."

Major Kim nodded.

"If we take it just as it approaches the wharf," McCoy said to Zimmerman, "it would be moving slowly. And it would be, I'd say, about two hundred yards from halfway up the hill."

"I'd make it two hundred yards," Zimmerman agreed.

"Hold fire until I fire," McCoy said.

Ten minutes later, from his firing position—behind a knee-high rock halfway up the hill—McCoy surveyed the village below him. There was no one in sight, no sign of activity at all.

He pulled the operating rod lever of his National Match Garand far enough back so that he could see the gleam of a cartridge halfway in the chamber, and then, after letting the operating rod slide forward again, hit it with the heel of his hand to make sure it was fully closed.

Then he took a quick sight—primarily to make sure he had a good firing position—at the end of the wharf, then carefully laid the rifle on the rock.

Then he put his binoculars to his eyes and took a good look at the junk, starting at the bow.

Then he said, "I'll be a sonofabitch."

"What?" Zimmerman asked from his position, twenty yards to McCoy's left.

"I was just about to shoot George," McCoy said, laughing, and got to his feet, picked up the Garand, put the safety back on, and started to go as fast as he could down the hill.

Zimmerman put his binoculars to his eyes and looked at the junk, then shook his head and got to his feet, and started after McCoy.

"Dispatch, Dispatch, H-1, H-1," Hart said into his microphone.

"H-1, Dispatch, Go."

"Five, I say again, Five," Hart said.

Five was a code phrase—one of eight hastily prepared in Pusan—that stood for: "In Tokchok-kundo. McCoy party safe."

"H-1, understand Five, Five, confirm."

"Confirm, confirm."

"Stand by."

"Standing by."

A new voice with a strong British accent came over the air.

"H-1, this is Saint Bernard. H-1, this is Saint Bernard."

"Jesus, who the hell is that?" Hart asked, and told McCoy what he had heard over his earphones.

McCoy gestured for him to hand over the headset and the microphone.

"Station calling H-1, go ahead," McCoy said.

"Delighted to hear you're all right, my friend," the voice said. "We were getting a bit concerned."

"It's Captain Jones-Fortin," McCoy said.

"My present position is Four Zero Three," Jones-Fortin said.

"Hold one," McCoy said. "George, give me your chart and the overlay."

"Understand Four Zero Three," McCoy said to the microphone.

It took Hart at least a minute to unfold the chart and get the overlay in place. It seemed like much longer.

"I have your location."

"Could you possibly come there at nine tonight? We need to talk."

"Dave, can you find that place in the dark?"

"I think so. It's about ten miles off the lighthouse, just about due west."

"Affirmative, affirmative," McCoy said.

"See you then," Jones-Fortin said. "Saint Bernard Clear."

"George, do you know anything about this?" McCoy asked.

Hart shook his shoulders helplessly.

XXI

[ONE]
Aboard Wind of Good Fortune
37 Degrees 36 Minutes North Latitude, 126 Degrees 53
  Minutes East Longitude
The Yellow Sea
2055 25 August 1950

"You understand this is dead-reckoning navigation," Lieutenant David Taylor, USNR, said to Captain Kenneth R. McCoy, USMCR. "Sometimes known as by-guess-and-by-golly navigation."

They were standing by the forward rail of the "bridge" on the high stern of the *Wind of Good Fortune* with Major Kim. A Korean seaman had the tiller, and two more had been posted as lookouts, one high on the rearward mast, the other on the forecastle.

They had been at sea since shortly after their radio contact with HMS *Charity* at 1800. McCoy hadn't wanted to have the *Wind of Good Fortune* at the wharf in Tokchok-kundo, where it might be seen, and Taylor said the simplest way of concealing her would be to sail her back down the Flying Fish Channel into the Yellow Sea, out of sight of the Korean peninsula.

McCoy had again left Zimmerman in charge on Tokchok-kundo, because he was obviously better qualified to have that command than George Hart, but after thinking about taking Hart with them on the *Wind of Good Fortune*, realized that Hart would be more useful on the island with Zimmerman, if for no other reason than Zimmerman could bring him up to date on what was planned. Hart was a Marine, and all Marines can fire rifles, and when they finally went to seize Taemuui-do and Yonghung-do, Hart would be needed.

Only after it had grown dark had Taylor set a course that would take them to the rendezvous at sea with HMS *Charity*.

"I'm afraid you're going to tell me what that means," McCoy said.

"We don't know precisely where we are," Taylor said. "We have been sailing a compass course, which may or may not have taken us precisely where we want to go. There may be—probably are—currents moving us off course."

"What do we have to do to establish 'precisely'?" McCoy asked.

"Shoot the stars with a sextant is the usual means," Taylor said. "But we don't have a sextant."

A few minutes later, there was a flash of white light to port. It seemed to be pointed right at them. It was followed at ten-second intervals by a flash of light that seemed to be pointed ahead of them, then directly away from them, then behind them.

Then the light went out and stayed out.

"Are you trying to make this exciting for me, or don't you know what that is?" McCoy asked.

"Make for the lights," Taylor called in Korean to the Korean on the tiller.

"That's the *Charity?*" McCoy asked.

"God, I hope so," Taylor said, piously.

Taylor reached into the control compartment and came up with a four-cell flashlight. He flashed it—sending, McCoy realized after a moment, the Morse code short and long flashes spelling M C—to port.

"Is that the flashlight Dunn dropped to us?" McCoy asked.

"All it needed was one battery, and it was as good as new," Taylor said, somewhat smugly. "I had batteries."

Now there came a light aimed directly at them, spelling C.

The C message was repeated once every sixty seconds after that. Five minutes later, just as McCoy began to think he could make out the ship on the horizon, floodlights mounted fore, aft, and amidship on the *Charity* lit the hull for five seconds and then went off again. It was now possible to judge the distance—no more than two hundred yards—separating the sleek, dead-in-the-water destroyer from the junk.

A small spotlight flashed on and off at them until they were quite close to the *Charity,* and then floodlights illuminated a ladder swung over her side.

"Why do they call that a ladder when it's really a flight of stairs?" McCoy wondered aloud.

"Jesus, Ken!" Taylor said.

Two seamen, under the supervision of the diminutive chief petty officer who had supervised putting the lifeboats over the side of the *Charity,* was standing on the platform at the lower end of the stairs. He was wearing immaculate whites.

"Captain," he called, as the *Wind of Good Fortune* drew quite close, "the captain suggests you gentlemen come aboard, and that your vessel circle astern of us."

"Got you, Chief," Taylor called, and issued the necessary orders to the helmsman.

McCoy saw that he also handed him the flashlight Colonel Dunn had dropped into the mud.

McCoy jumped from the deck of the *Wind of Good Fortune* onto the platform first, followed by Major Kim and finally Taylor.

"Right up the ladder, if you please, gentlemen," the chief ordered.

As McCoy reached the level of the deck, the sea pushed the *Wind of Good Fortune* into the ladder, and the noise made him look down to see what had happened.

There didn't seem to be any damage; the *Wind of Good Fortune* seemed to be backing away from the *Charity.*

McCoy climbed the last two steps of the ladder and stepped onto the deck, where the executive officer was standing in his crisp white uniform. And there were two rows of sailors, in whites, three to a row, saluting. Just as McCoy realized what was going on, there came the shrill sound of a bosun's pipe, and a voice called out.

"United States Marines, *board*-ing!"

McCoy saluted the executive officer, then faced the stern and saluted the British flag.

"Permission to come aboard, sir?"

"Granted."

The executive officer looked at Major Kim as he stepped onto the deck, dressed like McCoy and Taylor, in black pajamas, and for a moment a look of confusion crossed his face, but he rose to the occasion.

"South Korean officer, *board*-ing," he called out.

And Major Kim rose to the occasion by mimicking every step of McCoy's response perfectly.

And finally, Taylor stepped onto the deck in his black pajamas.

"United States Navy, *board*-ing!"

When Taylor had finished saluting the British colors, the bosun's piping died out and the executive officer put out his hand to Taylor.

"Nice to have you aboard again, Lieutenant," he said. "Will you follow me, please?"

He led them between the lines of saluting sailors—who seemed to find nothing strange, McCoy saw, in their rendering honors to three men in black pajamas—into the superstructure, and through interior passageways to the bridge.

Captain the Honorable Darwin Jones-Fortin waved them permission to come on the bridge.

"Your welcome overwhelms us, Captain," Taylor said.

"Well, the last time I rather sneaked you aboard. You're now here officially, and it seemed appropriate. First things first. I dislike sitting here dead in the water. How many knots can your magnificent vessel make? And do you have enough fuel?"

"Twelve to thirteen knots, sir," Taylor said, "in a sea like this. And there's plenty of fuel aboard."

"Good show," Jones-Fortin said. "Make turns for ten knots," he ordered. "Make a wide circle to port."

The helmsman repeated the order.

"You have the conn, Number One," Jones-Fortin ordered.

"I have the conn, sir," the executive officer said.

"Why don't we go to my cabin?" Jones-Fortin said, and motioned them ahead of him into an interior passageway.

There was already someone in the captain's cabin, a Royal Marine lieutenant in field clothing and web gear.

"Gentlemen, may I present Lieutenant Richard Diceworth, Royal Marines?" Jones-Fortin said. "Diceworth, this is Captain McCoy of the U.S. Marines, Lieutenant Taylor of the U.S. Navy, and I haven't had the privilege . . ."

"Major Kim Pak-Su, Korean national police."

The men shook hands.

"Admiral Matthews," Jones-Fortin explained, "apparently after consulting with your General Pickering at some length, and having decided that your Flying Fish Channel operation deserved a bit more support than he initially offered, sent Diceworth and fifteen Royal Marines from HMS *Jamaica,* his flagship."

"I don't know what to say," McCoy confessed.

"Let me tell you what we have to offer, and then you tell me if you think it would be helpful," Jones-Fortin said. "In addition to Diceworth and his men, we have the boats which brought them to *Charity* from the *Jamaica.* There's two of them, each with a coxswain, and they're a bit larger—about twice the size, I would guess—of the lifeboats. They're also a bit faster and more seaworthy."

McCoy just shook his head.

"And while we were waiting for you to join us, my Number One and my gunnery officer, after studying aerial photographs of the islands, have offered the opinion that they can bring all of them under our guns."

"You'd have to go into the Flying Fish to do that, Captain, wouldn't you?" Taylor asked.

"No, actually not. We can lay the cannon fire from a position seaward of the islands, and use the islands, so to speak, as rocks behind which to hide from possible enemy observation."

"Jesus!" McCoy said.

"Sir William made it quite clear to me, Captain McCoy, that the use of British elements in your operation is by no means an order. Using any, or all, of what we can offer is entirely up to you. What do you think?"

"I think if it wouldn't give Taylor the wrong idea about Marines, I'd kiss Lieutenant Diceworth," McCoy said.

"Well, perhaps there would be time for that later," Jones-Fortin said. "But right now, nose-to-the-grindstone, et cetera, right?"

[TWO]
Tokchok-kundo Island
0330 25 August 1950

"What the hell is going on?" Master Gunner Ernest W. Zimmerman asked when Captain Kenneth R. McCoy jumped off the *Wind of Good Fortune* onto the wharf. "I almost blew you out of the water when I saw you coming in with that light."

Another man jumped onto the wharf, and Zimmerman looked at him in absolute surprise.

"Lieutenant Diceworth, Royal Marines, Master Gunner Zimmerman," McCoy said.

"How do you do, Mr. Zimmerman?" Diceworth said, politely.

Zimmerman saluted, then looked at McCoy for an explanation.

"I want everybody who won't fit in Boat Two—including the militia—on the *Wind of Good Fortune* in ten minutes," McCoy said. "I want to be in the Flying Fish Channel in fifteen minutes."

"I asked you what's going on, Killer," Zimmerman pursued.

"There's been a slight change in the operation."

"What kind of a change?" Zimmerman asked, dubiously.

"I only want to do it once, Ernie," McCoy said. "Get everybody loaded up."

"Good morning, Lieutenant," Zimmerman said to Diceworth. "With respect, sir, may the gunner inquire where the hell the lieutenant came from?"

Diceworth smiled.

"From HMS *Jamaica,* actually," Diceworth said.

"He and fifteen more English Marines," McCoy added.

"Actually, Captain," Diceworth said, "that's *Royal* Marines."

"Sorry," McCoy said. "And two pretty good-sized boats with people who know how to drive them, and radios with which they can talk to *Charity,* the destroyer, who's laying just outside the lighthouse."

"No shit?"

"And can bring naval gunfire to bear on all the islands, and has aerial photos, so we can call in what we need when we need it."

"No shit?"

"And now, if your curiosity is settled for the moment, Mr. Zimmerman, would you please get your ass out of low gear, and start getting this circus on the road?"

The essential difference between the pre–Royal Marines and pre–HMS *Charity* plan, and what they were going to try to do now, was that the element of surprise wasn't nearly as important as it had been.

If the two-lifeboat "invasion fleet" had been detected and brought under fire by any of the North Korean forces, it would almost certainly have meant disaster. The North Koreans had both machine guns and rifles, and would have brought the lifeboats under fire the moment they saw they were filled with armed men.

Machine-gun and rifle fire from firm ground goes where it is directed. Machine-gun and rifle fire from crowded lifeboats bobbing in the rapidly receding tide waters of the Flying Fish Channel would have struck its targets only by wild coincidence.

So the element of surprise in the initial plan was of prime importance. Now it fell into the category of "nice to have if we can get away with it."

The plan now had a role for the *Wind of Good Fortune.* With the two boats from HMS *Jamaica* running to her starboard, where they could probably not be seen, and towing the lifeboat, she would move up the Flying Fish Channel past Taebu-do and Taemuui-do under both diesel and sail power. The sails probably would do very little to propel her forward, and their being raised might have the opposite effect, if there was a strong wind from the north—in which case they would be lowered.

All the Marines—Royal and U.S.—and most of Major Kim's national police would be in the boats. They were now divided into three teams, scattering the Royal Marines among the U.S. Marines.

The two larger teams, one commanded by Captain McCoy and the other by Lieutenant Diceworth, would, if everything went well, land undetected at the narrow point—the center of the hourglass—of Yonghung-do, and then split, and simultaneously move over land, Diceworth's team to take the village of Oe-Ri on the south end of the island, and McCoy's to take Nae-ri on the northern end.

The lifeboat would hold a seven-man team, commanded by Zimmerman, as the reserve.

Taylor, Hart, and Kim would be aboard *Wind of Good Fortune,* Kim to control the militia, and Hart to operate the radio to report what was going on—especially if something went wrong.

It was a good plan of operation, and it almost worked.

They managed to get past Taebu-do and Taemuui-do without, so far as they could tell, arousing any interest whatever.

But as they approached Oe-Ri on the south end of Yonghung-do, hoping to pass there, too, undetected, the junk sailing up the Flying Fish Channel attracted the attention of a North Korean sentry. First, there was a siren, and then the *Wind of Good Fortune* was in the light of a searchlight, and finally there came machine-gun fire, which, after a moment, walked its way through the water and into the hull of the *Wind of Good Fortune.*

And a moment after that, two rounds of five-inch naval gunfire landed on the machine-gun position. The searchlight went out, the machine gun stopped firing, and the outer of the two *Jamaica* boats—which held Lieutenant Diceworth's team—cut free from the *Wind of Good Fortune* and headed for the village.

As a Royal Marine handed twenty-round magazines to a U.S. Marine firing his Browning Automatic Rifle from the bow of the boat, two more rounds of five-inch from *Charity* landed in Oe-Ri.

The second boat from HMS *Jamaica*—carrying McCoy's team—now started to edge ahead of the *Wind of Good Fortune,* headed up the Flying Fish Channel for the north end of the island and the village of Nae-Ri.

With the loss of the element of surprise, there was no need now to land in the middle of Yonghung-do and go overland.

The distance was a little over three miles, and the boat was making—even against the rapidly receding tide—close to fifteen knots. It took them just over fifteen minutes to reach the end of the island, but that was apparently enough time for the North Koreans on the southern end of the island to notify the North Koreans on the northern end that they were under attack. When McCoy's boat turned out of the Flying Fish Channel toward the village of Nae-Ri, they were immediately brought under rifle fire.

They've probably laid a telephone line across the island, McCoy thought, as he watched a Royal Marine sergeant speak into the microphone of his field radio:

"Mother, Mother, Baby Two, Baby Two, Sixteen, Sixteen," he said, lowered the microphone, and turned to McCoy.

"On the way, sir," he said. "If the captain remembers, Sixteen is four rounds from *Charity*'s five-incher, sir."

"Good show, Sergeant!" Captain McCoy said, in the best English accent he could muster.

A few moments later, there was the *thruttle-thruttle* sound of a large-caliber round moving in the air, and then an enormous explosion in the village of Nae-Ri. And then another, and another, and another.

McCoy, who was riding in the bow, gestured to the coxswain to make for the shore, and then to Sergeant Jennings to get on the bow with his Browning Automatic Rifle.

THREE

TOP SECRET

0500 GREENWICH 25 AUGUST 1950

FROM OFFICER COMMANDING HMS CHARITY

TO HMS JAMAICA
PERSONAL AND IMMEDIATE ATTENTION VICE ADMIRAL SIR
WILLIAM MATTHEWS, RN

SIR

I HAVE THE HONOR TO REPORT, BASED ON INFORMATION
FURNISHED ME BY CAPTAIN GEORGE F. HART, USMC, THE
FOLLOWING:

(1) THE ISLANDS OF YONGHUNG-DO AND TAEMUUI-DO WERE
    SUCCESSFULLY INVESTED BY US AND ROYAL MARINE FORCES
    EARLY THIS MORNING AND ALL RESISTANCE WAS ENDED AT
    1500 LOCAL TIME THIS AFTERNOON.

(2) US AND BRITISH CASUALTIES ZERO KILLED AND ZERO
    WOUNDED.

(3) ENEMY CASUALTIES SEVEN KILLED SIX WOUNDED NINE
    PRISONERS.

(4) IT IS THE INTENTION OF CAPTAIN K.R. MCCOY USMC TO
    INVADE THE ISLAND OF TAEBU-DO AS SOON AS TIDAL
    CONDITIONS PERMIT. HE REPORTS WHITE FLAGS HAVE BEEN
    HOISTED PRESUMABLY INDICATING A DESIRE OF THE ENEMY
    TO SURRENDER. CAPTAIN MCCOY REQUESTS THAT BRIGADIER
    GENERAL PICKERING, USMC, BE APPRISED BY YOU OF
    THESE DEVELOPMENTS.

```
MOST RESPECTFULLY SUBMITTED


DARWIN JONES-FORTIN, RN
COMMANDING HMS CHARITY


TOP   SECRET
```

[FOUR]
The Residence of the Supreme Commander UN
Command/Allied Forces in Japan
The Embassy of the United States
Tokyo, Japan
1930 25 August 1950

"Oh, Fleming," MacArthur said, rising from an armchair in the upstairs sitting room, "there you are. Thank you for coming."

"It was good of you to receive me on such short notice," Pickering said, "and even kinder to ask me to supper. I know I'm intruding . . ."

He walked to Jean MacArthur and kissed her cheek.

"Don't be silly," she said. "We don't see enough of you socially, Fleming."

"This isn't exactly social, Jean," Pickering said.

"For the next ten minutes, it will be, while we have a cocktail and hors d'oeuvres," MacArthur said.

A Filipino steward offered Pickering a tray, on which sat a squat crystal glass dark with whiskey.

"Your health," Pickering said, as he picked it up.

"Do you hear often from Patricia?" Jean asked.

"I call her, or she calls me, just about every day," Pickering said.

"And how, poor dear, is she bearing up?"

"The tough part is not knowing," Pickering replied, honestly.

"And there's still no word about your son?" MacArthur asked.

"Only in the sense that my station chief in Pusan reports that there is no word that Pick has been captured."

"And would he know?" Jean MacArthur asked.

"He would," Pickering said. "Actually, he's very good at what he does."

"Forgive me," MacArthur said. "He didn't—the CIA didn't—seem to be able to give us advance knowledge of what happened on June 26."

My God, if I get into that, I'll really be in trouble.

"Yes, I know," Pickering said. "That's one of the reasons I was sent here, to see if I can prevent a blunder like that from happening again."

"And I can think of no one better able to do that," MacArthur said. "Your report will be to Admiral Hillenkoetter, I presume?"

"I haven't even begun to prepare a report," Pickering said. "But when I do, it will go to the President."

"Despite the perhaps unkind things I have said about the OSS in the past, I questioned President Truman's decision to abolish it immediately after the war," MacArthur said.

"He seems to have quickly realized his mistake," Pickering replied. "He formed the CIA several months later."

"I sometimes wonder . . . ," MacArthur said. "Let me phrase it this way: President Truman seems to understand what a threat Joseph Stalin and company pose to the world. Frankly, I have often wondered if many of those close to President Roosevelt were similarly concerned. Many of those were still in the upper echelons around President Truman when he abolished the OSS."

"I'm sure it pleased those people, General," Pickering said. "But my best information was that it was senior officers of the military who wanted to bury the OSS, and successfully urged Truman to do so."

"Why would they want to do that?"

"Because they couldn't control it themselves."

"That's a hell of an accusation, Fleming," MacArthur said, "and let me quickly and emphatically disassociate myself from any group of senior officers . . . I was never asked what I thought should happen to the OSS. Had I been asked, I would have said I felt it to be quite valuable to the nation. And when the CIA was formed, I was delighted when they sent their experts to assist me here."

Oh, what the hell. I'm going to infuriate him anyway. Why put it off for ten minutes?

"General, the point there is that the CIA wasn't here to assist you," Pickering said. "Not in the sense you're implying. You're suggesting that you considered them part of your staff, and that implies you controlled them."

"And you find something wrong with that?"

"To do their job properly, CIA people cannot be subordinate to the local commander," Pickering said.

"Even to someone like Douglas?" Jean MacArthur said, loyally. "I can understand your position, I think, at division level, or corps level, but Douglas is the Supreme Commander!"

"That's the point, Jean," Pickering said. "The more important, the more imposing, the local commander is—and I submit that your husband is the most important and most imposing of all the commanders I know of—the less likely the CIA man is to challenge his judgment. And he is supposed to think, and act, independently."

"Would you say that applies to our relationship?" MacArthur asked.

"Yes, sir, I would," Pickering said. "Our friendship aside, I really think you were happier before I came here, when the CIA station chief thought of himself—and you thought of him—as a member of your staff, and you both behaved accordingly."

"You apparently don't think much of your CIA station chief," MacArthur said.

"Or maybe Douglas, either," Jean said. "Fleming, I never thought I'd hear you talk like this—"

"Jean, you know better than that," Pickering interrupted. "My admiration for Douglas is bottomless, as an officer and a man."

"It certainly doesn't sound like it," she said.

Pickering turned to face MacArthur.

"The only reason I haven't relieved the station chief is that I'm afraid his replacement might be even worse."

"In what sense?" MacArthur said, icily. "That he would be even more cooperative with the local commander?"

"I think it's perfectly natural for any senior officer—including you—to be uncomfortable with the notion of having people playing on their fields whom they do not control. And to do whatever they can to get that control. In the case of the Tokyo CIA station chief, you did just that. Or Charley Willoughby did, which is the same thing."

MacArthur stared at him icily for a moment.

"Granting, for the sake of argument, that I did, or General Willoughby did, manage, so to speak, to bring your station chief to think of himself as a member of the team, what harm was done?"

"I was less than completely honest a moment ago when I implied I'm going to relieve the station chief for having allowed himself to be sucked into Charley Willoughby's—and your—orbit. The fact is that he was derelict—even criminally derelict—in the performance of his duties."

"That certainly deserves amplification," MacArthur said.

"In his case, it was an act of what I have to believe was intentional failure to do his job properly. It was either that, or he was, literally, so inept or so stupid that he didn't know what was going on."

"And what was going on?"

"A report was prepared by an intelligence officer on the staff of the Naval Element, SCAP, strongly indicating that the North Koreans had prepared an invasion force."

"I know of no such report, and, frankly, Pickering—"

"General, there was a report. I've seen it. You apparently didn't get to see it because General Willoughby ordered it destroyed."

"That's an outrageous accusation!"

"Unfortunately, it's true," Pickering said.

"What intelligence officer?" MacArthur said. "What we are going to do right now, General Pickering, tonight, is get General Willoughby and this intelligence officer of yours in here and get to the bottom of this. After which I will take whatever action seems appropriate."

"You can get Charley Willoughby in here, General, if you like, and I will repeat to him what I just told you. If that is your desire, I would suggest that you also summon Captain Edward C. Wilkerson—"

"Who's he?" MacArthur interrupted.

"The Chief of the Naval Element, SCAP. He's the other villain in this sad affair. He acquiesced when General Willoughby ordered the report destroyed."

"I don't believe any of this," Jean MacArthur said.

From the look on Douglas MacArthur's face, neither did he.

"We will start with the intelligence officer who allegedly prepared this report," MacArthur said. "And then . . ."

"Unfortunately, he's not available tonight," Pickering said.

"Why not? Where is he?"

"On Tokchok-kundo Island," Pickering said.

"Where?"

"From which, early this morning, he launched an invasion of Taemuui-do, Yonghung-do, and Taebu-do islands in the Flying Fish Channel, which, as of 1500 this afternoon, are under our control."

MacArthur stared at him in disbelief.

"Do I understand you correctly, General Pickering, that you have launched an operation—without any consultation, much less permission from myself or anyone on my staff—that may—without question will—seriously impact on the Inchon invasion?"

Pickering didn't immediately reply. But he smiled, which caused MacArthur's face to turn white.

"I fail to see the humor in any of this, so perhaps you would be good enough to tell me why you are smiling?"

"Forgive me," Pickering said. "I was thinking about General Patton's reply to General Bradley during the Sicilian campaign. . . ."

MacArthur, after a moment, chuckled and then laughed.

"I don't understand," Jean MacArthur said.

"Bradley was concerned, darling," MacArthur explained, "that the mutual dislike between George Patton and General Montgomery would see Georgie take extraordinary—possibly too risky—steps to be in Palermo before Montgomery could get there. So he messaged him words to the effect, 'Do not do not take Palermo without my permission.' To which Georgie replied, 'I hold Palermo, should I give it back?' "

She chuckled. "I'd never heard that before," she said.

"Would that this situation were as amusing," MacArthur said to Pickering.

"General, I think I should tell you that President Truman was aware of my plan," Pickering said.

"Would you tell me why you did it?" MacArthur asked.

"General, I've been privileged to be in on the planning of many of your invasions," Pickering said. "I like to think I learned from watching you."

"Why didn't you come to me?"

"Your staff was determined to take the islands on D Minus One," Pickering said. "You agreed. I thought doing so would give the enemy twenty-four hours' notice of our intentions. That question had come up and been decided in favor of D Minus One. If I had come to you with this, you would have been forced to choose between your trusted staff and an amateur challenging their—and your—judgment."

"I have overridden my staff before, and you know that."

"I wasn't sure I could carry it off. Not me. Captain McCoy. I thought it was worth the risk. If we failed, only a few men would be lost. If we succeeded . . ."

"And what makes you think the enemy won't immediately take action to retake the islands?"

"The hope is that the enemy will believe it's nothing more than the South Koreans improving their positions along the Flying Fish Channel. They may not even take action. If they do, all they're going to find on the three islands are South Korean national police."

"And when the invasion doesn't take place in the next three or four days, you think they will relax?"

"Yes, sir," Pickering said. "I spoke with Captain McCoy on the radio shortly before I came here. He said the North Koreans on the islands were not in radio contact with the mainland. So they could not have reported they were under attack by U.S. and Royal Marines. He believes the deception worked."

"Royal Marines?"

"Yes, sir. From HMS *Jamaica.* And HMS *Charity* provided naval gunfire for the assaults."

"So Admiral Matthews also felt D Minus One for the assault on the islands was not a good idea," MacArthur said. "I wonder why he didn't come to me with his objections."

"I can only guess that he felt much as I felt, sir."

MacArthur looked at him for a long moment, then asked, thoughtfully, "We have no idea what will happen between now and the invasion, do we?"

"No, sir. But McCoy feels—and I concur—that if there is an attack on the islands, and we refrain from using gunfire from the *Charity* to repel it, it would lend credence to the idea that the whole thing was a South Korean operation, nothing more."

"In which case, we would lose the islands."

"Not necessarily, sir. There're thirty South Korean police already on the islands, and we intend to reinforce them. If an attack doesn't come for several days, we should have enough South Koreans in place to repel anything but a major effort."

"That's a pretty iffy situation," MacArthur said. "So iffy that I don't consider it wise to throw this equation—what if we already held the islands?—into the last-minute planning just yet. Right now, the fewer people who know about this, the better, and we will take things as they develop. Wouldn't you agree, Fleming?"

"Yes, sir."

Don't tell me that's it?

We're back to "Fleming"? And he just wants to sit on this, "take things as they develop"?

"Would you like another little drop before we go into supper, Fleming?" the Supreme Commander asked. "Or not?"

"I think another one would go down nicely, sir. Thank you."

[FIVE]
Tokchok-kundo Island
0530 26 August 1950

"I can stay," Lieutenant David Taylor, USNR, said to Captain Kenneth R. McCoy, USMC. "Kim is as good a skipper for the *Wind of Good Fortune* as I am, and Major Kim will be aboard."

"What, are there two last names in all of Korea—Kim and Lee?" Master Gunner Ernest W. Zimmerman observed, rhetorically.

Taylor and McCoy chuckled.

"Don't let this go to your head, Taylor," McCoy said. "But I disagree, and right now we can't afford to get in trouble with the *Wind of Good Fortune.* You go. We'll be all right."

"Says the eternal optimist," Zimmerman said.

"The sooner we get the militia off the islands, and Kim's national police on them, the better off we're going to be," McCoy said.

"What makes you so sure there's going to be more national police?" Zimmerman asked.

"Because we now hold the islands, and I don't think any national police commander would want to take the chance of becoming known as the guy who was responsible for us losing them again, simply because he was afraid to reinforce them."

Zimmerman's shrug indicated he accepted the logic.

"I wish we could have kept the Limeys," Zimmerman said. "At least the boats."

"They couldn't swim back to the *Charity,*" McCoy said. "They left us one of their boats, and the radio . . ."

"But not the guy to drive it," Zimmerman argued.

". . . and we'll have to do with that," McCoy went on, ignoring him. And then he changed his mind.

"I want you to have this straight in your mind, Ernie, so I'll go over it one more time. There is no way we can hold any of these islands if the North Koreans really want to take them back. And if they tried they would become damned curious if we put up a hell of a fight—"

"So what we're going to do is hope they stay stupid," Zimmerman interrupted.

"You're getting close to the line, Ernie," McCoy said, very coldly. "What we're going to do is when they send a couple of boats—and they will—to see what happened on Taemuui-do and Yonghung-do, is have the militia fire on them with rifles. They may get lucky—none of the militia can really shoot, and all they have is the Japanese Arisakas—and kill a couple of the NKs. But even if they don't, bullets will be flying, and nobody likes that. The first time that happens, the NKs may pull back. But they'll come back, and when they do, the militia takes a couple more shots at them, and then takes off into the hills. The NKs, we hope, will take a look around, see no evidence of anybody but Koreans being there, and maybe, maybe, go into the hills after them. More likely, they'll just get back in the boats. They won't have enough men, we don't think, to leave enough men on the islands to garrison them. And why should they? There's nothing on the islands but a bunch of South Koreans armed with some Jap rifles, pissing in the wind against the inevitable triumph of the Armies of Socialism. Their misguided brethren can be left there to be dealt with later, by somebody else."

"And when they come here? They'll know Americans are here."

"We'll deal with that when it happens," McCoy said. "And pray it doesn't happen in the next two weeks. What we have to do now is buy time. You got all that straight, now?"

"I got it," Zimmerman said.

"What I was hoping to get, Mr. Zimmerman, was the expected response of a Marine who has been given an order."

Zimmerman met his eyes.

"Aye, aye, sir," he said.

"Thank you, Mr. Zimmerman."

"Jesus, Killer, all I was doing was asking."

"I'll leave you lovebirds now," Lieutenant Taylor said. "With a little luck, I'll be back in forty-eight hours."

"With fresh eggs, chickens, and bread, right?" Zimmerman asked.

"With fresh eggs, chickens, and bread," Taylor said.

He saluted, which surprised McCoy, and walked down onto the wharf, gestured to the crew of the *Wind of Good Fortune* to let loose her lines, and climbed aboard. The ebbing tide immediately started to pull her away from the wharf and toward the Flying Fish Channel, even before Taylor made it to the stern and started her engine.

"Can I say something?" Zimmerman said.

"Why not?"

"Remember Guadalcanal? The Navy dumped the First Division on the beach, and then they took off with the heavy artillery and the rations, leaving the Division on the beach?"

"I remember hearing something about that," McCoy said.

"I used to wonder how those guys felt about getting dumped on some island and watching the Navy sail away. Now I know."

[SIX]
U.S. Navy Base Sasebo
Sasebo, Kyushu, Japan
1500 5 September 1950

LST stands for Landing Ship, Tank, which means the vessel was designed to deposit tracked armored fighting vehicles directly onto beaches. When approaching a beach, the less draft—the portion of the vessel extending underwater—the better. So the design for the LST had provided for a flat bottom. It was known by the Naval architects, of course, that a flat-bottomed oceangoing vessel was, in any but the calmest of waters, going to toss and turn and twist and otherwise move in such a manner that passengers aboard were liable to be very uncomfortable and possibly, even probably, suffer mal de mer, but passenger comfort was not a design criterion, and getting tanks as close to the beach as possible was.

The first Marine of B Company, 5th Marines, to suffer mal de mer became nauseous ten minutes after LST-450 left Pusan for Sasebo. By the time LST-450 tied up at Sasebo, all but three members of B Company had suffered mal de mer to one degree or another, including Captain Howard Dunwood, USMCR, the company commander.

He found this both depressing and professionally humiliating. A commanding officer tossing his cookies countless times hardly stands as an example for his men to follow.

The commanding officer of LST-450, Lieutenant John X. McNear—a thirty-year-old naval reservist who six weeks before had been the golf professional at Happy Hollow Country Club, Phoenix, Arizona—extended to Captain Dunwood the privilege of his bridge, and between bouts of nausea, Captain Dunwood learned from Lieutenant McNear that while this—the weather, the seas—was pretty bad, it was nothing like the weather he had experienced sailing the sonofabitch from San Diego, California, to Pusan.

He also informed Captain Dunwood that their destination was the U.S. Navy Base, Sasebo, Japan.

This caused Captain Dunwood to think that at Sasebo, his company would be brought back up to strength—Baker was down to 101 men and three officers, including Captain Dunwood—and that they would probably be partici-

pating in the supposedly secret invasion of some port—Inchon, he had heard—
up the Korean peninsula.

He was very curious, however, about why—literally on the pier at Pusan,
about to board one of the attack transports—Baker Company had been separated from the battalion and ordered aboard the LST.

It was only scuttlebutt, of course, but the word on the pier had been that
the attack transports were headed for Yokohama, near Tokyo. If that was so, why
was Baker Company going to Sasebo?

Captain Dunwood had unpleasant memories of Sasebo. It was at Sasebo that
that candy-ass "Marine" captain who had done the job on his finger had debarked from the aircraft in his splendidly tailored uniform.

Lieutenant McNear couldn't even hazard a guess about why Baker Company
was going by itself on LST-450—which could have easily transported, for the
relatively short voyage, four times that many men—or what would happen to
them in Sasebo. His own orders were to remain in Sasebo until further orders;
he had expected to be ordered right back to Pusan.

On docking at Sasebo, Baker Company was marched into an aircraft hangar
that had been hastily converted to a temporary barracks by the installation of
long rows of folding canvas cots, a row of toilets, and a row of showerheads.

The enlisted Marines were stripped, showered, and then given a rudimentary physical examination—which included a "short-arm inspection" to detect
gonorrhea, which showed, in Captain Dunwood's judgment, that the Navy
had no fucking idea what was going on in Korea—and then were issued three
sets of underwear and stockings and two sets of new utilities. Privates through
corporal were then given a partial pay of twenty dollars, sergeants and up of
thirty, and officers of fifty.

Baker Company was then informed that, due to the special circumstances,
the Officer Commanding Sasebo Naval Base had waived the standing uniform
regulations, and they would be permitted to have liberty in Sasebo from 1700
until 2330.

A Navy chaplain and a Navy surgeon then spoke almost emotionally about
the dangers to body and soul the Marines would encounter in Sasebo, unless
they remembered their mothers and other female loved ones who were waiting
for them at home and trusted them to behave like the Christian—or Jewish, as
the case might be—gentlemen they were supposed to be.

This was followed by a twenty-minute color motion picture of individuals
in the terminal stages of syphilis, and of other individuals whose genitalia were
covered with suppurating scabs. Captain Dunwood had seen the film before, at

Camp Drake, when he had first arrived in Japan, and at Camp Pendleton, California, when he reported on active duty.

Then a bus appeared to take whichever of the Marines desired to avail themselves of a little local culture to town.

Captain Dunwood then debated whether it would be wiser to take dinner in the mess, which had a section for officers, but no intoxicants, or in the Officers' Club, which did. If he went to the O Club, and had a couple of drinks, and that candy-ass sonofabitch who'd done the job on his finger was there, he was likely to get himself in trouble.

A couple of drinks and the sudden insight—*If I do knock out some of the bastard's teeth, which he deserves, the fucking finger's still not right, what are they going to do to me, send me to Korea?*—saw Captain Dunwood take both his dinner and breakfast the next morning in the Officers' Club.

He did not see the candy-ass sonofabitch during either meal, and couldn't decide whether that was a good thing or not.

At 0800 their first morning ashore at Sasebo, two Marine officers, a major and a lieutenant, and a technical sergeant, came into the "temporary barracks," ordered guards posted at all doors, set up a blackboard and a tripod, and announced they were from the G-3 section of what was now the First Marine Division, and that they were here to brief Baker Company on its very special role in the first amphibious invasion by the United States Marine Corps since World War II.

Using maps—and the surprisingly skillful technical sergeant, who drew on the blackboard whatever needed to be illustrated—it was explained to the men and officers of Baker Company that to reach the landing beaches at Inchon, the invasion fleet would have to traverse the Flying Fish Channel, and that in the Flying Fish Channel were two islands, Taemuui-do and Yonghung-do.

These islands, the major went on in a manner that reminded Captain Dunwood of the district sales manager of the Chrysler Corporation urging the salesmen to greater heights, were so located that any artillery on them could be brought to bear on ships of the invasion fleet moving down the Flying Fish Channel.

This situation, of course, could not be permitted. Commencing at 0400 14 September, both islands (and other islands in the immediate vicinity) would be brought under an intense naval artillery barrage by various vessels of the invasion fleet, probably including the battleship USS *Missouri,* which had been hastily demothballed and rushed to Japan from the West Coast.

Whether or not the *Missouri* actually turned its fifteen-inch naval cannon on the islands, the briefing officer had said, there was enough firepower on the other men-of-war, cruisers, and destroyers, to wipe the islands clean. Company B should encounter virtually no resistance when they went ashore on Taemuui-do and Yonghung-do.

That was so much bullshit, Captain Dunwood believed. He had gone ashore at Tarawa and Iwo Jima, and on each occasion had been assured that following the massive pre-invasion barrages of naval artillery to be laid on those islands, resistance would be minimal.

He of course kept his personal—or was it, he wondered, professional?—opinion to himself, and went so far as to correct another Marine, who had also been on Okinawa, who said "Bullshit, I've heard that before" aloud when told of the awesome resistance-destroying naval artillery barrage to be laid down.

The next five days, said the major from First Marine Division G-3, would be devoted to training Baker Company for, and equipping it for, the seizure of the islands of Taemuui-do and Yonghung-do in the Flying Fish Channel.

Then they would reboard LST-450 and sail for the channel itself.

The training was good—Captain Dunwood had to admit that—and it was necessary. It had been a long time since anybody moved from an LST into a Higgins boat, and some of his men had never done so.

Captain Dunwood took dinner every night in the O Club, but he never saw the candy-ass sonofabitch who'd done the job on his finger so long as he was at Sasebo. But he often thought about him, and hoped he would.

XXII

[ONE]

Tokchok-kundo Island
1530 13 September 1950

The last message from General Pickering to McCoy—with the date and time stamp 1200 12 Sep—had included the cryptic line "will be out of town for the next few days," which McCoy correctly interpreted to mean that he was leaving Tokyo to board the command ship USS *Mount McKinley.*

That suggested the invasion was still on, that there had been no delays.

Taylor had told him that because of the tides, the only time and date the invasion could take place was in the early-morning hours of 15 September.

With that criterion, if there had been serious problems in mounting the invasion, the options available had not included a delay while the problem was being solved. Rather, the options had been to solve the problem, live with it, or call the invasion off. The invasion, McCoy was sure, was on.

And, in the absence of word to the contrary, that meant the D Minus 1 assault on Taemuui-do, Yonghung-do, and Tokchok-kundo itself was on.

Over the past week, as Major Kim had infiltrated national police onto Taemuui-do and Yonghung-do, he had exfiltrated the militia. That hadn't been nearly as difficult as McCoy thought it would be. The militia had been local fishermen before being issued Arisaka rifles and bandoliers of ammunition and told what was expected of them.

With the arrival of the national police, they had become local fishermen again, turned the weapons over to the national police, and left. For example, the small local fishing boats that touched ashore during the day at Nae-Ri with two fishermen aboard, left with three. Or four.

McCoy had been personally uncomfortable with militia, since he thought of them as—knew they were—civilians, and his entire life in the Corps had taught him to keep civilians out of the line of fire.

Now he was personally uncomfortable with the notion of just over 120 national policemen on the three islands they held. Intellectually, he understood they were more like gendarmerie, a paramilitary force, organized and trained more like soldiers than policemen, but emotionally, Captain K. R. McCoy, USMCR, thought of them as "Kim's Cops."

And if the artillery started landing, as it inevitably would unless Pickering could get MacArthur to call it off, Kim's Cops were going to get blown off Taemuui-do and Yonghung-do. Major Kim's assurances to McCoy that he had instructed his men precisely what to do if they came under naval gunfire, and that he was sure they would be all right, did absolutely nothing to reassure McCoy.

Privately, he agreed with what Zimmerman had to say after Kim had given his "I have given the men precise instructions" speech and then gone off somewhere.

"Step Three," Zimmerman had said, "bend over, with your hands over your ears and your ears between your knees. Step Four, kiss your ass goodbye."

"Come on, Ernie," McCoy had said. "Kim's a good officer. He's done a good job."

"Yeah," Zimmerman admitted. It was true.

By the time the North Koreans had made their first investigation of the village of Nae-Ri, for example, Kim had managed to infiltrate enough national policemen and exfiltrate enough of the militia so that seventy percent of the "fishermen" the North Koreans had seen as they nosed their thirty-five-foot power launch into the harbor were in fact national policemen—

—who knew how to use their Japanese Arisaka rifles, and killed or wounded three of the twenty North Korean soldiers on the launch before it could be turned around and gotten out of the line of fire.

The launch didn't come back for two days, and when it put troops ashore, it found Nae-Ri deserted.

The launch left a six-man squad under a corporal at Nae-Ri, and then went to the village of Oe-Ri, at the southern end of the island, where they landed unopposed. They left another six-man squad at Oe-Ri, and sailed off confident of having restored Socialist Rule.

Kim's Cops had had the North Korean troops at Nae-Ri disarmed and trussed and bound for shipment out aboard the next small fishing boats before the power launch had reached Oe-Ri, and the NKs left at Oe-Ri disarmed and trussed and bound fifteen minutes after the power launch left the harbor.

It took the North Koreans three days to discover that all was not right in Nae-Ri, and when they sailed back into that port, they were brought under a hail of fire that killed three more of their troops before the lieutenant in charge withdrew to reassess the situation.

With slight variations, the same scenes had played at Taemuui-do and Taebu-do. Both islands provided sufficient resistance for the North Koreans to have to really consider whether massing enough troops to overcome it would be worthwhile, or—since all it seemed to be was a group of misguided capitalist lackeys—whether it would be best to wait and see what happened.

It had been what McCoy had told Major Kim he wanted to happen, and it had happened, almost entirely because of Kim's control of his men.

And now, unless the D Minus 1 assault on the channel islands was called off, the national police were going to get blown away by a phrase Zimmerman confessed he never understood: "friendly fire."

The other thing that was worrying McCoy was that there had been no North Korean investigation at all of Tokchok-kundo. Not one boat, of any size, had nosed into their harbor, much less one of the thirty-five-foot power launches.

There were, McCoy decided, several possible reasons for that. One was that Tokchok-kundo was the farthest island from the NK positions on the mainland, except for the lighthouse island, and that was really not an island but a large rock jutting out of the water.

It was also possible that Tokchok-kundo was on a list, to be investigated, and if necessary—from their point of view—neutralized and pacified after Taemuui-do, Yonghung-do, and Taebu-do.

And it was also possible that one, or two, or a half-dozen of the friendly local fishermen who had been selling Kim information—or giving it to him—had also sold—or given—to the NKs the information that not only were there a bunch of Americans on Tokchok-kundo, but that they had a boat, and were, among other things, using the island as a temporary holding pen for North Korean prisoners.

McCoy made a joke of it, always smiling when he said, with great pomposity, "I devoutly believe that bad things inevitably happen, and when they happen, happen at the worst possible time, and therefore, we have to do thus and so."

But the truth was, he devoutly believed just that.

The bad that was inevitably going to happen was a North Korean investigation of the island of Tokchok-kundo, and the worst possible time for that to happen was right now.

So far, they had been lucky. Luck runs out.

The D Minus 1 assault of the islands was apparently on for first thing in the morning. If it wasn't on, there would have been word from General Pickering. The USS *Mount McKinley* had as good a commo center aboard as—probably better than—the one in the Dai Ichi Building. If he had something to say to them, George Hart would have heard it.

In this case, no news was bad news.

There was only one slim chance to avoid the gunfire: When the warships steamed up to the Flying Fish Channel in the early hours of tomorrow morning, the lighthouse had to be showing light.

The lighthouse keeper that Kim had talked about had not been on Tokchok-kundo when McCoy and Taylor arrived, so to get it up and running the way it should be was out of the question, but there was plenty of diesel fuel available, and diesel fuel burns.

Captain McCoy called an Officers' Call of his staff. It convened in the captain's cabin of the *Wind of Good Fortune*. Present were Lieutenant Taylor, Captain Hart, and Master Gunner Zimmerman.

"I have reason to believe the North Koreans may come into port tonight, probably just before dark," McCoy began

"Where'd you get that, Killer?" Zimmerman asked, curiously.

My worst-thing-at-the-worst-time theory, Ernie.

"I thought you knew, Mr. Zimmerman," McCoy said. "God tells me things."

"Oh, Jesus Christ, McCoy!" Taylor said, half in disgust, half laughing.

"And there have been two changes of plan," McCoy said. "The first is that if they do come in, we're going to have to kill everybody on board, or sink the launch, preferably both."

"Not just run them off, to come back and play later?" Taylor asked.

"The minute they come in the harbor, they're going to see the boat," McCoy said. "So the first thing we shoot on the boat is wherever the radio is likely to be, and anybody who looks like he has a microphone."

"Why are they going to see the boat?" Hart asked.

"Because the camouflage will be off it."

"Oh?"

"Because you and me, Hart, the moment we finish with the NKs, are going to go to the lighthouse. Maybe, just maybe, if that's lit up in the wee hours of the morning, they won't lay naval gunfire on the islands."

"No, you're not," Zimmerman said.

"What did you say, Mr. Zimmerman?" McCoy snapped icily.

"Hart and me'll go to the lighthouse," Zimmerman said. "We'll take two of the guys with us." He paused, then went on: "Who do you want to be here if the general gets on the radio?" Zimmerman said. "You or me?"

"Taylor will be here."

"He's right, Ken," Taylor said. "You can't leave here. But I don't think Ernie should, either. Hart and I can handle the lighthouse if you give us two men, and Ernie can work the radio."

"For what it's worth, I vote with the Navy," Hart said. "I'm a little uncomfortable with the idea of the Killer steering me around in the boat in the dark."

"OK," Taylor said. "That's settled. We just had a vote."

"A *vote?*" McCoy said. "What does this look like, Congress?"

"What I'd like to know, Ken," Taylor said, ignoring him, "is how you can be so sure the NKs are going to suddenly show up."

"I've got a gut feeling," McCoy admitted. "That's all."

"That's good enough for me, Killer," Zimmerman said, matter-of-factly. "I will go alert the troops to prepare to repel boarders."

He got up and walked out of the cabin.

Hart and McCoy looked at each other.

"You stick by the radio, George," McCoy ordered. "Tell Kim to turn the engine on and leave it running. Maybe, with a little luck, we'll hear from the general, and none of this John Wayne business will be necessary."

Hart nodded, and then said,

"Aye, aye, sir."

The John Wayne business proved to be necessary. Twenty minutes later, as Technical Sergeant Keller was hauling the camouflage netting off the boat, the lookout posted on the end of the wharf suddenly started to run down the wharf toward the shore.

Keller waved at him to stay where he was, and after another half-dozen steps, the lookout jumped to one side of the wharf and concealed himself in the rocks.

Keller dropped the camouflage net and jumped ashore, and, bent double, ran into the alley between the closest two houses. He ran behind the houses until he came to the one where he thought Captain McCoy would be.

He wasn't.

He ran to the next house.

McCoy was there, taking up the squatting firing position with his Garand as if he were on the range at Camp LeJeune.

"Captain!"

"I see them, Jennings," McCoy said.

Jennings looked through the window, and for the first time saw the boat, and the North Korean soldiers in their cotton uniforms manning what looked like an air-cooled .50 on her bow.

The partially uncovered boat caught their attention, and they fired a short burst at it.

"Shit," McCoy said. "I was hoping they'd try to capture it intact!"

Then his Garand went off, and then again, and then again, and Jennings saw the two Koreans on the machine gun fall, one backward, as if something had pushed him, and the other just collapse straight downward.

"If you remember how to use that rifle, Sergeant," McCoy said, "now would be a good time."

[TWO]
Aboard LST-450
37 Degrees 11 Minutes North Latitude, 125 Degrees 58 Minutes East Longitude
The Yellow Sea
1615 13 September 1950

LST-450 was now bobbling in a wide circle in the Yellow Sea about fifty miles off the lighthouse marking the entrance to the Flying Fish Channel. She was alone, in the sense that she was not escorted by—under the protection of—a destroyer or any other kind of warship, but there had always been some sort of aircraft more or less overhead since she had sailed from Sasebo, and the farther north they had moved, there seemed to be more ships just visible on all sides of her.

Not a convoy, Captain Howard Dunwood, USMCR, had reasoned, although there certainly was a convoy out there someplace, surrounded by men-of-war. What he was looking at were ships of the invasion fleet who someone had judged did not need protection as much as some *other* ships—an LST was not as valuable as an aircraft carrier or an assault transport, obviously—and had been placed, for the time being, far enough from where the action was likely to occur to keep them reasonably safe.

After reviewing with his men for the umpteenth time the role Baker Company was to play in the Inchon invasion, Dunwood turned them over to the first sergeant and went to the bridge. He would have a cup of coffee with the captain before the evening meal was called.

The major sent to Sasebo from Division G-3 had been—as Dunwood expected he would be—a bullshitter, but the more Dunwood thought about what Baker Company was going to be expected to do, the more he came to believe the major had been right about one thing. Baker Company's role in the invasion was going to be critical.

You just can't sail large unarmored vessels slowly past artillery, and that's exactly what was going to happen unless Baker Company could (a) seize the islands, and (b) hold them against counterattack long enough for the Navy to get some cruisers and destroyers down the channel past them.

And the more often Baker Company rehearsed its role, the more Dunwood was sure that Division G-3 had come up with a pretty good plan to do what had to be done, and that the plan—now changed by what they'd learned in rehearsal—was now as good as it was going to get.

What was going to happen now was that during the hours of darkness—probably meaning as soon as it really got dark—LST-450 would end its circling and move to a position just off the lighthouse marking the entrance to the Flying Fish Channel.

There, it would rendezvous with five Higgins boats put into the water from the USS *Pickaway* (APA-222).

Starting at 0330 the next morning—14 September—after they had had their breakfast, Company B would begin to transfer from LST-450 to the Higgins boats. There would be twenty men and one officer on three of the boats, and twenty men under the first sergeant on the fourth, and twenty men under a gunnery sergeant on the fifth.

The naval gunfire directed at the channel islands would begin at 0400 and end at 0430. As soon as it lifted, the Higgins boats would enter the Flying Fish Channel, move down it, and occupy, first, Taemuui-do and Yonghung-do Islands, and then, depending on the situation, other islands in the immediate vicinity.

They would then establish positions from which they could defend the islands from enemy counterattack. That was the plan.

What Captain Dunwood privately believed would happen was that when the Higgins boats appeared off Taemuui-do and Yonghung-do, North Korean troops would come up from the underground positions in which they had been—successfully—shielding themselves from the naval gunfire, unlimber their machine guns, and fire upon the Higgins boats approaching their shores.

Captain Dunwood's experience had been that light machine guns (the Japanese rough equivalent of the U.S. .30 caliber) would sometimes penetrate the sides of a Higgins boat and that heavy machine guns (the Japanese rough equivalent of the U.S. .50 caliber) almost always would do so.

With the result that if the projectiles did not immediately encounter a body inside the boat, they would often ricochet around the interior until they did.

To take his mind off that unpleasant probability for himself and his men, Captain Dunwood called to mind again the face of that candy-ass "Marine" captain who'd dislocated his finger, and was at that very moment probably having a predinner cocktail with his wife, the general's daughter, in the O Club at Sasebo. The sonofabitch had probably heard there were some real Marines on the base and been smart enough to make himself scarce while they were there.

Lieutenant John X. McNear, USNR, waved Dunwood onto the bridge.

"My orders are pretty open," McNear volunteered. " 'The hours of darkness' is a pretty vague term. I was thinking I'd wait until about 2100 and then start edging over."

"I was wondering," Dunwood said, as he helped himself to coffee.

"I'm supposed to check in with ComNavForce—the *Mount McKinley*—when I leave here. I expect that I'd hear from them soon enough if they thought I should have left earlier."

"I'm sure you would," Dunwood replied.

"Bridge, Radio," the intercom metallically announced.

McNear pressed the lever beside his chair.

"Go, Sparks," he said.

"Skipper, I'm getting an Urgent from ComNavForce."

"Well, then, when you have it typed up and logged in, why don't you bring it to the bridge?" McNear said, and turned to Dunwood. "See, I told you."

Two minutes later, the radio operator, a nineteen-year-old in blue dungarees, came onto the bridge and handed McNear a sheet of typewriter paper.

McNear read it and handed it to Dunwood.

```
SECRET

URGENT

1530 13 SEP 1950
FROM COMNAVFORCE

TO LST-450

REFERENCE OPS ORDER 12-222

PARA III B 6. IS CHANGED TO READ AS FOLLOWS:

LST-450 WILL DROP ANCHOR AT POSITION 23-23 NLT 0400 15
SEPTEMBER 1950 AND RENDEZVOUS WITH LANDING CRAFT FROM
USS PICKAWAY.

REMAINER OF ORIGINAL PARA III B 6 IS DELETED AS IS ALL
OF PARA III B-7

FURTHER AMENDMENTS TO FOLLOW.

END

SECRET
```

"What's it mean?" Captain Dunwood asked.

"You saw where it said the fifteenth?" McNear asked. Dunwood nodded.

"It used to read the fourteenth, tomorrow morning," McNear said. "For reasons ComNavFor has not chosen to share with me, it means he has changed his mind. Or MacArthur himself has. Specifically, it means we don't have to go to the mouth of the Flying Fish Channel until the day after tomorrow, and when we get there, you don't have to get in the Higgins boats—that we just sit there until they make up their minds what to do with us," the captain said.

[THREE]
Aboard LST-450
37 Degrees 36 Minutes North Latitude, 126 Degrees 53
Minutes East Longitude
The Yellow Sea
0320 15 September 1950

As oceangoing vessels go, LSTs are not very large, and LST-450 was moving at steerage speed, so ordinarily she would not be thought to be posing much of a threat to other vessels operating in the vicinity of the mouth of the Flying Fish Channel.

However, to the coxswain of one of the five Higgins boats bobbing in the water, the bulk of the LST approaching them, even barely moving, was a bit disturbing.

"Fuck him," the twenty-one-year-old coxswain of the nearest boat said to no one in particular, and then took action that he considered to be necessary and of paramount importance to the safety of his vessel and crew.

He took a powerful searchlight from its compartment, turned it on, and shined it directly at the bridge of LST-450.

"We're dead ahead of you, you dumb fuck!" the coxswain said. "See us now?"

On the bridge of LST-450, the sudden very bright light coming out of the blackness literally blinded the master, the helmsman, and Captain Howard Dunwood, USMCR.

"Full astern!" Captain McNear ordered. "Keep your eyes closed until that fucking light goes out! Where the fuck were the lookouts?"

"What the hell was that?" Captain Dunwood asked, his eyes tightly closed.

He now saw an almost painful red ball, which took a long time to fade, even after the white light went out.

"I think we were just about to run over the Higgins boats," McNear said.

In the next few minutes, it became apparent to Captain McNear that he had two choices regarding maintaining his position—three, if dropping anchor was included, something he did not want to do under any circumstances. One was to put his ship into reverse and try to hold it against the heavy tide now moving northward into the Flying Fish Channel. Backing any vessel is difficult, and backing an LST is very difficult. He elected his other option.

He went to his flying bridge and picked up the bullhorn.

"Ahoy, the Higgins boats, I am about to turn 180, into the current."

There was no reply.

"Anybody out there?" Captain McNear called over the bullhorn.

"We heard you, Captain," a voice unaided by a bullhorn replied, faintly, but audibly.

"Bring her around 180 to port," McNear ordered, as he went back on the bridge, and himself took over the controls to quickly turn his ship around.

"Hey, look at that!" Captain Dunwood called in surprise.

"Not now, for Christ's sake, Howard!" McNear said, angrily, disgustedly.

Captain Dunwood, more than a little embarrassed, fell silent, and then after a moment left the bridge and stood on the flying bridge.

And then, Captain McNear, as the bow of his ship finished its turn, said exactly the same thing Captain Dunwood had said.

"Hey, look at that!"

All along a quarter of the horizon, to port from dead ahead of LST-450, there were white flashes, immediately followed by fiery red glows. Ships—and in some cases, their naval cannon—appeared momentarily in the blackness, and then a moment later, the sound of projectiles passing overhead became continuous.

He turned to see Captain Dunwood's reaction. Dunwood was nowhere in sight.

Goddamn, now what? Did he fall overboard? Did I collide with one of those fucking Higgins boats?

"Take the wheel," McNair ordered. "Hold what we have!"

"Hold what we have, aye, aye, sir," the helmsman said.

McNear found Dunwood leaning on the aft rail of the flying bridge, looking down the Flying Fish Channel.

"Howard, I guess the naval gunfire has commenced," McNear said, dryly.

"Yeah," Dunwood said. But then he added what he had been thinking—this was not the first time he'd heard naval gunfire passing overhead—"but it's not landing on my islands. It's landing way the hell and gone down the Channel."

"Yeah," McNear agreed thoughtfully.

"And that light over there, the fire, whatever. What's that?" Dunwood asked, pointing.

McNear looked.

"Unless I'm a hell of a lot more lost than I think I am, that's the lighthouse that was supposed to be leveled yesterday by that massive naval gunfire barrage we heard so much about that didn't come until just now."

"I thought lighthouse lights went, you know, on and off," Captain Dunwood said.

"They *rotate,*" Captain McNear said. "That one's not rotating. But that's the lighthouse. Come back inside, Howard, I may need you."

Three minutes later as LST-450's chief boatswain (actually a petty officer second class) reported to Captain McNair that the Higgins boats were tied alongside, and McNair had been debating with himself whether he should make another 180-degree turn so that he would be pointed down the Flying Fish Channel again, the radio operator came onto the bridge with a new Urgent Message from ComNavFor.

McNair read it and handed it to Dunwood.

```
SECRET

URGENT

0335 13 SEP 1950
FROM COMNAVFORCE

TO LST-450
ON RECEIPT YOU WILL IMMEDIATELY DEPLOY FROM USMC
LANDING TEAM ABOARD AND LANDING CRAFT ATTACHED AS
FOLLOWS:
(1) ONE HIGGINS BOAT WITH MARINES ABOARD TO FLYING FISH
    CHANNEL LIGHTHOUSE PURPOSE OF GARRISONING ISLAND,
    MAINTAINING EXISTING LIGHTHOUSE FIRE UNTIL
```

DAYLIGHT, AND EVACUATING USMC PERSONNEL PRESENTLY
HOLDING LIGHTHOUSE.

(2) TWO HIGGINS BOATS WITH MARINES ABOARD TO TOKCHOK-
KUNDO ISLAND PURPOSE OF GARRISONING ISLAND, AND
EVACUATING USMC PERSONNEL PRESENTLY HOLDING ISLAND.

(3) USMC PERSONNEL EVACUATED WILL BE TRANSPORTED TO USS
MOUNT MCKINLEY.

(4) COMNAV FORCE WILL BE ADVISED MOST EXPEDITIOUS MEANS
OF DEPARTURE OR LANDING CRAFT; LANDINGS ON
LIGHTHOUSE AND TOKCHOK-KUNDO ISLAND, AND ETA
EVACUEES MT MCKINLEY.

END

SECRET

"What the hell is this all about?" Dunwood asked.

"Howard, I haven't a clue," Captain McNair confessed. "But it looks like somebody beat you to those islands."

Dunwood considered that.

"Yeah," he said, finally. "Maybe all we were was a backup force, in case something went wrong."

"Could be," McNair agreed.

They could have told us that, the sonsofbitches, Captain Dunwood thought, *instead of giving us the whole-invasion-depends-on-you-grabbing-those-islands bullshit.*

Goddamn the Marine Corps!

Dunwood felt a little better after he told his Marines about the change of orders. After he went through the "Any questions? Anything?" business, Staff Sergeant Schmidt raised his hand.

"OK, Sergeant?"

"Captain, right after we landed at Pusan, they put out a call for all former Marine Raiders. . . ."

"And?"

"Well, sir, grabbing these islands sounds like something the Raiders would do, sir. Just a thought, Captain."

"Well, we'll find out, won't we?" Dunwood said. "But you're right, Schmidt. Grabbing these islands does sound like something the Marine Raiders would do."

[FOUR]
Tokchok-kundo Island
0515 15 September 1950

"Captain, there's an American flag flying on the back of that junk," Staff Sergeant Schmidt called to Captain Howard Dunwood as the two Higgins boats closed on Tokchok-kundo.

"Yeah, I see it. Careful. I don't like the smell of this place."

"I think that's the drying fish, sir," Staff Sergeant Schmidt said.

"Very goddamn funny," Dunwood said. "I'll tell your widow you died with a smile on your face. Now be careful, goddamn it!"

The Higgins boat touched shore. The ramp fell onto the rocky shore with a loud clang.

The Marines ran down the ramp and turned right and left, spreading out, weapons at the ready. Captain Dunwood was in the center of what ultimately was a formation in the shape of a V, holding his carbine in one hand.

"Hold your fire! Hold your fire!" a voice shouted, an obviously American voice.

A figure appeared. He was in black pajamas, and had a band of the same material around his forehead. He held his hands over his head in a gesture of surrender.

"That's Jennings, Captain," Staff Sergeant Schmidt said.

"You know him?"

"Sir, when they put out the call for Marine Raiders . . ."

"He was one of them, huh?"

"Yes, sir," Schmidt said. "Jennings?"

"How they hanging, Smitty?" Technical Sergeant Jennings inquired.

"You're a Marine Raider, Sergeant?" Captain Dunwood asked. He'd never actually seen a Marine Raider before.

"No, sir, they put the Raiders out of business a long time ago. But it's like being a Marine, Captain. Once a Raider, always a Raider. There's a bunch of us here."

"You're in charge, Sergeant?"

"No, sir," Jennings said.

"I am," a voice said, and Dunwood saw another character in black pajamas with a black headband, his hands over his head in gesture of surrender. A Garand was hanging from his shoulder, and he had some kind of knife strapped to his wrist.

"You're a Marine officer?"

"Captain K. R. McCoy, USMCR, at your service, sir."

Captain Dunwood looked at Captain McCoy.

He didn't look much like what Dunwood thought a Marine Raider should look like, but there was something familiar about him.

"Don't I know you?"

"We've met," McCoy said, smiling, and then asked: "How's your finger?"

"I'll be a sonofabitch. You're the candy-ass on the airplane!"

"Is it safe to put my hands down now?" McCoy asked.

[FIVE]
USS *Mount McKinley*
The Flying Fish Channel
0610 15 September 1950

"Permission to come aboard, sir?" Captain K. R. McCoy inquired of the officer of the deck.

"Granted."

McCoy stepped onto the deck, saluted the OD and the national colors, and then Brigadier General Fleming Pickering.

"How are you, Ken?"

"In great need of a bath," McCoy said.

"I don't care how you smell," Miss Jeanette Priestly, of the *Chicago Tribune*, said. "I'll kiss you anyway."

She kissed his cheek and hugged him enthusiastically.

Pickering greeted every man as he stepped from the ladder on the deck. The next to the last to come aboard was Technical Sergeant Jennings.

"Jennings," McCoy ordered, and Jennings walked to them.

"Show her," McCoy ordered.

Jennings dug in the pocket of his black pajamas and out with three aluminum cans of 35-mm film.

"Jennings, in addition to his many other talents," McCoy said, "is an amateur photographer. I told him you'd probably give him a good price for those."

"If they're what I think they are, I damned sure will."

"I couldn't take money," Jennings said.

"The hell you can't," McCoy said.

"I don't know is they came out, Miss Priestly," Jennings said. "But I was in the lighthouse with Mr. Taylor when the barrage started."

"Like I said, Jeanette, a picture like that would be worth a lot of money," McCoy said.

Taylor came aboard last.

"General, I don't know what's going on. . . ."

"The 5th Marines are about to land on Wolmi-do," Pickering said.

"I've got some last-minute intel—fresh as of about 0500."

"Then we'll get it and you to General Willoughby," Pickering said.

"Dressed like this, sir?" Taylor said.

"Yes, Mr. Taylor, dressed just like that," Pickering said. "And you come along, too, McCoy."

In the passageway en route to the command center, Pickering put his hand on McCoy's arm.

"A heads-up, Ken," he said. "I told General MacArthur about your report."

McCoy seemed surprised.

"And?"

"I don't know, Ken," Pickering admitted. "I can't imagine him dumping Willoughby, but he knows. And I think he now believes."

"So you're telling me watch my back again?"

"Let me put it this way, Ken. Look surprised when MacArthur tells you he and the Commandant have decided you're entitled to put on the gold leaf again And I'm sure he'll tell you."

"What's MacArthur got to do with that?"

"He personally messaged the Commandant. Had a number of nice things to say about you."

"And you had nothing to do with that?"

"I'm a little ashamed—I should have done something about it a long time ago—to admit he beat me to it," Pickering said. "Anyway, it's effective today, Major McCoy."

General of the Army Douglas MacArthur was leaning on the map table in the command room, supporting himself on his hands, with his staff around him jockeying for position.

Pickering had the thought that it looked not unlike photographs he had seen of Hitler and his generals at Rastenburg.

"Ah," he said as Pickering, Taylor, and McCoy entered the room. "Gentlemen, for those of you who—for reasons I am sure you understand—I was not able to bring into the picture previously, these are the two officers, Lieutenant David Taylor, USN, and Major K. R. McCoy, USMC, who supervised, with great skill and courage, the covert operation I put into play to seize the Flying Fish Channel Islands."

[SIX]
Stateroom B-65
USS *Mount McKinley*
The Flying Fish Channel
0915 September 1950

"Very nice," McCoy said, as he, Taylor, Hart, and Zimmerman followed Pickering into the stateroom. "I've never been in this kind of officer's country before."

"There're two like this," Pickering said. "You fellows can decide who bunks with who. I put all the luggage in the one next door."

"These are flag officer's quarters," McCoy protested.

"They were assigned to me, and now I'm letting you use them," Pickering said. "The original idea was to put you all in sick bay."

"I thought you got one for you and one for Jeanette," Hart said, sitting down on the bed. "Jesus, that feels good."

"Jeanette batted her eyes at the captain," Pickering said, "whereupon he offered her his cabin, and I moved into General Howe's just before you came aboard."

"Where's he?"

"When last seen, headed for Inchon," Pickering said. "With the announced intention of hitching up with Chesty Puller and his First Marines."

"He must have a death wish," McCoy said.

Pickering picked up on the bitter tone. He started to say something, then changed his mind, and instead went to a metal chest of drawers, the top drawer of which had a combination lock. He worked the combination, opened it, and came out with a bottle of Famous Grouse wrapped in a towel.

"I suspect you can use one of these, Ken," Pickering said. "Or two."

"The last I heard booze aboard ships was an absolute no-no," McCoy said. "And thank you, General, but no."

"Speak for yourself, John Alden," Hart said. "You can hand me that, boss."

Pickering did so, then asked, "What's bothering you, Ken?"

McCoy shrugged.

"El Supremo taking credit for the operation?"

"That didn't surprise me at all," McCoy said. " 'Fertig the Crazy Man' became 'my brilliant guerrilla leader in the Philippines,' remember?"

"Very well," Hart said.

"I don't know that story," Taylor said.

"I guess what pisses me off is that Willoughby is going to walk," McCoy said. "Isn't he?"

"What did you think was going to happen to him? They'd march him to the door of the Dai Ichi Building, cut the stars and buttons off his uniform, and toss him into the gutter?"

"That would be one solution," McCoy said, and then said, "Oh, hell, George, hand me that."

"For one thing, Ken, he rendered long and faithful service to El Supremo. . . ."

"Covering his own ass, I suspect, every step of the way," McCoy said, and took a pull from the neck of the bottle. He handed it to Taylor, who looked for a moment as if he didn't know what to do with it, but then took a pull. And then handed it to Zimmerman.

"Ken," Pickering said, "look at it this way. MacArthur will never completely trust him again. That hurts both of them. MacArthur has learned that somebody he trusted completely was not trustworthy. And Willoughby will know for the rest of his life that the only reason MacArthur doesn't sack him, doesn't publicly humiliate him, is for the good of the service. And I know Douglas MacArthur well enough to know that's why he's acting as he has. I think he thinks Willoughby will now ask to retire, and he'll let him, and that will be the end of it, without getting into accusations and excuses or denials."

McCoy met Pickering's eyes for a long moment.

"If you say so, sir," he said after a moment.

"That was a speech, Ken, not an order," Pickering said.

McCoy opened his mouth to reply, and there came a knock at the door.

"Who is it?" Pickering asked, and gestured to Zimmerman to get the scotch bottle out of sight.

"Ship's doctor. Let me in, please," a male voice called.

"This is General Pickering, what is it?"

"Captain Arnold, General. Please let me in."

"Hold your hands in front of your mouths," Pickering ordered softly. "Just a moment, Doctor!"

"What are they going to do if they catch us, boss?" Hart asked. "Send us to bed without our supper?"

It wasn't that funny, but it produced chuckles, and very soon the chuckles were uncontrollable giggles.

Pickering, making a valiant effort not to smile, opened the door to the doctor, who was carrying a small cardboard carton. What the doctor, a silver-haired man Pickering's age, saw were four apparently hysterical men in black pajamas sitting on the two beds.

"General," the ship's doctor said, "General MacArthur asked me if I didn't think this was medically indicated for these gentlemen."

He held the box up. It contained twenty-four 1.5-ounce bottles of Kentucky Bourbon Whiskey FOR MEDICAL PURPOSES ONLY.

That pushed Pickering over the edge.

"Gentlemen," he said. "General MacArthur thinks you should have a drink." And then he was laughing so hard he had to hold on to the door.

The ship's doctor had practiced medicine long enough, and had been in the Navy long enough, to know when pursuing suspicions was neither sound medical nor naval practice.

"I'll leave these with you, General," the doctor said. "I'm sure you will dispense them with discretion."

"Doctor, what about my Marines?"

"You are?" the doctor asked.

"Major McCoy, sir."

Jesus, I said that without thinking. I really must have wanted that gold leaf back. And goddamn it, "Major" sounds good.

"I'll take care of your Marines, Major," the ship's doctor said. "Rest assured of that."

The hysteria—which Pickering had decided was just that, a condition induced by their sudden change from a life-threatening situation to one where they were relatively safe—had almost passed when, five minutes later, Jeanette Priestly knocked on the door of Stateroom B-65.

"I'd hate to tell you what it smells like in here," she said.

"What can we do for you, Jeanette?" Pickering asked.

"I need your influence," she said. "I want to go on the press Higgins boat when it goes to Inchon in two hours."

"And they won't let you go? They say why?"

"Because they don't have the personnel to properly protect me," she said. "I think maybe you owe me, General. I lived up to my end of the bargain."

"Go tell them you've got two Marines," McCoy said. "One of them a field-grade officer."

"Hey!" Pickering said. "How many of those little bottles have you had? You just came back from the war."

"General," McCoy said. "You know she's going whether or not they say she can. And we've done this before. And there're some people I really want to see in Seoul."

"See about what?" Pickering challenged.

McCoy hesitated.

"See about what, Ken?"

"Pick," McCoy said. "They might know where he is."

"That was below the belt, Ken," Pickering said. "How can I say no after that?"

"With respect, sir, I don't think you can."

Pickering exhaled audibly.

"George, grab a quick shower and shave and get into a decent uniform," he ordered, "and then go find whoever's in charge of this Higgins boat for the press, and tell them the CIA will require three spaces on it, and I don't care who gets bumped to provide them."

"Aye, aye, sir," Hart said, and pushed himself off the bed.

[SEVEN]

PRESS URGENT

FOR CHICAGO TRIBUNE

SLUG MACARTHUR RETURNS SEOUL TO SOUTH KOREAN PRESIDENT
SYNGMAN RHEE

BY JEANETTE PRIESTLY

CHICAGO TRIBUNE WAR CORRESPONDENT

SEOUL KOREA SEPTEMBER 29—

AT NOON TODAY, WITH A MESSAGE THAT MESMERIZED HIS
AUDIENCE OF SENIOR AMERICAN AND SOUTH KOREAN OFFICIALS,
GENERAL OF THE ARMY DOUGLAS MACARTHUR, IN THE NAME OF
THE UNITED NATIONS, RETURNED THE BATTERED CAPITAL OF
THIS WAR-RAVAGED NATION "IN GOD'S NAME" TO ITS
PRESIDENT, SYNGMAN RHEE. AS HE SPOKE, THE REVERBERATION
OF HEAVY CANNON FIRING ON THE OUTSKIRTS OF THE CITY
CAUSED PLASTER AND GLASS TO FALL FROM THE WALLS,
CEILING, AND WINDOWS OF THE BULLET-POCKED CAPITAL
BUILDING.

MACARTHUR AND RHEE FLEW INTO SEOUL'S KIMPO AIRPORT
ABOARD "THE BATAAN" SHORTLY AFTER 10 THIS MORNING,
TRAVELED ACROSS THE HAN RIVER ON A PONTOON BRIDGE, AND
THEN THROUGH THE DEVASTATED CITY TO ITS BATTERED
CAPITAL BUILDING. THERE THEY WERE MET BY US AMBASSADOR
JOHN J. MUCIO, MAJOR GENERAL EDWARD M. ALMOND,
COMMANDER OF THE INVASION, GENERAL "JOHNNIE" WALKER,
DEFENDER OF THE PUSAN PERIMETER AND OTHER SENIOR
OFFICERS.

MACARTHUR CONCLUDED HIS BRIEF REMARKS BY INVITING THOSE
PRESENT TO JOIN HIM IN OFFERING THE LORD'S PRAYER, AND

```
IMMEDIATELY FOLLOWING THE CEREMONY, DECORATED BOTH
ALMOND AND WALKER WITH THE DISTINGUISHED SERVICE CROSS,
THE NATION'S SECOND-HIGHEST AWARD "FOR PERSONAL VALOR
IN THE FACE OF THE ENEMY."

IMMEDIATELY AFTER THAT, HE RETURNED TO KIMPO FIELD,
BOARDED THE BATAAN, AND FLEW TO TOKYO. EN ROUTE HE
SPOKE TO THIS REPORTER MODESTLY OF HIS OWN ROLE IN THE
WAR, SAYING THE CREDIT BELONGED ENTIRELY TO THE YOUNG
MEN WITH RIFLES IN THEIR HANDS AND THE OFFICERS WHO
ACTUALLY LED THEM ON THE BATTLEFIELD.

END NOTHING FOLLOWS
```

[EIGHT]
The Residence of the Supreme Commander UN Command/Allied Forces in Japan
The Embassy of the United States
Tokyo, Japan
2030 29 September 1950

"Thank you for coming with me today, Fleming," General of the Army Douglas MacArthur said to Brigadier General Fleming Pickering.

"My God, I was honored to be there," Pickering said. "Thank you for taking me."

"You made your contribution to this campaign," MacArthur said. "You had every right to be there."

"That's unjustified, but thank you," Pickering said.

"I didn't see General Howe there," MacArthur said.

"He was there, sir."

And he said, "Liberated city, my ass. They're still shooting in the city limits," but somehow mentioning that doesn't seem appropriate.

The steward handed Pickering a glass of whiskey.

And it's now incumbent upon me to offer some kind of a toast. But I really can't think of one. This war's not over, and if the Chinese come in, which seems more likely every day, we'll be up to ears in a worse mess than we were before Inchon.

He raised his glass nevertheless, and said,

"I propose—"

The door opened and Colonel Huff came in.

"Sir, there's a Lieutenant Colonel Porter to see you."

"Ask him to be good enough to call upon me in the morning," MacArthur said. "Sid, I told you I didn't wish—"

"He's carrying a personal from General Ridgway, General."

"And I'll look at it in the morning. Thank you, Sid."

"Sir, the colonel is under orders to put General Ridgway's personal into your hands as soon as possible," Huff persisted.

"Ask him to come in, please," MacArthur said, impatiently.

A tall, good-looking young officer marched in, saluted, said, "General Ridgway's compliments, General," and handed him a squarish envelope.

"Thank you, Colonel," MacArthur said, "please be good enough to attend me tomorrow after ten at my headquarters."

"Yes, sir," Colonel Porter said, saluted again, did an about-face, and marched out of the room.

MacArthur tore the envelope open, glanced at it, then read it carefully again. Then he held it out at arm's length and sort of waved it until his wife had taken it from him.

Then he turned his back on Pickering and his wife, took a handkerchief from the hip pocket of his soft-washed khakis, and rather loudly blew his nose.

If I didn't know better, if anyone but Douglas MacArthur did that, I'd say he was crying. I wonder what the hell was in that note?

As if reading his mind, Jean MacArthur handed Pickering the note, went to her husband, and put her arms around him.

"Douglas," she said. "Darling, that's simply beautiful!"

Pickering looked at the note.

WASHINGTON, 26 SEPTEMBER 1950

BY OFFICER COURIER

MY DEAR GENERAL MACARTHUR:

UNDER GOD'S GUIDANCE, THE FULL FRUITS OF THE
INDOMITABLE COURAGE AND UNSHAKABLE PERSEVERANCE OF OUR
FORCES SEEM ABOUT TO REACH HARVEST.

THEY WILL ATTEST AGAIN TO THE INCOMPARABLE BRILLIANCE
OF YOUR UNSURPASSED LEADERSHIP AND JUDGMENT.

THEY WILL DEMONSTRATE AGAIN THE UNFAILING RESPONSE OF
AMERICAN FORCES TO TRUE LEADERSHIP, REGARDLESS OF ODDS.

WHAT A TRIBUTE, TO BE RECORDED IN OUR MILITARY HISTORY
TO OUR DEAD AND MAIMED.

SINCERELY,

M. B. Ridgway
MATTHEW RIDGWAY
VICE CHIEF OF STAFF
UNITED STATES ARMY

"A wonderful tribute," Pickering said, "and well-deserved."

"Thank you, Fleming," said MacArthur. There was a slight waver in his voice.

Jesus, I was right. MacArthur actually was crying!

Pickering read the note through again: "indomitable courage," "unshakable perseverance," "true leadership." He thought of McCoy and Zimmerman and Taylor and the South Koreans who had gone with them to the islands, and smiled. All these words applied there, too.

"Regardless of odds." He hadn't heard from McCoy since they'd said good-bye on the *Mount McKinley.* He'd tried to put the Killer's words out of his mind, but he'd failed miserably. "They might know where he is."

Goddamn him. I'm not sure hope is what I want right now.

Pickering felt a slight sting at the corners of his eyes.

Jesus Christ! Two generals, blubbering like babies.

He noticed the glass in his hand and raised it. "I never finished my toast, General," he said.

MacArthur looked at him.

"I'd like to do that now," Pickering went on. "To our men in Korea—wherever they are. God watch over them all."

"I'll drink to that," MacArthur said, and raised his glass to Pickering's.

For a moment, both men were silent. Then they drank, and their talk turned once more to war.

AFTERWORD

There really was a major general, a friend of President Harry S Truman since their service as captains, whom the President sent to the Far East immediately after the Korean War began, in a role very much like the one the fictional Major General Howe plays in this book. He landed at Inchon on D day, and immediately hooked up with the legendary Colonel "Chesty" Puller, USMC.

And there really was a naval reserve lieutenant, Eugene F. Clark, a Mustang like my fictional character Lieutenant David Taylor, USNR, in this book, who did in fact seize the islands in the Flying Fish Channel with the assistance of a handful of Marines, and Korean national policemen.

I learned of Lieutenant Clark's exploits from my friend Ed Ivanhoe, who is the historian *cum laude* of the Special Operations community, and who was himself involved in Korean War Special Operations. And some others, in other places.

The exploits of the real naval hero also came to the attention—from other sources—of the distinguished historian Thomas Fleming. He published an article based on what he had learned. Shortly after it was published, Lieutenant Clark's family got in touch with Mr. Fleming and told him that on his return from Korea, Lieutenant Clark, now deceased, had written a book about the Flying Fish Channel operation but never submitted it for publication.

Would Mr. Fleming have a look at it to see if a publisher might be interested? They thought it was a good story. When he read it, so did Mr. Fleming.

Several weeks later—*as he was actually editing the segment of this book that put my fictional character David Taylor on Tokchok-kundo Island*—Lieutenant Clark's manuscript landed on the desk of Putnam's publisher and editor-in-chief, Neil Nyren.

Putnam will publish Lieutenant Clark's memoirs of the Flying Fish Channel Operation, titled *The Secrets of Inchon,* in Spring 2002.

W. E. B. Griffin
Pilar, Buenos Aires Province, Argentina
August 23, 2001